THE COMPLETE J.G. REE
BY

Edgar Wallace

FOREWORD

Edgar Wallace was a British author who is best known for creating King Kong. Wallace was a very prolific writer despite his sudden death at age 56. In total Wallace is credited with over 170 novels, almost 1,000 short stories, and 18 stage plays. Wallace's works have been turned into well over 100 films. This edition of The Complete J.G. Reeder Series includes a table of contents.

Room 13

CHAPTER I

OVER the grim stone archway was carved the words:
PARCERE SUBJECTIS
In cold weather, and employing the argot of his companions Johnny Gray translated this as "Parky Subjects"—it certainly had no significance as "Spare the Vanquished" for he had been neither vanquished nor spared.
Day by day, harnessed to the shafts, he and Lal Morgon had pulled a heavy hand-cart up the steep slope, and day by day had watched absently the red-bearded gate-warder put his key in the big polished lock and snap open the gates. And then the little party had passed through, an armed warder leading, an armed warder behind, and the gate had closed.
And at four o'clock he had walked back under the archway and waited whilst the gate was unlocked and the handcart admitted.
Every building was hideously familiar. The gaunt "halls," pitch painted against the Dartmoor storms, the low-roofed office, the gas house, the big, barn-like laundry, the ancient bakery, the exercise yard with its broken asphalt, the ugly church, garishly decorated, the long, scrubbed benches with the raised seats for the warders...and the graveyard where the happily released lifers rested from their labours.
One morning in spring, he went out of the gate with a working-party. They were building a shed, and he had taken the style and responsibility of bricklayer's labourer. He liked the work because you can talk more freely on a job like that, and he wanted to hear all that Lal Morgon had to say about the Big Printer.
"Not so much talking to-day," said the warder in charge, seating himself on a sack-covered brick heap.
"No, sir," said Lal.
He was a wizened man of fifty and a lifer, and he had no ambition, which was to live long enough to get another "lagging."
"But not burglary, Gray," he said as he leisurely set a brick in its place; "and not shootin', like old Legge got his packet. And not faking Spider King, like you got yours."
"I didn't get mine for faking Spider King," said Johnny calmly. "I didn't know that Spider King had been rung in when I took him on the course, and was another horse altogether. They framed up Spider King to catch me. I am not complaining."
"I know you're innocent—everybody is," said Lal soothingly. "I'm the only guilty man in boob. That's what the governor says. 'Morgon,' he says, 'it does my heart good to meet a guilty man that ain't the victim of circumstantiality. Like everybody else is in boob,' he says."
Johnny did not pursue the subject. There was no reason why he should. This fact was beyond dispute. He had known all about the big racecourse swindles that were being worked, and had been an associate of men who backed the "rung in" horses. He accepted the sentence of three years' penal servitude that had been passed without appeal or complaint. Not because he was guilty of the act for which he was charged—there was another excellent reason.
"If they lumbered you with the crime, it was because you was a mug," said old Lal complacently. "That's what mugs are for—to be lumbered. What did old Kane say?"
"I didn't see Mr. Kane," said Johnny shortly.
"He'd think you was a mug, too," said Lal with satisfaction—"hand me a brick, Gray, and shut

up! That nosey screw's coming over." The "nosey screw" was no more inquisitive than any other warder. He strolled across, the handle of his truncheon showing from his pocket, the well-worn strap dangling. "Not so much talking," he said mechanically.

"I was asking for a brick, sir,-" said Lal humbly. "These bricks ain't so good as the last lot."

"I've noticed that," said the warder, examining a half-brick with a professional and disapproving eye.

"Trust you to notice that, sir," said the sycophant with the right blend of admiration and awe. And, when the warder had passed:

"That boss-eyed perisher don't know a brick from a gas-stove," said Lal without heat. "He's the bloke that old Legge got straightened when he was in here—used to have private letters brought in every other day. But then, old Legge's got money. Him and Peter Kane smashed the strong-room 'of the Orsonic and got away with a million dollars. They never caught Peter, but Legge was easy. He shot a copper and got life."

Johnny had heard Legge's biography a hundred times, but Lal Morgon had reached the stage of life when every story he told was new.

"That's why he hates Peter," said the garrulous bricklayer. "That's why young Legge and him are going to get Peter. And young Legge's hot! Thirty years of age by all accounts, and the biggest printer of slush in the world! And it's not ord'nary slush. Experts get all mixed up when they see young Legge's notes—can't tell 'em from real Bank of England stuff. And the police and the secret service after him for years—and then never got him!"

The day was warm, and Lal stripped off his red and blue striped working jacket. He wore, as did the rest of the party, the stained yellow breeches faintly stamped with the broad arrow. Around his calves were buttoned yellow gaiters. His shirt was of stout cotton, white with narrow blue stripes, and on his head was a cap adorned with mystic letters of the alphabet to indicate the dates of his convictions. A week later, when the letters were abolished, Lal Morgon had a grievance. He felt as a soldier might feel when he was deprived of his decorations.

"You've never met young Jeff?" stated rather than asked Lal, smoothing a dab of mortar with a leisurely touch.

"I've seen him—I have not met him," said Johnny grimly, and something in his tone made the old convict look up.

"He 'shopped' me," said Johnny, and Lal indicated his surprise with an inclination of his head that was ridiculously like a bow.

"I don't know why, but I do know that he 'shopped 'me," said Johnny. "He was the man who fixed up the fake, got me persuaded to bring the horse on to the course, and then squeaked. Until then I did not know that the alleged Spider King was in reality Boy Saunders cleverly camouflaged."

"Squeaking's hidjus," said the shocked Lal, and he seemed troubled. "And Emanuel Legge's boy, too! Why did he do it—did you catch him over money?"

Johnny shook his head.

"I don't know. If it's true that he hates Peter Kane he may have done it out of revenge, knowing that I'm fond of Peter, and...well, I'm fond of Peter. He warned me about mixing with the crowd I ran with—"

"Stop that talking, will you?" They worked for some time in silence. Then: "That screw will get somebody hung one of these days," said Lal in a tone of quiet despair. "He's the feller that little Lew Morse got a bashing for —over clouting him with a spanner in the blacksmith's shop. He was nearly killed. What a pity! Lew wasn't much account, an' he's often said he'd as soon be dead as sober."

At four o'clock the working-party fell in and marched or shuffled down the narrow road to the prison gates. Parcere Subjectis. Johnny looked up and winked at the grim jest, and he had the illusion that the archway winked back at him. At half-past four he turned into the deep-recessed doorway of his cell, and the yellow door closed on him with a metallic snap of a lock.

It was a big, vaulted cell, and the colour of the folded blanket ends gave it a rakish touch of gaiety. On a shelf in one corner was a photograph of a fox terrier, a pretty head turned inquiringly toward him. He poured out a mugful of water and drank it, looking up at the barred window. Presently his tea would come, and then the lock would be put on for eighteen and a half hours. And for eighteen and a half hours he must amuse himself as best he could. He could read whilst the light held—a volume of travel was on the ledge that served as a table. Or he could write on his slate, or draw horses and dogs, or work out interminable problems in mathematics, or write poetry...or think. That was the worst exercise of all. He crossed the cell and took down the photograph. The mount had worn limp with much handling, and he looked with a half-smile into the big eyes of the terrier.

"It is a pity you can't write, old Spot." he said. Other people could write, and did, he thought as he replaced the photograph. But Peter Kane never once mentioned Marney, and Marney had not written since...a long time. It was ominous, informative, in some ways decisive. A brief reference, "Marney is well," or "Marney thanks you for your inquiry," and that was all.

The whole story was clearly written in those curt phrases, the story of Peter's love for the girl, and his determination that she should not marry a man with the prison taint. Peter's adoration of his daughter was almost a mania—her happiness and her future came first, and must always be first. Peter loved him—Johnny had sensed that. He had given him the affection that a man might give his grown son. If this tragic folly of his had not led to the entanglement which brought him to a convict prison, Peter would have given Marney to him, as she was willing to give herself.

"That's that," said Johnny, in his role of philosopher. And then came tea and the final lock-up, and silence...and thoughts again.

Why did young Legge trap him? He had only seen the man once; they had never even met. It was only by chance that he had ever seen this young printer of forged notes. He could not guess that he was known to the man he "shopped," for Jeff Legge was an illusive person. One never met him in the usual rendezvous where the half-underworld foregather to boast and plot or drink and love.

A key rattled in the lock, and Johnny got up. He forgot that it was the evening when the chaplain visited him. "Sit down. Gray." The door closed on the clergyman, and he seated himself on Johnny's bed. It was curious that he should take up the thread of Johnny's interrupted thoughts.

"I want to get your mind straight about this man Legge...the son, I mean. It is pretty bad to brood on grievances, real or fancied, and you are nearing the end of your term of imprisonment, when your resentment will have a chance of expressing itself. And, Gray, I don't want to see you here again."

Johnny Gray smiled.

"You won't see me here!" he emphasised the word. "As to Jeff Legge, I know little about him, though I've done some fairly fluent guessing and I've heard a lot."

The chaplain shook his head thoughtfully.

"I have heard a little; he's the man they call the Big Printer, isn't he? Of course, I know all about the flooding of Europe with spurious notes, and that the police had failed to catch the man who was putting them into circulation. Is that Jeff Legge?"

Johnny did not answer, and the chaplain smiled a little sadly. "Thou shalt not squeak'—the eleventh commandment, isn't it?" he asked good-humouredly. "I am afraid I have been indiscreet. When does your sentence end?"

"In six months," replied Johnny, "and I'll not be sorry."

"What are you going to do? Have you any money?"

The convict's lips twitched.

"Yes, I have three thousand a year," he said quietly. "That is a fact which did not come out at the trial, for certain reasons. No, padre, money isn't my difficulty. I suppose I shall travel. I certainly shall not attempt to live down my grisly past."

"That means you're not going to change your name," said the chaplain with a twinkle in his eye.

"Well, with three thousand a year, I can't see you coming here again." Suddenly he remembered. Putting his hand in his pocket, he took out a letter. "The Deputy gave me this, and I'd nearly forgotten. It arrived this morning."

The letter was opened, as were all letters that came to convicts, and Johnny glanced carelessly at the envelope. It was not, as he had expected, a letter from his lawyer. The bold handwriting was Peter Kane's—the first letter he had written for six months. He waited until the door had closed upon the visitor, and then he took the letter from the envelope. There were only a few lines of writing.

'Dear Johnny, I hope you are not going to be very much upset by the news I am telling you. Marney is marrying Major Floyd, of Toronto, and I know that you're big enough and fine enough to wish her luck. The man she is marrying is a real good fellow who will make her happy.

Johnny put down the letter on to the ledge, and for ten minutes paced the narrow length of his cell, his hands clasped behind him. Marney to be married! His face was white, tense, his eyes dark with gloom. He stopped and poured out a mugful of water with a hand that shook, then raised the glass to the barred window that looked eastward.

"Good luck to you, Marney!" he said huskily, and drank the mug empty.

CHAPTER II

TWO days later, Johnny Gray was summoned to the Governor's office and heard the momentous news.
"Gray, I have good news for you. You are to be released immediately. I have just had the authority."
Johnny inclined his head.
"Thank you, sir," he said.
A warder took him to a bathroom, where he stripped, and, with a blanket about him, came out to a cubicle, where his civilian clothes were waiting. He dressed with a queer air of unfamiliarity, and went back to his cell. The warder brought him a looking-glass and a safety-razor, and he completed his toilet.
The rest of the day was his own. He was a privileged man, and could wander about the prison in his strangely-feeling attire, the envy of men whom he had come to know and to loathe; the half madmen who for a year had been whispering their futilities into his ear.
As he stood there in the hall at a loose end, the door was flung open violently, and a group of men staggered in. In the midst of them was a howling, shrieking thing that was neither man nor beast, his face bloody, his wild arms gripped by struggling warders.
He watched the tragic group as it made its way to the punishment cells.
"Fenner," said somebody under his breath. "He coshed a screw, but they can't give him another bashing."
"Isn't Fenner that twelve-year man, that's doing his full time?" asked Johnny, remembering the convict. "And he's going out to-morrow, too!"
"That's him," said his informant, one of the hall sweepers. "He'd have got out with nine, but old Legge reported him. Game to the last, eh? They can't bash him after to-morrow, and the visiting justices won't be here for a week."
Johnny remembered the case. Legge had been witness to a brutal assault on the man by one of the warders, who had since been discharged from the service. In desperation the unfortunate Fenner had hit back, and had been tried. Legge's evidence might have saved him from the flogging which followed, but Legge was too good a friend of the warders—or they were too good friends of his—to betray a "screw." So Fenner had gone to the triangle, as he would not go again.
He could not sleep the last night in the cell. His mind was on Marney. He did not reproach her for a second. Nor did he feel bitter toward her father. It was only right and proper that Peter Kane should do what was best for his girl. The old man's ever-present fear for his daughter's future was almost an obsession. Johnny guessed that when this presentable Canadian had come along, Peter had done all in his power to further the match.
Johnny Gray walked up the steep slope for the last time. A key turned in the big lock, and he stood outside the gates, a free man. The red-bearded head warder put out his hand.
"Good luck to you," he said gruffly. "Don't you come over the Alps again."
"I've given up mountain climbing," said Johnny.
He had taken his farewell of the Governor, and now the only thing to remind him of his association with the grim prison he had left was the warder who walked by his side to the station. He had some time to wait, and Johnny tried to get some information from another angle.

"No, I don't know Jeff Legge," said the warder, shaking his head. "I knew the old man: he was here until twelve months ago—you were here, too, weren't you, Gray?"

Johnny nodded.

"Mr. Jeff Legge has never been over the Alps, then?" he asked sardonically.

"No, not in this prison, and he wasn't in Parkhurst or Portland, so far as I can remember. I've been at both places. I've heard the men talking about him. They say he's clever, which means that he'll be putting out his tins one morning. Good-bye, Gray, and be good!"

Johnny gripped the outstretched hand of the man, and, when he was in the carriage, took out his silk handkerchief and wiped his hand of the last prison contact.

His servant was waiting for him at Paddington when he arrived that afternoon, and with him, straining at a leash, a small, lop-eared fox terrier, who howled his greeting long before Johnny had seen the group. In another second the dog was struggling in his arms, licking his face, his ears and his hair, and whining his joy at the reunion. There were tears in Johnny's eyes when he put the dog down on the platform.

"There are a number of letters for you, sir. Will you dine at home?"

The excellent Parker might have been welcoming his master from a short sojourn at Monte Carlo, so very unemotional was he.

"Yes, I'll dine at home," said Johnny. He stepped into the taxicab that Parker had hired, and Spot leapt after him.

"There is no baggage, sir?" asked Parker gravely through the open window.

"There is no baggage," said Johnny as gravely. "You had better ride back with me, Parker."

The man hesitated.

"It would be a very great liberty, sir," he said.

"Not so great a liberty as I have had taken with me during the past year and nine months," said Johnny.

As the cab came out into dismal Chapel Street, the greatly daring Parker asked:

"I hope you have not had too bad a time, sir?"

Johnny laughed.

"It has not been pleasant, Parker. Prisons seldom are."

"I suppose not, sir," agreed Parker, and added unnecessarily: "I have never been in prison, sir."

Johnny's flat was in Queen's Gate, and at the sight of the peaceful luxury of his study he caught his breath.

"You're a fool," he said aloud to himself.

"Yes, sir," said the obliging Parker.

That night many men came furtively to the flat in Queen's Gate, and Johnny, after admitting the first of these, called Parker into his small dining-room.

"Parker, I am told that during my absence in the country even staid men have acquired the habit of attending cinema performances?"

"Well, sir, I like the pictures myself," admitted Parker.

"Then go and find one that lasts until eleven o'clock," said Johnny.

"You mean, sir—?"

"I mean I don't want you here to-night."

Parker's face fell, but he was a good servant.

"Very good, sir," he said, and went out, wondering sorrowfully what desperate plans his master was hatching.

At half-past ten the last of the visitors took his leave.

"I'll see Peter to-morrow," said Johnny, tossing the end of his cigarette into the hall fireplace. "You know nothing of this wedding, when it is to take place?"

"No, Captain. I only know Peter slightly."

"Who is the bridegroom?"

"A swell, by all accounts—Peter is a plausible chap, and he'd pull in the right kind. A major in the Canadian Army, I've heard, and a very nice man. Peter can catch mugs easier than some people can catch flies—"

"Peter was never a mug-catcher," said John Gray sharply.

"I don't know," said the other. "There's one born every minute."

"But they take a long time to grow up, and the women get first pluck," said Johnny good-humouredly.

Parker, returning at 11.15, found his master sitting before a fireplace which was choked with burnt paper.

Johnny reached Horsham the next afternoon soon after lunch, and none who saw the athletic figure striding up the Horsham Road would guess that less than two days before he had been the inmate of a convict cell.

He had come to make his last desperate fight for happiness. How it would end, what argument to employ, he did not know. There was one, and one only, but that he could not use.

As he turned into Down Road he saw two big limousines standing one behind the other, and wondered what social event was in progress.

Manor Hill stood aloof from its suburban neighbours, a sedate, red-brick house, its walls gay with clematis. Johnny avoided the front gates and passed down a side path which, as he knew, led to the big lawn behind, where Peter loved to sun himself at this hour.

He paused as he emerged into the open. A pretty parlourmaid was talking to an elderly man, who wore without distinction the livery of a butler. His lined face was puckered uncomfortably, and his head was bent in a listening attitude, though it was next to impossible for a man totally deaf to miss hearing all that was said.

"I don't know what sort of houses you've been in, and what sort of people you've been working for, but I can tell you that if I find you in my room again, looking in my boxes, I shall tell Mr. Kane. I won't have it, Mr. Ford!"

"No, miss," said the butler, huskily.

It was not, Johnny knew, emotion which produced the huskiness. Barney Ford had been husky from his youth—probably squawked huskily in his cradle.

"If you are a burglar and trying to keep your hand in, I understand it," the girl continued hotly, "but you're supposed to be a respectable man! I won't have this underhand prying and sneaking. Understand that! I won't have it!"

"No, miss," said the hoarse Barney. John Gray surveyed the scene with amusement. Barney he knew very well. He had quitted the shadier walks of life when Peter Kane had found it expedient to retire from his hazardous calling. Ex-convict, ex-burglar and ex-prizefighter, his seamy past was in some degree redeemed by his affection for the man whose bread he ate and in whose service he pretended to be, though a worse butler had never put on uniform than Barney.

The girl was pretty, with hair of dull gold and a figure that was both straight and supple. Now her face was flushed with annoyance, and the dark eyes were ablaze. Barney certainly had prying habits, the heritage of his unregenerate days. Other servants had left the house for the same reason, and Peter had cursed and threatened without wholly reforming his servitor.

The girl did not see him as she turned and flounced into the house, leaving the old man to stare after her. "You've made her cross," said John, coming up behind him. Barney Ford spun round and stared. Then his jaw dropped. "Good Lord, Johnny, when did you come down from college?" The visitor laughed softly.

"Term ended yesterday," he said. "How is Peter?"

Before he replied the servant blew his nose violently, all the time keeping his eye upon the newcomer. "How long have you bin here?" he asked at length. "I arrived at the tail-end of your conversation," said Johnny, amused. "Barney, you haven't reformed!" Barney Ford screwed up his face into an expression of scorn. "They think you're a hook even if you ain't one," he said. "What does she know about life? You ain't seen Peter? He's in the house; I'll tell him in a minute. He's all right. All beans and bacon about the girl. That fellow adores the ground she walks on. It's not natural, being fond of your kids like that. I never was." He shook his head despairingly. "There's too much lovey-dovey and not enough strap nowadays. Spare the rod and spoil the child, as the good old poet says."

John Grey turned his head at the sound of a foot upon a stone step. It was Peter, Peter radiant yet troubled. Straight as a ramrod, for all his sixty years and white hair. He was wearing a morning coat and pearl-grey waistcoat —an innovation. For a second he hesitated, the smile struck from his- face, frowning, and then he came quickly his hand outstretched.

"Well, Johnny boy, had a rotten time?"

His hand fell on the young man's shoulder, his voice had the old pleasure of pride and affection.

"Fairly rotten," said Johnny; "but any sympathy with me is wasted. Personally, I prefer Dartmoor to Parkhurst—it is more robust, and there are fewer imbeciles."

Peter took his arm and led him to a chair beneath the big Japanese umbrella planted on the lawn. There was something in his manner, a certain awkwardness which the newcomer could not understand.

"Did you meet anybody...there...that I know, Johnny boy?"

"Legge," said the other laconically, his eyes on Peter's face.

"That's the man I'm thinking of. How is he?"

The tone was careless, but Johnny was not deceived. Peter was intensely interested.

"He's been out six months—didn't you know?"

The other's face clouded.

"Out six months? Are you sure?"

Johnny nodded.

"I didn't know."

"I should have thought you would have heard from him," said John quietly. "He doesn't love you!"

Peter's slow smile broadened.

"I know he doesn't; did you get a chance of talking with him?"

"Plenty of chances. He was in the laundry, and he straightened a couple of screws so that he could do what he liked. He hates you, Peter. He says you shopped him."

"He's a liar," said Peter calmly. "I wouldn't shop my worst enemy, Ho shopped himself. Johnny, the police get a reputation for smartness, but the truth is, every other criminal arrests himself. Criminals aren't clever. They wear gloves to hide fingerprints, and then write their names in the visitors book. Legge and I smashed the strong-room of the Orsonic and got away with a hundred and twenty thousand pounds in American currency—it was the last job I did. It was dead easy getting away, but Emanuel started boasting what a clever fellow he was; and he drank a bit. An honest man can drink and wake up in his own bed. But a crook who drinks says good morning to the gaoler."

He dropped the subject abruptly, and again his hand fell on the younger man's shoulder.

"Johnny, you're not feeling sore, are you?"

Johnny did not answer.

"Are you?"

And now the fight was to begin. John Gray steeled himself for the forlorn hope.

"About Marney? No, only—"

"Old boy, I had to do it." Peter's voice was urgent, pleading. "You know what she is to me. I liked you well enough to take a chance, but after they dragged you I did some hard thinking. It would have smashed me, Johnny, if she'd been your wife then. I couldn't bear to see her cry even when she was quite a little baby. Think what it would have meant to her. It was bad enough as it was. And then this fellow came along—a good, straight, clean, cheery fellow—a gentleman. And well, I'll tell you the truth— I helped him. You'll like him. He's the sort of man anybody would like. And she loves him, Johnny."

There was a silence.

"I don't bear him any ill-will. It would be absurd if I did. Only, Peter, before she marries I want to say—"

"Before she marries?" Peter Kane's voice shook. "John, didn't Barney tell you? She was married this morning."

CHAPTER III

"MARRIED?"

Johnny repeated the word dully.

Marney married...! It was incredible, impossible to comprehend. For a moment the stays and supports of existence dissolved into dust, and the fabric of life fell into chaos.

"Married this morning, Johnny. You'll like him. He isn't one of us, old boy. He's as straight as...well, you understand, Johnny boy? I've worked for her and planned for her all these years; I'd have been rotten if I took a chance with her future."

Peter Kane was pleading, his big hand on the other's shoulder, his fine face clouded with anxiety and the fear that he had hurt this man beyond remedy.

"I should have wired..."

"It would have made no difference," said Peter Kane almost doggedly. "Nothing could have been changed, Johnny, nothing. It had to be. If you had been convicted innocently—I don't say you weren't—I couldn't have the memory of your imprisonment hanging over her; I couldn't have endured the uncertainty myself. Johnny, I've been crook all my life— up to fifteen years ago. I take a broader view than most men because I am what I am. But she doesn't know that. Craig's here to-day—"

"Craig—the Scotland Yard man?"

Peter nodded, a look of faint amusement in his eyes.

"We're good friends; we have been for years. And do you know what he said this morning? He said, 'Peter, you've done well to marry that girl into the straight way,' and I know he's right."

Johnny stretched back in the deep cane chair, his hand shading his eyes, as though he found the light too strong for him.

"I'm not going to be sorry for myself," he said with a smile, and stretching out his hand, gripped Kane's arm. "You'll not have another vendetta on your hands, Peter. I have an idea that Emanuel Legge will keep you busy—"

He stopped suddenly. The ill-fitted butler had made a stealthy appearance.

"Peter," he began in his husky whisper, "he's come. Do you want to see him?"

"Who?"

"Emanuel Legge—uglier than ever."

Peter Kane's face set, mask-like.

"Where is Miss Marney—Mrs. Floyd?"

"She's gettin' into her weddin' things and falderals for the photogrypher," said Barney. "She had 'em off once, but the photogrypher's just come, and he's puttin' up his things in the front garden. I sez to Marney—"

"You're a talkative old gentleman," said Peter grimly. "Send Emanuel through. Do you want to see him, Johnny?"

John Gray rose.

"No," he said. "I'll wander through your alleged rosary. I want nothing to remind me of The Awful Place, thank you."

Johnny had disappeared through an opening of the box hedge at the lower end of the lawn when Barney returned with the visitor.

Mr. Emanuel Legge was a man below middle height, thin of body and face, grey and a little bald.

On his nose perched a pair of horn-rimmed spectacles. He stood for a second or two surveying the scene, his chin lifted, his thin lips drawn in between his teeth. His attire was shabby, a steel chain served as a watch-guard, and, as if to emphasise the rustiness of his wrinkled suit, he wore boots that were patently new and vividly yellow. Hat in hand, he waited, his eyes slowly sweeping the domain of his enemy, until at last they came to rest upon his host.

It was Peter Kane who broke the deadly silence.

"Well, Emanuel? Come over and sit down."

Legge moved slowly toward his host. "Quite a swell place, Peter. Everything of the best, eh? Trust you! Still got old Barney, I see. Has he reformed too? That's the word, ain't it—'reformed'?"

His voice was thin and complaining. His pale blue eyes blinked coldly at the other.

"He doesn't go thieving any more, if that is what you mean," said Peter shortly, and a look of pain distorted the visitor's face.

"Don't use that word; it's low—"

"Let me take your hat." Peter held out his hand, but the man drew his away.

"No, thanks. I promised a young friend of mine that I wouldn't lose anything while I was here. How long have you been at this place, Peter?"

"About fourteen years."

Peter sat down, and the unwelcome guest followed his example, pulling his chair round so that he faced the other squarely.

"Ah!" he said thoughtfully. "Living very comfortable, plenty to eat, go out and come in when you like. Good way of spending fourteen years. Better than having the key on you four o'clock in the afternoon. Princetown's the same old place—oh, I forgot you'd never been there."

"I've motored through," said Peter coolly, deliberately, and knew that he had touched a raw place before the lips of the man curled back in a snarl.

"Oh, you've motored through!" he sneered. "I wish I'd known; I'd have hung my flags out! They ought to have decorated Princetown that day. Peter. You drove through!" he almost spat the words.

"Have a cigar?"

Emanuel Legge waved aside the invitation.

"No, thanks. I've got out of the habit—you do in fifteen years. You can get into some, too. Fifteen years is a long time out of a life."

So Emanuel had come to make trouble, and had chosen his day well. Peter took up the challenge.

"The man you shot would have been glad of a few—he died two years after," he said curtly, and all the pent fury of his sometime comrade flamed in his eyes.

"I hope he's in hell," he hissed, "the dirty flattie!" With an effort he mastered himself. "You've had a real good time, Peter? Nice house, that wasn't bought for nothing. Servants and whatnot and motoring through the moor! You're clever!"

"I admit it."

The little man's hands were trembling, his thin lips twitched convulsively.

"Leave your pal in the lurch and get away yourself, eh? Every man for himself—well, that's the law of nature, ain't it? And if you think he's going to squeak, send a line to the busies in charge of the case and drop a few hundred to 'em and there you are!" He paused, but no reply came. "That's how it's done, ain't it, Peter?"

Kane shrugged his shoulders indifferently.

"I don't know—I'm never too old to learn."

"But that's the way it's done?" insisted the man, showing his teeth again. "That's the way you keep out of boob, ain't it?"

Peter looked at his tormentor, outwardly untroubled.

"I won't argue with you," he said.

"You can't," said the other. "I'm logical." He gazed around. "This house cost a bit of money. What's half of two hundred thousand? I'm a bad counter!" Peter did not accept the opening. "It's a hundred thousand, ain't it? I got sixty thousand—you owe me forty."

"We got less than a hundred and twenty thousand pounds, if you're talking about the ship job. You got sixty thousand, which was more than your share. I paid it into your bank the day you went down."

Legge smiled sceptically.

"The newspapers said a million dollars," he murmured.

"You don't believe what you read in the newspapers, do you? Emanuel, you're getting childish." Then suddenly: "Are you trying to put the 'black' on me?"

"Blackmail?" Emanuel was shocked. "There's honour amongst—friends surely, Peter. I only want what's right and fair."

Peter laughed softly, amusedly.

'Comic, is it? You can afford to laugh at a poor old fellow who's been in 'stir' for fifteen years." The master of Manor Hill snapped round on him.

"If you'd been in hell for fifty I should still laugh."

Emanuel was sorry for himself. That was ever a weakness of his; he said as much.

"You wouldn't, would you? You've got a daughter, haven't you? Young? Married to-day, wasn't she?"

"Yes."

"Married money—a swell?"

"Yes. She married a good man."

"He doesn't know what you are, Peter?" Emanuel asked the question carelessly, and his host fixed him with a steely glance.

"No. What's the idea? Do you think you'll get forty thousand that way?"

"I've got a boy. You've never sat in a damp cell with the mists of the moor hanging on the walls and thought and thought till your heart ached? You can get people through their children." He paused. "I could get you that way."

In a second Peter Kane was towering above him, an ominous figure.

"The day my heart ached," he said slowly, "yours would not beat! You're an old man, and you're afraid of death! I can see it in your eyes. I am afraid of nothing. I'd kill you!"

Before the ferocity of voice and mien, Legge shrank farther into his chair.

"What's all this talk about killing? I only want what's fair. Fond of her, ain't you, Peter? I'll bet you are. They say that you're crazy about her. Is she pretty? I don't suppose she takes after you. Young Johnny Gray was sweet on her too. Peter, I'll get you through her—"

So far he got, and then a hand like a steel clamp fell on his neck, and he was jerked from his chair.

Peter spoke no word but, dragging the squirming figure behind him, as if it had neither weight nor resistance, he strode up the narrow pathway by the side of the house, across the strip of garden, through the gate and into the road. A jerk of his arm, and Emanuel Legge was floundering in the dusty road.

"Don't come back, Emanuel," he said, and did not stop to listen to the reply.

John Gray passed out of sight and hearing of the two men, being neither curious to know Legge's business nor anxious to renew a prison acquaintance.

Below the box hedge were three broad terraces, blazing with colour, blanketed with the subtle fragrance of flowers. Beyond that, a sloping meadow leading to a little river. Peter had bought his property wisely. A great cedar of Lebanon stood at the garden's edge; to the right, massed bushes were patched with purple and heliotrope blooms.

He sat down on a marble seat, glad of the solitude which he shared only with a noisy thrush and a lark invisible in the blue above him.

Marney was married. That was the beginning and the end of him. But happy. He recognised his very human vanity in the instant doubt that she could be happy with anybody but him.

How dear she was! And then a voice came to him, a shrill, hateful voice. It was Legge's—he was threatening the girl, and Johnny's blood went cold. Here was the vulnerable point in Peter Kane's armour; the crevice through which he could be hurt.

He started to his feet and went up the broad steps of the terrace, three at a time. The garden was empty, save for Barney setting a table. Kane and his guest had disappeared. He was crossing the lawn when he saw something white shining in the gloom beyond the open French windows of a room. Something that took glorious shape. A girl in bridal white, and her hands were outstretched to him. So ethereal, so unearthly was her beauty, that at first he did not recognise her.

"Johnny!"

A soldierly figure was at her side, Peter Kane was behind her, but he had no eyes for any but Marney.

She came flying toward him, both his hands were clasped in her warm palm.

"Oh, Johnny...Johnny!"

Then he looked up into the smiling face of the bridegroom, that fine, straight man to whom Peter had entrusted his beloved girl. For a second their eyes met, the debonair Major Floyd and his. Not by a flicker of eyelash did Johnny Gray betray himself.

The husband of the woman he loved was Jeff Legge, forger and traitor, the man sworn with his father to break the heart of Peter Kane.

CHAPTER IV

HAD he betrayed himself, he wondered? All his willpower was exercised to prevent such a betrayal. Though a tornado of fury swept through and through him, though he saw the face of the man distorted and blurred, and brute instinct urged his limbs to savage action, he remained outwardly unmoved. It was impossible for the beholder to be sure whether he had paled, for the sun and wind of Dartmoor had tanned his lean face the colour of mahogany. For a while so terrific was the shock that he was incapable of speech or movement.

"Major Floyd" was Jeff Legge! In a flash he realised the horrible plot. This was Emanuel's revenge—to marry his crook son to the daughter of Peter Kane.

Jeff was watching him narrowly, but by no sign did Johnny betray his recognition. It was all over in a fraction of a second. He brought his eyes back to the girl, smiling mechanically. She seemed oblivious to her surroundings. That her new husband stood by, watching her with a gleam of amusement in his eyes, that Peter was frowning anxiously, and that even old Barney was staring open-mouthed, meant nothing. "Johnny, poor Johnny! You aren't hating me, are you?"

John smiled and patted the hand that lay in his. "Are you happy?" he asked in a low voice.

"Yes, oh yes, I'm happily married—that's what you mean, isn't it? I'm very happy...Johnny, was it terrible? I haven't stopped thinking about you, I haven't. Though I didn't write...after...Don't you think I was a beast? I know I was. Johnny, didn't it hurt you, old boy?"

He shook his head.

"There's one thing you mustn't be in Dartmoor—sorry for yourself. Are you happy?"

She did not meet his eyes.

"That is twice you've asked in a minute! Isn't it disloyal to say that I am? Don't you want to meet Jeffrey?"

"Why, of course, I want to meet Jeffrey."

He crossed to the man, and Jeff Legge watched him.

"I want you to meet Captain Gray, a very old friend of mine," she said with a catch in her voice.

Jeffrey Legge's cold hand gripped his.

"I'm glad to meet you, Captain Gray."

Had he been recognised? Apparently not, for the face turned to him was puckered in an embarrassed smile.

"You've just come back from East Africa, haven't you? Get any shooting?"

"No, I didn't do any shooting," said Johnny.

"Lots of lions, aren't there?" said Jeff.

The lips of the ex-convict twitched.

"In that part of the country where I was living, the lions are singularly tame," he said dryly.

"Marney, darling, you're glad to see Gray on your wedding day, aren't you? —it was good of you to come, Gray. Mrs. Floyd has often spoken about you."

He put his arm about the girl, his eyes never leaving Johnny's face. He designed to hurt—to hurt them both. She stood rigidly, neither yielding nor resisting, tense, breathless, pale. She knew! The realisation came to John Gray like a blow. She knew that this man was a liar and a villain. She knew the trick that had been played upon her father!

"Happy, darling?"

"Very—oh, very."

There was a flutter in her voice, and now Johnny was hurt and the fight to hold himself in became terrific. It was Peter who for the moment saved the situation.

"Johnny, I want you to know this boy. The best in the world. And I want you to think with me that he's the best husband in the world for Marney."

Jeff Legge laughed softly. "Mr. Kane, you embarrass me terribly. I'm not half good enough for her—I'm just an awkward brute that doesn't deserve my good luck."

He bent and kissed the white-faced girl. Johnny did not take his eyes from the man. "Happy, eh? I'll bet you're happy; you rascal," chuckled Kane.

Marney pulled herself away from the encircling arm. "Daddy, I don't think this is altogether amusing Johnny."

Her voice shook. The man from Dartmoor knew that she was on the verge of tears.

"It takes a lot to bore me." John Gray found his voice. "Indeed, the happiness of young people—I feel very old just now—is a joy. You're a Canadian, Major Floyd?"

"Yes—a French Canadian, though you wouldn't guess that from my name. My people were habitant and went west in the 'sixties—to Alberta and Saskatchewan, long before the railway came. You ought to go to Canada; you'd like it better than the place you've been to."

"I'm sure I should."

Peter had strolled away, the girl's arm in his.

"No lions in Canada, tame or wild," said Jeff, regarding him from under his drooped eyelids.

Gray had lit a cigarette. He was steady now, steady of nerve and hand.

"I should feel lonely without lions," he said coolly, and then: "If you will forgive my impertinence, Major Floyd, you have married a very nice girl."

"The very, very best."

"I would go a long way to serve her—a long way. Even back to the lions." Their eyes met. In the bridegroom's was a challenge; in Johnny Gray's cold murder. Jeff Legge's eyes fell and he shivered. "I suppose you like —hunting?" he said. "Oh, no, you said you didn't. I wonder why a man of your—er—character went abroad?"

"I was sent," said Johnny, and he emphasised every word. "Somebody had a reason for sending me abroad—they wanted me out of the way. I should have gone, anyhow, but this man hurried the process."

"Do you know who it was?"

The East African pretence had been tacitly dropped. Jeff might do so safely, for he would know that the cause of John Gray's retirement from the world was no secret.

"I don't know the man. He was a stranger to me. Very few people know him personally. In his set—our set—not half a dozen people could identify him. Only one man in the police knows him—"

"Who is that?" interrupted the other quickly.

"A man named Reeder. I heard that in prison—of course you knew I had come from Dartmoor?" Jeff nodded with a smile.

"That is the fellow who is called The Great Unknown," he said, striving to thin the contempt from his voice. "I've heard about him in the club. He is a very stupid person of middle age, who lives in Peckham. So he isn't as much unknown as your mystery man."

"It is very likely," said the other. "Convicts invest their heroes and enemies with extraordinary gifts and qualities. I only know what I have been told. At Dartmoor they say Reeder knows everything. The Government gave him carte blanche to find the Big Printer—"

"And has he found him?" asked Jeff Legge innocently.

"He'll find him," said Johnny. "Sooner or later there will be a squeak."
"May I be there to hear it," said Jeff Legge, and showed his white teeth in a mirthless smile.

CHAPTER V

JOHNNY was alone in the lower garden, huddled up on a corner of the marble bench, out of sight but not out of hearing of the guests who were assembling on the lawn. He had to think, and think quickly. Marney knew! But Marney had not told, and Johnny guessed why.

When had Jeff Legge told her? On the way back from the church, perhaps. She would not let Peter know—Peter, who deemed her future assured, her happiness beyond question. What had Jeff said? Not much, Johnny guessed. He had given her just a hint that the charming Major Floyd she had married was not the Major Floyd with whom she was to live.

Johnny was cool now—icy cold was a better description. He must be sure, absolutely sure, beyond any question of doubt. There might be some resemblance between Jeff Legge and this Major Floyd. He had only seen the crook once, and that at a distance.

He heard the rustle of skirts and looked round quickly. It was the maid he had seen quarrelling with Barney.

"Mr. Kane says, would you care to be in the group that is being photographed, Captain Gray?" she asked.

He did not immediately reply. His eyes were scanning her with a new interest.

"Tell him I'd rather not, and come back."

"Come back, sir?" she repeated in astonishment.

"Yes, I want to talk to you," said Johnny with a smile. "Have mercy on a disgruntled guest, who can find nobody to entertain him."

She stood, hesitating. He could see the indecision in her face.

"I don't know if Mr. Kane would like that," she said, and a smile trembled at the corner of her mouth. "Very well, I'll come back."

It was not till ten minutes later, when he judged the photograph had been taken and the guests had gone again to the house, that she appeared, demure but curious.

"Sit down," said Johnny. He threw away his cigarette and moved to the end of the stone bench.

"Don't stop smoking for me, Captain Gray," she said.

"How long have you been here?" he asked.

"With Mr. Kane? About six months," she said.

"Pretty good job?" he asked carelessly.

"Oh, yes, sir, very."

"What is your name?"

"My name is Lila. Why do you ask?"

"I think you and I ought to get better acquainted, Lila," he said, and took her unresisting hand. Secretly she was amused; on the surface she showed some sign of being shocked.

"I didn't know you were that type of flirting man, Mr. Gray—you're a Captain, though, aren't you?"

"'Captain' is a purely honorary title, Lila," said Johnny. "I suppose you'll miss your lady?"

"Yes, I shall miss her," said Lila.

"A nice girl, eh?" bantered Johnny.

"And a very nice husband," she said tartly.

"Do you think so?"

"Yes, I suppose he is a nice fellow. I don't know much about him."

"Good-looking?" suggested Johnny.

The woman shrugged her shoulders.

"I suppose he is."

"And very much in love with Miss Kane. That fellow adores her," said Johnny. "In fact, I don't know that I've ever seen a man so much in love with a woman."

She suppressed a sigh.

"Oh, yes, I suppose he is," she said impatiently. "Do you want me any more, Captain Gray, because I've a lot of work to do?"

"Don't run away," said Johnny in his most gentle voice, "Weddings always make me romantic." He took up the thread where it was interrupted. "I don't expect the Major will have eyes for any other girl for years," he said. "He's head over heels in love, and why shouldn't he be? I suppose," he said reminiscently, avoiding her eyes, "he is the sort of man who would have had many love affairs in the past." He shrugged his shoulders. "With the kind of girls that one picks up and puts down at pleasure."

Now a flush, deep and even, had come to her face, and her eyes held a peculiar brightness.

"I don't know anything about Major Floyd," she said shortly, and was rising, but his hand fell upon her arm.

"Don't run away, Lila."

"I'm not going to stay," she said with sudden vehemence. "I don't want to discuss Major Floyd or anybody else. If you want me to talk to you—"

"I want to talk to you about the honeymoon. Can't you picture them, say, on Lake Como, in a bower of roses? Can't you imagine him forgetting all that's past, all the old follies, all the old girls—?"

She wrenched her arm from his grip and stood up, and her face was deadly white.

"What are you getting at, Gray?" she asked, all the deference, all the demureness, gone from her voice.

"I'm getting at you, Miss Lila Sain," he said, "and if you attempt to get away from me, I'll throttle you!"

She stared at him, her breath coming quickly. "You were supposed to be a gentleman, too," she said.

"I'm supposed to be Johnny Gray from Dartmoor. Sit down. What's the graft, Lila?"

"I don't understand what you're talking about."

"What's the graft?" asked Johnny with deadly calm. "Jeff Legge put you here to nose the house for him, and keep him wise as to what was going on."

"I don't know Jeff Legge," she faltered.

"You're a liar," said Johnny ungently. "I know you, Lila. You run with Legge and you're a cheap squeak. I've seen you a dozen times. Who is Major Floyd?"

"Go and ask him," she said defiantly.

"Who is Major Floyd?"

The grip on her arm tightened.

"You know," she said sullenly. "It's Jeff Legge."

"Now listen, Lila. Come here." He had released her, and now he crooked his finger. "Go and blow to Jeff, and I'll squeak on you both—you understand that? I'll put Jeff just where I want him to be—there's a vacant cell at Dartmoor, anyway. That gives you a twinge, doesn't it? You're keen on Jeff?"

She did not reply.

"I'll put him where I want him to be," he repeated slowly and deliberately, "unless you do as I tell you."

"You're going to put the 'black' on him?" she said, her lips curling.

"'Black' doesn't mean anything in my young life," said Johnny. "But I tell you this, that I'll find Reeder and squeak the whole pageful unless I have my way."

"What do you want?" she asked.

"I want to know where they're going, and where they're staying. I want to know their plans for the future. Are you married to him, by any chance?"

A glance at her face gave him the answer.

"You're not? Well, you may be yet, Lila. Aren't you tired of doing his dirty work?"

"Perhaps I am and perhaps I'm not," she replied defiantly. "You can do nothing to him now, anyway, Johnny Gray. He's got your girl, and if you squeaked like a garden of birds you couldn't undo what that old God-man did this morning! Jeff's too clever for you. He'll get you, Gray—"

"If he knows," said Johnny quietly. "But if he knows, Reeder knows too. Do you get that?"

"What are you going to do?" she asked after a silence.

"I'm having one of my little jokes," said Johnny between his teeth. "A real good joke! It is starting now. I can't tell Peter, because he'd kill your young man, and I have a particular objection to Peter going to the drop. And you can't tell Jeff, because there'd be a case for a jury, and when Jeff came out you'd be an old woman. That's not a good prospect, eh? Now tell me all you've got to tell, and speak slowly, because I don't write shorthand."

He whipped a small notebook from his pocket, and as she spoke, reluctantly, sulkily, yet fearfully, he wrote rapidly. When he had finished: "You can go now, my gentle child," he said, and she stood up, her eyes blazing with rage.

"If you squeak, Johnny Gray, I'll kill you. I never was keen on this marriage business—naturally. I knew old Legge wanted him to marry Peter's daughter, because Legge wanted to get one back on him. But Jeff's been good to me; and the day the busies come for Legge I'll come for you, and I'll shoot you stone dead, Johnny, as God's my judge!"

"Beat it!" said Johnny tersely.

He waited till she was gone through one of the openings in the box hedge, then passed along to the other and stopped. Peter Kane was standing in the open, shielded from view by the thin box bush, and Peter's face was inscrutable.

CHAPTER VI

"HALLO, Johnny! Running for the compensation stakes?"
Johnny laughed.
"You mean the maid? She is rather pretty, isn't she?"
"Very," said the other.
Had he heard? That was a question and a fear in Johnny's mind. The marble bench was less than six feet from the bush where Peter Kane stood. If he had been there any time—
"Been waiting long for me, Peter?" he asked.
"No! I just saw you take a farewell of Lila—very nice girl, that, Johnny—an extraordinarily nice girl. I don't know when I've seen a nicer. What did you find to talk about?"
"The weather, dicky-birds and the course of true love," said Johnny, as Kane took his arm and led him across the lawn.
"Everything variable and flighty, eh?" said Peter with a little smile. "Come and eat, Johnny. These people are going away soon. Marney is changing now. What do you think of my new son-in-law, eh?"
His old jovial manner held. When they came into the big reception-room, and Peter Kane's arm went round his son-in-law's shoulder, Johnny breathed a sigh of relief. Thank God he did not know! He had sweated in his fear of what might follow a discovery.
Thirty-six people sat down in the dining-room, and, contrary to convention, Marney, who sat at the head of the table, was wearing her going-away dress. John shot a quick glance at her as he came in, but she averted her eyes. Her father sat on her left; next to him was the clergyman who had performed the ceremony. Next came a girl friend, and then a man, by whose side Johnny sat. He recognised the leathery features instantly.
"Been away, Johnny?" Detective-Superintendent Craig asked the question in a voice so carefully pitched that it did not reach any farther than the man to whom he spoke.
The chatter and buzz of conversation, the little ripples of laughter that ran up and down the table, did something to make the privacy of their talk assured.
As Old Barney bent over to serve a dish, Craig gave a sidelong glance at his companion.
"Peter's got old Barney still—keeping honest, Barney?"
"I'm naturally that way," said Barney sotto voce. "It's not meeting policemen that keeps me straight."
The hard features of the detective relaxed.
"There are lots of other people who could say that, Barney," he said, and when the man had passed to the next guest: "He's all right. Barney never was a bad man. I think he only did one stretch—he wouldn't have done that if he'd had Peter's imagination, Johnny."
"Peter's imagination?"
"I'm not referring to his present imagination, but the gift he had fourteen—fifteen years ago. Peter was the cleverest of them all. The brilliant way his attack was planned, the masterly line of retreat, the wonderful alibis, so beautifully dovetailed into one another that, if we had pinched him, he'd not only have been discharged, but he would have got something from the poor box! It used to be the life ambition of every young officer to catch him, to find some error of judgment, some flaw in his plan. But it was police-proof and foolproof."
"He'd blush to hear you," said the other dryly.

"But it's true, Johnny! The clever letters he used to write, all to fool us. He did a lot of work with letters—getting people together, luring 'em to the place he wanted 'em and where their presence served him best. I remember how he got my chief to be at Charing Cross under the clock at ten-past nine, and showed up himself and made him prove-his alibi!" He laughed gently.

"I suppose," said Gray, "people would think it remarkable that you and he are such good friends?"

"They wouldn't say it was remarkable; they'd say it was damned suspicious!" growled the other. "Having a drink?" he said suddenly, and pulled a wine bottle across the table.

"No, thanks—I seldom drink. We have to keep a very clear head in our business. We can't afford to dream."

"We can't afford anything else," said Craig. "Why 'our business,' old man? You're out of that?"

Johnny saw the girl look toward him. It was only a glance—but in that brief flash he saw all that he feared to see—the terror, the bewilderment, the helplessness. He set his teeth and turned abruptly to the detective.

"How is your business?" he asked.

"Quiet."

"I'm sorry to hear that," said John Gray with mock concern, "But trade's bad everywhere, isn't it?"

"What sort of time did you have—in the country?" asked Craig, and his companion grinned.

"Wonderful! My bedroom wanted papering, but the service was quite good."

Craig sighed.

"Ah well, we live and learn," he said heavily. "I was sorry about it, Johnny, very sorry. It's a misfortune, but there's no use grieving about it. You were one of the unlucky ones. If all the people who deserved prison were in prison—why, there wouldn't be any housing problems. I hear there were quite a lot of stars there," Craig went on. "Harry Becker, and young Lew Storing—why, old Legge must have been there in your time. And another fellow—now, what's his name? The slush man—ah. Carper, that's it. Ever see him?"

"Yes; he and I were once harnessed to the same cart."

"Ah!" said Craig encouragingly. "I'll bet you heard a few things. He'd talk to you."

"He did."

Craig bent toward him, lowering his voice.

"Suppose I told you a certain party coppered you, and suppose I said I've reason to believe that your copper is the man I want. Now couldn't we exchange confidences?" he asked.

"Yes, we might squeak together, and it would sound like one of those syncopated orchestras. But we won't. Honestly, Craig, I can't tell you about the Big Printer. Reeder ought to know all about him!"

"Reeder!" said the other scornfully. "An amateur! All this fal-de-lal about secret service men gets my goat! If they'd left the matter to the police, we'd have had the Big Printer—ever seen him, Johnny?"

"No," said Johnny untruthfully.

"Reeder, eh?" said the thoughtful detective. "They used to have an office man named Golden once, an old fellow that thought he could catch slushers by sitting in an office and thinking hard. Reeder isn't much better by all accounts. I saw him once, a soft fellow on the edge of senile decay!"

Craig sighed deeply, looked up and down the happy board with a bleak and grudging glance, and then: "Just for a little heart-to-heart talk, I know where you could get an easy 'monkey,' Johnny," he said softly.

Johnny did not smile.

"It would have to be a monkey on a stick, Craig—"

"We're both men of the world," interrupted the detective imploringly.

"Yes," said Johnny Gray, "but not the same world, Craig."

One last despairing effort the detective made, though he knew that, in angling for a squeak, he might as well have tried Peter himself.

"The Bank of England will pay a thousand pounds for the information I want."

"And who can afford it better?" said Johnny heartily. "Now, shut up, Craig; somebody's going to make a speech."

It was a mild and beatific oration delivered by the officiating clergyman. When it came to its machine-made peroration Craig, who was intensely interested in the sonorous platitudes, looked round and saw that his companion had gone from his side—later he saw him leaning over Peter's chair, and Peter was nodding vigorously. Then Johnny passed through the door.

Somebody else was watching him. The bridegroom, twiddling the stem of his wineglass between his fingers, saw him go, and was more than ordinarily interested. He was sufficiently curious, at any rate, to catch the eye of the pretty maid and look significantly at the door. At that signal Lila followed Johnny Gray. He was not in the hall, and she went out into the road, but here saw no sign of the man she sought. There was, however, somebody else, and she obeyed his call to her.

"Tell Jeff I want him before he starts on that honeymoon of his," snarled Emanuel Legge, glaring at her through the glasses. "He's been talking to that girl—I saw her face. What did he say?"

"How do I know?" she Snapped back. "You and your Jeff! I wish to the Lord I'd never come into this job. What's the graft, anyway? That flash crook knows all about it, Legge."

"Wh—Johnny Gray? Is he here? He did come, then?"

She nodded.

"What do you mean—'he knows'?"

"He knows Jeff—recognised him first pop," said the girl inelegantly, and Emanuel Legge whistled.

"Have you told Jeff that he has been recognised?"

The harsh features of Emanuel Legge were drawn and tense.

"What is the use of asking me? I haven't had a word with him. He's so taken up with this girl—"

"Forget it," said Legge with a gesture. "Tell me what this Johnny Gray says."

"I'll tell you one thing that amused me," said the girl grimly. "He said he'd throttle me if I squeaked! And he's got a fascinating pair of hands. I shouldn't like to play rough with that fellow—there's no use in tut-tutting me, Emanuel. I've told you all he said. He knows Jeff; he must have seen him before he went 'over the Alps'."

The old man was thinking, his brow furrowed, his lips pursed.

"It's pretty bad if he guesses, because he's sweet on the girl, and there's going to be trouble. Get Jeff out quick!"

"If you stay here, Peter will see you," she warned him. "Go down the lane and turn into the private path. I'll send Jeff to you in the lower garden." Nodding, he hurried away. It took her some time to find an opportunity, but presently she signalled the man with her eyes, and he followed her to the lawn.

"The old man's waiting down in the lower garden," she said in a low voice. "Hurry."

"What is wrong?" he asked quickly, sensing trouble.

"He'll tell you."

With a glance round Jeff hurried on to the terrace just as his father reached the rendezvous.

"Jeff, Gray knows."

The man drew a quick breath. "Me?" he said incredulously. "He didn't so much as bat a lid when I met him."

Emanuel nodded.

"That fellow's hell cool—the most dangerous crook in the world. I was in the Awful Place with him, and I know his reputation. There's nothing he's afraid of. If he tells Peter...shoot first! Peter won't be carrying a gun, but he's sure to have one within travelling distance—and Peter is a quick mover. I'll cover you; I've got two boys handy that 'mind' me, and Johnny...well, he'll get what's coming."

"What am I to do?"

Jeff Legge was biting his nails thoughtfully.

"Get the girl away—you're due to leave by car, ain't you? Get her to the Charlton Hotel. You're supposed to stay there a week—make it a day. Clear to Switzerland to-morrow and atop her writing. I'll fix Peter. He'll pay."

"For what?"

"To get his girl back; forty thousand—maybe more."

Jeff Legge whistled.

"I didn't see that side of the graft before. It's a new variety of 'black'."

"It's what I choose to call it!" hissed his father. "You're in fifty-fifty. You can have the lot so far as I care. You make that girl eat dirt, d'ye hear? Put her right down to earth, Jeff...Peter will pay."

"I promised Lila..." began the other, hesitant.

"Promise your Aunt Rebecca Jane!" Emanuel almost screamed. "Lila! That trash, and you the big man, too—what are ye running? A girls' refuge society? Get!"

"What about Gray?"

"I'll fix Gray!"

CHAPTER VII

THE old man made his way back to the road and passed quickly along until he came to the main highway. Two men were seated in the shade of a bush, eating bread and cheese. They came quickly enough when he whistled them, tall, broad-shouldered men whose heavy jowls had not felt a lather-brush for days.

"Either of you boys know Johnny Gray?" he asked.

"I was on the 'moor' with him," said one gruffly, "if he's the fellow that went down for 'ringing in 'horses?"

Emanuel nodded.

"He's in the house, and it's likely he'll walk to the station, and likely enough take the short cut across the fields. That'll be easy for you. He's got to be coshed—you understand? Get him good, even if you have to do it in the open. If there's anybody with him, get him in London. But get him."

Emanuel came back to his observation post as the first of the cars went into the drive. Jeff was moving quickly—and there was need.

Presently the car came out. Emanuel caught a glimpse of Jeff and the frightened face of the girl, and rubbed his hands in an ecstasy of satisfaction. Peter was standing in the middle of the road, watching the car. If he knew! The smile vanished from the old man's face. Peter did not know; he had not been told. Why? Johnny would not let her go, knowing. Perhaps Lila was lying. You can never trust women of that kind; they love sensation. Johnny...dangerous. The two words left one impression. And there was Johnny, standing, one hand in pocket, the other waving at the car as it came into brief view on the Shoreham road, as unconcerned as though he were the least interested.

A second car went in and came out. Some guests were leaving. Now, if Johnny had sense, he would be driven to London with a party. But Johnny hadn't sense. He was just a poor sucker, like all cheap crooks are. He came out alone, crossed the road and went down the narrow passage that led to the field path.

Emanuel looked backward. His bulldogs had seen and were moving parallel to the unconscious Gray.

From the road two paths led to the field, forming a Y where they met. Johnny had passed the fork when he heard the footsteps behind him. Glancing back, he saw a familiar face and did some shrewd guessing. He could run and easily outdistance these clumsy men. He preferred to face them, and turned, holding his malacca cane in both hands.

"Lo, Gray," said the bigger of the men. "Where'n thunder are you going in such a hurry? I want to talk with you, you dirty squeaker! You're the fellow that told the deputy I was getting tobacco in through a screw!"

It was a crude invention, but good enough to justify the rough house that was booked to follow. They carried sticks in their hands, pliable canes, shotted at the end.

The blow missed Johnny as he stepped back, and then something long and bright glittered in the afternoon sun. The scabbard of the sword cane he held defensively before him, the sword, thin and deadly, was pointed to the nearer of his enemies. They stopped, Saxon-like, appalled by the sight of steel. "Bad boy!" said Johnny reproachfully.

The razor-pointed rapier flickered from face to face, and the men stumbled back, getting into one another's way. One of the men felt something wet on his cheek, and put up his hand. When it came down it was wet and red.

"Beast, you have my brand!" said Johnny with deadly pleasantry. "Come when I call you."

He clicked the sword back in its wooden sheath and strode away. His indifference, his immense superiority, was almost as tremendously impressive as his cold toleration.

"He's ice, that fellow," said the man with the cut cheek. A sob of rage softened the rasp of his voice. "By...I'll kill him for that!"

But he made no attempt to follow, and his companion was glad.

John Gray increased his pace, and after a while emerged into the outskirts of the town. Here he found a Ford cab and reached the station in time to see the train pull out. He had made a mistake; the time-table had been changed that day, but in half an hour there was a fast train from Brighton that stopped only at Horsham.

He crossed the station yard to an hotel and was in the telephone booth for a quarter of an hour before he emerged, his collar limp, perspiration streaming down his face.

There was no sign of a familiar face when he came back to the platform. He expected to see Emanuel eventually, and here he was not disappointed, for Emanuel arrived a few minutes before the Brighton train came in.

Officially, it was their first meeting since they had been members of the same farm gang at Dartmoor, and Legge's expression of surprise was therefore appropriate.

"Why, if it isn't Gray! Well, fancy meeting you, old man! Well, this is a surprise! When did you come out?"

"Cease your friendly badinage," said Johnny shortly. "If we can get an empty compartment, I've got a few words to say to you, Emanuel."

"Been down to the wedding?" asked the old man slyly. "Nice girl, eh? Done well for herself? They tell me he's a Canadian millionaire. Ain't that Peter's luck! That fellow would fall off rock and drop in feathers, he's that lucky."

Johnny made no answer. When the train stopped and he found himself opposite a first-class carriage, he opened the door and Emanuel hopped in.

"If you're short of money—" began Legge.

"I'm not," said the other curtly. "I'm short of nothing except bad company. Now listen, Emanuel,"—the train was puffing slowly from the station when he spoke again—"I'm going to give you a chance."

The wide-eyed astonishment of Emanuel Legge was very convincing, but Johnny was not open to conviction at the moment.

"I don't get you, Johnny," he said. "What's all this talk about giving me a chance? Have you been drinking?"

Johnny had seated himself opposite the man, and now he leant forward and placed his hand upon the other's knee.

"Emanuel," he said gently, "call off that boy, and there'll be no squeak. Take that wounded fawn look from your face, because I haven't any time for fooling. You call off Jeff and send the girl back home to-night, or I squeak. Do you understand that?"

"I understand your words, Johnny Gray, but what they mean is a mystery to me." Emanuel Legge shook his head. "What boy are you talking about? I've only got one boy, and he's at college—"

"You're a paltry old liar. I'm talking about Jeff Legge, who married Peter's daughter to-day. I've tumbled to your scheme, Emanuel. You're getting even with Peter. Well, get even with him, but try some other way."

"She's married him of her own free will," began the man. "There's no law against that, is there, Johnny? Fell in love with him right on the spot! That's what I like to see, Johnny—young people in love."

If he hoped to rattle his companion he was disappointed.

"Now he can unmarry of his own free will," said Johnny calmly. "Listen to me, Emanuel Legge. When you arrive in London, you'll go straight away to the Charlton Hotel and talk very plainly to your son. He, being a sensible man, will carry out your instructions—"

"Your instructions," corrected Emanuel, his mouth twisted in a permanent smile. "And what happens if I don't, Johnny?"

"I squeak," said Johnny, and the smile broadened.

"They are married, old man. You can't divorce 'em. You can turn a brown horse into a black 'un, but you can't turn Mrs. Jeffrey Legge into Miss Marney Kane, clever as you are."

Johnny leant forward.

"I can turn Mr. Jeffrey Legge into Dartmoor Jail," he said unpleasantly, "and that's what I propose to do."

"On what charge?" Emanuel raised his eyebrows. "Give us a little rehearsal of this squeal of yours, Gray."

"He's the Big Printer," said Johnny, and the smile slowly dissolved. "The Government has spent thousands to catch him; they've employed the best secret service men in the world to pull him down, and I can give them just the information they want. I know where his stuff is planted. I know where it is printed; I know at least four of his agents. You think Jeff's secret is his own and yours, but you're mistaken, Emanuel. Craig knows he's the Big Printer; he told me so at lunch. All he wants is evidence, and the evidence I can give him. Old Reeder knows—you think he's a fool, but he knows. I could give him a squeak that would make him the cleverest lad in the world."

Emanuel Legge licked his dry lips.

"Going in for the 'con business, Johnny?" he asked banteringly. There was no amusement in his voice. "What a confidence man you'd make! You look like a gentleman, and talk like one. Why, they'd fall for you and never think twice! But that confidence stuff doesn't mean anything to me, Johnny. I'm too old and too wide to be bluffed—"

"There's no bluff here," interrupted Johnny. "I have got your boy like that!" He held out his hand and slowly clenched it.

For fully five minutes Emanuel Legge sat huddled in a corner of the compartment, staring out upon the flying scenery.

"You've got him like that, have you, Johnny boy?" he said gently. "Well, there's no use deceiving you, I can see. Slush is funny stuff—they call it 'phoney 'in America. Did you know that? I guess you would, because you're well educated. But it's good slush, Johnny. Look at this. He's a note. Is it good or bad?"

His fingers had gone into his waistcoat pocket and withdrew a thin pad of paper an inch square. Fold by fold he opened it out and showed a five-pound note. He caressed the paper with finger and thumb. The eyes behind the powerful glasses gleamed; the thin-lined face softened with pride.

"Is it good or bad, Johnny?"

Though the day was bright and hot, and not a cloud was in the sky, the four electric lamps in the carriage lit up suddenly. In the powerful light of day they seemed pale ghosts of flame, queerly dim. As the sunshine fell upon them their shadows were cast upon the white cornice of the carriage.

"There's a tunnel coming," said Emanuel. "It will give you a chance of seeing them at their best—feel 'em, Johnny! The real paper; bankers have fallen for 'em..."

With a roar the train plunged into the blackness of the tunnel. Emanuel stood with his back to the carriage door, the note held taut between his hands.

"There's only one flaw—the watermark. I'm giving away secrets, eh? Look!"

He stretched his arms up until he held the note against one of the bracket lamps. To see, John Gray had to come behind him and peer over his shoulder. The thunder of the train in the narrow tunnel was almost deafening.

"Look at the 'F'," shouted Emanuel. "See...that 'F' in 'Five'— it's printed too shallow..."

As Johnny bent forward the old man thrust at him with his shoulder, and behind that lurch of his was all the weight and strength of his body. Taken by surprise, John Gray was thrown from his balance. He staggered back against the carriage door, felt it give and tried to recover his equilibrium. But the thrust was too well timed. The door flew open, and he dropped into the black void, clutching as he did so the window ledge. For a second he swayed with the in and out swinging of the door. Then Legge's clenched fist hammered down on his fingers, and he dropped...

CHAPTER VIII

HE struck a layer of thick sand and turned a complete somersault. The wall of the tunnel caught and almost dislocated his arm, and he rebounded toward the whirling wheels. One wheel flicked him back against the wall, and he slid, his arms covering his face, the flint ballast of the road ripping his sleeves to ribbons...

He was alive. The train had passed. He saw the red tail-lights closing to one another. Gingerly he moved first one leg and then the other; then he rolled over toward the wall and lay on his back without further movement. His heart was pounding furiously; he felt a soreness working through the numb overlay of shock. Shock...shock sometimes killed men. His heart was going faster yet; he experienced a horrible nausea, and he found himself trembling violently.

The proper thing to do was to inject a solution of gum-acacia into his veins (his thoughts were curiously well ordered). Doctors did that; he remembered the doctor telling him at Dartmoor. But there was no gum-acacia to be had...Ten minutes later he lifted his body on his elbow and struggled to a sitting position. His head swam, but it did not ache; his arms...he felt them carefully. They were very sore, but no bones were broken.

A roadman at the exit of the tunnel nearly dropped with amazement as a grimy young man whose clothes were in rags emerged, limping.

"I fell out," said Johnny. "Can you tell me if there is anywhere I can hire a car?"

The roadman was going off duty and was willing to act as guide. Johnny hobbled up the steep slopes of the railway cutting, and with the assistance of the interested workman, traversed a wide field to the road. And then came a blessed sportsman on his way back from Gatwick Races, and he was alone in his car.

At first he looked suspicious at the bruised and ragged figure that had held him up. In the end he flung open the door by his side.

"Step up," he said.

To the railway worker Johnny had a few words to say.

"Here's five," he said. "Two for your help and three to stop your talking. I don't want this business to be reported, you understand? The truth is, I had been looking on the wine when it was red and gaveth its colour aright."

Johnny had evidently touched a sympathetic chord.

"You mean you was boozed?" said the man. "You can trust me."

The angel who drove him to London was not a talkative angel. Beyond expressing the wish that something drastic had happened to him before he went racing, and the advancement of his view that all racing was crooked and all jockeys thieves, he contributed little to the entertainment of his passenger, and the passenger was glad.

At the first cab-rank they struck—it was in Sutton—Johnny insisting upon alighting.

"I'll take you home if you like," said his gloomy benefactor.

Gently the other declined.

"My name is Lawford," said the motorist in a sudden outburst of confidence. "I've got an idea I know your face. Haven't I seen you on the track?"

"Not for some time," said Johnny.

"Rather like a fellow I once met...well, introduced to...fellow named Gay or Gray...regular rascal. He got time."

"Thanks," said Johnny, "that was I!" and the hitherto reticent Mr. Lawford became almost conversational in his apologies.

The young man finished the journey in a Sutton taxi and reached Queen's Gate late in the afternoon. Parker, who opened the door to him, asked no questions. "I have laid out another suit for you, sir," he returned to the study to say—the only oblique reference he made to his employer's disorder.

As he lay in a hot bath, soaking the stiffness out of his limbs, Johnny examined his injuries. They were more or less superficial, but he had had a terribly narrow escape from death, and he was not wholly recovered from the violence of it. Emanuel had intended his destruction. The attempt did not surprise him. Men of Legge's type worked that way. He met them in Dartmoor. They would go to a killing without fire of rage or frenzy of despair. Once he had seen a convict select with deliberation and care a large jagged stone and drop it upon the head of a man working in the quarry below. Fortunately, a warder had seen the act, and his shout saved the intended victim from mutilation. The assailant had only one excuse. The man he had attacked had slighted him in some way.

In the hearts of these men lived a cold beast. Johnny often pictured it, an obscene shape with pale, lidless eyes and a straight slit of a mouth. He had seen the beast staring at him from a hundred distorted faces, had heard its voice, had seen its hatefulness expressed in actions that he shivered to recall. Something of the beast had saturated into his own soul.

When he came from his bath, the masseur whom Parker had summoned was waiting, and for half an hour he groaned under the kneading hands.

The evening newspaper that Parker procured contained no news of the "accident"—Emanuel was hardly likely to report the matter, even for his own protection. There were explanations he could offer—Johnny thought of several.

Free from the hands of the masseur, he rested in his dressing-gown.

"Has anybody called?" he asked.

"A Mr. Reeder, sir."

Johnny frowned.

"Mr. Reeder?" he repeated. "What did he want?"

"I don't know, sir. He merely asked for you. A middle-aged man, with rather a sad face," said Parker. "I told him you were not at home, and that I would take any message for you, but he gave none."

His employer made no reply. For some reason, the call of the mysterious Mr. Reeder worried him more than the memory of the tragic happening of that afternoon, more, for the moment, than the marriage of Marney Kane.

CHAPTER IX

MARNEY made her journey to London that afternoon in almost complete silence. She sat in a corner of the limousine, and felt herself separated from the man she had married by a distance which was becoming immeasurable. Once or twice she stole a timid glance at him, but he was so preoccupied with his thoughts that he did not even notice. They were not pleasant thoughts, to judge by his unchanging scowl. All the way up he nibbled at his nails; a wrinkle between his eyes.

It was not until the big car was bowling across one of the river bridges that the strain was relieved, and he turned his head, regarding her coldly.

"We're going abroad to-morrow," he said, and her heart sank.

"I thought you were staying in town for a week, Jeff," she asked, trouble in her eyes. "I told father—"

"Does it matter?" he said roughly, and then she found courage to ask him a question that had been in her mind during that dreary ride.

"Jeff, what did you mean this morning, on the way back from the church... ? You frightened me."

Jeff Legge chuckled softly.

"I frightened you, did I?" he sneered. "Well, if that's all that's going to happen to you, you're a lucky girl!"

"But you're so changed..." she was bewildered. "I—I didn't want to marry you...I thought you wanted...and father was so very anxious... "

"Your father was very anxious that you should marry a man in good society with plenty of money," he said, emphasising every word. "Well, you've married him, haven't you? When I told you this morning that I'd got your father like that "—he put out his thumb suggestively—"I meant it. I suppose you know your father's a crook?"

The beautiful face flushed and went pale again.

"How dare you say that?" she asked, her voice trembling with anger. "You know it isn't true. You know!"

Jeffrey Legge closed his eyes wearily. "There's a whole lot of revelations coming to you, my good girl," he said, "but I guess we'd better wait till we reach the hotel."

Silence followed, until the car drew up before the awning of the Charlton, and then Jeff became his smiling, courteous self, and so remained until the door of their sitting-room closed upon them.

"Now, you've got to know something, and you can't know it too soon," he said, throwing his hat upon a settee. "My name isn't Floyd at all. I'm Jeffrey Legge. My father was a convict until six months ago. He was put in prison by Peter Kane."

She listened, open-mouthed, stricken dumb with amazement and fear.

"Peter Kane is a bank robber—or he was till fifteen years ago, when he did a job with my father, got away with a million dollars, and squeaked on his pal."

"Squeaked?" she said, bewildered.

"Your father betrayed him," said Jeffrey patiently. "I'm surprised that Peter hasn't made you acquainted with the technical terms of the business. He squeaked on his pal, and my father went down for twenty years."

"It is not true," she said indignantly. "You are inventing this story. My father was a broker. He never did a dishonest thing in his life. And if he had, he would never have betrayed his friend!" The answer seemed to amuse Legge.

"Broker, was he? I suppose that means he's a man who's broken into strong-rooms? That's the best joke I've heard for a long time! Your father's crook! Johnny knows he's crook. Craig knows he's crook. Why in hell do you think a broker should be a pal of a 'busy'? And take that look off your face— a 'busy' is a detective. Peter has certainly neglected your education!"

"Johnny knows?" she said, horror-stricken. "Johnny knows father is— I don't believe it! All you have told me is lies. If it were so, why should you want to marry me?"

Suddenly she realised the truth, and stood, frozen with horror, staring back at the smiling man.

"You've guessed, eh? We've been waiting to get under Peter's skin for years. And I guess we've got there. And now, if you like, you can tell him. There's a telephone; call him up. Tell him I'm Jeff Legge, and that all the wonderful dreams he has had of seeing you happy and comfortable are gone! Phone him! Tell him you never wanted to marry me, and it was only to make him happy that you did—you've got to break his heart, anyway. You might as well start now."

"He'd kill you," she breathed.

"Maybe he would. And that'd be a fine idea too. We'd have Peter on the trap. It would be worth dying for. But I guess he wouldn't kill me. At the sight of a gun in his hands, I'd shoot him like a dog. But don't let that stop you telling him, Marney darling."

He stretched out his hand, but she recoiled from him to horror and loathing.

"You planned it all...this was your revenge?"

He nodded.

"But Johnny...Johnny doesn't know."

She saw the change in the man's face, that suave assurance of his vanish.

"He does know." She pointed an accusing finger at him. "He knows!"

"He knows, but he let you go, honey," said Jeff. "He's one of us, and we never squeak. One of us!" he repeated the words mechanically.

She sat down and covered her face with her hands, and Jeffrey, watching her, thought at first that she was crying. When she raised her face, her eyes were dry. And, more extraordinary to him, the fear that he had seen there was no longer there.

"Johnny will kill you," she said simply. "He wouldn't let me go...like that...if he knew. It isn't reasonable to suppose that he would, is it?"

It was Jeff Legge's turn to be uncomfortable. Not at the menace of Johnny's vengeance, but at her utter calmness. She might have been discussing the matter impartially with a third person. For a moment he lost his grip of the situation. All that she said was so obviously, so patently logical, and instinctively he looked round as though he expected to find Johnny Gray at his elbow. The absurdity of the situation struck him, and he chuckled nervously.

"Johnny!" he sneered. "What do you expect Johnny to do, eh? He's just out of 'bird'—that's jail; it is sometimes called 'boob'—I see there's a whole lot of stuff you've got to learn before you get right into the family ways."

He lounged toward her and dropped his hands on her shoulders.

"Now, old girl," he said, "there are two things you can do. You can call up Peter and put him wise, or you can make the best of a bad job."

"I'll call father," she said, springing up. Before she could reach the telephone, his arm was round her, and he had swung her back.

"You'll call nothing," he said. "There's no alternative, my little girl. You're Mrs. Legge, and I lowered myself to marry the daughter of such a squealing old hound! Marney, give me a kiss."

You've not been very free with your tokens of affection, and I haven't pressed you, for fear of scaring you off. Always the considerate gentleman—that's Jeff Legge."

Suddenly she was in his arms, struggling desperately. He tried to reach her lips, but she buried her face in his coat, until, with a savage jerk that almost dislocated her shoulder, he had flung her at arm's distance. She looked up at the inflamed face and shuddered.

"I've got you, Marney." His voice was hoarse with triumph. "I've got you properly...legally. You're my wife! You realise that? No man can come between you and me."

He pulled her toward him, caught her pale face between his hands, and turned it up to his. With all the strength of utter horror and loathing, she tore herself free, fled to the door, flung it open, and stood back, wide-eyed with amazement.

In the doorway stood a tall, broad woman, with vividly red hair and a broad, good-humoured face. From her costume she was evidently one of the chambermaids of the hotel. From her voice she was most obviously Welsh.

"What are you doing here?" demanded Jeff. "Get out, damn you!"

"Why do you talk so at me now, look you? I will not have this bad language. The maid of this suite I am!"

Marney saw her chance of escaping, and, running into the room, slammed the door and locked it.

CHAPTER X

FOR a moment Jeff Legge stood, helpless with rage. Then he flung all his weight against the door, but it did not yield. He took up the telephone, but changed his mind. He did not want a scandal. Least of all did he wish to be advertised as Jeffrey Legge. Compromise was a blessed word —he knocked at the door.

"Marney, come out and be sensible," he said, "I was only joking. The whole thing was just to try you—"

She offered no reply. There was probably a telephone in the bedroom, he thought. Would she dare call her father? He heard another door unlocked. The bedroom gave on to the corridor, and he went out, to see the big chambermaid emerging. She was alone, and no sooner was she outside the door than it was locked upon her.

"I'll report you to the management," he said furiously. He could have murdered her without compunction. But his rage made no impression upon the phlegmatic Welsh woman.

"A good character I have, look you, from all my employers. To be in the bedroom, it was my business. You shall not use bad language to me, look you, or I will have the law on you!"

Jeffrey thought quickly. He waited in the corridor until the woman had disappeared, then he beckoned from the far end a man who was evidently the floor waiter.

"Go down to the office and ask the manager, with my compliments, if I can have a second set of keys to my rooms," he said suavely. "My wife wishes to have her own."

He slipped a bill into the man's hand, of such magnitude that the waiter was overwhelmed.

"Certainly, sir. I think I can arrange," he said.

"And perhaps you would lend me your pass key," said Jeff carelessly.

"I haven't a pass key, sir. Only the management have that," replied the man; "but I believe I can get you what you want."

He came back in a few minutes to the sitting-room with many apologies. There were no duplicate sets of keys.

Jeff closed the sitting-room door on the man and locked it. Then he went over to the bedroom door.

"Marney!" he called, and this time she answered him. "Are you going to be sensible?"

"I think I'm being very sensible," was her reply.

"Come out and talk to me."

"Thank you, I would rather remain here."

There was a pause.

"If you go to your father, I will follow and kill him. I've got to shoot first, you know, Marney, after what you've told me."

There was a silence, and he knew that his words had impressed her.

"Think it over," he suggested. "Take your time about it."

"Will you promise to leave me alone?" she asked.

"Why, sure, I'll promise anything," he said, and meant it. "Come out, Marney," he wheedled. "You can't stay there all day. You've got to eat."

"The woman will bring me my dinner," was the instant reply, and Jeffrey cursed her softly.

"All right, have it your own way," he said. "But I tell you this, that if you don't come out to-night, there will be trouble in your happy family."

He was satisfied, even though she did not answer him, that Marney would make no attempt to communicate with her father—that night, at least. After that night, nothing mattered.

He got on to the telephone, but the man he sought had not arrived. A quarter of an hour later, as he was opening his second bottle of champagne, the telephone bell tinkled and Emanuel Legge's voice answered him.

"She's giving me trouble," he said in a low voice, relating what had happened.

He heard his father's click of annoyance and hastened to excuse his own precipitancy.

"She had to know sooner or later."

"You're a fool," snarled the old man. "Why couldn't you leave it?"

"You've got to cover me here," said Jeff urgently. "If she phones to Peter, there is going to be trouble. And Johnny—"

"Don't worry about Johnny," said Emanuel Legge unpleasantly. "There will be no kick coming from him."

He did not offer any explanation, and Jeff was too relieved by the assurance in his father's voice to question him on the subject.

"Take a look at the keyhole," said Emanuel, "and tell me if the key's in the lock. Anyway, I'll send you a couple of tools, and you'll open that door in two jiffs—but you've got to wait until the middle of the night, when she's asleep."

Half an hour later a small package arrived by district messenger, and Jeffrey, cutting the sealed cord, opened the little box and picked out two curiously wrought instruments. For an hour he practised on the door of the second bedroom leading from the saloon, and succeeded in turning the key from the reverse side. Toward dinner-time he heard voices in Marney's bedroom, and, creeping to the door, listened. It was the Welsh woman, and there came to his ears the clatter of plates and cutlery, and he smiled. He had hardly got back to his chair and his newspaper when the telephone bell rang. It was the reception clerk.

"There's a lady to see you. She asked if you'd come down. She says it is very important."

"Who is it?" asked Jeffrey, frowning.

"Miss Lila."

"Lila!" He hesitated. "Send her up, please," he said, and drew a heavy velvet curtain across the door of Marney's room.

At the first sight of Peter Kane's maid he knew that she had left Horsham in a hurry. Under the light coat she wore he saw the white collar of her uniform.

"What's the trouble with you, Lila?" he asked.

"Where is Marney?" she asked.

He nodded to the curtained room.

"Have you locked her in?"

"To be exact, she locked herself in," said Jeff with a twisted smile.

The eyes of the woman narrowed. "Oh, it's like that, is it?" she asked harshly. "You haven't lost much time, Jeff."

"Don't get silly ideas in your nut," he said coolly. "I told her who I was, and there was a row—that's all there is to it. Now, what's the trouble?"

"Peter Kane's left Horsham with a gun in his pocket, that's all," she said, and Jeffrey paled.

"Sit down and tell me just what you mean."

"After you'd gone I went up to my room, because I was feeling mighty bad," she said. "I've got my feelings, and there isn't a woman breathing that can see a man go away with another girl—"

"Cut out all the sentiment and let's get right down to the facts," commanded Jeff.

"I'll tell it in my own way if you don't mind, Jeffrey Legge," said Lila.

"Well, get on with it," he said impatiently.

"I wasn't there long before I heard Peter in his room—it is underneath mine—and he was talking to himself. I guess curiosity got the better of my worry, and I went down and listened. I couldn't hear what he was saying, and so I opened the door of his room a little bit. He had just changed. The moment I went in he was slipping the magazine in the butt of a Browning—I saw him put it in his coat pocket, and then I went downstairs. After a while he came down too, and, Jeff, I didn't like the look of his face. It was all grey and pinched, and if ever I saw a devil in a man's eyes I saw it in Peter Kane's. I heard him order the car, and then I went down into the kitchen, thinking he was going at once. But he didn't leave for about half an hour."

"What was he doing?"

"He was in his own room, writing. I don't know what he was writing, because he always uses a black blotting-pad. He must have written a lot, because I know there were half a dozen sheets of stationery in the rack, and when I went in after he'd left they had all gone. There was nothing torn up in the waste-paper basket, and he'd burnt nothing, so he must have taken all the stuff with him. I tried to get you on the phone, but you hadn't arrived, and I decided to come up."

"How did you come up—by train or car?"

"By taxi. There wasn't a train for nearly two hours."

"You didn't overtake Peter by any chance?" She shook her head.

"I wouldn't. He was driving himself; his machine is a Spanz, and it moves!"

Jeff bit his nails. "That gun of Peter's worries me a little," he said after a while, "because he isn't a gunman. Wait."

He took up the telephone and again called his father, and in a few words conveyed the story which Lila had brought.

"You'll have to cover me now," he said anxiously. "Peter knows."

A long pause. "Johnny must have told him. I didn't dream he would," said Emanuel. "Keep to the hotel, and don't go out. I'll have a couple of boys watching both entrances, and if Peter shows his nose in Pall Mall he's going to be hurt."

Jeff hung up the receiver slowly and turned to the girl. "Thank you, Lila. That's all you can do for me."

"It is not all you can do for me," said Lila. "Jeff, what is going to happen now? I've tried to pin you down, but you're a little too shifty for me. You told me that this was going to be one of those high-class platonic marriages which figure in the divorce courts, and, Jeff, I'm beginning to doubt."

"Then you're a wise woman," said Jeffrey calmly. For a moment she did not understand the significance of the words.

"I'm a wise woman?" she repeated. "Jeff, you don't mean—"

"I'm entitled to my adventures," said Jeffrey, settling himself comfortably in the big armchair and crossing his legs. "I have a dear little wife, and for the moment, Lila, our little romance is finished."

"You don't mean that?" she asked unsteadily. "Jeff, you're kidding. You told me that all you wanted was to get a share of Peter's money, and Emanuel told me the same. He said he was going to put the 'black' on Peter and get away with forty thousand."

"In the meantime I've got away with the girl," said Jeffrey comfortably, "and there's no sense in kicking up a fuss, Lila. We've had a good time, and change is everything in life."

She was on her feet now, glaring down at him.

"And have I been six months doing slavey work, nosing for you, Jeffrey Legge, to be told that our little romance is finished?" she asked shrilly. "You've double-crossed me, you dirty thief! And if I don't fix you, my name's not Lila."

"It isn't," said Jeffrey. He reached for a cigar and lit it. "And never was. Your name's Jane—that is, if you haven't been telling me lies. Now, Lila, be an intelligent human being. I've put aside five hundred for you—"

"Real money, I hope," she sneered. "No, you're not going to get away with it so easy, Mr. Jeffrey Legge. You've fooled me from beginning to end, and you either carry out your promise or I'll—"

"Don't say you'll squeak," said Jeffrey, closing his eyes in mock resignation. "You're all squeakers. I'm tired of you! You don't think I'd give you anything to squeak about, do you? That I'd trust you farther than I could fling you? No, my girl, I'm four kinds of a fool, but not that kind. You know just as much about me as the police know, or as Johnny Gray knows. You can't tell my new wife, because she knows too. And Peter knows—in fact, I shouldn't be surprised if somebody didn't write a story about it in the newspapers to-morrow!"

He took out his pocket-case, opened it, and from a thick wad of notes peeled five, which he flung on to the table. "There's your 'monkey,' and au revoir, beauteous maiden,'" he said.

She took up the notes slowly, folded them, and slipped them into her bag. Her eyes were burning fires, her face colourless. If she had flown at him in a fury he would have understood, and was, in fact, prepared. But she said nothing until she stood, the knob of the door in her hand.

"There are three men after you, Jeffrey Legge," she said, "and one will get you. Reeder, or Johnny, or Peter—and if they fail, you look out for me!"

And on this threat she took her departure, slamming the door behind her, and Jeffrey settled down again to his newspaper, with the feeling of satisfaction which comes to a man who has got through a very unpleasant task.

CHAPTER XI

IN a long sedate road in suburban Brockley lived a man who had apparently no fixed occupation. He was tall, thin, somewhat cadaverous, and he was known locally as a furtive night-bird. Few had seen him in the daytime, and the inquisitive who, by skilful cross-examination, endeavoured to discover his business from a reticent housekeeper learnt comparatively little, and that little inaccurate. Policemen on night duty, morning wayfarers had seen him walking up Brockley Road in the early hours, coming apparently from the direction of London. He was known as Mr. J.G. Reeder. Letters in that name came addressed to him—large blue letters, officially stamped and sealed, and in consequence it was understood in postal circles that he held a Government position.

The local police force never troubled him. He was one of the subjects which it was not permissible to discuss. Until the advent of Emanuel Legge that afternoon, nobody ever remembered Mr. Reeder having a caller.

Emanuel had come from prison to the affairs of the everyday world with a clearer perception of values than his son. He was too old a criminal to be under any illusions. Sooner or later, the net of the law would close upon Jeffrey, and the immunity which he at present enjoyed would be at an end. To every graft came its inevitable lagging. Emanuel, wise in his generation, had decided upon taking the boldest step of his career. And that he did so was not flattering to the administration of justice; nor could it be regarded as a tribute to the integrity of the police.

Emanuel had "straightened" many a young detective, and not a few advanced in years. He knew the art of "dropping" to perfection. In all his life he had only met three or four men who were superior to the well-camouflaged bribe. A hundred here and there makes things easier for the big crook; a thousand will keep him out of the limelight; but, once the light is on him, not a million can disturb the inevitable march of justice. Emanuel was working in the pre-limelight stage, and hoped for success.

If his many inquiries were truthfully answered, the police had not greatly changed since his young days. Secret service men were new to him. He had thought, in spite of the enormous sums allocated to that purpose in every year's budget, that secret service was an invention of the sensational novelist and even now, he imagined Mr. Reeder to be one who was subsidised from the comparatively private resources of the banks rather than from the Treasury.

It was Emanuel's action to grasp the nettle firmly. "Infighting is not much worse than hugging," was a favourite saying of his, and once he had located Mr. J.G. Reeder, the night-hawk—and that had been the labour of months—the rest was easy. Always providing that Mr. Reeder was amenable to argument.

The middle-aged woman who opened the door to him gave him an unpromising reception.

"Mr. Reeder is engaged," she said, "and he doesn't want to see any visitors."

"Will you kindly tell him," said Emanuel with his most winning smile and a beam of benevolence behind his thick glasses, "that Mr. Legge from Devonshire would like to see him on a very particular matter of business?"

She closed the door in his face, and kept him so long waiting that he decided that even the magic of his name and its familiar association (he guessed) had not procured him an entry. But here he was mistaken. The door was opened for him, closed and bolted behind him, and he was led up a flight of stairs to the first floor.

The house was, to all appearance, well and comfortably furnished. The room into which he was ushered, if somewhat bare and official-looking, had an austerity of its own. Sitting behind a large writing-table, his back to the fireplace, was a man whom he judged to be between fifty and sixty. His face was thin, his expression sad. Almost on the end of his nose was clipped a pair of large, circular pince-nez. His hair was of that peculiar tint, red turning to grey, and his ears were large and prominent, seeming to go away from his head at right angles. All this Emanuel noted in a glance.

"Good morning, or good afternoon, Mr. Legge," said the man at the desk. He half rose and offered a cold and lifeless hand. "Sit down, will you?" he said wearily. "I don't as a rule receive visitors, but I seem to remember your name. Now where have I heard it?"

He dropped his chin to his breast and looked over his spectacles dolefully. Emanuel's expansive smile struck against the polished surface of his indifference and rebounded. He felt for the first time the waste of expansiveness.

"I had a little piece of information I thought I'd bring to you, Mr. Reeder," he said. "I suppose you know that I'm one of those unfortunate people who, through the treachery of others, have suffered imprisonment?"

"Yes, yes, of course," said Mr. Reeder in his weak voice, his chin still bent, his pale blue eyes fixed unwaveringly on the other. "Of course, I remember. You were the man who robbed the strong-room. Of course you were. Legge, Legge? I seem to remember the name too. Haven't you a son?"

"I have a son, the best boy in the world," said Emanuel fervently.

There was a telephone receiver at Mr. Reeder's right hand and throughout the interview he was polishing the black stem with the cuff of his alpaca coat, a nervous little trick which first amused and then irritated the caller.

"He has never been in trouble, Mr. Legge? Ah, that's a blessing," he sighed. "So many young people get into trouble nowadays."

If there was one person whom Legge did not want to discuss it was his son. He got off the subject as well as he could.

"I understand, Mr. Reeder, that you're doing special work for the Government—in the police department?"

"Not in the police department," murmured the other. "No, no, certainly not—not in the police department. I scarcely know a policeman. I see them often in the streets, and very picturesque figures they are. Mostly young men in the vigour and prime of youth. What a wonderful thing is youth, Mr. Legge! I suppose you're very proud of your son?"

"He's a good boy," said Emanuel shortly, and Mr. Reeder sighed again. "Children are a great expense," he said. "I often wonder whether I ought to be glad that I never married. What is your son by occupation, Mr. Legge?"

"An export agent," said Emanuel promptly.

"Dear, dear!" said the other, and shook his head. Emanuel did not know whether he was impressed or only sympathising.

"Being in Dartmoor, naturally I met a number of bad characters," said the virtuous Emanuel; "men who did not appeal to me, since I was perfectly innocent and only got my stretch—lagging—imprisonment through a conspiracy on the part of a man I've done many a good turn to—"

"Ingratitude," interrupted Mr. Reeder, drawing in his breath. "What a terrible thing is ingratitude! How grateful your son must be that he has a father who looks after him, who has properly

educated him and brought him up in the straight way, in spite of his own deplorable lapses!"
"Now, look here, Mr. Reeder." Emanuel thought it was time to get more definitely to business. "I'm a very plain man, and I'm going to speak plainly to you. It has come to my knowledge that the gentlemen you are acting for are under the impression that my boy's got to do with the printing of 'slush' —counterfeit notes. I was never more hurt in my life than when I heard this rumour. I said to myself: 'I'll go straight away to Mr. Reeder and discuss the matter with him. I know he's a man of the world, and he will understand my feelings as a father Some people, Mr. Reeder "—his elbows were on the table and he leant over and adopted a more confidential tone—"some people get wrong impressions. Only the other day somebody was saying to me: 'That Mr. Reeder is broke. He's got three county court summonses for money owed—"
"A temporary embarrassment," murmured Mr. Reeder. "One has those periods of financial—er—depression." He was polishing the stem of the telephone more vigorously.
"I don't suppose you're very well paid? I'm taking a liberty in making that personal statement, but as a man of the world you'll understand. I know what it is to be poor. I've had some of the best society people in my office,"—Emanuel invented the office on the spur of the moment —"the highest people in the land, and if they've said: 'Mr. Legge, can you oblige me with a thousand or a couple of thousand?' why, I've pulled it out, as it were, like this."
He put his hand in his pocket and withdrew it, holding a large roll of money fastened with a rubber band.
For a second Mr. J.G. Reeder allowed his attention to be distracted, and surveyed the pile of wealth with the same detached interest which he had given to Emanuel. Then, reaching out his hand cautiously, he took the note from the top, felt it, fingered it, rustled it, and looked quickly at the watermark.
"Genuine money," he said in a hushed voice, and handed the note back with apparent reluctance.
"If a man is broke," said Legge emphatically, "I don't care who he is or what he is, I say: 'Is a thousand or two thousand any good to you?"
"And is it?" asked Mr. Reeder.
"Is what?" said Emanuel, taken off his guard.
"Is it any good to him?"
"Well, of course it is," said Legge. "My point is this; a gentleman may be very hard pressed, and yet be the most solvent person in the world. If he can only get a couple of thousand just when he wants it—why, there's no scandal, no appearance in court which might injure him in his job—"
"How very true! How very, very true!" Mr. Reeder seemed profoundly touched. "I hope you pass on these wise and original statements to your dear son, Mr. Legge?" he said. "What a splendid thing it is that he has such a father!"
Emanuel cursed him under his breath.
"Two thousand pounds," mused Mr. Reeder. "Now, if you had said five thousand pounds—"
"I do say five thousand," said Emanuel eagerly. "I'm not going to spoil the ship for a ha'porth of tar."
"If you had said five thousand pounds," Mr. Reeder went on, "I should have known that three thousand was 'slush,' or shall we say 'phoney'— because you only drew two thousand from the City and Birmingham Bank this morning, all in hundred pound notes, series GI.19721 to 19740. Correct me if I'm wrong. Of course, you might have some other genuine money stowed away in your little hotel, Mr. Legge; or your dear boy may have given you another three thousand as a sort of wedding present—I forgot, though, a bridegroom doesn't give wedding presents, does he? He receives them. How foolish of me! Put away your money, Mr. Legge. This room is very

draughty, and it might catch cold. Do you ever go to the Hilly Fields? It is a delightful spot. You must come to tea with me one Sunday, and we will go up and hear the band. It is a very inexpensive but satisfactory method of spending two hours. As to those judgment summonses,"—he coughed, and rubbed his nose with his long forefinger—"those summonses were arranged in order to bring you here, I did so want to meet you, and I knew the bait of my impecuniosity would be almost irresistible."

Emanuel Legge sat, dumbfounded.

"Do you know a man named 'Golden'? Ah, he would be before your time. Have you ever heard of him? He was my predecessor. I don't think you met him. He had a great saying—set a 'brief' to catch a thief. We called a note a 'brief' in those days. Good afternoon, Mr. Legge. You will find your way down."

Legge rose, and with that the sad-faced man dropped his eyes and resumed the work he had been at when the visitor had interrupted him.

"I only want to say this, Mr. Reeder——" began Legge.

"Tell my housekeeper," pleaded Reeder weakly, and he did not look up. "She's frightfully interested in fairy stories—I think she must be getting towards her second childhood. Good afternoon, Mr. Legge."

CHAPTER XII

EMANUEL LEGGE was half-way home before he could sort out his impressions. He went back to the Bloomsbury Hotel where he was staying. There was no message for him, and there had been no callers. It was now seven o'clock. He wondered whether Jeff had restrained his impatience. Jeff must be told and warned. Johnny Gray, dead or maimed in a hospital, had ceased to be a factor. Peter Kane, for all his cunning and his vengefulness, might be dismissed as a source of danger. It was Mr. J.G. Reeder who filled his thoughts, the bored Civil Servant with a weak voice, who had such a surprising knowledge of things, and whose continuous pointed references to Jeffrey filled him with unquiet. Jeffrey must clear out of the country, and must go while the going was good. If he hadn't been such a fool, he would have moved that night. Now, that was impossible.

Peter had not arrived at the Charlton, or the men whom Legge had set to watch would have reported. If it had not been for the disturbing interview he had had with Reeder, he would have been more worried about Peter Kane; for when Peter delayed action, he was dangerous.

At eight o'clock that night, a small boy brought him a note to the hotel. It was addressed "E. Legge," and the envelope was grimy with much handling. Emanuel took the letter to his room and locked the door before he opened it. It was from a man who was very much on the inside of things, one of Jeff's shrewd but illiterate assistants, first lieutenant of the Big Printer, and a man to be implicitly trusted.

There were six closely written pages, ill-spelt and blotted. Emanuel read the letter a dozen times, and when he finished, there was panic in his heart.

"Johnny Gray got out of the tunnel all right, and he's going to squeak to Reeder," was the dramatic beginning, and there was a great deal more...

Emanuel knew a club in the West End of London, and his name was numbered amongst the members, even in the days when he had little opportunity of exercising his membership. It was a club rather unlike any other, and occupied the third and fourth floor of a building, the lower floors being in the possession of an Italian restaurateur. Normally, the proprietor of a fairly popular restaurant would not hire out his upper floors to so formidable a rival; but the proprietors of the club were also proprietors of the building, the restaurant keeper being merely a tenant.

It suited the membership of the Highlow Club to have their premises a little remote. It suited them better that no stairway led from the lower to the upper floors. Members of the club went down a narrow passage by the side of the restaurant entrance. From the end of the passage ran a small elevator, which carried them to the third floor. The County Council, in granting this concession, insisted upon a very complete fire escape system outside the building—a command which very well suited the members. Some there were who found it convenient to enter the premises by this latter method and a window leading into the club was left unfastened day and night against such a contingency.

On the flat roof of the building was a small superstructure, which was never used by the club members; whilst another part of the building, which also belonged exclusively to the Highlow, was the basement, to which the restaurant proprietor had no access—much to his annoyance, since it necessitated the building of a wine storage room in the limited space in the courtyard behind.

Stepping out of the elevator into a broad passage, well carpeted, its austere walls hung with etchings, Emanuel Legge was greeted respectfully by the liveried porter who sat behind a desk within sight of the lift. There was every reason why Emanuel should be respected at the Highlow, for he was, in truth, the proprietor of the club, and his son had exercised control of the place during many of the years his father had been in prison.

The porter, who was a big ex-prize fighter, expressly engaged for the purpose for which he was frequently required, hurried from his tiny perch to stand deferentially before his master.

"Anybody here?" asked Legge.

The man mentioned a few names.

"Let me see the engagement book," said the other, and the man produced from beneath the ledge of his desk a small, red book, and Emanuel turned the pages. The old man's hand ran down the list, and suddenly stopped.

"Oh, yes," he said softly, closing the book and handing it back.

"Are you expecting anybody, Mr. Legge?" asked the porter.

"No, I'm not expecting anybody...only I wondered..."

"Mr. Jeffrey got married to-day, I hear, sir? I'm sure all the staff wish him joy."

All the staff did not wish Mr. Jeffrey Legge joy, for neither he nor his father were greatly popular, even in the tolerant society of the Highlow, and moreover, strange as it may appear, very few people knew him by sight.

"That's very good of you, very good indeed," murmured Emanuel absently.

"Are you dining here, sir?"

"No, no, I'm not dining here. I just looked in, that is all." He stepped back into the elevator, and the porter watched it drop with pleasure. It was half-past eight; the glow was dying in the sky, and the lights were beginning to twinkle in the streets, as Emanuel walked steadily towards Shaftesbury Avenue.

Providentially, he was at the corner of a side street when he saw Peter Kane. He was near enough to note that under his thin overcoat Peter was in evening dress. Slipping into the doorway, he watched the man pass. Peter was absorbed in thought; his eyes were on the ground, and he had no interest for anything but the tremendous problem which occupied his mind.

Legge came back to the corner of the street and watched him furtively. Opposite the club, Peter stopped, looked up for a while, and passed on. The watcher laughed to himself. That club could have no pleasant memories for Peter Kane that night; it was in the Highlow that he had met the "young Canadian officer" and had "rescued" him, as he had thought, from his dangerous surroundings. There had Peter been trapped, for the introduction of Jeff Legge was most skilfully arranged. Going into the club one night, Peter saw, as he thought, a young, good-looking soldier boy in the hands of a gang of cardsharpers, and the "rescued officer" had been most grateful, and had called upon Peter at the earliest opportunity. So simple, so very simple, to catch Peter. It would be a more difficult matter, thought Emanuel, for Peter to catch him.

He waited until the figure had disappeared in the gloom of the evening, and then walked back to the Avenue. This comedy over, there remained the knowledge of stark tragedy, of danger to his boy, and the upsetting of all his plans, and, the most dreadful of all possibilities, the snaring of the Big Printer. This night would the battle be fought, this night of nights would victory or defeat be in his hands. Reeder—Johnny—Peter Kane—all opposed him, innocent of their co-operation, and in his hands a hostage beyond price—the body and soul of Marney Legge.

He had scarcely disappeared when another person known to him came quickly along the quiet street, turned into the club entrance, and, despite the expostulations of the elevator man, insisted upon being taken up. The porter had heard the warning bell and stood waiting to receive her when the door of the elevator opened.

"Where's Emanuel?" she asked.

"Just gone," said the porter.

"That's a lie. I should have seen him if he'd just gone."

She was obviously labouring under some emotion, and the porter, an expert on all stages of feminine emotionalism, shrewdly diagnosed the reason for her wildness of manner and speech. "Been a wedding to-day, hasn't there?" he asked with heavy jocularity. "Now, Lila, what's the good of kicking up a fuss? You know you oughtn't to come here. Mr. Legge gave orders you weren't to be admitted whilst you were at Kane's."

"Where is Emanuel?" she asked.

"I tell you he's just gone out," said the porter in a tone of ponderous despair. "What a woman you are! You don't believe anything!"

"Has he gone back to his hotel?"

"That's just where he has gone. Now be wise, girl, and beat it. Anybody might be coming here—Johnny Gray was in last night, and he's a pal of Peter's."

"Johnny knows all about me," she said impatiently. "Besides, I've left Peter's house."

She stood undecidedly at the entrance of the open elevator, and then, when the porter was preparing some of his finest arguments for her rapid disappearance, she stepped into the lift and was taken down.

The Highlow was a curious club, for it had no common room. Fourteen private dining-rooms and a large and elegantly furnished card-room constituted the premises. Meals were served from the restaurant below, being brought up by service lift to a small pantry. The members of the club had not the club feeling in the best sense of the word. They included men and women, but the chief reason for the club's existence was that it afforded a safe and not unpleasant meeting-place for members of the common class, and gave necessary seclusion for the slaughter of such innocents as came within the influence of its more dexterous members. How well its inner secrets were kept is best illustrated by the fact that Peter Kane had been a member for twenty years without knowing that his sometime companion in crime had any official connection with its control. Nor was it ever hinted to him that the man who was directing the club's activities during Emanuel's enforced absence, was his son.

Peter was a very infrequent visitor to the Highlow; and indeed, on the occasion of his first meeting with the spurious Major Floyd, he had been tricked into coming, though this he did not know.

The porter was busy until half-past nine. Little parties came, were checked off in the book, and then—he looked at his watch.

"Twenty-five to ten," he said, and pushed a bell button.

A waiter appeared from the side passage.

"Put a bottle of wine in No. 13," he said.

The waiter looked at him surprised.

"No. 13?" he said, as if he could not believe his ears.

"I said it," confirmed the porter.

Jeffrey ate a solitary dinner. The humour of the situation did not appeal to him. On his honeymoon, he and his wife were dining, a locked door between them. But he could wait. Again he tried the queer-shaped pliers upon the key of the second bedroom. The key turned readily. He put the tool into his pocket with a sense of power. The clatter of a table being cleared came to him from the other room, and presently he heard the outer door close and a click of the key turning. He lit his fourth cigar and stepped out on to the balcony, surveying the crowded street with a dispassionate interest. It was theatre time. Cars were rolling up to the Haymarket; the long queue that he had seen waiting at the doors of the cheaper parts of the house had disappeared; a restaurant immediately opposite was blazing with lights; and on a corner of the street a band of ex-soldiers were playing the overture of "Lohengrin."

Glancing down into the street, he distinguished one of the "minders" his father had put there for his protection, and grinned. Peter could not know; he would have been here before. As to Johnny...? Emanuel had been very confident that Johnny presented no danger, and it rather looked as though Emanuel's view was right. But if Peter knew, why hadn't he come?

He strolled back to the room, looked at the girl's door and walked toward it.

"Marney!" he called softly.

There was no answer. He knocked on the panel.

"Marney, come along. I want to talk to you. You needn't open the door. I just wanted to ask you something."

Still there was no answer. He tried the door; it was locked.

"Are you there?" he called sharply, but she did not reply.

He pulled the pliers from his pocket, and, pushing the narrow nose into the keyhole, gripped the end of the key and turned it. Then, flinging open the door, he rushed in.

The room was empty, and the big bathroom that led out of the suite was empty also. He ran to the passage door: it was locked—locked from the outside. In a sweat of fear he flew through the saloon into the corridor, and the first person he saw was the floor waiter.

"Madam, sir? Yes, she went out a little time ago."

"Went out, you fool? Where?" stormed Jeff.

"I don't know, sir. She just went out. I saw her going along the corridor."

Jeff seized his hat and went down the stairs three at a time. The reception clerk had not seen the girl, nor had any of the pages, or the porter on the door. Oblivious to any immediate danger, he dashed out into the street, and, looking up and down, saw the minder and called him.

"She hasn't come out this entrance. There's another in "Pall Mall," he explained. "Jimmy Low's there."

But the second man on the Pall Mall entrance had not seen her either. Jeff went back to interview the manager.

"There is no other way out. Sir, unless she went down the service stairs."

"It was that cursed maid, the Welsh woman," snarled Jeffrey. "Who is she? Can I see her?"

"She went off duty this afternoon, sir," said the manager. "Is there anything I can do? Perhaps the lady has gone out for a little walk? Does she know London?"

Jeff did not stop to reply: he fled up the stairs, back to the room, and made a quick search. The girl's dressing-case, which he knew had been taken into the bedroom, was gone. Something on the floor attracted his attention. He picked it up, and read the few scribbled lines, torn from a notebook; and as he read, a light came into his eyes. Very carefully he folded the crumpled sheet and put it into his pocket. Then he went back to his sitting-room, and sat for a long time in the big arm-chair, his legs thrust out before him, his hands deep in his trousers pockets, and his thoughts were not wholly unpleasant.

The light was now nearly gone, and he got up. "Room thirteen," he said. "Room thirteen is going to hold a few surprises to-night!"

CHAPTER XIII

TO Parker, the valet, as he laid out Johnny's dress clothes, there was a misfortune and a tragedy deeper than any to which Johnny had been a spectator. Johnny, loafing into his bedroom, a long, black, ebonite cigarette-holder between his teeth, found his man profoundly agitated.
"The buckle of your white dress waistcoat has in some unaccountable way disappeared," he said in a hushed voice. "I'm extremely sorry, sir, because this is the only white dress waistcoat you have."
"Be cheerful," said Johnny. "Take a happier view of life. You can tie the tapes behind. You could even sew me together, Parker. Are you an expert needle worker, or do you crochet?"
"My needlework has been admired, sir," said Parker complacently. "I think yours is an excellent suggestion. Otherwise, the waistcoat will not sit as it should. Especially in the case of a gentleman with your figure."
"Parker," said Johnny, as he began to dress leisurely, "have you ever killed a man?"
"No, sir, I have never killed a man," said Parker gravely. "When I was a young man, I once ran over a cat—I was a great cyclist in my youth."
"But you never killed a man? And, what is more, you've never even wanted to kill a man?"
"No, sir, I can't say that I ever have," said Parker after a few moments' consideration, as though it were possible that some experience had been his which had been overlooked in the hurry of his answering.
"It is quite a nice feeling, Parker. Is there a hip pocket to these —yes, there is," he said, patting his trousers.
"I'm sorry there is," said Parker, "very sorry indeed. Gentlemen get into the habit of carrying their cigarette cases in the hip pocket, with the result that the coat tail is thrown out of shape. That is where the dinner jacket has its advantages—the Tuxedo, as an American gentleman once called it, though I've never understood why a dinner jacket should be named after a Scottish town."
"Tuxedo is in Dixie," said Johnny humorously, "and Dixie is America's lost Atlantis. Don't worry about the set of my coat tail. I am not carrying my cigarette case there."
"Anything more bulky would of course be worse, sir," said Parker, and Johnny did not carry the discussion any farther.
"Get me a cab," he ordered.
When Parker returned, he found his master was fully dressed.
"You will want your cane, sir. Gentlemen are carrying them now in evening dress. There is one matter I would like to speak to you about before you go —it is something that has been rather worrying me for the past few days."
Johnny was leaving the room, and turned.
"Anything serious?" he asked, for a moment deceived.
"I don't like telling you, sir, but I have discussed the matter with very knowledgeable people, and they are agreed that French shapes are no longer worn in silk hats. You occasionally see them in theatrical circles—"|
Johnny put up a solemn hand.
"Parker, do not let us discuss my general shabbiness. I didn't even know I had a hat of French shape." He took off his hat and looked at it critically. "It is a much better shape than the hat I was

wearing a week ago, Parker, believe me!"

"Of course I believe you, sir," agreed Parker, and turned to the door.

Johnny dismissed his cab in Shaftesbury Avenue and walked down toward the club. It was dark now; half-past nine had chimed as he came along Piccadilly.

It was a point of honour with all members of the Highlow that nobody drove up to the club, and its very existence was unknown to the taximen. That was a rule that had been made, and most faithfully adhered to; and the members of the Highlow observed their rules, for, if a breach did not involve a demand for their resignation, it occasionally brought about a broken head.

Just before he reached the club, he saw somebody cross the road. It was not difficult to recognise Jeff Legge. Just at that moment it would have been rather embarassing for Johnny to have met the man. He turned and walked back the way he had come, to avoid the chance of their both going up in the elevator together.

Jeff Legge was in a hurry: the elevator did not move fast enough for him, and he stepped out on to the third floor and asked a question.

"No, sir, nobody has come. If they do, I'll send them along to you. Where will you be? You haven't a room engaged—your own room is taken. We don't often let it, but we're full to-night, and Mr. Legge raised no objection."

"No, I don't object," said Jeff; "but don't you worry about that. Let me see the book."

Again the red-covered engagement book was opened. Jeff read and nodded.

"Fine," he said. "Now tell me again who is here."

"There is Mr. George Kurlu, with a party of friends in No. 3; there's Mr. Bob Albutt and those two young ladies he goes about with—they're in No. 4." And so he recited until he came to No. 13.

"I know all about No. 13," said Jeff Legge between his teeth. "You needn't bother about me, however. That will do."

He strode along the carpeted hallway, turned abruptly into the right-angled passage, and presently stopped before a door with a neat golden "13" painted on its polished panel. He opened the door and went in. On the red-covered table was a bottle of wine and two glasses.

It was a moderately large room, furnished with a sofa, four dining chairs and a deep easy chair, whilst against one wall was a small buffet. The room was brilliantly lighted. Six bracket lamps were blazing; the centre light above the table, with its frosted bulbs, was full on. He did not shut the door, leaving it slightly ajar. There was too much light for his purpose. He first switched out the bracket lamps, and then all but one of the frosted bulbs in the big shaded lamp over the table. Then he sat down, his back to the door, his eyes on the empty fire-grate.

Presently he heard a sound, the whining of the elevator, and smiled. Johnny stepped out to the porter's desk with a friendly nod.

"Good evening, Captain," said the porter with a broad grin. "Glad to see you back, sir. I wasn't here last night when you came in. Hope you haven't had too bad a time in the country?"

"Abroad, my dear fellow, abroad," murmured the other reproachfully, and the porter chuckled.

"Same old crowd, I suppose?"

"Yes, sir."

"Same old bolt down the fire-escape when the 'busies' call—or have you got all the 'busies' straightened?"

"I don't think there's much trouble, sir," said the porter. "We often have a couple of those gentlemen in here to dinner. The club's very convenient sometimes. I shouldn't think they'll ever shut us up."

"I shouldn't think so, either," said Johnny. "Which of the 'busies' do you get?"

"Well, sir, we get Mr. Craig, and—once we had that Reeder. He came here alone, booked a table and came alone! Can you beat it? Came and had his dinner, saw nobody and went away again. I don't think he's right up there "—he tapped his forehead significantly. "Anything less like a 'busy' I've never seen."

"I don't know whether he is a detective," said Johnny carelessly. "From all I've heard, he has nothing whatever to do with the police."

"Private, is he?" said the other in a tone of disappointment.

"Not exactly private. Anyway," with a smile, "he's not going to bother you or our honourable members. Anybody here?"

The porter looked to left and right, and lowered his voice.

"A certain person you know is here," he said meaningly.

Johnny laughed.

"It would be a funny club if there wasn't somebody I knew," he said. "Don't worry about me; I'll find a little corner for myself..."

* * * * *

Jeff looked at his watch; it was a quarter to ten, and he glanced up at the light; catching a glimpse of himself in the mirror of the buffet, was satisfied.

Room 13! And Marney was his wife! The blood surged up into his face, gorging the thick veins in his temples at the thought. She should pay! He had helped the old man, as he would help him in any graft, but he had never identified himself so completely with the plan as he did at that moment.

"Put her down to the earth," had said Emanuel, and by God he would do it. As for Johnny Gray... The door opened stealthily, and a hand came in, holding a Browning. He heard the creak of the door but did not look round, and then: "Bang!"

Once the pistol fired. Jeff felt a sharp twitch of pain, exquisite, unbearable, and fell forward on his knees.

Twice he endeavoured to rise, then with a groan fell in a huddled heap, his head in the empty fireplace.

CHAPTER XIV

THE doors and the walls of the private dining-rooms were almost sound-proof. No stir followed the shot. In the hall outside, the porter lifted his head and listened.
"What was that?" he asked the waiting elevator man.
"Didn't hear anything," said the other laconically. "Somebody slammed a door."
"Maybe," said the porter, and went back to his book. He was filling in the names of that night's visitors, an indispensable record in such a club, and he was filling them in with pencil, an equally necessary act of caution, for sometimes the club members desired a quick expungement of this evidence.
In Room 13 silence reigned. A thin blue cloud floated to the ceiling; the door opened a little farther, and Johnny Gray came in, his right hand in his overcoat pocket.
Slowly he crossed the room to where the huddled figure lay, and, stooping, turned it upon its back. Then, after a brief scrutiny, his quick hands went through the man's pockets. He found something, carried to it the light, read with a frown and pushed the paper into his own pocket. Going out, he closed the door carefully behind him and strolled back to the hall.
"Not staying, Captain?" asked the porter in surprise.
"No, nobody I know here. Queer how the membership changes."
The man on duty was too well trained to ask inconvenient questions.
"Excuse me. Captain." He went over to Johnny and bent down. "You've got some blood on your cuff."
He took out his handkerchief and wiped the stain clean. Then his frowning eyes met the young man's.
"Anything wrong, Captain?"
"Nothing that I can tell you about," said Johnny; "Good night."
"Good night, sir," said the porter.
He stood by his desk, looking hard at the glass doors of the elevator, heard the rattle of the gate as it opened, and the whine of the lift as it rose again.
"Just stay here, and don't answer any rings till I come back," he said.
He hurried along the corridor into the side passage and, coming to No. 13, knocked. There was no answer. He turned the handle. One glance told him all he wanted to know. Gently he closed the door and hurried back to the telephone on his desk.
Before he raised the receiver he called the gaping lift-boy.
"Go to all the rooms, and say a murder has been committed. Get everybody out."
He was still clasping the telephone with damp hands when the last frightened guest crowded into the elevator, then:
"Highlow Club speaking. Is that the Charing Cross Hospital?...I want an ambulance here...Yes, 38, Boburn Street...There's been an accident."
He rung off and called another number.
"Highlow Club. Is that the police station?...It's the porter at the Highlow Club speaking, sir. One of our members has shot himself."
He put down the instrument and turned his face to the scared elevator man who had returned to the high level. At the end of the passage stood a crowd of worried waiters.
"Benny," he said, "Captain Gray hasn't been here to-night. You understand? Captain—Gray—

has—not—been—here—to-night."

The guest-book was open on the desk. He took his pencil and wrote, on the line where Johnny Gray's name should have been, "Mr. William Brown of Toronto."

CHAPTER XV

THE last of the guests had escaped, when the police came, and, simultaneously with the ambulance, Divisional-Inspector Craig, who had happened to be making a call in the neighbourhood. The doctor who came with the ambulance made a brief examination.
"He is not dead, though he may be before he reaches hospital," he said.
"Is it a case of suicide?"
The doctor shook his head.
"Suicides do not, as a rule, shoot themselves under the right shoulder-blade. It would be a difficult operation: try it yourself. I should say he'd been shot from the open doorway."
He applied a rough first dressing, and Jeffrey was carried into the elevator. In the bottom passage a stretcher was prepared, and upon this he was laid, and, covered with a blanket, carried through the crowd which had assembled at the entrance.
"Murder, or attempted murder, as the case may be," said Craig. "Someone has tipped off the guests. You, I suppose, Stevens? Let me see your book."
The inspector ran his finger down the list, and stopped at Room 13.
"Mr. William Brown of Toronto, Who is Mr. Brown of Toronto?"
"I don't know, sir. He engaged a room by telephone, I didn't see him go."
"That old fire-escape of yours still working?" asked Craig sardonically. "Anybody else been here? Who is the wounded man? His face seemed familiar to me."
"Major Floyd, sir."
"Who?" asked Craig sharply. "Impossible! Major Floyd is—" It was Floyd! He remembered now. Floyd, with whom he had sat that day—that happily-married man!
"What was he doing here?" he asked. "Now, spill it, Stevens, unless you want to get yourself into pretty bad trouble."
"I've spilled all I know, sir," said Stevens doggedly. "It was Major Floyd."
And then an inspiration came to him.
"If you want to know who it was, it was Jeff Legge. Floyd's his fancy name."
"Who?"
Craig had had many shocks in his life, but, this was the greatest he had had for years.
"Jeff Legge? Old Legge's son?"
Stevens nodded.
"Nobody knows that but a couple of us," he said. "Jeff doesn't work in the light."
The officer nodded slowly.
"I've never seen him," he admitted. "I knew Legge had a son, but I didn't know he was running crook. I thought he was a bit of a boy."
"He's some boy, let me tell you!" said Stevens.
Craig sat down, his chin in his hands.
"Mrs. Floyd will have to be told. Good God! Peter Kane's daughter! Peter didn't know that he'd married her to Legge's son?"
"I don't know whether he knew or not," said Stevens, "but if I know old Peter, he'd as soon know that she'd gone to the devil as marry her to a son of Emanuel Legge's. I'm squeaking in a way," he said apologetically, "but you've got to know—Emanuel will tell you as soon as he gets the news."

"Come here," said Craig. He took the man's arm and led him to the passage where the detectives were listening, opened the door of a private room, the table giving evidence of the hasty flight of the diners. "Now," he said, closing the door, "what's the strength of this story?"

"I don't know it all, Mr. Craig, but I know they were putting a point on Peter Kane a long time ago. Then one night they brought Peter along and kidded him into thinking that Jeff was a sucker in the hands of the boys. Peter had never seen Jeff before—as a matter of fact, I didn't know he was Jeff at the time; I'd heard a lot about him, but, like a lot of other people, I hadn't seen him. Well, they fooled Peter all right. He took the lad away with him. Jeff was wearing a Canadian officer's uniform, and, of course, Jeff told the tale. He wouldn't be the son of his father if he didn't. That's how he got to know the Kanes, and was taken to their home. When I heard about the marriage, I thought Peter must have known. I never dreamt they were playing a trick on him."

"Peter didn't know," said Craig slowly. "Where's the girl?"

"I can't tell you. She's in London somewhere."

"At the Charlton," nodded the other. "Now, you've got to tell me, Stevens, who is Mr. Brown of Toronto? It's written differently from your usual hand —written by a man who has had a bad scare. In other words, it was written after you'd found the body."

Stevens said nothing.

"You saw him come out; who was he?"

"If I die this minute—" began Stevens.

"You might in a few months, as 'accessory after,'" said the other ominously; "and that's what you'll do if you conceal a murderer. Who is Mr. Brown?"

Stevens was struggling with himself, and after a while it came out.

"Johnny was here to-night," he said huskily. "Johnny Gray."

Craig whistled.

There was a knock at the door. A police officer, wanting instructions.

"There's a woman down below, pretty nigh mad. I think you know her, sir."

"Not Lila?" blurted Stevens.

"That's the girl. Shall I let her come up?"

"Yes," said Craig. "Bring her in here."

She came in a minute, distracted, incoherent, her hair dishevelled, her hands trembling.

"Is he dead?" she gasped. "For God's sake tell me. I see it in your face —he's dead. Oh, Jeff, Jeff!"

"Now you sit down," said the kindly Craig. "He's no more dead than you or I are. Ask Stevens. Jeff's doing very well indeed. Just a slight wound, my dear—nothing to worry about. What was the trouble? Do you know anything about it?"

She could not answer him.

"He's dead," she moaned. "My God, I killed him! I saw him and followed him here!"

"Give her a glass of wine, Stevens."

The porter poured out a glass of white wine from one of the many deserted bottles on the table, and put it to her chattering teeth.

"Now, Lila, let's get some sense out of you. I tell you, Jeff's not dead. What is he to you, anyway?"

"Everything," she muttered. She was shivering from head to foot. "I married him three years ago. No, I didn't," she said in a sudden frenzy.

"Go on; tell us the truth," said Craig. "We're not going to pull him for bigamy, anyway."

"I married him three years ago," she said. "He wasn't a bad fellow to me. It was the old man's idea, his marrying this girl, and there was a thousand for me in it. He put me down in Horsham to look after her, and see that there were no letters going to Johnny. There wasn't any need of that, because she never wrote. I didn't like the marriage idea, but he swore to me that it was only to get Peter's money, and I believed him. Then to-night he told me the truth, knowing I wouldn't squeak. I wish to God I had now, I wish I had! He is dead, isn't he? I know he's dead!"

"He's not dead, you poor fish," said Craig impatiently. "I might be congratulating you if he was. No, he's got a bit of a wound."

"Who shot him?"

"That's just what I want to know," said Craig. "Was it you?"

"Me!" Her look of horror supplied a satisfactory answer to his question. "No, I didn't. I didn't know he was here, or coming here. I thought he was at the hotel, till I saw him. Yet I had a feeling that he was coming here to-night, and I've been waiting about all evening. I saw Peter and dodged him."

"Peter? Has he been near the club?"

She shook her head.

"I don't know. He was on his way. I thought he was going to the Highlow. There's nowhere else he'd go in this street—I saw him twice."

Craig turned his bright, suspicious eyes upon the porter.

"Peter been here? I didn't see anything about Mr. Brown of Montreal?" he asked sarcastically.

"No, he hasn't. I haven't seen Peter since the Lord knows when," said the porter emphatically. "That's the truth. You can give the elevator boy permission to tell you all he knows, and if Peter was here to-night you can hang me."

Craig considered for a long time.

"Does Peter know his way in by the easy route?" he asked.

"You mean the fire-escape? Yes, Peter knows that way, but members never come in by the back nowadays. They've got nothing to hide."

Craig went out of the room and walked down the passage stopping at No. 13. Immediately opposite the door was a window, and it was wide open. Beyond was the grille of the fire-escape landing. He stepped out through the window and peered down into the dark yard where the escape ended. By the light of a street lamp he saw a stout gate, in turn pierced by a door, and this led to the street. The door was open, a fact which might be accounted for by the presence in the yard of two uniformed policemen, the flash of whose lanterns he saw. He came back into the corridor and to Stevens.

"Somebody may have used the fire-escape to-night, and they may not," he said. "What time did Gray come in? Who came in first?"

"Jeff came first, about five minutes before Gray."

"Then what happened?"

"I had a chat with Captain Gray," said the porter, after a second's hesitation. "He went round into the side passage—"

"The same way that Jeff had gone?"

The porter nodded.

"About a minute later—in fact, it was shorter than a minute —I heard what I thought was a door slammed. I remarked upon the fact to the elevator man."

"And then?"

"I suppose four or five minutes passed after that, and Captain Gray came out. Said he might look in later."

"There was no sign of a struggle in Captain Gray's clothes?"

"No, sir. I'm sure there was no struggle."

"I should think not," agreed Craig. "Jeff Legge never had a chance of showing fight."

The girl was lying on the sofa, her head buried in her arms, her shoulders shaking, and the sound of her weeping drew the detective's attention to her.

"Has she been here before to-night?"

"Yes, she came, and I had to throw her out—Emanuel told me she was not to be admitted."

Craig made a few notes in his book, closed it with a snap and put it in his pocket.

"You understand, Stevens, that, if you're not under arrest, you're under open arrest. You'll close the club for to-night and admit no more people. I shall leave a couple of men on the premises."

"I'll lock up the beer," said Stevens facetiously.

"And you needn't be funny," was the sharp retort. "If we close this club you'll lose your job—and if they don't close it now they never will."

He took aside his assistant.

"I'm afraid Johnny's got to go through the hoop to-night," he said. "Send a couple of men to pull him in. He lives at Albert Mansions. I'll go along and break the news to the girl, and somebody'll have to tell Peter—I hope there's need for Peter to be told," he added grimly.

CHAPTER XVI

A SURPRISE awaited him when he came to the Charlton. Mrs. Floyd had gone—nobody knew whither. Her husband had followed her some time afterwards, and neither had returned. Somebody had called her on the telephone, but had left no name.

"I know all about her husband not returning," said Craig. "But haven't you the slightest idea where the lady is?"

"No."

The negative reply was uncompromising.

"Her father hasn't been here?"

His informant hesitated.

"Yes, sir; he was on Mrs. Floyd's floor when she was missing—in fact, when Major Floyd was down here making inquiries. The floor waiter recognised him, but did not see him come or go."

Calling up the house at Horsham he learnt, what he already knew, that Peter was away from home. Barney, who answered him, had heard nothing of the girl; indeed, this was the first intimation he had had that all was not well. And a further disappointment lay in store for him. The detective he had sent to find Johnny returned with the news that the quarry had gone. According to the valet, his master had returned and changed in a hurry, and, taking a small suit-case, had gone off to an unknown destination.

An inquiry late that night elicited the fact that Jeff was still living, but unconscious. The bullet had been extracted, and a hopeful view was taken of the future. His father had arrived early in the evening, and was half mad with anxiety and rage. "And if he isn't quite mad by the morning, I shall be surprised," said the surgeon. "I'm going to keep him here and give him a little bromide to ease him down."

"Poison him," suggested Craig.

When the old detective was on the point of going home, there arrived a telephone message from the Horsham police, whom he had enlisted to watch Peter's house.

"Mr. Kane and his daughter arrived in separate motorcars at a quarter past twelve," was the report. "They came within a few minutes of one another."

Craig was on the point of getting through to the house, but thought better of it. A fast police car got him to Horsham under the hour, the road being clear and the night a bright one. Lights were burning in Peter's snuggery, and it was he himself who, at the sound of the motor wheels, came to the door.

"Who's that?" he asked, as Craig came up the dark drive, and, at the sound of the detective's voice, he came half-way down the drive to meet him. "What's wrong, Craig? Anything special?"

"Jeff's shot. I suppose you know who Jeff is?"

"I know, to my sorrow," said Peter Kane promptly. "Shot? How? Where?"

"He was shot this evening between a quarter to ten and ten o'clock, at the Highlow Club."

"Come in. You'd better not tell my girl—she's had as much as she can bear tonight. Not that I'm worrying a damn about Jeff Legge. He'd better die, and die quick, for if I get him—"

He did not finish his sentence, and the detective drew the man's arm through his.

"Now, listen, Peter, you've got to go very slow on this case, and not talk such a darned lot. You're under suspicion too, old man. You were seen in the vicinity of the club."

"Yes, I was seen in the vicinity of the club," repeated Peter, nodding. "I was waiting there—well,

I was waiting there for a purpose. I went to the Charlton, but my girl had gone—I suppose they told you— and then I went on to the Highlow, and saw that infernal Lila—by the way, she's one of Jeff's women, isn't she?"

"To be exact," said the other quietly, "she's his wife."

Peter Kane stopped dead.

"His wife?" he whispered. "Thank God for that! Thank God for that! I forgive her everything. Though she is a brute—how a woman could allow —but I can't judge her. That graft has always been dirty to me. It is hateful and loathsome. But, thank God she's his wife, Craig!" Then: "Who shot this fellow?"

"I don't know. I'm going to pull Johnny for it."

They were in the hall, and Peter Kane spun round, open-mouthed, terror in his eyes.

"You're going to pull Johnny?" he said. "Do you know what you're saying, Craig? You're mad! Johnny didn't do it. Johnny was nowhere near—"

"Johnny was there. And, what is more, Johnny was in the room, either at the moment of the shooting or immediately after. The elevator boy has spoken what's in his mind, which isn't much, but enough to convict Johnny if this fellow dies."

"Johnny there!" Peter's voice did not rise above a whisper.

"I tell you frankly, Peter, I thought it was you."

Craig was facing him squarely, his keen eyes searching the man's pallid face. "When I heard you were around, and that you had got to know that this fellow was a fake. Why were you waiting?"

"I can't tell you that—not now," said the other, after turning the matter over in his mind. "I should have seen Johnny if he was there. I saw this girl Lila, and I was afraid she'd recognise me. I think she did, too. I went straight on into Shaftesbury Avenue, to a bar I know. I was feeling queer over this—this discovery of mine. I can prove I was there from a quarter to ten till ten, if you want any proof. Oh, Johnny, Johnny!"

All this went on in the hall. Then came a quick patter of footsteps, and Marney appeared in the doorway.

"Who is it—Johnny? Oh, it is you, Mr. Craig? Has any-thing happened?" She looked in alarm from face to face. "Nothing has happened to Johnny?"

"No, nothing has happened to Johnny," said Craig soothingly. He glanced at Peter. "You ought to know this, Marney," he said. "I can call you Marney —I've known you since you were five. Jeff Legge has been shot."

He thought she was going to faint, and sprang to catch her, but with an effort of will she recovered.

"Jeff shot?" she asked shakily. "Who shot him?"

"I don't know. That's just what we are trying to discover. Perhaps you can help us. Why did you leave the hotel. Was Johnny with you?"

She shook her head. "I haven't seen Johnny," she said, "but I owe him —everything. There was a woman in the hotel." She glanced timidly at her father. "I think she was an hotel thief or something of the sort. She was there to—to steal. A big Welsh woman."

"A Welsh woman?" said Craig quickly. "What is her name?"

"Mrs. Gwenda Jones. Johnny knew about her, and telephoned her to tell her to take care of me until he could get to me. She got me out of the hotel, and then we walked down the Duke of York steps into the Mall. And then a curious thing happened—I was just telling daddy when you came. Mrs. Jones —she's such a big woman—"

"I know the lady," said Craig.

"Well, she disappeared. She wasn't exactly swallowed up by the earth," she said with a faint smile, "and she didn't go without warning. Suddenly she said to me: 'I must leave you now, my dear. I don't want that man to see me.' I looked round to find who it was that she was so terribly afraid of, and there seemed to be the most harmless lot of people about. When I turned, Mrs. Jones was running up the steps. I didn't wish to call her back, I felt so ridiculous. And then a man came up to me, a middle-aged man with the saddest face you could imagine. I told you that, daddy?"

He nodded.

"He took his hat off—his hair was almost white—and asked me if my name was Kane. I didn't tell him the other name," she said with a shiver. "'May I take you to a place of safety, Miss Kane?' he said. 'I don't think you ought to be seen with that raw-boned female.' I didn't know what to do, I was so frightened, and I was glad of the company and protection of any man, and, when he called a cab, I got in without the slightest hesitation. He was such a gentle soul, Mr. Craig. He talked of nothing but the weather and chickens! I think we talked about chickens all the way to Lewisham."

"Are you sure it was Lewisham?"

"It was somewhere in that neighbourhood. What other places are there?"

"New Cross, Brockley—" began Craig.

"That's the place—Brockley. It was the Brockley Road. I saw it printed on the corner of the street. He took me into his house. There was a nice, motherly old woman whom he introduced to me as his housekeeper."

"And what did he talk about?" asked the fascinated Craig.

"Chickens," she said solemnly. "Do you know what chickens lay the best eggs? I'm sure you don't. Do you know the best breed for England and the best for America? Do you know the most economical chickens to keep? I do! I wondered what he was going to do with me. I tried to ask him, but he invariably turned me back to the question of incubators and patent feeds, and the cubic space that a sitting hen requires as compared with an ordinary hen. It was the quaintest, most fantastic experience. It seems now almost like one of Alice's dreams! Then, at ten o'clock, I found a motor-car had come for me. 'I'm sending you home, young lady,' he said."

"Were you with him all the time, by the way?" asked Craig.

She shook her head.

"No, some part of the time I was with his housekeeper, who didn't even talk about chickens, but knitted large and shapeless jumpers, and sniffed. That was when he was telephoning. I knew he was telephoning because I could hear the drone of his voice."

"He didn't bring you back?"

"No, he just put me into the car and told me that I should be perfectly safe. I arrived just a few minutes ahead of daddy."

The detective scratched his chin, irritated and baffled.

"That's certainly got me," he said. "The raw-boned lady I know, but the chicken gentleman is mysterious. You didn't hear his name, by any chance?"

She shook her head.

"Do you know the number of the house?"

"Yes," she said frankly, "but he particularly asked me to forget it, and I've forgotten it." Then, in a more serious tone: "Is my— my—"

"Your nothing," interrupted Peter. "The blackguard was married— married to Lila. I think I must have gone daft, but I didn't realise this woman was planted in my house for a purpose. That type of girl wouldn't come at the wages she did if she had been genuine. Barney was always suspicious of her, by the way."

"Have you seen Johnny?" the girl asked Craig.

"No, I haven't seen him," said Craig carefully. "I thought of calling on him pretty soon."

Then it came to her in a flash, and she gasped.

"You don't think Johnny shot this man? You can't think that?"

"Of course he didn't shoot him," said Peter loudly. "It is a ridiculous idea. But you'll understand that Mr. Craig has to make inquiries in all sorts of unlikely quarters. You haven't been able to get hold of Johnny to-night?"

A glance passed between them, and Peter groaned.

"What a fool! What a fool!" he said. "Oh, my God, what a fool!"

"Father, Johnny hasn't done this? It isn't true, Mr. Craig. Johnny wouldn't shoot a man. Did anybody see him? How was he shot?"

"He was shot in the back."

"Then it wasn't Johnny." she said. "He couldn't shoot a man in the back!"

"I think, young lady," said Craig with a little smile, "that you'd better go to bed and dream about butterflies. You've had a perfect hell of a day, if you'll excuse my language. Say the firm word to her, Peter. Who's that?" He turned his head, listening.

"Barney," said Peter. "He has a distressing habit of wearing slippers. You can hear him miles away. He's opening the door to somebody—one of your people, perhaps. Or he's taking your chauffeur a drink. Barney has an enormous admiration for chauffeurs. They represent mechanical genius to him."

The girl was calmer now.

"I have too much to thank God for to-day, for this terrible thing to be true," she said in a low voice. "Mr. Craig, there is a mistake, I'm sure. Johnny couldn't have committed such a crime. It was somebody else—one of Jeffrey Legge's associates, somebody who hated him. He told me once that lots of people hated him, and I thought he was joking; he seemed so nice, so considerate. Daddy, I was mad to go through that, even to make you happy."

Peter Kane nodded.

"If you were mad, I was criminal, girlie," he said. "There was only one man in the world for you—"

The door opened slowly, and Barney sidled in. "Johnny to see you folks," he said, and pulled the door wider.

John Gray was standing in the passage, and his eyes fell upon Craig with a look of quiet amusement.

CHAPTER XVII

IN another second the girl was in his arms, clinging to him, weeping convulsively on his shoulder, her face against his, her clasped hands about his neck.
Craig could only look, wondering and fearing. Johnny would not have walked into the net unwarned. Barney would have told him that he was there. What amazed Craig, as the fact slowly dawned upon him, was that Johnny was still in evening dress. He took a step toward him, and gently Johnny disengaged the girl from his arms.
"I'll like to see the right cuff of your shirt, Johnny," said Craig.
Without a word, Gray held up his arm, and the inspector scrutinised the spotless linen, for spotless it was. No sign of a stain was visible.
"Either somebody's doing some tall lying, or you're being extraordinarily clever, Johnny. I'll see that other cuff if I may."
The second scrutiny produced no tangible result.
"Didn't you go home and change to-night?"
"No, I haven't been near my flat," he said.
Craig was staggered.
"But your man said that you came in, changed, took a suit-case and went away."
"Then Parker has been drinking," was the calm reply "I have been enjoying the unusual experience of dining with the detective officer who was responsible for my holiday in Devonshire."
Craig took a step back.
"With Inspector Flaherty?" he asked.
Johnny nodded.
"With the good Inspector Flaherty. We have been exchanging confidences about our mutual acquaintances."
"But who was it went to your flat?" asked the bewildered Craig.
"My double. I've always contended that I have a double," said Johnny serenely.
He stood in the centre of the astounded group. Into Marney's heart had crept a wild hope.
"Johnny," she said, "was it this man who committed the crime for which you were punished?"
To her disappointment he shook his head.
"No, I am the gentleman who was arrested and sent to Dartmoor—my double stops short of these unpleasant experiences, and I can't say that I blame him."
"But do you mean to say that he deceived your servant?"
"Apparently," said Johnny, turning again to the detective who had asked the question.
"I take your word, of course, Johnny, as an individual."
Johnny chuckled.
"I like the pretty distinction. As an official, you want corroboration. Very well, that is not hard to get. If you take me back to Flaherty, he will support all I have told you."
Peter and the detective had the good taste to allow him to take leave of the girl without the embarrassment of their presence.
"It beats me—utterly beats me. Have you ever heard of this before, Peter?"
"That Johnny had a double? No, I can't say that I have."
"He may have invented the story for the sake of the girl. But there is the fact: he's in evening

dress, whilst his servant distinctly described him as wearing a grey tweed suit. There is no mark of blood on his cuff, and I'm perfectly certain that Stevens wouldn't have tried to get Johnny in bad. He is very fond of the boy. Of course, he may be spinning this yarn for the sake of Marney, but it'll be easy enough to corroborate. I'll use your phone, Peter," he said suddenly. "I've got Flaherty's number in my book."

The biggest surprise of the evening came when a sleepy voice, undeniably Flaherty's, answered him.

"Craig's speaking. Who have you been dining with tonight, Flaherty?"

"You don't mean to tell me that you've called me up in the middle of the night," began the annoyed Irishman, "to ask me who I've been dining with?"

"This is serious, Flaherty. I want to know."

"Why, with Johnny, of course—Johnny Gray. I asked him to come to dinner."

"What time did he leave you?"

"Nearer eleven than ten," was the reply. "No, it was after eleven."

"And he was with you all that time? He didn't leave for a quarter of an hour?"

"Not for a quarter of a minute. We just talked and talked..."

Craig hung up the receiver and turned away from the instrument, shaking his head.

"Any other alibi would have hanged you, Johnny. But Flaherty's the straightest man in the C.I.D."

In view of what followed when Johnny reached his flat in the early hours of the morning, this testimony to the integrity of Inspector Flaherty seemed a little misguided.

"Nobody else been here?"

"No, sir," said Parker.

"What did you do with the shirt I took off?"

"I cut off the cuffs and burnt them, sir. I did it with a greater pleasure, because the rounded corner cuff is just a little demode, if you do not mind my saying so, just a little—how shall I call it?— theatrical."

"The rest of the shirt—?"

"The rest of the shirt, sir," said Parker deferentially, "I am wearing. It is rather warm to wear two shirts, but I could think of no other way of disposing of it, sir. Shall I put your bath ready?"

Johnny nodded.

"If you will forgive the impertinence, did you succeed in persuading the gentleman you were going to see, to support your statement?"

"Flaherty? Oh, yes. Flaherty owes me a lot. Good night, Parker."

"Good night, sir. I hope you sleep well. Er—may I take that pistol out of your pocket, sir? It is spoiling the set of your trousers. Thank you very much."

He took the Browning gingerly between his finger and thumb and laid it on Johnny's writing-table.

"You don't mind my being up a little late, sir?" he said. "I think I would like to clean this weapon before I retire."

CHAPTER XVIII

JEFF LEGGE reclined in a long cane chair on a lawn which stretched to the edge of a cliff. Before him were the blue waters of the Channel, and the more gorgeous blue of an unflecked sky. He reached out his hand and took a glass that stood on the table by his side, sipped it with a wry face and called a name pettishly.

It was Lila who came running to his side.

"Take this stuff away, and bring me a whisky-and-soda," he said.

"The doctor said you weren't to have anything but lime juice. Oh, Jeff, you must do as he tells you," she pleaded.

"I'll break your head for you when I get up," he snarled. "Do as you're told. Where's the governor?"

"He's gone into the village to post some letters."

He ruminated on this, and then:

"If that busy comes, you can tell him I'm too ill to be seen."

"Who—Craig?"

"Yes," he growled, "the dirty, twisting thief! Johnny would have been in boob for this if he hadn't straightened Craig. If he didn't drop a thousand to keep off the moor, I'm a dead man!"

She pulled up a low chair to his side.

"I don't think Johnny did it," she said. "The old man thinks it was Peter. The window was found open after. He could have come in by the fire-escape—he knows the way."

He grumbled something under his breath, and very discreetly she did not press home her view.

"Where's Marney—back with her father?"

She nodded.

"Who told him I was married to you?"

"I don't know, Jeff," she said.

"You liar! You told him; nobody else could have known. If I get 'bird' for this marriage, I'll kill you, Lila. That's twice you've squeaked on me."

"I didn't know what I was saying. I was half mad with worry."

"I wish you'd gone the whole journey," he said bitterly. "It isn't the woman—I don't care a damn about that. It's the old man's quarrel, and he's got to get through with it. It's the other business being disorganised that's worrying me. Unless it's running like clockwork, you'll get a jam; and when you've got a jam, you collect a bigger crowd than I want to see looking at my operations. You didn't squeak about that, I suppose?"

"No, Jeff, I didn't know."

"And that's the reason you didn't squeak, eh?"

He regarded her unfavourably. And now she turned on him.

"Listen, Jeff Legge. I'm a patient woman, up to a point, and I'll stand for all your bad temper whilst you're ill. But you're living in a new age, Jeff, and you'd better wake up to the fact. All that Bill Sikes and Nancy stuff never did impress me. I'm no clinger. If you got really rough with me, I'd bat you, and that's a fact. It may not be womanly, but it's wise. I never did believe in the equality of the sexes, but no girl is the weaker vessel if she gets first grip of the kitchen poker."

Very wisely he changed the subject.

"I suppose they searched the club from top to bottom?" he said.

"They did."

"Did they look in the loft?"

"I believe they did. Stevens told me that they turned everything inside out."

He grunted.

"They're clever," he said. "It must be wonderful to be clever. Who's this?" He scowled across the lawn at a strange figure that had appeared, apparently by way of the cliff gate.

She rose and walked to meet the stooping stranger, who stood, hat in hand, waiting for her and smiling awkwardly.

"I'm so sorry to intrude," he said. "This is a beautiful place, is it not? If I remember rightly, this is the Dellsea Vicarage? I used to know the vicar —a very charming man. I suppose you have taken the house from him?"

She was half amused, half annoyed.

"This is Dellsea Vicarage," she said curtly. "Do you want to see anybody?"

"I wanted to see Mr. Jeffrey"—he screwed up his eyes and stared at the sky, as though trying to withdraw from some obscure cell of memory a name that would not come without special effort—"Mr. Jeffrey Legge— that is the name—Mr. Jeffrey Legge."

"He is very ill and can't be seen."

"I'm sorry to hear that," said the stranger, his mild face expressing the intensest sympathy. "Very sorry indeed."

He fixed his big, round glasses on the tip of his nose, for effect apparently, because he looked over them at her.

"I wonder if he would see me for just a few minutes. I've called to inquire about his health."

"What is your name?" she asked.

"Reeder—J.G. Reeder."

The girl felt her colour go, and turned quickly.

"I will ask him," she said.

Jeff heard the name and pursed his lips.

"That's the man the bank are running—or maybe it's the Government —to trail me," he said in a low tone. "Slip him along, Lila."

Mr. Reeder was beckoned across the lawn, and came with quick, mincing steps.

"I'm so sorry to see that you're in such a deplorable condition, Mr. Legge," he said. "I hope your father is well?"

"Oh, you've met the old man, have you?" said Jeffrey in surprise.

Mr. Reeder nodded.

"Yes; I have met your father," he said. "A very entertaining and a very ingenious man. Very!"

The last word was spoken with emphasis.

Jeff was silent at this tribute to his parent's amiability.

"There has been a lot of talk in town lately about a certain nefarious business that is being carried on—surreptitiously, of course," said Mr. Reeder, choosing his words with care. "I who live out of the world, and in the backwater of life, hear strange rumours about the distribution of illicit money—I think the cant term is 'slush' or 'slosh'— probably it is 'slush'."

"It is 'slush,'" agreed Jeff, not knowing whether to be amused or alarmed, and watching the man all the time.

"Now I feel sure that the persons who are engaged in this practice cannot be aware of the enormously serious nature of their offence," said Mr. Reeder confidentially.

He broke off his lecture to look around the lawn and well-stocked garden that flanked it on either side.

"How beautiful is the world, Mr. Jeff—I beg your pardon, Mr. Legge," he said. "How lovely those flowers are! I confess that the sight of bluebells always brings a lump to my throat. I don't suppose they are bluebells," he added, "for it is rather late in the year. But that peculiar shade of blue! And those wonderful roses—I can smell them from here."

He closed his eyes, raised his nose and sniffed loudly—a ludicrous figure; but Jeff Legge did not laugh.

"I know very little, but I understand that in Dartmoor Prison there are only a few potted flowers, and that those are never seen by the prisoners, except by one privileged man whose task it is to tend them. A lifer, generally. Life without flowers must be very drab, Mr. Legge."

"I'm not especially fond of flowers," said Jeffrey.

"What a pity!" said the other regretfully. "What a thousand pities! But there is no sea view from that establishment, no painted ships upon a painted ocean—which is a quotation from a well-known poem; no delightful sense of freedom; nothing really that makes life durable for a man under sentence, let us say, of fifteen or twenty years."

Jeff did not reply.

"Do you love rabbits?" was the surprising question that was put to him.

"No, I can't say that I do."

Lila sat erect, motionless, all her senses trained to hear and understand.

Mr. Reeder sighed.

"I am very fond of rabbits. Whenever I see a rabbit in a cage or in a hutch, I buy it, take it to the nearest wood and release it. It may be a foolish kindness, because, born and reared in captivity, it may not have the necessary qualities to support itself amongst its wilder fellows. But I like letting rabbits loose; other people like putting rabbits in cages." He shook his finger in Jeffrey's face. "Never be a rabbit in a cage, Mr. Jeffrey —or is it Mr. Legge? Yes, Mr. Legge."

"I am neither a rabbit, nor a chicken, nor a fox, nor a skylark," said Jeffrey. "The cage hasn't been built that could hold me."

Again Mr. Reeder sighed.

"I remember another gentleman saying that some years ago. I forget in what prison he was hanged. Possibly it was Wandsworth—yes, I am sure it was Wandsworth. I saw his grave the other day. Just his initials. What a pity! What a sad end to a promising career! He is better off, I think, for twenty long years in a prison cell, that is a dreadful fate, Mr. Legge! And it is a fate that would never overtake a man who decided to reform. Suppose, let us say, he was forging Bank of England notes, and decided that he would burn his paper and his water-markers, dismiss all his agents...I don't think we should worry very much about that type of person. We should meet him generously and liberally, especially if his notes were of such excellent quality that they were difficult for the uninitiated to detect."

"What has happened to Golden?" asked Jeffrey boldly.

The eyes of the elderly man twinkled.

"Golden was my predecessor," he said. "A very charming fellow, by some accounts—"

Again Jeffrey cut him short.

"He used to be the man who was looking after the 'slush' for the police. Is he dead?"

"He has gone abroad," said Mr. Reeder gravely. "Yes, Mr. Golden could not stand this climate. He suffered terribly from asthma, or it may have been sciatica. I know there was an 'a 'at the end of it. Did you ever meet him? Ah! You missed a very great opportunity," said Mr. Reeder.

"Golden was a nice fellow—not as smart, perhaps, as he might have been, or as he should have been, but a very nice fellow. He did not work, perhaps, so much in the open as I do; and there I think he was mistaken. It is always an error to shut yourself up in an office and envelop yourself in an atmosphere of mystery. I myself am prone to the same fault. Now, my dear Mr. Legge, I am sure you will take my parable kindly, and will give it every thought and consideration."

"I would, if I were a printer of 'slush,' but, unfortunately, I'm not," said Jeffrey Legge with a smile.

"You're not, of course," the other hastened to say. "I wouldn't dream of suggesting you were. But with your vast circle of acquaintances—and, I'm sure, admirers—you may perhaps be able to convey my simple little illustration. I don't like to see rabbits in cages, or birds in cages, or anything else behind bars. And I think that Dartmoor is so—what shall I say?—unaesthetic. And it seems such a pity to spend all the years in Devonshire. In the spring, of course, it is delightful; in the summer it is hot; in the winter, unless you're at Torquay, it is deplorable. Good morning, Mr. Legge."

He bowed low to the girl, and, bowing, his spectacles fell off. Stooping, he picked them up with an apology and backed away and they watched him in silence till he had disappeared from view.

CHAPTER XIX

"WHAT do you think of him for a busy?" asked Jeffrey contemptuously.

She did not answer. Contact with the man had frightened her. It was not like Lila to shiver in the presence of detectives.

"I don't know what he is," she said a little breathlessly. "He's something like a...good-natured snake. Didn't you feel that, Jeffrey?"

"Good-natured nothing," said the other with a curl of his lip. "He's worse than Golden. These big corporations fall for that kind of man. They never give a chance to a real clever busy."

"Who was Golden?" she asked.

"He was an old fellow too. They fired him." He chuckled to himself. "And I was responsible for firing him. Then they brought in Mr. J.G. Reeder with a flourish of trumpets. He's been on the game three years, and he's just about as near to making a pull as he ever was."

"Jeff, isn't there danger?" Her voice was very serious.

"Isn't there always danger? No more danger than usual," he said. "They can't touch me. Don't worry! I've covered myself so that they can't see me for overcoats! Once the stuff's printed, they can never put it back on me."

"Once it's printed." She nodded slowly. "Then you are the Big Printer, Jeff?"

"Talk about something else," he said.

When Emanuel returned, as he did soon after, Lila met him at the gate and told him of Reeder's visit. To her surprise, he took almost the same view as Jeff had taken.

"He's a fool, but straight—up to five thousand, anyway. No man is straight when you reach his figure."

"But why did he come to Jeff?" she asked.

"Doesn't everybody in the business know that Jeff's the Big Printer? Haven't they been trying to put it on him for years? Of course he came. It was his last, despairing stroke. How's the boy?" he asked.

"He's all right, but a little touchy."

"Of course he's a little touchy," said Emanuel indignantly. "You don't suppose he's going to get better in a day, do you? The club's running again."

"Has it been closed?"

"It hasn't exactly been closed, but it has been unpopular," he said, showing his teeth in that smile of his. "Listen." He caught her arm on the edge of the lawn. "Get your mind off that shooting, will you? I'll fix the man responsible for that."

"Do you know?" she asked.

It was the first time he had ever discussed the matter calmly, for the very mention of the attack upon Jeff had hitherto been sufficient to drive him to an incoherent frenzy.

"Yes, I know," he said gratingly. "It was Peter Kane, but you needn't say anything about that—I'll fix him, I tell you."

"Jeff thinks it was—"

"Never mind what Jeff thinks," he said impatiently. "Do as I tell you."

He sent her into the house to brew him a cup of tea—Emanuel was a great drinker of tea—and in her absence he had something to say to his son.

"Jeff, there's a big call for your stuff," he said. "I've had a letter from Harvey. He says there's another man started in the north of England, and he's turning out pretty good material. But they want yours—they can place half a million on the Continent right away. Jeff, what Harvey says is right. If there's a slackening of supply while you're ill, the busy fellows are going to tumble to you."

"I've thought of that," said Jeffrey. "You can tell anybody who's interested that there'll be a printing next week."

"Are you well enough to go up?" asked his father anxiously.

Jeffrey nodded, and shifted himself more erect, but winced in the process.

"Reeder's been here: did she tell you?"

Emanuel nodded.

"I'm not worried much about Reeder. Down in Dartmoor he's a bogey, but then, they bogey any man they don't know. And they've got all sorts of stories about him. It's very encouraging to get near to the real thing."

They laughed together, and for the rest of the day discussed ways and means.

Jeffrey had said no more than was true when he had told the girl he was well covered. In various parts of the country he had twelve banking accounts, each in a different name, and in one of the safe deposits, an enormous sum in currency, ready for emergency.

"You've got to stop some time, I suppose," said his father, "but it is mighty tempting to carry on with those profits. It's a bigger graft than I ever attempted, Jeff." And his son accepted this respectful tribute with a smirk.

The old man sat, his clasped hands between his knees, staring, out over the sea.

"It has got to end some day, and that would be a fine end, but I can't quite see how it could be done."

"What are you talking about?" asked the other curiously.

"I'm thinking about Peter—the respectable Mr. Peter Kane. Not quite so respectable in that girl's eyes as he used to be, but respectable enough to have busies to dinner, and that crook, Johnny Gray—Johnny will marry the girl, Jeff."

Jeffrey Legge winced.

"She can marry the devil so far as I'm concerned," he said.

"But she can't marry without divorcing you. Do you realise that, my son? That's the law. And she can't divorce you without shopping you for bigamy. That's the law too. And the question is, will she delay her action until Johnny's made a bit, or will she start right in? If she gives me just the time I want, Jeff, you'll have your girl and I'll have Peter Kane. She's your wife in the eyes of the law."

There was a significance in his words that made the other man look at him quickly.

"What's the great idea?" he asked.

"Suppose Peter was the Big Printer?" said Emanuel, speaking in a tone that was little above a whisper. "Suppose he was caught with the goods? It could be done. I don't mean by planting the stuff in his house—nobody would accept that; but getting him right on the spot, so that his best friend at Scotland Yard couldn't save him? How's that for an idea?"

"It couldn't be done," said the other immediately.

"Oh, couldn't it?" sneered Emanuel. "You can do any old thing you want, if you make up your mind to do it. Or if you're game to do it."

"That wouldn't get me the girl."

Emanuel turned his head slowly toward his heir.

"If they found the Big Printer, they'll have to find the big printing," he said deliberately. "That means we should all have to skip, and skip lively. We might have a few hours start, and in these days of aeroplanes, three hours is four hundred miles. Jeff, if we are caught, and they guess I've been in this printing all the time, I shall never see outside again. And you'll go down for life. They can't give you any worse than that—not if you took the girl away with you."

"By force?" asked the other in surprise. The idea had not occurred to him.

The father nodded.

"If we have to skip, that's the only thing for you to do, son. It's no offence—remember that. She's your wife." He looked to left and right, to see if there was the faintest shadow of a chance that he would be overheard, and then: "Suppose we ask Peter and his girl and Johnny Gray to dinner? A nice little dinner party, eh?"

"Where?" asked the other suspiciously.

"In Room 13," said Emanuel Legge. "In Room 13, Jeff, boy! A nice little dinner. What do you think? And then two whiffs of sleep stuff—"

"You're mad," said the other angrily. "What's the good of talking that way? Do you think he's going to come to dinner and bring his girl? Oh, you're nutty to think it!"

"Trust me," said Emanuel Legge.

CHAPTER XX

WALKING down Regent Street one morning, Johnny Gray saw a familiar face—a man standing on the kerb selling penny trinkets. The face was oddly familiar, but he had gone on a dozen paces before he could recall where he had seen him before, and turned back. The man knew him; at any rate, his uncouth features twisted in a smile.

"Good morning, my lord," he said. "What about a toy balloon for the baby?"

"Your name is Fenner, isn't it?" said Johnny with a good-humoured gesture of refusal.

"That's me. Captain. I didn't think you'd recognised me. How's business?"

"Quiet," said Johnny conventionally. "What are you doing?"

The man shrugged his enormous shoulders.

"Selling these, and filling in the time with a little sluicing."

Johnny shook his head reprovingly. "'Sluicing' in the argot indicates a curious method of livelihood. In public wash-places, where men strip off their coats to wash their hands for luncheon, there are fine pickings to be had by a man with quick fingers and a knowledge of human nature."

"Did you ever get your towelling*?"

[*Flogging]

"No," said the other contemptuously and with a deep growl. "I knew they couldn't, that's why I coshed the screw. I was too near my time. If I ever see old man Legge, by God I'll—"

Jimmy raised his fingers. A policeman was strolling past, and was eyeing the two suspiciously. Apparently, if he regarded Fenner with disfavour, Johnny's respectability redeemed the association.

"Poor old 'flattie'!" said Fenner as the officer passed. "What a life!"

The man looked him up and down amusedly.

"You seem to have struck it, Gray," he said, with no touch of envy. "What's your graft?"

Johnny smiled faintly.

"It is one you'll find difficult to understand, Fenner. I am being honest!"

"That's certainly a new one on me," said the other frankly. "Have you seen old Emanuel?" His voice was now quite calm. "Great fellow, Emanuel! And young Emanuel—Jeffrey—what a lad!"

There was a glint in his eyes as he scrutinised Johnny that told that young man he knew much more of recent happenings than he was prepared to state. And his next words supported that view.

"You keep away from the Legge lot, Captain," he said earnestly. "They are no good to anybody, and least of all to a man who's had an education like yours. I owe Legge one, and I'll pet him, but I'm not thinking about that so much as young Jeff. You're the fellow he would go after, because you dress like a swell and you look like a swell—the very man to put 'slush' about without anybody tumbling."

"The Big Printer, eh?" said Johnny, with that quizzical smile of his.

"The Big Printer," repeated the other gravely. "And he is a big printer. You hear all sorts of lies down on the moor, but that's true. Jeff's got the biggest graft that's ever been worked in this country. They'll get him sooner or later, because there never was a crook game yet that hadn't got a squeak about it somewhere. And the squeak has started, judging by what I can read in the papers. Who shot him?" he asked bluntly.

Johnny shook his head.

"That is what is known as a mystery," he said, and, seeing the man's eyes keenly searching his face, he laughed aloud. "It wasn't me, Fenner. I'll assure you on that point. And as to me being a friend of Jeff"—he made a wry little face—"that isn't like me either. How are you off for money?"

"Rotten," said the other laconically, and Johnny slipped a couple of Treasury notes on to the tray. He was turning away when the man called him back. "Keep out of boob," he said significantly. "And don't think I'm handing round good advice. I'm not thinking of Dartmoor. There are other boobs that are worse—I can tell you that, because I've seen most of them."

He gathered up the money on the tray without so much as a word of thanks, and put it in his waistcoat pocket.

"Keytown Jail is the worst prison in England," he said, not looking at his benefactor but staring straight ahead. "The very worst—don't forget that, Gray. Keytown Prison is the worst boob in England; and if you ever find yourself there, do something to get out. So-long!"

The mentality of the criminal had been a subject for vicarious study during Johnny's stay in Dartmoor, and he mused on the man's words as he continued his walk along Regent Street. Here was a man offering advice which he himself had never taken. The moral detachment of old lags was no new phenomenon to Johnny. He had listened for hours to the wise admonitions and warnings of convicts, who would hardly be free from the fusty cell of the prison before they would be planning new villainies, new qualifications for their return.

He had never heard of Keytown Jail before, but it was not remarkable that Fenner should have some special grudge against a particular jail. The criminal classes have their likes and their dislikes; they loathed Wandsworth and preferred Pentonville, or vice versa, for no especial reason. There were those who swore by Parkhurst; others regarded Dartmoor as home, and bitterly resented any suggestion that they should be transferred to the island prison.

So musing, he bumped into Craig. The collision was not accidental, for Craig had put himself in the way of the abstracted young man.

"What are you planning, Johnny—a jewel robbery, or just ringing the changes on the Derby favourite?"

Johnny chuckled.

"Neither. I was at that moment wondering what there was particularly bad about Keytown Jail. Where is Keytown Jail, by the way?"

"Keytown? I don't remember—oh, yes, I do. Just outside Oxford. Why?"

"Somebody was telling me it was the worst prison in England."

"They are all the worst, Johnny," said Craig. "And if you're thinking out a summer holiday, I can't recommend either. Keytown was pretty bad," he admitted. "It is a little country jail, but it is no longer in the Prison Commissioners' hands. They sold it after the war, when they closed down so many of these little prisons. The policy now is to enlarge the bigger places and cut out these expensive little boobs that cost money to staff. They closed Hereford Jail in the same way, and half a dozen others, I should think. So you needn't bother about Keytown," he smiled bleakly.

"One of your criminal acquaintances has been warning you, I guess?"

"You've guessed right," said Johnny, and advanced no information, knowing that, if Craig continued his walk, he would sooner or later see the toy pedlar.

"Mr. Jeffrey Legge is making a good recovery," said the detective, changing the subject: "and there are great rejoicings at Scotland Yard. If there is one man we want to keep alive until he is hanged in a scientific and lawful manner, it is Mr. Jeffrey Legge. I know what you're going to say—we've got nothing on him. That is true. Jeffrey has been too clever for us. He has got his father skinned to death in that respect. He makes no mistakes—a rare quality in a forger; he carries no 'slush,' keeps none in his lodgings. I can tell you that, because we've pulled him in twice on suspicion, and searched him from occiput to tendo achilles. Forgive the anatomical terms, but anatomy is my hobby. Hallo!"

He was looking across the street at a figure which was not unfamiliar to Johnny. Mr. Reeder wore a shabby frock-coat and a somewhat untidy silk hat on the back of his head. Beneath his arm he carried a partially furled umbrella. His hands, covered in grey cotton gloves (at a distance Johnny thought they were suede), were clasped behind him. His spectacles were, as usual, so far down his nose that they seemed in danger of slipping over.

"Do you know that gentleman?"

"Man named Reeder, isn't it? He's a 'busy'."

Craig's lips twitched.

"He's certainly a 'busy 'of sorts," he said dryly, "but not of our sort."

"He is a bank-man, isn't he?" asked Johnny, watching Mr. Reeder's slow and awkward progress.

"He is in the employ of the bank," said the detective, "and he's not such a fool as he looks. I happen to know. He was down seeing young Legge yesterday. I was curious enough to put a man on to trail him. And he knows more about young Legge than I gave him credit for."

When Johnny parted from the detective, Mr. Reeder had passed out of sight. Crossing Piccadilly Circus, however, he saw the elderly man waiting in a bus queue, and interestedly stood and watched him until the bus arrived and Mr. Reeder boarded the machine and disappeared into its interior. As the bus drew away, Johnny raised his eyes to the destination board and saw that it was Victoria.

"I wonder," said Johnny, speaking his thought aloud.

For Victoria is the railway station for Horsham.

CHAPTER XXI

MR. REEDER descended from the bus at Victoria Station, bought a third- class return ticket to Horsham, and, going on to the bookstall, purchased a copy of the Economist and the Poultry World, and, thus fortified for the journey, passed through the barrier, and finding an empty carriage, ensconced himself in one corner. From thence onward, until the train drew into Horsham Station, he was apparently alternately absorbed in the eccentricities of Wyandottes and the fluctuations of the mark.

There were many cabs at the station, willing and anxious to convey him to his destination for a trifling sum; but apparently Mr. Reeder was deaf to all the urgent offers which were made to him, for he looked through the taxi- men, or over their heads, as though there were no such things as grim mechanicians or drivers of emaciated horses; and, using his umbrella as a walking- stick, he set out to walk the distance intervening between the station and Peter Kane's residence.

Peter was in his snuggery, smoking a meditative cigar, when Barney came in with the news. "There's an old guy wants to see you, Peter. I don't know who he is, but he says his name's Reeder."

Peter's brows met.

"Reeder?" he said sharply. "What sort of man is he?"

"An old fellow," said Barney. "Too shaky for a 'busy'. He looks as if he's trying to raise subscriptions for the old chapel organ."

It was not an unfair description, as Peter knew.

"Bring him here, Barney, and keep your mouth shut. And bear in mind that this is the busiest 'busy' you are ever likely to meet."

"A copper?" said Barney incredulously.

Peter nodded.

"Where's Marney?" he asked quickly.

"Up in her boojar," said Barney with relish. "She's writing letters. She wrote one to Johnny. It started 'Dear old boy'."

"How do you know?" asked Peter sharply.

"Because I read it," said Barney without shame. "I'm a pretty good reader: I can read things upside down, owing to me having been in the printing business when I was a kid."

"Bring in Mr. Reeder," interrupted Peter ominously. "And remember, Barney, that if ever I catch you reading anything of mine upside down, you will be upside down! And don't argue."

Barney left the room, uttering a mechanical defiance which such threats invariably provoked. Mr. Reeder came in, his shabby hat in one hand, his umbrella in the other, and a look of profound unhappiness on his face.

"Good morning, Mr. Kane," he said, laying down his impedimenta. "What a beautiful morning it is for a walk! It is a sin and a shame to be indoors on a day like this. Give me a garden, with roses, if I may express a preference, and just a faint whiff of heliotrope..."

"You'd like to see me in the garden, eh?" said Peter. "Perhaps you're wise."

Barney, his inquisitive ears glued to the keyhole, cursed softly.

"I was in a garden yesterday," murmured Mr. Reeder, as they walked across the lawn toward the sunken terraces. "Such a lovely garden! One bed was filled with blue flowers. There is something about a blue flower that brings a lump into my throat. Rhododendrons infuriate me: I have never understood why. There is that about a clump of rhododendrons which rouses all that is evil in my nature. Daffodils, on the other hand, and especially daffodils intermingled with hyacinths, have a most soothing effect upon me. The garden to which I refer had the added attraction of being on the edge of the sea —a veritable Garden of Eden, Mr. Kane, although "—he wagged his head from side to side disparagingly—"there were more snakes than is customary. There was a snake in a chair, and a snake who was posting letters in the village, and another official snake who was hiding behind a clump of bushes and had followed me all the way from London—sent, I think, by that misguided gentleman, Mr. Craig."

"Where were you, Mr. Reeder?"

"At a seaside villa, a beautiful spot. A truly earthly paradise," sighed Mr. Reeder. "The very place an intelligent man would go to if he were convalescent, and the gentleman on the chair was certainly convalescent."

"You saw Jeff Legge, eh? Sit down."

He pointed to the marble bench where Johnny had sat and brooded unhappily on a certain wedding day.

"I think not," said Mr. Reeder, shaking his head as be stared at the marble seat. "I suffer from rheumatism, with occasional twinges of sciatica. I think I would rather walk with you, Mr. Kane." He glanced at the hedge. "I do not like people who listen. Sometimes one listens and hears too much. I heard the other day of a very charming man who happened to be standing behind a bush, and heard the direful character of his son-in-law revealed. It was not good for him to hear so much."

Peter knew that the man was speaking about him, but gave no sign.

"I owe you something, Mr. Reeder, for the splendid way you treated my daughter—"

Mr. Reeder stopped him with a gesture.

"A very charming girl. A very lovely girl," he said with mild enthusiasm. "And so interested in chickens! One so seldom meets with women who take a purely sincere interest in chickens."

They had reached a place where it was impossible they could be overheard. Peter, who realised that the visitor would not have called unless he had something important to say, waited for the next move. Mr. Reeder returned to the subject of eavesdropping.

"My friend—if I may call him my friend—who learnt by accident that his son-in-law was an infernal rascal—if you will excuse that violent expression—might have got himself into serious trouble, very serious trouble." He shook his head solemnly. "For you see," he went on, "my friend—I do hope he will allow me to call him my friend? —has something of a criminal past, and all his success has been achieved by clever strategy. Now, was it clever strategy"—he did not look at Peter, and his faded eyes surveyed the landscape gloomily— "was it clever of my friend to convey to Mr. Emanuel Legge the astounding information that at a certain hour, in a certain room—I think its number was thirteen, but I am not sure—Mr. John Gray was meeting Mr. J.G. Reeder to convey information which would result in Emanuel Legge's son going to prison for a long period of penal servitude? Was it wise to forge the handwriting of one of Emanuel Legge's disreputable associates, and induce the aforesaid Emanuel to mount the fire-escape at the Highlow Club and shoot, as he thought, Mr. John Gray, who wasn't Mr. Gray at all, but his own son? I ask you, was it wise?"

Peter did not answer.

"Was it discreet, when my friend went to the hotel where his daughter was staying, and found her gone, to leave a scribbled note on the floor, which conveyed to Mr. Jeffrey Legge the erroneous

information that the young lady was meeting Johnny Gray in Room 13 at nine-thirty? I admit," said Mr. Reeder handsomely, "that by these clever manoeuvres, my friend succeeded in getting Jeffrey Legge just where he wanted him at the proper time; for Jeffrey naturally went to the Highlow Club in order to confront and intimidate his wife. You're a man of the world, Mr. Kane, and I am sure you will see how terribly indiscreet my friend was. For Jeffrey might have been killed." He sighed heavily. "His precious life might have been lost; and if the letters were produced at the trial, my friend himself might have been tried for murder."
He dusted the arm of his frock-coat tenderly.
"The event had the elements of tragedy," he said, "and it was only by accident that Jeff's face was turned away from the door; and it was only by accident that Emanuel was not seen going out. And it was only by the sheerest and cleverest perjury that Johnny Gray was not arrested."
"Johnny was not there," said Peter sharply.
"On the contrary, Johnny was there—please admit that he was there?" pleaded Mr. Reeder. "Otherwise, all my theories are valueless. And a gentleman in my profession hates to see his theories suffer extinction."
"I'll not admit anything of the sort," said Peter sharply. "Johnny spent that evening with a police officer. It must have been his double."
"His treble perhaps," murmured the other. "Who knows? Humanity resembles, to a very great extent, the domestic fowl, gallus domesticus. One man resembles another—it is largely a matter of plumage."
He looked up to the sky as though he were seeking inspiration from heaven itself.
"Mr. Jeffrey Legge has not served you very well, Mr. Kane," he said. "In fact, I think he has served you very badly. He is obviously a person without principle or honour, and deserves anything that may come to him."
Peter waited, and suddenly the man brought his eyes to the level of his.
"You must have heard, in the course of your travels, a great deal about Mr. Legge?" he suggested. "Possibly more has come to you since this unfortunate—indeed, dastardly—happening, of which I cannot remind you without inflicting unnecessary pain. Now, Mr. Kane, don't you think that you would be rendering a service to human society if—"
"If I squeaked," said Peter Kane quietly. "I'll put your mind at rest on that subject immediately. I know nothing of Jeffrey Legge except that he's a blackguard. But if I did, if I had the key to his printing works, if I had evidence in my pocket of his guilt—" he paused.
"And if you had all these?" asked Mr. Reeder gently.
"I should not squeak," said Peter with emphasis, "because that is not the way. A squeak is a squeak, whether you do it in cold blood or in the heat of temper."
Again Mr. Reeder sighed heavily, took off his glasses, breathed on them and polished them with gentle vigour, and did not speak until he had replaced them.
"It is all very honourable," he said sadly. "This—er—faith and—er—integrity. Again the poultry parallel comes to my mind. Certain breeds of chickens hold together and have nothing whatever to do with other breeds, and, though they may quarrel amongst themselves, will fight to the death for one another. Your daughter is well, I trust?"
"She is very well," said Peter emphatically, "surprisingly so. I thought she would have a bad time—here she is." He turned at that moment and waved his hand to the girl, who was coming down the steps of the terrace. "You know Mr. Reeder?" said Peter as the girl came smiling toward the chicken expert with outstretched hand.
"Why, of course I know him," she said warmly. "Almost you have persuaded me to run a poultry

farm!"

"You might do worse," said Mr. Reeder gravely. "There are very few women who take an intelligent interest in such matters. Men are ever so much more interested in chickens."

Peter looked at him sharply. There was something in his tone, a glint of unsuspected humour in his eyes, that lit and died in a second, and Peter Kane was nearer to understanding the man at that moment than he had ever been before.

And here Peter took a bold step.

"Mr. Reeder is a detective," he said, "employed by the banks to try and track down the people who have been putting so many forged notes on the market."

"A detective!"

Her eyes opened wide in surprise, and Mr. Reeder hastened to disclaim the appellation.

"Not a detective. I beg of you not to misunderstand, Miss Kane. I am merely an investigator, an inquiry agent, not a detective. 'Detective' is a term which is wholly repugnant to me. I have never arrested a man in my life, nor have I authority to do so."

"At any rate, you do not look like a detective, Mr. Reeder," smiled the girl.

"I thank you," said Mr. Reeder gratefully. "I should not wish to be mistaken for a detective. It is a profession which I admire, but do not envy."

He took from his pocket a large note-case and opened it. Inside, fastened by a rubber band in the centre, was a thick wad of bank-notes. Seeing them, Peter's eyebrows rose.

"You're a bold man to carry all that money about with you, Mr. Reeder," he said.

"Not bold," disclaimed the investigator. "I am indeed a very timid man."

He slipped a note from under the elastic band and handed it to his wondering host. Peter took it.

"A fiver," he said.

Mr. Reeder took another. Peter saw it was a hundred before he held it in his hand.

"Would you cash that for me?"

Peter Kane frowned.

"What do you mean?"

"Would you cash it for me?" asked Mr. Reeder. "Or perhaps you have no change? People do not keep such large sums in their houses."

"I'll change it for you with pleasure," said Peter, and was taking out his own note-case when Mr. Reeder stopped him with a gesture.

"Forged," he said briefly.

Peter looked at the note in his hand.

"Forged? Impossible! That's a good note."

He rustled it scientifically and held it up to the light. The watermark was perfect. The secret marks on the face of the note which he knew very well were there. He moistened the corner of the note with his thumb.

"You needn't trouble," said Reeder. "It answers all the tests."

"Do you mean to tell me this is 'slush'—I mean a forgery?"

The other nodded, and Peter examined the note again with a new interest. He who had seen so much bad money had to admit that it was the most perfect forgery he had ever handled.

"I shouldn't have hesitated to change that for you. Is all the other money the same?"

Again the man nodded.

"But is that really bad money?" asked Marney, taking the note from her father. "How is it made?"

Before the evasive answer came she guessed. In a flash she pieced together the hints, the vague scraps of gossip she had heard about the Big Printer.

"Jeffrey Legge!" she gasped, going white. "Oh!"

"Mr. Jeffrey Legge," nodded Reeder. "Of course we can prove nothing. Now perhaps we can sit down."

It was he who suggested that they should go back to the garden seat. Not until, in his furtive way, he had circumnavigated the clump of bushes that hid the lawn from view did he open his heart.

"I am going to tell you a lot, Mr. Kane," he said, "because I feel you may be able to help me, in spite of your principles. There are two men who could have engraved this note, one man who could manufacture the paper. Anybody could print it—anybody, that is to say, with a knowledge of printing. The two men are Lacey and Burns. They have both been in prison for forgery; they were both released ten years ago, and since then have not been seen. The third man is a paper maker, who was engaged in the bank-note works at Wellington. He went to penal servitude for seven years for stealing banknote paper. He also has been released a very considerable time, and he also has vanished."

"Lacey and Burns? I have heard of them. What is the other man's name?" asked Peter.

Mr. Reeder told him.

"Jennings? I never heard of him."

"You wouldn't because he is the most difficult type of criminal to track. In other words, he is not a criminal in the ordinary sense of the word. I am satisfied that he is on the Continent because, to be making paper, it is necessary that one should have the most up-to-date machinery. The printing is done here."

"Where?" asked the girl innocently, and for the first time she saw Mr. Reeder smile.

"I want this man very badly, and it is a matter of interest for you, young lady, because I could get him to-morrow—for bigamy." He saw the girl flush. "Which I shall not do. I want Jeff the Big Printer, not Jeff the bigamist. And oh, I want him badly!"

A sound of loud coughing came from the lawn, and Barney appeared at the head of the steps.

"Anybody want to see Emanuel Legge?"

They looked at one another.

"I don't want to see him," said Mr. Reeder decidedly. He nodded at the girl. "And you don't want to see him. I fear that leaves only you, Mr. Kane."

CHAPTER XXII

PETER was as cool as ice when he came into the drawing-room and found Emanuel examining the pictures on the wall with the air of a connoisseur. He turned, and beamed a benevolent smile upon the man he hated.

"I didn't think you'd come here again, Legge," said Peter with dangerous calm.

"Didn't you now?" Emanuel seemed surprised. "Well, why not? And me wanting to fix things up, too! I'm surprised at you, Peter."

"You'll put nothing right," said the other. "The sooner you recognise that fact and clear, the better it will be for everybody."

"If I'd known," Emanuel went on, unabashed, "if only I'd dreamt that the young woman Jeffrey had taken up with was your daughter, I would have stopped it at once, Peter. The boy had been brought up straight and never had met you. It is funny the number of straight people that never met Peter Kane. Of course, if he'd been on the crook, he'd have known at once. Do you think my boy would have married the daughter of a man who twisted his father? Is it likely, Peter? However, it's done now, and what's done can't be undone. The girl's fond of him, and he's fond of the girl—"

"When you've finished being comic, you can go," said Peter "I never laugh before lunch."

"Don't you, Peter? And not after? I've come at a very bad time, it seems to me. Now listen, Peter. Let's talk business."

"I've no business with you." Peter opened the door.

"Haste was always your weakness, Peter," said Emanuel, not budging from where he stood. "Never lose your temper. I lost my temper once and shot a copper, and did fifteen years for it. Fifteen years, whilst you were sitting here in luxury, entertaining the lords and ladies of the neighbourhood, and kidding 'em you were straight. I'm going to ask you a favour, Peter."

"It is granted before you ask," said the other sardonically.

"I'm going to ask you and Johnny boy to come and have a bit of dinner with me and Jeffrey, and let us fix this thing up. You're not going to have this girl brought into the divorce court, are you? And you've got to get a divorce, whether he's married or whether he isn't. As a matter of fact, he isn't married at all. I never dreamt you'd be such a mug as to fall for the story that Lila was properly married to Jeff. All these girls tell you the same thing. It's vanity, Peter, a human weakness, if I may so describe it."

"Perhaps it was the vanity of the registrar who signed their marriage certificate, and the vanity of the people who witnessed the marriage," said Peter. "Your son was married to this girl at the Greenwich Registry Office; I've got a copy of the certificate—you can see it if you like."

Still the smile on Emanuel's face did not fade.

"Ain't you smart?" he said admiringly. "Ain't you the quickest grafter that ever grafted? Married or not, Peter, the girl's got to go into the court for the marriage to be—what do you call it?—annulled, that's the word. And she can't marry till she does. And they'll never annul the marriage until you get my boy caught for bigamy, and that you won't do, Peter, because you don't want to advertise what a damned fool you are. Take my advice, come and talk it over. Bring Johnny with you—"

"Why should I bring Johnny? I can look after myself."

"Johnny's an interested party," said the other. "He's interested in anything to do with Marney, eh?" He chuckled, and for a second Peter Kane had all his work to maintain his calm.

"I'm not going to discuss Marney with you. I'll meet you and the Printer, and I don't suppose Johnny will mind either. Though what you can do that the law can't do, I don't know."

"I can give you evidence that you can't get any other way," said the other. "The fact is, Peter, my poor boy has realised he's made a mistake. He married a girl who was the daughter of a respectable gentleman, and when I broke it to him, Peter, that he'd married into a crook family, he was upset! He said I ought to have told him."

"I don't know what funny business you're going to try," said Peter Kane, "but I'm not going to run away from it. You want me to meet you and your son —where?"

"What about the old Highlow?" suggested Emanuel. "What about Room 13, where a sad accident nearly occurred?"

"Where you shot your son?" asked Peter coolly, and only for a second did the man's self-possession leave him. His face turned a dusky red and then a pale yellow.

"I shot my son there, did I? Peter, you're getting old and dopy! You've been dreaming again, Peter. Shot my son!"

"I'll come to this fool dinner of yours."

"And Marney?" suggested the other.

"Marney doesn't put her foot inside the doors of the Highlow," said Peter calmly. "You're mad to imagine I would allow that. I can't answer for Johnny, but I'll be there."

"What about Thursday?" suggested the old man.

"Any day will suit me," said Peter impatiently. "What time do you want us?"

"Half-past eight. Just a snack and a talk. We may as well have a bit of food to make it cheerful, eh, Peter? Remember that dinner we had a few days before we smashed the Southern Bank? That must be twenty years ago. You split fair on that, didn't you? I'll bet you did—I had the money! No taking a million dollars and calling it a hundred and twenty thousand pounds, eh, Peter?"

This time Peter stood by the door, and the jerk of his head told Emanuel Legge that the moment for persiflage had passed.

"I want to settle this matter." The earnestness of his manner did not deceive Peter. "You see, Peter, I'm getting old, and I want to go abroad and take the boy with me. And I want to give him a chance too—a good- looking lad like that ought to have a chance. For I'll tell you the truth —he's a single man."

Peter smiled.

"You can laugh! He married Lila—you've got a record of that, but have you taken a screw at the divorce list? That takes the grin off your face. They were divorced a year after they were married. Lila got tired of the other man and came back to Jeff. You're a looker-up; go and look up that! Ask old Reeder—"

"Ask him yourself," said Peter "He's in the garden."

He had no sooner said the words than he regretted them. Emanuel was silent for a while.

"So Reeder's here, in the garden, is he? He's come for a squeak. But you can't, because you've nothing to squeak about. What does he want?"

"Why don't you ask him?"

"That fellow spends his life wandering about other people's gardens," grumbled Emanuel. A disinterested observer might have imagined that Mr. Reeder's passion for horticulture was the only grievance against him. "He was round my garden yesterday. I dare say he told you? Came worrying poor Jeff to death. But you always were fond of busies, weren't you, Peter? How's your old friend Craig? I can't stand them myself, but then I am a crook. Thursday will suit you, Peter?

That gives you six days."

"Thursday will suit me," said Peter. "I hope it will suit you."

As he came back on to the lawn Reeder and the girl were coming into view up the steps, and without preliminary he told them what had passed.

"I fear," said Mr. Reeder, shaking his head sadly, "that Emanuel is not as truthful a man as he might be. There was no divorce. I was sufficiently interested in the case to look up the divorce court records." He rubbed his chin thoughtfully. "I think your dinner party at the Highlow—is that the name?—will be an interesting one," he said. "Are you sure he did not invite me?" And again Peter saw that glint of humour in his eyes.

CHAPTER XXIII

MR. EMANUEL LEGGE had a great deal of business to do in London. The closing of the club had sadly interfered with the amenities of the Highlow, for many of its patrons and members were, not unnaturally, reluctant to be found on premises subject, at any moment, to the visitation of inquisitive police officers. Stevens, the porter, had been reinstated, though his conduct, in Emanuel's opinion, had been open to the gravest suspicion. In other ways he was a reliable man, and one whose services were not lightly to be dispensed with. To his surprise, when he had come to admonish the porter, that individual had taken the wind out of his sails by announcing his intention of retiring unless the staff was changed. And he had his way, the staff in question being the elevator boy, Benny.

"Benny squeaked on me," said Stevens briefly, "and I'm not going to have a squeaker round."

"He squeaked to me, my friend," said Emanuel, showing his teeth unpleasantly. "He told me you tried to shield Johnny Gray."

"He's a member, ain't he?" asked the porter truculently. "How do I know what members you want put away, and what members you want hidden? Of course, I helped the Captain—or thought I was trying to help him. That's my job."

There was a great deal of logic in this. Benny, the elevator boy, was replaced.

Stepping out of the lift, Emanuel saw the prints of muddy boots in the hall, and they were wet.

"Who is here?" he asked.

"Nobody in particular."

Legge pointed to the footprints.

"Somebody has been here recently," he said.

"They're mine," said Stevens without hesitation. "I went out to get a cab for Monty Ford."

"Are there any mats?" snapped Emanuel.

Stevens did not answer.

There was a great deal of work for Emanuel to do. For example, there was the matter of a certain house in Berkeley Square to be cleared off. Though he was no longer in active work, he did a lot of crooked financing, and the house had been taken with his money. It was hired furnished for a year, and it was the intention of his associates to run an exclusive gambling club. Unfortunately, the owner, who had a very valuable collection of paintings and old jewellery, discovered the character of the new tenant (a dummy of Legge's) and had promptly cancelled the agreement. Roughly, the venture had cost Emanuel a thousand, and he hated losing good money.

It was late that night when he left the club. He was sleeping in town, intending to travel down to his convalescent son by an early train in the morning. It had been raining heavily, and the street was empty when he went out of the club, pulling the collar of his macintosh about his neck.

He had taken two strides when a man stepped out of the shadow of a doorway and planted himself squarely in his path. Emanuel's hand dropped to his pocket, for he was that rarest variety of criminal, an English gunman.

"Keep your artillery out of action, Legge," said a voice that was strangely familiar.

He peered forward, but in the shadow he could not distinguish the stranger's face.

"Who are you?"

"An old friend of yours," was the reply. "Don't tell me you've forgotten all your pals! Why, you'll be passing a screw in the street one of these days without touching your hat to him."

And then it dawned upon Emanuel.

"Oh...you're Fenner, aren't you?"

"I'm Fenner," admitted the man. "Who else could I be? I've been waiting to see you, Mr. Emanuel Legge. I wondered if you would remember a fellow you sent to the triangle...fifteen lashes I had. You've never had a 'bashing,' have you, Legge? It's not so nice as you'd think. When they'd took me back to my cell and put that big bit of lint on my shoulder, I laid on my face for a week. Naturally, that interfered with my sleeping, though it helped me a whole lot to think. And what I thought was this, Emanuel, that a thousand a stroke wouldn't be too much to ask from the man who got it for me."

Legge's lip twisted in a sneer.

"Oh, it's 'the black' you're after, is it? Fifteen thousand pounds, is that your price?"

"I could do a lot with fifteen thousand, Legge. I can go abroad and have a good time—maybe, take a house in the country."

"What's the matter with Dartmoor?" snarled Emanuel. "You'll get no fifteen thousand from me—not fifteen thousand cents, not fifteen thousand grains of sand. Get out of my way!"

He lurched forward, and the man slipped aside. He had seen what was in the old man's hand. Legge turned as he passed, facing him and walking sideways, alert to meet any attempt which was launched.

"That's a pretty gun of yours, Legge," drawled the convict. "Maybe I shall meet you one of these days when you won't be in a position to pull it."

A thought struck Emanuel Legge, and he walked slowly back to the man, and his tone was mild, even conciliatory.

"What's the good of making a fuss, Fenner? I didn't give you away. Half a dozen people saw you cosh that screw."

"But half a dozen didn't come forward, did they?" asked Fenner wrathfully. "You were the only prisoner; there was not a screw in sight."

"That's a long time ago," said Emanuel after a pause. "You're not going to make any trouble now, are you? Fifteen thousand pounds is out of the question. It is ridiculous to ask me for that. But if a couple of hundred will do you any good, why, I'll send it to you."

"I'll have it now," said Fenner.

"You won't have it now, because I haven't got it," replied Emanuel. "Tell me where you're to be found, and I'll send a boy along with it in the morning."

Fenner hesitated. He was surprised even to touch for a couple of hundred.

"I'm staying at Rowton House, Wimborne Street, Pimlico."

"In your own name?"

"In the name of Fenner," the other evaded, "and that's good enough for you."

Emanuel memorised the address.

"It will be there at ten o'clock," he said. "You're a mug to quarrel with me. I could put you on to a job where you could have made not fifteen, but twenty thousand."

All the anger had died out of the burglar's tone when he asked:

"Where?"

"There's a house in Berkeley Square," said Emanuel quickly, and gave the number.

It was providential that he had remembered that white elephant of his. And he knew, too, that at that moment the house was empty but for a caretaker.

"Just wait here," he said, and went back into the club and to his little office on the third floor. Opening a drawer of his desk, he took out a small bunch of keys, the duplicates that had been made during the brief period that the original keys had been in his possession. He found Fenner waiting where he had left him.

"Here are the keys. The house is empty. One of our people borrowed the keys and got cold feet at the last minute. There's about eight thousand pounds' worth of jewellery in a safe—you can't miss it. It is in the principal drawing-room—in show cases—go and take a look at it. And there's plate worth a fortune."

The man jingled the keys in his hand.

"Why haven't you gone after it, Emanuel?"

"Because it's not my graft," said Emanuel. "I'm running straight now. But I want my cut, Fenner. Don't run away with any idea that you're getting this for nothing. You've got a couple of nights to do the job; after that, you haven't the ghost of a chance, because the family will be coming back."

"But why do you give it to me?" asked Fenner, still suspicious.

"Because there's nobody else," was the almost convincing reply. "It may be that the jewellery is not there at all," went on Emanuel frankly. "It may have been taken away. But there is plenty of plate. I wouldn't have given it to you if I'd got the right man—I doubt whether I'm going to get my cut from you."

"You'll get your cut," said the other roughly. "I'm a fool to go after this, knowing what a squeaker you are, but I'll take the risk. If you put a point on me over this, Emanuel, I'll kill you. And I mean it."

"I'm sick of getting news about my murder," said Emanuel calmly. "If you don't want to do it, leave it. I'll send you up a couple of hundred in the morning, and that's all I'll do for you. Give me back those keys."

"I'll think about it," said the man, and turned away without another word.

It was one o'clock, and Emanuel went back to the club, working the automatic lift himself to the second floor.

"Everybody gone, Stevens?" he asked.

The porter stifled a yawn and shook his head.

"There's a lady and a gentleman"—he emphasised the word— "in No. 8. They've been quarrelling since nine o'clock. They ought to be finished by now."

"Put my office through to the exchange," said Emanuel. Behind the porter's desk was a small switchboard, and he thrust in the two plugs. Presently the disc showed him that Emanuel was through.

Mr. Legge had many friends amongst the minor members of the Criminal Investigation Department. They were not inexpensive acquaintances, but they could on occasion be extremely useful. That night, in some respects, Emanuel's luck was in, when he found Sergeant Shilto in his office. There had been a jewel theft at one of the theatres, which had kept the sergeant busy.

"Is that you, Shilto?" asked Legge in a low voice. "It's Manileg." He gave his telegraphic address, which also served as a nom de plume when such delicate negotiations as these were going through.

"Yes, Mr. Manileg?" said the officer, alert, for Emanuel did not call up police headquarters unless there was something unusual afoot.

"Do you want a cop—a real one?" asked Legge in a voice little above a whisper. "There's a man named Fenner—"

"The old lag?" asked Shilto. "Yes, I saw him to-day. What's he doing?"

"He's knocking off a little silver, from 973, Berkeley Square. Be at the front door: you'll probably see him go in. You want to be careful, because he's got a gun. If you hurry, you'll get

there in front of him. Good-night."
He hung up the receiver and smiled. The simplicity of the average criminal always amused Emanuel Legge.

CHAPTER XXIV

PETER wrote to tell of the invitation which Legge had extended to him. Johnny Gray had the letter by the first post. He sat in his big armchair, his silk dressing-gown wrapped around him, his chin on his fists; and seeing him thus, the discreet Parker did not intrude upon his thoughts until Johnny, reading the letter again, tore it in pieces and threw it into the wastepaper-basket. He had a whimsical practice of submitting most of his problems, either in parable form or more directly, to his imperturbable manservant.
"Parker, if you were asked to take dinner in a lion's den, what dress would you wear?"
Parker looked down at him thoughtfully, biting his lip.
"It would largely depend, sir, on whether there were ladies to be present," he said. "Under those extraordinary circumstances, one should wear full dress and a white tie."
Johnny groaned.
"There have been such dinners, sir," Parker hastened to assure him in all seriousness. "I recall that, when I was a boy, a visiting menagerie came to our town, and one of the novelties was a dinner which was served in a den of ferocious lions; and I distinctly remember that the lion-tamer wore a white dress bow and a long tail coat. He also wore top boots," he said after a moment's consideration, "which, of course, no gentleman could possibly wear in evening dress. But then, he was an actor."
"But supposing the lion-tamer had a working arrangement with the lions? Wouldn't you suggest a suit of armour?" asked Johnny without smiling, and Parker considered the problem for a moment.
"That would rather turn it into a fancy-dress affair, sir," he said, "where, of course, any costume is permissible. Personally," he added, "I should never dream of dining in a den of lions under any circumstances."
"That's the answer I've been waiting for; it is the most intelligent thing you've said this morning," said Johnny. "Nevertheless, I shall not follow your excellent advice. I will be dining at the Highlow Club on Thursday. Get me the morning newspaper: I haven't seen it."
He turned the pages apathetically, for the events which were at the moment agitating political London meant nothing in his life. On an inner page he found a brief paragraph which, however, did interest him. It was in the latest news column, and related to the arrest of a burglar, who had been caught red handed breaking into a house in Berkeley Square. The man had given his name as Fenner. Johnny shook his head sadly. He had no doubt as to the identity of the thief, for burglary was Fenner's graft. Since the news had come in the early hours of the morning, there were no details, and he put the paper aside and fell into a train of thought.
Poor Fenner! He must go back to that hell, which was only better than Keytown Jail. He would be spared the ordeal of Keytown, at any rate, if what Craig had said was true. Glancing at the clock, he saw that it was nearly eleven and jumped up. He was taking Marney to lunch and a matinee that day. Peter was bringing her up, and he was to meet them at Victoria.
Since his release from Dartmoor, Johnny had had no opportunity of a quiet talk with the girl, and this promised to be a red-letter day in his life. He had to wait some time, for the train was late; and as he stood in the broad hall, watching with abstracted interest the never-ceasing rush and movement and life about him, he observed, out of the corner of his eye, a man sidling toward him.

Johnny had that sixth sense which is alike the property of the scientist, the detective and the thief. He was immediately sensitive to what he called the approaching spirit, and long before the shabby stranger had spoken to him, he knew that he was the objective. Nearer at hand, he recognised the stranger as a man he had seen in Dartmoor, and remembered that he had come to prison at the same time as Fenner and for the same offence, though he had been released soon after Johnny had passed through that grim gateway.

"I followed you down here, Mr. Gray, but I didn't like to talk to you in the street," said the stranger, apparently immersed in an evening newspaper, and talking, as such men talk, without moving his lips.

Johnny waited, wondering what was the communication, and not doubting that it had to do with Fenner.

"Old Fenner's been 'shopped 'by Legge," said the man, "He went to knock off some silver from a house in Berkeley Square, and Shilto was waiting in the hall for him."

"How do you know Legge shopped him?" asked Johnny, interested.

"It was a 'shop' all right," said the other without troubling to explain. "If you can put in a good word for Fenner, he'd be much obliged."

"But, my dear fellow," said John with a little smile, "to whom can I put in a good word? In the present circumstances I couldn't put a word in for my own maiden aunt. I'll see what I can do."

There was no need to tell the furtive man to go. With all a thief's keen perceptions he had seen the eyes of Johnny Gray light up, and with a sidelong glance assured himself as to the cause. Johnny went toward the girl with long strides, and, oblivious to curious spectators and Peter Kane alike, took both her hands in his. Her loveliness always came to him in the nature of a glorious surprise. The grace and poise of her were indefinite quantities that he could not keep exactly in his mind, and inevitably she surpassed his impressions of her.

After he had handed the girl into a taxi, the older man beckoned him aside.

"I'm not any too sure about this Highlow dinner," he said. "Love feasts are not Emanuel's specialities, and there's a kick coming somewhere, Johnny. I hope you're prepared for it?"

Johnny nodded.

"Emanuel isn't usually so obvious," he said. "In fact, the whole thing is so patent and so crude that I can't suspect anything more than an attempt to straighten matters as far as Marney is concerned."

Peter's face clouded.

"There will be no straightening there," he said shortly. "If he has committed bigamy, he goes down for it. Understand that, Johnny. It will be very unpleasant because of Marney's name being dragged into the light, but I'm going through with it."

He turned away with a wave of his hand, and Johnny returned to the girl.

"What is the matter with father?" she asked as the taxi drew out of the station. "He is so quiet and thoughtful these days. I suppose the poor dear's worrying about me, though he needn't, for I never felt happier."

"Why?" asked Johnny, indiscreetly.

"Because—oh, well, because," she said, her face flushing the faintest shade of pink. "Because I'm unmarried, for one thing. I hated the idea, Johnny. You don't know how I hated it. I understand now poor daddy's anxiety to get me married into respectable society." Her sense of humour, always irrepressible, overcame her anxiety. "I wonder if you understand my immoral sense of importance at the discovery that poor father has done so many illegal things! I suppose it is the kink that he has transmitted to me."

"Was it a great shock to you, Marney?" interrupted the young man quietly.

She nodded. "Yes, but shocks are like blows—they hurt and they fade. It isn't pleasant to be twisted violently to another angle of view. It pains horribly, Johnny. But I think when I found—" She hesitated.

"When you found that I was a thief."

"When I found that you were—oh, Johnny, why did you? You had so many advantages; you were a University man, a gentleman—Johnny, it wasn't big of you. There's an excuse for daddy; he told me about his youth and his struggles and the fearful hardness of living. But you had opportunities that he never had. Easy money isn't good money, is it, Johnny?"

He was silent, and then, with a quick, breath-catching sigh, she smiled again.

"I haven't come out to lecture you, and I shall not even ask you if, for my sake, you will go straight in the future. Because, Johnny"—she dropped a cool palm on the back of his hand—"I'm not going to do anything like the good fairy in the storybooks and try to save you from yourself."

"I'm saved," said Johnny, with a quizzical smile. "You're perfectly right: there was no reason why I should be a thief. I was the victim of circumstances. It was possibly the fascination of the game—no, no, it wasn't that. One of these days I will tell you why I left the straight path of virtue. It is a long and curious story."

She made no further reference to his fall, and throughout the lunch was her own gay self. Looking down at her hand, Johnny saw, with satisfaction, that the platinum wedding-ring she had worn had been replaced by a small, plain gold ring, ornamented with a single turquoise, and his breath came faster. He had first met her at a gymkhana, a country fair which had been organised for charity, and the ring had been the prize he had won at a shooting match, one of the gymkhana features—though it was stretching terminology to absurd lengths so to describe the hotch-potch of contests which went to the making of the programme—and had offered it to her as whimsically as it had been accepted. Its value was something under a pound. To Johnny, all the millions in the world would not have given him the joy that its appearance upon her finger gave him now.

After luncheon she returned to the unpleasant side of things.

"Johnny, you're going to be very careful, aren't you? Daddy says that Jeff Legge hates you, and he is quite serious about it. He says that there are no lengths to which Jeffrey and his father will not go to hurt you—and me," she added.

Johnny bent over the table, lowering his voice. "Marney, when this matter is settled—I mean, the release from your marriage—will you take me—whatever I am?"

She met his eyes steadily and nodded. It was the strangest of all proposals, and Jeffrey Legge, who had watched the meeting at the station, had followed her, and now was overlooking them from one of the balconies of the restaurant, flushed a deeper red, guessing all that that scene meant.

CHAPTER XXV

ON Thursday afternoon, Emanuel Legge came out of the elevator at the Highlow Club, and, with a curt nod to Stevens, walked up the heavily carpeted corridor, unlocked the door of his tiny office and went in. For half an hour he sat before his desk, his hands clasped on the blotting-pad before him, motionless, his mind completely occupied by his thoughts. At last he opened his desk, pressed a bell by his side, and he had hardly taken his fingers from the push when the head waiter of the establishment, a tall, unpleasant-looking Italian, came in.
"Fernando, you have made all the arrangements about the dinner to-night?"
"Yes," said the man.
"All the finest wines, eh? The best in the house?"
He peered at the waiter, his teeth showing in a smile.
"The very best," said Fernando briskly.
"There will be four: myself and Major Floyd, Mr. Johnny Gray and Peter Kane."
"The lady is not coming?" asked Fernando.
"No, I don't think she'll be dining with us to-night," said Emanuel carefully.
When the waiter had gone, he rose and bolted the door and returned to an idle examination of the desk. He found extraordinary pleasure in opening the drawers and looking through the little works of reference which filled a niche beneath the pigeon-holes. This was Jeffrey's desk, and Jeff was the apple of his eye.
Presently he rose and walked to a nest of pigeon-holes which stood against the wall, and, putting his hand into one, he turned a knob and pulled. The nest opened like a door, exposing a narrow, spiral staircase which led upward and downward. He left the secret door open and pulled down a switch, which gave him light above and below. For a second he hesitated whether he should go up or down, and decided upon the latter course.
At the foot of the stairs was another door, which he opened, passing into the cellar basement of the house. As the door moved, there came to him a wave of air so super-heated that for a moment he found difficulty in breathing. The cellar in which he found himself was innocent of furnishing, except for a table placed under a strong light, and a great, enclosed furnace which was responsible for the atmosphere of the room. It was like a Turkish bath, and he had not gone two or three paces before the perspiration was rolling down his cheeks.
A broad-shouldered, undersized man was sitting at the table, a big book open before him. He had turned at the sound of the key in the door, and now he came toward the intruder. He was a half-caste, and, beyond the pair of blue dungaree trousers, he wore no clothing. His yellow skin and his curiously animal face gave him a particularly repulsive appearance.
"Got the furnace going, eh, Pietro?" said Emanuel mildly, taking off his spectacles to wipe the moisture which had condensed upon the lenses.
Pietro grunted something and, picking up an iron bar, lifted open the big door of the furnace. Emanuel put up his hands to guard his face from the blast of heat that came forth.
"Shut it, shut it!" he said testily, and when this was done, he went nearer to the furnace.
Two feet away there ran a box-like projection, extending from two feet above the floor to the ceiling. A stranger might have imagined that this was an air shaft, introduced to regulate the ventilation. Emanuel was not a stranger. He knew that the shaft ran to the roof, and that it had a very simple explanation.

"That's a good fire you've got, eh, Pietro? You could burn up a man there?"

"Burn anything," growled the other, "but not man."

Emanuel chuckled.

"Scared I'm going to put a murder point on you, are you? Well, you needn't be," he said. "But it's hot enough to melt copper, eh, Pietro?"

"Melt it down to nothing."

"Burnt any lately?"

The man nodded, rubbing his enormous arms caressingly.

"They came last Monday week, after the boss had been shot," said the other. He had a curious impediment in his speech which made his tone harsh and guttural. "The fellows upstairs knew they were coming, so there was nothing to see. The furnace was nearly out."

Emanuel nodded.

"The boss said the furnace was to be kept going for a week," said Pietro complainingly. "That's pretty tough on me, Mr. Legge. I feel sometimes I'd nearly die, the heat's so terrible."

"You get the nights off," said Emanuel, "and there are weeks when you do no work. To-night I shall want you...Mr. Jeff has told you?"

The dwarf nodded. Emanuel passed through the door, closing it behind him; and, contrasted with the heat of the room, it seemed that he had walked into an ice wall. His collar was limp, his clothes were sticking to him, as he made his way up the stairs, and, passing the open door of his office, continued until he reached the tiny landing which scarcely gave him foothold. He knocked twice on the door, for of this he had no key. After a pause came an answering knock, a small spyhole opened and an inquiring and suspicious eye examined him.

When at last the door was opened, he found he was in a small room with a large skylight, heavily barred. At one end of the skylight was a rolled blind, which could be drawn across at night and effectively veil the glare of light which on occasions rose from this room.

The man who grinned a welcome was little and bald. His age was in the region of sixty, and the grotesqueness of his appearance was due less to his shabby attire and diminutive stature than to the gold-rimmed monocle fixed in his right eye.

In the centre of the room was a big table littered with paraphernalia, ranging from a small microscope to a case filled with little black bottles. Under the brilliant overhead light which hung above the table, and clamped to the wood by glass-headed pins, was an oblong copper plate, on which the engraver had been working—the engraving tool was in his hand as he opened the door.

"Good morning, Lacey. What are you working at now?" asked Emanuel with a benevolent air of patronage appropriate to the proprietor in addressing a favourite workman.

"The new fives," said the other. "Jeff wants a big printing. Jeff's got brains. Anybody else would have said, 'Work from a photographic plate' —you know what that means. After a run of a hundred, the impression goes wrong, and before you know where you are, there's a squeak. But engraving is engraving," he said with pride. "You can get all the new changes without photography. I never did hold with this new method—'boobs' are full of fellows who think they can make slush with a camera and a zinc plate!"

It was good to hear praise of Jeffrey, and Emanuel Legge purred. He examined the half-finished plate through his powerful glasses, and though the art of the engraver was one with which he was not well acquainted, he could admire the fine work which this expert forger was doing.

To the left of the table was an aperture like the opening of a service lift. It was a continuation of the shaft which led from the basement, and it had this value, that, however clever the police might be, long before they could break into the engraver's room all evidence of his guilt would have been flung into the opening and consumed in the furnace fire. Jeffrey's idea. "What a mind!" said the admiring Lacey. "It reduces risk to what I might term a minimum. It is a pleasure working for Jeff, Mr. Legge. He takes no chances."

"I suppose Pietro is always on the spot?"

Mr. Lacey smiled. He took up a plate from the table and examined it back and front.

"That is one I spoilt this morning," he said. "Spilt some acid on it. Look!"

He went to the opening, put in his hand, and evidently pressed a bell, for a faint tinkle came from the mouth of the shaft. When he withdrew his hand, the plate that it held had disappeared. There came the buzz of a bell from beneath the table.

"That plate's running like water by now," he said. "There's no chance of a squeak if Pietro's all right. Wide! That's Jeffrey! As wide as Broad Street! Why, Mr. Legge, would you believe that I don't know to this day where the stuff's printed? And I'll bet the printer hasn't got the slightest idea where the plates are made. There isn't a man in this building who has got so much as a smell of it."

Emanuel passed down to his own office, a gratified father, and, securely closing the pigeon-hole door, he went out into the club premises to look at Room 13. The table was already laid. A big rose-bowl, overflowing with the choicest blooms, filled the centre; an array of rare glass, the like of which the habitues of the club had never seen on their tables, stood before each plate.

His brief inspection of the room satisfied him, and he returned, not to his office but to Stevens, the porter.

"What's the idea of telling the members that all the rooms are engaged to-night?" asked Stevens. "I've had to put off Lew Brady, and he pays."

"We're having a party, Stevens," said Emanuel, "and we don't want any interruption. Johnny Gray is coming. And you can take that look off your face; if I thought he was a pal of yours, you wouldn't be in this club two minutes. Peter Kane's coming too."

"Looks to me like a rough house," said Stevens. "What am I to do?" he asked sarcastically. "Bring in the police at the first squeal?"

"Bring in your friend from Toronto," snapped Emanuel, and went home to change.

CHAPTER XXVI

JOHNNY was the first of the guests to arrive, and Stevens helped him to take off his raincoat. As he did so, he asked in a low voice: "Got a gun, Captain?"
"Never carry one, Stevens. It is a bad habit to get into."
"I never thought you were a mug," said Stevens in the same voice.
"Any man who has been in prison is, ex officio, one of the Ancient Order of Muggery," said Johnny, adjusting his bow in the mirror by the porter's desk. "What's going?"
"I don't know," said the other, bending down to wipe the mud from Johnny's boots. "But curious things have happened in No. 13; and don't sit with your back to the buffet. Do you get that?"
Johnny nodded.
He had reached the end of the corridor when he heard the whine of the ascending lift, and stopped. It was Peter Kane, and to him in a low voice, Johnny passed on the porter's advice.
"I don't think they'll start anything," said Peter under his breath. "But if they do, there's a nurse at Charing Cross Hospital who's going to say: 'What, you here again?'"
As Johnny had expected, his two hosts were waiting in Room 13. The silence which followed their arrival was, for one member of the party, an awkward one.
"Glad to see you, Peter," said Emanuel at last, though he made no pretence of shaking hands. "Old friends ought to keep up acquaintances. There's my boy, Jeffrey. I think you've met him," he said with a grin.
"I've met him," said Peter, his face a mask.
Jeffrey Legge had apparently recovered fully from his unpleasant experience.
"Now sit down, everybody," said Emanuel, bustling around, pulling out the chairs. "You sit here, Johnny."
"I'd rather face the buffet; I like to see myself eat," said Johnny, and, without invitation, sat down in the position he had selected.
Not waiting, Peter seated himself on Johnny's left, and it was Emanuel himself, a little ruffled by this preliminary upset to his plans, who sat with his back to the buffet. Johnny noticed the quick exchange of glances between father and son; he noticed, too, that the buffet carried none of the side dishes for which it was designed, and wondered what particular danger threatened from that end of the room.
By the side of the sideboard, in one corner, hung a long, blue curtain, which, he guessed, hid a door leading to No. 12. Peter, who was better acquainted with the club, knew that No. 12 was the sitting-room, and that the two made one of those suites which were very much in request when a lamb was brought to the killing.
"Now, boys," said Emanuel with spurious joviality, "there is to be no bickering and quarrelling. We're all met round the festive board, and we've nothing to do but find a way out that leaves my boy's good name unsullied, if I may use that word."
"You can use any word you like," said Peter. "It'll take more than a dinner party to restore his tarnished reputation."
"What long words you use, Peter!" said Emanuel admiringly. "It's my own fault that I don't know them, because I had plenty of time to study when I was away 'over the Alps'. Never been over the Alps, have you, Peter? Well, when they call it 'time,' they use the right word. The one thing you've got there is time!"

Peter did not answer, and it was Jeffrey who took up the conversation.

"See here, Peter," he said, "I'm not going to make a song about this business of mine. I'm going to put all my cards on the table. I want my wife."

"You know where Lila is better than I," said Peter. "She's not in my employment now."

"Lila nothing!" retorted Jeffrey. "If you fall for that stuff, you're getting soft. I certainly married Lila, but she was married already, and I can give you proof of it."

The conversation flagged here, for the waiter came in to serve the soup.

"What wine will you have, sir?"

"The same as Mr. Emanuel," said Peter.

Emanuel Legge chuckled softly.

"Think I'm going to 'knock you out,' eh, Peter? What a suspicious old man you are!"

"Water," said Johnny softly when the waiter came to him.

"On the water-wagon, Johnny? That's good. A young man in your business has got to keep his wits about him. I'll have champagne, Fernando, and so will Major Floyd. Nothing like champagne to keep your heart up," he said.

Peter watched, all his senses alert, as the wine came, bubbling and frothing, into the long glasses.

"That will do, Fernando," said Emanuel, watching the proceedings closely.

As the door closed, Johnny could have sworn he heard an extra click.

"Locking us in?" he asked pleasantly, and Emanuel's eyebrows rose.

"Locking you in, Johnny? Why, do you think I'm afraid of losing you, like you're afraid of losing Marney?"

Johnny sipped the glass of water, his eyes fixed on the old man's face. What was behind that buffet? That was the thought which puzzled him. It was a very ordinary piece of furniture, of heavy mahogany, a little shallow, but this was accounted for by the fact that the room was not large, and, in furnishing, the proprietors of the club had of necessity to economise space. There were two cupboard doors beneath the ledge on which the side dishes should have been standing. Was it his imagination that he thought he saw one move the fraction of an inch?

"Ever been in 'bird' before, Johnny?"

It was Emanuel who did most of the talking.

"I know they gave you three years, but was that your first conviction?"

"That was my first conviction," said Johnny.

The old man looked up at the ceiling, pulling at his chin.

"Ever been in Keytown?" he demanded. "No good asking you, Peter, I know. You've never been in Keytown or any bad boob, have you? Clever old Peter!"

"Let us talk about something else," said Peter. "I don't believe for one moment the story you told me about Lila having been married before. You've told me a fresh lie every time the matter has been discussed. I'm going to give you a show, Emanuel, for old times' sake. You've been a swine, and you've been nearer to death than you know, for, if your plan had come off as you expected it would, I'd have killed you."

Emanuel chuckled derisively.

"Old Peter's going to be a gunman," he said. "And after all the lectures you've given me! I'm surprised at you, Peter. Now I'll tell you what I'm going to do." He rested his elbows on the table and cupped his chin in his hands, his keen eyes, all the keener for the magnification of his spectacles, fixed hardly upon his sometime friend. "By my reckoning, you owe me forty thousand pounds, and I know I'm not going to get it without a struggle. Weigh in with that money, and I'll make things easy for my son's wife." He emphasised the last word.

"You can cut that out!"

It was Jeffrey whose rough interruption checked his father's words.

"There's no money in the world that's going to get Marney from me. Understand that." He brought his hand down with a crash upon the table. "She belongs to me, and I want her, Peter. Do you get it? And what is more, I'm going to take her."

Johnny edged a little farther from the table, and folding his arms across his chest, his lips parted in a smile. His right hand reached for the gun that he carried under his armpit: a little Browning, but a favourite one of Johnny's in such crises as these. For the cupboard door had moved again, and the door of the room was locked: of that he was certain. All this talk of Marney was sheer blind to keep them occupied.

It had long passed the time when the plates should have been cleared and the second course make its appearance. But there was to be no second course, at that dinner. Emanuel was speaking chidingly, reproachfully.

"Jeffrey, my boy, you mustn't spoil a good deal," he said. "The truth is—"

And then all the lights of the room went out. Instantly Johnny was on his feet, his back to the wall, his gun fanning the dark.

"What's the game?" asked Peter's voice sharply. "There'll be a real dead man here if you start fooling."

"I don't know," said Emanuel, speaking from the place where he had been. "Ring the bell, Jeff. I expect the switch has gone."

There was somebody else in the room: Johnny felt the presence instinctively—a stealthy somebody who was moving toward him. Holding out one hand, ready to pounce the moment it touched, he waited. A second passed—five seconds—ten seconds—and then the lights went on again.

Peter was also standing with his back to the wall, and in his hand a murderous looking Webley. Jeffrey and his father were side by side in the places they had been when the lights went out. There was no fifth man in the room.

"What's the game?" asked Peter suspiciously.

"The game, my dear Peter? What a question to ask! You don't make me responsible for the fuses, do you? I'm not an electrician. I'm a poor old crook who has done time that other people should have done—that's all," said Emanuel pleasantly. "And look at the hardware! Bad idea, carrying guns. Let an old crook give you a word of advice, Peter," he bantered. "I'm not surprised at Johnny, because he might be anything. Sit down, you damned fools," he said jocularly. "Let's talk."

"I'll talk when you open that door," said Johnny quietly. "And I'll put away my gun on the same condition."

In three strides, Emanuel was at the door. There was a jerk of his wrist, and it flew open.

"Have the door open if you're frightened," he said contemptuously. "I guess it's being in boob that makes you scared of the dark. I got that way myself."

As he had turned the handle, Johnny had heard a second click. He was confident that somebody stood outside the door, and that the words Legge had uttered were intended for the unknown sentry. What was the idea?

Peter Kane was sipping his champagne, with an eye on his host. Had he heard the noise, too? Johnny judged that he had. The extinguishing of the lights had not been an accident. Some secret signal had been given, and the lights cut off from the controlling switchboard. The doors of the buffet cupboard were still. Turning his head, Johnny saw that Jeffrey's eyes were fixed on his

with a hard concentration which was significant. What was he expecting?
The climax, whatever it might be, was at hand.
"It's a wonder to me, Gray, that you've never gone in for slush." Jeffrey was speaking slowly and deliberately. "It's a good profession, and you can make money that you couldn't dream of getting by faking racehorses."
"Perhaps you will tell me how to start in that interesting profession," said Johnny coolly.
"I'll put it on paper for you, if you like. It'll be easier to make a squeak about. Or, better still, I'll show you how it's done. You'd like that?"
"I don't know that I'm particularly interested, but I'm sure my friend Mr. Reeder—"
"Your friend Mr. Reeder!" sneered the other. "He's a pal of yours too, is he?"
"All law-abiding citizens are pals of mine," said Johnny gravely.
He had put his pistol back in his jacket pocket, and his hand was on it.
"Well, how's this for a start?"
Jeffrey rose from the table and went to the buffet. He bent down and must have touched some piece of mechanism; for, without any visible assistance, the lid of the buffet turned over on some invisible axis, revealing a small but highly complicated piece of machinery, which Johnny recognised instantly as one of those little presses employed by banknote printers when a limited series of notes, generally of a high denomination, were being made.
The audacity of this revelation momentarily took his breath away.
"You could pull that buffet to pieces," continued Jeffrey, "and then not find it."
He pressed a switch, and the largest of the wheels began to spin, and with it a dozen tiny platens and cylinders. Only for a few minutes, and then he cut off the current, pressed the hidden mechanism again, and the machine turned over out of sight, and the two astonished men stared at the very ordinary looking surface of a very ordinary buffet.
"Easy money, eh, Gray?" said Emanuel, with an admiring smirk at his son. "Now listen, boys," His tone grew suddenly practical and businesslike as he came back to his chair. "I want to tell you something that's going to be a lot of good to both of you, and we'll leave Marney out of it for the time being."
Johnny raised his glass of water, still watchful and suspicious.
"The point is—" said Emanuel, and at that moment Johnny took a long sip from the glass.
The liquid had hardly reached his throat when he strove vainly to reject it. The harsh tang of it he recognised, and, flinging the glass to the floor, jerked out his gun.
And then some tremendous force within him jerked at his brain, and the pistol dropped from his paralysed hand.
Peter was on his feet, staring from one to the other.
"What have you done?"
He leapt forward, but before he could make a move, Emanuel sprang at him like a cat. He tried to fight clear, but he was curiously lethargic and weak. A vicious fist struck him on the jaw, and he went down like a log.
"Got you!" hissed Emanuel, glaring down at his enemy. "Got you, Peter, my boy! Never been in boob, have you? I'll give you a taste of it!"
Jeffrey Legge stooped and jerked open the door of the cupboard, and a man came stooping into the light. It was a catlike Pietro, grinning from ear to ear in sheer enjoyment of the part he had played. Emanuel dropped his hand on his shoulder.
"Good boy," he said. "The right stuff for the right man, eh? To every man his dope, Jeff. I knew that this Johnny Gray was going to be the hardest, and if I'd taken your advice and given them

both a knock-out, we'd have only knocked out one. Now they know why the lights went out. Pick 'em up."

The little half-caste must have been enormously strong, for he lifted Peter without an effort and propped him into an armchair. This done, he picked up the younger man and laid him on the sofa, took a little tin box from his pocket, and, filling a hypodermic syringe from a tiny phial, looked round for instructions.

Jeffrey nodded, and the needle was driven into the unfeeling flesh. This done, he lifted the eyelid of the drugged man and grinned again.

"He'll be ready to move in half an hour," he said. "My knock-out doesn't last longer."

"Could you get him down the fire-escape into the yard?" asked Emanuel anxiously. "He's a pretty heavy fellow, that Peter. You'll have to help him, Jeff boy. The car's in the yard. And, Jeff, don't forget you've an engagement at two o'clock."

His son nodded.

Again the half-caste swung up Peter Kane, and Jeffrey, holding the door wide, helped him to carry the unconscious man through the open window and down the steel stairway, though he needed very little help, for the strength of the man was enormous.

He came back, apparently unmoved by his effort, and hoisted Johnny on to his back. Again unassisted, he carried the young man to the waiting car below, and flung him into the car. He was followed this time by Jeffrey, wrapped from head to foot in a long waterproof, a chauffeur's cap pulled down over his eyes. They locked both doors of the machine, and Peitro opened the gate and glanced out. There were few people about, and the car swung out and sped at full speed toward Oxford Street.

Closing and locking the gate, the half-caste went up the stairs of the fire-escape two at a time and reported to his gratified master.

Emanuel was gathering the coats and hats of his two guests into a bundle. This done, he opened a cupboard and flung them in, and they immediately disappeared.

"Go down and burn them," he said laconically. "You've done well, Pietro. There's fifty for you to-night."

"Good?" asked the other laconically.

Emanuel favoured him with his benevolent smile. He took the two glasses from which the men had drunk, and these followed the clothes. A careful search of the room brought to light no further evidence of their presence. Satisfied, Emanuel sat down and lit a long, thin cigar. His night's work was not finished. Jeff had left to him what might prove the hardest of all the tasks. From a small cupboard he took a telephone, and pushed in the plug at the end of a long flex. He had some time to wait for the number, but presently he heard a voice which he knew was Marney's.

"Is that you, Marney?" he asked softly, disguising his voice so cleverly that the girl was deceived.

"Yes, daddy. Are you all right? I've been so worried about you."

"Quite all right, darling. Johnny and I have made a very interesting discovery. Will you tell Barney to go to bed, and will you wait up for me —open the door yourself?"

"Is Johnny coming back with you?"

"No, no, darling; I'm coming alone."

"Are you sure everything is all right?" asked the anxious voice.

"Now, don't worry, my pet. I shall be with you at two o'clock. When you hear the car stop at the gate, come out. I don't want to come into the house. I'll explain everything to you."

"But—"

"Do as I ask you, darling," he said, and before she could reply had rung off.

But could Jeff make it? He would like to go himself, but that would mean the employment of a chauffeur, and he did not know one he could trust. He himself was not strong enough to deal with the girl, and, crowning impossibility, motor-car driving was a mystery—that was one of the accomplishments which a long stay in Dartmoor had denied to him.

But could Jeff make it? He took a pencil from his pocket and worked out the times on the white tablecloth. Satisfied, he put away his pencil, and was pouring out a glass of champagne when there was a gentle tap-tap-tap at the door. He looked up in surprise. The man had orders not under any circumstances to come near Room 13, and it was his duty to keep the whole passage clear until he received orders to the contrary.

Tap-tap-tap.

"Come in," he said.

The door opened. A man stood in the doorway. He was dressed in shabby evening clothes; his bow was clumsily tied one stud was missing from his white shirt-front.

"Am I intruding upon your little party?" he asked timidly.

Emanuel said nothing. For a long time he sat staring at this strange apparition. As if unconscious of the amazement and terror he had caused, the visitor sought to read just his frayed shirt-cuffs, which hung almost to the knuckles of his hands. And then:

"Come in, Mr. Reeder," said Emanuel Legge a little breathlessly.

CHAPTER XXVII

MR. REEDER sidled into the room apologetically, closing the door behind him.

"All alone, Mr. Legge?" he asked. "I thought you had company?"

"I had some friends, but they've gone."

"Your son gone, too?" Reeder stared helplessly from one corner of the room to the other. "Dear me, this is a disappointment, a great disappointment."

Emanuel was thinking quickly. In all probability the shabby detective had been watching the front of the house, and would know that they had not left that way. He took a bold step.

"They left a quarter of an hour ago. Peter and Johnny went down the fire-escape—my boy's car was in the yard. We never like to have a car in front of the club premises; people talk so much. And after the publicity we've had—"

Mr. Reeder checked him with a mild murmur of agreement.

"That was the car, was it? I saw it go and wondered what it was all about—Number XC. 9712, blue-painted limousine—Daimler—I may be wrong, but it seemed like a Daimler to me. I know so little about motor-cars that I could be very easily mistaken, and my eyesight is not as good as it used to be."

Emanuel cursed him under his breath.

"Yes, it was a Daimler," he said, "one we bought cheap at the sales."

The absent-minded visitor's eyes were fixed on the table.

"Took their wine-glasses with them?" he asked gently. "I think it is a pretty custom, taking souvenirs of a great occasion. I'm sure they were very happy."

How had he got in, wondered Emanuel? Stevens had strict orders to stop him, and Fernando was at the end of the L-shaped passage. As if he divined the thought that was passing through Legge's mind, Mr. Reeder answered the unspoken question.

"I took the liberty of coming up the fire-escape, too," he said. "It was an interesting experience. One is a little old to begin experiments, and I am not the sort of man that cares very much for climbing, particularly at night."

Following the direction of his eyes, Emanuel saw that a small square of the rusty trousers had been worn, and through the opening a bony white knee.

"Yes, I came up the fire-escape, and fortunately the window was open. I thought I would give you a pleasant surprise. By the way, the escape doesn't go any higher than this floor? That is curious, because, you know, my dear Mr. Legge, it might well happen, in the event of fire, that people would be driven to the roof. If I remember rightly, there is nothing on the roof but a square superstructure—store-room, isn't it? Let me think. Yes, it's a store-room, I'm sure."

"The truth is," interrupted Emanuel, "I had two old acquaintances here, Johnny Gray and Peter Kane. I think you know Peter?"

The other inclined his head gently.

"And they got just a little too merry. I suppose Johnny's not used to wine, and Peter's been a teetotaller for years." He paused. "In fact, they were rather the worse for drink."

"That's very sad." Mr. Reeder shook his head. "Personally, I am a great believer in prohibition. I would prohibit wine and beer, and crooks and forgers, tale-tellers, poisoners"—he paused at the word— "druggers would be a better word," he said. "They took their glasses with them, did they? I hope they will return them. I should not like to think that people I—er—like would be

guilty of so despicable a practice as—er—the petty theft of—er— wine-glasses."
Again his melancholy eyes fell on the table.
"And they only had soup! It is very unusual to get bottled before you've finished the soup, isn't it? I mean, in respectable circles," he added apologetically.
He looked back at the open door over his spectacles.
"I wonder," he mused, "how they got down that fire-escape in the dark in such a sad condition?"
Again his expressionless eyes returned to Emanuel.
"If you see them again, will you tell them that I expect both Mr. Kane and Mr. Johnny—what is his name?—Gray, that is it! to keep an appointment they made with me for to-morrow morning? And that if they do not turn up at my house at ten o'clock..."
He stopped, pursing up his lips as though he were going to whistle. Emanuel wondered what was coming next, and was not left long in doubt.
"Did you feel the cold very much in Dartmoor? They tell me that the winters are very trying, particularly for people of an advanced age. Of course," Mr. Reeder went on, "one can have friends there; one can even have relations there. I suppose it makes things much easier if you know your son or some other close relative is living on the same landing—there are three landings, are there not? But it is much nicer to live in comfort in London, Mr. Legge—to have a cosy little suite in Bloomsbury, such as you have got; to go where you like without a screw following you—I think 'screw' is a very vulgar word, but it means 'warder,' does it not?"
He walked to the door and turned slowly.
"You won't forget that I expect to meet Mr. Peter Kane and Mr. John Gray tomorrow at my house at half-past ten—you won't forget, will you?"
He closed the door carefully behind him, and, with his great umbrella hooked on to his arm, passed along the corridor into the purview of the astounded Fernando, astounding the jailers on guard at the end.
"Good evening," murmured Mr. Reeder as he passed.
Fernando was too overcome to make a courteous reply.
Stevens saw him as he came into the main corridor, and gasped.
"When did you come in, Mr. Reeder?"
"Nobody has ever seen you come in, but lots of people see you go out," said Reeder good-humouredly. "On the other hand, there are people who are seen coming into this club whom nobody sees go out. Mr. Gray didn't pass this way, or Mr. Kane?"
"No, sir," said Stevens in surprise. "Have they gone?"
Reeder sighed heavily.
"Yes, they've gone," he said. "I hope not for long, but they've certainly gone. Good night, Stevens. By the way, your name isn't Stevens, is it? I seem to remember you"—he screwed up his eyes as though he had difficulty in recalling the memory—" I seem to remember your name wasn't Stevens, let us say, eight years ago."
Stevens flushed.
"It is the name I'm known as now, sir."
"A very good name, too, an excellent name," murmured Mr. Reeder as he stepped into the elevator. "And after all, we must try to live down the past. And I'd be the last to remind you of your—er—misfortune."
When he reached the street, two men who had been standing on the opposite sidewalk crossed to him.
"They've gone," said Mr. Reeder. "They were in that car, as I feared. All stations must be

warned, and particularly the town stations just outside of London, to hold up the car. You have its number. You had better watch this place till the morning," he said to one of them.

"Very good, sir."

"I want you especially to follow Emanuel, and keep him under observation until to-morrow morning."

The detective left on duty waited with that philosophical patience which is the greater part of the average detective's equipment, until three o'clock in the morning; and at that hour, when daylight was coming into the sky, Emanuel had not put in an appearance. Stevens went off duty half an hour after Mr. Reeder's departure. At two o'clock the head waiter and three others left, Fernando locking the door. Then, a few minutes before three, the squat figure of Pietro, muffled up in a heavy overcoat, and he too locked the door behind him, disappearing in the direction of Shaftesbury Avenue. At half-past three the detective left a policeman to watch the house, and got on the 'phone to Mr. Reeder, who was staying in town.

"Dear me!" said Mr. Reeder, an even more incongruous sight in pyjamas which were a little too small for him, though happily there were no spectators of his agitation. "Not gone, you say? I will come round."

It was daylight when he arrived. The gate in the yard was opened with a skeleton key (the climb so graphically described by Mr. Reeder was entirely fictitious, and the cut in his trousers was due to catching a jagged nail in one of the packing-cases with which the yard was littered), and he mounted the iron stairway to the third floor.

The window through which he had made his ingress on the previous evening was closed and fastened, but, with the skill of a professional burglar, Mr. Reeder forced back the catch and, opening the window, stepped in.

There was enough daylight to see his whereabouts. Unerringly he made for Emanuel's office. The door had been forced, and there was no need to use the skeleton key. There was no sign of Emanuel, and Reeder came out to hear the report of the detective, who had made a rapid search of the club.

"All the doors are open except No. 13, sir," he said. "That's bolted on the inside. I've got the lock open."

"Try No. 12," said Reeder. "There are two ways in—one by way of a door, which you'll find behind a curtain in the corner of the room, and the other way through the buffet, which communicates with the buffet in No. 13. Break nothing if you can help it, because I don't want my visit here advertised."

He followed the detective into No. 12, and found that there was no necessity to use the buffet entrance, for the communicating door was unlocked. He stepped into No. 13; it was in complete darkness.

"Humph!" said Mr. Reeder, and sniffed. "One of you go along this wall and find the switch. Be careful you don't step on something."

"What is there?"

"I think you'll find...however, turn on the light."

The detective felt his way along the wall, and presently his finger touched a switch and he turned it down. And then they saw all that Mr. Reeder suspected. Sprawled across the table was a still figure—a horrible sight, for the man who had killed Emanuel Legge had used the poker which, twisted and bloodstained, lay amidst the wreckage of rare glass and once snowy napery.

CHAPTER XXVIII

IT was unnecessary to call a doctor to satisfy the police. Emanuel Legge had passed beyond the sphere of his evil activities.
"The poker came from—where?" mused Mr. Reeder, examining the weapon thoughtfully. He glanced down at the little fireplace. The poker and tongs and shovel were intact, and this was of a heavier type than was used in the sitting-rooms.
Deftly he searched the dead man's pockets, and in the waistcoat he found a little card inscribed with a telephone number, "Horsham 98753." Peter's. That had no special significance at the moment, and Reeder put it with the other documents that he had extracted from the dead man's pockets. Later came an inspector to take charge of the case.
"There was some sort of struggle, I imagine," said Mr. Reeder. "The right wrist, I think you'll find, is broken. Legge's revolver was underneath the table. He probably pulled it, and it was struck from his hand. I don't think you'll want me any more, inspector."
He was examining the main corridor when the telephone switchboard at the back of Stevens's little desk gave him an idea. He put through a call to Horsham, and, in spite of the earliness of the hour, was almost immediately answered.
"Who is that?" he asked.
"I'm Mr. Kane's servant," said a husky Voice.
"Oh, is it Barney? Is your master at home yet?"
"No, sir. Who is it speaking?"
"It is Mr. Reeder...Will you tell Miss Kane to come to the telephone?"
"She's not here either. I've been trying to get on to Johnny Gray all night, but his servant says he's out."
"Where is Miss Kane?" asked Reeder quickly.
"I don't know, sir. Somebody came for her in the night in a car, and she went away, leaving the door open. It was the wind slamming it that woke me up."
It was so long before Mr. Reeder answered that Barney thought he had gone away.
"Did nobody call for her during the evening? Did she have any telephone messages?"
"One, sir, about ten o'clock. I think it was her father, from the way she was speaking."
Again a long interval of silence, and then: "I will come straight down to Horsham," said Mr. Reeder, and from the pleasant and conversational quality of his voice, Barney took comfort; though, if he had known the man better, he would have realised that Mr. Reeder was most ordinary when he was most perturbed.
Mr. Reeder pushed the telephone away from him and stood up.
So they had got Marney. There was no other explanation. The dinner party had been arranged to dispose of the men who could protect her. Where had they been taken?
He went back to the old man's office, which was undergoing a search at the hands of a police officer.
"I particularly want to see immediately any document referring to Mr Peter Kane," he said "any road maps which you may find here, and especially letters address to Emanuel Legge by his son. You know, of course, that this office was broken into? There should be something in the shape of clues."
The officer shook his head. "I'm afraid, Mr. Reeder, we won't find much here," he said. "So far,

I've only come across old bills and business letters which you might find in any office."

The detective looked round.

"There is no safe?" he asked.

All the timidity and deference in his manner had gone. He was patently a man of affairs.

"Yes, sir, the safe's behind that panelling. I'll get it open this morning. But I shouldn't imagine that Legge would leave anything compromising on the premises. Besides, his son has had charge of the Highlow for years. Previous to that, they had a manager who is now doing time. Before him, if I remember right, that fellow Fenner, who has been in boob for burglary."

"Fenner?" said the other sharply. "I didn't know he ever managed this club."

"He used to, but he had a quarrel with the old man. I've got an idea they were in jug together."

Fenner's was not the type of mentality one would expect to find among the officers of a club, even a club of the standing of the Highlow: but there was this about the Highlow, that it required less intelligence than sympathy with a certain type of client.

Reeder was assisting the officer by taking out the contents of the pigeon-holes, when his hand touched a knob.

"Hallo, what is this?" he said, and turned it.

The whole desk shifted slightly, and, pulling, he revealed the door to the spiral staircase.

"This is very interesting," he said. He ascended as far as the top landing. There was evidently a door here, but every effort he made to force it ended in failure. He came down again, continuing to the basement, and this time he was joined by the inspector in charge of the case.

"Rather hot," said Mr. Reeder, as he opened the door. "I should say there is a fire burning here."

It took him some time to discover the light connections, and when he did, he whistled. For, lying by the side of the red-hot stove, he saw a piece of shining metal and recognised it. It was an engraver's plate, and one glance told him that it was the finished plate from which £5 notes could be printed.

The basement was empty, and for a second the mystery of the copper plate baffled him.

"We may not have found the Big Printer, but we've certainly found the Big Engraver," he said. "This plate was engraved somewhere upstairs." He pointed to the shaft. "What is it doing down here? Of course!" He slapped his thigh exultantly. "I never dreamt he was right—but he always is right!"

"Who?" asked the officer.

"An old friend of mine, whose theory was that the plates from which the slush was printed were engraved within easy reach of a furnace, into which, in case of a police visitation, they could be pushed and destroyed. And, of course, the engraving plant is somewhere upstairs. But why they should throw down a perfectly new piece of work, and at a time when the attendant was absent, is beyond me. Unless...Get me an axe; I want to see the room on the roof."

The space was too limited for the full swing of an axe, and it was nearly an hour before at last the door leading to the engraver's room was smashed in. The room was flooded with sunshine, for the skylight had not been covered. Reeder's sharp eyes took in the table with a glance, and then he looked beyond, and took a step backward. Lying by the wall, dishevelled, mud-stained, his white dress-shirt crumpled to a pulp, was Peter Kane, and he was asleep!

They dragged him to a chair, bathed his face with cold water, but even then he took a long time to recover.

"He has been drugged: that's obvious," said Mr. Reeder, and scrutinised the hands of the unconscious man for a sign of blood. But though they were covered with rust and grime, Reeder found not so much as one spot of blood; and the first words that Peter uttered, on recovering consciousness, confirmed the view that he was ignorant of the murder.

"Where is Emanuel?" he asked drowsily. "Have you got him?"

"No; but somebody has got him," said Reeder gently, and the shock of the news brought Peter Kane wide awake.

"Murdered!" he said unbelievingly. "Are you sure? Of course, I'm mad to ask you that." He passed his hand wearily across his forehead. "No, I know nothing about it. I suppose you suspect me, and I don't mind telling you that I was willing to murder him if I could have found him." Briefly he related what had happened at the dinner.

"I knew that I was doped, but dope works slowly on me, and the only chance I had was to sham dead. Emanuel gave me a thump in the jaw, and that was my excuse for going out. They got me downstairs into the yard and put me into the car first. I slipped out the other side as soon as the nigger went up to get Johnny. There were a lot of old cement sacks lying about, and I threw a couple on to the floor, hoping that in the darkness they would mistake the bundle for me. Then I lay down amongst the packing-cases and waited. I guessed they'd brought down Johnny, but I was powerless to help him. When the car had gone, and Pietro had gone up again, I followed. I suppose the dope was getting busy, and if I'd had any sense, I should have got over the gate. My first thought was that they might have taken my gun away and left it in the room. I tried to open the door, but it was locked."

"Are you sure of that, Peter?"

"Absolutely sure."

"How long after was this?"

"About half an hour. It took me all that time to get up the stairs, because I had to fight the dope all the way. I heard somebody moving about, and slipped into one of the other rooms, and then I heard the window pulled down and locked. I didn't want to go to sleep, for fear they discovered me; but I must have dozed, for when I woke up, it was dark and cold, and I heard no sound at all. I tried the door of thirteen again, but could make no impression on it. So I went to Emanuel's office. I know the place very well: I used to go in there in the old days, before Emanuel went to jail, and I knew all about the spiral staircase to the roof. All along I suspected that the hut they'd put on the roof was the place where the slush was printed. But here I was mistaken, for I had no sooner got into the room than I saw that it was where the engraver worked. There was a plate on the edge of a shaft. I suppose I was still dizzy, because I fumbled at it. It slipped through my hand, and I heard a clang come up from somewhere below."

"How did you get into this room?"

"The door was open," was the surprising reply. "I have an idea that it is one of those doors that can only be opened and closed from the inside. The real door of the room is in the room in Emanuel's office. It is the only way in, and the only way out, both from the basement and the room on the roof. I don't know what happened after that. I must have lain down, for by now the dope was working powerfully. I ought to let Marney know I'm all right. She'll be worried..."

He saw something in the detective's face, something that made his heart sink.

"Marney! Is anything wrong with Marney?" he asked quickly.

"I don't know. She went out last night—or rather, early this morning—and has not been seen since."

Peter listened, stricken dumb by the news. It seemed to Mr. Reeder that he aged ten years in as few minutes.

"Now, Kane, you've got to tell me all you know about Legge," said Reeder kindly. "I haven't any doubt that Jeffrey's taken her to the big printing place. Where is it?"

Peter shook his head.

"I haven't the least idea," he said. "The earlier slush was printed in this building; in fact, it was printed in Room 13. I've known that for a long time. But as the business grew, young Legge had to find another works. Where he has found it is a mystery to me, and to most other people."

"But you must have heard rumours?" persisted Reeder.

Again Peter shook his head.

"Remember that I mix very little with people of my own profession, or my late profession," he said. "Johnny and old Barney are about the only crooks I know, outside of the Legge family. And Stevens, of course—he was in jail ten years ago. I've lost touch with all the others, and my news has come through Barney, though most of Barney's gossip is unreliable."

They reached Barney by telephone, but he was unable to give any information that was of the slightest use. All that he knew was that the printing works were supposed to be somewhere in the West.

"Johnny knows more about it than I do, or than anybody. All the boys agree as to that," said Barney. "They told him a lot in 'boob'."

Leaving Peter to return home, Mr. Reeder made a call at Johnny's flat. Parker was up. He had been notified earlier in the morning of his master's disappearance, but he had no explanation to offer.

He was preparing to give a list of the clothes that Johnny had been wearing, but Reeder cut him short impatiently.

"Try to think of Mr. Gray as a human being, and not as a tailor's dummy," he said wrathfully. "You realise that he is in very grave danger?"

"I am not at all worried, sir," said the precise Parker. "Mr. Gray was wearing his new sock suspenders—"

For once Mr. Reeder forgot himself.

"You're a damned fool, Parker," he said.

"I hope not, sir." said Parker as he bowed him out.

CHAPTER XXIX

IT was five minutes past two in the morning when Marney, sitting in the drawing-room at the front of the house, heard the sound of a motor-car stop before the house. Going into the hall, she opened the door, and, standing on the step, peered into the darkness.
"Is that you, father?" she asked.
There was no reply, and she walked quickly up the garden path to the gate. The car was a closed coupe, and as she looked over the gate, she saw a hand come out and beckon her, and heard a voice whisper:
"Don't make a noise. Come in here; I want to talk to you. I don't want Barney to see me."
Bewildered, she obeyed. Jerking open the door, she jumped into the dark interior, by the side of the man at the wheel.
"What is it?" she asked.
Then, to her amazement, the car began to move toward the main road. It had evidently circled before it had stopped.
"What is the matter, father?" she asked.
And then she heard a low chuckle that made her blood run cold.
"Go into the back and stay there. If you make a row, I'll spoil that complexion of yours, Marney Legge!"
"Jeffrey!" she gasped.
She gripped the inside handle of the door and had half turned it when he caught her with his disengaged hand and flung her into the back of the car.
"I'll kill you if you make me do that again." There was a queer little sob of pain in his voice, and she remembered his wound.
"Where are you taking me?" she asked.
"I'm taking you to your father," was the unexpected reply. "Will you sit quiet? If you try to get away, or attempt to call assistance, I'll drive you at full speed into the first tree I see and we'll finish the thing together."
From the ferocity of his tone she did not doubt that he would carry his threat into execution. Mile after mile the car sped on, flashing through villages, slowing through the sparsely peopled streets of small towns. It was nearing three o'clock when they came into the street of a town and, looking through the window, she saw a grey facade and knew she was in Oxford.
In ten minutes they were through the city and traversing the main western road. And now, for the first time, Jeffrey Legge became communicative.
"You've never been in 'boob', have you, angel?" he asked.
She did not answer.
"Never been inside the little bird-house with the other canaries, eh? Well, that's an experience ahead of you. I am going to put you in jail, kid. Peter's never been in jail either, but he nearly had the experience to-night."
"I don't believe you," she said. "My father has not broken the law."
"Not for a long time, at any rate," agreed Jeffrey, dexterously lighting a cigarette with one hand. "But there's a little 'boob' waiting for him all right now."
"A prison," she said, incredulously. "I don't believe you."
"You've said that twice, and you're the only person living that's called me a liar that number of

times."

He turned off into a side road, and for a quarter of an hour gave her opportunity for thought.

"It might interest you to know that Johnny is there," he said. "Dear little Johnny! The easiest crook that ever fell—and this time he's got a lifer."

The car began to move down a sharp declivity, and, looking through the rain-spattered windscreen, she saw a squat, dark building ahead.

"Here we are," he said, as the car stopped.

Looking through the window she saw, with a gasp of astonishment, that he had spoken the truth. They were at the door of a prison. The great, black, iron-studded gates were opening as she looked, and the car passed through under the deep archway and stopped.

"Get down," said Jeff, and she obeyed.

A narrow black door led from the archway, and, following her, he caught her by the arm and pushed her through. She was in a narrow room, the walls of which were covered with stained and discoloured whitewash. A large fireplace, overflowing with ashes, a rickety chair and a faded board screwed to the wall were the only furniture. In the dim light of a carbon lamp she saw the almost indistinguishable words: "His Majesty's Prison, Keytown," and beneath, row after row of closely set regulations. A rough-looking, powerfully-built man had followed her into the room, which was obviously the gate-keeper's lodge.

"Have you got the cell ready?"

"Yes, I have." said the man. "Does she want anything to eat?"

"If she does, she'll want," said Jeff curtly.

He took off his greatcoat and hung it on a nail, and then, with Jeffrey's hand gripping her arm, she was led again into the archway and across a small courtyard, through an iron grille gate and a further door. A solitary light that burnt in a bracket near the door, showed her that she was in a small hall. Around this, at the height of about nine feet from the ground, ran a gallery, which was reached by a flight of iron stairs. There was no need to ask what was the meaning of those two rows of black doors that punctured the wall. They were cells. She was in a prison!

While she was wondering what it all meant, a door near at hand was unlocked, and she was pushed in. The cell was a small one, the floor of worn stone, but a new bedstead had been fitted up in one corner. There was a washstand; and, as she was to discover, the cell communicated with another containing a stone bath and washplace.

"The condemned cell," explained Jeffrey Legge with relish. "You'll have plenty of ghosts to keep you company to-night, Marney."

In her heart she was panic-stricken, but she showed none of her fear as she faced him.

"A ghost would be much less repulsive to me than you, Jeffrey Legge," she said, and he seemed taken aback by the spirit she displayed.

"You will have both," he said, as he slammed the door on her and locked it.

The cell was illuminated by a feeble light that came through an opaque pane of glass by the side of the door. Presently, when her eyes grew accustomed to the semi-darkness, she was able to take stock of her surroundings. The prison must have been a very old one, for the walls were at one place worn smooth, probably by the back of some condemned unfortunate who had waited day after day for the hour of doom. She shuddered, as her imagination called to her the agony of soul which these four walls had held.

By standing on the bed she could reach a window. That also was of toughened glass, set in small, rusty frames. Some of the panes were missing, but she guessed that the outlook from the window would not be particularly promising, even supposing she could force the window.

The night had been unusually cold and raw for the time of year, and, pulling a blanket from the bed, she wrapped it about her and sat down on the stool, waiting for the light to grow.

And so, sitting, her weary eyes closing involuntarily, she heard a stealthy tapping. It came from above, and her heart fluttered at the thought that possibly, in the cell above her, her father was held...or Johnny.

Climbing on to the bed, she rapped with her knuckles on the stone ceiling. Somebody answered. They were tapping a message in Morse, which she could not understand. Presently the tapping ceased. She heard footsteps above. And then, looking by chance at the broken pane of the window, she saw something come slowly downward and out of view. She leapt up, gripping the window pane, and saw a piece of black silk.

With difficulty two fingers touched it at last and drew it gently in through the window pane. She pulled it up, and, as she suspected, found a piece of paper tied to the end. It was a bank-note. Bewildered, she gazed at it until it occurred to her that there might be a message written on the other side. The pencil marks were faint, and she carried the note as near to the light as she could get.

"Who is there? Is it you, Peter? I am up above. Johnny."

She suppressed the cry that rose to her lips. Both Johnny and her father were there. Then Jeffrey had not lied.

How could she answer? She had no pencil. Then she saw that the end of the cotton was weighted by a small piece of pencil, the kind that is found attached to a dance programme. With this unsatisfactory medium she wrote a reply and pushed it through the window, and after a while she saw it drawn up. Johnny was there—and Johnny knew. She felt strangely comforted by his presence, impotent though he was.

For half an hour she waited at the window, but now the daylight had come, and evidently Johnny thought it was too dangerous to make any further communications.

Exhausted, she lay down on the bed, intending to remain awake, but within five minutes she was sleeping heavily. The sound of a key in the lock made her spring to her feet. It was the man she had seen in the early morning; he was carrying a big tray, set with a clumsy cup and saucer, six slices of bread and butter, and an enormous teapot. He put it down on the bed, for want of a table, and without a word went out. She looked at the little platinum watch on her wrist: it was ten o'clock. Half an hour later the man came and took away the tray.

"Where am I?" she asked.

"You're in 'boob,'" he said with quiet amusement. "But it is better than any other 'boob' you've ever been in, young lady. And don't try to ask me questions, because you'll not get a civil answer if you do."

At two o'clock came another meal, a little more tastily served this time. It seemed, from the appearance of the plate, that Jeffrey had sent into Oxford for a new service specially for her benefit. Again she attempted to discover what had happened to her father, but with no more satisfactory result.

The weary day dragged through; every minute seemed an hour, every hour interminable. Darkness had fallen again when the last of the visits was made, and this time it was Jeffrey Legge. At the sight of his face, all her terror turned to wonder. He was ghastly pale, his eyes burnt strangely, and the hand that came up to his lips was trembling as though he were suffering from a fever. "What do you want?" she asked.

"I want you," he said brokenly. "I want you for the life of my father!"

"What do you mean?" she gasped.

"Peter Kane killed my father last night," he said.

"You're mad," she gasped. "My father is here—you told me."

"I told you a lie. What does it matter what I told you, anyway? Peter Kane escaped on the way to Keytown, and he went back to the club and killed my father!"

CHAPTER XXX

THE girl looked at him, speechless.

"It isn't true!" she cried.

"It's not true, isn't it?" Jeffrey almost howled the words. He was mad with hate, with grief, with desire for cruel vengeance. "I'll show you whether it's not true, my lady. You're my wife—do you understand that? If you don't, you're going to."

He flung out of the cell, turning to voice his foul mind, and then the door clanged on her, and he strode out of the hall into the little house that was once the Governor's residence, and which was now the general headquarters of the Big Printer.

He poured himself out a stiff dose of whisky and drank it undiluted, and the man who had accompanied him watched him curiously.

"Jeff, it looks to me as if it's time to make a get-away. We can't keep these people here very long. The men are scared, too."

"Scared, are they?" sneered Jeffrey Legge. "I guess they'd be more scared if they were in front of a judge and jury."

"That's the kind of scare they're anxious to avoid," said his lieutenant calmly. "Anyway, Jeff, we're getting near the end, and it seems to me that it's the time for all sensible men to find a little home on the other side of the water."

Legge thought for a long time, and when he spoke his voice was more calm.

"Perhaps you're right," he said. "Tell them they can clear to-night."

The other man was taken aback by the answer.

"To-night?" he said. "Well, I don't know that there's that hurry."

"Tell 'em to clear to-night. They've got all the money they want. I'm shutting this down."

"Who killed your father?"

"Peter Kane," snarled Legge. "I've got the full strength of it. The police are hiding him up, but he did the killing all right. They found him on the premises in the morning."

He sat awhile, staring moodily at the glass in his hand.

"Let them go to-night," he said, "every one of them. I'll tell them myself."

"Do you want me to go?" asked the other.

Legge nodded.

"Yes; I want to be alone. I'm going to fix two people tonight," he said, between his teeth, "and I'm fixing them good."

"Some of the men like Johnny Gray; they were in boob with him," suggested his assistant, but Jeffrey stopped him with an oath.

"That's another reason they can get out," he said, "and they can't know too soon."

He jumped to his feet and strode out of the room, the man following at a distance.

There were two halls to the prison, and it was into the second that he turned. This was brilliantly illuminated. The doors had been removed from most of the cells, and several of them were obviously sleeping-rooms for the half a dozen men who sat about a table playing cards. At only four places were the cell doors intact, for behind these were the delicate printing presses which from morning till night were turning out and numbering French, American and English paper currency. There was not one of the men at the table, or who came to the doors of their cubicles, attracted by the unusual appearance of Legge, who had not served long terms of imprisonment on forgery charges. Jeffrey had recruited them as carefully as a theatrical producer recruits his beauty chorus. They were men without homes, without people, mainly without hope; men inured to the prison system, and who found, in this novel method of living, a delightful variation of the life to which they were most accustomed.

It was believed by the authorities that Keytown Jail was in the hands of a syndicate engaged in experimental work of a highly complicated character, and no obstacle had been placed in the way of laying power cables to the "laboratories." Jeff had found the safest asylum in the land, and one which was more strongly guarded than any he could have built.

His speech was short and to the point.

"Boys, I guess that the time has come when we've got to make the best of our way home. You've all enough money to live comfortably on for the rest of your lives, and I advise you to get out of the country as soon as you can. You have your passports; you know me way; and there's no time like the present."

"Do you mean that we've got to go to-night, Jeff?" asked a voice.

"I mean to-night. I'll have a car run you into London; but you'll have to leave your kit behind, but you can afford that."

"What are you going to do with the factory?"

"That's my business," said Jeff.

The proposal did not find universal favour, but they stood in such awe of the Big Printer that, though they demurred, they obeyed. By ten o'clock that night the prison was empty, except for Jeffrey and his assistant.

"I didn't see Bill Holliss go," said the latter; but Jeffrey Legge was too intent upon his plans to give the matter a moment's thought.

"Maybe you'll see yourself go now, Jenkins," said he "You can take your two-seater and run anywhere you like."

"Let me stay till the morning," asked the man.

"You'll go to-night. Otherwise, what's the use of sending the other fellows away?"

He closed the big gate upon the car. He was alone with his wife and with the man he hated. He could think calmly now. The madness of rage had passed. He made a search of a little storeroom and found what he was looking for. It was a stout rope. With this over his arm, and a storm-lamp in his hand, he went out into the yard and came to a little shed built against the wall. Unlocking the rusty padlock, he pulled the doors apart. The shed was empty; the floor was inches thick with litter, and, going back, he found a broom and swept it clean. With the aid of a ladder he mounted to a beam that ran transversely across the roof, and fastened one end of the rope securely.

Coming down, he spent half an hour in making a noose.

He was in the death-house. Under his feet was the fatal trap that a pull of the rusty lever would spring. He wanted to make the experiment, but the trap would take a lot of time to pull up. His face was pouring with perspiration when he had finished. The night was close, and a flicker of lightning illuminated for a second the gloomy recesses of the prison yard.

As he entered the hall a low growl of thunder came to him, but the storm in his heart was more violent than any nature could provide.

He tiptoed up the iron stairs to the landing, and came at last to No. 4 and hesitated. His enemy could wait. Creeping down the stairs again, his heart beating thunderously, he stood outside the door of the condemned cell. The key trembled as he inserted it in the lock. No sound broke the stillness as the door opened stealthily, and he slipped into the room.

He waited, holding his breath, not knowing whether she were awake or asleep, and then crept

forward to the bed. He saw the outline of a figure.
"Marney," he said huskily, groping for her face.
And then two hands like steel clamps caught him by the throat and flung him backward.
"I want you, Jeffrey Legge," said a voice—the voice of Johnny Gray.

CHAPTER XXXI

JOHNNY GRAY came to consciousness with a violent headache and a sense of suffocating restriction, which he discovered was due to his wing collar holding tightly in spite of the rough usage that had been his. This fact would have been pleasing to Parker, but was intensely discomforting to the wearer, and in a minute he had stripped the offending collar from his throat and had risen unsteadily to his feet.

The room in which he was had a familiar appearance. It was a cell, and —Keytown Jail! He remembered Fenner's warning. So Fenner knew! Keytown Jail, sold by the Government to—Jeffrey Legge! The idea was preposterous; but why not? A timber merchant had bought a jail at Hereford; a firm of caterers had purchased an old prison in the North of England, and were serving afternoon teas in the cells.

Now he understood. Keytown Prison was the headquarters of the Big Printer. The one place in the world that the police would never dream of searching, particularly if, as he guessed, Jeffrey Legge had offered some specious excuse for his presence and the presence of his company in this isolated part of the world.

The sound of voices came faintly up to him, and he heard a door bang and the clicking of locks; and with that sound he recalled the happenings of the evening. It must be Peter: they had got him too. In spite of his discomfiture, in spite of the awful danger in which he knew he was, he laughed softly to himself.

Above his bed was a window with scarcely a whole pane. But there was no escape that way. A thought struck him, and, leaning down, he tapped a Morse message on the floor. If it was Peter, he could understand. He heard the answering tap which came feebly, and when he signalled again he knew that whoever was in the cell below had no knowledge of the Morse code. He searched his pockets and found a tiny scrap of pencil, but could find no paper, except a bundle of five-pound notes, which his captors had not troubled to remove. Here was both stationery and the means of writing, but how could he communicate with the occupant of the cell below? Presently a plan suggested itself, and he tore off the lapel of his dinner-jacket and unravelled the silk. Tying the pencil to the end to give it weight, he slowly lowered his message, hoping, though it seemed unlikely, that his fellow-prisoner would be able to see the paper.

To his joy he felt a tug, and when, a few minutes later, he carefully drew up the message, it was to find, written underneath his own, one which left him white and shaking. Marney here! He groaned aloud at the thought. It was too light now to risk any further communication. There was a ewer of water and a basin in the cell, and with this he relieved the aching in his head; and when breakfast came, he was ready.

The man who brought in the tray was a stranger to him, as also was the man who stood on guard at the door, revolver in hand.

"What's the great idea?" asked Johnny coolly, sitting on the bed and swinging his legs. "Has Jeff bought a jail to practise in? Wouldn't it have been cheaper to have gone over the Alps?"

"You shut up, Johnny Gray," growled the man. "You'll be sorry for yourself before you're out of here."

"Who isn't?" asked Johnny. "How is Peter?"

"You know damned well Peter has escaped," said the other before he could check himself.

"Escaped!" said the delighted Johnny. "You don't mean that?"

"Never mind what I mean," growled the man, realising he had said too much. "You keep a civil tongue in your head, Gray, and you'll be treated square. If you don't, there are plenty of men on the spot to make Dartmoor a paradise compared with Keytown."

The door slammed in Johnny Gray's face, but he was so absorbed in the news which the man had unwillingly given to him that he had to force himself to eat.

Soon after the man came to take away the tray.

"What's your name, bo', anyway?" said Johnny carelessly. "I hate calling you 'face'—it's low."

"Bill's my name," said the man, "and you needn't call me Bill either. You say 'sir' to me."

"Woof!" said Johnny admiringly. "You're talking like a real screw!"

The door slammed in his face. He had further time to consider his plans. They had taken away his watch and chain, his gold cigarette-case and the small penknife he carried, but these losses did not worry him in the slightest. His chief anxiety was to know the exact character of Keytown Prison. And that he determined to learn at the earliest opportunity.

It was late in the afternoon; he guessed it was somewhere in the neighbourhood of four when his lunch came, and he was quite ready to eat it, though a little suspicious of its possible accessories.

"No poison in this, Bill?" he asked pleasantly as he took the bread and cheese from the man's hand.

"There's no need to poison you; we could starve you, couldn't we?" said the other. "If Jeff was here, maybe I'd get a rapping for giving you anything."

"Gone away, has he? Well, prisons are more pleasant when the governor's away. Am I right, Bill? Now, what do you say to a couple of hundred of real money?"

"For what?" asked the man, stopping at the door. "If you mean it's for letting you make a get-away, why, you're silly! You're going to stay here till Jeff fixes you."

All the day Johnny had heard, or rather felt, a peculiar whirr of sound coming from some remote quarter of the prison.

"Got electric light here, Bill?" he said conversationally.

"Yes, we have," said the other. "This is a model boob, this is."

"I'll bet it is," said Johnny grimly. "Are you running any electric radiators in my cell to-night, or do you want all the power for the press?" He saw the man's face twitch. "Of course, you're running the slush factory here —everybody knows that. Take my advice, Bill—go whilst the going's good. Or the bulls will have you inside the realest boob you've seen." He had made the guard more than a little uncomfortable, as he saw, and sought to press home the impression he had created. "Jeffrey's going to shop you sooner or later, because he's a natural born shopper. And he's got the money, Bill, to get away with, and the motor-cars and aeroplanes. You haven't got that. You'll have to walk on your own pads. And the bulls will get you half-way over the field."

"Oh, shut up!" said the man uncomfortably, and the conversation ended, as in the morning, with the slamming of the door.

Presently a little spy-hole in the cell door opened.

"What made you think this is a print-shop?" asked Bill's voice.

"I don't think anything about it; I know," said Johnny decisively. "If you like to come to me this evening I'll tell you the name of every worker here, the position of every press, and the length of the lagging you'll get."

The cover of the spy-hole dropped.

Jeffrey was away; that was all to the good. If he remained away for the whole of the night...He was worried about Marney, and it required all his strength of will not to fret himself into a state of nerves.

In an hour Bill returned, and this time he brought no guard but himself, but, for safety's sake, carried on his conversation through a little grille in the door.

"You're bluffing, Johnny Gray. We've got a fellow here who was in boob with you, and he says you're the biggest bluffer that ever lived. You don't know anything."

"I know almost everything," said Johnny immodestly. "For instance, I know you've got a young lady in the cell below. How's she doing?"

The man was taken aback for a moment.

"Who told you?" he asked suspiciously. "Nobody else has been here, have they?"

"Nobody at all. It is part of my general knowledge. Now listen, Bill. How are you treating that lady? And your life hangs on your answer—don't forget it."

"She's all right," said Bill casually. "They've given her the condemned cell, with a bathroom and all, and a proper bed—not like yours. And you can't scare me, Gray."

"I'll bet I can't," said Johnny. "Bring me some water."

But the water was not forthcoming, and it was dark before the man made his reappearance. Johnny listened at the door; he was coming alone. Johnny pulled up the leg of his trousers and showed those suspenders which were Parker's pride. But they were not ordinary suspenders. Strapped to the inside of the calf was a small holster. The automatic it carried was less than four inches in length, but its little blunt-nosed bullets were man-stoppers of a peculiarly deadly kind. The door swung open, and Bill stepped in.

"Jeff's back—" he began, and then: "Step in, and step lively," said Johnny.

His arm had shot out, and the pistol hand of the jailer was pinned to his side.

"This gun may look pretty paltry, but it would blow a square inch out of your heart, and that's enough to seriously inconvenience you for the remainder of your short life." With a turn of his wrist he wrenched the revolver from the man's grasp. "Sit over there," he said. "Is anybody in the hall?"

"For God's sake, don't let Jeff see you. He'll kill me," pleaded the agitated prisoner.

"I'd hate for him to do that," said Johnny. He peeped out into the hall: it was empty, and he went back to his prisoner. "Stand against the wall. I'm going to give you the twice-over."

His hands searched quickly but effectively. The key he was putting in his pocket when he noticed the design of the ward. "Pass-key, I fancy. Now, don't make a fuss, Bill, because you'll be let out first thing in the morning, and maybe I'll have a good word to say for you at the Oxford Assizes. There's something about you that I like. Give me the simple criminal, and the Lord knows you're simple enough!"

He stepped out of the cell, snapped the lock of the door, and, keeping in the shadow, walked swiftly along the gallery until he came to the open stairway on to the floor below.

The hall was untenanted. Apparently Bill was the only jailer. He had reached the floor when the door at the end of the hall opened and somebody came in. He flattened himself in one of the recessed cell doorways. Two men entered, and one, he guessed, was Jeff. One, two, three, four—the fourth door from the end. That was Marney's door, immediately under his own. He saw Jeffrey stop, heard the too-familiar grind of the lock, and his enemy disappeared, leaving the second man on guard outside.

If Jeffrey had made an attempt to close the door behind him, Johnny would have shot down the guard and taken the consequences. But the man was absent for only a few minutes. When he came out, he was shouting incoherently threats that made the hair rise on Johnny Gray's neck. But they were only threats.

The hall door closed on Jeffrey Legge and Johnny moved swiftly to No. 4. As the door opened, the girl shrank back against the wall.

"Don't touch me!" she cried.

"Marney!"

At the sound of his voice she stood, rooted to the spot. The next second she was laughing and weeping in his arms.

"But, Johnny, how did you get here?...where were you?...you won't leave me?"

He soothed her and quietened her as only Johnny Gray could. "I'll stay... I think this fellow will come back. If he does, he will wish he hadn't!" And Jeffrey came. As the grip of strong hands closed on his throat, and the hateful voice of his enemy came to his ears, Johnny's prophecy was justified.

CHAPTER XXXII

FOR a second Legge was paralysed with rage and fear. Then, in the wildness of his despair, he kicked at the man, who had slipped from the bed and was holding him. He heard an exclamation, felt for a second the fingers relax; and, slipping like an eel from the grasp, flew to the door and closed it. He stood, breathless and panting by the doorway, until he heard the sound of steel against the inner keyhole, and in a flash realised that Johnny had secured the pass-key. Quick as lightning, he slipped his own key back into the lock and turned it slightly, so that it could not be pushed out from the other side.

Johnny Gray! How had he got there? He fled up the stairs and hammered on the door of the cell where he thought his prisoner was held safe. A surly voice replied to him.

"You swine!" he howled. "You let him go! You twister! You can stay there and starve, damn you!"

"I didn't let him go. He held me up. Look out, Jeff, he's got a gun."

The news staggered the man. The search of Johnny's clothing had been of a perfunctory nature, but he had thought that it was impossible that any kind of weapon could have been concealed.

"Let me out, guv'nor," pleaded the prisoner. "You've got a key."

There was a third key in his house, Jeffrey remembered. Perhaps this man might be of use to him. He was still weak from his wound, and would need assistance.

"All right, I'll get the key. But if you shopped me—"

"I didn't shop you, I tell you. He held me up—"

Legge went back to his room, found the key, and, taking another stiff dose of whisky, returned and released his man.

"He's got my gun, too," explained Bill. "Where are all the fellows? We'll soon settle with him."

"They've gone," said Jeffrey.

What a fool he had been! If he had had the sense to keep the gang together only for a few hours—But he was safe, unless Johnny found a means of getting through the window.

"In my room you'll find a pistol; it is in the top right-hand corner of my desk," he said quickly. "Take it and get outside Johnny's cell—on the yard side. If he tries to escape that way, shoot. Because, if he escapes, you're going a long journey, my friend."

Inside the cell, a chagrined Johnny Gray sat down on the girl's bed to consider the possibilities of the position.

"My dear, there's going to be serious trouble here, and I don't want you to think otherwise," he said. "I should imagine there were quite a number of men in this prison, in which case, though I shall probably get two or three of them, they'll certainly get me in the end."

She sat by his side, holding his hand, and the pressure of her fingers was eloquent of the faith she had in him.

"Johnny, dear, does it matter very much what happens now? They can't come in, and we can't get out. How long will it take to starve us to death?"

Johnny had already considered that problem.

"About three days," he said, in such a matter-of-fact tone that she laughed. "My only hope, Marney, is that your father, who, as I told you, has escaped, may know more about this place than he has admitted."

"Did you know anything about it?" she asked.

He hesitated.

"Yes, I think I did. I wasn't sure, though I was a fool not to locate it just as soon as Fenner warned me against Keytown Jail. These chaps like to speak in parables, and mystery is as the breath of their nostrils. Besides, I should have been certain that Fenner knew the jail had been taken over from the Government."

He made a careful examination of the bars about the window, but without instruments or tools to force them, he knew that escape that way was impossible. When, in the early hours of the morning, he saw the patient figure of Bill, he realised the extent of the impossibility.

"Good morning, William. I see you're out," he greeted the scowling sentry, who immediately jumped to cover, flourishing his long-barrelled weapon.

"Don't you show your nose, or I'll blow it off," he threatened. "We've got you, Mr. Gray."

"They've got you, alas, my poor William," said Johnny sadly. "The busies will be here at nine o'clock—you don't suppose that I should have let myself come into a trap like this? Of course, I didn't. I squeaked! It was my only chance, William. And your only chance is to sneak away at the earliest opportunity, and turn State's evidence. I'm addressing you as a friend."

"You'll never get away from here alive," said the man. "Jeff's going to fix you."

"Indeed?" the prisoner began politely, when a scream made him turn.

"Johnny!"

The shutter which hid the grille in the door was swung back, and the muzzle of Jeffrey's Browning had been pushed through one of the openings. As Johnny dropped flat on the bed, he was stunned by the deafening sound of an explosion. Something hit the wall, ricochetted to the roof, and fell almost at the girl's feet. Before the pistol could be withdrawn, Johnny Gray had fired. A jagged end of iron showed where his bullet struck.

"The time for persiflage," said Johnny cheerfully, "is past. Now you will sit in that corner, young lady, and will not budge without permission." He pointed to the wall nearest the door, which afforded perfect cover, and, dragging up a stool, he seated himself by her side. "Jeffrey's got quite a tough proposition," he said in his conversational tone. "He can't burn the prison, because there's nothing to burn. He can't come in, and he mustn't go out. If he would only for one moment take away that infernal key—"

"There is another door going out from the bathroom," she said suddenly. "I think it leads to an exercise ground. You can just see a little railed- off space through the window."

Johnny went into the bathroom and examined the door. Screwing his head, he could see, through a broken pane, ten square yards of space, where in olden times a condemned prisoner took his exercise, removed from the gaze of his fellows. He tried the key, and to his delight, it turned. Another minute and he was in the little paved yard.

Looking round, he saw a high and narrow gateway, which seemed to be the only exit from the courtyard. And on the other side of that gateway was William, the sentry, well armed and sufficiently terrified to be dangerous. Slipping off his boots, Johnny crept to the gate and listened. The sound of the man's footsteps pacing the flagged walk came to him. Stooping, he squinted through the keyhole, and saw Bill standing, his back toward him, some six yards away. There was no time to be lost. He inserted the key, and the gate was opened before the man could turn to face the levelled revolver.

"Don't shout," whispered Johnny. "You're either discreet or dead. Hand over that gun, you unfortunate man." He moved swiftly toward the terrified criminal, and relieved him of his weapon. With a gesture, Johnny directed him to the exercise yard. "Get in and stay," he said, and locked the door, and for the second time. Bill (his other name, Johnny never discovered, was

Holliss) was a prisoner.

Skirting the building, he came to the entrance of the hall. The door was open, and with his hand on the uplifted hammer of the gun, and his finger pressing the trigger, Johnny leapt into the building. "Hands up!" he shouted.

At the words, Jeffrey Legge spun round. There was a boom of sound, something whistled past Gray's face, and he fired twice. But now the man was running, zigzagging to left and right, and Johnny hesitated to fire. He disappeared through the door at the farther end of the hall, shutting it behind him, and Johnny raced after him.

He was in the courtyard now, facing the grille-covered archway. As he came into view, Jeffrey disappeared through the lodge-keeper's door. Johnny tried the grille, but in vain, for a pass-key operates on all locks save the lock of the entrance gate of a prison. That alone is distinct, and may not be opened save by the key that was cut for it.

Covering the lodge-keeper's door with his gun, Johnny waited, and, waiting, heard a rumbling sound. Something was coming down the centre of the archway. The straight line of it came lower and lower. A hanging gate! He had forgotten that most old country prisons were so equipped. Under the cover of this ancient portcullis, Legge could escape, for it masked the entrance of the lodge.

He turned back to the girl.

"Keep out of sight. He's got away," he warned her. "This fellow isn't finished yet."

The gate was down. Jeffrey put on the overcoat he had left in the lodge, slipped his pistol into his pocket and opened the great gates. He had at least a dozen hours' start, he thought, as he stepped into the open...

"Please do not put your hand in your pocket, Mr. Jeffrey," said a plaintive voice. "I should so hate to shoot a fellow-creature. It would be a deed utterly repugnant to my finest feelings."

Jeffrey raised his hands to their fullest extent, for Mr. Reeder was not alone. Behind him were four armed policemen, a cordon of mounted constabulary, spread in a semicircle, cutting off all avenues of escape. And, most ominous of all, was the deadly scrutiny of Peter Kane, who stood at Feeder's right hand.

CHAPTER XXXIII

FOR the first time Jeffrey Legge felt the cold contact of handcuffs. He was led back to the porter's lodge, whilst two of the policemen worked at the windlass that raised the hanging gate.
"It's a cop, Craig," he said, for the inspector in charge was that redoubtable thief-catcher. "But I'm going to squeak all I know. Johnny Gray is in this. He's been working my slush for years. You'll find the presses in the second hall, but the other birds have done some quick flying."
"They've all flown into the police station at Oxford," said Craig, "and they're singing their pretty little songs merrily. The Oxford police took a whole carload of them about eleven o'clock last night. Unfortunately, they weren't so ready to squeak as you."
"Johnny Gray's in it, I tell you."
"Oh, how can you say such a thing?" said the shocked Mr. Reeder. "I'm perfectly sure Mr. Gray is quite innocent."
Jeffrey regarded him with a sneer of contempt.
"You're a pretty funny 'busy'. I suppose Craig brought you here?"
"No," murmured Mr. Reeder, "I brought myself here."
"The only thing I can say about you," said Jeffrey Legge, "is that you're smarter than old Golden—and that's not saying much."
"Not very much," murmured Mr. Reeder."
"But you're not smart enough to know that Johnny Gray has been in this business for years."
"Even while he was in prison?" suggested Mr. Reeder innocently. "The opportunities are rather restricted, don't you think? But don't let us quarrel, Mr. Jeffrey."
The portcullis was raised now, and in a few minutes the girl was in her father's arms.
"Johnny, you've had a narrow squeak," said Craig, as he shook the man's hand, "and there's some talk about you being in this slush business, but I'll not believe it till I get proof."
"Who killed old Legge?" asked Johnny.
The detective shook his head.
"We don't know. But Stevens has disappeared, and Stevens was Fenner's brother. I got it from Mr. Reeder, who seems to have remarkable sources of information."
"Not at all," disclaimed the apologetic Reeder. "I certainly have a remarkable source of information, and to that all credit must go. But I think you will confirm my statement, John, that Stevens is Fenner's brother?"
To Peter's surprise, Johnny nodded. "Yes, I knew they were brothers; and it is unnecessary to say that their name was neither Stevens nor Fenner. It is pretty well established that the old man gave away Fenner—shopped him for the Berkeley Square job—and possibly Stevens got to know of this, and had been waiting his opportunity to settle accounts with Emanuel. Have you caught him?"
"Not yet," said Craig.
"I hope you won't," said Johnny. "What are you going to do about me, Peter?"
He put his arm round the girl's shoulder, and Peter smiled. "I suppose I'll have to let her marry you, Johnny, whether you're a crook or honest. I want you to go straight, and I'll make it worth while—"
"That I can promise you." It was Mr. Reeder who spoke. "And may I offer an apology. I'm rather a wolf in sheep's clothing, or a sheep in wolf's clothing. The truth is, my name is Golden."

"Golden!" gasped Craig. "But I thought Golden was out of this business?"

"He is out of it, and yet he is in it," explained Mr. Reeder carefully. "I am an excellent office man," he confessed, in that mincing manner of his, staring owlishly over his glasses, "but a very indifferent seeker of information, and although, when Mr. John Gray Reeder was appointed over me as chief inspector of my department—'

"Here, stop!" said the dazed Craig. "John Gray Reeder? Who is Inspector John Gray Reeder?"

Mr. Golden's hand went out in the direction of the smiling Johnny.

"Johnny! You a 'busy'!" said the bewildered Peter. "But you went to jail sure enough?"

"I certainly went to jail," said Johnny. "It was the only place I could get any news about the Big Printer, and I found out all I wanted to know. It was a trying two years, but well worth it, though I nearly lost the only thing in the world that made life worth living," he said. "You've got to forgive me, Peter, because I spied on you—a good spy doesn't play favourites. I've been watching you and every one of your pals, and I watched Marney most of all. And now I'm going to watch her for years and years!"

"You see," said Mr. Golden, who seemed most anxious to exculpate himself from any accusation of cleverness, "I was merely the listener-in, if I may use a new-fangled expression, to the information which John broadcasted. I knew all about this marriage, and I was the person who appointed a woman detective to look after her at the Charlton Hotel—but on Johnny's instructions. That is why he was able to prove his alibi, because naturally, that section of the police which knows him, is always ready to prove alibis for other officers of the police who are mistakenly charged with being criminals."

"How did you guess about the prison?"

"Fenner squeaked," said Mr. Golden with a gesture of deprecation. "'Squeak' is not a word I like, but it is rather expressive. Yes, Fenner squeaked."

Two happy people drove home together in the car which had brought Marney to Keytown. The country between Oxford and Horsham is the most beautiful in the land. The road passes through great aisles of tall trees, into which a car may be turned and be hidden from the view of those who pass along the road. Johnny slowed the machine at an appropriate spot, and put it toward the thickest part of the wood. And Marney, who sat with folded hands by his side, did not seek any explanation for his eccentricity.

The Mind of Mr. J.G. Reeder

I. — THE POETICAL POLICEMAN

First published under the title "The Strange Case of the Night Watchman" in
The Grand Magazine, Vol. 46, Sep 1924-Feb 1925, as part of the J.G. Reeder series
"The Man Who Saw Evil"

THE day Mr. Reeder arrived at the Public Prosecutor's office was indeed a day of fate for Mr. Lambton Green, Branch Manager of the London Scottish and Midland Bank.

That branch of the bank which Mr. Green controlled was situate at the corner of Pell Street and Firling Avenue on the 'country side' of Ealing. It is a fairly large building and, unlike most suburban branch offices, the whole of the premises were devoted to banking business, for the bank carried very heavy deposits, the Lunar Traction Company, with three thousand people on its pay-roll, the Associated Novelties Corporation, with its enormous turnover, and the Laraphone Company being only three of the L.S.M.'s customers.

On Wednesday afternoons, in preparation for the pay days of these corporations, large sums in currency were brought from the head office and deposited in the steel and concrete strong-room, which was immediately beneath Mr. Green's private office, but admission to which was gained through a steel door in the general office. This door was observable from the street, and to assist observation there was a shaded lamp fixed to the wall immediately above, which threw a powerful beam of light upon the door. Further security was ensured by the employment of a night watchman, Arthur Malling, an army pensioner.

The bank lay on a restricted police beat which had been so arranged that the constable on patrol passed the bank every forty minutes. It was his practice to look through the window and exchange signals with the night watchman, his orders being to wait until Malling appeared.

On the night of October 17th Police Constable Burnett stopped as usual before the wide peep-hole and glanced into the bank. The first thing he noticed was that the lamp above the strong-room door had been extinguished. The night watchman was not visible, and, his suspicions aroused, the officer did not wait for the man to put in an appearance as he would ordinarily have done, but passed the window to the door, which, to his alarm, he found ajar. Pushing it open, he entered the bank, calling Malling by name.

There was no answer.

Permeating the air was a faint, sweet scent which he could not locate. The general offices were empty and, entering the manager's room in which a light burnt, he saw a figure stretched upon the ground. It was the night watchman. His wrists were handcuffed, two straps had been tightly buckled about his knees and ankles.

The explanation for the strange and sickly aroma was now clear. Above the head of the prostrate man was suspended, by a wire hooked to the picture-rail, an old tin can, the bottom of which was perforated so that there fell an incessant trickle of some volatile liquid upon the thick cotton pad which covered Malling's face.

Burnett, who had been wounded in the war, had instantly recognised the smell of chloroform and, dragging the unconscious man into the outer office, snatched the pad from his face and, leaving him only long enough to telephone to the police station, sought vainly to bring him to consciousness.

The police reserves arrived within a few minutes, and with them the divisional surgeon who, fortunately, had been at the station when the alarm came through. Every effort to restore the unfortunate man to life proved unavailing.

'He was probably dead when he was found,' was the police doctor's verdict. 'What those scratches are on his right palm is a mystery.'

He pulled open the clenched fist and showed half a dozen little scratches. They were recent, for there was a smear of blood on the palm.

Burnett was sent at once to arouse Mr. Green, the manager, who lived in Firling Avenue, at the corner of which the bank stood; a street of semi- detached villas of a pattern familiar enough to the Londoner. As the officer walked through the little front garden to the door he saw a light through the panels, and he had hardly knocked before the door was opened and Mr. Lambton Green appeared, fully dressed and, to the officer's discerning eye, in a state of considerable agitation. Constable Burnett saw on a hall chair a big bag, a travelling rug and an umbrella.

The little manager listened, pale as death, whilst Burnett told him of his discovery.

'The bank robbed? Impossible!' he almost shrieked. 'My God! this is awful!'

He was so near the point of collapse that Burnett had to assist him into the street.

'I — I was going away on a holiday,' he said incoherently, as he walked up the dark thoroughfare towards the bank premises. 'The fact is — I was leaving the bank. I left a note explaining to the directors.'

Into a circle of suspicious men the manager tottered. He unlocked the drawer of his desk, looked and crumbled up.

'They're not here!' he said wildly. 'I left them here — my keys — with the note!'

And then he swooned. When the dazed man recovered he found himself in a police cell and, later in the day, he drooped before a police magistrate, supported by two constables and listened, like a man in a dream, to a charge of causing the death of Arthur Malling, and further, of converting to his own use the sum of £100,000.

It was on the morning of the first remand that Mr. John G. Reeder, with some reluctance for he was suspicious of all Government departments, transferred himself from his own office on Lower Regent Street to a somewhat gloomy bureau on the top floor of the building which housed the Public Prosecutor. In making this change he advanced only one stipulation: that he should be connected by private telephone wire with his old bureau.

He did not demand this — he never demanded anything. He asked, nervously and apologetically. There was a certain wistful helplessness about John G. Reeder that made people feel sorry for him, that caused even the Public Prosecutor a few uneasy moments of doubt as to whether he had been quite wise in substituting this weak-appearing man of middle age for Inspector Holford — bluff, capable and heavily mysterious.

Mr. Reeder was something over fifty, a long-faced gentleman with sandy- grey hair and a slither of side whiskers that mercifully distracted attention from his large outstanding ears. He wore half-way down his nose a pair of steel-rimmed pince-nez, through which nobody had ever seen him look — they were invariably removed when he was reading. A high and flat-crowned bowler hat matched and yet did not match a frockcoat tightly buttoned across his sparse chest. His boots were square-toed, his cravat—of the broad, chest-protector pattern—was ready-made and buckled into place behind a Gladstonian collar. The neatest appendage to Mr. Reeder was an umbrella rolled so tightly that it might be mistaken for a frivolous walking cane. Rain or shine, he carried this article hooked to his arm, and within living memory it had never been unfurled.

Inspector Holford (promoted now to the responsibilities of Superintendent) met him in the office to hand over his duties, and a more tangible quantity in the shape of old furniture and fixings.

'Glad to know you, Mr. Reeder. I haven't had the pleasure of meeting you before, but I've heard a lot about you. You've been doing Bank of England work, haven't you?'

Mr. Reeder whispered that he had had that honour, and sighed as though he regretted the drastic sweep of fate that had torn him from the obscurity of his labours. Mr. Holford's scrutiny was full of misgivings.

'Well,' he said awkwardly, 'this job is different, though I'm told that you are one of the best informed men in London, and if that is the case this will be easy work. Still, we've never had an outsider—I mean, so to speak, a private detective—in this office before, and naturally the Yard is a bit—'

'I quite understand,' murmured Mr. Reeder, hanging up his immaculate umbrella. 'It is very natural. Mr. Bolond expected the appointment. His wife is annoyed—very properly. But she has no reason to be. She is an ambitious woman. She has a third interest in a West End dancing club that might be raided one of these days.'

Holford was staggered. Here was news that was little more than a whispered rumour at Scotland Yard.

'How the devil do you know that?' he blurted.

Mr. Reeder's smile was one of self-depreciation.

'One picks up odd scraps of information,' he said apologetically. 'I—I see wrong in everything. That is my curious perversion—I have a criminal mind!'

Holford drew a long breath.

'Well—there is nothing much doing. That Ealing case is pretty clear. Green is an exconvict, who got a job at the bank during the war and worked up to manager. He has done seven years for conversion.'

'Embezzlement and conversion,' murmured Mr. Reeder. 'I—er—I'm afraid I was the principal witness against him: bank crimes were rather—er—a hobby of mine. Yes, he got into difficulties with moneylenders. Very foolish—extremely foolish. And he doesn't admit his error.' Mr. Reeder sighed heavily. 'Poor fellow! With his life at stake one may forgive and indeed condone his pitiful prevarications.'

The inspector stared at the new man in amazement.

'I don't know that there is much "poor fellow" about him. He has cached £100,000 and told the weakest yarn that I've ever read—you'll find copies of the police reports here, if you'd like to read them. The scratches on Malling's hand are curious—they've found several on the other hand. They are not deep enough to suggest a struggle. As to the yarn that Green tells—'

Mr. J.G. Reeder nodded sadly.

'It was not an ingenious story,' he said, almost with regret. 'If I remember rightly, his story was something like this: he had been recognised by a man who served in Dartmoor with him, and this fellow wrote a blackmailing letter telling him to pay or clear out. Sooner than return to a life of crime, Green wrote out all the facts to his directors, put the letter in the drawer of his desk with his keys, and left a note for his head cashier on the desk itself, intending to leave London and try to make a fresh start where he was unknown.'

'There were no letters in or on the desk, and no keys,' said the inspector decisively. 'The only true part of the yarn was that he had done time.'

'Imprisonment,' suggested Mr. Reeder plaintively. He had a horror of slang. 'Yes, that was true.'

Left alone in his office, he spent a very considerable time at his private telephone, communing with the young person who was still a young person, although the passage of time had dealt unkindly with her. For the rest of the morning he was reading the depositions which his predecessor had put on the desk.

It was late in the afternoon when the Public Prosecutor strolled into his room and glanced at the big pile of manuscript through which his subordinate was wading.

'What are you reading—the Green business?' he asked, with a note of satisfaction in his voice.

'I'm glad that is interesting you, though it seems a fairly straightforward case. I have had a letter from the president of the man's bank, who for some reason seems to think Green was telling the truth.'

Mr. Reeder looked up with that pained expression of his which he invariably wore when he was puzzled.

'Here is the evidence of Policeman Burnett,' he said. 'Perhaps you can enlighten me, sir. Policeman Burnett stated in his evidence—let me read it:

"Some time before I reached the bank premises I saw a man standing at the corner of the street, immediately outside the bank. I saw him distinctly in the light of a passing mail van. I did not attach any importance to his presence, and I did not see him again. It was possible for this man to have gone round the block and come to 120, Firling Avenue without being seen by me. Immediately after I saw him, my foot struck against a piece of iron on the sidewalk. I put my lamp on the object and found it was an old horseshoe. I had seen children playing with this particular shoe earlier in the evening. When I looked again towards the corner, the man had disappeared. He would have seen the light of my lamp. I saw no other person, and so far as I can remember, there was no light showing in Green's house when I passed it."

Mr. Reeder looked up.

'Well?' said the Prosecutor. 'There's nothing remarkable about that. It was probably Green, who dodged round the block and came in at the back of the constable.'

Mr. Reeder scratched his chin.

'Yes,' he said thoughtfully, 'ye--es.' He shifted uncomfortably in his chair. 'Would it be considered indecorous if I made a few inquiries, independent of the police?' he asked nervously. 'I should not like them to think that a mere dilettante was interfering with their lawful functions.'

'By all means,' said the Prosecutor heartily. 'Go down and see the officer in charge of the case: I'll give you a note to him—it is by no means unusual for my officer to conduct a separate investigation, though I am afraid you will discover very little. The ground has been well covered by Scotland Yard.'

'It would be permissible to see the man?' hesitated Reeder.

'Green? Why, of course! I will send you up the necessary order.'

The light was fading from a grey, blustering sky, and rain was falling fitfully, when Mr. Reeder, with his furled umbrella hooked to his arm, his coat collar turned up, stepped through the dark gateway of Brixton Prison and was led to the cell where a distracted man sat, his head upon his hands, his pale eyes gazing into vacancy.

'It's true; it's true! Every word.' Green almost sobbed the words.

A pallid man, inclined to be bald, with a limp yellow moustache, going grey. Reeder, with his extraordinary memory for faces, recognised him the moment he saw him, though it was some time before the recognition was mutual.

'Yes, Mr. Reeder, I remember you now. You were the gentleman who caught me before. But I've been as straight as a die. I've never taken a farthing that didn't belong to me. What my poor girl will think—'

'Are you married?' asked Mr. Reeder sympathetically.

'No, but I was going to be—rather late in life. She's nearly thirty years younger than me, and the best girl that ever—'

Reeder listened to the rhapsody that followed, the melancholy deepening in his face.

'She hasn't been into the court, thank God, but she knows the truth. A friend of mine told me that she has been absolutely knocked out.'
'Poor soul!' Mr. Reeder shook his head.
'It happened on her birthday, too,' the man went on bitterly.
'Did she know you were going away?'
'Yes, I told her the night before. I'm not going to bring her into the case. If we'd been properly engaged it would be different; but she's married and is divorcing her husband, but the decree hasn't been made absolute yet. That's why I never went about with her or saw much of her. And of course, nobody knew about our engagement, although we lived in the same street.'
'Firling Avenue?' asked Reeder, and the bank manager nodded despondently.
'She was married when she was seventeen to a brute. It was pretty galling for me, having to keep quiet about it—I mean, for nobody to know about our engagement. All sorts of rotten people were making up to her, and I had just to grind my teeth and say nothing. Impossible people! Why, that fool Burnett, who arrested me, he was sweet on her; used to write her poetry—you wouldn't think it possible in a policeman, would you?'
The outrageous incongruity of a poetical policeman did not seem to shock the detective.
'There is poetry in every soul, Mr. Green,' he said gently, 'and a policeman is a man.'
Though he dismissed the eccentricity of the constable so lightly, the poetical policeman filled his mind all the way home to his house in the Brockley Road, and occupied his thoughts for the rest of his waking time.
It was a quarter to eight o'clock in the morning, and the world seemed entirely populated by milkmen and whistling newspaper boys, when Mr. J.G. Reeder came into Firling Avenue.
He stopped only for a second outside the bank, which had long since ceased to be an object of local awe and fearfulness, and pursued his way down the broad avenue. On either side of the thoroughfare ran a row of pretty villas—pretty although they bore a strong family resemblance to one another; each house with its little forecourt, sometimes laid out simply as a grass plot, sometimes decorated with flower-beds. Green's house was the eighteenth in the road on the right-hand side. Here he had lived with a cook-housekeeper, and apparently gardening was not his hobby, for the forecourt was covered with grass that had been allowed to grow at its will.
Before the twenty-sixth house in the road Mr. Reeder paused and gazed with mild interest at the blue blinds which covered every window. Evidently Miss Magda Grayne was a lover of flowers, for geraniums filled the window-boxes and were set at intervals along the tiny border under the bow window. In the centre of the grass plot was a circular flower-bed with one flowerless rose tree, the leaves of which were drooping and brown.
As he raised his eyes to the upper window, the blind went up slowly, and he was dimly conscious that there was a figure behind the white lace curtains. Mr. Reeder walked hurriedly away, as one caught in an immodest act, and resumed his peregrinations until he came to the big nursery gardener's which formed the corner lot at the far end of the road.
Here he stood for some time in contemplation, his arm resting on the iron railings, his eyes staring blankly at the vista of greenhouses. He remained in this attitude so long that one of the nurserymen, not unnaturally thinking that a stranger was seeking a way into the gardens, came over with the laborious gait of the man who wrings his living from the soil, and asked if he was wanting anybody.
'Several people,' sighed Mr. Reeder; 'several people!'
Leaving the resentful man to puzzle out his impertinence, he slowly retraced his steps. At No. 412 he stopped again, opened the little iron gate and passed up the path to the front door. A small

girl answered his knock and ushered him into the parlour.

The room was not well furnished; it was scarcely furnished at all. A strip of almost new linoleum covered the passage; the furniture of the parlour itself was made up of wicker chairs, a square of art carpet and a table. He heard the sound of feet above his head, feet on bare boards, and then presently the door opened and a girl came in.

She was pretty in a heavy way, but on her face he saw the marks of sorrow. It was pale and haggard; the eyes looked as though she had been recently weeping.

'Miss Magda Grayne?' he asked, rising as she came in.

She nodded.

'Are you from the police?' she asked quickly.

'Not exactly the police,' he corrected carefully. 'I hold an—er—an appointment in the office of the Public Prosecutor, which is analogous, to, but distinct from, a position in the Metropolitan Police Force.'

She frowned, and then:

'I wondered if anybody would come to see me,' she said. 'Mr. Green sent you?'

'Mr. Green told me of your existence: he did not send me.'

There came to her face in that second a look which almost startled him. Only for a fleeting space of time, the expression had dawned and passed almost before the untrained eye could detect its passage.

'I was expecting somebody to come,' she said. Then: 'What made him do it?' she asked.

'You think he is guilty?'

'The police think so.' She drew a long sigh. 'I wish to God I had never seen this place!'

He did not answer; his eyes were roving round the apartment. On a bamboo table was an old vase which had been clumsily filled with golden chrysanthemums, of a peculiarly beautiful variety. Not all, for amidst them flowered a large Michaelmas daisy that had the forlorn appearance of a parvenu that had strayed by mistake into noble company.

'You're fond of flowers?' he murmured.

She looked at the vase indifferently.

'Yes, I like flowers,' she said. 'The girl put them in there.' Then: 'Do you think they will hang him?'

The brutality of the question, put without hesitation, pained Reeder.

'It is a very serious charge,' he said. And then: 'Have you a photograph of Mr. Green?'

She frowned.

'Yes; do you want it?'

He nodded.

She had hardly left the room before he was at the bamboo table and had lifted out the flowers. As he had seen through the glass, they were roughly tied with a piece of string. He examined the ends, and here again his first observation had been correct: none of these flowers had been cut; they had been plucked bodily from their stalks. Beneath the string was the paper which had been first wrapped about the stalks. It was a page torn from a notebook; he could see the red lines, but the pencilled writing was indecipherable.

As her foot sounded on the stairs, he replaced the flowers in the vase, and when she came in he was looking through the window into the street.

'Thank you,' he said, as he took the photograph from her.

It bore an affectionate inscription on the back.

'You're married, he tells me, madam?'

'Yes, I am married, and practically divorced,' she said shortly.
'Have you been living here long?'
'About three months,' she answered. 'It was his wish that I should live here.'
He looked at the photograph again.
'Do you know Constable Burnett?'
He saw a dull flush come to her face and die away again.
'Yes, I know the sloppy fool!' she said viciously. And then, realising that she had been surprised into an expression which was not altogether ladylike, she went on, in a softer tone: 'Mr. Burnett is rather sentimental, and I don't like sentimental people, especially — well, you understand, Mr.—'
'Reeder,' murmured that gentleman.
'You understand, Mr. Reeder, that when a girl is engaged and in my position, those kind of attentions are not very welcome.'
Reeder was looking at her keenly. Of her sorrow and distress there could be no doubt. On the subject of the human emotions, and the ravages they make upon the human countenance, Mr. Reeder was almost as great an authority as Mantegazza.
'On your birthday,' he said. 'How very sad! You were born on the seventeenth of October. You are English, of course?'
'Yes, I'm English,' she said shortly. 'I was born in Walworth—in Wallington. I once lived in Walworth.'
'How old are you?'
'Twenty-three,' she answered.
Mr. Reeder took off his glasses and polished them on a large silk handkerchief.
'The whole thing is inexpressibly sad,' he said. 'I am glad to have had the opportunity of speaking with you, young lady. I sympathise with you very deeply.'
And in this unsatisfactory way he took his departure.
She closed the door on him, saw him stop in the middle of the path and pick up something from a border bed, and wondered, frowning, why this middle-aged man had picked up the horseshoe she had thrown through the window the night before. Into Mr. Reeder's tail pocket went this piece of rusted steel and then he continued his thoughtful way to the nursery gardens, for he had a few questions to ask.
The men of Section 10 were parading for duty when Mr. Reeder came timidly into the charge room and produced his credentials to the inspector in charge.
'Oh, yes, Mr. Reeder,' said that officer affably. 'We have had a note from the P.P.'s office, and I think I had the pleasure of working with you on that big slush* case a few years ago. Now what can I do for you?...Burnett? Yes, he's here.'
[* Slush—forged Bank of England notes.]
He called the man's name and a young and good-looking officer stepped from the ranks.
'He's the man who discovered the murder—he's marked for promotion,' said the inspector. 'Burnett, this gentleman is from the Public Prosecutor's office and he wants a little talk with you. Better use my office, Mr. Reeder.'
The young policeman saluted and followed the shuffling figure into the privacy of the inspector's office. He was a confident young man: already his name and portrait had appeared in the newspapers, the hint of promotion had become almost an accomplished fact, and before his eyes was the prospect of a supreme achievement.
'They tell me that you are something of a poet, officer,' said Mr. Reeder.

Burnett blushed.

'Why, yes, sir. I write a bit,' he confessed.

'Love poems, yes?' asked the other gently. 'One finds time in the night—er—for such fancies. And there is no inspiration like—er—love, officer.'

Burnett's face was crimson.

'I've done a bit of writing in the night, sir,' he said, 'though I've never neglected my duty.'

'Naturally,' murmured Mr. Reeder. 'You have a poetical mind. It was a poetical thought to pluck flowers in the middle of the night—'

'The nurseryman told me I could take any flowers I wanted,' Burnett interrupted hastily. 'I did nothing wrong.'

Reeder inclined his head in agreement.

'That I know. You picked the flowers in the dark—by the way, you inadvertently included a Michaelmas daisy with your chrysanthemums—tied up your little poem to them and left them on the doorstep with—er—a horseshoe. I wondered what had become of that horseshoe.'

'I threw them up on to her—to the lady's window-sill,' corrected the uncomfortable young man. 'As a matter of fact, the idea didn't occur to me until I had passed the house—'

Mr. Reeder's face was thrust forward.

'This is what I want to confirm,' he said softly. 'The idea of leaving the flowers did not occur to you until you had passed her house? The horseshoe suggested the thought? Then you went back, picked the flowers, tied them up with the little poem you had already written, and tossed them up to her window—we need not mention the lady's name.'

Constable Burnett's face was a study.

'I don't know how you guessed that, but it is a fact. If I've done anything wrong—'

'It is never wrong to be in love,' said Mr. J.G. Reeder soberly. 'Love is a very beautiful experience—I have frequently read about it.'

Miss Magda Grayne had dressed to go out for the afternoon and was putting on her hat, when she saw the queer man who had called so early that morning, walking up the tessellated path. Behind him she recognised a detective engaged in the case. The servant was out; nobody could be admitted except by herself. She walked quickly behind the dressing-table into the bay of the window and glanced up and down the road. Yes, there was the taxicab which usually accompanies such visitations, and, standing by the driver, another man, obviously a 'busy.' She pulled up the overlay of her bed, took out the flat pad of bank-notes that she found, and thrust them into her handbag, then, stepping on tiptoe, she went out to the landing, into the unfurnished back room, and, opening the window, dropped to the flat roof of the kitchen. In another minute she was in the garden and through the back gate. A narrow passage divided the two lines of villas that backed on one another. She was in High Street and had boarded a car before Mr. Reeder grew tired of knocking. To the best of his knowledge Mr. Reeder never saw her again.

At the Public Prosecutor's request, he called at his chief's house after dinner and told his surprising story.

'Green, who had the unusual experience of being promoted to his position over the heads of his seniors, for special services he rendered during the war, was undoubtedly an ex-convict, and he spoke the truth when he said that he had received a letter from a man who had served a period of imprisonment with him. The name of this blackmailer is, or rather was, Arthur George Crater, whose other name was Malling!'

'Not the night watchman?' said the Public Prosecutor, in amazement.

Mr. Reeder nodded.

'Yes, sir, it was Arthur Malling. His daughter, Miss Magda Crater, was, as she very truly said, born at Walworth on the 17th of October, 1900. She said Wallington after, but Walworth first. One observes that when people adopt false family names, they seldom change their given names, and the 'Magda' was easy to identify.

'Evidently Malling had planned this robbery of the bank very carefully. He had brought his daughter, in a false name, to Ealing, and had managed to get her introduced to Mr. Green. Magda's job was to worm her way into Green's confidence and learn all that she could. Possibly it was part of her duty to secure casts of the keys. Whether Malling recognised in the manager an old prison acquaintance, or whether he obtained the facts from the girl, we shall never know. But when the information came to him, he saw, in all probability, an opportunity of robbing the bank and of throwing suspicion upon the manager.

The girl's role was that of a woman who was to be divorced, and I must confess this puzzled me until I realised that in no circumstances would Malling wish his daughter's name to be associated with the bank manager.

'The night of the seventeenth was chosen for the raid. Malling's plan to get rid of the manager had succeeded. He saw the letter on the table in Green's private office, read it, secured the keys—although he had in all probability a duplicate set—and at a favourable moment cleared as much portable money from the bank vaults as he could carry, hurried them round to the house in Firling Avenue, where they were buried in the central bed of the front garden, under a rose bush—I rather imagined there was something interfering with the nutrition of that unfortunate bush the first time I saw it. I can only hope that the tree is not altogether dead, and I have given instructions that it shall be replanted and well fertilised.'

'Yes, yes,' said the Prosecutor, who was not at all interested in horticulture.

'In planting the tree, as he did in some haste, Malling scratched his hand. Roses have thorns—I went to Ealing to find the rose bush that had scratched his hand. Hurrying back to the bank, he waited, knowing that Constable Burnett was due at a certain time. He had prepared the can of chloroform, the handcuffs and straps were waiting for him, and he stood at the corner of the street until he saw the flash of Burnett's lamp; then, running into the bank and leaving the door ajar, he strapped himself, fastened the handcuffs and lay down, expecting that the policeman would arrive, find the open door and rescue him before much harm was done.

'But Constable Burnett had had some pleasant exchanges with the daughter. Doubtless she had received instructions from her father to be as pleasant to him as possible. Burnett was a poetical young man, knew it was her birthday, and as he walked along the street his foot struck an old horseshoe and the idea occurred to him that he should return, attach the horseshoe to some flowers, which the nurseryman had given him permission to pick, and leave his little bouquet, to so speak, at his lady's feet—a poetical idea, and one worthy of the finest traditions of the Metropolitan Police Force. This he did, but it took some time; and all the while this young man was philandering—Arthur Crater was dying!

In a few seconds after lying down he must have passed from consciousness...the chloroform still dripped, and when the policeman eventually reached the bank, ten minutes after he was due, the man was dead!'

The Public Prosecutor sat back in his padded chair and frowned at his new subordinate.

'How on earth did you piece together all this?' he asked in wonder.

Mr. Reeder shook his head sadly.

"I have that perversion," he said. 'It is a terrible misfortune, but it is true. I see evil in everything...in dying rose bushes, in horseshoes — in poetry even. I have the mind of a criminal. It is deplorable!"

II. — THE TREASURE HUNT

First published in The Grand Magazine, Vol. 46, Sep 1924-Feb 1925,
as part of the J.G. Reeder series "The Man Who Saw Evil"

THERE is a tradition in criminal circles that even the humblest of detective officers is a man of wealth and substance, and that his secret hoard was secured by thieving, bribery and blackmail. It is the gossip of the fields, the quarries, the tailor's shop, the laundry and the bakehouse of fifty county prisons and three convict establishments, that all highly placed detectives have by nefarious means laid up for themselves sufficient earthly treasures to make work a hobby and their official pittance the most inconsiderable portion of their incomes.

Since Mr. J.G. Reeder had for over twenty years dealt exclusively with bank robbers and forgers, who are the aristocrats and capitalists of the underworld, legend credited him with country houses and immense secret reserves. Not that he would have a great deal of money in the bank. It was admitted that he was too clever to risk discovery by the authorities. No, it was hidden somewhere: it was the pet dream of hundreds of unlawful men that they would some day discover the hoard and live happily ever after. The one satisfactory aspect of his affluence (they all agreed) was that, being an old man—he was over 50—he couldn't take his money with him, for gold melts at a certain temperature and gilt-edged stock is seldom printed on asbestos paper.

The Director of Public Prosecutions was lunching one Saturday at his club with a judge of the King's Bench—Saturday being one of the two days in the week when a judge gets properly fed. And the conversation drifted to a certain Mr. J.G. Reeder, the chief of the Director's sleuths.

'He's capable,' he confessed reluctantly, 'but I hate his hat. It is the sort that So-and-so used to wear,' he mentioned by name an eminent politician; 'and I loathe his black frock-coat, people who see him coming into the office think he's a coroner's officer, but he's capable. His side-whiskers are an abomination, and I have a feeling that, if I talked rough to him, he would burst into tears—a gentle soul. Almost too gentle for my kind of work. He apologises to the messenger every time he rings for him!'

The judge, who knew something about humanity, answered with a frosty smile.

'He sounds rather like a potential murderer to me,' he said cynically.

Milord, in his extravagance, he did Mr. J.G. Reeder an injustice, for Mr. Reeder was capable of breaking the law—quite. At the same time there were many people who formed an altogether wrong conception of J.G.'s harmlessness as an individual. And one of these was a certain Lew Kohl, who mixed bank-note printing with elementary burglary.

Threatened men live long, a trite saying but, like most things trite, true. In a score of cases, when Mr. J.G. Reeder had descended from the witness stand, he had met the baleful eye of the man in the dock and had listened with mild interest to divers promises as to what would happen to him in the near or the remote future. For he was a great authority on forged bank-notes and he had sent many men to penal servitude.

Mr. Reeder, that inoffensive man, had seen prisoners foaming at the mouth in their rage, he had seen them white and livid, he had heard their howling execrations and he had met these men after their release from prison and had found them amiable souls half ashamed and half amused at their nearly forgotten outbursts and horrific threats.

But when, in the early part of 1914, Lew Kohl was sentenced for ten years, he neither screamed his imprecations nor registered a vow to tear Mr. Reeder's heart, lungs and important organs from his frail body.

Lew just smiled and his eyes caught the detective's for the space of a second—the forger's eyes were pale blue and speculative, and they held neither hate nor fury. Instead, they said in so many words:

'At the first opportunity I will kill you.'

Mr. Reeder read the message and sighed heavily, for he disliked fuss of all kinds, and resented, in so far as he could resent anything, the injustice of being made personally responsible for the performance of a public duty.

Many years had passed, and considerable changes had occurred in Mr. Reeder's fortune. He had transferred from the specialised occupation of detecting the makers of forged bank-notes to the more general practice of the Public Prosecutor's bureau, but he never forgot Lew's smile.

The work in Whitehall was not heavy and it was very interesting. To Mr. Reeder came most of the anonymous letters which the Director received in shoals. In the main they were self-explanatory, and it required no particular intelligence to discover their motive. Jealousy, malice, plain mischief-making, and occasionally a sordid desire to benefit financially by the information which was conveyed, were behind the majority. But occasionally:

'Sir James is going to marry his cousin, and it's not three months since his poor wife fell overboard from the Channel steamer crossing to Calais. There's something very fishy about this business. Miss Margaret doesn't like him, for she knows he's after her money. Why was I sent away to London that night? He doesn't like driving in the dark, either. It's strange that he wanted to drive that night when it was raining like blazes.'

This particular letter was signed 'A Friend.' Justice has many such friends.

'Sir James' was Sir James Tithermite, who had been a director of some new public department during the war and had received a baronetcy for his services.

'Look it up,' said the Director when he saw the letter. 'I seem to remember that Lady Tithermite was drowned at sea.'

'On the nineteenth of December last year,' said Mr. Reeder solemnly. 'She and Sir James were going to Monte Carlo, breaking their journey in Paris. Sir James, who has a house near Maidstone, drove to Dover, garaging the car at the Lord Wilson Hotel. The night was stormy and the ship had a rough crossing—they were half-way across when Sir James came to the purser and said that he had missed his wife. Her baggage was in the cabin, her passport, rail ticket and hat, but the lady was not found, indeed was never seen again.'

The Director nodded.

'I see, you've read up the case.'

'I remember it,' said Mr. Reeder. 'The case is a favourite speculation of mine. Unfortunately I see evil in everything and I have often thought how easy—but I fear that I take a warped view of life. It is a horrible handicap to possess a criminal mind.'

The Director looked at him suspiciously. He was never quite sure whether Mr. Reeder was serious. At that moment, his sobriety was beyond challenge.

'A discharged chauffeur wrote that letter, of course,' he began.

'Thomas Dayford, of 179, Barrack Street, Maidstone,' concluded Mr. Reeder. 'He is at present in the employ of the Kent Motor-Bus Company, and has three children, two of whom are twins and bonny little rascals.'

The Chief laughed helplessly.

"I'll take it that you know!" he said. 'See what there is behind the letter. Sir James is a big fellow in Kent, a Justice of the Peace, and he has powerful political influences. There is nothing in this letter, of course. Go warily, Reeder—if any kick comes back to this office, it goes on to you—intensified!'

Mr. Reeder's idea of walking warily was peculiarly his own. He travelled down to Maidstone the next morning, and, finding a bus that passed the lodge gates of Elfreda Manor, he journeyed comfortably and economically, his umbrella between his knees. He passed through the lodge gates, up a long and winding avenue of poplars, and presently came within sight of the grey manor house.

In a deep chair on the lawn he saw a girl sitting, a book on her knees, and evidently she saw him, for she rose as he crossed the lawn and came towards him eagerly.

'I'm Miss Margaret Letherby—are you from—?' She mentioned the name of a well-known firm of lawyers, and her face fell when Mr. Reeder regretfully disclaimed connection with those legal lights.

She was as pretty as a perfect complexion and a round, not too intellectual, face could, in combination, make her.

'I thought—do you wish to see Sir James? He is in the library. If you ring, one of the maids will take you to him.'

Had Mr. Reeder been the sort of man who could be puzzled by anything, he would have been puzzled by the suggestion that any girl with money of her own should marry a man much older than herself against her own wishes. There was little mystery in the matter now. Miss Margaret would have married any strong-willed man who insisted.

'Even me,' said Mr. Reeder to himself, with a certain melancholy pleasure.

There was no need to ring the bell. A tall, broad man in a golfing suit stood in the door-way. His fair hair was long and hung over his forehead in a thick flat strand; a heavy tawny moustache hid his mouth and swept down over a chin that was long and powerful.

'Well?' he asked aggressively.

'I'm from the Public Prosecutor's office,' murmured Mr. Reeder. 'I have had an anonymous letter.' His pale eyes did not leave the face of the other man.

'Come in,' said Sir James gruffly. As he closed the door he glanced quickly first to the girl and then to the poplar avenue. 'I'm expecting a fool of a lawyer,' he said, as he flung open the door of what was evidently the library.

His voice was steady; not by a flicker of eyelash had he betrayed the slightest degree of anxiety when Reeder had told his mission.

'Well—what about this anonymous letter? You don't take much notice of that kind of trash, do you?'

Mr. Reeder deposited his umbrella and flat-crowned hat on a chair before he took a document from his pocket and handed it to the baronet, who frowned as he read. Was it Mr. Reeder's vivid imagination, or did the hard light in the eyes of Sir James soften as he read?

'This is a cock and bull story of somebody having seen my wife's jewellery on sale in Paris,' he said. 'There is nothing in it. I can account for every one of my poor wife's trinkets. I brought back the jewel case after that awful night. I don't recognise the handwriting: who is the lying scoundrel who wrote this?'

Mr. Reeder had never before been called a lying scoundrel, but he accepted the experience with admirable meekness.

"I thought it untrue,' he said, shaking his head. 'I followed the details of the case very thoroughly. You left here in the afternoon—'

'At night,' said the other brusquely. He was not inclined to discuss the matter, but Mr. Reeder's appealing look was irresistible. 'It is only eighty minutes' run to Dover. We got to the pier at eleven o'clock, about the same time as the boat train, and we went on board at once. I got my cabin key from the purser and put her ladyship and her baggage inside.'

'Her ladyship was a good sailor?'

'Yes, a very good sailor; she was remarkably well that night. I left her in the cabin dozing, and went for a stroll on the deck—'

'Raining very heavily and a strong sea running,' nodded Reeder, as though in agreement with something the other man had said.

'Yes—I'm a pretty good sailor—anyway, that story about my poor wife's jewels is utter nonsense. You can tell the Director that, with my compliments.'

He opened the door for his visitor, and Mr. Reeder was some time replacing the letter and gathering his belongings.

'You have a beautiful place here. Sir James—a lovely place. An extensive estate?'

'Three thousand acres.' This time he did not attempt to disguise his impatience. 'Good afternoon.'

Mr. Reeder went slowly down the drive, his remarkable memory at work.

He missed the bus which he could easily have caught, and pursued an apparently aimless way along the winding road which marched with the boundaries of the baronet's property. A walk of a quarter of a mile brought him to a lane shooting off at right angles from the main road, and marking, he guessed, the southern boundary. At the corner stood an old stone lodge, on the inside of a forbidding iron gate. The lodge was in a pitiable state of neglect and disrepair. Tiles had been dislodged from the roof, the windows were grimy or broken, and the little garden was overrun with docks and thistles. Beyond the gate was a narrow, weed-covered drive that trailed out of sight into a distant plantation.

Hearing the clang of a letter-box closing, he turned to see a postman mounting his bicycle.

'What place is this?' asked Mr. Reeder, arresting the postman's departure.

'South Lodge—Sir James Tithermite's property. It's never used now. Hasn't been used for years—I don't know why; it's a short cut if they happen to be coming this way.'

Mr. Reeder walked with him towards the village, and he was a skilful pumper of wells, however dry; and the postman was not dry by any means.

'Yes, poor lady! She was very frail—one of those sort of invalids that last out many a healthy man.'

Mr. Reeder put a question at random and scored most unexpectedly.

'Yes, her ladyship was a bad sailor. I know because every time she went abroad she used to get a bottle of that stuff people take for sea-sickness. I've delivered many a bottle till Raikes the chemist stocked it—"Pickers' Travellers' Friend," that's what it was called. Mr. Raikes was only saying to me the other day that he'd got half a dozen bottles on hand and he didn't know what to do with them. Nobody in Climbury ever goes to sea.'

Mr. Reeder went on to the village and idled his precious time in most unlikely places. At the chemist's, at the blacksmith's shop, at the modest building yard. He caught the last bus back to Maidstone, and by great good luck the last train to London.

And, in his vague way, he answered the Director's query the next day with:

'Yes, I saw Sir James: a very interesting man.'

This was on the Friday. All day Saturday he was busy. The Sabbath brought him a new interest. On this bright Sunday morning, Mr. Reeder, attired in a flowered dressing-gown, his feet encased in black velvet slippers, stood at the window of his house in Brockley Road and surveyed the deserted thoroughfare. The bell of a local church, which was accounted high, had rung for early Mass, and there was nothing living in sight except a black cat that lay asleep in a patch of sunlight on the top step of the house opposite. The hour was 7.30, and Mr. Reeder had been at his desk since six, working by artificial light, the month being March towards the close. From the half-moon of the window bay he regarded a section of the Lewisham High Road and as much of Tanners Hill as can be seen before it dips past the railway bridge into sheer Deptford. Returning to his table, he opened a carton of the cheapest cigarettes and, lighting one, puffed in an amateurish fashion. He smoked cigarettes rather like a woman who detests them but feels that it is the correct thing to do.

'Dear me,' said Mr. Reeder feebly.

He was back at the window, and he had seen a man turn out of Lewisham High Road. He had crossed the road and was coming straight to Daffodil House—which frolicsome name appeared on the door-posts of Mr. Reeder's residence. A tall, straight man, with a sombre brown face, he came to the front gate, passed through and beyond the watcher's range of vision.

'Dear me!' said Mr. Reeder, as he heard the tinkle of a bell.

A few minutes later his housekeeper tapped on the door.

'Will you see Mr. Kohl, sir?' she asked.

Mr. J.G. Reeder nodded.

Lew Kohl walked into the room to find a middle-aged man in a flamboyant dressing-gown sitting at his desk, a pair of pince-nez set crookedly on his nose.

'Good morning. Kohl.'

Lew Kohl looked at the man who had sent him to seven and a half years of hell, and the corner of his thin lips curled.

'Morning, Mr. Reeder.' His eyes flashed across the almost bare surface of the writing-desk on which Reeder's hands were lightly clasped. 'You didn't expect to see me, I guess?'

'Not so early,' said Reeder in his hushed voice, 'but I should have remembered that early rising is one of the good habits which are inculcated by penal servitude.'

He said this in the manner of one bestowing praise for good conduct.

'I suppose you've got a pretty good idea of why I have come, eh? I'm a bad forgetter, Reeder, and a man in Dartmoor has time to think.'

The older man lifted his sandy eyebrows, the steel-rimmed glasses on his nose slipped further askew.

'That phrase seems familiar,' he said, and the eyebrows lowered in a frown. 'Now let me think—it was in a melodrama, of course, but was it "Souls in Harness" or "The Marriage Vow"?'

He appeared genuinely anxious for assistance in solving this problem.

'This is going to be a different kind of play,' said the long-faced Lew through his teeth. 'I'm going to get you, Reeder—you can go along and tell your boss, the Public Prosecutor. But I'll get you sweet! There will be no evidence to swing me. And I'll get that nice little stocking of yours, Reeder!'

The legend of Reeder's fortune was accepted even by so intelligent a man as Kohl.

'You'll get my stocking! Dear me, I shall have to go barefooted,' said Mr. Reeder, with a faint show of humour.

'You know what I mean—think that over. Some hour and day you'll go out, and all Scotland Yard won't catch me for the killing! I've thought it out—'

'One has time to think in Dartmoor,' murmured Mr. J.G. Reeder encouragingly. 'You're becoming one of the world's thinkers, Kohl. Do you know Rodin's masterpiece—a beautiful statue throbbing with life—'

'That's all.' Lew Kohl rose, the smile still trembling at the corner of his mouth. 'Maybe you'll turn this over in your mind, and in a day or two you won't be feeling so gay.'

Reeder's face was pathetic in its sadness. His untidy sandy-grey hair seemed to be standing on end; the large ears, that stood out at right angles to his face, gave the illusion of quivering movement.

Lew Kohl's hand was on the door-knob.

'Womp!'

It was the sound of a dull weight striking a board; something winged past his cheek, before his eyes a deep hole showed in the wall, and his face was stung by flying grains of plaster. He spun round with a whine of rage.

Mr. Reeder had a long-barrelled Browning in his hand, with a barrel-shaped silencer over the muzzle, and he was staring at the weapon open-mouthed.

'Now how on earth did that happen?' he asked in wonder.

Lew Kohl stood trembling with rage and fear, his face yellow-white.

'You—you swine!' he breathed. 'You tried to shoot me!'

Mr. Reeder stared at him over his glasses.

'Good gracious—you think that? Still thinking of killing me, Kohl?'

Kohl tried to speak but found no words, and, flinging open the door, he strode down the stairs and through the front entrance. His foot was on the first step when something came hurtling past him and crashed to fragments at his feet. It was a large stone vase that had decorated the window-sill of Mr. Reeder's bedroom. Leaping over the debris of stone and flower mould, he glared up into the surprised face of Mr. J.G. Reeder.

'I'll get you!' he spluttered.

'I hope you're not hurt?' asked the man at the window in a tone of concern. 'These things happen. Some day and some hour—'

As Lew Kohl strode down the street, the detective was still talking.

Mr. Stan Bride was at his morning ablutions when his friend and sometime prison associate came into the little room that overlooked Fitzroy Square.

Stan Bride, who bore no resemblance to anything virginal, being a stout and stumpy man with a huge, red face and many chins, stopped in the act of drying himself and gazed over the edge of the towel.

'What's the matter with you?' he asked sharply. 'You look as if you'd been chased by a busy. What did you go out so early for?'

Lew told him, and the jovial countenance of his room-mate grew longer and longer—

'You poor fish!' he hissed. 'To go after Reeder with that stuff! Don't you think he was waiting for you? Do you suppose he didn't know the very moment you left the Moor?'

'I've scared him, anyway,' said the other, and Mr. Bride laughed.

'Good scout!' he sneered. 'Scare that old person!' (He did not say 'person.') 'If he's as white as you, he is scared! But he's not. Of course he shot past you—if he'd wanted to shoot you, you'd have been stiff by now. But he didn't. Thinker, eh—he's given you somep'n' to think about.'

'Where that gun came from I don't—'

There was a knock at the door and the two men exchanged glances.

'Who's there?' asked Bride, and a familiar voice answered.

'It's that busy from the Yard,' whispered Bride, and opened the door.

The 'busy' was Sergeant Allford, C.I.D., an affable and portly man and a detective of some promise.

'Morning, boys—not been to church, Stan?'

Stan grinned politely.

'How's trade, Lew?'

'Not so bad.' The forger was alert, suspicious.

'Come to see you about a gun—got an idea you're carrying one. Lew- Colt automatic R.7/94318. That's not right. Lew-guns don't belong to this country.'

'I've got no gun,' said Lew sullenly.

Bride had suddenly become an old man, for he also was a convict on licence, and the discovery might send him back to serve his unfinished sentence.

'Will you come a little walk to the station, or will you let me go over you?'

'Go over me,' said Lew, and put out his arms stiffly whilst the detective rubbed him down.

'I'll have a look round,' said the detective, and his 'look round' was very thorough.

'Must have been mistaken,' said Sergeant Allford. And then, suddenly: 'Was that what you chucked into the river as you were walking along the Embankment?'

Lew started. It was the first intimation he had received that he had been 'tailed' that morning. Bride waited till the detective was visible from the window crossing Fitzroy Square; then he turned in a fury on his companion.

'Clever, ain't you! That old hound knew you had a gun—knew the number. And if Allford had found it you'd have been "dragged" and me too!'

'I threw it in the river,' said Lew sulkily.

'Brains—not many but some!' said Bride, breathing heavily. 'You cut out Reeder—he's hell and poison, and if you don't know it you're deaf! Scared him? You big stiff! He'd cut your throat and write a hymn about it.'

'I didn't know they were tailing me,' growled Kohl; 'but I'll get him! And his money too.'

'Get him from another lodging,' said Bride curtly. 'A crook I don't mind, being one; a murderer I don't mind, but a talking jackass makes me sick. Get his stuff if you can—I'll bet it's all invested in real estate, and you can't lift houses—but don't talk about it. I like you, Lew, up to a point; you're miles before the point and out of sight. I don't like Reeder—I don't like snakes, but I keep away from the Zoo.'

So Lew Kohl went into new diggings on the top floor of an Italian's house in Dean Street, and here he had leisure and inclination to brood upon his grievances and to plan afresh the destruction of his enemy. And new plans were needed, for the schemes which had seemed so watertight in the quietude of a Devonshire cell showed daylight through many crevices.

Lew's homicidal urge had undergone considerable modification. He had been experimented upon by a very clever psychologist—though he never regarded Mr. Reeder in this light, and, indeed, had the vaguest idea as to what the word meant. But there were other ways of hurting Reeder, and his mind fell constantly back to the dream of discovering this peccant detective's hidden treasure.

It was nearly a week later that Mr. Reeder invited himself into the Director's private sanctum, and that great official listened spellbound while his subordinate offered his outrageous theory about Sir James Tithermite and his dead wife. When Mr. Reeder had finished, the Director pushed back his chair from the table.

'My dear man,' he said, a little irritably, 'I can't possibly give a warrant on the strength of your surmises—not even a search warrant. The story is so fantastic, so incredible, that it would be more at home in the pages of a sensational story than in a Public Prosecutor's report.'

'It was a wild night, and yet Lady Tithermite was not ill,' suggested the detective gently. 'That is a fact to remember, sir.'

The Director shook his head.

'I can't do it—not on the evidence,' he said. 'I should raise a storm that'd swing me into Whitehall. Can't you do anything—unofficially?'

Mr. Reeder shook his head.

'My presence in the neighbourhood has been remarked,' he said primly. 'I think it would be impossible to—er—cover up my traces. And yet I have located the place, and could tell you within a few inches—'

Again the Director shook his head.

'No, Reeder,' he said quietly, 'the whole thing is sheer deduction on your part. Oh, yes, I know you have a criminal mind—I think you have told me that before. And that is a good reason why I should not issue a warrant. You're simply crediting this unfortunate man with your ingenuity. Nothing doing!'

Mr. Reeder sighed and went back to his bureau, not entirely despondent, for there had intruded a new element into his investigations.

Mr. Reeder had been to Maidstone several times during the week, and he had not gone alone; though seemingly unconscious of the fact that he had developed a shadow, for he had seen Lew Kohl on several occasions, and had spent an uncomfortable few minutes wondering whether his experiment had failed.

On the second occasion an idea had developed in the detective's mind, and if he were a laughing man he would have chuckled aloud when he slipped out of Maidstone station one evening and, in the act of hiring a cab, had seen Lew Kohl negotiating for another.

Mr. Bride was engaged in the tedious but necessary practice of so cutting a pack of cards that the ace of diamonds remained at the bottom, when his former co-lodger burst in upon him, and there was a light of triumph in Lew's cold eye which brought Mr. Bride's heart to his boots.

'I've got him!' said Lew.

Bride put aside the cards and stood up.

'Got who?' he asked coldly. 'And if it's killing, you needn't answer, but get out!'

'There's no killing.'

Lew sat down squarely at the table, his hands in his pockets, a real smile on his face.

'I've been trailing Reeder for a week, and that fellow wants some trailing!'

'Well?' asked the other, when he paused dramatically.

'I've found his stocking!'

Bride scratched his chin, and was half convinced.

'You never have?'

Lew nodded.

'He's been going to Maidstone a lot lately, and driving to a little village about five miles out. There I always lost him. But the other night, when he came back to the station to catch the last train, he slipped into the waiting-room and I found a place where I could watch him. What do you think he did?'

Mr. Bride hazarded no suggestion.

'He opened his bag,' said Lew impressively, 'and took out a wad of notes as thick as that! He'd been drawing on his bank! I trailed him up to London. There's a restaurant on the station and he went in to get a cup of coffee, with me keeping well out of his sight. As he came out of the restaurant he took out his handkerchief and wiped his mouth. He didn't see the little book that dropped, but I did. I was scared sick that somebody else would see it, or that he'd wait long enough to find it himself. But he went out of the station and I got that book before you could say "knife." Look!'

It was a well-worn little notebook, covered with faded red morocco. Bride put out his hand to take it.

'Wait a bit,' said Lew. 'Are you in this with me fifty-fifty, because I want some help?'

Bride hesitated.

'If it's just plain thieving, I'm with you,' he said.

'Plain thieving—and sweet,' said Lew exultantly, and pushed the book across the table.

For the greater part of the night they sat together talking in low tones, discussing impartially the methodical book-keeping of Mr. J.G. Reeder and his exceeding dishonesty.

The Monday night was wet. A storm blew up from the south-west, and the air was filled with falling leaves as Lew and his companion footed the five miles which separated them from the village. Neither carried any impedimenta that was visible, yet under Lew's waterproof coat was a kit of tools of singular ingenuity, and Mr. Bride's coat pockets were weighted down with the sections of a powerful jemmy.

They met nobody in their walk, and the church bell was striking eleven when Lew gripped the bars of the South Lodge gates, pulled himself up to the top and dropped lightly on the other side. He was followed by Mr. Bride, who, in spite of his bulk, was a singularly agile man. The ruined lodge showed in the darkness, and they passed through the creaking gates to the door and Lew flashed his lantern upon the keyhole before he began manipulation with the implements which he had taken from his kit.

The door was opened in ten minutes and a few seconds later they stood in a low-roofed little room, the principal feature of which was a deep, grateless fire-place. Lew took off his mackintosh and stretched it over the window before he spread the light in his lamp, and, kneeling down, brushed the debris from the hearth, examining the joints of the big stone carefully.

'This work's been botched,' he said. 'Anybody could see that.'

He put the claw of the jemmy into a crack and levered up the stone, and it moved slightly. Stopping only to dig a deeper crevice with a chisel and hammer he thrust the claw of the jemmy farther down. The stone came up above the edge of the floor and Bride slipped the chisel underneath.

'Now together,' grunted Lew.

They got their fingers beneath the hearth-stone and with one heave hinged it up. Lew picked up the lamp and, kneeling down, flashed a light into the dark cavity. And then:

'Oh, my God!' he shrieked.

A second later two terrified men rushed from the house into the drive. And a miracle had happened, for the gates were open and a dark figure stood squarely before them.

'Put up your hands, Kohl!' said a voice, and hateful as it was to Lew Kohl, he could have fallen on the neck of Mr. Reeder.

At twelve o'clock that night Sir James Tithermite was discussing matters with his bride-to-be: the stupidity of her lawyer, who wished to safeguard her fortune, and his own cleverness and foresight in securing complete freedom of action for the girl who was to be his wife.

'These blackguards think of nothing but their fees,' he began, when his footman came in unannounced, and behind him the Chief Constable of the county and a man he remembered seeing before.

'Sir James Tithermite?' said the Chief Constable unnecessarily, for he knew Sir James very well.

'Yes, Colonel, what is it?' asked the baronet, his face twitching.

'I am taking you into custody on a charge of wilfully murdering your wife, Eleanor Mary Tithermite.'

'The whole thing turned upon the question as to whether Lady Tithermite was a good or a bad sailor,' explained J.G. Reeder to his chief. 'If she were a bad sailor, it was unlikely that she would be on the ship, even for five minutes, without calling for the stewardess. The stewardess did not see her ladyship, nor did anybody on board, for the simple reason that she was not on board! She was murdered within the grounds of the Manor; her body was buried beneath the hearthstone of the old lodge, and Sir James continued his journey by car to Dover, handing over his packages to a porter and telling him to take them to his cabin before he returned to put the car into the hotel garage. He had timed his arrival so that he passed on board with a crowd of passengers from the boat train, and nobody knew whether he was alone or whether he was accompanied, and, for the matter of that, nobody cared. The purser gave him his key, and he put the baggage, including his wife's hat, into the cabin, paid the porter and dismissed him. Officially, Lady Tithermite was on board, for he surrendered her ticket to the collector and received her landing voucher. And then he discovered she had disappeared. The ship was searched, but of course the unfortunate lady was not found. As I remarked before—'

'You have a criminal mind,' said the Director good-humouredly. 'Go on, Reeder.'

'Having this queer and objectionable trait, I saw how very simple a matter it was to give the illusion that the lady was on board, and I decided that, if the murder was committed, it must have been within a few miles of the house. And then the local builder told me that he had given Sir James a little lesson in the art of mixing mortar. And the local blacksmith told me that the gate had been damaged, presumably by Sir James's car—I had seen the broken rods and all I wanted to know was when the repairs were effected. That she was beneath the hearth in the lodge I was certain. Without a search warrant it was impossible to prove or disprove my theory, and I myself could not conduct a private investigation without risking the reputation of our department—if I may say "our,"' he said apologetically.

The Director was thoughtful.

'Of course, you induced this man Kohl to dig up the hearth by pretending you had money buried there. I presume you revealed that fact in your notebook? But why on earth did he imagine that you had a hidden treasure?'

Mr. Reeder smiled sadly.

'The criminal mind is a peculiar thing,' he said, with a sigh. 'It harbours illusions and fairy stories. Fortunately, I understand that mind. As I have often said — '

III. — THE TROUPE

First published under the title "A Place on the River" in
The Grand Magazine, Vol. 46, Sep 1924-Feb 1925, as part of the J.G. Reeder series
"The Man Who Saw Evil"

THERE was a quietude and sedateness about the Public Prosecutor's office which completely harmonised with the tastes and inclinations of Mr. J.G. Reeder. For he was a gentleman who liked to work in an office where the ticking of a clock was audible and the turning of a paper produced a gentle disturbance.

He had before him one morning the typewritten catalogue of Messrs. Willoby, the eminent estate agents, and he was turning the leaves with a thoughtful expression. The catalogue was newly arrived, a messenger having only a few minutes before placed the portfolio on his desk.

Presently he smoothed down a leaf and read again the flattering description of a fairly unimportant property, and his scrutiny was patently a waste of time, for, scrawled on the margin of the sheet in red ink was the word 'Let,' which meant that 'Riverside Bower' was not available for hire. The ink was smudged, and 'Let' had been obviously written that morning.

'Humph!' said Mr. Reeder.

He was interested for many reasons. In the heat of July riverside houses are at a premium: at the beginning of November they are somewhat of a drug on the market. And transatlantic visitors do not as a rule hire riverside cottages in a month which is chiefly distinguished by mists, rain and general discomfort.

Two reception: two bedrooms: bath, large dry cellars, lawn to river, small skiff and punt. Gas and electric light. Three guineas weekly or would be let for six months at 2 guineas.

He pulled his table telephone towards him and gave the agents' number.

'Let, is it—dear me! To an American gentleman? When will it be available?'

The new tenant had taken the house for a month. Mr. Reeder was even more intrigued, though his interest in the 'American gentleman' was not quite as intensive as the American gentleman's interest in Mr. Reeder.

When the great Art Lomer came on a business trip from Canada to London, a friend and admirer carried him off one day to see the principal sight of London.

'He generally comes out at lunch time,' said the friend, who was called 'Cheep,' because his name was Sparrow.

Mr. Lomer looked up and down Whitehall disparagingly, for he had seen so many cities of the world that none seemed as good as the others.

'There he is!' whispered Cheep, though there was no need for mystery or confidence.

A middle-aged man had come out of one of the narrow doorways of a large grey building. On his head was a high, flat-crowned hat, his body was tightly encased in a black frock coat. A weakish man with yellowy-white side-whiskers and eyeglasses, that were nearer to the end than the beginning of his nose.

'Him?' demanded the amazed Art.

'Him,' said the other, incorrectly but with emphasis.

'Is that the kind of guy you're scared about? You're crazy. Why, that man couldn't catch a cold! Now, back home in T'ronto—'

Art was proud of his home town, and in that spirit of expansiveness which paints even the unpleasant features of One's Own with the most attractive hues, he had even a good word to say about the Royal Canadian Police—a force which normally, and in a local atmosphere, he held in the greatest detestation.

Art 'operated'—he never employed a baser word—from Toronto, which, by its proximity to Buffalo and the United States border, gave him certain advantages. He had once 'operated' in Canada itself, but his line at that period being robbery of a kind which is necessarily accompanied by assault, he had found himself facing a Canadian magistrate, and a Canadian magistrate wields extraordinary powers. Art had been sent down for five years and, crowning horror, was ordered to receive twenty-five lashes with a whip which has nine tails, each one of which hurts. Thereafter he cut out violence and confined himself to the formation of his troupe—and Art Lomer's troupe was famous from the Atlantic to the Pacific.

He had been plain Arthur Lomer when he was rescued from a London gutter and a career of crime and sent to Canada, the charitable authorities being under the impression that Canada was rather short on juvenile criminals. By dint of great artfulness, good stage management and a natural aptitude for acquiring easy money, he had gained for himself a bungalow on the islands, a flat in Church Street, a six-cylinder car and a New England accent which would pass muster in almost any place except New England.

'I'll tell the world you fellows want waking up! So that's your Reeder? Well, if Canada and the United States was full of goats like him, I'd pack more dollars in one month than Hollywood pays Chaplin in ten years. Yes, sir. Listen, does that guy park a clock?'

His guide was a little dazed.

'Does he wear a watch? Sure!'

Mr. Art Lomer nodded.

'Wait—I'll bring it back to you in five minutes—I'm goin' to show you sump'n'.'

It was the maddest fool thing he had ever done in his life; he was in London on business, and was jeopardising a million dollars for the sake of the cheap applause of a man for whose opinion he did not care a cent.

Mr. Reeder was standing nervously on the sidewalk, waiting for what he described as 'the vehicular traffic' to pass, when a strange man bumped against him.

'Excuse me, sir,' said the stranger.

'Not at all,' murmured Mr. Reeder. 'My watch is five minutes fast—you can see the correct time by Big Ben.'

Mr. Lomer felt a hand dip into his coat pocket, saw, like one hypnotised, the watch go back to J.G. Reeder's pocket.

'Over here for long?' asked Mr. Reeder pleasantly.

'Why—yes.'

'It's a nice time of the year.' Mr. Reeder removed his eyeglasses, rubbed them feebly on his sleeve and replaced them crookedly. 'But the country is not quite so beautiful as Canada in the fall. How is Leoni?'

Art Lomer did not faint; he swayed slightly and blinked hard, as if he were trying to wake up. Leoni was the proprietor of that little restaurant in Buffalo which was the advanced base of those operations so profitable to Art and his friends.

'Leoni? Say, mister—'

'And the troupe—are they performing in England or—er—resting? I think that is the word.'

Art gaped at the other. On Mr. Reeder's face was an expression of solicitude and inquiry. It was as though the well-being of the troupe was an absorbing preoccupation.

'Say—listen—' began Art huskily.

Before he could collect his thoughts, Reeder was crossing the road with nervous glances left and right, his umbrella gripped tightly in his hand.

'I guess I'm crazy,' said Mr. Lomer, and walked back very slowly to where he had left his anxious cicerone.

'No—he got away before I could touch him,' he said briefly, for he had his pride. 'Come along, we'll get some eats, it's nearly twel—'

He put his hand to his pocket, but his watch was gone! So also was the expensive platinum albert. Mr. Reeder could be heavily jocular on occasions.

'Art Lomer—is there anything against him?' asked the Director of Public Prosecutions, whose servant Mr. J.G. Reeder was.

'No, sir, there is no complaint here. I have come into—er—possession of a watch of his, which I find, by reference to my private file, was stolen in Cleveland in 1921—it is in the police file of that date. Only—um—it seems remarkable that this gentleman should be in London at the end of the tourist season.'

The Director pursed his lips dubiously.

'M--m. Tell the people at the Yard. He doesn't belong to us. What is his speciality?'

'He is a troupe leader—I think that is the term. Mr. Lomer was once associated with a theatrical company in—er—a humble capacity.'

'You mean he is an actor?' asked the puzzled Director.

'Ye--es, sir; a producer rather than actor. I have heard about his troupe, though I have never had the pleasure of seeing them perform. A talented company.'

He sighed heavily and shook his head. 'I don't quite follow you about the troupe. How did his watch come into your possession, Reeder?'

Mr. Reeder nodded. 'That was a little jest on my part,' he said, lowering his voice. 'A little jest.'

The Director knew Mr. Reeder too well to pursue the subject.

Lomer was living at the Hotel Calfort, in Bloomsbury. He occupied an important suite, for, being in the position of a man who was after big fish, he could not cavil at the cost of the groundbait. The big fish had bitten much sooner than Art Lomer had dared to hope. Its name was Bertie Claude Staffen, and the illustration was apt, for there was something very fishlike about this young man with his dull eyes and his permanently opened mouth. Bertie's father was rich beyond the dreams of actresses. He was a pottery manufacturer, who bought cotton mills as a side-line, and he had made so much money that he never hired a taxi if he could take a bus, and never took a bus if he could walk. In this way he kept his liver (to which he frequently referred) in good order and hastened the degeneration of his heart.

Bertie Claude had inherited all his father's meanness and such of his money as was not left to faithful servants, orphan homes and societies for promoting the humanities, which meant that Bertie inherited almost every penny. He had the weak chin and sloping forehead of an undeveloped intellect, but he knew there were twelve pennies to a shilling and that one hundred cents equalled one dollar, and that is more knowledge than the only sons of millionaires usually acquire.

He had one quality which few would suspect in him: the gift of romantic dreaming. When Mr. Staffen was not occupied in cutting down overhead charges or speeding up production, he loved to sit at his ease, a cigarette between his lips, his eyes half closed, and picture himself in heroic situations. Thus, he could imagine dark caves stumbled upon by acident, filled with dusty boxes bulging with treasure; or he saw himself at Deauville Casino, with immense piles of mille notes before him, won from fabulously rich Greeks, Armenians—in fact, anybody who is fabulously rich. Most of his dreams were about money in sufficient quantities to repay him the death duties on his father's estate which had been iniquitously wrung from him by thieving revenue officers. He was a very rich man, but ought to be richer—this was his considered view.

When Bertie Claude arrived at the Calfort Hotel and was shown into Art's private sitting-room, he stepped into a world of heady romance. For the big table in the centre of the room was covered with specimens of quartz of every grade, and they had been recovered from a brand-new mine located by Art's mythical brother and sited at a spot which was known only to two men, one of whom was Art Lomer and the other Bertie Claude Staffen.

Mr. Staffen took off his light overcoat and, walking to the table, inspected the ore with sober interest.

'I've had the assay,' he said. 'The johnny who did it is a friend of mine and didn't charge a penny; his report is promising—very promising.'

'The company—' began Art, but Mr. Staffen raised a warning finger.

'I think you know, and it is unnecessary for me to remind you, that I do not intend speculating a dollar in this mine. I'm putting up no money. What I'm prepared to do is to use my influence in the promotion for a quid pro quo. You know what that means?'

'Something for nothing!' said Art, and in this instance was not entirely wide of the mark.

'Well, no—stock in the company. Maybe I'll take a directorship later, when the money is up and everything is plain sailing. I can't lend my name to a—well, unknown quantity.'

Art agreed.

'My friend has put up the money,' he said easily. 'If that guy had another hundred dollars he'd have all the money in the world—he's that rich. Stands to reason, Mr. Staffen, that I wouldn't come over here tryin' to get money from a gentleman who is practically a stranger. We met in Canada—sure we did! But what do you know about me? I might be one large crook—I might be a con man or anything!'

Some such idea had occurred to Bertie Claude, but the very frankness of his friend dispelled something of his suspicions.

'I've often wondered since what you must have thought of me, sittin' in a game with that bunch of thugs,' Art went on, puffing a reflective cigar. 'But I guess you said to yourself, "This guy is a man of the world—he's gotta mix." An' that's true. In these Canadian mining camps you horn in with some real tough boys—yes, sir. They're sump'n' fierce.'

'I quite understood the position,' said Bertie Claude, who hadn't. 'I flatter myself I know men. If I haven't shown that in "Homo Sum" then I've failed in expression.'

'Sure,' said Mr. Lomer lazily, and added another 'Sure!' to ram home the first. 'That's a pretty good book. When you give it to me at King Edward Hotel I thought it was sump'n' about arithmetic. But 'tis mighty good poetry, every line startin' with big letters an' the end of every line sounding like the end word in the line before. I said to my secretary, "That Mr. Staffen must have a brain." How you get the ideas beats me. That one about the princess who comes out of a clam—'

'An oyster—she was the embodiment of the pearl,' Bertie hastened to explain. 'You mean "The White Maiden"?'

Lomer nodded lazily.

'That was grand. I never read poetry till I read that; it just made me want to cry like a great big fool! If I had your gifts I wouldn't be loafin' round Ontario prospecting. No, sir.'

'It is a gift,' said Mr. Staffen after thought. 'You say you have the money for the company?'

'Every cent. I'm not in a position to offer a single share—that's true. Not that you need worry about that. I've reserved a few from promotion. No, sir, I never had any intention of allowing you to pay a cent.'

He knocked off the ash of his cigar and frowned.

'You've been mighty nice to me, Mr. Staffen,' he said slowly, 'and though I don't feel called upon to tell every man my business, you're such a square white fellow that I feel sort of confident about you. This mine means nothing.'

Bertie Claude's eyebrows rose.

'I don't quite get you,' he said.

Art's smile was slow and a little sad.

'Doesn't it occur to you that if I've got the capital for that property, it was foolish of me to take a trip to Europe?'

Bertie had certainly wondered why.

'Selling that mine was like selling bars of gold. It didn't want any doing; I could have sold it if I'd been living in the Amaganni Forest. No, sir, I'm here on business that would make your hair stand up if you knew.'

He rose abruptly and paced the room with quick, nervous strides, his brow furrowed in thought.

'You're a whale of a poet,' he said suddenly. 'Maybe you've got more imagination than most people. What does the mine mean for me? A few hundred thousand dollars' profit.' He shrugged his shoulders. 'What are you doing on Wednesday?'

The brusqueness of the question took Bertie Claude aback.

'On Wednesday? Well, I don't know that I'm doing anything.'

Mr. Lomer bit his lip thoughtfully.

'I've got a little house on the river. Come down and spend a night with me, and I'll let you into a secret that these newspapers would give a million dollars to know. If you read it in a book you wouldn't believe it. Maybe one day you can write it. It would take a man with your imagination to put it over. Say, I'll tell you now.'

And then, with some hesitation, Mr. Lomer told his story.

'Politics, and all that, I know nothing about. There has been a sort of revolution in Russia by all accounts, and queer things have been happenin'. I'm not such a dunce that I don't know that. My interest in Russia was about the same as yours in Piketown, Saskatchewan. But about six months ago I got in touch with a couple of Russkis. They came out of the United States in a hurry, with a sheriff's posse behind them, and I happened to be staying on a farm near the border when they turned up. And what do you think they'd been doing?'

Mr. Staffen shook his head.

'Peddling emeralds,' said the other soberly.

'Emeralds? Peddling? What do you mean—trying to sell emeralds?'

Art nodded.

'Yes, sir. One had a paper bag full of 'em, all sizes. I bought the lot for twelve thousand dollars, took 'em down to T'ronto and got them valued at something under a million dollars.'

Bertie Claude was listening open-mouthed.

'These fellows had come from Moscow. They'd been peddlin' jewellery for four years. Some broken-down Prince was acting as agent for the other swells—I didn't ask questions too closely, because naturally I'm not inquisitive.'

He leant forward and tapped the other's knee to emphasise his words.

'The stuff I bought wasn't a twentieth of their stock. I sent them back to Russia for the rest of the loot, and they're due here next I week.'

'Twenty million dollars!' gasped Bertie Claude. 'What will it cost you?'
'A million dollars--two hundred thousand pounds. Come down to my place at Marlow, and I'll show you the grandest emeralds you ever saw—all that I've got left, as a matter of fact. I sold the biggest part to a Pittsburg millionaire for—well, I won't give you the price, because you'll think I robbed him! If you like any stone you see—why, I'll let you buy it, though I don't want to sell. Naturally, I couldn't make profit out of a friend.'
Bertie Claude listened, dazed, while his host catalogued his treasures with an ease and a shrewd sense of appraisement. When Mr. Staffen left his friend's room, his head was in a whirl, though he experienced a bewildered sense of familiarity with a situation which had often figured in his dreams.
As he strode through the hall, he saw a middle-aged man with a flat-topped felt hat, but beyond noticing that he wore a ready-made cravat, that his shoes were square-toed and that he looked rather like a bailiff's officer, Bertie Claude would have passed him, had not the old-fashioned gentleman stood in his way.
'Excuse me, sir. You're Mr. Staffen, are you not?'
'Yes,' said Bertie shortly.
'I wonder if I could have a few moments' conversation with you on—er—a matter of some moment?'
Bertie waved an impatient hand.
'I've no time to see anybody,' he said brusquely. 'If you want an appointment you'd better write for it.'
And he walked out, leaving the sad-looking man to gaze pensively after him.
Mr. Lomer's little house was an isolated stone bungalow between Marlow and the Quarry Wood, and if he had sought diligently, Mr. Lomer could not have found a property more suitable for his purpose. Bertie Claude, who associated the river with sunshine and flannelled ease, shivered as he came out of the railway station and looked anxiously up at the grey sky. It was raining steadily, and the station cab that was waiting for him dripped from every surface.
'Pretty beastly month to take a bungalow on the river,' he grumbled.
Mr. Lomer, who was not quite certain in his mind what was the ideal month for riverside bungalows, agreed.
'It suits me,' he said. 'This house of mine has got the right kind of lonesomeness. I just hate having people looking over me.'
The road from the station to the house followed parallel with the line of the river. Staring out of the streaming windows, Mr. Staffen saw only the steel-grey of water and the damp grasses of the meadows through which the road ran. A quarter of an hour's drive, however, brought them to a pretty little cottage which stood in a generous garden. A bright fire burnt in the hall fire-place, and there was a general air of cosiness and comfort about the place that revived Bertie's flagging spirits. A few seconds later they were sitting in a half-timbered dining-room, where tea had been laid.
Atmosphere has an insensible appeal to most people, and Bertie found himself impressed alike by the snugness of the place and the unexpected service, for there was a trim, pretty waiting maid, a sedate, middle-aged butler, and a sober-faced young man in footman's livery, who had taken off his wet mackintosh and had rubbed his boots dry before he entered the dining-room.
'No, the house isn't mine: it is one I always hire when I'm in England,' said Mr. Lomer, who never told a small and unnecessary lie; because small and unnecessary lies are so easily detected. 'Jenkins, the butler, is my man, so is the valet; the other people I just hired with the house.'

After tea he showed Bertie up to his bedroom, and, opening a drawer of his bureau, took out a small steel box, fastened with two locks. These he unfastened and lifted out a shallow metal tray covered with a layer of cotton-wool.

'You can have any of these, that take your eye,' he said. 'Make me an offer and I'll tell you what they're worth.'

He rolled back the cotton-wool and revealed six magnificent stones.

'That one?' said Mr. Lomer, taking the largest between his finger and thumb. 'Why that's worth six thousand dollars—about twelve hundred pounds. And if you offered me that sum for it, I'd think you were a fool, because the only safe way of getting emeralds is to buy 'em fifty per cent. under value. I reckon that cost me about'—he made a mental calculation—'ninety pounds.'

Bertie's eyes shone. On emeralds he was something of an expert, and that these stones were genuine, he knew.

'You wouldn't like to sell it for ninety pounds?' he asked carelessly.

Art Lomer shook his head.

'No, sir. I've gotta make some profit even from my friends! I'll let you have it for a hundred.'

Bertie's hand sought his inside pocket.

'No, I don't want paying now. What do you know about emeralds anyway? They might be a clever fake. Take it up to town, show it to an expert—'

'I'll give you the cheque now.'

'Any time will do.'

Art wrapped up the stone carefully, put it in a small box and handed it to his companion.

'That's the only one I'm going to sell,' he explained as he led the way back to the dining-room.

Bertie went immediately to the small secretaire, wrote the cheque and, tearing it out, handed it to Mr. Lomer. Art looked at the paper and frowned.

'Why, what do I do with this?' he asked. 'I've got no bank account here. All my money's in the Associated Express Company.'

'I'll make it "pay bearer,"' said Bertie obligingly.

Still Mr. Lomer was dubious.

'Just write a note telling the President, or whoever he is, to cash that little bit of paper. I hate banks anyway.'

The obliging Bertie Claude scribbled the necessary note. When this was done, Bertie came to business, for he was a business man. 'Can I come in on this jewel deal?'

Art Lomer shook his head reluctantly. 'Sorry, Mr. Staffen, but that's almost impossible. I'll be quite frank with you, because I believe in straightforward dealing. When you ask to come in on that transaction, you're just asking me for money!'

Bertie made a faint noise of protest.

'Well, that's a mean way of putting it, but it comes to the same thing. I've taken all the risk, I've organised the operation—and it's cost money to get that guy out of Russia: aeroplanes and special trains and everything. I just hate to refuse you, because I like you, Mr. Staffen. Maybe if there's any little piece to which you might take a fancy, I'll let you have it at a reasonable price.'

Bertie thought for a moment, his busy mind at work.

'What has the deal cost you up to now?' he asked.

Again Mr. Lomer shook his head. 'It doesn't matter what it's cost me—if you offered me four times the amount of money I've spent—and that would be a considerable sum—I couldn't let you in on this deal. I might go so far as giving you a small interest, but I wouldn't take money for that.'

'We'll talk about it later,' said Bertie, who never lost hope.
The rain had ceased, and the setting sun flooded the river with pale gold, and Bertie was walking in the garden with his host, when from somewhere above them came the faint hum of an aeroplane engine. Presently he saw the machine circling and disappearing behind the black crown of Quarry Wood. He heard an exclamation from the man at his side and, turning, saw Art's face puckered in a grimace of annoyance and doubt.
'What's the matter?' he asked.
'I'm wondering,' said Art slowly. 'They told me next week...why, no, I'm foolish.'
It was dark. The butler had turned on the lights and drawn the blinds when they went indoors again, and it was not difficult for Bertie to realise that something had happened which was very disturbing to his host. He was taciturn, and for the next half-hour scarcely spoke, sitting in front of the fire gazing into the leaping flames and starting at every sound.
Dinner, a simple meal, was served early, and whilst the servants were clearing away, the two men strolled into the tiny drawing-room.
'What's the trouble, Lomer?'
'Nothing,' said the other with a start, 'only—'
At that moment they heard the tinkle of a bell, and Art listened tensely. He heard the parley of voices in the hall, and then the footman came.
'There's two men and a lady to see you, sir,' he said.
Bertie saw the other bite his lip.
'Show them in,' said Art curtly, and a second later a tall man, wearing the leather coat and helmet of an airman, walked into the room.
'Marsham! What in hell — !'
The girl who followed instantly claimed Bertie Claude's attention. She was slim and dark, and her face was beautiful, despite the pallor of her cheeks and the tired look in her eyes. The second of the men visitors was hardly as prepossessing: a squat, foreign-looking individual with a short-clipped beard, he was wrapped to his neck in an old fur overcoat, and his wild-looking head was bare.
Art closed the door.
'What's the great idea?' he asked.
'There's been trouble,' said the tall man sulkily. 'The Prince has had another offer. He has sent some of the stuff, but he won't part with the pearls or the diamonds until you pay him half of the money you promised. This is Princess Pauline Dimitroff, the Prince's daughter,' he explained.
Art shot an angry look at the girl.
'Say, see here, young lady,' he said, 'I suppose you speak English?'
She nodded.
'This isn't the way we do business in our country. Your father promised—'
'My father has been very precipitate,' she said, with the slightest of foreign accent, which was delightful to Bertie's ear. 'He has taken much risk. Indeed, I am not sure that he has been very honest in the matter. It is very simple for you to pay. If he has your money to-night—'
'To-night?' boomed Art. 'How can I get the money for him to-night?'
'He is in Holland,' said the girl. 'We have the aeroplane waiting.'
'But how can I get the money to-night?' repeated the Canadian angrily. 'Do you think I carry a hundred thousand pounds in my pistol pocket?'
Again she shrugged, and, turning to the unkempt little man, said something to him in a language which was unintelligible to Mr. Staffen. He replied in his hoarse voice, and she nodded.

'Pieter says my father will take your cheque. He only wishes to be sure that there is no—' She paused, at a loss for an English word.

'Did I ever double-cross your father?' asked Art savagely. 'I can't give you either the money or the cheque. You can call off the deal—I'm through!'

By this time the aviator had unrolled the package he carried under his arm, placed it on the table, and Bertie Claude grew breathless at the sight of the glittering display that met his eyes. There were diamonds, set and unset; quaint and ancient pieces of jewellery that must have formed the heirlooms of old families; but their historical value did not for the moment occur to him. He beckoned Art aside.

'If you can keep these people here tonight,' he said in a low voice, 'I'll undertake to raise all the money you want on that collection alone.'

Art shook his head.

'It's no use, Mr. Staffen. I know this guy. Unless I can send him the money to-night, we'll not smell the rest of the stuff.'

Suddenly he clapped his hands.

'Gee!' he breathed. 'That's an idea! You've got your cheque-book.'

Cold suspicion showed in the eyes of Bertie Claude.

'I've got my cheque-book, certainly,' he said, 'but—'

'Come into the dining-room.' Art almost ran ahead of him, and when they reached the room he closed the door. 'A cheque can't be presented for two or three days. It certainly couldn't be presented to-morrow,' he said, speaking rapidly. 'By that time we could get this stuff up to town to your bankers, and you could keep it until I redeem it. What's more, you can stop payment of the cheque tomorrow morning if the stones aren't worth the money.'

Bertie looked at the matter from ten different angles in as many seconds.

'Suppose I gave them a post-dated cheque to make sure?' he said.

'Post-dated?' Mr. Lomer was puzzled. 'What does that mean?' And when Bertie explained, his face brightened. 'Why, sure!' he said. 'That's a double protection. Make it payable the day after to-morrow.'

Bertie hesitated no more. Sitting down at the table he took out his cheque-book and a fountain pen, and verified the date.

'Make it "bearer",' suggested Art, when the writer paused, 'same as you did the other cheque.'

Bertie nodded and added his signature, with its characteristic underlining.

'Wait a second.'

Art went out of the room and came back within a minute.

'They've taken it!' he said exultantly. 'Boy,' he said, as he slapped the gratified young man on the shoulder, 'you've gotta come in on this now and I didn't want you to. It's fifty-fifty—I'm no hog. Come along, and I'll show you something else that I never intended showing a soul.'

He went out into the passage, opened a little door that led down a flight of stone steps to the cellar, switching on the light as he went down the stairs. Unlocking a heavy door, he threw it open.

'See here,' he said, 'did you ever see anything like this?'

Bertie Claude peered into the dark interior.

'I don't see—' he began, when he was so violently pushed into the darkness that he stumbled. In another second the door closed on him; he heard the snap of a lock and shrieked: 'I say, what's this!'

'I say, you'll find out in a day or two,' said the mocking voice of Mr. Lomer.

Art closed the second door, ran lightly up the stairs and joined footman, butler, trim maid and the three visitors in the drawing-room.

'He's well inside. And he stays there till the cheque matures—there's enough food and water in the cellar to last him a week.'

'Did you get him?' asked the bearded Russian.

'Get him! He was easy,' said the other scornfully. 'Now, you boys and girls, skip, and skip quick! I've got a letter from this guy to his bank manager, telling him to—' he consulted the letter and quoted—'"to cash the attached cheque for my friend Mr. Arthur Lomer."'

There was a murmur of approval from the troupe.

'The aeroplane's gone back, I suppose?'

The man in the leather coat nodded.

'Yes,' he said, 'I only hired it for the afternoon.'

'Well, you can get back too. Ray and Al, you go to Paris and take the C.P. boat from Havre. Slicky, you get those whiskers off and leave honest from Liverpool. Pauline and Aggie will make Genoa, and we'll meet at Leoni's on the fourteenth of next month and cut the stuff all ways!'

Two days later Mr. Art Lomer walked into the noble offices of the Northern Commercial Bank and sought an interview with the manager. That gentleman read the letter, examined the cheque and touched a bell.

'It's a mighty big sum,' said Mr. Lomer, in an almost awe-stricken voice.

The manager smiled. 'We cash fairly large cheques here,' he said, and, to the clerk who came at his summons: 'Mr. Lomer would like as much of this in American currency as possible. How did you leave Mr. Staffen?'

'Why, Bertie and I have been in Paris over that new company of mine,' said Lomer. 'My! it's difficult to finance Canadian industries in this country, Mr. Soames, but we've made a mighty fine deal in Paris.'

He chatted on purely commercial topics until the clerk returned and laid a heap of bills and banknotes on the table. Mr. Lomer produced a wallet, enclosed the money securely, shook hands with the manager and walked out into the general office. And then he stopped, for Mr. J.G. Reeder stood squarely in his path.

'Pay-day for the troupe, Mr. Lomer—or do you call it "treasury"? My theatrical glossary is rather rusty.'

'Why, Mr. Reeder,' stammered Art, 'glad to see you, but I'm rather busy just now—'

'What do you think has happened to our dear friend, Mr. Bertie Claude Staffen?' asked Reeder anxiously.

'Why, he's in Paris.'

'So soon!' murmured Reeder. 'And the police only took him out of your suburban cellar an hour ago! How wonderful are our modern systems of transportation! Marlow one minute, Paris the next, and Moscow, let us say, the next.'

Art hesitated no longer. He dashed past, thrusting the detective aside, and flew for the door. He was so annoyed that the two men who were waiting for him had the greatest difficulty in putting the handcuffs on his wrists.

'Yes, sir,' said Mr. Reeder to his chief, 'Art always travels with his troupe. The invisibility of the troupe was to me a matter for grave suspicion, and of course I've had the house under observation ever since Mr. Staffen disappeared. It is not my business, of course,' he said apologetically, 'and really I should not have interfered. Only, as I have often explained to you, the curious workings of my mind —'

IV. — THE STEALER OF MARBLE

First published under the title "The Telephone Box" in
The Grand Magazine, Vol. 46, Sep 1924-Feb 1925, as part of the J.G. Reeder series
"The Man Who Saw Evil"

MARGARET BELMAN'S chiefest claim to Mr. Reeder's notice was that she lived in the Brockley Road, some few doors from his own establishment. He did not know her name, being wholly incurious about law-abiding folk, but he was aware that she was pretty, that her complexion was that pink and white which is seldom seen away from a magazine cover. She dressed well, and if there was one thing that he noted about her more than any other, it was that she walked and carried herself with a certain grace that was especially pleasing to a man of aesthetic predilections.

He had, on occasions, walked behind her and before her, and had ridden on the same street car with her to Westminster Bridge. She invariably descended at the corner of the Embankment, and was as invariably met by a good-looking young man and walked away with him. The presence of that young man was a source of passive satisfaction to Mr. Reeder, for no particular reason, unless it was that he had a tidy mind, and preferred a rose when it had a background of fern and grew uneasy at the sight of a saucerless cup.

It did not occur to him that he was an object of interest and curiosity to Miss Belman.

'That was Mr. Reeder—he has something to do with the police, I think,' she said.

'Mr. J.G. Reeder?'

Roy Master looked back with interest at the middle-aged man scampering fearfully across the road, his unusual hat on the back of his head, his umbrella over his shoulder like a cavalryman's sword.

'Good Lord! I never dreamt he was like that.'

'Who is he?' she asked, distracted from her own problem.

'Reeder? He's in the Public Prosecutor's Department, a sort of a detective—there was a case the other week where he gave evidence. He used to be with the Bank of England—'

Suddenly she stopped, and he looked at her in surprise.

'What's the matter?' he asked.

'I don't want you to go any farther, Roy,' she said. 'Mr. Telfer saw me with you yesterday, and he's quite unpleasant about it.'

'Telfer?' said the young man indignantly. 'That little worm! What did he say?'

'Nothing very much,' she replied, but from her tone he gathered that the 'nothing very much' had been a little disturbing.

'I am leaving Telfers,' she said unexpectedly. 'It is a good job, and I shall never get another like it—I mean, so far as the pay is concerned.'

Roy Master did not attempt to conceal his satisfaction.

'I'm jolly glad,' he said vigorously. 'I can't imagine how you've endured that boudoir atmosphere so long. What did he say?' he asked again, and, before she could answer: 'Anyway, Telfers are shaky. There are all sorts of queer rumours about them in the City.'

'But I thought it was a very rich corporation!' she said in astonishment.

He shook his head.

'It was—but they have been doing lunatic things—what can you expect when a halfwitted weakling like Sidney Telfer is at the head of affairs? They underwrote three concerns last year that no brokerage business would have touched with a barge-pole, and they had to take up the shares. One was a lost treasure company to raise a Spanish galleon that sank three hundred years ago! But what really did happen yesterday morning?'

'I will tell you to-night,' she said, and made her hasty adieux.

Mr. Sidney Telfer had arrived when she went into a room which, in its luxurious appointments, its soft carpet and dainty etceteras, was not wholly undeserving of Roy Masters' description. The head of Telfers Consolidated seldom visited his main office on Threadneedle Street. The atmosphere of the place, he said, depressed him; it was all so horrid and sordid and rough. The founder of the firm, his grandfather, had died ten years before Sidney had been born, leaving the business to a son, a chronic invalid, who had died a few weeks after Sidney first saw the light. In the hands of trustees the business had flourished, despite the spasmodic interferences of his eccentric mother, whose peculiarities culminated in a will which relieved him of most of that restraint which is wisely laid upon a boy of sixteen.

The room, with its stained-glass windows and luxurious furnishing, fitted Mr. Telfer perfectly, for he was exquisitely arrayed. He was tall and so painfully thin that the abnormal smallness of his head was not at first apparent. As the girl came into the room he was sniffing delicately at a fine cambric handkerchief, and she thought that he was paler than she had ever seen him—and more repellent.

He followed her movements with a dull stare, and she had placed his letters on his table before he spoke.

'I say, Miss Belman, you won't mention a word about what I said to you last night?'

'Mr. Telfer,' she answered quietly, 'I am hardly likely to discuss such a matter.'

'I'd marry you and all that, only...clause in my mother's will,' he said disjointedly. 'That could be got over—in time.'

She stood by the table, her hands resting on the edge.

'I would not marry you, Mr. Telfer, even if there were no clause in your mother's will; the suggestion that I should run away with you to America—'

'South America,' he corrected her gravely. 'Not the United States; there was never any suggestion of the United States.'

She could have smiled, for she was not as angry with this rather vacant young man as his startling proposition entitled her to be.

'The point is,' he went on anxiously, 'you'll keep it to yourself? I've been worried dreadfully all night. I told you to send me a note saying what you thought of my idea—well, don't!'

This time she did smile, but before she could answer him he went on, speaking rapidly in a high treble that sometimes rose to a falsetto squeak:

'You're a perfectly beautiful girl, and I'm crazy about you, but... there's a tragedy in my life...really. Perfectly ghastly tragedy. An' everything's at sixes an' sevens. If I'd had any sense I'd have brought in a feller to look after things. I'm beginning to see that now.'

For the second time in twenty-four hours this young man, who had almost been tongue-tied and had never deigned to notice her, had poured forth a torrent of confidences, and in one had, with frantic insistence, set forth a plan which had amazed and shocked her. Abruptly he finished, wiped his weak eyes, and in his normal voice:

'Get Billingham on the 'phone; I want him.'

She wondered, as her busy fingers flew over the keys of her typewriter, to what extent his agitation and wild eloquence was due to the rumoured 'shakiness' of Telfers Consolidated.

Mr. Billingham came, a sober little man, bald and taciturn, and went in his secretive way into his employer's room. There was no hint in his appearance or his manner that he contemplated a great crime. He was stout to a point of podginess; apart from his habitual frown, his round face, unlined by the years, was marked by an expression of benevolence.

Yet Mr. Stephen Billingham, managing director of the Telfer Consolidated Trust, went into the office of the London and Central Bank late that afternoon and, presenting a bearer cheque for one hundred and fifty thousand pounds, which was duly honoured, was driven to the Credit Lilloise. He had telephoned particulars of his errand, and there were waiting for him seventeen packets, each containing a million francs, and a smaller packet of a hundred and forty-six mille notes. The franc stood at 74.55 and he received the eighteen packages in exchange for a cheque on the Credit Lilloise for £80,000 and the 150 thousand-pound notes which he had drawn on the London and Central.

Of Billingham's movements thenceforth little was known. He was seen by an acquaintance driving through Cheapside in a taxicab which was traced as far as Charing Cross—and there he disappeared. Neither the airways nor the waterways had known him, the police theory being that he had left by an evening train that had carried an excursion party via Havre to Paris.

'This is the biggest steal we have had in years,' said the Assistant Director of Public Prosecutions. 'If you can slip in sideways on the inquiry, Mr. Reeder, I should be glad. Don't step on the toes of the City police—they are quite amiable people where murder is concerned, but a little touchy where money is in question. Go along and see Sidney Telfer.'

Fortunately, the prostrated Sidney was discoverable outside the City area. Mr. Reeder went into the outer office and saw a familiar face.

'Pardon me, I think I know you, young lady,' he said, and she smiled as she opened the little wooden gate to admit him.

'You are Mr. Reeder—we live in the same road,' she said, and then quickly: 'Have you come about Mr. Billingham?'

'Yes.' His voice was hushed, as though he were speaking of a dead friend. 'I wanted to see Mr. Telfer, but perhaps you could give me a little information.'

The only news she had was that Sidney Telfer had been in the office since seven o'clock and was at the moment in such a state of collapse that she had sent for the doctor.

'I doubt if he is in a condition to see you,' she said.

'I will take all responsibility,' said Mr. Reeder soothingly. 'Is Mr. Telfer—er—a friend of yours. Miss — ?'

'Belman is my name.' He had seen the quick flush that came to her cheek: it could mean one of two things. 'No, I am an employee, that is all.'

Her tone told him all he wanted to know. Mr. J.G. Reeder was something of an authority on office friendships.

'Bothered you a little, has he?' he murmured, and she shot a suspicious look at him. What did he know, and what bearing had Mr. Telfer's mad proposal on the present disaster? She was entirely in the dark as to the true state of affairs; it was, she felt, a moment for frankness.

'Wanted you to run away! Dear me!' Mr. Reeder was shocked. 'He is married?'

'Oh, no—he's not married,' said the girl shortly. 'Poor man, I'm sorry for him now. I'm afraid that the loss is a very heavy one—who would suspect Mr. Billingham?'

'Ah! who indeed!' sighed the lugubrious Reeder, and took off his glasses to wipe them; almost she suspected tears. 'I think I will go in now—that is the door?'

Sidney jerked up his face and glared at the intruder. He had been sitting with his head on his arms for the greater part of an hour.

'I say...what do you want?' he asked feebly. 'I say...I can't see anybody...Public Prosecutor's Department?' He almost screamed the words. 'What's the use of prosecuting him if you don't get the money back?'

Mr. Reeder let him work down before he began to ply his very judicious questions.

'I don't know much about it,' said the despondent young man. 'I'm only a sort of figurehead. Billingham brought the cheques for me to sign and I signed 'em. I never gave him instructions; he got his orders. I don't know very much about it. He told me, actually told me, that the business was in a bad way—half a million or something was wanted by next week...Oh, my God! And then he took the whole of our cash.'

Sidney Telfer sobbed his woe into his sleeve like a child. Mr. Reeder waited before he asked a question in his gentlest manner.

'No, I wasn't here: I went down to Brighton for the week-end. And the police dug me out of bed at four in the morning. We're bankrupt. I'll have to sell my car and resign from my club—one has to resign when one is bankrupt.'

There was little more to learn from the broken man, and Mr. Reeder returned to his chief with a report that added nothing to the sum of knowledge. In a week the theft of Mr. Billingham passed from scare lines to paragraphs in most of the papers—Billingham had made a perfect getaway.

In the bright lexicon of Mr. J.G. Reeder there was no such word as holiday. Even the Public Prosecutor's office has its slack time, when juniors and sub-officials and even the Director himself can go away on vacation, leaving the office open and a subordinate in charge. But to Mr. J.G. Reeder the very idea of wasting time was repugnant, and it was his practice to brighten the dull patches of occupation by finding a seat in a magistrate's court and listening, absorbed, to cases which bored even the court reporter.

John Smith, charged with being drunk and using insulting language to Police Officer Thomas Brown; Mary Jane Haggitt, charged with obstructing the police in the execution of their duty; Henry Robinson, arraigned for being a suspected person, having in his possession housebreaking tools, to wit, one cold chisel and a screwdriver; Arthur Moses, charged with driving a motor-car to the common danger--all these were fascinating figures of romance and legend to the lean man who sat between the press and railed dock, his square- crowned hat by his side, his umbrella gripped between his knees, and on his melancholy face an expression of startled wonder.

On one raw and foggy morning, Mr. Reeder, self-released from his duties, chose the Marylebone Police Court for his recreation. Two drunks, a shop theft and an embezzlement had claimed his rapt attention, when Mrs. Jackson was escorted to the dock and a rubicund policeman stepped to the witness stand, and, swearing by his Deity that he would tell the truth and nothing but the truth, related his peculiar story.

'P.C. Ferryman No. 9717 L. Division,' he introduced himself conventionally. 'I was on duty in the Edgware Road early this morning at 2.30 a.m. when I saw the prisoner carrying a large suit-case. On seeing me she turned round and walked rapidly in the opposite direction. Her movements being suspicious, I followed and, overtaking her, asked her whose property she was carrying. She told me it was her own and that she was going to catch a train. She said that the case contained her clothes. As the case was a valuable one of crocodile leather I asked her to show me the inside. She refused. She also refused to give me her name and address and I asked her to accompany me to the station.'

There followed a detective sergeant.

'I saw the prisoner at the station and in her presence opened the case. It contained a considerable quantity of small stone chips—'

'Stone chips?' interrupted the incredulous magistrate. 'You mean small pieces of stone—what kind of stone?'

'Marble, your worship. She said that she wanted to make a little path in her garden and that she had taken them from the yard of a monumental mason in the Euston Road. She made a frank statement to the effect that she had broken open a gate into the yard and filled the suit-case without the mason's knowledge.'

The magistrate leant back in his chair and scrutinised the charge sheet with a frown.

'There is no address against her name,' he said.

'She gave an address, but it was false, your worship—she refuses to offer any further information.'

Mr. J.G. Reeder had screwed round in his seat and was staring open-mouthed at the prisoner. She was tall, broad-shouldered and stoutly built. The hand that rested on the rail of the dock was twice the size of any woman's hand he had ever seen. The face was modelled largely, but though there was something in her appearance which was almost repellent, she was handsome in her large way. Deep-set brown eyes, a nose that was large and masterful, a well-shaped mouth and two chins—these in profile were not attractive to one who had his views on beauty in women, but Mr. J.G. Reeder, being a fair man, admitted that she was a fine-looking woman. When she spoke it was in a voice as deep as a man's, sonorous and powerful.

'I admit it was a fool thing to do. But the idea occurred to me just as I was going to bed and I acted on the impulse of the moment. I could well afford to buy the stone—I had over fifty pounds in my pocket-book when I was arrested.'

'Is that true?' and, when the officer answered, the magistrate turned his suspicious eyes to the woman. 'You are giving us a lot of trouble because you will not tell your name and address. I can understand that you do not wish your friends to know of your stupid theft, but unless you give me the information, I shall be compelled to remand you in custody for a week.'

She was well, if plainly, dressed. On one large finger flashed a diamond which Mr. Reeder mentally priced in the region of two hundred pounds. 'Mrs. Jackson' was shaking her head as he looked.

'I can't give you my address,' she said, and the magistrate nodded curtly.

'Remanded for inquiry,' he said, and added, as she walked out of the dock: 'I should like a report from the prison doctor on the state of her mind.'

Mr. J.G. Reeder rose quickly from his chair and followed the woman and the officer in charge of the case through the little door that leads to the cells.

'Mrs. Jackson' had disappeared by the time he reached the corridor, but the detective-sergeant was stooping over the large and handsome suit-case that he had shown in court and was now laying on a form.

Most of the outdoor men of the C.I.D. knew Mr. J.G. Reeder, and Sergeant Mills grinned a cheerful welcome.

'What do you think of that one, Mr. Reeder? It is certainly a new line on me! Never heard of a tombstone artist being burgled before.'

He opened the top of the case, and Mr. Reeder ran his fingers through the marble chips.

'The case and the loot weighs over a hundred pounds,' said the officer. 'She must have the strength of a navvy to carry it. The poor officer who carried it to the station was hot and melting when he arrived.'

Mr. J.G. was inspecting the case. It was a handsome article, the hinges and locks being of oxidised silver. No maker's name was visible on the inside, or owner's initials on its glossy lid. The lining had once been of silk, but now hung in shreds and was white with marble dust.

'Yes,' said Mr. Reeder absently, 'very interesting—most interesting. Is it permissible to ask whether, when she was searched, any—er—document?' The sergeant shook his head. 'Or unusual possession?'

'Only these.'

By the side of the case was a pair of large gloves. These also were soiled, and their surfaces cut in a hundred places.

'These have been used frequently for the same purpose,' murmured Mr. J.G. 'She evidently makes—er—a collection of marble shavings. Nothing in her pocket-book?'

'Only the bank-notes: they have the stamp of the Central Bank on their backs. We should be able to trace 'em easily.'

Mr. Reeder returned to his office and, locking the door, produced a worn pack of cards from a drawer and played patience—which was his method of thinking intensively. Late in the afternoon his telephone bell rang, and he recognised the voice of Sergeant Mills.

'Can I come along and see you? Yes, it is about the bank-notes.'

Ten minutes later the sergeant presented himself.

'The notes were issued three months ago to Mr. Telfer,' said the officer without preliminary, 'and they were given by him to his housekeeper, Mrs. Welford.'

'Oh, indeed?' said Mr. Reeder softly, and added, after reflection: 'Dear me!'

He pulled hard at his lip.

'And is "Mrs. Jackson" that lady?' he asked.

'Yes. Telfer—poor little devil—nearly went mad when I told him she was under remand—dashed up to Holloway in a taxi to identify her. The magistrate has granted bail, and she'll be bound over to-morrow. Telfer was bleating like a child—said she was mad. Gosh! that fellow is scared of her—when I took him into the waiting-room at Holloway Prison she gave him one look and he wilted. By the way, we have had a hint about Billingham that may interest you. Do you know that he and Telfer's secretary were very good friends?'

'Really?' Mr. Reeder was indeed interested. 'Very good friends? Well, well!'

'The Yard has put Miss Belman under general observation: there may be nothing to it, but in cases like Billingham's it is very often a matter of cherchez la femme.'

Mr. Reeder had given his lip a rest and was now gently massaging his nose.

'Dear me!' he said. 'That is a French expression, is it not?'

He was not in court when the marble stealer was sternly admonished by the magistrate and discharged. All that interested Mr. J.G. Reeder was to learn that the woman had paid the mason and had carried away her marble chips in triumph to the pretty little detached residence in the Outer Circle of Regent's Park. He had spent the morning at Somerset House, examining copies of wills and the like; his afternoon he gave up to the tracing of Mrs. Rebecca Alamby Mary Welford.

She was the relict of Professor John Welford of the University of Edinburgh, and had been left a widow after two years of marriage. She had then entered the service of Mrs. Telfer, the mother of Sidney, and had sole charge of the boy from his fourth year. When Mrs. Telfer died she had made the woman sole guardian of her youthful charge. So that Rebecca Welford had been by turns nurse and guardian, and was now in control of the young man's establishment.

The house occupied Mr. Reeder's attention to a considerable degree. It was a red-brick modern dwelling consisting of two floors and having a frontage on the Circle and a side road. Behind and beside the house was a large garden which, at this season of the year, was bare of flowers. They were probably in snug quarters for the winter, for there was a long green-house behind the garden.

He was leaning over the wooden palings, eyeing the grounds through the screen of box hedge that overlapped the fence with a melancholy stare, when he saw a door open and the big woman come out. She was bare-armed and wore an apron. In one hand she carried a dust box, which she emptied into a concealed ash-bin, in the other was a long broom.

Mr. Reeder moved swiftly out of sight. Presently the door slammed and he peeped again. There was no evidence of a marble path. All the walks were of rolled gravel.

He went to a neighbouring telephone booth, and called his office.

'I may be away all day,' he said.

There was no sign of Mr. Sidney Telfer, though the detective knew that he was in the house. Telfer's Trust was in the hands of the liquidators, and the first meeting of creditors had been called. Sidney had, by all accounts, been confined to his bed, and from that safe refuge had written a note to his secretary asking that 'all papers relating to my private affairs' should be burnt. He had scrawled a postscript: 'Can I possibly see you on business before I go?' The word 'go' had been scratched out and 'retire' substituted. Mr. Reeder had seen that letter—indeed, all correspondence between Sidney and the office came to him by arrangement with the liquidators. And that was partly why Mr. J.G. Reeder was so interested in 904, The Circle.

It was dusk when a big car drew up at the gate of the house. Before the driver could descend from his seat, the door of 904 opened, and Sidney Telfer almost ran out. He carried a suit-case in each hand, and Mr. Reeder recognised that nearest him as the grip in which the housekeeper had carried the stolen marble.

Reaching over, the chauffeur opened the door of the machine and, flinging in the bags, Sidney followed hastily. The door closed, and the car went out of sight round the curve of the Circle.

Mr. Reeder crossed the road and took up a position very near the front gate, waiting.

Dusk came and the veil of a Regent's Park fog. The house was in darkness, no flash of light except a faint glimmer that burnt in the hall, no sound. The woman was still there—Mrs. Sidney Telfer, nurse, companion, guardian and wife. Mrs. Sidney Telfer, the hidden director of Telfers Consolidated, a masterful woman who, not content with marrying a weakling twenty years her junior, had applied her masterful but ill-equipped mind to the domination of a business she did not understand, and which she was destined to plunge into ruin. Mr. Reeder had made good use of his time at the Records Office: a copy of the marriage certificate was almost as easy to secure as a copy of the will.

He glanced round anxiously. The fog was clearing, which was exactly what he did not wish it to do, for he had certain acts to perform which required as thick a cloaking as possible.

And then a surprising thing happened. A cab came slowly along the road and stopped at the gate.

'I think this is the place, miss,' said the cabman, and a girl stepped down to the pavement.

It was Miss Margaret Belman.

Reeder waited until she had paid the fare and the cab had gone, and then, as she walked towards the gate, he stepped from the shadow.

'Oh!—Mr. Reeder, how you frightened me!' she gasped. 'I am going to see Mr. Telfer—he is dangerously ill—no, it was his housekeeper who wrote asking me to come at seven.'

'Did she now! Well, I will ring the bell for you.'

She told him that that was unnecessary—she had the key which had come with the note.

'She is alone in the house with Mr. Telfer, who refuses to allow a trained nurse near him,' said Margaret, 'and—'

'Will you be good enough to lower your voice, young lady?' urged Mr. Reeder in an impressive whisper. 'Forgive the impertinence, but if our friend is ill—'

She was at first startled by his urgency.

'He couldn't hear me,' she said, but spoke in a lower tone.

'He may—sick people are very sensitive to the human voice. Tell me, how did this letter come?'

'From Mr. Telfer? By district messenger an hour ago.'

Nobody had been to the house or left it—except Sidney. And Sidney, in his blind fear, would carry out any instructions which his wife gave to him.

'And did it contain a passage like this?' Mr. Reeder considered a moment. '"Bring this letter with you"?'

'No,' said the girl in surprise, 'but Mrs. Welford telephoned just before the letter arrived and told me to wait for it. And she asked me to bring the letter with me because she didn't wish Mr. Telfer's private correspondence to be left lying around. But why do you ask me this, Mr. Reeder—is anything wrong?'

He did not answer immediately. Pushing open the gate, he walked noiselessly along the grass plot that ran parallel with the path.

'Open the door, I will come in with you,' he whispered and, when she hesitated: 'Do as I tell you, please.'

The hand that put the key into the lock trembled, but at last the key turned and the door swung open. A small night-light burnt on the table of the wide panelled hall. On the left, near the foot of the stairs, only the lower steps of which were visible, Reeder saw a narrow door which stood open, and, taking a step forward, saw that it was a tiny telephone-room.

And then a voice spoke from the upper landing, a deep, booming voice that he knew.

'Is that Miss Belman?'

Margaret, her heart beating faster, went to the foot of the stairs and looked up.

'Yes, Mrs. Welford.'

'You brought the letter with you?'

'Yes.'

Mr. Reeder crept along the wall until he could have touched the girl.

'Good,' said the deep voice. 'Will you call the doctor—Circle 743—and tell him that Mr. Telfer has had a relapse—you will find the booth in the hall: shut the door behind you, the bell worries him.'

Margaret looked at the detective and he nodded.

The woman upstairs wished to gain time for something—what?

The girl passed him: he heard the thud of the padded door close, and there was a click that made him spin round. The first thing he noticed was that there was no handle to the door, the second that the keyhole was covered by a steel disc, which he discovered later was felt-lined. He heard the girl speaking faintly, and put his ear to the keyhole.

'The instrument is disconnected—I can't open the door.'

Without a second's hesitation, he flew up the stairs, umbrella in hand, and as he reached the landing he heard a door close with a crash. Instantly he located the sound. It came from a room on the left immediately over the hall. The door was locked.

'Open this door,' he commanded, and there came to him the sound of a deep laugh.

Mr. Reeder tugged at the stout handle of his umbrella. There was a flicker of steel as he dropped the lower end, and in his hand appeared six inches of knife blade.

The first stab at the panel sliced through the thin wood as though it were paper. In a second there was a jagged gap through which the black muzzle of an automatic was thrust.

'Put down that jug or I will blow your features into comparative chaos!' said Mr. Reeder pedantically.

The room was brightly lit, and he could see plainly. Mrs. Welford stood by the side of a big square funnel, the narrow end of which ran into the floor. In her hand was a huge enamelled iron jug, and ranged about her were six others. In one corner of the room was a wide circular tank, and beyond, at half its height, depended a large copper pipe.

The woman's face turned to him was blank, expressionless.

'He wanted to run away with her,' she said simply, 'and after all I have done for him!'

'Open the door.'

Mrs. Welford set down the jug and ran her huge hand across her forehead.

'Sidney is my own darling,' she said. 'I've nursed him, and taught him, and there was a million—all in gold—in the ship. But they robbed him.'

She was talking of one of the ill-fated enterprises of Telfers Consolidated Trust—that sunken treasure ship to recover which the money of the company had been poured out like water. And she was mad. He had guessed the weakness of this domineering woman from the first.

'Open the door; we will talk it over. I'm perfectly sure that the treasure ship scheme was a sound one.'

'Are you?' she asked eagerly, and the next minute the door was open and Mr. J.G. Reeder was in that room of death.

'First of all, let me have the key of the telephone-room—you are quite wrong about that young lady: she is my wife.'

The woman stared at him blankly.

'Your wife?' A slow smile transfigured the face. 'Why—I was silly. Here is the key.'

He persuaded her to come downstairs with him, and when the frightened girl was released, he whispered a few words to her, and she flew out of the house.

'Shall we go into the drawing-room?' he asked, and Mrs. Welford led the way.

'And now will you tell me how you knew—about the jugs?' he asked gently.

She was sitting on the edge of a sofa, her hands clasped on her knees, her deep-set eyes staring at the carpet.

'John—that was my first husband—told me. He was a professor of chemistry and natural science, and also about the electric furnace. It is so easy to make if you have power—we use nothing but electricity in this house for heating and everything. And then I saw my poor darling being ruined through me, and I found how much money there was in the bank, and I told Billingham to draw it and bring it to me without Sidney knowing. He came here in the evening. I sent Sidney away—to Brighton, I think. I did everything—put the new lock on the telephone box and fixed the shaft from the roof to the little room—it was easy to disperse everything with all the doors open and an electric fan working on the floor—'

She was telling him about the improvised furnace in the green-house when the police arrived with the divisional surgeon, and she went away with them, weeping because there would be nobody to press Sidney's ties or put out his shirts.

Mr. Reeder took the inspector up to the little room and showed him its contents.

'This funnel leads to the telephone box—' he began.

'But the jugs are empty,' interrupted the officer.

Mr. J.G. Reeder struck a match and, waiting until it burnt freely, lowered it into the jug. Half an inch lower than the rim the light went out.

'Carbon monoxide,' he said, 'which is made by steeping marble chips in hydrochloric acid—you will find the mixture in the tank. The gas is colourless and odourless—and heavy. You can pour it out of a jug like water. She could have bought the marble, but was afraid of arousing suspicion. Billingham was killed that way. She got him to go to the telephone box, probably closed the door on him herself, and then killed him painlessly.'

'What did she do with the body?' asked the horrified officer.

'Come out into the hot-house,' said Mr. Reeder, 'and pray do not expect to see horrors: an electric furnace will dissolve a diamond to its original elements.'

Mr. Reeder went home that night in a state of mental perturbation, and for an hour paced the floor of his large study in Brockley Road.

Over and over in his mind he turned one vital problem: did he owe an apology to Margaret Belman for saying that she was his wife?

V. — SHEER MELODRAMA

First published under the title "The Man from the East" in
The Grand Magazine, Vol. 47, Mar-Aug 1925, as part of the J.G. Reeder series
"The Man Who Saw Evil"

IT was Mr. Reeder who planned the raid on Tommy Fenalow's snide shop and worked out all the details except the composition of the raiding force. Tommy had a depot at Golders Green whither trusted agents came, purchasing Treasury notes for £7 10s. per hundred, or £70 a thousand. Only experts could tell the difference between Tommy's currency and that authorised by and printed for H.M. Treasury. They were the right shades of brown and green, the numbers were of issued series, the paper was exact. They were printed in Germany at £3 a thousand, and Tommy made thousands per cent. profit.

Mr. Reeder discovered all about Tommy's depot in his spare time, and reported the matter to his chief, the Director of Public Prosecutions. From Whitehall to Scotland Yard is two minutes' walk, and in just that time the information got across.

'Take Inspector Greyash with you and superintend the raid,' were his instructions.

He left the inspector to make all the arrangements, and amongst those who learnt of the projected coup was a certain detective officer who made more money from questionable associations than he did from Government. This officer 'blew' the raid to Tommy, and when Mr. Reeder and his bold men arrived at Golders Green, there was Tommy and three friends playing a quiet game of auction bridge, and the only Treasury notes discoverable were veritable old masters.

'It is a pity,' sighed J.G. when they reached the street; 'a great pity. Of course I hadn't the least idea that Detective-Constable Wilshore was in our party. He is—er—not quite loyal.'

'Wilshore?' asked the officer, aghast. 'Do you mean he "blew" the raid to Tommy?'

Mr. Reeder scratched his nose and said gently, that he thought so.

'He has quite a big income from various sources—by the way, he banks with the Midland and Derbyshire, and his account is in his wife's maiden name. I tell you this in case—er—it may be useful.'

It was useful enough to secure the summary ejection of the unfaithful Wilshore from the force, but it was not sufficiently useful to catch Tommy, whose parting words were:

'You're clever, Reeder; but you've got to be lucky to catch me!'

Tommy was in the habit of repeating this scrap of conversation to such as were interested. It was an encounter of which he was justifiably proud, for few dealers in 'slush' and 'snide' have ever come up against Mr. J.G. and got away with it.

'It's worth a thousand pounds to me—ten thousand! I'd pay that money to make J.G. look sick, anyway, the old dog! I guess the Yard will think twice before it tries to shop me again, and that's the real kick in the raid. J.G.'s name is Jonah at head-quarters, and if I can do anything to help, it will be mud!'

To a certain Ras Lal Punjabi, an honoured (and paying) guest, Mr. Fenalow told this story, with curious results.

A good wine tastes best in its own country, and a man may drink sherry by the cask in Jerez de la Frontena and take no ill, whereas if he attempted so much as a bottle in Fleet Street, he would suffer cruelly. So also does the cigarette of Egypt preserve its finest bouquet for such as smoke it in the lounge of a Cairo hotel.

Crime is yet another quantity which does not bear transplanting. The American safe-blower may flourish in France just so long as he acquires by diligent study, and confines himself to, the Continental method. It is possible for the European thief to gain a fair livelihood in oriental countries, but there is no more tragic sight in the world than the Eastern mind endeavouring to adapt itself to the complexities of European roguery.

Ras Lal Punjabi enjoyed a reputation in Indian police circles as the cleverest native criminal India had ever produced. Beyond a short term in Poona Jail, Ras Lal had never seen the interior of a prison, and such was his fame in native circles that, during this short period of incarceration, prayers for his deliverance were offered at certain temples, and it was agreed that he would never have been convicted at all but for some pretty hard swearing on the part of the police commissioner sahib—and anyway, all sahibs hang together, and it was a European judge who sent him down.

He was a general practitioner of crime, with a leaning towards specialisation in jewel thefts. A man of excellent and even gentlemanly appearance, with black and shiny hair parted at the side and curling up over one brow in an inky wave, he spoke English, Hindustani and Tamil very well indeed, had a sketchy knowledge of the law (on his visiting cards was the inscription 'Failed LL.B.') and a very full acquaintance with the science of precious stones.

During Mr. Ras Las Punjabi's brief rest in Poona, the police commissioner sahib, whose unromantic name was Smith, married a not very good-looking girl with a lot of money. Smith Sahib knew that beauty was only skin deep and that she had a kind heart, which is notoriously preferable to the garniture of coronets. It was honestly a love match. Her father owned jute mills in Calcutta, and on festive occasions, such as the Governor-General's ball, she carried several lakhs of rupees on her person; but even rich people are loved for themselves alone.

Ras Lal owed his imprisonment to an unsuccessful attempt he had made upon two strings of pearls the property of the lady in question, and when he learnt, on his return to freedom, that Smith Sahib had married the resplendent girl and had gone to England, he very naturally attributed the hatred and bitterness of Smith Sahib to purely personal causes, and swore vengeance.

Now in India the business of every man is the business of his servants. The preliminary inquiries, over which an English or American jewel thief would spend a small fortune, can be made at the cost of a few annas. When Ras Lal came to England he found that he had overlooked this very important fact.

Smith, sahib and memsahib, were out of town; they were, in fact, on the high seas en route for New York when Ras Lal was arrested on the conventional charge of 'being a suspected person.' Ras had shadowed the Smiths' butler, and, having induced him to drink, had offered him immense sums to reveal the place, receptacle, drawer, safe, box or casket wherein 'Mrs. Commissioner Smith's' jewels were kept. His excuse for asking, namely, that he had had a wager with his brother that the jewels were kept under the Memsahib's bed, showed a lamentable lack of inventive power. The butler, an honest man, though a drinker of beer, informed the police. Ras Lal and his friend and assistant Ram were arrested, brought before a magistrate, and would have been discharged but for the fact that Mr. J.G. Reeder saw the record of the case and was able to supply from his own files very important particulars of the dark man's past. Therefore Mr. Ras Lal was sent down to hard labour for six months, but, what was more maddening, the story of his ignominious failure was, he guessed, broadcast throughout India.

This was the thought which distracted him in his lonely cell at Wormwood Scrubbs. What would

India think of him?—he would be the scorn of the bazaars, 'the mocking point of third-rate mediocrities,' to use his own expression. And automatically he switched his hate from Smith Sahib to one Mr. J.G. Reeder. And his hate was very real, more real because of the insignificance and unimportance of this Reeder Sahib, whom he likened to an ancient cow, a sneaking weasel, and other things less translatable. And in the six months of his durance he planned desperate and earnest acts of reprisal.

Released from prison, he decided that the moment was not ripe for a return to India. He wished to make a close study of Mr. J.G. Reeder and his habits, and, being a man with plenty of money, he could afford the time, and, as it happened, could mix business with pleasure.

Mr. Tommy Fenalow found means of getting in touch with the gentleman from the Orient whilst he was in Wormwood Scrubs, and the handsome limousine that met Ras Lal at the gates of the Scrubbs when he came out of jail was both hired and occupied by Tommy, a keen business man, who had been offered by his German printer a new line of one-hundred-rupee notes that might easily develop into a most profitable side-line.

'You come along and lodge at my expense, boy,' said the sympathetic Tommy, who was very short, very stout, and had eyes that bulged like a pug dog's. 'You've been badly treated by old Reeder, and I'm going to tell you a way of getting back on him, with no risk and a ninety per cent profit. Listen, a friend of mine—'

It was never Tommy who had snide for sale: invariably the hawker of forged notes was a mysterious 'friend.'

So Ras was lodged in a service flat which formed part of a block owned by Mr. Fenalow, who was a very rich man indeed. Some weeks after this, Tommy crossed St. James's Street to intercept his old enemy.

'Good morning, Mr. Reeder.'

Mr. J.G. Reeder stopped and turned back.

'Good morning, Mr. Fenalow,' he said, with that benevolent solicitude which goes so well with a frock coat and square-toed shoes. 'I am glad to see that you are out again, and I do trust that you will now find a more—er—legitimate outlet for your undoubted talents.'

Tommy went angrily red.

'I haven't been in "stir" and you know it, Reeder! It wasn't for want of trying on your part. But you've got to be something more than clever to catch me—you've got to be lucky! Not that there's anything to catch me over—I've never done a crook thing in my life, as you well know.'

He was so annoyed that the lighter exchanges of humour he had planned slipped from his memory.

He had an appointment with Ras Lal, and the interview was entirely satisfactory. Mr. Ras Lal made his way that night to an uncomfortably situated rendezvous and there met his new friend.

'This is the last place in the world old man Reeder would dream of searching,' said Tommy enthusiastically, 'and if he did he would find nothing. Before he could get into the building, the stuff would be put out of sight.'

'It is a habitation of extreme convenience,' said Ras Lal.

'It is yours, boy,' replied Tommy magnificently. 'I only keep this place to get-in and put-out. The stuff's not here for an hour and the rest of the time the store's empty. As I say, old man Reeder has gotta be something more than clever—he's gotta be lucky!'

At parting he handed his client a key, and with that necessary instrument tendered a few words of advice and warning.

'Never come here till late. The police patrol passes the end of the road at ten, one o'clock and four. When are you leaving for India?'

'On the twenty-third,' said Ras, 'by which time I shall have uttered a few reprisals on that cad Reeder.'

'I shouldn't like to be in his shoes,' said Tommy, who could afford to be sycophantic, for he had in his pocket two hundred pounds' worth of real money which Ras had paid in advance for a vaster quantity of money which was not so real.

It was a few days after this that Ras Lal went to the Orpheum Theatre, and it was no coincidence that he went there on the same night that Mr. Reeder escorted a pretty lady to the same place of amusement.

When Mr. J.G. Reeder went to the theatre (and his going at all was contingent upon his receiving a complimentary ticket) he invariably chose a melodrama, and preferably a Drury Lane melodrama, where to the thrill of the actors' speeches was added the amazing action of wrecked railway trains, hair-raising shipwrecks and terrific horse-races in which the favourite won by a nose. Such things may seem wildly improbable to blase dramatic critics—especially favourites winning—but Mr. Reeder saw actuality in all such presentations.

Once he was inveigled into sitting through a roaring farce, and was the only man in the house who did not laugh. He was, indeed, such a depressing influence that the leading lady sent a passionate request to the manager that 'the miserable-looking old man in the middle of the front row' should have his money returned and be requested to leave the theatre. Which, as Mr. Reeder had come in on a free ticket, placed the manager in a very awkward predicament.

Invariably he went unaccompanied, for he had no friends, and fifty-two years had come and gone without bringing to his life romance or the melting tenderness begot of dreams. In some manner Mr. Reeder had become acquainted with a girl who was like no other girl with whom he had been brought into contact. Her name was Belman, Margaret Belman, and he had saved her life, though this fact did not occur to him as frequently as the recollection that he had imperilled that life before he had saved it. And he had a haunting sense of guilt for quite another reason.

He was thinking of her one day—he spent his life thinking about people, though the majority of these were less respectable than Miss Margaret Belman. He supposed that she would marry the very good-looking young man who met her street car at the corner of the Embankment every morning and returned with her to the Lewisham High Road every night. It would be a very nice wedding, with hired motor-cars, and the vicar himself performing the ceremony, and a wedding breakfast provided by the local caterer, following which bride and bridegroom would be photographed on the lawn surrounded by their jovial but unprepossessing relatives. And after this, one specially hired car would take them to Eastbourne for an expensive honeymoon. And after that all the humdrum and scrapings of life, rising through villadom to a little car of their own and Saturday afternoon tennis parties.

Mr. Reeder sighed deeply. How much more satisfactory was the stage drama, where all the trouble begins in the first act and is satisfactorily settled in the last. He fingered absently the two slips of green paper that had come to him that morning. Row A, seats 17 and 18. They had been sent by a manager who was under some obligation to him. The theatre was the Orpheum, home of transpontine drama, and the play was 'The Fires of Vengeance.' It looked like being a pleasant evening.

He took an envelope from the rack, addressed it to the box office, and had begun to write the accompanying letter returning the surplus voucher, when an idea occurred to him. He owed Miss Margaret Belman something, and the debt was on his conscience. He had once, for reasons of expediency, described her as his wife. This preposterous claim had been made to appease a mad woman, it is true, but it had been made. She was now holding a good position—a secretaryship at one of the political head-quarters, for which post she had to thank Mr. J.G. Reeder, if she only knew it.

He took up the 'phone and called her number, and, after the normal delay, heard her voice.

'Er—Miss Belman,' Mr. Reeder coughed, 'I have—er—two tickets for a theatre tonight. I wonder if you would care to go?'

Her astonishment was almost audible.

'That is very nice of you, Mr. Reeder. I should love to come with you.'

Mr. J.G. Reeder turned pale.

'What I mean is, I have two tickets—I thought perhaps that your—er—your—er—that somebody else would like to go—what I mean was—'

He heard a gentle laugh at the other end of the phone.

'What you mean is that you don't wish to take me,' she said, and for a man of his experience he blundered badly.

'I should esteem it an honour to take you,' he said, in terror that he should offend her, 'but the truth is, I thought—'

'I will meet you at the theatre—which is it? Orpheum—how lovely! At eight o'clock.'

Mr. Reeder put down the instrument, feeling limp and moist. It is the truth that he had never taken a lady to any kind of social function in his life, and as there grew upon him the tremendous character of this adventure he was overwhelmed and breathless. A murderer waking from dreams of revelry to find himself in the condemned cell suffered no more poignant emotions than Mr. Reeder, torn from the smooth if treacherous currents of life and drawing nearer and nearer to the horrid vortex of unusualness.

'Bless me,' said Mr. Reeder, employing a strictly private expression which was reserved for his own crises.

He employed in his private office a young woman who combined a meticulous exactness in the filing of documents with a complete absence of those attractions which turn men into gods, and in other days set the armies of Perseus moving towards the walls of Troy. She was invariably addressed by Mr. Reeder as 'Miss.' He believed her name to be 'Oliver.' She was in truth a married lady with two children, but her nuptials had been celebrated without his knowledge.

To the top floor of a building in Regent Street Mr. Reeder repaired for instruction and guidance.

'It is not—er—a practice of mine to—er—accompany ladies to the theatre, and I am rather at a loss to know what is expected of me, the more so since the young lady is—er—a stranger to me.'

His frosty-visaged assistant sneered secretly. At Mr. Reeder's time of life, when such natural affections as were not atrophied should in decency be fossilised!

He jotted down her suggestions.

'Chocolates indeed? Where can one procure — ? Oh, yes, I remember seeing the attendants sell them. Thank you so much, Miss—er—'

And as he went out, closing the door carefully behind him, she sneered openly.

'They all go wrong at seventy,' she said insultingly.

Margaret hardly knew what to expect when she came into the flamboyant foyer of the Orpheum. What was the evening equivalent to the square-topped derby and the tightly-buttoned frock coat of ancient design which he favoured in the hours of business? She would have passed the somewhat elegantly dressed gentleman in the correct pique waistcoat and the perfectly tied butterfly bow, only he claimed her attention.

'Mr. Reeder!' she gasped.

It was indeed Mr. Reeder: with not so much as a shirt-stud wrong; with a suit of the latest mode, and shoes glossy and V-toed. For Mr. Reeder, like many other men, dressed according to his inclination in business hours, but accepted blindly the instructions of his tailor in the matter of fancy raiment. Mr. J.G. Reeder was never conscious of his clothing, good or bad—he was, however, very conscious of his strange responsibility.

He took her cloak (he had previously purchased programmes and a large box of chocolates, which he carried by its satin ribbon). There was a quarter of an hour to wait before the curtain went up, and Margaret felt it incumbent upon her to offer an explanation.

'You spoke about "somebody" else; do you mean Roy—the man who sometimes meets me at Westminster?'

Mr. Reeder had meant that young man. 'He and I were good friends,' she said, 'no more than that—we aren't very good friends anymore.'

She did not say why. She might have explained in a sentence if she had said that Roy's mother held an exalted opinion of her only son's qualities, physical and mental, and that Roy thoroughly endorsed his mother's judgment, but she did not.

'Ah!' said Mr. Reeder unhappily. Soon after this the orchestra drowned further conversation, for they were sitting in the first row near to the noisiest of the brass and not far removed from the shrillest of the wood-wind. In odd moments, through the thrilling first act, she stole a glance at her companion. She expected to find this man mildly amused or slightly bored by the absurd contrast between the realities which he knew and the theatricalities which were presented on the stage. But whenever she looked, he was absorbed in the action of the play; she could almost feel him tremble when the hero was strapped to a log and thrown into the boiling mountain stream, and when the stage Jove was rescued on the fall of the curtain, she heard, with something like stupefaction, Mr. Reeder's quivering sigh of relief.

'But surely, Mr. Reeder, this bores you?' she protested, when the lights in the auditorium went up.

'This—you mean the play—bore me? Good gracious, no! I think it is very fine, remarkably fine.'

'But it isn't life, surely? The story is so wildly improbable, and the incidents—oh, yes, I'm enjoying it all; please don't look so worried! Only I thought that you, who knew so much about criminology—is that the word?—would be rather amused.'

Mr. Reeder was looking very anxiously at her.

'I'm afraid it is not the kind of play—'

'Oh, but it is—I love melodrama. But doesn't it strike you as being—far-fetched? For instance, that man being chained to a log, and the mother agreeing to her son's death?'

Mr. Reeder rubbed his nose thoughtfully.

'The Bermondsey gang chained Harry Salter to a plank, turned it over and let him down, just opposite Billingsgate Market. I was at the execution of Tod Rowe, and he admitted it on the scaffold. And it was "Lee" Pearson's mother who poisoned him at Teddington to get his insurance money so that she could marry again. I was at the trial and she took her sentence laughing—now what else was there in that act? Oh, yes, I remember: the proprietor of the saw-mill tried to get the young lady to marry him by threatening to send her father to prison. That has been done hundreds of times—only in a worse way. There is really nothing very extravagant about a melodrama except the prices of the seats, and I usually get my tickets free!'

She listened, at first dumbfounded and then with a gurgle of amusement.

'How queer—and yet—well, frankly, I have only met melodrama once in life, and even now I cannot believe it. What happens in the next act?'

Mr. Reeder consulted his programme.

'I rather believe that the young woman in the white dress is captured and removed to the harem of an Eastern potentate,' he said precisely, and this time the girl laughed aloud.

'Have you a parallel for that?' she asked triumphantly, and Mr. Reeder was compelled to admit that he knew no exact parallel, but—

'It is rather a remarkable coincidence,' he said, 'a very remarkable coincidence!'

She looked at her programme, wondering if she had overlooked anything so very remarkable.

'There is at this moment, watching me from the front row of the dress circle—I beg you not to turn your head—one who, if he is not a potentate, is undoubtedly Eastern; there are, in fact, two dark-complexioned gentlemen, but only one may be described as important.'

'But why are they watching you?' she asked in surprise.

'Possibly,' said Mr. Reeder solemnly, 'because I look so remarkable in evening dress.'

One of the dark-complexioned gentlemen turned to his companion at this moment.

'It is the woman he travels with every day; she lives in the same street, and is doubtless more to him than anybody in the world, Ram. See how she laughs in his face and how the old so-and-so looks at her! When men come to his great age they grow silly about women. This thing can be done to-night. I would sooner die than go back to Bombay without accomplishing my design upon this such-and-such and so-forth.'

Ram, his chauffeur, confederate and fellow jail-bird, who was cast in a less heroic mould, and had, moreover, no personal vendetta, suggested in haste that the matter should be thought over.

'I have cogitated every hypothesis to its logical conclusions,' said Ras Lal in English.

'But, master,' said his companion urgently, 'would it not be wise to leave this country and make a fortune with the new money which the fat little man can sell to us?'

'Vengeance is mine,' said Ras Lal in English.

He sat through the next act which, as Mr. Reeder had truly said, depicted the luring of an innocent girl into the hateful clutches of a Turkish pasha and, watching the development of the plot, his own scheme underwent revision. He did not wait to see what happened in the third and fourth acts—there were certain preparations to be made.

'I still think that, whilst the story is awfully thrilling, it is awfully impossible,' said Margaret, as they moved slowly through the crowded vestibule. 'In real life—in civilised countries, I mean—masked men do not suddenly appear from nowhere with pistols and say "Hands up!"—not really, do they, Mr. Reeder?' she coaxed.

Mr. Reeder murmured a reluctant agreement.

'But I have enjoyed it tremendously!' she said with enthusiasm, and looking down into the pink face Mr. Reeder felt a curious sensation which was not entirely pleasure and not wholly pain.

'I am very glad,' he said.

Both the dress-circle and the stalls disgorged into the foyer, and he was looking round for a face he had seen when he arrived. But neither Ras Lal nor his companion in misfortune was visible. Rain was falling dismally, and it was some time before he found a cab.

'Luxury upon luxury,' smiled Margaret, when he took his place by her side. 'You may smoke if you wish.'

Mr. Reeder took a paper packet of cigarettes from his waistcoat pocket, selected a limp cylinder, and lit it.

'No plays are quite like life, my dear young lady,' he said, as he carefully pushed the match through the space between the top of the window and the frame. 'Melodramas appeal most to me because of their idealism.'

She turned and stared at him.
'Idealism?' she repeated incredulously.
He nodded.
'Have you ever noticed that there is nothing sordid about a melodrama? I once saw a classical drama—"Oedipus"—and it made me feel sick. In melodrama even the villains are heroic and the inevitable and unvarying moral is "Truth crushed to earth will rise again"—isn't that idealism? And they are wholesome. There are no sex problems; unpleasant things are never shown in an attractive light—you come away uplifted.'
'If you are young enough,' she smiled.
'One should always be young enough to rejoice in the triumph of virtue,' said Mr. Reeder soberly.
They crossed Westminster Bridge and bore left to the New Kent Road. Through the rain-blurred windows J.G. picked up the familiar landmarks and offered a running commentary upon them in the manner of a guide. Margaret had not realised before that history was made in South London.
'There used to be a gibbet here—this ugly-looking goods station was the London terminus of the first railways—Queen Alexandra drove from there when she came to be married—the thoroughfare on the right after we pass the Canal bridge is curiously named Bird-in-Bush Road—'
A big car had drawn level with the cab, and the driver was shouting something to the cabman. Even the suspicious Mr. Reeder suspected no more than an exchange of offensiveness, till the cab suddenly turned into the road he had been speaking about. The car had fallen behind, but now drew abreast.
'Probably the main road is up,' said J.G., and at that moment the cab slowed and stopped.
He was reaching out for the handle when the door was pulled open violently, and in the uncertain light Mr. Reeder saw a broad-shouldered man standing in the road.
'Alight quickly!'
In the man's hand was a long, black Colt, and his face was covered from chin to forehead by a mask.
'Quickly—and keep your hands erect!'
Mr. Reeder stepped out into the rain and reached to close the door.
'The female also—come, miss!'
'Here—what's the game—you told me the New Cross Road was blocked.' It was the cabman talking.
'Here is a five—keep your mouth shut.'
The masked man thrust a note at the driver.
'I don't want your money—'
'You require my bullet in your bosom perchance, my good fellow?' asked Ras Lal sardonically.
Margaret had followed her escort into the road by this time. The car had stopped just behind the cab. With the muzzle of the pistol stuck into his back, Mr. Reeder walked to the open door and entered. The girl followed, and the masked man jumped after them and closed the door. Instantly the interior was flooded with light.
'This is a considerable surprise to a clever and intelligent police detective?'
Their captor sat on the opposite seat, his pistol on his knees. Through the holes of the black mask a pair of brown eyes gleamed malevolently. But Mr. Reeder's interest was in the girl. The shock had struck the colour from her face, but he observed with thankfulness that her chief emotion was not fear. She was numb with amazement, and was stricken speechless.

The car had circled and was moving swiftly back the way they had come. He felt the rise of the Canal bridge, and then the machine turned abruptly to the right and began the descent of a steep hill. They were running towards Rotherhithe—he had an extraordinary knowledge of London's topography.
The journey was a short one. He felt the car wheels bump over an uneven roadway for a hundred yards, the body rocking uncomfortably, and then with a jar of brakes the machine stopped suddenly.
They were on a narrow muddy lane. On one side rose the arches of a railway aqueduct, on the other an open space bounded by a high fence. Evidently the driver had pulled up short of their destination, for they had to squelch and slide through the thick mud for another fifty yards before they came to a narrow gateway in the fence. Through this they struck a cinder-path leading to a square building, which Mr. Reeder guessed was a small factory of some kind. Their conductor flashed a lamp on the door, and in weatherworn letters the detective read:
'The Storn-Filton Leather Company.'
'Now!' said the man, as he turned a switch. 'Now, my false-swearing and corrupt police official, I have a slight bill to settle with you.'
They were in a dusty lobby, enclosed on three sides by matchboard walls.
'"Account" is the word you want, Ras Lal,' murmured Mr. Reeder.
For a moment the man was taken aback, and then, snatching the mask from his face:
'I am Ras Lal! And you shall repent it! For you and for your young missus this is indeed a cruel night of anxiety!'
Mr. Reeder did not smile at the quaint English. The gun in the man's hand spoke all languages without error, and could be as fatal in the hands of an unconscious humorist as if it were handled by the most savage of purists.
And he was worried about the girl: she had not spoken a word since their capture. The colour had come back to her cheeks, and that was a good sign. There was, too, a light in her eyes which Reeder could not associate with fear.
Ras Lal, taking down a long cord that hung on a nail in the wooden partition, hesitated.
'It is not necessary,' he said, with an elaborate shrug of shoulder; 'the room is sufficiently reconnoitred—you will be innocuous there.'
Flinging open a door, he motioned them to pass through and mount the bare stairs which faced them. At the top was a landing and a large steel door set in the solid brickwork.
Pulling back the iron bolt, he pushed at the door, and it opened with a squeak. It was a large room, and had evidently been used for the storage of something inflammable, for the walls and floor were of rough-faced concrete and above a dusty desk an inscription was painted, 'Danger. Don't smoke in this store.' There were no windows except one some eighteen inches square, the top of which was near the ceiling. In one corner of the room was a heap of grimy paper files, and on the desk a dozen small wooden boxes, one of which had been opened, for the nail-bristling lid was canted up at an angle.
'Make yourself content for half an hour or probably forty minutes,' said Ras Lal, standing in the doorway with his ostentatious revolver. 'At that time I shall come for your female; to-morrow she will be on a ship with me, bound for—ah, who knows where?'
'Shut the door as you go out,' said Mr. J.G. Reeder; 'there is an unpleasant draught.'
Mr. Tommy Fenalow came on foot at two o'clock in the morning and, passing down the muddy lane, his electric torch suddenly revealed car marks. Tommy stopped like a man shot. His knees trembled beneath him and his heart entered his throat at the narrowest end. For a while he was

undecided whether it would be better to run or walk away. He had no intention of going forward. And then he heard a voice. It was Ras Lal's assistant, and he nearly swooned with joy. Stumbling forward, he came up to the shivering man.

'Did that fool boss of yours bring the car along here?' he asked in a whisper.

'Yas—Mr. Ras Lal,' said Ram with whom the English language was not a strong point.

'Then he's a fool!' growled Tommy. 'Gosh! he put my heart in my mouth!'

Whilst Ram was getting together sufficient English to explain what had happened, Tommy passed on. He found his client sitting in the lobby, a black cheroot between his teeth, a smile of satisfaction on his dark face.

'Welcome!' he said, as Tommy closed the door. 'We have trapped the weasel.'

'Never mind about the weasel,' said the other impatiently. 'Did you find the rupees?'

Ras Lal shook his head.

'But I left them in the store—ten thousand notes. I thought you'd have got them and skipped before this,' said Mr. Fenalow anxiously.

'I have something more important in the store—come and see my friend.'

He preceded the bewildered Tommy up the stairs, turned on the landing light and threw open the door.

'Behold—' he said, and said no more.

'Why, it is Mr. Fenalow!' said Mr. J.G.

One hand held a packet of almost life-like rupee notes; as for the other hand—

'You oughter known he carried a gun, you dam' black baboon,' hissed Tommy. 'An' to put him in a room where the stuff was, and a telephone!'

He was being driven to the local police station, and for the moment was attached to his companion by links of steel.

'It was a mere jest or a piece of practical joking, as I shall explain to the judge in the morning,' said Ras airily.

Tommy Fenalow's reply was unprintable.

Three o'clock boomed out from St. John's Church as Mr. Reeder accompanied an excited girl to the front door of her boarding-house.

'I can't tell you how I—I've enjoyed tonight,' she said.

Mr. Reeder glanced uneasily at the dark face of the house.

'I hope — er — your friends will not think it remarkable that you should return at such an hour —'

Despite her assurance, he went slowly home with an uneasy feeling that her name had in some way been compromised. And in melodrama, when a heroine's name is compromised, somebody has to marry her.

That was the disturbing thought that kept Mr. Reeder awake all night.

VI. — THE GREEN MAMBA

First published under the title "The Dangerous Reptile" in
The Grand Magazine, Vol. 47, Mar-Aug 1925, as part of the J.G. Reeder series
"The Man Who Saw Evil"

THE spirit of exploration has ruined more promising careers than drink, gambling or the smiles of women. Generally speaking, the beaten tracks of life are the safest, and few men have adventured into the uncharted spaces in search of easy money who have not regarded the discovery of the old hard road whence they strayed as the greatest of their achievements.

Mo Liski held an assured position in his world, and one acquired by the strenuous and even violent exercise of his many qualities. He might have gone on until the end of the chapter, only he fell for an outside proposition, and, moreover, handicapped himself with a private feud, which had its beginning in an affair wholly remote from his normal operations.

There was a Moorish grafter named El Rahbut, who had made several visits to England, travelling by the banana boats which make the round trip from London River to Funchal Bay, Las Palmas, Tangier and Oporto. He was a very ordinary, yellow-faced Moor, pock-marked and undersized, and he spoke English, having in his youth fallen into the hands of a well-meaning American missionary. This man Rahbut was useful to Mo because quite a lot of German drugs are shipped via Trieste to the Levant, and many a crate of oranges has been landed in the Pool that had, squeezed in their golden interiors, little metal cylinders containing smuggled saccharine, heroin, cocaine, hydrochlorate and divers other noxious medicaments.

Rahbut brought such things from time to time, was paid fairly and was satisfied. One day, in the saloon bar of 'The Four Jolly Seamen,' he told Mo of a great steal. It had been carried out by a group of Anghera thieves working in Fez, and the loot was no less than the Emeralds of Suliman, the most treasured possession of Morocco. Not even Abdul Aziz in his most impecunious days had dared to remove them from the Mosque of Omar; the Anghera men being what they were, broke into the holy house, killed two guardians of the treasure, and had got away with the nine green stones of the great king. Thereafter arose an outcry which was heard from the bazaars of Calcutta to the mean streets of Marsi-Karsi. But the men of Anghera were superior to the voice of public opinion and they did no more than seek a buyer. El Rahbut, being a notorious bad character, came into the matter, and this was the tale he told to Mo Liski at 'The Four Jolly Seamen' one foggy October night.

'There is a million pesetas profit in this for you and me, Mr. Good Man,' said Rahbut (all Europeans who paid on the nail were 'Mr. Good Man' to El Rahbut). 'There is also death for me if this thing becomes known.'

Mo listened, smoothing his chin with a hand that sparkled and flashed dazzlingly. He was keen on ornamentation. It was a little outside his line, but the newspapers had stated the bald value of the stolen property, and his blood was on fire at the prospect of earning half a million so easily. That Scotland Yard and every police head-quarters in the world were on the look-out for the nine stones of Suliman did not greatly disturb him. He knew the subterranean way down which a polished stone might slide; and if the worst came to the worst, there was a reward of £5,000 for the recovery of the jewels.

'I'll think it over; where is the stuff?'

'Here,' said Rahbut, to the other's surprise. 'In ten—twenty minutes I could lay them on your hands, Mr. Good Man.'

Here seemed a straightforward piece of negotiation; it was doubly unfortunate that at that very period he should find himself mixed up in an affair which promised no profit whatever—the feud of Marylou Plessy, which was to become his because of his high regard for the lady.

When a woman is bad, she is usually very bad indeed, and Marylou Plessy was an extremely malignant woman. She was rather tall and handsome, with black sleek hair, boyishly shingled, and a heavy black fringe that covered a forehead of some distinction.

Mr. Reeder saw her once: he was at the Central Criminal Court giving evidence against Bartholomew Xavier Plessy, an ingenious Frenchman who discovered a new way of making old money. His forgeries were well-nigh undetectable, but Mr. Reeder was no ordinary man. He not only detected them, but he traced the printer, and that was why Bartholomew Xavier faced an unimpassioned judge, who told him in a hushed voice how very wrong it was to debase the currency; how it struck at the very roots of our commercial and industrial life. This the debonair man in the dock did not resent. He knew all about it. It was the judge's curt postscript which made him wince.

'You will be kept in penal servitude for twenty years.'

That Marylou loved the man is open to question. The probabilities are that she did not; but she hated Mr. Reeder, and she hated him not because he had brought her man to his undoing, but because, in the course of his evidence, he had used the phrase 'the woman with whom the prisoner is associated.' And Mr. John Reeder could have put her beside Plessy in the dock had he so wished: she knew this too and loathed him for his mercifulness.

Mrs. Plessy had a large flat in Portland Street. It was in a block which was the joint property of herself and her husband, for their graft had been on the grand scale, and Mr. Plessy owned race-horses before he owned a number in Parkhurst Convict Establishment. And here Marylou entertained lavishly.

A few months after her husband went to prison, she dined tête-à-tête with Mo Liski, the biggest of the gang leaders and an uncrowned emperor of the underworld. He was a small, dapper man who wore pince-nez and looked rather like a member of one of the learned professions. Yet he ruled the Strafas and the Sullivans and the Birklows, and his word was law on a dozen race-tracks, in a score of spieling clubs and innumerable establishments less liable to police supervision. People opposing him were incontinently 'coshed'—rival leaders more or less paid tribute and walked warily at that. He levied toll upon bookmakers and was immune from police interference by reason of their two failures to convict him.

Since there are white specks on the blackest coat, he had this redeeming feature, that Marylou Plessy was his ideal woman, and it is creditable in a thief to possess ideals, however unworthily they may be disposed.

He listened intently to Marylou's views, playing with his thin watchguard, his eyes on the embroidery of the tablecloth. But though he loved her, his native caution held him to reason.

'That's all right, Marylou,' he said. 'I dare say I could get Reeder, but what is going to happen then? There will be a squeak louder than a bus brake! And he's dangerous. I never worry about the regular busies, but this old feller is in the Public Prosecutor's office, and he wasn't put there because he's silly. And just now I've got one of the biggest deals on that I've ever touched. Can't you "do" him yourself? You're a clever woman: I don't know a cleverer.'

'Of course, if you're scared of Reeder — !' she said contemptuously, and a tolerant smile twisted his thin lips.

'Me? Don't be silly, dearie! Show him a point yourself. If you can't get him, let me know. Scared of him! Listen! That old bird would lose his feathers and be skinned for the pot before you could say "Mo Liski" if I wanted!'

In the Public Prosecutor's office they had no doubt about Mr. Reeder's ability to take care of himself, and when Chief Inspector Pyne came over from the Yard to report that Marylou had been in conference with the most dangerous man in London, the Assistant Prosecutor grinned his amusement.

'No—Reeder wants no protection. I'll tell him if you like, but he probably knows all about it. What are you people doing about the Liski crowd?'

Pyne pulled a long face.

'We've had Liski twice, but well organised perjury has saved him. The Assistant Commissioner doesn't want him again till we get him with the blood on his hands, so to speak. He's dangerous.'

The Assistant Prosecutor nodded.

'So is Reeder,' he said ominously. 'That man is a genial mamba! Never seen a mamba? He's a nice black snake, and you're dead two seconds after he strikes!'

The chief inspector's smile was one of incredulity.

'He never impressed me that way—rabbit, yes, but snake, no!'

Later in the morning a messenger brought Mr. Reeder to the chief's office, and he arrived with that ineffable air of apology and diffidence which gave the uninitiated such an altogether wrong idea of his calibre. He listened with closed eyes whilst his superior told him of the meeting between Liski and Marylou.

'Yes, sir,' he sighed, when the narrative came to an end. 'I have heard rumours. Liski? He is the person who associates with unlawful characters? In other days and under more favourable conditions he would have been the leader of a Florentine faction. An interesting man. With interesting friends.'

'I hope your interest remains impersonal,' warned the lawyer, and Mr. Reeder sighed again, opened his mouth to speak, hesitated, and then: 'Doesn't the continued freedom of Mr. Liski cast—um—a reflection upon our department, sir?' he asked.

His chief looked up: it was an inspiration which made him say:

'Get him!'

Mr. Reeder nodded very slowly.

'I have often thought that it would be a good idea,' he said. His gaze deepened in melancholy. 'Liski has many acquaintances of a curious character,' he said at last. 'Dutchmen, Russians, Jewish persons—he knows a Moor.'

The chief looked up quickly.

'A Moor—you're thinking of the Nine Emeralds? My dear man, there are hundreds of Moors in London and thousands in Paris.'

'And millions in Morocco,' murmured Mr. Reeder. 'I only mention the Moor in passing, sir. As regards my friend Mrs. Plessy—I hope only for the best.'

And he melted from the room.

The greater part of a month passed before he showed any apparent interest in the case. He spent odd hours wandering in the neighbourhood of Lambeth, and on one occasion he was seen in the members' enclosure at Hurst Park race-track—but he spoke to nobody, and nobody spoke to him. One night Mr. Reeder came dreamily back to his well-ordered house in Brockley Road, and found waiting on his table a small flat box which had arrived, his housekeeper told him, by post that afternoon. The label was addressed in typewritten characters 'John Reeder, Esq.' and the postmark was Central London.

He cut the thin ribbon which tied it, stripped first the brown paper and then the silver tissue, and exposed a satiny lid, which he lifted daintily. There, under a layer of paper shavings, were roll upon roll of luscious confectionery. Chocolate, with or without dainty extras, had an appeal for Mr. Reeder, and he took up a small globule garnished with crystallised violets and examined it admiringly.

His housekeeper came in at that moment with his tea-tray and set it down on the table. Mr. Reeder looked over his large glasses.

'Do you like chocolates, Mrs. Kerrel?' he asked plaintively.

'Why, yes, sir,' the elderly lady beamed. 'So do I,' said Mr. Reeder. 'So do I!' and he shook his head regretfully, as he replaced the chocolate carefully in the box. 'Unfortunately,' he went on, 'my doctor—a very excellent man—has forbidden me all sorts of confectionery until they have been submitted to the rigorous test of the public analyst.'

Mrs. Kerrel was a slow thinker, but a study of current advertisement columns in the daily newspaper had enlarged to a very considerable extent her scientific knowledge.

'To see if there is any vitamines in them, sir?' she suggested.

Mr. Reeder shook his head.

'No, I hardly think so,' he said gently. 'Vitamines are my sole diet. I can spend a whole evening with no other company than a pair of these interesting little fellows, and take no ill from them. Thank you, Mrs. Kerrel.'

When she had gone, he replaced the layer of shavings with punctilious care, closed down the lid, and as carefully re-wrapped the parcel. When it was finished he addressed the package to a department at Scotland Yard, took from a small box a label printed redly 'Poison.' When this was done, he scribbled a note to the gentleman affected, and addressed himself to his muffins and his large teacup.

It was a quarter-past six in the evening when he had unwrapped the chocolates. It was exactly a quarter-past eleven, as he turned out the lights preparatory to going to bed, that he said aloud:

'Marylou Plessy—dear me!'

Here began the war.

This was Wednesday evening; on Friday morning the toilet of Marylou Plessy was interrupted by the arrival of two men who were waiting for her when she came into the sitting-room in her negligee. They talked about fingerprints found on chocolates and other such matters.

Half an hour later a dazed woman sat in the cells at Harlboro Street and listened to an inspector's recital of her offence. At the following sessions she went down for two years on a charge of 'conveying by post to John Reeder a poisonous substance, to wit aconite, with intent to murder.'

To the last Mo Liski sat in court, his drawn haggard face testifying to the strength of his affection for the woman in the dock. After she disappeared from the dock he went outside into the big, windy hall, and there and then made his first mistake.

Mr. Reeder was putting on his woollen gloves when the dapper man strode up to him.

'Name of Reeder?'

'That is my name, sir.'

Mr. Reeder surveyed him benevolently over his glasses. He had the expectant air of one who has steeled himself to receive congratulations.

'Mine is Mo Liski. You've sent down a friend of mine—'

'Mrs. Plessy?'

'Yes—you know! Reeder, I'm going to get you for that!'

Instantly somebody behind him caught his arm in a vice and swung him round. It was a City detective.

'Take a walk with me,' he said.

Mo went white. Remember that he owed the strength of his position to the fact that never once had he been convicted: the register did not bear his name.

'What's the charge?' he asked huskily.

'Intimidation of a Crown witness and using threatening language,' said the officer.

Mo came up before the Aldermen at the Guildhall the next morning and was sent to prison for three weeks, and Mr. Reeder, who knew the threat would come and was ready to counter with the traditional swiftness of the mamba, felt that he had scored a point. The gang leader was, in the parlance of the law, 'a convicted person.'

'I don't think anything will happen until he comes out,' he said to Pyne, when he was offered police protection. 'He will find a great deal of satisfaction in arranging the details of my—um—"bashing," and I feel sure that he will postpone action until he is free. I had better have that protection until he comes out—'

'After he comes out, you mean?'

'Until he comes out,' insisted Mr. Reeder carefully. 'After—well—um—I'd rather like to be unhampered by—um—police protection.'

Mo Liski came to his liberty with all his senses alert. The cat-caution which had, with only one break, kept him clear of trouble, dominated his every plan. Cold-bloodedly he cursed himself for jeopardising his emerald deal, and his first step was to get into touch with El Rahbut.

But there was a maddening new factor in his life: the bitter consciousness of his fallibility and the fear that the men he had ruled so completely might, in consequence, attempt to break away from their allegiance. There was something more than sentiment behind this fear. Mo drew close on fifteen thousand a year from his racecourse and club-house victims alone. There were pickings on the side: his 'crowd' largely controlled a continental drug traffic worth thousands a year. Which may read romantic and imaginative, but was true. Not all the 'bunce' came to Mo and his men. There were pickings for the carrion fowl as well as for the wolves.

He must fix Reeder. That was the first move. And fix him so that there was no recoil. To beat him up one night would be an easy matter, but that would look too much like carrying into execution the threat which had put him behind bars. Obviously some ingenuity was called for; some exquisite punishment more poignant than the shock of clubs.

Men of Mr. Liski's peculiar calling do not meet their lieutenants in dark cellars, nor do they wear cloaks or masks to disguise their identities. The big six who controlled the interests serving Mo Liski came together on the night of his release, and the gathering was at a Soho restaurant, where a private dining-room was engaged in the ordinary way.

'I'm glad nobody touched him whilst I was away,' said Mo with a little smile. 'I'd like to manage this game myself. I've been doing some thinking whilst I was in bird, and there's a good way to deal with him.'

'He had two coppers with him all the time, or I'd have coshed him for you, Mo,' said Teddy Alfield, his chief of staff.

'And I'd have coshed you, Teddy,' said Mr. Liski ominously. 'I left orders that he wasn't to be touched, didn't I? What do you mean by "you'd have coshed him"?'

Alfield, a big-shouldered man whose speciality was the 'knocking-off' of unattended motor-cars, grew incoherent.

'You stick to your job,' snarled Mo. 'I'll fix Reeder. He's got a girl in Brockley; a young woman who is always going about with him—Belman's her name and she lives nearly opposite his house. We don't want to beat him up—yet. What we want to do is to get him out of his job, and that's easy. They fired a man in the Home Office last week because he was found at the "95" Club after drinking hours.'

He outlined a simple plan.

Margaret Belman left her office one evening and, walking to the corner of Westminster Bridge and the Embankment, looked around for Mr. Reeder. Usually, if his business permitted, he was to be found hereabouts, though of late the meetings had been very few, and when she had seen him he was usually in the company of two glum men who seated themselves on either side of him.

She let one car pass, and had decided to catch the second which was coming slowly along the Embankment, when a parcel dropped at her feet. She looked round to see a pretty, well-dressed woman swaying with closed eyes, and had just time to catch her by the arm before she half collapsed. With her arm round the woman's waist she assisted her to a seat providentially placed hereabouts.

'I'm so sorry—thank you ever so much. I wonder if you would call me a taxi?' gasped the fainting lady.

She spoke with a slightly foreign accent, and had the indefinable manner of a great lady; so Margaret thought.

Beckoning a cab, she assisted the woman to enter.

'Would you like me to go home with you?' asked the sympathetic girl.

'It would be good of you,' murmured the lady, 'but I fear to inconvenience you—it was so silly of me. My address is 105, Great Claridge Street.'

She recovered sufficiently on the journey to tell Margaret that she was Madame Lemaire, and that she was the widow of a French banker. The beautiful appointments of the big house in the most fashionable part of Mayfair suggested that Madame Lemaire was a woman of some wealth. A butler opened the door, a liveried footman brought in the tea which Madame insisted on the girl taking with her.

'You are too good. I cannot be thankful enough to you, mademoiselle. I must know you better. Will you come one night to dinner? Shall we say Thursday?'

Margaret Belman hesitated. She was human enough to be impressed by the luxury other surroundings, and this dainty lady had the appeal of refinement and charm which is so difficult to resist.

'We will dine tête-à-tête, and after—some people may come for dancing. Perhaps you have a friend you would like to come?'

Margaret smiled and shook her head. Curiously enough, the word 'friend' suggested only the rather awkward figure of Mr. Reeder, and somehow she could not imagine Mr. Reeder in this setting.

When she came out into the street and the butler had closed the door behind her, she had the first shock of the day. The object of her thoughts was standing on the opposite side of the road, a furled umbrella hooked to his arm.

'Why, Mr. Reeder!' she greeted him.

'You had seven minutes to spare,' he said, looking at his big-faced watch. 'I gave you half an hour—you were exactly twenty-three minutes and a few odd seconds.'

'Did you know I was there?' she asked unnecessarily.

'Yes—I followed you. I do not like Mrs. Annie Feltham—she calls herself Madame something or other. It is not a nice club.'

'Club!' she gasped.

Mr. Reeder nodded.

'They call it the Muffin Club. Curious name—curious members. It is not nice.'

She asked no further questions, but allowed herself to be escorted to Brockley, wondering just why Madame had picked upon her as a likely recruit to the gaieties of Mayfair.

And now occurred the succession of incidents which at first had so puzzled Mr. Liski. He was a busy man, and almost regretted that he had not postponed putting his plan of operation into movement. That he had failed in one respect he discovered when by accident, as it seemed, he met Mr. Reeder face to face in Piccadilly.

'Good morning, Liski,' said Mr. Reeder, almost apologetically. 'I was so sorry for that unfortunate contretemps, but believe me, I bear no malice. And whilst I realise that in all probability you do not share my sentiments, I have no other wish than to live on the friendliest terms with you.'

Liski looked at him sharply. The old man was getting scared, he thought. There was almost a tremble in his anxious voice when he put forward the olive branch.

'That's all right, Mr. Reeder,' said Mo, with his most charming smile. 'I don't bear any malice either. After all, it was a silly thing to say, and you have your duty to do.'

He went on in this strain, stringing platitude to platitude, and Mr. Reeder listened with evidence of growing relief.

'The world is full of sin and trouble,' he said, shaking his head sadly; 'both in high and low places vice is triumphant, and virtue thrust, like the daisies, underfoot. You don't keep chickens, do you, Mr. Liski?'

Mo Liski shook his head.

'What a pity!' sighed Mr. Reeder. 'There is so much one can learn from the domestic fowl! They are an object lesson to the unlawful. I often wonder why the Prison Commissioners do not allow the convicts at Dartmoor to engage in this harmless and instructive hobby. I was saying to Mr. Pyne early this morning, when they raided the Muffin Club—what a quaint title it has—'

'Raided the Muffin Club?' said Mo quickly. 'What do you mean? I've heard nothing about that.'

'You wouldn't. That kind of institution would hardly appeal to you. Only we thought it was best to raid the place, though in doing so I fear I have incurred the displeasure of a young lady friend of mine who was invited to dinner there to-morrow night. As I say, chickens—'

Now Mo Liski knew that his plan had miscarried. Yet he was puzzled by the man's attitude.

'Perhaps you would like to come down and see my Buff Orpingtons, Mr. Liski? I live in Brockley.' Reeder removed his glasses and glared owlishly at his companion. 'Say at nine o'clock to-night; there is so much to talk about. At the same time, it would add to the comfort of all concerned if you did not arrive—um—conspicuously: do you understand what I mean? I should not like the people of my office, for example, to know.'

A slow smile dawned on Liski's face. It was his faith that all men had their price, whether it was paid in cash or terror; and this invitation to a secret conference was in a sense a tribute to the power he wielded.

At nine o'clock he came to Brockley, half hoping that Mr. Reeder would go a little farther along the road which leads to compromise. But, strangely enough, the elderly detective talked of nothing but chickens. He sat on one side of the table, his hands clasped on the cloth, his voice vibrant with pride as he spoke of the breed that he was introducing to the English fowl-house, and, bored to extinction, Mo waited.

'There is something I wanted to say to you, but I fear that I must postpone that until another meeting,' said Mr. Reeder, as he helped his visitor on with his coat. 'I will walk with you to the corner of Lewisham High Road: the place is full of bad characters, and I shouldn't like to feel that I had endangered your well-being by bringing you to this lowly spot.'

Now, if there is one place in the world which is highly respectable and free from the footpads which infest wealthier neighbourhoods, it is Brockley Road. Liski submitted to the company of his host, and walked to the church at the end of the road.

'Good-bye, Mr. Liski,' said Reeder earnestly. 'I shall never forget this pleasant meeting. You have been of the greatest help and assistance to me. You may be sure that neither I nor the department I have the honour to represent will ever forget you.'

Liski went back to town, a frankly bewildered man. In the early hours of the morning the police arrested his chief lieutenant, Teddy Alfield, and charged him with a motor-car robbery which had been committed three months before.

That was the first of the inexplicable happenings. The second came when Liski, returning to his flat off Portland Place, was suddenly confronted by the awkward figure of the detective.

'Is that Liski?' Mr. Reeder peered forward in the darkness. 'I'm so glad I've found you. I've been looking for you all day. I fear I horribly misled you the other evening when I was telling you that Leghorns are unsuitable for sandy soil. Now on the contrary—'

'Look here, Mr. Reeder, what's the game?' demanded the other brusquely.

'The game?' asked Reeder in a pained tone.

'I don't want to know anything about chickens. If you've got anything to tell me worth while, drop me a line and I'll come to your office, or you can come to mine.'

He brushed past the man from the Public Prosecutor's Department and slammed the door of his flat behind him. Within two hours a squad from Scotland Yard descended upon the house of Harry Merton, took Harry and his wife from their respective beds, and charged them with the unlawful possession of stolen jewellery which had been traced to a safe deposit.

A week later, Liski, returning from a vital interview with El Rahbut, heard plodding steps overtaking him, and turned to meet the pained eye of Mr. Reeder.

'How providential meeting you!' said Reeder fervently. 'No, no, I do not wish to speak about chickens, though I am hurt a little by your indifference to this noble and productive bird.'

'Then what in hell do you want?' snapped Liski. 'I don't want anything to do with you, Reeder, and the sooner you get that into your system the better. I don't wish to discuss fowls, horses—'

'Wait!' Mr. Reeder bent forward and lowered his voice. 'Is it not possible for you and me to meet together and exchange confidences?'

Mo Liski smiled slowly.

'Oh, you're coming to it at last, eh? All right. I'll meet you anywhere you please.'

'Shall we say in the Mall near the Artillery statue, to-morrow night at ten? I don't think we shall be seen there.'

Liski nodded shortly and went on, still wondering what the man had to tell him. At four o'clock he was wakened by the telephone ringing furiously, and learnt, to his horror, that O'Hara, the most trustworthy of his gang leaders, had been arrested and charged with a year-old burglary. It was Carter, one of the minor leaders, who brought the news.

'What's the idea, Liski?' And there was a note of suspicion in the voice of his subordinate which made Liski's jaw drop.

'What do you mean—what's the idea? Come round and see me. I don't want to talk over the phone.'

Carter arrived half an hour later, a scowling, suspicious man.

'Now what do you want to say?' asked Mo, when they were alone.

'All I've got to say is this,' growled Carter; 'a week ago you're seen talking to old Reeder in Lewisham Road, and the same night Teddy Alfield is pinched. You're spotted having a quiet talk with this old dog, and the same night another of the gang goes west. Last night I saw you with my own eyes having a confidential chat with Reeder—and now O'Hara's gone!'

Mo looked at him incredulously.

'Well, and what about it?' he asked.

'Nothing—except that it's a queer coincidence, that's all,' said Carter, his lip curling. 'The boys have been talking about it: they don't like it, and you can't blame them.'

Liski sat pinching his lip, a far-away look in his eyes. It was true, though the coincidence had not struck him before. So that was the old devil's game! He was undermining his authority, arousing a wave of suspicion which, if it were not checked, would sweep him from his position.

'All right, Carter,' he said, in a surprisingly mild tone. 'It never hit me that way before. Now I'll tell you, and you can tell the other boys just what has happened.'

In a few words he explained Mr. Reeder's invitations.

'And you can tell 'em from me that I'm meeting the old fellow to-morrow night, and I'm going to give him something to remember me by.'

The thing was clear to him now, as he sat, after the man's departure, going over the events of the past week. The three men who had been arrested had been under police suspicion for a long time, and Mo knew that not even he could have saved them. The arrests had been made by arrangement with Scotland Yard to suit the convenience of the artful Mr. Reeder.

'I'll "artful" him!' said Mo, and spent the rest of the day making his preparations.

At ten o'clock that night he passed under the Admiralty Arch. A yellow mist covered the park, a drizzle of rain was falling, and save for the cars that came at odd intervals towards the palace, there was no sign of life.

He walked steadily past the Memorial, waiting for Mr. Reeder. Ten o'clock struck and a quarter past, but there was no sign of the detective.

'He's smelt a rat,' said Mo Liski between his teeth, and replaced the short life-preserver he had carried in his pocket.

It was at eleven o'clock that a patrolling police-constable fell over a groaning something that lay across the sidewalk, and, flashing his electric lamp upon the still figure, saw the carved handle of a Moorish knife before he recognised the pain-distorted face of the stricken Mo Liski.

'I don't quite understand how it all came about,' said Pyne thoughtfully. (He had been called into consultation from head-quarters.) 'Why are you so sure it was the Moor Rahbut?'

'I am not sure,' Mr. Reeder hastened to correct the mistaken impression. 'I mentioned Rahbut because I had seen him in the afternoon and searched his lodgings for the emeralds—which I am perfectly sure are still in Morocco, sir.' He addressed his chief. 'Mr. Rahbut was quite a reasonable man, remembering that he is a stranger to our methods.'

'Did you mention Mo Liski at all, Mr. Reeder?' asked the Assistant Public Prosecutor.

Mr. Reeder scratched his chin.

'I think I did—yes, I'm pretty certain that I told him that I had an appointment with Mr. Liski at ten o'clock. I may even have said where the appointment was to be kept. I can't remember exactly how the subject of Liski came up. Possibly I may have tried to bluff this indigenous native—"Bluff" is a vulgar word, but it will convey what I mean—into the belief that unless he gave me more information about the emeralds, I should be compelled to consult one who knew so many secrets. Possibly I did say that. Mr. Liski will be a long time in hospital, I hear? That is a pity. I should never forgive myself if my incautious words resulted in poor Mr. Liski being taken to the hospital—alive!'

When he had gone, the chief looked at Inspector Pyne. Pyne smiled.

'What is the name of that dangerous reptile, sir?' asked the inspector. '"Mamba," isn't it? I must remember that.'

VII. — THE STRANGE CASE

First published under the title "The Weak Spot" in
The Grand Magazine, Vol. 47, Mar-Aug 1925, as part of the J.G. Reeder series
"The Man Who Saw Evil"

IN the days of Mr. Reeder's youth, which were also the days when hansom cabs plied for hire and no gentleman went abroad without a nosegay in the lapel of his coat, he had been sent, in company with another young officer from Scotland Yard, to arrest a youthful inventor of Nottingham who earned more than a competence by methods which were displeasing to Scotland Yard. Not machines nor ingenious contrivances for saving labour did this young man invent—but stories. And they were not stories in the accepted sense of the word, for they were misstatements designed to extract money from the pockets of simple-minded men and women. Mr. Eiter employed no fewer than twenty-five aliases and as many addresses in the broadcasting of his fiction, and he was on the way to amassing a considerable fortune when a square-toed Nemesis took him by the arm and led him to the seat of justice. An unsympathetic judge sent Mr. Eiter to seven years' penal servitude, describing him as an unconscionable swindler and a menace to society—at which Willie Eiter smiled, for he had a skin beside which the elephant's was gossamer silk.

Mr. Reeder remembered the case chiefly because the prosecuting attorney, commenting upon the various disguises and subterfuges which the prisoner had adopted, remarked upon a peculiarity which was revealed in every part which the convict had played—his inability to spell 'able' which he invariably wrote as though he were naming the victim of Cain's envy.

'There is this identity to be discovered in every criminal, however ingenious he may be,' the advocate had said. 'Whatever his disguise, no matter how cleverly he dissociates one role or pose from another, there is a distinguishable weakness common to every character he affects, and especially is this observable in criminals who live by fraud and trickery.'

This Mr. Reeder remembered throughout his useful life. Few people knew that he had ever been associated with Scotland Yard. He himself evaded any question that was put to him on the subject. It was his amiable trait to pretend that he was the veriest amateur and that his success in the detection of wrongdoing was to be traced to his own evil mind that saw wrong very often where no wrong was.

He saw wrong in so many apparently innocent acts of man that it was well for his reputation that those who were acquainted with and pitied him because of his seeming inadequacy and unattractive appearance did not know what dark thoughts filled his mind.

There was a very pretty girl who lived in Brockley Road at a boarding-house. He did not like Miss Margaret Belman because she was pretty, but because she was sensible: two terms which are as a rule antagonistic. He liked her so well that he often travelled home on the cars with her, and they used to discuss the Prince of Wales, the Labour Government, the high cost of living, and other tender subjects with great animation. It was from Miss Belman that he learned about her fellow-boarder, Mrs. Carlin, and once he travelled back with her to Brockley—a frail, slim girl with experience in her face and the hint of tragedy in her fine eyes.

So it happened that he knew all about Mr. Harry Carlin long before Lord Sellington sent for him, for Mr. Reeder had the gift of evoking confidences by the suggestion rather than the expression of his sympathy.

She spoke of her husband without bitterness—but also without regret. She knew him—rather well, despite the shortness of their married life. She hinted once, and inadvertently, that there was a rich relation to whose wealth her husband would be heir if he were a normal man. Her son would, in due course, be the possessor of a great title—and penniless. She was at such pains to rectify her statement that Mr. Reeder, suspicious of peerages that come to Brockley, was assured of her sincerity, however great might be her error. Later he learned that the title was that borne by the Right Honourable the Earl of Sellington and Manford.

There came a slack time for the Public Prosecutor's office, when it seemed that sin had gone out of the world; and Mr. Reeder sat for a week on end in his little room, twiddling his thumbs or reading the advertisement columns of The Times, or drawing grotesque men upon his blotting-pad, varying these performances with the excursions he was in the habit of making to those parts of London which very few people choose for their recreation. He loved to poke about the slum areas which lie in the neighbourhood of the Great Surrey Docks; he was not averse from frequenting the north side of the river, again in the dock areas; but when his chief asked him whether he spent much time at Limehouse, Mr. Reeder replied with a pathetic smile.

'No, sir,' he said gently, 'I read about such places—I find them infinitely more interesting in the pages of a—er—novel. Yes, there are Chinese there, and I suppose Chinese are romantic, but even they do not add romance to Limehouse, which is the most respectable and law-abiding corner of the East End.'

One morning the Public Prosecutor sent for his chief detective, and Mr. Reeder obeyed the summons with a light step and a pleasant sense of anticipation.

'Go over to the Foreign Office and have a talk with Lord Sellington,' said the Prosecutor. 'He is rather worried about a nephew of his. Harry Carlin. Do you know the name?'

Mr. Reeder shook his head; for the moment he did not associate the pale girl who typed for her living.

'He's a pretty bad lot,' explained the Prosecutor, 'and unfortunately he's Sellington's heir. I rather imagine the old gentleman wants you to confirm his view.'

'Dear me!' said Mr. Reeder, and stole forth.

Lord Sellington, Under-Secretary of State for Foreign Affairs, was a bachelor and an immensely rich man. He had been rich in 1912 when, in a panic due to certain legislation which he thought would affect him adversely as a great landowner, he sold his estates and invested the larger bulk of his fortune (against all expert advice) in American industrial stocks. The war had trebled his possessions. Heavy investments in oil lands had made him many times a millionaire. He was a philanthropist, gave liberally to institutions devoted to the care of young children; he was the founder of the Eastleigh Children's Home, and subscribed liberally to other similar institutions. A thin, rather sour-faced man, he glared up under his shaggy eyebrows as Mr. Reeder sidled apologetically into his room.

'So you're Reeder, eh?' he grumbled, and was evidently not very much impressed by his visitor. 'Sit down, sit down,' he said testily, walked to the door as though he were not certain that Mr. Reeder had closed it, and came back and flopped into his chair on the other side of the table. 'I have sent for you in preference to notifying the police,' he said. 'Sir James speaks of you, Mr. Reeder, as a gentleman of discretion.'

Mr. Reeder bowed slightly, and there followed a long and awkward pause, which the Under-Secretary ended in an abrupt, irritable way.

'I have a nephew—Harry Carlin. Do you know him?'

'I know of him,' said Mr. Reeder truthfully; in his walk to the Foreign Office he had remembered the deserted wife.

'Then you know nothing good of him!' exploded his lordship. 'The man is a blackguard, a waster, a disgrace to the name he bears! If he were not my brother's son I would have him under lock and key to-night—the scoundrel! I have four bills in my possession—'

He stopped himself, pulled open a drawer savagely, took out a letter and slammed it on the table. 'Read that,' he snapped.

Mr. Reeder pulled his glasses a little farther up his nose (he always held them very tight when he was really using them) and perused the message. It was headed 'The Eastleigh Home for Children,' and was a brief request for five thousand pounds, which the writer said he would send for that evening, and was signed 'Arthur Lassard.'

'You know Lassard, of course?' said his lordship. 'He is the gentleman associated with me in my philanthropic work. Certain monies were due for land which we purchased adjoining the home. As you probably know, there are lawyers who never accept cheques for properties they sell on behalf of their clients, and I had the money ready and left it with my secretary, and one of Lassard's people was calling for it. That it was called for, I need hardly tell you,' said his lordship grimly. 'Whoever planned the coup planned it well. They knew I would be speaking in the House of Lords last night; they also knew that I had recently changed my secretary and had engaged a gentleman to whom most of my associates are strangers. A bearded man came for the money at half-past six, produced a note from Mr. Lassard, and that was the end of the money, except that we have discovered that it was changed this morning into American bills. Of course, both letters were forged: Lassard never signed either, and made no demand whatever for the money, which was not needed for another week.'

'Did anybody know about this transaction?' asked Mr. Reeder.

His lordship nodded slowly.

'My nephew knew. He came to my house two days ago to borrow money. He has a small income from his late mother's estate, but insufficient to support him in his reckless extravagance. He admitted frankly to me that he had come back from Aix broke. How long he had been in London I am unable to tell you, but he was in my library when my secretary came in with the money which I had drawn from the bank in preparation for paying the bill when it became due. Very foolishly I explained why I had so much cash in the house and why I was unable to oblige him with the thousand pounds which he wanted to borrow,' he added dourly.

Mr. Reeder scratched his chin.

'What am I to do?' he asked.

'I want you to find Carlin,' Lord Sellington almost snarled. 'But most I want that money back— you understand, Reeder? You're to tell him that unless he repays—'

Mr. Reeder was gazing steadily at the cornice moulding.

'It almost sounds as if I am being asked to compound a felony, my lord,' he said respectfully. 'But I realise, in the peculiar circumstances, we must adopt peculiar methods. The black-bearded gentleman who called for the money would appear to have been'—he hesitated—'disguised?'

'Of course he was disguised,' said the other irritably.

'One reads of such things,' said Mr. Reeder with a sigh, 'but so seldom does the bearded stranger appear in real life! Will you be good enough to tell me your nephew's address?'

Lord Sellington took a card from his pocket and threw it across the table. It fell to the floor, but he did not apologise. He was that kind of man.

'Jermyn Mansions,' said Mr. Reeder as he rose. 'I will see what can be done.'

Lord Sellington grunted something which might have been a tender farewell, but probably was not.

Jermyn Mansions is a very small, narrow-fronted building and, as Mr. Reeder knew—and he knew a great deal—was a block of residential flats, which were run by an ex-butler who was also the lessee of the establishment. By great good fortune, as he afterwards learned, Harry Carlin was at home, and in a few minutes the man from the Public Prosecutor's office was ushered into a shabby drawing-room that overlooked Jermyn Street.

A tall young man stood by the window, looking disconsolately into that narrow and lively thoroughfare, and turned as Mr. Reeder was announced. Thin-faced, narrow-headed, small-eyed, if he possessed any of the family traits and failings, the most marked was perhaps his too ready irritation.

Mr. Reeder saw, through an open door, a very untidy bedroom, caught a glimpse of a battered trunk covered with Continental labels.

'Well, what the devil do you want?' demanded Mr. Carlin. Yet, in spite of his tone, there was an undercurrent of disquiet which Mr. Reeder detected.

'May I sit down?' said the detective and, without waiting for an invitation, pulled a chair from the wall and sat down gingerly, for he knew the quality of lodging-house chairs.

His self-possession, the hint of authority he carried in his voice, increased Mr. Harry Carlin's uneasiness; and when Mr. Reeder plunged straight into the object of his visit, he saw the man go pale.

'It is a difficult subject to open,' said Mr. Reeder, carefully smoothing his knees, 'and when I find myself in that predicament I usually employ the plainest language.'

And plain language he employed with a vengeance. Half-way through Carlin sat down with a gasp.

'What—what!' he stammered. 'Does that old brute dare —! I thought you came about the bills—I mean—'

'I mean,' said Mr. Reeder carefully, 'that if you have had a little fun with your relative, I think that jest has gone far enough. Lord Sellington is prepared, on the money being refunded, to regard the whole thing as an over-elaborate practical joke on your part—'

'But I haven't touched his beastly money!' the young man almost screamed. 'I don't want his money—'

'On the contrary, sir,' said Reeder gently, 'you want it very badly. You left the Hotel Continental without paying your bill; you owe some six hundred pounds to various gentlemen from whom you borrowed that amount; there is a warrant out for you in France for passing cheques which are usually described by the vulgar as—er—"dud." Indeed'—again Mr. Reeder scratched his chin and looked thoughtfully out of the window—'indeed I know no gentleman in Jermyn Street who is so badly in need of money as your good self.'

Carlin would have stopped him, but the middle-aged man went on remorselessly.

'I have been for an hour in the Record Department of Scotland Yard, where your name is not unknown, Mr. Carlin. You left London rather hurriedly to avoid—er—proceedings of an unpleasant character. "Bills," I think you said? You are known to have been the associate of people with whom the police are a little better acquainted than they are with Mr. Carlin. You were also associated with a race-course fraud of a peculiarly unpleasant character. And amongst your minor delinquencies there is—er—a deserted young wife, at present engaged in a City office as typist, and a small boy for whom you have never provided.'

Carlin licked his dry lips.

'Is that all?' he asked, with an attempt at a sneer, though his voice shook and his trembling hands betrayed his agitation.

Reeder nodded.

'Well, I'll tell you something. I want to do the right thing by my wife. I admit I haven't played square with her, but I've never had the money to play square. That old devil has always been rolling in it, curse him! I'm the only relation he has, and what has he done? Left every bean to these damned children's homes of his! If somebody has caught him for five thousand I'm glad! I shouldn't have the nerve to do it myself, but I'm glad if they did—whoever they may be. Left every penny to a lot of squalling, sticky-faced brats, and not a bean to me!'

Mr. Reeder let him rave on without interruption, until at last, almost exhausted by his effort, he dropped down into a deep chair and glared at his visitor.

'Tell him that,' he said breathlessly; 'tell him that!'

Mr. Reeder made time to call at the little office in Portugal Street wherein was housed the headquarters of Lord Sellington's various philanthropic enterprises. Mr. Arthur Lassard had evidently been in communication with his noble patron, for no sooner did Reeder give his name than he was ushered into the plainly furnished room where the superintendent sat.

It was not unnatural that Lord Sellington should have as his assistant in the good work so famous an organiser as Mr. Arthur Lassard. Mr. Lassard's activities in the philanthropic world were many. A broad-shouldered man with a jolly red face and a bald head, he had survived all the attacks which come the way of men engaged in charitable work, and was not particularly impressed by a recent visit he had had from Harry Carlin.

'I don't wish to be unkind,' he said, 'but our friend called here on such a lame excuse that I can't help feeling that his real object was to secure a sheet of my stationery. I did, in fact, leave him in the room for a few minutes, and he had the opportunity to purloin the paper if he desired.'

'What was his excuse?' asked Mr. Reeder, and the other shrugged.

'He wanted money. At first he was civil and asked me to persuade his uncle; then he grew abusive, said that I was conspiring to rob him—I and my "infernal charities"!'

He chuckled, but grew grave again.

'The situation is mysterious to me,' he said. 'Evidently Carlin has committed some crime against his lordship, for he is terrified of him!'

'You think Mr. Carlin forged your name and secured the money?'

The superintendent spread out his arms in despair.

'Who else can I suspect?' he asked.

Mr. Reeder took the forged letter from his pocket and read it again.

'I've just been on the phone to his lordship,' Mr. Lassard went on. 'He is waiting, of course, to hear your report, and if you have failed to make this young man confess his guilt, Lord Sellington intends seeing his nephew tonight and making an appeal to him. I can hardly believe that Mr. Carlin could have done this wicked thing, though the circumstances seem very suspicious. Have you seen him, Mr. Reeder?'

'I have seen him,' said Mr. Reeder shortly. 'Oh, yes, I have seen him!'

Mr. Arthur Lassard was scrutinising his face as though he were trying to read the conclusion which the detective had reached, but Mr. Reeder's face was notoriously expressionless.

He offered a limp hand and went back to the Under-Secretary's house. The interview was short and on the whole disagreeable.

'I never dreamt he would confess to you,' said Lord Sellington with ill-disguised contempt. 'Harry needs somebody to frighten him, and, my God! I'm the man to do it! I'm seeing him to-night.'

A fit of coughing stopped him and he gulped savagely from a little medicine bottle that stood on his desk.

'I'll see him to-night,' he gasped, 'and I'll tell him what I intend doing! I've spared him hitherto because of his relationship and because he inherits the title. But I'm through. Every cent I have goes to charity. I'm good for twenty years yet, but every penny—'

He stopped. He was a man who never disguised his emotion, and Mr. Reeder, who understood men, saw the struggle that was going on in Sellington's mind.

'He says he hasn't had a chance. I may have treated him unfairly—we shall see.' He waved the detective from his office as though he were dismissing a strange dog that had intruded upon his privacy, and Mr. Reeder went out reluctantly, for he had something to tell his lordship.

It was peculiar to him that, in his more secretive moments, he sought the privacy of his old-fashioned study in Brockley Road. For two hours he sat at his desk calling a succession of numbers—and curiously enough, the gentlemen to whom he spoke were bookmakers. Most of them he knew. In the days when he was the greatest expert in the world on forged currency notes, he had been brought into contact with a class which is often the innocent medium by which the forger distributed his handicraft—and more often the instrument of his detection.

It was a Friday, a day on which most of the principals were in their offices till a late hour. At eight o'clock he finished, wrote a note and, phoning for a messenger, sent his letter on its fateful errand.

He spent the rest of the evening musing on past experiences and in refreshing his memory from the thin scrap-books which filled two shelves in his study.

What happened elsewhere that evening can best be told in the plain language of the witness-box. Lord Sellington had gone home after his interview with Mr. Reeder suffering from a feverish cold, and was disposed, according to the evidence of his secretary, to put off the interview which he had arranged with his nephew. A telephone message had been sent through to Mr. Carlin's hotel, but he was out. Until nine o'clock his lordship was busy with the affairs of his numerous charities, Mr. Lassard being in attendance. Lord Sellington was working in a small study which opened from his bedroom.

At a quarter-past nine Carlin arrived and was shown upstairs by the butler, who subsequently stated that he heard voices raised in anger. Mr. Carlin came downstairs and was shown out as the clock struck half-past nine, and a few minutes later the bell rang for Lord Sellington's valet, who went up to assist his master to bed.

At half-past seven the next morning, the valet, who slept in an adjoining apartment, went into his master's room to take him a cup of tea. He found his employer lying face downward on the floor; he was dead, and had been dead for some hours. There was no sign of wounds, and at first glance it looked as though this man of sixty had collapsed in the night. But there were circumstances which pointed to some unusual happening. In Lord Sellington's bedroom was a small steel wall-safe, and the first thing the valet noticed was that this was open, papers were lying on the floor, and that in the grate was a heap of paper which, except for one corner, was entirely burnt.

The valet telephoned immediately for the doctor and for the police, and from that moment the case went out of Mr. Reeder's able hands.

Later that morning he reported briefly to his superior the result of his inquiries.

'Murder, I am afraid,' he said sadly. 'The Home Office pathologist is perfectly certain that it is a case of aconitine poisoning. The paper in the hearth has been photographed, and there is no doubt whatever that the burnt document is the will by which Lord Sellington left all his property to various charitable institutions.'

He paused here.

'Well?' asked his chief, 'what does that mean?'

Mr. Reeder coughed.

'It means that if this will cannot be proved, and I doubt whether it can, his lordship died intestate. The property goes with the title—'

'To Carlin?' asked the startled Prosecutor.

Mr. Reeder nodded.

'There were other things burnt; four small oblong slips of paper, which had evidently been fastened together by a pin. These are quite indecipherable.' He sighed again. The Public Prosecutor looked up.

'You haven't mentioned the letter that arrived by district messenger after Lord Sellington had retired for the night.'

Mr. Reeder rubbed his chin.

'No, I didn't mention that,' he said reluctantly.

'Has it been found?'

Mr. Reeder hesitated.

'I don't know. I rather think that it has not been,' he said.

'Would it throw any light upon the crime, do you think?'

Mr. Reeder scratched his chin with some sign of embarrassment.

'I should think it might,' he said. 'Will you excuse me, sir? Inspector Salter is waiting for me.'

And he was out of the room before the Prosecutor could frame any further inquiry.

Inspector Salter was striding impatiently up and down the little room when Mr. Reeder came back. They left the building together. The car that was waiting for them brought them to Jermyn Street in a few minutes. Outside the flat three plain-clothes men were waiting, evidently for the arrival of their chief, and the Inspector passed into the building, followed closely by Mr. Reeder. They were half-way up the stairs when Reeder asked:

'Does Carlin know you?'

'He ought to,' was the grim reply. 'I did my best to get him penal servitude before he skipped from England.'

'Humph!' said Mr. Reeder. 'I'm sorry he knows you.'

'Why?' The Inspector stopped on the stairs to ask the question.

'Because he saw us getting out of the cab. I caught sight of his face, and—'

He stopped suddenly. The sound of a shot thundered through the house, and in another second the Inspector was racing up the stairs two at a time and had burst into the suite which Carlin occupied.

A glimpse of the prostrate figure told them they were too late. The Inspector bent over the dead man.

'That has saved the country the cost of a murder trial,' he said.

'I think not,' said Mr. Reeder gently, and explained his reasons.

Half an hour later, as Mr. Lassard walked out of his office, a detective tapped him on the shoulder.

'Your name is Eiter,' he said, 'and I want you for murder.'

'It was a very simple case really, sir,' explained Mr. Reeder to his chief. 'Eiter, of course, was known to me personally, but I remembered especially that he could not spell the word "able," and I recognised this peculiarity in our friend the moment I saw the letter which he wrote to his patron asking for the money. It was Eiter himself who drew the five thousand pounds; of that I am convinced. The man is, and always has been, an inveterate gambler, and I did not have to make many inquiries before I discovered that he was owing a large sum of money and that one bookmaker had threatened to bring him before Tattersall's Committee unless he paid. That would have meant the end of Mr. Lassard, the philanthropic custodian of children. Which, by the way, was always Eiter's role. He ran bogus charitable societies—it is extraordinarily easy to find dupes who are willing to subscribe for philanthropic objects. Many years ago, when I was a young man, I was instrumental in getting him seven years. I'd lost sight of him since then until I saw the letter he sent to Lord Sellington. Unfortunately for him, one line ran: "I shall be glad if you are abel to let my messenger have the money"—and he spelt "able" in the Eiter way. I called on him and made sure. And then I wrote to his lordship, who apparently did not open the letter till late that night.

'Eiter had called on him earlier in the evening and had had a long talk with him. I only surmise that Lord Sellington had expressed a doubt as to whether he ought to leave his nephew penniless, scoundrel though he was; and Eiter was terrified that his scheme for getting possession of the old man's money was in danger of failing. Moreover, my appearance in the case had scared him. He decided to kill Lord Sellington that night, took aconitine with him to the house and introduced it into the medicine, a bottle of which always stood on Sellington's desk. Whether the old man destroyed the will which disinherited his nephew before he discovered he had been poisoned, or whether he did it after, we shall never know. When I had satisfied myself that Lassard was Eiter, I sent a letter by special messenger to Stratford Place—'

'That was the letter delivered by special messenger?'

Mr. Reeder nodded.

'It is possible that Sellington was already under the influence of the drug when he burnt the will, and burnt too the four bills which Carlin had forged and which the old man had held over his head as a threat. Carlin may have known his uncle was dead; he certainly recognised the Inspector when he stepped out of the cab, and, thinking he was to be arrested for forgery, shot himself.'

Mr. Reeder pursed his lips and his melancholy face grew longer.

'I wish I had never known Mrs. Carlin—my acquaintance with her introduces that element of coincidence which is permissible in stories but is so distressing in actual life. It shakes one's confidence in the logic of things.'

VIII. — THE INVESTORS

First published in The Grand Magazine, Vol. 47, Mar-Aug 1925,
as part of the J.G. Reeder series "The Man Who Saw Evil"

THERE are seven million people in Greater London and each one of those seven millions is in theory and practice equal under the law and commonly precious to the community. So that, if one is wilfully wronged, another must be punished; and if one dies of premeditated violence, his slayer must hang by the neck until he be dead.

It is rather difficult for the sharpest law-eyes to keep tag of seven million people, at least one million of whom never keep still and are generally unattached to any particular domicile. It is equally difficult to place an odd twenty thousand or so who have domiciles but no human association. These include tramps, aged maiden ladies in affluent circumstances, peripatetic members of the criminal classes and other friendless individuals.

Sometimes uneasy inquiries come through to head-quarters. Mainly they are most timid and deferential. Mr. X. has not seen his neighbour, Mr. Y. for a week. No, he doesn't know Mr. Y. Nobody does. A little old man who had no friends and spent his fine days pottering in a garden overlooked by his more gregarious neighbour. And now Mr. Y. potters no more. His milk has not been taken in; his blinds are drawn. Comes a sergeant of police and a constable who breaks a window and climbs through, and Mr. Y. is dead somewhere—dead of starvation or a fit or suicide. Should this be the case, all is plain sailing. But suppose the house empty and Mr. Y. disappeared. Here the situation becomes difficult and delicate.

Miss Elver went away to Switzerland. She was a middle-aged spinster who had the appearance of being comfortably circumstanced. She went away, locked up her house and never came back. Switzerland looked for her; the myrmidons of Mussolini, that hatefully efficient man, searched North Italy from Domodossola to Montecattini. And the search did not yield a thin-faced maiden lady with a slight squint.

And then Mr. Charles Boyson Middlekirk, an eccentric and overpowering old man who quarrelled with his neighbours about their noisy children, he too went away. He told nobody where he was going. He lived alone with his three cats and was not on speaking terms with anybody else. He did not return to his grimy house.

He too was well off and reputedly a miser. So was Mrs. Athbell Marting, a dour widow who lived with her drudge of a niece. This lady was in the habit of disappearing without any preliminary announcement of her intention. The niece was allowed to order from the local tradesmen just sufficient food to keep body and soul together, and when Mrs. Marling returned (as she invariably did) the bills were settled with a great deal of grumbling on the part of the payer, and that was that. It was believed that Mrs. Marting went to Boulogne or to Paris or even to Brussels. But one day she went out and never came back. Six months later her niece advertised for her, choosing the cheapest papers—having an eye to the day of reckoning.

'Queer sort of thing,' said the Public Prosecutor, who had before him the dossiers of four people (three women and a man) who had so vanished in three months.

He frowned, pressed a bell and Mr. Reeder came in. Mr. Reeder took the chair that was indicated, looked owlishly over his glasses and shook his head as though he understood the reason for his summons and denied his understanding in advance. 'What do you make of these disappearances?' asked his chief.

'You cannot make any positive of a negative,' said Mr. Reeder carefully. 'London is a large place full of strange, mad people who live such—um—commonplace lives that the wonder is that more of them do not disappear in order to do something different from what they are accustomed to doing.'

'Have you seen these particulars?'

Mr. Reeder nodded.

'I have copies of them,' he said. 'Mr. Salter very kindly—'

The Public Prosecutor rubbed his head in perplexity.

'I see nothing in these cases—nothing in common, I mean. Four is a fairly low average for a big city—'

'Twenty-seven in twelve months,' interrupted his detective apologetically.

'Twenty-seven—are you sure?' The great official was astounded.

Mr. Reeder nodded again.

'They were all people with a little money; all were drawing a fairly large income, which was paid to them in bank-notes on the first of every month—nineteen of them were, at any rate. I have yet to verify eight—and they were all most reticent as to where their revenues came from. None of them had any personal friends or relatives who were on terms of friendship, except Mrs. Marting. Beyond these points of resemblance there was nothing to connect one with the other.'

The Prosecutor looked at him sharply, but Mr. Reeder was never sarcastic. Not obviously so, at any rate.

'There is another point which I omitted to mention,' he went on. 'After their disappearance no further money came for them. It came for Mrs. Marting when she was away on her jaunts, but it ceased when she went away on her final journey.'

'But twenty-seven—are you sure?'

Mr. Reeder reeled off the list, giving name, address and date of disappearance.

'What do you think has happened to them?'

Mr. Reeder considered for a moment, staring glumly at the carpet.

'I should imagine that they were murdered,' he said, almost cheerfully, and the Prosecutor half rose from his chair.

'You are in your gayest mood this morning, Mr. Reeder,' he said sardonically. 'Why on earth should they be murdered?'

Mr. Reeder did not explain. The interview took place in the late afternoon, and he was anxious to be gone, for he had a tacit appointment to meet a young lady of exceeding charm who at five minutes after five would be waiting on the corner of Westminster Bridge and Thames Embankment for the Lee car.

The sentimental qualities of Mr. Reeder were entirely unknown. There are those who say that his sorrow over those whom fate and ill-fortune brought into his punitive hands was the veriest hypocrisy. There were others who believed that he was genuinely pained to see a fellow-creature sent behind bars through his efforts and evidence.

His housekeeper, who thought he was a woman-hater, told her friends in confidence that he was a complete stranger to the tender emotions which enlighten and glorify humanity. In the ten years which she had sacrificed to his service he had displayed neither emotion nor tenderness except to inquire whether her sciatica was better or to express a wish that she should take a holiday by the sea. She was a woman beyond middle age, but there is no period of life wherein a woman gives up hoping for the best. Though the most perfect of servants in all respects, she secretly despised him, called him, to her intimates, a frump, and suspected him of living apart from an ill-treated wife. This lady was a widow (as she had told him when he first engaged her) and she had seen better—far better—days.

Her visible attitude towards Mr. Reeder was one of respect and awe. She excused the queer character of his callers and his low acquaintances. She forgave him his square-toed shoes and high, flat-crowned hat, and even admired the ready-made Ascot cravat he wore and which was fastened behind the collar with a little buckle, the prongs of which invariably punctured his fingers when he fastened it. But there is a limit to all hero-worship, and when she discovered that Mr. Reeder was in the habit of waiting to escort a young lady to town every day, and frequently found it convenient to escort her home, the limit was reached.

Mrs. Hambleton told her friends—and they agreed—that there was no fool like an old fool, and that marriages between the old and the young invariably end in the divorce court (December v. May and July). She used to leave copies of a favourite Sunday newspaper on his table, where he could not fail to see the flaring head-lines:

OLD MAN'S WEDDING ROMANCE
WIFE'S PERFIDY BRINGS GREY HAIR
IN SORROW TO THE LAW COURTS.

Whether Mr. Reeder perused these human documents she did not know. He never referred to the tragedies of ill-assorted unions, and went on meeting Miss Belman every morning at nine o'clock, and at five-five in the afternoons whenever his business permitted.

He so rarely discussed his own business or introduced the subject that was exercising his mind that it was remarkable he should make even an oblique reference to his work. Possibly he would not have done so if Miss Margaret Belman had not introduced (unwillingly) a leader of conversation which traced indirectly to the disappearances.

They had been talking of holidays: Margaret was going to Cromer for a fortnight.

'I shall leave on the second. My monthly dividends (doesn't that sound grand?) are due on the first—'

'Eh?'

Reeder slued round. Dividends in most companies are paid at half-yearly intervals.

'Dividends, Miss Margaret?'

She flushed a little at his surprise and then laughed.

'You didn't realise that I was a woman of property?' she bantered him. 'I receive ten pounds a month—my father left me a little house property when he died. I sold the cottages two years ago for a thousand pounds and found a wonderful investment.'

Mr. Reeder made a rapid calculation.

'You are drawing something like 12 and a half per cent.,' he said. 'That is indeed a wonderful investment. What is the name of the company?'

She hesitated.

'I'm afraid I can't tell you that. You see—well, it's rather secret. It is to do with a South American syndicate that supplies arms to—what do you call them—insurgents! I know it is rather dreadful to make money that way—I mean out of arms and things, but it pays terribly well and I can't afford to miss the opportunity.'

Reeder frowned.

'But why is it such a terrible secret?' he asked. 'Quite a number of respectable people make money out of armament concerns.'

Again she showed reluctance to explain her meaning.

'We are pledged—the shareholders, I mean—not to divulge our connection with the company,' she said. 'That is one of the agreements I had to sign. And the money comes regularly. I have had nearly £300 of my thousand back in dividends already.'

'Humph!' said Mr. Reeder, wise enough not to press his question. There was another day tomorrow.

But the opportunity to which he looked forward on the following morning was denied to him. Somebody played a grim 'joke' on him—the kind of joke to which he was accustomed, for there were men who had good reason to hate him, and never a year passed but one or the other sought to repay him for his unkindly attentions.

'Your name is Reeder, ain't it?'

Mr. Reeder, tightly grasping his umbrella with both hands, looked over his spectacles at the shabby man who stood at the bottom of the steps. He was on the point of leaving his house in the Brockley Road for his office in Whitehall, and since he was a methodical man and worked to a time-table, he resented in his mild way this interruption which had already cost him fifteen seconds of valuable time.

'You're the fellow who shopped Ike Walker, ain't you?'

Mr. Reeder had indeed 'shopped' many men. He was by profession a shopper, which, translated from the argot, means a man who procures the arrest of an evildoer. Ike Walker he knew very well indeed. He was a clever, a too clever, forger of bills of exchange, and was at that precise moment almost permanently employed as orderly in the convict prison at Dartmoor, and might account himself fortunate if he held this easy job for the rest of his twelve years' sentence.

His interrogator was a little hard-faced man wearing a suit that had evidently been originally intended for somebody of greater girth and more commanding height. His trousers were turned up noticeably; his waistcoat was full of folds and tucks which only an amateur tailor would have dared, and only one superior to the criticism of his fellows would have worn. His hard, bright eyes were fixed on Mr. Reeder, but there was no menace in them so far as the detective could read.

'Yes, I was instrumental in arresting Ike Walker,' said Mr. Reeder, almost gently.

The man put his hand in his pocket and brought out a crumpled packet enclosed in green oiled silk. Mr. Reeder unfolded the covering and found a soiled and crumpled envelope.

'That's from Ike,' said the man. 'He sent it out of stir by a gent who was discharged yesterday.'

Mr. Reeder was not shocked by this revelation. He knew that prison rules were made to be broken, and that worse things have happened in the best regulated jails than this item of a smuggled letter. He opened the envelope, keeping his eyes on the man's face, took out the crumpled sheet and read the five or six lines of writing.

DEAR REEDER — Here is a bit of a riddle for you.

What other people have got, you can have. I haven't got it, but it is coming to you. It's red-hot when you get it, but you're cold when it goes away.

Your loving friend,

IKE WALKER (doing a twelve stretch because you went on the witness stand and told a lot of lies.)

Mr. Reeder looked up and their eyes met. 'Your friend is a little mad, one thinks?' he asked politely.

'He ain't a friend of mine. A gent asked me to bring it,' said the messenger.

'On the contrary,' said Mr. Reeder pleasantly, 'he gave it to you in Dartmoor Prison yesterday. Your name is Mills; you have eight convictions for burglary, and will have your ninth before the year is out. You were released two days ago—I saw you reporting at Scotland Yard.'

The man was for the moment alarmed and in two minds to bolt. Mr. Reeder glanced along Brockley Road, saw a slim figure, that was standing at the corner, cross to a waiting tramcar, and, seeing his opportunity vanish, readjusted his time-table.

'Come inside, Mr. Mills.'

'I don't want to come inside,' said Mr. Mills, now thoroughly agitated. 'He asked me to give this to you and I've give it. There's nothing else—'

Mr. Reeder crooked his finger.

'Come, birdie!' he said, with great amiability. 'And please don't annoy me! I am quite capable of sending you back to your friend Mr. Walker. I am really a most unpleasant man if am upset.'

The messenger followed meekly, wiped his boots with great vigour on the mat and tiptoed up the carpeted stairs to the big study where Mr. Reeder did most of his thinking.

'Sit down, Mills.'

With his own hands Mr. Reeder placed a chair for his uncomfortable visitor, and then, pulling another up to his big writing table, he spread the letter before him, adjusted his glasses, read, his lips moving, and then leaned back in his chair.

'I give it up,' he said. 'Read me this riddle.'

'I don't know what's in the letter—' began the man.

'Read me this riddle.'

As he handed the letter across the table, the man betrayed himself, for he rose and pushed back his chair with a startled, horrified expression that told Mr. Reeder quite a lot. He laid the letter down on his desk, took a large tumbler from the sideboard, inverted it and covered the scrawled paper. Then:

'Wait,' he said, 'and don't move till I come back.'

And there was an unaccustomed venom in his tone that made the visitor shudder.

Reeder passed out of the room to the bathroom, pulled up his sleeves with a quick jerk of his arm and, turning the faucet, let hot water run over his hands before he reached for a small bottle on a shelf, poured a liberal portion into the water and let his hands soak. This done, for three minutes he scrubbed his fingers with a nail-brush, dried them, and, removing his coat and waistcoat carefully, hung them over the edge of the bath. He went back to his uncomfortable guest in his shirt-sleeves.

'Our friend Walker is employed in the hospital?' he stated rather than asked. 'What have you had there—scarlet fever or something worse?'

He glanced down at the letter under the glass.

'Scarlet fever, of course,' he said, 'and the letter has been systematically infected. Walker is almost clever.'

The wood of a fire was laid in the grate. He carried the letter and the blotting-paper to the hearth, lit the kindling and thrust paper and letter into the flames.

'Almost clever,' he said musingly. 'Of course, he is one of the orderlies in the hospital. It was scarlet fever, I think you said?'

The gaping man nodded.

'Of a virulent type, of course. How very fascinating!'

He thrust his hands in his pockets and looked down benevolently at the wretched emissary of the vengeful Walker.

'You may go now, Mills,' he said gently. 'I rather think that you are infected. That ridiculous piece of oiled silk is quite inadequate—which means "quite useless"—as a protection against wandering germs. You will have scarlet fever in three days, and will probably be dead at the end of the week. I will send you a wreath.'

He opened the door, pointed to the stairway and the man slunk out.

Mr. Reeder watched him through the window, saw him cross the street and disappear round the corner into the Lewisham High Road, and then, going up to his bedroom, he put on a newer frock-coat and waistcoat, drew on his hands a pair of fabric gloves and went forth to his labours. He did not expect to meet Mr. Mills again, never dreaming that the gentleman from Dartmoor was planning a 'bust' which would bring them again into contact. For Mr. Reeder the incident was closed.

That day news of another disappearance had come through from police head-quarters, and Mr. Reeder was waiting at ten minutes before five at the rendezvous for the girl who, he instinctively knew, could give him a thread of the clue. He was determined that this time his inquiries should bear fruit; but it was not until they had reached the end of Brockley Road, and he was walking slowly up towards the girl's boarding-house, that she gave him a hint.

'Why are you so persistent, Mr. Reeder?' she asked, a little impatiently. 'Do you wish to invest money? Because, if you do, I'm sorry I can't help you. That is another agreement we made, that we would not introduce new shareholders.'

Mr. Reeder stopped, took off his hat and rubbed the back of his head (his housekeeper, watching him from an upper window, was perfectly certain he was proposing and had been rejected).

'I am going to tell you something, Miss Belman, and I hope—er—that I shall not alarm you.'

And very briefly he told the story of the disappearances and the queer coincidence which marked every case—the receipt of a dividend on the first of every month. As he proceeded, the colour left the girl's face.

'You are serious, of course?' she said, serious enough herself. 'You wouldn't tell me that unless—. The company is the Mexico City Investment Syndicate. They have offices in Portugal Street.'

'How did you come to hear of them?' asked Mr. Reeder.

'I had a letter from their manager, Mr. de Silvo. He told me that a friend had mentioned my name, and gave full particulars of the investment.'

'Have you that letter?'

She shook her head.

'No; I was particularly asked to bring it with me when I went to see them. Although, in point of fact, I never did see them,' smiled the girl. 'I wrote to their lawyers—will you wait? I have their letter.'

Mr. Reeder waited at the gate whilst the girl went into the house and returned presently with a small portfolio, from which she took a quarto sheet. It was headed with the name of a legal firm, Bracher & Bracher, and was the usual formal type of letter one expects from a lawyer.

'DEAR MADAM,' it ran, 'Re--Mexico City Investment Syndicate: We act as lawyers to this syndicate, and so far as we know it is a reputable concern. We feel that it is only due to us that we should say that we do not advise investments in any concern which offers such large profits, for usually there is a corresponding risk. We know, however, that this syndicate has paid 12 and a half per cent. and sometimes as much as 20 per cent., and we have had no complaints about them. We cannot, of course, as lawyers, guarantee the financial soundness of any of our clients, and can only repeat that, in so far as we have been able to ascertain, the syndicate conducts a genuine business and enjoys a very sound financial backing.

'Yours faithfully,
'BRACHER & BRACHER.'
'You say you never saw de Silvo?'
She shook her head.
'No; I saw Mr. Bracher, but when I went to the office of the syndicate, which is in the same building, I found only a clerk in attendance. Mr. de Silvo had been called out of town. I had to leave the letter because the lower portion was an application for shares in the syndicate. The capital could be withdrawn at three days' notice, and I must say that this last clause decided me; and when I had a letter from Mr. de Silvo accepting my investment, I sent him the money.'
Mr. Reeder nodded.
'And you've received your dividends regularly ever since?' he said.
'Every month,' said the girl triumphantly. 'And really I think you're wrong in connecting the company with these disappearances.'
Mr. Reeder did not reply. That afternoon he made it his business to call at 179, Portugal Street. It was a two-story building of an old-fashioned type. A wide flagged hall led into the building; a set of old-fashioned stairs ran up to the 'top floor,' which was occupied by a China merchant; and from the hall led three doors. That on the left bore the legend 'Bracher & Bracher, Solicitors,' and immediately facing was the office of the Mexican Syndicate. At the far end of the passage was a door which exhibited the name 'John Baston,' but as to Mr. Baston's business there was no indication.
Mr. Reeder knocked gently at the door of the syndicate and a voice bade him come in. A young man, wearing glasses, was sitting at a typewriting table, a pair of dictaphone receivers in his ears, and he was typing rapidly.
'No, sir, Mr. de Silvo is not in. He only comes in about twice a week,' said the clerk. 'Will you give me your name?'
'It is not important,' said Reeder gently, and went out, closing the door behind him.
He was more fortunate in his call upon Bracher & Bracher, for Mr. Joseph Bracher was in his office: a tall, florid gentleman who wore a large rose in his buttonhole. The firm of Bracher & Bracher was evidently a prosperous one, for there were half a dozen clerks in the outer office, and Mr. Bracher's private sanctum, with its big partner desk, was a model of shabby comfort.
'Sit down, Mr. Reeder,' said the lawyer, glancing at the card.
In a few words Mr. Reeder stated his business, and Mr. Bracher smiled.
'It is fortunate you came to-day,' he said. 'If it were to-morrow we should not be able to give you any information. The truth is, we have had to ask Mr. de Silvo to find other lawyers. No, no, there is nothing wrong, except that they constantly refer their clients to us, and we feel that we are becoming in the nature of sponsors for their clients, and that, of course, is very undesirable.'
'Have you a record of the people who have written to you from time to time asking your advice?'
Mr. Bracher shook his head.
'It is a curious thing to confess, but we haven't,' he said; 'and that is one of the reasons why we have decided to give up this client. Three weeks ago, the letter-book in which we kept copies of all letters sent to people who applied for a reference most unaccountably disappeared. It was put in the safe overnight, and in the morning, although there was no sign of tampering with the lock, it had vanished. The circumstances were so mysterious, and my brother and I were so deeply concerned, that we applied to the syndicate to give us a list of their clients, and that request was never complied with.'
Mr. Reeder sought inspiration in the ceiling.

'Who is John Baston?' he asked, and the lawyer laughed.

'There again I am ignorant. I believe he is a very wealthy financier, but, so far as I know, he only comes to his office for three months in the year, and I have never seen him.'

Mr. Reeder offered him his flabby hand and walked back along Portugal Street, his chin on his breast, his hands behind him dragging his umbrella, so that he bore a ludicrous resemblance to some strange tailed animal.

That night he waited again for the girl, but she did not appear, and although he remained at the rendezvous until half-past five he did not see her. This was not very unusual, for sometimes she had to work late, and he went home without any feeling of apprehension. He finished his own frugal dinner and then walked across to the boarding-house. Miss Belman had not arrived, the landlady told him, and he returned to his study and telephoned first to the office where she was employed and then to the private address of her employer.

'She left at half-past four,' was the surprising news. 'Somebody telephoned to her and she asked me if she might go early.'

'Oh!' said Mr. Reeder blankly.

He did not go to bed that night, but sat up in a small room at Scotland Yard, reading the brief reports which came in from the various divisions. And with the morning came the sickening realisation that Margaret Belman's name must be added to those who had disappeared in such extraordinary circumstances.

He dozed in the big Windsor chair. At eight o'clock he returned to his own house and shaved and bathed, and when the Public Prosecutor arrived at his office he found Mr. Reeder waiting for him in the corridor. It was a changed Mr. Reeder, and the change was not due entirely to lack of sleep. His voice was sharper; he had lost some of that atmosphere of apology which usually enveloped him.

In a few words he told of Margaret Belman's disappearance.

'Do you connect de Silvo with this?' asked his chief.

'Yes, I think I do,' said the other quietly, and then: 'There is only one hope, and it is a very slender one—a very slender one indeed!'

He did not tell the Public Prosecutor in what that hope consisted, but walked down to the offices of the Mexican Syndicate.

Mr. de Silvo was not in. He would have been very much surprised if he had been. He crossed the hallway to see the lawyer, and this time he found Mr. Ernest Bracher present with his brother. When Reeder spoke to the point, it was very much to the point.

'I am leaving a police officer in Portugal Street to arrest de Silvo the moment he puts in an appearance. I feel that you, as his lawyers, should know this,' he said.

'But why on earth — ?' began Mr. Bracher, in a tone of astonishment.

'I don't know what charge I shall bring against him, but it will certainly be a very serious one,' said Reeder. 'For the moment I have not confided to Scotland Yard the basis for my suspicions, but your client has got to tell a very plausible story and produce indisputable proof of his innocence to have any hope of escape.'

'I am quite in the dark,' said the lawyer, mystified. 'What has he been doing? Is his syndicate a fraud?'

'I know nothing more fraudulent,' said the other shortly. 'To-morrow I intend obtaining the necessary authority to search his papers and to search the room and papers of Mr. John Baston. I have an idea that I shall find something in that room of considerable interest to me.'

It was eight o'clock that night before he left Scotland Yard, and he was turning towards the familiar corner, when he saw a car come from Westminster Bridge towards Scotland Yard. Somebody leaned out of the window and signalled him, and the car turned. It was a two-seater coupe and the driver was Mr. Joseph Bracher.

'We've found de Silvo,' he said breathlessly as he brought the car to a standstill at the kerb and jumped out.

He was very agitated and his face was pale. Mr. Reeder could have sworn that his teeth were chattering.

'There's something wrong—very badly wrong,' he went on. 'My brother has been trying to get the truth from him—my God! if he has done these terrible things I shall never forgive myself.'

'Where is he?' asked Mr. Reeder.

'He came just before dinner to our house at Dulwich. My brother and I are bachelors and we live there alone now, and he has been to dinner before. My brother questioned him and he made certain admissions which are almost incredible. The man must be mad.'

'What did he say?'

'I can't tell you. Ernest is detaining him until you come.'

Mr. Reeder stepped into the car and in a few minutes they were flying across Westminster Bridge towards Camberwell. Lane House, an old-fashioned Georgian residence, lay at the end of a countrified road which was, he found, a cul de sac. The house stood in grounds of considerable size, he noted as they passed up the drive and stopped before the porch. Mr. Bracher alighted and opened the door, and Reeder passed into a cosily furnished hall. One door was ajar.

'Is that Mr. Reeder?' He recognised the voice of Ernest Bracher, and walked into the room.

The younger Mr. Bracher was standing with his back to the empty fire-place; there was nobody else in the room.

'De Silvo's gone upstairs to lie down,' explained the lawyer. 'This is a dreadful business, Mr. Reeder.'

He held out his hand and Reeder crossed the room to take it. As he put his foot on the square Persian rug before the fire-place, he realised his danger and tried to spring back, but his balance was lost. He felt himself falling through the cavity which the carpet hid, lashed out and caught for a moment the edge of the trap, but as the lawyer came round and raised his foot to stamp upon the clutching fingers, Reeder released his hold and dropped.

The shock of the fall took away his breath, and for a second he sprawled, half lying, half sitting, on the floor of the cellar into which he had fallen. Looking up, he saw the older of the two leaning over. The square aperture was diminishing in size. There was evidently a sliding panel which covered the hole in normal times.

'We'll deal with you later, Reeder,' said Joseph Bracher with a smile. 'We've had quite a lot of clever people here—'

Something cracked in the cellar. The bullet seared the lawyer's cheek, smashed a glass chandelier to fragments, and he stepped back with a yell of fear. In another second the trap was closed and Reeder was alone in a small brick-lined cellar. Not entirely alone, for the automatic pistol he held in his hand was a very pleasant companion in that moment of crisis.

From his hip pocket he took a flat electric hand-lamp, switched on the current and surveyed his prison. The walls and floor were damp; that was the first thing he noticed. In one corner was a small flight of brick steps leading to a locked steel door, and then:

'Mr. Reeder.'

He spun round and turned his lamp upon the speaker. It was Margaret Belman, who had risen from a heap of sacks where she had been sleeping.

'I'm afraid I've got you into very bad trouble,' she said, and he marvelled at her calm.
'How long have you been here?'
'Since last night,' she answered. 'Mr. Bracher telephoned me to see him and he picked me up in his car. They kept me in the other room until to-night, but an hour ago they brought me here.'
'Which is the other room?'
She pointed to the steel door. She offered no further details of her capture, and it was not a moment to discuss their misfortune. Reeder went up the steps and tried the door; it was fastened from the other side, and opened inward, he discovered. There was no sign of a keyhole. He asked her where the door led and she told him that it was to an underground kitchen and coal-cellar. She had hoped to escape, because only a barred window stood between her and freedom in the 'little room' where she was kept.
'But the window was very thick,' she said, 'and of course I could do nothing with the bars.'
Reeder made another inspection of the cellar, then sent the light of his lamp up at the ceiling. He saw nothing there except a steel pulley fastened to a beam that crossed the entire width of the cellar.
'Now what on earth is he going to do?' he asked thoughtfully, and as though his enemies had heard the question and were determined to leave him in no doubt as to their plans, there came the sound of gurgling water, and in a second he was ankle-deep.
He put the light on to the place whence the water was coming. There were three circular holes in the wall, from each of which was gushing a solid stream.
'What is it?' she asked in a terrified whisper.
'Get on to the steps and stay there,' he ordered peremptorily, and made investigation to see if it was possible to staunch the flow. He saw at a glance that this was impossible. And now the mystery of the disappearances was a mystery no longer.
The water came up with incredible rapidity, first to his knees, then to his thighs, and he joined her on the steps.
There was no possible escape for them. He guessed the water would come up only so far as would make it impossible for them to reach the beam across the roof or the pulley, the dreadful purpose of which he could guess. The dead must be got out of this charnel house in some way or other. Strong swimmer as he was, he knew that in the hours ahead it would be impossible to keep afloat.
He slipped off his coat and vest and unbuttoned his collar.
'You had better take off your skirt,' he said, in a matter-of-fact tone. 'Can you swim?'
'Yes,' she answered in a low voice.
He did not ask her the real question which was in his mind: for how long could she swim? There was a long silence; the water crept higher; and then: 'Are you very much afraid?' he asked, and took her hand in his.
'No, I don't think I am,' she said. 'It is wonderful having you with me—why are they doing this?'
He said nothing, but carried the soft hand to his lips and kissed it.
The water was now reaching the top step. Reeder stood with his back to the iron door, waiting. And then he felt something touch the door from the other side. There was a faint click, as though a bolt had been slipped back. He put her gently aside and held his palms to the door. There was no doubt now: somebody was fumbling on the other side. He went down a step and presently he felt the door yield and come towards him, and there was a momentary gleam of light. In another second he had wrenched the door open and sprung through.
'Hands up!'

Whoever it was had dropped his lamp, and now Mr. Reeder focused the light of his own torch and nearly dropped.

For the man in the passage was Mills, the ex-convict who had brought the tainted letter from Dartmoor!

'All right, guv'nor, it's a cop,' growled the man.

And then the whole explanation flashed upon the detective. In an instant he had gripped the girl by the hand and dragged her through the narrow passage, into which the water was now steadily overrunning.

'Which way did you get in, Mills?' he demanded authoritatively.

'Through the window.'

'Show me—quick!'

The convict led the way to what was evidently the window through which the girl had looked with such longing. The bars had been removed; the window sash itself lifted from its rusty hinges; and in another second the three were standing on the grass, with the stars twinkling above them.

'Mills,' said Mr. Reeder, and his voice shook, 'you came here to "bust" this house.'

'That's right,' growled Mills. 'I tell you it's a cop. I'm not going to give you any trouble.'

'Skip!' hissed Mr. Reeder. 'And skip quick! Now, young lady, we'll go for a little walk.'

A few seconds later a patrolling constable was smitten dumb by the apparition of a middle-aged man in shirt and trousers, and a lady who was inadequately attired in a silk petticoat.

* * * * *

'The Mexican company was Bracher & Bracher,' explained Reeder to his chief. 'There was no John Baston. His room was a passage-way by which the Brachers could get from one room to the other. The clerk in the Mexican Syndicate's office was, of course, blind; I spotted that the moment I saw him. There are any number of blind typists employed in the City of London. A blind clerk was necessary if the identity of de Silvo with the Brachers was to be kept a secret.

'Bracher & Bracher had been going badly for years. It will probably be found that they have made away with clients' money; and they hit upon this scheme of inducing foolish investors to put money into their syndicate on the promise of large dividends. Their victims were well chosen, and Joseph—who was the brains of the organisation—conducted the most rigorous investigation to make sure that these unfortunate people had no intimate friends. If they had any suspicion about an applicant, Brachers would write a letter deprecating the idea of an investment and suggesting that the too-shrewd dupe should find another and a safer method than the Mexican syndicate afforded.

'After they had paid one or two years' dividends the wretched investor was lured to the house at Dulwich and there scientifically killed. You will probably find an unofficial cemetery in their grounds. So far as I can make out, they have stolen over a hundred and twenty thousand pounds in the past two years by this method.'

'It is incredible,' said the Prosecutor, 'incredible!'

Mr. Reeder shrugged.

'Is there anything more incredible than the Burke and Hare murders? There are Burkes and Hares in every branch of society and in every period of history.'

'Why did they delay their execution of Miss Belman?'

Mr. Reeder coughed.

'They wanted to make a clean sweep, but did not wish to kill her until they had me in their hands. I rather suspect'—he coughed again—'that they thought I had an especial interest in the young

lady.'
'And have you?' asked the Public Prosecutor.
Mr. Reeder did not reply.

Terror Keep

FOREWORD

RIGHTLY speaking, it is improper, not to say illegal, for those sadly privileged few who go in and out of Broadmoor Criminal Lunatic Asylum, to have pointed out to them any particular character, however notorious he may have been or to what heights of public interest his infamy had carried him, before the testifying doctors and a merciful jury consigned him to this place without hope. But often had John Flack been pointed out as he shuffled about the grounds, his hands behind him, his chin on his breast, a tall, lean old man in an ill-fitting suit of drab clothing, who spoke to nobody and was spoken to by few.

"That is Flack—THE Flack—the cleverest crook in the world.... Crazy John Flack ... nine murders..."

In their queer, sane moments, men who were in Broadmoor for isolated homicides were rather proud of Old John. The officers who locked him up at night and watched him as he slept had little to say against him, because he gave no trouble, and through all the six years of his incarceration had never once been seized of those frenzies which so often end in the hospital for some poor innocent devil, and a rubber-padded cell for the frantic author of misfortune.

He spent most of his time writing and reading, for he was something of a genius with his pen, and wrote with extraordinary rapidity. He filled hundreds of little exercise books with his great treatise on crime. The governor humoured him; allowed him to retain the books, expecting in due course to add them to his already interesting museum.

Once, as a great concession, Old Jack gave him a book to read, and the governor read and gasped. It was entitled "Method of robbing a bank vault when only two guards are employed." The governor, who had been a soldier, read and read, stopping now and then to rub his head; for this document, written in the neat, legible hand of John Flack, was curiously reminiscent of a divisional order for attack. No detail was too small to be noted; every contingency was provided for. Not only were the constituents of the drug to be employed to "settle the outer watchman" given, but there was an explanatory note which may be quoted:

"If this drug is not procurable, I advise that the operator should call upon a suburban doctor and describe the following symptoms.... The doctor will then prescribe the drug in a minute quantity. Six bottles of this medicine should be procured and the following method adopted to extract the drug...."

"Have you written much like this, Flack?" asked the wondering officer.

"This?" John Flack shrugged his lean shoulders. "I am doing this for amusement, just to test my memory. I have already written sixty-three books on the subject, and those works are beyond improvement. During the six years I have been here, I have not been able to think of a single improvement on my old system."

Was he jesting? Was this a flight of a disordered mind? The governor, used as he was to his patients and their peculiar ways, was not certain.

"You mean you have written an encyclopædia of crime?" he asked incredulously. "Where is it to be found?"

Old Flack's thin lips curled in a disdainful smile, but he made no answer.

Sixty-three hand-written volumes represented the life work of John Flack. It was the one achievement upon which he prided himself.

On another occasion, when the governor referred to his extraordinary literary labours, he said: "I have put a huge fortune in the hands of any clever man—providing, of course," he mused, "that he is a man of resolution and the books fall into his hands at a very early date. In these days of scientific discovery, what is a novelty to-day is a commonplace to-morrow."

The governor had his doubts as to the existence of these deplorable volumes, but very soon after the conversation took place he had to revise his judgment. Scotland Yard, which seldom if ever chases chimeras, sent down one Chief Inspector Simpson, who was a man entirely without imagination and had been promoted for it.

His interview with Crazy John Flack was a brief one. "About these books of yours, Jack," he said. "It would be terrible if they fell into wrong hands. Ravini says you've got a hundred volumes hidden somewhere."

"Ravini?" Old John Flack showed his teeth. "Listen, Simpson! You don't think you're going to keep me in this awful place all my life, do you? If you do, you've got another guess coming. I'll skip one of these odd nights—you can tell the governor if you like—and then Ravini and I are going to have a little talk."

His voice grew high and shrill. The old mad glitter that Simpson had seen before came back to his eyes.

"Do you ever have daydreams, Simpson? I have three! I've got a new method of getting away with a million: that's one, but it's not important. Another one is Reeder: you can tell J.G. what I say. It's a dream of meeting him alone one nice, dark, foggy night, when the police can't tell which way the screams are coming. And the third is Ravini: George Ravini's got one chance, and that is for him to die before I get out!"

"You're mad," said Simpson.

"That's what I'm here for," said John Flack truthfully.

This conversation with Simpson and that with the governor were two of the longest he ever had, all the six years he was in Broadmoor. Mostly when he wasn't writing he strolled about the grounds, his chin on his chest, his hands clasped behind him. Occasionally, he reached a certain place near the high wall, and it is said that he threw letters over, though this is very unlikely. What is more possible is that he found a messenger who carried his many and cryptic letters to the outer world and brought in exchange monosyllabic replies. He was very friendly with the officer in charge of his ward, and one early morning this man was discovered with his throat cut. The ward door was open, and John Flack had gone out into the world to realize his daydreams.

CHAPTER I

THERE were two subjects which irritated the mind of Margaret Belman as the Southern Express carried her toward Selford Junction and the branch line train which crawled from the junction to Siltbury. The first of these was, not unnaturally, the drastic changes she now contemplated, the second the effect they already had had upon Mr. J.G. Reeder, that mild and middle-aged man. When she had announced that she was seeking a post in the country, he might at least have shown some evidence of regret; a certain glumness would have been appropriate, at any rate. Instead, he had brightened visibly at the prospect.

"I am afraid I shan't be able to come to London very often," she had said.

"That is good news," said Mr. Reeder, and added some banality about the value of periodical changes of air and the beauty of getting near to nature.

In fact, he had been more cheerful than he had been for a week—which was rather exasperating. Margaret Belman's pretty face puckered as she recalled her disappointment and chagrin. All thoughts of dropping this application of hers disappeared. Not that she imagined for one moment that a six-hundred-a-year secretaryship was going to drop into her lap for the mere asking. She was wholly unsuited to the job; she had had no experience in hotel work; and the chances of her being accepted were remote.

As to the Italian who had made so many attempts to make her acquaintance—he was one of the unpleasant commonplaces so familiar to a girl who worked for her living that in ordinary circumstances she would not have given him a second thought.

But that morning he had followed her to the station, and she was certain that he had heard her tell the girl who came with her that she was returning by the 6:15. A policeman would deal effectively with him—if she cared to risk the publicity. But a girl, however annoyed, shrinks from such an ordeal; she must deal with him in her own way.

That was not a happy prospect, and the two matters in combination were sufficient to spoil what otherwise might have been a very happy or interesting afternoon.

As to Mr. Reeder—

Margaret Belman frowned. She was twenty-three, an age when youngish men are rather tiresome. On the other hand, men in the region of fifty are not especially attractive. She loathed Mr. Reeder's side whiskers; they made him look rather like a Scottish butler. Of course, he was a dear....

Here the train reached the junction and she found herself at the surprisingly small station of Siltbury before she had quite made up her mind whether she was in love with Mr. Reeder or merely annoyed with him.

The driver of the station cab stopped his unhappy-looking horse before the small gateway and pointed with his whip.

"This is the best way in for you, miss," he said. "Mr. Daver's office is at the end of the path."

He was a shrewd old man, who had driven many applicants for the post of secretary at Larmes Keep, and he guessed that this one, the prettiest of all, did not come as a guest. In the first place, she brought no baggage, and then, too, the ticket collector had come running after her to hand back the return half of her railway ticket, which she had absent-mindedly surrendered.

"I'd better wait for you, miss?"

"Oh, yes, please," said Margaret Belman hastily as she got down from the dilapidated victoria.

"You got an appointment?"

The cabman was a local character, and local characters assume privileges.

"I ast you," he explained carefully, "because lots of young wimmin have come up to Larmes without appointments and Mr. Daver wouldn't see 'em. They just cut out the advertisement and come along, but the 'ad' says write. I suppose I've made a dozen journeys with young wimmin who ain't got appointments. I'm telling you for your own good."

The girl smiled.

"You might have warned them before they left the station," she said with good-humour, "and saved them the cab fare. Yes, I have an appointment."

From where she stood by the gate, she had a clear view of Larmes Keep. It bore no resemblance to a hotel and less to the superior boarding house that she knew it to be. That part of the house which had been the original Keep was easily distinguished, though the gray, straight walls were masked with ivy that covered also part of the buildings which had been added in the course of the years.

She looked across a smooth green lawn, on which were set a few wicker chairs and tables, to a rose garden which, even in autumn, was a blaze of colour. Behind this was a belt of pine trees that seemed to run to the cliff's edge. She had a glimpse of a gray-blue sea and a blur of dim smoke from a steamer invisible below the straight horizon. A gentle wind carried the fragrance of the pines to her, and she sniffed ecstatically.

"Isn't it gorgeous!" she breathed.

The cabman said it "wasn't bad" and pointed with his whip again.

"It's that little square place—only built a few years ago. Mr. Daver is more of a writing gentleman than a boarding-house gentleman."

She unlatched the oaken gate and walked up the stone path toward the sanctum of the writing gentleman. On either side of the crazy pavement was a deep border of flowers—she might have been passing through a cottage garden.

There was a long window and a small green door to the annex. Evidently she had been seen, for, as her hand went up to the brass bell-push, the door opened.

It was obviously Mr. Daver himself. A tall, thin man of fifty, with a yellow, elflike face and a smile that brought all her sense of humour into play. Very badly she wanted to laugh. The long upper lip overhung the lower, and except that the face was thin and lined, he had the appearance of some grotesque and foolish mascot. The staring, round brown eyes, the puckered forehead, and a twist of hair that stood upright on the crown of his head made him more brownie-like than ever.

"Miss Belman?" he asked, with a certain eagerness.

He lisped slightly and had a trick of clasping his hands as if he were in an agony of apprehension lest his manner should displease.

"Come into my den," he said, and gave such emphasis to the last word that she nearly laughed again.

The "den" was a very comfortably furnished study, one wall of which was covered with books. Closing the door behind her, he pushed up a chair with a little nervous laugh.

"I'm so very glad you came. Did you have a comfortable journey? I'm sure you did. And is London hot and stuffy? I'm afraid it is. Would you like a cup of tea? Of course you would."

He fired question and answer so rapidly that she had no chance of replying, and he had taken up a telephone and ordered the tea before she could express a wish on the subject.

"You are young, very young." He shook his head sadly, "Twenty-four—no? Do you use the typewriter? What a ridiculous question to ask!"

"It is very kind of you to see me, Mr. Daver," she said, "and I don't suppose for one moment that I shall suit you, I have had no experience in hotel management, and I realize, from the salary you offer—"

"Quiet," said Mr. Daver, shaking his head solemnly: "that is what I require. There is very little work, but I wished to be relieved even of that little. My own labours"—he waved his hand to a pedestal desk littered with paper—"are colossal. I need a lady to keep accounts—to watch my interests. Somebody I can trust. I believe in faces, do you? I see that you do. And in character shown in handwriting? You believe in that also. I have advertised for three months and have interviewed thirty-five applicants. Impossible! Their voices—terrible! I judge people by their voices. So do you. On Monday, when you telephoned, I said to myself, 'The Voice!'"

He was clasping his hands together so tightly that his knuckles showed whitely, and this time her laughter was almost beyond arrest.

"Although, Mr. Daver, I know nothing of hotel management, I think I could learn, and I want the position, naturally. The salary is terribly generous."

"'Terribly generous,'" repeated the man, in a murmur. "How curious those words sound in juxtaposition!"

The door opened and a woman bearing a silver tray came in. She was dressed very neatly in black. The faded eyes scarcely looked at Margaret as she stood meekly waiting while Mr. Daver spoke.

"My housekeeper. How kind of you to bring the tea, Mrs. Burton!—Mrs. Burton, this is the new secretary to the company. She must have the best room in the Keep—the Blue Room. But—ah!"—he pinched his lip anxiously—"blue may not be your colour?"

Again Margaret laughed.

"Any colour is my colour," she said. "But I haven't decided—"

"Go with Mrs. Burton; see the house—your office—your room."

He pointed to the door, and before the girl knew what she was doing she had followed the housekeeper through the door. A narrow passage connected the private office of Mr. Daver with the house, and Margaret was ushered into a large and lofty room which covered the superficial area of the Keep.

"The banquittin' 'all," said Mrs. Burton in a thin cockney voice remarkable for its monotony. "It's used as a lounge. We've only got three boarders. Mr. Daver's very partic'lar. We get a lot in for the winter."

"Three boarders isn't a very paying proposition," said the girl.

Mrs. Burton sniffed.

"Mr. Daver don't want it to pay. It's the company he likes. He only turned it into a boardin' 'ouse because he likes to see people come and go without having to talk to 'em. It's a nobby."

"A what?" asked the puzzled girl. "Oh, you mean a hobby?"

"I said a nobby," said Mrs. Burton, in her listless, uncomplaining way.

Beyond the hall was a small and cosy sitting room with French windows opening on to the lawn. Outside the windows, three people sat at tea. One was an elderly clergyman with a strong, hard face. He was eating toast and reading a church paper, oblivious of his companion. The second member of the party was a pale-faced girl about Margaret's own age. In spite of her pallor she was extraordinarily beautiful. A pair of big, dark eyes surveyed the visitor for a moment and then returned to her companion, a military-looking man of forty.

Mrs. Burton waited until they were ascending the broad stairway to the upper floor before she

"introduced" them. "The clergyman's a Reverend Dean from South Africa, the young lady's Miss Olga Crewe, the other gent is Colonel Hothling—they're boarders.—This is your room, miss."
It was indeed a gem of an apartment; the sort of room that Margaret Belman had dreamed about. It was exquisitely furnished, and, like all the other rooms at Larmes Keep (as she discovered later), was provided with its private bathroom. The walls were panelled to half their height; the ceilings heavily beamed. She guessed that beneath the parquet was the original stone-flagged floor.
Margaret looked and sighed. It was going to be very hard to refuse this post. Why she should think of refusing it at all she could not for the life of her understand.
"It's a beautiful room," she said.
Mrs. Burton cast an apathetic eye round the apartment.
"It's old," she said. "I don't like old houses. I used to live in Brixton—"
She stopped abruptly, sniffed in a deprecating way, and jingled the keys that she carried in her hand.
"You're suited, I suppose?"
"Suited? You mean, am I taking the appointment? I don't know yet."
Mrs. Burton looked round vaguely. The girl had the impression that she was trying to say something in praise of the place—-something that would prejudice her in favour of accepting the appointment. Then she spoke.
"The food's good," she said, and Margaret smiled.
When she came back through the hall she saw the three people she had seen at tea. The Colonel was walking by himself; the clergyman and the pale-faced girl were strolling across the lawn talking to one another.
Mr. Daver was sitting at his desk, his high forehead resting on his palm, and he was biting the end of a pen as Mrs. Burton closed the door on them.
"You like the room: naturally. You will start—when? Next Monday week, I think. What a relief! You have seen Mrs. Burton." He wagged a finger at her roguishly. "Ah! Now you know! It is impossible! Can I leave her to meet the duchess and speed the duke? Can I trust her to adjust the little quarrels that naturally arise between guests? You are right—I can't. I must have a lady here—I must! I must!"
He nodded emphatically, his impish brown eyes fixed on hers, the bulging upper lip grotesquely curved in a delighted grin.
"My work suffers, as you see; constantly to be brought from my studies to settle such matters as the fixing of a tennis net—intolerable!"
"You write a great deal?" she managed to ask.
She felt she must postpone her decision to the last possible moment.
"A great deal. On crime. Ah, you are interested? I am preparing an encyclopædia of crime!"
He said this impressively, dramatically.
"On crime?"
He nodded.
"It is one of my hobbies. I am a rich man and can afford hobbies. This place is a hobby. I lose four thousand a year, but I am satisfied. I pick and choose my own guests. If one bores me I tell him to go—that his room has been taken. Could I do that if they were my friends? No! They interest me; they fill the house; they give me company and amusement. When will you come?"
She hesitated.
"I think—"

"Monday week? Excellent!" He shook her hand vigorously.

"You need not be lonely. If my guests bore you, invite your own friends. Let them come as the guests of the house. Until Monday!"

She was walking down the garden path to the waiting cabman, a little dazed, more than a little undecided.

"Did you get the place, miss?" asked the friendly cabman.

"I suppose I did," replied Margaret.

She looked back toward Larmes Keep. The lawns were empty, but near at hand she had a glimpse of a woman. Only for a second, and then she disappeared in a belt of laurel that ran parallel with the boundary wall of the property. Evidently there was a rough path through the bushes, and Mrs. Burton had sought this hiding place. Her hands covered her face as she staggered forward blindly, and the faint sound of her sobs came back to the astonished girl.

"That's the housekeeper—she's a bit mad," said the cabman calmly.

CHAPTER II

GEORGE RAVINI was not an unpleasant looking man. From his own point of view, which was naturally prejudiced, he was extremely attractive, with his crisp brown hair, his handsome Neapolitan features, his height and his poise. And when to his natural advantages were added the best suit that Savile Row could create, the most spotless of gray hats, and the malacca swordstick on which one kid-gloved hand rested as upon the hilt of a foil, the shiniest of enamelled shoes, and the finest of gray silk socks, the picture was well framed and embellished.

Greatest embellishment of all were George Ravini's luck rings. He was a superstitious man and addicted to charms. On the little finger of his right hand were three gold rings, and in each ring three large diamonds. The luck stones of Ravini were one of the traditions of Saffron Hill. Most of the time he had the half-amused, half-bored smile of a man for whom life held no mysteries and could offer in experience little that was new. And the smile was justified, for George knew most of the things that were happening in London or likely to happen.

He had worked outward from a one-room house in Saffron Hill, where he first saw the light; had enlarged the narrow horizons which surrounded his childhood so that now, in place of the poverty-stricken child who had shared a bed with his father's performing monkey, he was not only the possessor of a classy flat in Half Moon Street, but the owner of the block in which it was situated. His balance at the Continental Bank was a generous one; he had securities which brought him an income beyond his needs, and a larger revenue from the two night clubs and gambling houses which he controlled, to say nothing of the perquisites which came his way from a score of other sources.

The word of Ravini was law from Leyton to Clerkenwell; his fiats were obeyed within a mile radius of Fitzroy Square; and no other gang leader in London might raise his head without George's permission save at the risk of waking in the casualty ward of the Middlesex Hospital entirely surrounded by bandages.

He waited patiently on the broad space of Waterloo Station, occasionally consulting his gold wrist watch, and surveyed with a benevolent and proprietorial eye the stream of life that flowed from the barriers.

The station clock showed a quarter after six. He glanced at his watch and scanned the crowd that was debouching from No. 7 platform. After a few minutes' scrutiny, he saw the girl, and with a pat to his cravat and a touch to the brim of his hat which set it tilting, he strolled to meet her. Margaret Belman was too intent with her own thoughts to be thinking about the debonair and youngish man who had so often sought an introduction by the conventional method of pretending they had met before. Indeed, in the excitement of her visit to Larmes Keep, she had forgotten that this pestiferous gallant existed or was likely to be waiting for her on her return from the country. George Ravini stopped and waited for her approach, smiling his approval. He liked slim girls of her colouring: girls who dressed rather severely and wore rather nice stockings and plain little hats. He raised his hat; the luck stones glittered beautifully.

"Oh!" said Margaret Belman, and stopped, too.

"Good-evening, Miss Belman," said George, flashing his white teeth. "Quite a coincidence, meeting you again."

As she attempted to walk past him, he fell in by her side.

"I wish I had my car here, I might have driven you home," he said conversationally. "I've got a new 20 Rolls—rather a neat little machine. I don't use it a great deal—I like to walk from Half Moon Street."

"Are you walking to Half Moon Street now?" she asked quietly.

But George was a man of experience.

"Your way is my way," he said.

She stopped.

"What is your name?" she asked.

"Smith—Anderton Smith," he answered readily. "Why do you want to know?"

"I want to tell the next policeman we meet," she said, and Mr. Ravini, not unaccustomed to such threats, was amused.

"Don't be a silly little girl," he said. "I'm doing no harm and you don't want to get your name in the newspapers. Besides, I should merely say that you asked me to walk with you and that we were old friends."

She looked at him steadily.

"I may meet a friend very soon who will need a lot of convincing," she said. "Will you please go away?"

George was pleased to stay, as he explained.

"What a foolish young lady you are!" he began. "I'm merely offering you the common courtesies—"

A hand gripped his arm and slowly pulled him round—and this in broad daylight on Waterloo Station, under the eyes of at least two of his own tribe. Mr. Ravini's dark eyes snapped dangerously.

And yet seemingly his assailant was a most inoffensive man. He was tall and rather melancholy-looking. He wore a frock coat buttoned tightly across his breast and a high, flat-crowned, hard felt hat. On his biggish nose a pair of steel-rimmed pince-nez were set at an awkward angle. A slither of sandy side whiskers decorated his cheek, and hooked to his arm was a lightly furled umbrella. Not that George examined these details with any care: they were rather familiar to him. He knew Mr. J.G. Reeder, detective to the Public Prosecutor's office, and the fight went out of his eyes.

"Why, Mr. Reeder!" he said, with a geniality that almost sounded sincere. "This is a pleasant surprise. Meet my young lady friend Miss Belman—I was just taking her along—"

"Not to the Flotsam Club for a cup of tea?" murmured Mr. Reeder in a tone of pain. "Not to Harraby's Restaurant? Don't tell me that, Giorgio! Dear me! How interesting either experience would be!"

He beamed upon the scowling Italian.

"At the Flotsam," he went on, "you would have been able to show the young lady where your friends caught young Lord Fallen for three thousand pounds only the night before last—so they tell me. At Harraby's you might have shown her that interesting little room where the police come in by the back way whenever you consider it expedient to betray one of your friends. She has missed a treat!"

George Ravini's smile did not harmonize with his sudden pallor.

"Now, listen, Mr. Reeder—"

"I'm sorry I can't, Giorgio." Mr. Reeder shook his head mournfully. "My time is precious. Yet, I will spare you one minute to tell you that Miss Belman is a very particular friend of mine. If her experience of to-day is repeated, who knows what might happen, for I am, as you probably know, a malicious man." He eyed the Italian thoughtfully. "Is it malice, I wonder, which inhibits a most interesting revelation which I have on the tip of my tongue? I wonder. The human mind, Mr. Ravini, is a curious and complex thing. Well, well, I must be getting along. Give my regards to your criminal associates, and if you find yourself shadowed by a gentleman from Scotland Yard, bear him no resentment. He is doing his duty. And do not lose sight of my—um—warning about this lady."

"I have said nothing to this young lady that a gentleman shouldn't."

Mr. Reeder peered at Ravini.

"If you have," he said, "you may expect to see me some time this evening—and I shall not come alone. In fact"—this in a most confidential tone—"I shall bring sufficient strong men with me to take from you the keys of your box in the Fetter Lane Safe Deposit."

That was all he said, and Ravini reeled under the threat.

Before he had quite recovered, Mr. J.G. Reeder and his charge had disappeared into the throng.

CHAPTER III

"AN interesting man," said Mr. Reeder, as the cab crossed Westminster Bridge. "He is, in fact, the most interesting man I know at this particular moment. It was fate that I should walk into him as I did. But I wish he wouldn't wear diamond rings!"
He stole a sidelong glance at his companion.
"Well, did you—um—like the place?"
"It is very beautiful," she said; without enthusiasm, "but it is rather far away from London."
His face fell.
"Have you declined the post?" he asked anxiously.
She half turned in the seat and looked at him.
"Mr. Reeder, I honestly believe you wish to see the back of me!"
To her surprise, Mr. Reeder went very red.
"Why—um—of course I do—I don't, I mean. But it seems a very good position, even as a temporary position." He blinked at her. "I shall miss you, I really shall miss you, Miss—um—Margaret. We have become such"—here he swallowed something—"good friends, but the—a certain business is on my mind—I mean, I am rather perturbed."
He looked from one window to the other as though he suspected an eavesdropper riding on the step of the cab, and then, lowering his voice:
"I have never discussed with you, my dear Miss—um—Margaret, the rather unpleasant details of my trade; but there is, or was, a gentleman named Flack—F-l-a-c-k," he spelt it. "You remember?" he asked anxiously, and when she shook her head: "I hoped that you would. One reads about these things in the public press. But five years ago you would have been a child—"
"You're very flattering," she smiled. "I was, in fact, a grown-up young lady of eighteen."
"Were you really?" asked Mr. Reeder in a hushed voice. "You surprise me! Well, Mr. Flack was the kind of person one so frequently reads about in the pages of the sensational novelist—who has not too keen a regard for the probabilities and facts of life. A master criminal, the organizer of—um—a confederation, or, as vulgar people would call it, gang."
He sighed and closed his eyes, and she thought for one moment he was praying for the iniquitous criminal.
"A brilliant criminal—it is a terrible thing to confess, but I have had a reluctant admiration for him. You see, as I have so often explained to you, I am cursed with a criminal mind. But he was mad."
"All criminals are mad: you have explained that so often," she said, a little tartly, for she was not anxious that the conversation should drift from her immediate affairs.
"But he was really mad," said Mr. Reeder with great earnestness, and tapped his forehead deliberately. "His very madness was his salvation. He did daring things, but with the cunning of a madman. He shot down two policemen in cold blood—he did this at midday in a crowded City street and got away. We caught him at last, of course. People like that are always caught in this country. I—um—assisted. In fact, I—well, I assisted! That is why I am thinking of our friend Giorgio; for it was Mr. Ravini who betrayed him to us for two thousand pounds. I negotiated the deal, Mr. Ravini being a criminal—"
She stared at him open-mouthed.
"That Italian? You don't mean that?"

Mr. Reeder nodded.

"Mr. Ravini had dealings with the Flack gang, and by chance learned of Old John's whereabouts. We took old John Flack in his sleep." Mr. Reeder sighed again. "He said some very bitter things about me. People, when they are arrested, frequently exaggerate the shortcomings of their—er—captors."

"Was he tried?" she asked.

"He was tried," said Mr. Reeder, "on a charge of murder. But of course he was mad. 'Guilty but insane' was the verdict, and he was sent to Broadmoor Criminal Lunatic Asylum."

He searched feebly in his pockets, produced a very limp packet of cigarettes, extracted one, and asked permission to smoke. She watched the damp squib of a thing drooping pathetically from his lower lip. His eyes were staring sombrely through the window at the green of the park through which they were passing, and he seemed entirely absorbed in his contemplation of nature.

"But what has that to do with my going into the country?"

Mr. Reeder brought his eyes round to survey her.

"Mr. Flack was a very vindictive man," he said, "a very brilliant man—I hate confessing this. And he has—um—a particular grudge against me, and being what he is, it would not be long before he discovered that I—er—I—am rather attached to you, Miss—Margaret."

A light dawned on her, and her whole attitude toward him changed as she gripped his arm.

"You mean, you want me out of London in case something happens? But what could happen? He's in Broadmoor, isn't he?"

Mr. Reeder scratched his chin and looked up at the roof of the cab.

"He escaped a week ago—hum! He is, I think, in London at this moment."

Margaret Belman gasped.

"Does this Italian—this Ravini man—know?"

"He does not know," said Mr. Reeder carefully, "but I think he will learn—yes, I think he will learn."

A week later, after Margaret Belman had gone, with some misgivings, to take up her new appointment, all Mr. Reeder's doubts as to the location of John Flack were dissipated.

* * * * *

There was some slight disagreement between Margaret Belman and Mr. Reeder, and it happened at lunch on the day she left London. It started in fun—not that Mr. Reeder was ever kittenish—by a certain suggestion she made. Mr. Reeder demurred. How she ever summoned the courage to tell him he was old-fashioned, Margaret never knew—but she did.

"Of course you could shave them off," she said scornfully. "It would make you look ten years younger."

"I don't think, my dear—Miss—um—Margaret, that I wish to look ten years younger," said Mr. Reeder.

A certain tenseness followed, and she went down to Siltbury feeling a little uncomfortable. Yet her heart warmed to him as she realized that his anxiety to get her out of London was dictated by a desire for her own safety. It was not until she was nearing her destination that she realized that he himself was in no ordinary danger. She must write and tell him she was sorry. She wondered who the Flacks were; the name was familiar to her, though in the days of their activity she gave little or no attention to people of their kind.

Mr. Daver, looking more impish than ever, gave her a brief interview on her arrival. It was he who took her to her office and very briefly explained her duties. They were neither heavy nor complicated, and she was relieved to discover that she had practically nothing whatever to do with the management of Larmes Keep. That was in the efficient hands of Mrs. Burton.

The staff of the hotel were housed in two cottages about a quarter of a mile from the Keep, only Mrs. Burton living on the premises.

"This keeps us more select," said Mr. Daver. "Servants are an abominable nuisance. You agree with me? I thought you would. If they are needed in the night, both cottages have telephones, and Grainger, the porter, has a pass-key to the outer door. That is an excellent arrangement—of which you approve? I am sure you do."

Conversation with Mr. Daver was a little superfluous. He supplied his own answers to all questions.

He was leaving the office when she remembered his great study.

"Mr. Daver, do you know anything about the Flacks?"

He frowned.

"Flax? Let me see, what is flax?"

She spelled the name.

"A friend of mine told me about them the other day," she said. "I thought you would know the name. They are a gang of criminals."

"Flack! To be sure—to be sure! Dear me, how very interesting! Are you also a criminologist? John Flack, George Flack, Augustus Flack"—he spoke rapidly, ticking them off on his long, tobacco-stained fingers. "John Flack is in a criminal lunatic asylum; his two brothers ... Terrible fellows, terrible, terrible fellows! What a marvellous institution is our police force! How wonderful is Scotland Yard! You agree with me? I was sure you would. Flack!" He frowned and shook his head. "I thought of dealing with the Flacks in a short monograph, but my data is not complete. Do you know them?"

She shook her head smilingly.

"No, I haven't that advantage."

"Terrible creatures," said Mr. Daver. "Amazing creatures. Who is your friend, Miss Belman? I should like to meet him. Perhaps he could tell me something more about them."

Margaret received the suggestion with dismay.

"Oh, no, you're not likely to meet him," she said hurriedly, "and I don't think he would talk even if you met him—perhaps it was indiscreet of me to mention him at all."

The conversation must have weighed on Mr. Daver's mind, for just as she was leaving her office that night for her room, a very tired girl, he knocked at the door, opened it at her invitation, and stood in the doorway.

"I have been going into the records of the Flacks," he said, "and it is surprising how little information there is. I have a newspaper cutting which says that John Flack is dead. He was the man who went into Broadmoor. Is he dead?"

Margaret shook her head.

"I couldn't tell you," she replied untruthfully. "I only heard a casual reference to him."

Mr. Daver scratched his round chin.

"I thought possibly somebody might have told you a few facts which you, so to speak, a laywoman"—he giggled—"might have regarded as unimportant, but which I—"

He hesitated expectantly.

"That is all I know, Mr. Daver," said Margaret.

She slept soundly that night; the distant hush-hush of the waves as they rolled up the long beach of Siltbury Bay lulling her to dreamless slumber.

Her duties did not begin till after breakfast, which she had in her office, and the largest part was the checking of the accounts. Apparently, Mrs. Burton attended to that side of the management, and it was only at the month's end, when checks were to be drawn, that her work was likely to be heavy. In the main, her day was taken up with correspondence. There were some one hundred and forty applicants for her post, who had to be answered; there were, in addition, a number of letters from persons who desired accommodation at Larmes Keep. All these had to be taken to Mr. Daver, and it was remarkable how fastidious he was. For example:

"The Reverend John Quinton? No, no; we have one parson in the house, that is enough. Tell him we are very sorry but we are full up. Mrs. Bagley wishes to bring her daughter? Certainly not! I cannot have children distracting me with their noise. You agree? I see you do. Who is this woman—'coming for a rest cure'? That means she's ill. I cannot have Larmes Keep turned into a sanitarium. You may tell them all that there will be no accommodations until after Christmas. After Christmas they can all come—I am going abroad."

The evenings were her own. She could, if she desired, go into Siltbury, which boasted two cinemas and a pierrot party, and Mr. Daver put the hotel car at her disposal for the purpose. She preferred, however, to wander through the grounds. The estate was much larger than she had supposed. Behind, to the south of the house, it extended for half a mile, the boundary to the east being represented by the cliffs, along which a breast-high rubble wall had been built, and with excellent reason, for here the cliff fell sheer two hundred feet to the rocks below. At one place there had been a little landslide; the wall had been carried away and the gap had been temporarily filled by a wooden fence. Some attempt had been made to create a nine-hole golf course, she saw, as she wandered round, but evidently Mr. Daver had grown tired of this enterprise, for the greens were knee-high in waving grasses.

At the southwest corner of the house, and distant about a hundred yards, was a big clump of rhododendrons, and this she explored, following a twisting path that led to the heart of the bushes. Quite unexpectedly she came upon an old well. The brickwork about it was in ruins; the well itself was boarded in. On the weather-beaten roof-piece above the windlass was a small wooden notice board, evidently fixed for the enlightenment of visitors:

"This well was used from 935 to 1794. It was filled in by the present owners of the property in May, 1914, 135 cartloads of rock and gravel being used for the purpose."

It was a pleasant occupation, standing by that ancient well and picturing the collar serfs and barefooted peasants who through the ages had stood where she was standing. As she came out of the bushes she saw the pale-faced Olga Crewe.

Margaret had not spoken either to the Colonel or to the clergyman; either she had avoided them, or they her. Olga Crewe she had not seen, and now she would have turned away, but the girl moved across to intercept her.

"You are the new secretary, aren't you?"

Her voice was musical, rather alluring. "Custardy" was Margaret's mental classification.

"Yes, I'm Miss Belman."

The girl nodded.

"My name you know, I suppose? Are you going to be terribly bored here?"

"I don't think so," smiled Margaret. "It is a beautiful spot."

The eyes of Olga Crewe surveyed the scene critically.

"I suppose it is—very beautiful, yes, but one gets very tired of beauty after a few years."

Margaret listened in astonishment.

"Have you been here so long?"

"I've practically lived here since I was a child. I thought Joe would have told you that: he's an inveterate old gossip."

"Joe?" She was puzzled.

"The cab driver, news-gatherer and distributor."

She looked at Larmes Keep and frowned.

"Do you know what they used to call this place, Miss Belman? The House of Tears—the Château des Larmes."

"Why ever?" asked Margaret.

Olga Crewe shrugged her pretty shoulders.

"Some sort of tradition, I suppose, that goes back to the days of Baron Augernvert, who built it. The locals have corrupted the name to Larmes Keep. You ought to see the dungeons."

"Are there dungeons?" asked Margaret in surprise, and Olga nodded. For the first time she seemed amused.

"If you saw them and the chains and the rings in the walls and the stone floors worn thin by bare feet, you might guess how its name arose."

Margaret stared back toward the Keep. The sun was setting behind it, and silhouetted as it was against the red light there was something ominous and sinister in that dark, squat pile.

"How very unpleasant!" she said, and shivered.

Olga Crewe laughed.

"Have you seen the cliffs?" she said, and led the way back to the long wall, and for a quarter of an hour they stood, their arms resting on the parapet, looking down into the gloom.

"You ought to get someone to row you round the face of the cliff. It's simply honeycombed with caves," she said. "There's one at the water's edge that tunnels right under the Keep. When the tides are unusually high they are flooded. I wonder Daver doesn't write a book about it."

There was just the faintest hint of a sneer in her tone, but it did not escape Margaret's attention.

"That must be the entrance," she said, pointing down to a swirl of water that seemed to run right up to the face of the cliff.

Olga nodded.

"At high tide you wouldn't notice that," she said, and then, turning abruptly, she asked the girl if she had seen the bathing pool.

This was an oblong bath, sheltered by high box hedges and lined throughout with blue tiles; a delightfully inviting plunge.

"Nobody uses it but myself. Daver would die at the thought of jumping in."

Whenever she referred to Mr. Daver it was in a scarcely veiled tone of contempt. She was not more charitable when she referred to the other guests. As they were nearing the house, Olga said, apropos of nothing:

"I shouldn't talk too much to Daver if I were you. Let him do the talking: he likes it."

"What do you mean?" asked Margaret quietly, but at that moment Olga left her side without any word of farewell and went toward the Colonel, who was standing, a cigar between his teeth, watching their approach.

The House of Tears!

Margaret remembered the title as she was undressing that night, and, despite her self-possession, shivered a little.

CHAPTER IV

THE policeman who stood on the corner where Bennett Street meets Hyde Lane had the world to himself. It was nearing three o'clock on a chilly morning of early fall. The good and bad of Mayfair slept—all, apparently, except Mr. J.G. Reeder, Friend of the Law and Terror of Criminals. Police Officer Dyer saw the yellow light behind the casemented window and smiled benevolently.

The night was so still that when he heard a key turn in a lock, he looked over his shoulder, thinking the noise was from the house immediately behind him. But the door did not move. Instead he saw a woman appear on the top doorstep five houses away.

"Officer!"

The voice was low, cultured, very urgent. He moved more quickly toward her than policemen usually move.

"Anything wrong, miss?"

Her face, he noticed in his worldly way, was "made up"; the cheeks heavily rouged, the lips a startling red for one who was afraid. He supposed her to be pretty in normal circumstances, but was doubtful as to her age. She wore a long black dressing gown, fastened up to her chin. Also he saw that the hand that gripped the railing which flanked the steps glittered in the lights of the street lamps.

"I don't know—quite. I am—alone in the—house and I—thought I heard—something."

Three words to a breath. Obviously she was terrified.

"Haven't you any servants in the house?"

The constable was surprised, a little shocked.

"No. I only came back from Paris at midnight—we took the house furnished—I think the servants I engaged mistook the date of my return. I am Mrs. Granville Fornese."

In a dim way he remembered the name. It had that value of familiarity which makes even the most assured hesitate to deny acquaintance. It sounded grand, too—the name of a Somebody. And Bennett Street was a place where Somebodies live.

The officer peered into the dark hall.

"If you would put the light on, madam, I will look round."

She shook her head; he almost felt the shiver of her.

"The lights aren't working. That is what frightened me. They were quite all right when I went to bed at one o'clock. Something woke me—I don't know what—and I switched on the lamp by the side of my bed, but there was no light. I keep a little portable battery lamp in my bag. I found this and turned it on."

She stopped, set her teeth in a mirthless smile. Police Officer Dyer saw the dark eyes were staringly wide.

"I saw—I don't know what it was—just a patch of black, like somebody crouching by the wall. Then it disappeared. And the door of my room was wide open. I closed and locked it when I went to bed."

The officer pushed open the door wider, sent a white beam of light along the passage. There was a small hall table against the wall, where a telephone instrument stood. Striding into the hall, he took up the instrument and lifted the hook: the 'phone was dead.

"Does this—"

So far he got with the question, and then stopped. From somewhere above him he heard a fault but sustained creak—the sound of a foot resting on a faulty floor board. Mrs. Fornese was still standing in the open doorway, and he went back to her.

"Have you a key to this door?" he asked, and she shook her head.

He felt along the inner surface of the lock and found a stop-catch, pushed it up.

"I'll have to 'phone from somewhere. You'd better—"

What had she best do? He was a plain police constable and was confronted with a delicate situation.

"Is there anywhere you could go—friends?"

"No." There was no indecision in that word. And then: "Doesn't Mr. Reeder live opposite? Somebody told me—"

In the house opposite a light showed. Mr. Dyer surveyed the lighted window dubiously. It stood for the elegant apartment of one who held a post superior to chief constables. No. 7 Bennett Street had been at a recent period converted into flats, and into one of these Mr. Reeder had moved from his suburban home. Why he should take a flat in that exclusive and interesting neighbourhood, nobody knew. He was credited by criminals with being fabulously rich; he was undoubtedly a snug man.

The constable hesitated, searched his pocket for the smallest coin of the realm, and, leaving the lady on the doorstep, crossed the road and tossed a ha'penny to the window. A second later the casement window was pushed open.

"Excuse me, Mr. Reeder, could I see you for a second?"

The head and shoulders disappeared, and in a very short time Mr. Reeder appeared in the doorway. He was so fully dressed that he might have been expecting the summons. The frock coat was tightly buttoned, on the back of his head his flat-topped felt hat, on his nose the pince-nez through which he never looked were askew.

"Anything wrong, constable?" he asked gently.

"Could I use your 'phone? There is a lady over there—Mrs. Fornese—alone—heard somebody in the house. I heard it, too—"

He heard a short scream—a crash—and jumped round. The door of No. 4 was closed. Mrs. Fornese had disappeared.

In six strides Mr. Reeder had crossed the road and was at the door. Stooping, he pressed in the flap of the letter box and listened. No noise but the ticking of a clock—a faint sighing sound.

"Hum!" said Mr. Reeder, scratching his long nose thoughtfully. "Hum—would you be so kind as to tell me all about this—um—happening?"

The police constable repeated the story, more coherently.

"You fastened the spring lock so that it would not move? A wise precaution."

Mr. Reeder frowned. Without another word he crossed the street and disappeared into his flat. There was a small drawer at the back of his writing desk. This he unlocked and, taking out a leather hold-all, unrolled this and selecting three curious steel instruments that were not unlike small hooks, fitted one into a wooden handle and returned to the constable.

"This, I fear, is—I will not say 'unlawful,' for a gentleman of my position is incapable of an unlawful act—shall I say 'unusual'?"

All the time he talked in his soft, apologetic way, he was working at the lock, turning the instrument first one way and then the other. Presently, with a click, the lock turned and Mr. Reeder pushed open the door.

"I think I had better borrow your lamp—thank you."

He took the electric lamp from the constable's hand and flung a white circle of light into the hall. There was no sign of life. He cast the beam up the stairs, and, stooping his head, listened. There came to his ear no sound, and noiselessly he stepped farther into the hall.

The passage continued beyond the foot of the stairs, and at the end was a door which apparently gave to the domestic quarters of the house. To the policeman's surprise, it was the door which Mr. Reeder examined. He turned the handle, but the door did not move, and, stooping, he squinted at the keyhole.

"There was somebody—upstairs," began the policeman with respectful hesitation.

"There was somebody upstairs," repeated Mr. Reeder absently. "You heard a creaky board, I think."

He came slowly back to the foot of the stairs and looked up. Then he cast his lamp along the floor of the hall.

"No sawdust," he said, speaking to himself, "so it can't be that."

"Shall I go up, sir?" said the policeman, and his foot was on the lower tread when Mr. Reeder, displaying unexpected strength in so weary-looking a man, pushed him back.

"I think not, constable," he said firmly. "If the lady is upstairs she will have heard our voices. But the lady is not upstairs."

"Do you think she's in the kitchen, sir?" asked the puzzled policeman.

Mr. Reeder shook his head sadly.

"Alas! how few modern women spend their time in a kitchen!" he said, and made an impatient clucking noise, but whether this was a protest against the falling off of woman's domestic qualities, or whether he "tchk'd" for some other reason, it was difficult to say, for he was a very preoccupied man.

He swung the lamp back to the door.

"I thought so," he said, with a note of relief in his voice. "There are two walking sticks in the hall stand. Will you get one of them, constable?"

Wondering, the officer obeyed, and came back, handing a long cherry-wood stick with a crooked handle to Mr. Reeder, who examined it in the light of his lamp.

"Dust-covered and left by the previous owner. The spike in place of the ferrule shows that it was purchased in Switzerland. Probably you are not interested in detective stories and have never read of the gentleman whose method I am plagiarizing?"

"No, sir," said the mystified officer.

Mr. Reeder examined the stick again.

"It is a thousand pities that it is not a fishing rod," he said. "Will you stay here, and don't move." And then he began to crawl up the stairs on his knees, waving his stick in front of him in the most eccentric manner. He held it up, lifting the full length of his arm, and as he crawled upward he struck at imaginary obstacles. Higher and higher he went, silhouetted against the reflected light of the lamp he carried, and Police Constable Dyer watched him open-mouthed.

"Don't you think I'd better—"

He got as far as this when the thing happened. There was an explosion that deafened him; the air was suddenly filled with flying clouds of smoke and dust; he heard the crackle of wood and the pungent scent of something burning. Dazed and stupefied, he stood stock still, gaping up at Mr. Reeder, who was sitting on a stair, picking little splinters of wood from his coat.

"I think you may come up in perfect safety," said Mr. Reeder, with great calmness.

"What—what was it?" asked the officer.

The enemy of criminals was dusting his hat tenderly, though this the officer could not see.

"You may come up."

Police Constable Dyer ran up the stairs and followed the other along the broad landing till he stopped and focussed in the light of his lamp a queer-looking and obviously home-made spring gun, the muzzle of which was trained through the banisters so that it covered the stairs up which he had ascended.

"There was," said Mr. Reeder carefully, "a piece of black thread stretched across the stairs, so that any person who bulged or broke that thread was certain to fire the gun."

"But—but the lady?"

Mr. Reeder coughed.

"I do not think she is in the house," he said, ever so gently. "I rather imagine that she went through the back. There is a back entrance to the mews, is there not? And that by this time she is a long way from the house. I sympathize with her—this little incident has occurred too late for the morning newspapers and she will have to wait for the sporting editions before she learns that I am still alive."

The police officer drew a long breath.

"I think I'd better report this, sir."

"I think you had," sighed Mr. Reeder. "And will you ring up Inspector Simpson and tell him that, if he comes this way, I should like to see him?"

Again the policeman hesitated.

"Don't you think we'd better search the house? They may have done away with this woman."

Mr. Reeder shook his head.

"They have not done away with any woman," he said decisively. "The only thing they have done away with is one of Mr. Simpson's pet theories."

"But, Mr. Reeder, why did this lady come to the door?"

Mr. Reeder patted him benignantly on the arm, as a mother might pat a child who asks a foolish question.

"The lady had been standing at the door for half an hour," he said gently; "on and off for half an hour, constable, hoping against hope, one imagines, that she would attract my attention. But I was looking at her from a room that was not—er—illuminated. I did not show myself because I—er—have a very keen desire to live!"

On this baffling note Mr. Reeder went into his house.

CHAPTER V

MR. REEDER sat at his ease, wearing a pair of grotesquely painted velvet slippers, a cigarette hanging from his lips, and explained to the detective inspector who had called in the early hours of the morning his reason for adopting a certain conclusion.

"I do not imagine for one moment that it was my friend Ravini. He is less subtle, in addition to which he has little or no intelligence. You will find that this coup has been planned for months, though it has only been put into execution to-day. No. 4 Bennett Street is the property of an old gentleman who spends most of his time in Italy. He has been in the habit of letting the house furnished for years; in fact, it was only vacated a month ago."

"You think, then," said the puzzled Simpson, "That the people, whoever they were, rented the house—"

Mr. Reeder shook his head.

"Even that I doubt," he said. "They have probably an order in view, and in some way got rid of the caretaker. They knew I would be at home last night, because I am always at home—um—on most nights since—" Mr. Reeder coughed in his embarrassment. "A young friend of mine has recently left London—I do not like going out alone."

And to Simpson's horror, a pinkish flush suffused the sober countenance of Mr. Reeder.

"A few weeks ago," he went on, with a pitiable attempt at airiness, "I used to dine out, attend a concert or one of those exquisite melodramas which have such an appeal to me."

"Whom do you suspect?" interrupted Simpson, who had not been called from his bed in the middle of the night to discuss the virtue of melodrama. "The Gregorys or the Donovans?" He named two groups that had excellent reason to be annoyed with Mr. Reeder and his methods.

J.G. Reeder shook his head.

"Neither," he said. "I think—indeed I am sure—that we must go back to ancient history for the cause."

Simpson opened his eyes.

"Not Flack?" he asked incredulously. "He's hiding—he wouldn't start anything so soon."

Mr. Reeder nodded.

"John Flack. Who else could have planned such a thing? The art of it! And, Mr. Simpson"—he leaned over and tapped the inspector on the breast—"there has not been a big robbery in London since Flack went to Broadmoor. You'll get the biggest of all in a week! The coup of coups! His mad brain is planning it now!"

"He's finished," said Simpson with a frown.

Mr. Reeder smiled wanly.

"We shall see. This little affair of to-night is a sighting shot—a mere nothing. But I am rather glad I am not—er—dining out in these days. On the other hand, our friend Giorgio Ravini is a notorious diner-out. Would you mind calling up Vine Street police station and finding out whether they have any casualties to report?"

Vine Street, which knew the movements of so many people, replied instantly that Mr. Giorgio Ravini was out of town; it was believed he was in Paris.

"Dear me!" said Mr. Reeder, in his feeble, aimless way. "How very wise of Giorgio—and how much wiser it will be if he stays there!"

Inspector Simpson rose and shook himself. He was a stout, hearty man who had that habit.

"I'll get down to the Yard and report this," he said. "It may not have been Flack, after all. He's a gang leader and he'd be useless without his crowd, and they are scattered. Most of them are in the Argentine."

"Ha-ha!" said Mr. Reeder, without any evidence of joy.

"What the devil are you laughing about?"

The other was instantly apologetic.

"It was what I would describe as a sceptical laugh. The Argentine! Do criminals really go to the Argentine except in those excellent works of fiction which one reads on trains? A tradition, Mr. Simpson, dating back to the ancient times when there was no extradition treaty between the two countries. Scattered, yes. I look forward to the day when I shall gather them all together under one roof. It will be a very pleasant morning for me, Mr. Simpson, when I can walk along the gallery, looking through the little peep-holes and watch them sewing mail bags—I know of no more sedative occupation than a little needlework! In the meantime, watch your banks—Old John is seventy years of age and has no time to waste. History will be made in the City of London before many days are past! I wonder where in Paris I could find Ravini?"

George Ravini was not the type of man whose happiness depended upon the good opinion which others held of him. Otherwise, he might well have spent his life in abject misery. As for Mr. Reeder—he discussed that interesting police official over a glass of wine and a good cigar in his Half Moon Street flat.

It was a showy, even a flashy, little ménage, for Mr. Ravini's motto was everything of the best and as much of it as possible, and his drawing room was rather like an over-ornamented French clock—all gilt and enamel where it was not silk and damask.

To his subordinate, one Lew Steyne, Mr. Ravini revealed his mind.

"If that old so-and-so knew half he pretends to know, I'd be taking the first train to Bordighera," he said. "But Reeder's a bluff. He's clever up to a point, but you can say that about almost any bogey you ever met."

"You could show him a few points," said the sycophantic Lew, and Mr. Ravini smiled and stroked his trim moustache.

"I wouldn't be surprised if the old nut is crazy about that girl. May and December—can you beat it!"

"What's she like?" asked Lew. "I never got a proper look at her face."

Mr. Ravini kissed the tips of his fingers ecstatically and threw the caress to the painted ceiling.

"Anyway, he can't frighten me, Lew. You know what I am. If I want anything I go after it, and I keep going after it till I get it! I've never seen anybody like her. Quite the lady and everything, and what she can see in an old such-and-such like Reeder licks me!"

"Women are funny," mused Lew. "You wouldn't think that a typist would chuck a man like you—"

"She hasn't chucked me," said Mr. Ravini curtly. "I'm simply not acquainted with her, that's all. But I'm going to be. Where's this place?"

"Siltbury," said Lew.

He took a piece of paper from his waistcoat pocket, unfolded it, and read the pencilled words.

"Larmes Keep, Siltbury—it's on the Southern. I trailed her when she left London with her boxes. Old Reeder came down to see her off, and looked about as happy as a wet cat."

"A boarding house," mused Ravini. "That's a queer sort of job."

"She's secretary," reported Lew. (He had conveyed this information at least four times, but Mr. Lew Steyne was one of those curious people who like to treat old facts as new sensations.)

"It's a posh place, too," said Lew. "Not like the ordinary boarding house—only swells go there. They charge twenty guineas a week for a room, and you're lucky if you get in."
Ravini thought on this, fondling his chin.
"This is a free country," he said. "What's to stop me staying at—what's the name of the place? Larmes Keep? I've never taken 'No' from a woman in my life. Half the time they don't mean it. Anyway, she's got to give me a room if I've the money to pay for it."
"Suppose she writes to Reeder?" suggested Lew.
"Let her write!" Ravini's tone was defiant, whatever might be the state of his mind. "What'll he have on me? It's no crime to pay your rent at a boarding house, is it?"
"Try her with one of your luck rings," grinned Lew.
Ravini looked at them admiringly.
"I couldn't get 'em off," he said, "and I'd never dream of parting with my luck that way. She'll be easy as soon as she knows me—don't you worry."
By a curious coincidence, as he was turning out of Half Moon Street the next morning, he met the one man in the world he did not wish to see. Fortunately, Lew had taken his suitcase on to the station, and there was nothing in Mr. Ravini's appearance to suggest that he was setting forth on an affair of gallantry.
Mr. Reeder looked at the man's diamonds glittering in the daylight. They seemed to exercise a peculiar fascination on the detective.
"The luck still holds, Giorgio," he said, and Georgio smiled complacently. "And whither do you go on this beautiful September morning? To bank your nefarious gains, or to get a quick visa to your passport?"
"Strolling round," said Ravini airily. "Just taking a little constitutional." And then, with a spice of mischief: "What's happened to that busy you were putting on to tail me up? I haven't seen him."
Mr. Reeder looked past him to the distance.
"He has never been far from you, Giorgio," he said gently. "He followed you from the Flotsam last night to that peculiar little party you attended in Maida Vale, and he followed you home at 2:15 A.M."
Giorgio's jaw dropped.
"You don't mean he's—" He looked round. The only person visible was a benevolent-looking man who might have been a doctor, from his frock coat and top hat.
"That's not him?" frowned Ravini.
"He,'" corrected Mr. Reeder. "Your English is not yet perfect."
Ravini did not leave London immediately. It was two o'clock before he had shaken off the watcher, and five minutes later he was on the Southern Express. The same old cabman who had brought Margaret Belman to Larmes Keep carried him up the long, winding hill road through the broad gates to the front of the house, and deposited him under the portico. An elderly porter, in a smart, well-fitting uniform, came out to greet the stranger.
"Mr.—"
"Ravini," said that gentleman. "I haven't booked a room."
The porter shook his head.
"I'm afraid we have no accommodation," he said. "Mr. Daver makes it a rule not to take guests unless they've booked their rooms in advance. I will see the secretary."
Ravini followed him into the spacious hall and sat down on one of the beautiful chairs. This, he decided, was something outside the usual run of boarding houses. It was luxurious even for a hotel. No other guests were visible. Presently he heard a step on the flagged floor and rose to

meet the eyes of Margaret Belman. Though they were unfriendly, she betrayed no sign of recognition. He might have been the veriest stranger.

"The proprietor makes it a rule not to accept guests without previous correspondence," she said. "In those circumstances, I am afraid we cannot offer you accommodation."

"I've already written to the proprietor," said Ravini, never at a loss for a glib lie. "Go along, young lady, be a sport and see what you can do for me."

Margaret hesitated. Her own inclination was to order his suitcase to be put in the waiting cab; but she was part of the organization of the place, and she could not let her private prejudices interfere with her duties.

"Will you wait?" she said, and went in search of Mr. Daver.

That great criminologist was immersed in a large book and looked up over his horn-rimmed spectacles.

"Ravini? A foreign gentleman? Of course he is. A stranger within our gate, as you would say. It is very irregular, but in the circumstances—yes, I think so."

"He isn't the type of man you ought to have here, Mr. Daver," she said firmly. "A friend of mine who knows these people says he is a member of the criminal classes."

Mr. Daver's ludicrous eyebrows rose.

"The criminal classes! What an extraordinary opportunity to study, as it were, at first hand! You agree? I knew you would! Let him stay. If he bores me, I will send him away."

Margaret went back, a little disappointed, feeling rather foolish, if the truth be told. She found Ravini waiting, caressing his moustache, a little less assured than he had been when she had left him.

"Mr. Daver says you may stay. I will send the housekeeper to you," she said, and went in search of Mrs. Burton and gave that doleful woman the necessary instructions.

She was angry with herself that she had not been more explicit in dealing with Mr. Daver. She might have told him that if Ravini stayed she would leave. She might even have explained the reason why she did not wish the Italian to remain in the house. She was in the fortunate position, however, that she had not to see the guests unless they expressed a wish to interview her, and Ravini was too wise to pursue his advantage.

That night, when she went to her room, she sat down and wrote a long letter to Mr. Reeder, but thought better of it and tore it up. She could not run to J.G. Reeder every time she was annoyed. He had a sufficiency of trouble, she decided, and here she was right. Even as she wrote, Mr. Reeder was examining with great interest the spring gun which had been devised for his destruction.

CHAPTER VI

TO do Ravini justice, he made no attempt to approach the girl, though she had seen him at a distance. The second day after his arrival, he had passed her on the lawn with no more than a nod and a smile, and indeed he seemed to have found another diversion, if not another objective, for he was scarcely away from Olga Crewe's side. Margaret saw them in the evening, leaning over the cliff wall, and George Ravini seemed remarkably pleased with himself. He was exhibiting his famous luck stones to Olga. Margaret saw her examine the rings and evidently made some remark upon them which sent Ravini into fits of laughter.

It was on the third day of his stay that he spoke to Margaret. They met in the big hall, and she would have passed on, but he stood in her way.

"I hope we're not going to be bad friends, Miss Belman," he said. "I'm not giving you any trouble, and I'm ready to apologize for the past. Could a gentleman be fairer than that?"

"I don't think you've anything to apologize for, Mr. Ravini," she said, a little relieved by his tone, and more inclined to be civil. "Now that you have so obviously found another interest in life, are you enjoying your stay?"

"It's perfectly marvellous," he said conventionally, for he was a man who loved superlatives.

"And say, Miss Belman, who is this young lady staying here, Miss Olga Crewe?"

"She's a guest: I know nothing about her."

"What a peach!" he said enthusiastically, and Margaret was amused.

"And a lady, every inch of her," he went on. "I must say I'm putty in the hands of real ladies! There's something about 'em that's different to shop girls and typists and people of that kind. Not that you're a typist," he went on hastily. "I regard you as a lady, too. Every inch of one. I'm thinking about sending for my Rolls to take her for a drive round the country. You're not jealous?"

Anger and amusement struggled for expression, but Margaret's sense of humour won, and she laughed long and silently all the way to her office.

Soon after this Mr. Ravini disappeared. So also did Olga. Margaret saw them coming into the hall about eleven, and the girl looked paler than usual and sweeping past her without a word, ran up the stairs. Margaret surveyed the young man curiously. His face was flushed, his eyes of an unusual brightness.

"I'm going up to town to-morrow," he said. "Early train—you needn't 'phone for a cab. I can walk down the hill."

He was almost incoherent.

"You're tired of Larmes Keep?"

"Eh? Tired? No, I'm not! This is the place for me!"

He smoothed back his dark hair and she saw his hand trembling so much that the luck stones flickered and flashed like fire. She waited until he had disappeared, and then she went upstairs and knocked at Olga's door. The girl's room was next to hers.

"Who's that?" asked a voice sharply.

"Miss Belman."

The key turned, the door opened. Only one light was burning in the room, so that her face was in shadow.

"Do you want anything?" she asked.

"May I come in?" asked Margaret. "There's something I wish to say to you."

Olga hesitated. Then:

"Come in," she said. "I've been snivelling. I hope you don't mind."

Her eyes were red, the stains of tears were still on her face.

"This damned place depresses me awfully," she excused herself as she dabbed her cheeks with a handkerchief. "What do you want to see me about?"

"Mr. Ravini. I suppose you know he is a—crook?"

Olga stared at her and her eyes went hard.

"I don't know that I am particularly interested in Mr. Ravini," she said slowly. "Why do you come to tell me this?"

Margaret was in a dilemma.

"I don't know—I thought you were getting rather friendly with him—it was very impertinent of me."

"I think it was," said Olga Crewe coldly, and the rebuff was such that Margaret's face went scarlet.

She was angry with herself when she went into her own room that night, and anger is a bad bedmate, and the most wakeful of all human emotions. She tossed from side to side in her bed, tried to forget there were such persons as Olga Crewe and George Ravini, tried every device she could think of to induce sleep, and was almost successful when—

She sat up in bed. Fingers were scrabbling on the panel of her door; not exactly scratching or tapping. She switched on the light, and, getting out of bed, walked to the door and listened. Somebody was there. The handle turned in her hand.

"Who's there?" she asked.

"Let me in, let me in!"

It was a frantic whisper, but she recognized the voice—Ravini!

"I can't let you in. Go away, please, or I'll telephone—"

She heard a sound, a curious muffled sound—sobbing—a man! And then the voice ceased. Her heart racing madly, she stood by the door, her ear to the panel, listening, but no other sound came.

She spent the rest of the night sitting up in bed, a quilt about her shoulders, listening, listening—Day broke grayly; the sun came up. She lay down and fell asleep. It was the maid bringing tea that woke her, and, getting out of bed, she opened the door.

"A nice morning, miss," said the fresh-faced country girl brightly.

Margaret nodded. As soon as the girl was gone she opened the door again to examine more closely the thing she had seen. It was a triangular patch of stuff that had been torn and caught in one of the splinters of the old oaken door. She took it off carefully and laid it in the palm of her hand. A jagged triangle of pink silk. She put it on her dressing table wonderingly. There must be an end to this. If Ravini was not leaving that morning, or Mr. Daver would not ask him to go, she would leave for London that night.

As she left her room, she met the housemaid.

"That man in No. 7 has gone, miss," the woman reported, "but he's left his pajamas behind."

"Gone already?"

"Must have gone last night, miss. His bed hasn't been slept in."

Margaret followed her along the passage to Ravini's room. His bag was gone, but on the pillow, neatly folded, was a suit of pink silk pajamas, and, bending over, she saw that the front of the coat was torn. A little triangular patch of pink silk had been ripped out!

CHAPTER VII

WHEN a nimble old man dropped from a high wall at midnight and, stopping only to wipe the blood from his hands—for he had come upon a guard patrolling the grounds in his flight—and walked briskly toward London, peering into every side lane for the small car that had been left for him, he brought a new complication into many lives, and for three people at least marked the date of their passing in the Book of Fate.

Police Headquarters were not slow to employ the press to advertise their wants. But the escape from Broadmoor of a homicidal maniac is something which is not to be rushed immediately into print. Not once but many times had the help of the public been enlisted in a vain endeavour to bring Old John Flack to justice. His description had been circulated, his haunts had been watched, without there being any successful issue to the search.

There was a conference at Scotland Yard, which Mr. Reeder attended; and they were five very serious men who gathered round the superintendent's desk, and mainly the talk was of bullion and of "noses," by which inelegant term is meant the inevitable police informer.

Crazy John "fell" eventually through the treachery of an outside helper. Ravini, the most valuable of gang leaders, had been employed to "cover" a robbery at the Leadenhall Bank. Bullion was John Flack's specialty; it was not without its interest for Mr. Ravini.

The theft had been successful. One Sunday morning two cars drove out of the courtyard of the Leadenhall Bank. By the side of the driver of each car sat a man in the uniform of the Metropolitan Police; inside each car was another officer. A City policeman saw the cars depart, but accepted the presence of the uniformed men and did not challenge the drivers. It was not an unusual event; transfers of gold or stocks on Sunday morning had been witnessed before, but usually the City authorities had been notified. He called Old Jewry station on the telephone to report the occurrence, but by this time John Flack was well away.

It was Ravini, cheated, as he thought, of his fair share of the plunder, who betrayed the old man; the gold was never recovered.

England had been ransacked to find John Flack's headquarters, but without success. There was not a hotel or boarding-house keeper who had not received his portrait, or one who recognized him in any guise.

The exhaustive inquiries which followed his arrest did little to increase the knowledge of the police. Flack's lodgings were found—a furnished room in Bloomsbury which he had occupied at rare intervals for years. But here were discovered no documents which gave the slightest clue to the real headquarters of the gang. Probably they had none. They were chosen and discarded as opportunity arose or emergency dictated, though it was clear that the old man had something in the nature of a general staff to assist him.

"Anyway," said Big Bill Gordon, chief of the Big Five, "he'll not start anything in the way of a bullion steal. His mind will be fully occupied with ways and means of getting out of the country."

It was Mr. Reeder's head that shook.

"The nature of criminals may change, but their vanities persist," he said, in his precise, grandiloquent way. "Mr. Flack prides himself not upon his murders but upon his robberies, and he will signify his return to freedom in the usual manner."

"His gang is scattered—" began Simpson.

J.G. Reeder silenced him with a sad, sweet smile.

"There is plenty of evidence, Mr. Simpson, that the gang has coagulated again. It is—um—an ugly word, but I can think of no better. Mr. Flack's escape from the—er—public institution where he was confined shows evidence of good team work. The rope, the knife with which he killed the unfortunate warder, the kit of tools, the almost certainty that there was a car waiting to take him away, are all symptomatic of gang work. And what has Mr. Flack—"

"I wish to God you wouldn't call him 'Mr.' Flack!" said Big Bill explosively.

J.G. Reeder blinked.

"I have an ineradicable respect for age," he said in a hushed voice, "but a greater respect for the dead. I am hoping to increase my respect for Mr. Flack in the course of the next month."

"If it's gang work," interrupted Simpson, "who are with him? The old crowd is either jailed or out of the country. I know what you're thinking about, Mr. Reeder: you've got your mind on what happened last night. I've been thinking it over, and it's quite likely that the man trap wasn't fixed by Flack at all, but by one of the other crowd. Do you know Donovan's out of Dartmoor? He has no reason for loving you."

Mr. Reeder raised his hand in protest.

"On the contrary, Joe Donovan, when I saw him in the early hours this morning, was a very affable and penitent man who deeply regretted the unkind things he said of me as he left the Old Bailey dock. He lives at Kilburn and spent last evening at a local cinema with his wife and daughter. No, it wasn't Donovan. He is not a brainy man. Only John Flack, with his dramatic sense, could have staged that little comedy which was so nearly a tragedy."

"You were nearly killed, they tell me, Reeder?" said Big Bill.

Mr. Reeder shook his head.

"I was not thinking of that particular tragedy. It was in my mind before I went up the stairs to force the door into the kitchen. If I had done that, I think I should have shot Mr. Flack, and there would have been an end of all our speculations and troubles."

Mr. Simpson was examining some papers that were on the table before him.

"If Flack's going after bullion, he's got very little chance. The only big movement is that of a hundred and twenty thousand sovereigns for Australia which goes by way of Tilbury to-morrow morning or the next day from the Bank of England, and it is impossible that Flack could organize a steal at such short notice."

Mr. Reeder was suddenly alert and interested.

"A hundred and twenty thousand sovereigns," he murmured, rubbing his chin irritably. "Ten tons. It goes by train?"

"By lorry, with ten armed men—one per ton," said Simpson humorously. "I don't think you need worry about that."

Mr. J.G. Reeder's lips were pursed as though he were whistling, but no sound issued. Presently he spoke.

"Flack was originally a chemist," he said slowly. "I don't suppose there is a better criminal chemist in England than Mr. Flack."

"Why do you say that?" asked Simpson with a frown.

Mr. Reeder shrugged his shoulders.

"I have a sixth sense," he said, almost apologetically, "and invariably I associate some peculiar quality with every man and woman who—um—passes under review. For example, Mr. Simpson, when I think of you, I have an instinctive, shadowy thought of a prize ring where I first had the pleasure of seeing you." (Simpson, who had been an amateur welterweight, grinned appreciatively.) "And my mind never rests upon Mr. Flack except in the surroundings of a laboratory with test tubes and all the paraphernalia of experimental chemistry. As for the little affair last night, I was not unprepared for it, but I suspected a trap—literally a—um—trap. Some evilly disposed person once tried the very same trick upon me; cut away the landing so that I should fall upon very unpleasant sharp spikes. I looked for sawdust the moment I went into the house, and when that was not present I guessed the gun."

"But how did you know there was anything?" asked Big Bill curiously.

Mr. Reeder smiled.

"I have a criminal mind," he said.

He went back to his flat in Bennett Street, his mind equally divided between Margaret Belman, safe in Sussex, and the ability of one normal lorry to carry a hundred and twenty thousand sovereigns. Such little details interested Mr. Reeder. Almost the first thing he did when he reached his flat was to call up a haulage contractor to discover whether such trucks were in use. For somehow he knew that, if the Flack gang were after this shipment to Australia, it was necessary that the gold should be carried in one vehicle. Why he should think this, not even Mr. Reeder knew. But he had, as he said, a criminal mind.

That afternoon he addressed himself to a novel and not unpleasing task. It was a letter, the first letter he had written to Margaret Belman, and in its way it was a curiosity.

It began:

"My Dear Miss Margaret:

"I trust you will not be annoyed that I should write to you; but certain incidents which disfigured perhaps our parting, and which may cause you (I say this knowing your kind heart) a little unhappiness, induce this letter—"

Mr. Reeder paused here to discover a method by which he could convey his regret at not seeing her without offering an embarrassing revelation of his more secret thoughts. At five o'clock when his servant brought in his tea, he was still sitting before the unfinished letter. Mr. Reeder took up the cup, carried it to his writing table, and stared at it as though for inspiration.

And then he saw on the surface of the steaming cup a thread-like formation of froth which had a curious metallic look. He dipped his forefinger delicately in the froth and put his finger to his tongue.

"Hum!" said Mr. Reeder, and rang the bell.

His man came instantly.

"Is there anything you want, sir?" He bent his head respectfully, and for a long time Mr. Reeder did not answer.

"The milk, of course!" he said.

"The milk, sir?" said the puzzled servant. "The milk's fresh, sir; it came this afternoon."

"You did not take it from the milkman, naturally. It was in a bottle outside the door."

The man nodded.

"Yes, sir."

"Good!" said Mr. Reeder, almost cheerfully. "In the future will you arrange to receive the milk from the milkman's own hands? You have not drunk any yourself, I see?"

"No, sir. I have had my tea, but I don't take milk with it, sir," said the servant, and Mr. Reeder favoured him with one of his rare smiles.

"That, Peters," he said, "is why you are alive and well. Bring the rest of the milk to me, and a new cup of tea. I also will dispense with the lacteal fluid."

"Don't you like milk, sir?" said the bewildered man.

"I like milk," replied Mr. Reeder gently, "but I prefer it without strychnine. I think, Peters, we're going to have a very interesting week. Have you any dependants?"

"I have an old mother, sir," said the mystified man.

"Are you insured?" asked Mr. Reeder, and Peters nodded dumbly.

"You have the advantage of me," said J.G. Reeder. "Yes, I think we are going to have an interesting week."

And his prediction was fully justified.

CHAPTER VIII

LONDON heard the news of John Flack's escape and grew fearful or indignant according to its several temperaments. A homicidal planner of great and spectacular thefts was in its midst. It was not very pleasant hearing for law-abiding citizens. And the news was more than a week old. Why had Scotland Yard not taken the public into its confidence? Why suppress this news of such vital interest? Who was responsible for the suppression of this important information? Headlines asked these questions in the more sensational sheets. The news of the Bennett Street outrage was public property. To his enormous embarrassment Mr. Reeder found himself an object of public interest.

Mr. Reeder used to sit alone at his desk at the Public Prosecutor's office and for hours on end do little more than twiddle his thumbs and gaze disconsolately at the virgin white of his blotting pad.

In what private daydreams he indulged, whether they concerned fabulous fortunes and their disposition, or whether they centred about a very pretty pink-and-white young lady, or whether indeed he thought at all and his mind was not a complete blank, those who interrupted his reveries and had the satisfaction of seeing him start guiltily had no means of knowing.

At this particular moment his mind was, in truth, completely occupied by his newest as well as his oldest enemy.

There were three members of the Flack gang originally—John, George, and Augustus. They had begun operations in the days when it was considered scientific and a little wonderful to burn out the lock of a safe. Augustus Flack was killed by the night watchman of Carrs Bank in Lombard Street during an attempt to rob the gold vault; George Flack, the youngest of the three, was sent to penal servitude for ten years as a result of a robbery in Bond Street, and died there; and only John, the mad master mind of the family, escaped detection and arrest.

It was he who brought into the organization one O. Sweizer, the Swiss-American bank robber; he who recruited Adolphe Victoire; and they brought others to the good work. For this was Crazy John's peculiar asset—that he could attract to himself, almost at a minute's notice, the best brains of the underworld. Though the rest of the Flacks were either dead or jailed, the organization was stronger than ever, and stronger because lurking somewhere in the background was this kinky brain.

Thus matters stood when Mr. J.G. Reeder came into the case—being brought into the matter not so much because the London police had failed, but because the Public Prosecutor recognized that the breaking up of the Flacks was going to be a lengthy business, occupying one man's complete attention.

Cutting the tentacles of the organization was an easy matter, comparatively.

Mr. Reeder took O. Sweizer, that stocky Swiss-American, when he and a man unknown were engaged in removing a safe from the Bedford Street Post Office one Sunday morning. Sweizer was ready for fight, but Mr. Reeder grabbed him just a little too quickly.

"Let up!" gasped Sweizer in French. "You're choking me, Reeder."

Mr. Reeder turned him onto his face and handcuffed him behind; then he went to the assistance of his admirable colleagues who were taking the other two men.

Victoire was arrested one night at the Charlton, where he was dining with Denver May. He gave no trouble, because the police took him on a purely fictitious charge and one which he knew he could easily disprove.

"My dear Mr. Reeder," said he in his elegant, languid way, "you are making quite an absurd mistake, but I will humour you. I can prove that when the pearls were taken from Hertford Street I was in Nice."

This was on the way to the station.

They put him in the dock and searched him, discovering certain lethal weapons handily disposed about his person, but he was only amused. He was less amused when he was charged with smashing the Bank of Lena, the attempted murder of a night watchman, and one or two other little matters which need not be particularized.

They got him into a cell, and as he was carried, struggling and raving like a lunatic, Mr. Reeder offered him a piece of advice which he rejected with considerable violence.

"Say you were in Nice at the time," he said gently.

Then one day the police pulled in a man in Somers Town, on the very prosaic charge of beating his wife in public. When they searched him, they found a torn scrap of a letter which was sent at once to Mr. Reeder. It read:

"Any night about eleven in Whitehall Avenue. Reeder is a man of medium height, elderly-looking, sandy-grayish hair and side whiskers rather thick, always carries an umbrella. Recommend you to wear rubber boots and take a length of iron to him. You can easily find out who he is and what he looks like. Take your time ... fifty on acc ... der when the job is finished...."

This was the first hint Mr. Reeder had that he was especially unpopular with the mysterious John Flack.

The day Crazy John Flack was sent down to Broadmoor had been a day of mild satisfaction for Mr. Reeder. He was not exactly happy or even relieved about it. He had the comfort of an accountant who had signed a satisfactory balance sheet, or the builder who was surveying his finished work. There were other balance sheets to be signed, other buildings to be erected—they differed only in their shapes and quantities.

One thing was certain, that on what other project Flack's mind was fixed, he was devoting a considerable amount of thought to J.G. Reeder—whether in reprisal for events that had passed or as a precautionary measure to check his activities in the future, the detective could only guess; but he was a good guesser.

The telephone bell, set in a remote corner of the room, rang sharply. Mr. Reeder took up the instrument with a pained expression. The operator of the office exchange told him that there was a call from Horsham. He pulled a writing pad toward him and waited. And then a voice spoke, and hardly was the first word uttered than he knew his man, for J.G. Reeder never forgot voices.

"That you, Reeder? Know who I am?"

The same thin, tense voice that had babbled threats from the dock of Old Bailey, the same little chuckling laugh that punctured every second.

Mr. Reeder touched a bell and began to write rapidly on his pad.

"Know who I am?—I'll bet you do! Thought you'd got rid of me, didn't you, but you haven't! Listen, Reeder, you can tell the Yard I'm busy—I'm going to give them the shock of their lives. Mad, am I? I'll show you whether I'm mad or not. And I'll get you, Reeder—"

A messenger came in. Mr. Reeder tore off the slip and handed it to him with an urgent gesture. The man read and bolted from the room.

"Is that Mr. Flack?" asked Reeder softly.

"Is it Mr. Flack, you old hypocrite! Have you got the parcel? I wondered if you had. What do you think of it?"

"The parcel?" asked Reeder, more gently than ever, and before the man could reply: "You will get into serious trouble for trying to hoax the Public Prosecutor's office, my friend," said Mr. Reeder reproachfully. "You are not Crazy John Flack—I know his voice. Mr. Flack spoke with a curious cockney accent which is not easy to imitate, and Mr. Flack at this moment is in the hands of the police."

He counted on the effect of this provocative speech, and he had made no mistake.

"You lie!" screamed the voice. "You know I'm Flack—Crazy John, eh?—Crazy Old John Flack—mad, am I? You'll learn!—You put me in that hell upon earth, and I'm going to serve you worse than I treated that damned Dago—"

The voice ceased abruptly. There was a click as the receiver was put down.

Reeder listened expectantly, but no other call came through. Then he rang the bell again and the messenger returned.

"Yes, sir, I got through straight away to the Horsham police station. The inspector is sending three men in a car to the post office."

Mr. Reeder gazed at the ceiling.

"Then I fear he has sent them too late," he said. "The venerable bandit will have gone."

A quarter of an hour later came confirmation of his prediction. The police had arrived at the post office, but the bird had flown. The clerk did not remember anybody old or wild-looking booking a call; he thought that the message had not come from the post office itself, which was also the telephone exchange, but from an outlying call box.

Mr. Reeder went in to report to the Public Prosecutor, but neither he nor his assistant was in the Office. He rang up Scotland Yard and passed on his information to Simpson.

"I respectfully suggest that you should get into touch with the French police and locate Ravini. He may not be in Paris at all."

"Where do you think he is?" asked Simpson.

"That," replied Mr. Reeder in a hushed voice, "is a question which has never been definitely settled in my mind. I should not like to say that he was in heaven, because I cannot imagine Giorgio Ravini with his luck stones—

"Do you mean that he's dead?" asked Simpson quickly.

"It is very likely; in fact, it is extremely likely."

There was a long silence at the other end of the telephone.

"Have you had the parcel?"

"That I am awaiting with the greatest interest," said Mr. Reeder, and went back to his office to twiddle his thumbs and stare at his white blotting pad.

The parcel came at three o'clock that afternoon, when Mr. Reeder had returned from his frugal lunch, which he invariably took at a large and popular tea shop in Whitehall. It was a very small parcel, about three inches square; it was registered and had been posted in London. He weighed it carefully, shook it and listened, but the lightness of the package precluded any possibility of there being concealed behind the paper wrapping anything that bore a resemblance to an infernal machine. He cut the paper tape that fastened it, took off the paper, and there was revealed a small cardboard box such as jewellers use. Removing the lid, he found a small pad of cotton-wool, and in the midst of this three gold rings, each with three brilliant diamonds. He put them on his blotting pad and gazed at them for a long time.

They were George Ravini's luck stones, and for ten minutes Mr. Reeder sat in a profound reverie, for he knew that George Ravini was dead, and it did not need the card which accompanied the rings to know who was responsible for the drastic and gruesome ending to Mr. Ravini's life. The sprawling "J.F." on the little card was in Mr. Flack's writing, and the three words, "Your turn next," were instructive, even if they were not, as they were intended to be, terrifying.

Half an hour later Mr. Reeder met Inspector Simpson by appointment at Scotland Yard. Simpson examined the rings curiously and pointed out a small, dark-brown speck at the edge of one of the luck stones.

"I don't doubt that Ravini is dead," he said. "The first thing to discover is where he went when he said he was going to Paris."

This task presented fewer difficulties than Simpson had imagined. He remembered one Lew Steyne and his association with the Italian, and a telephone call put through to the City police located Lew in five minutes.

"Bring him along in a taxi," said Simpson, and, as he hung up the receiver: "The question is, what is Crazy John's coup—murder on a large scale, or just picturesque robbery?"

"I think the latter," said Mr. Reeder thoughtfully. "Murder, with Mr. Flack, is a mere incident to the—er—more important business of money-making."

He pinched his lip thoughtfully.

"Forgive me if I seem to repeat myself, but I would again remind you that Mr. Flack's specialty is bullion, if I remember aright," he said. "Didn't he smash the strong room of the Megantic ... bullion, hum!" He scratched his chin and looked up over his glasses at Simpson.

The inspector shook his head.

"I only wish Crazy John was crazy enough to try to get out of the country by steamer—he won't. And the Leadenhall Bank stunt couldn't be repeated to-day. No, there's no chance of a bullion steal."

Mr. Reeder looked unconvinced.

"Would you ring up the Bank of England and find out if the money has gone to Tilbury?" he pleaded.

Simpson pulled the instrument toward him, gave a number and, after five minutes' groping through various departments, reached an exclusive personage. Mr. Reeder sat, with his hands clasped about the handle of his umbrella, a pained expression on his face, his eyes closed, and seemingly oblivious of the conversation. Presently Simpson hung up the receiver.

"The consignment should have gone this morning, but the sailing of the Olanic has been delayed by a stevedore strike—it goes to-morrow morning," he reported. "The gold is taken on a lorry to Tilbury with a guard. At Tilbury it is put into the Olanic's strong room, which is the newest and safest of its kind. I don't suppose that John will begin operations there."

"Why not?" J.G. Reeder's voice was almost bland; his face was screwed into its nearest approach to a smile. "On the contrary, as I have said before, that is the very consignment I should expect Mr. Flack to go after."

"I pray that you're a true prophet," said Simpson grimly. "I could wish for nothing better."

They were still talking of Flack and his passion for ready gold when Mr. Lew Steyne arrived in the charge of a local detective. No crook, however hardened, can step into the gloomy approaches of Scotland Yard without experiencing some uneasiness, and Lew's attempt to display his indifference was rather pathetic.

"What's the idea, Mr. Simpson?" he asked, in a grieved tone. "I've done nothing."

He scowled at Reeder, who was known to him, and whom he regarded, very rightly, as being responsible for his appearance at this most hated spot.

Simpson put a question, and Mr. Lew Steyne shrugged his shoulders.

"I ask you, Mr. Simpson, am I Ravini's keeper? I know nothing about the Italian crowd, and Ravini's scarcely an acquaintance."

Mr. Reeder shook his head.

"You spent two hours with him last Thursday evening," he said, and Lew was a little taken aback.

"I had a little bit of business with him, I admit," he said. "Over a house I'm trying to rent—"

His shifty eyes had become suddenly steadfast; he was looking open-mouthed at the three rings that lay on the table. Reeder saw him frown, and then:

"What are those?" asked Lew huskily. "They're not Giorgio's luck stones?"

Simpson nodded and pushed the little square of white paper on which they lay toward the visitor.

"Do you know them?" he asked.

Lew picked up one of the rings and turned it round in his hand.

"What's the idea?" he asked suspiciously. "Ravini told me himself he could never get these off."

And then, as the significance of their presence dawned upon him, he gasped.

"What's happened to him?" he asked quickly. "Is he—"

"I fear," said Mr. Reeder soberly, "that Giorgio Ravini is no longer with us."

"Dead?" Lew almost shrieked the word. His yellow face went a chalky white. "Where—who did it?"

"That is exactly what we want to know," said Simpson. "Now, Lew, you've got to spill it. Where is Ravini? He said he was going to Paris, I know, but, actually, where did he go?"

The thief's eyes strayed to Mr. Reeder.

"He was after that bird, that's all I know," he said sullenly.

"Which bird?" asked Simpson, but Mr. Reeder had no need to have its identity explained.

"He was after—Miss Belman?"

Lew nodded.

"Yes, a girl he knew—she went down into the country to take a job as hotel manager or something. I saw her go, as a matter of fact. Ravini wanted to get better acquainted, so he went down to stay at the hotel."

Even as he spoke, Mr. Reeder had reached for the telephone, and had given the peculiar code word which is equivalent to a command for a clear line.

A high-pitched voice answered him.

"I am Mr. Daver, the proprietor.... Miss Belman? I'm afraid she is out just now. She will be back in a few minutes. Who is it speaking?"

Mr. Reeder replied diplomatically. He was anxious to get into touch with George Ravini, and for two minutes he allowed the voluble Mr. Daver to air a grievance.

"Yes, he went in the early morning, without paying his bill..."

"I will come down and pay it," said Mr. Reeder.

CHAPTER IX

"THE point is," said Mr. Daver, "the only point—I think you will agree with me here—that really has any interest for us is that Mr. Ravini left without paying his bill. This was the point I emphasized to a friend of his who called me on the telephone this morning. That is to me the supreme mystery of his disappearance—he left without paying his bill!"

He leaned back in his chair and beamed at the girl in the manner of one who had expounded an unanswerable problem. With his finger-tips together, he had an appearance which was oddly reminiscent.

"The fact that he left behind a pair of pajamas which are practically valueless merely demonstrates that he left in a hurry. You agree with me? I am sure you do. Why he should leave in a hurry is naturally beyond my understanding. You say he was a crook; possibly he received information that he had been detected."

"He had no telephone calls and no letters while he was here," insisted Margaret.

Mr. Daver shook his head.

"That proves nothing. Such a man would have associates. I am sorry he has gone. I hoped to have an opportunity of studying his type. And, by the way, I have discovered something about Flack—the famous John Flack—did you know that he had escaped from the lunatic asylum? I gather from your alarm that you didn't. I am an observer, Miss B. Years of study of this fascinating subject have produced in me a sixth sense—the sense of observation, which is atrophied in ordinary individuals."

He took a long envelope from his drawer and pulled out a small bundle of press cuttings. These he sorted on his table, and presently unfolded a newspaper portrait of an elderly man and laid it before her.

"Flack," he said briefly.

She was surprised at the age of the man: the thin face, the grizzled moustache and beard, the deep-set intelligent eyes suggested almost anything rather than that confirmed and dangerous criminal.

"My press-cutting agency supplied these," he said. "And here is another portrait which may interest you, and in a sense the arrival of this photograph is a coincidence. I am sure you will agree with me when I tell you why. It is a picture of a man called Reeder."

Mr. Daver did not look up, or he would have seen the red come to the girl's face.

"A clever old gentleman attached to the Public Prosecutor's Department."

"He is not very old," said Margaret coldly.

"He looks old," said Mr. Daver, and Margaret had to agree that the newspaper portrait was not a very flattering one.

"This is the gentleman who was instrumental in arresting Flack, and the coincidence—now what do you imagine the coincidence is?"

She shook her head.

"He's coming here this day!"

Margaret Belman's mouth opened in amazement.

"I had a wire from him this afternoon saying he was coming to-night, and asking if I could accommodate him. But for my interest in this case, I should not have known his name or had the slightest idea of his identity. In all probability, I should have refused him a room."

He looked up suddenly.

"You say he is not so old. Do you know him? I see that you do. That is even a more remarkable coincidence. I am looking forward with the utmost delight to discussing with him my pet subject. It will be an intellectual treat."

"I don't think Mr. Reeder discusses crime," she said. "He is rather reticent on the subject."

"We shall see," said Mr. Daver, and from his manner she guessed that he, at any rate, had no doubt that the man from the Public Prosecutor's office would respond instantly to a sympathetic audience.

Mr. Reeder came just before seven, and to her surprise he had abandoned his frock coat and curious hat and was almost jauntily attired in gray flannels. He brought with him two very solid and heavy-looking steamer trunks.

The meeting was not without its moment of embarrassment.

"I trust you will not think, Miss—um—Margaret, that I am being indiscreet. But the truth is, I—um—am in need of a holiday."

He never looked less in need of a holiday; compared with the Reeder she knew, this man was most unmistakably alert.

"Will you come to my office?" she said, a little unsteadily.

When they reached her office, Mr. Reeder opened the door reverently. She had a feeling that he was holding his breath, and she was seized with an almost uncontrollable desire to laugh. Instead, she preceded him into her sanctum. When the door closed:

"I was an awful pig to you, Mr. Reeder," she began rapidly. "I ought to have written—the whole thing was so absurd—the quarrel, I mean."

"The disagreement," murmured Mr. Reeder. "I am old-fashioned, I admit, but an old man—"

"Forty-eight isn't old," she scoffed. "And why shouldn't you wear side whiskers? It was unpardonable of me—feminine curiosity: I wanted to see how you looked."

Mr. Reeder raised his hand. His voice was almost gay.

"The fault was entirely mine, Miss Margaret. I am old-fashioned. You do not think—er—it is indecorous, my paying a visit to Larmes Keep?"

He looked round at the door and lowered his voice.

"When did Mr. Ravini leave?" he asked.

She looked at him, amazed.

"Did you come down about that?"

He nodded slowly.

"I heard he was here. Somebody told me. When did he go?"

Very briefly she told him the story of her night's experience, and he listened, his face growing longer and longer, until she had finished.

"Before that, can you remember what happened? Did you see him the night before he left?"

She knit her forehead and tried to remember.

"Yes," she said suddenly, "he was in the grounds, walking with Miss Crewe. He came in rather late—"

"With Miss Crewe?" asked Reeder quickly. "Miss Crewe? Was that the rather interesting young lady I saw playing croquet with a clergyman as I came across the lawn?"

She looked at him in surprise.

"Did you come across the lawn? I thought you drove up to the front of the house."

"I descended from the vehicle at the top of the hill," Mr. Reeder hastily explained. "At my age, a little exercise is vitally necessary. The approaches to the Keep are charming. A young lady, rather pale, with dark eyes ... hum!"

He was looking at her searchingly, his head a little on one side.

"So she and Ravini went out. Were they acquainted?"

She shook her head.

"I don't think Ravini had met her until he came here."

She went on to tell him of Ravini's agitation, and of how she had found Olga Crewe in tears.

"Weeping—ah!" Mr. Reeder fondled his nose. "You have seen her since?"

And when the girl shook her head:

"She got up late the next morning—had a headache possibly?" he asked eagerly, and her eyes opened in astonishment.

"Why, yes. How did you know?"

But Mr. Reeder was not in an informative mood.

"The number of your room is—?"

"No. 4. Miss Crewe's is No. 5."

Reeder nodded.

"And Ravini was in No. 7—that is two doors away." Then, suddenly: "Where have you put me?"

She hesitated.

"In No. 7. Those were Mr. Daver's orders. It is one of the best rooms in the house. I warn you, Mr. Reeder, the proprietor is a criminologist and is most anxious to discuss his hobby."

"Delighted," murmured Mr. Reeder, but he was thinking of something else. "Could I see Mr. Daver?"

The quarter-of-an-hour gong had already sounded, and she took him along to the office in the annex. Mr. Daver's desk was surprisingly tidy. He was surveying an account book through large horn-rimmed spectacles and looked up inquiringly as she came in.

"This is Mr. Reeder," she said, and withdrew.

For a second they looked at one another, the detective and the Puck-faced little proprietor; and then, with a magnificent wave of his hand, Mr. Daver invited his visitor to a seat.

"This is a very proud moment for me, Mr. Reeder," he said, and bent himself double in a profound bow. "As a humble student of those great authorities whose works, I have no doubt, are familiar to you, I am honoured at this privilege of meeting one whom I may describe as a modern Lombroso. You agree with me? I was certain you would."

Mr. Reeder looked up at the ceiling.

"Lombroso?" he repeated slowly. "An—um—Italian gentleman, I think? The name is almost familiar."

Margaret Belman had not quite closed the door, and Mr. Daver rose and shut it; returned to his chair with an outflung hand and seated himself.

"I am glad you have come. In fact, Mr. Reeder, you have relieved my mind of a great uneasiness. Ever since yesterday morning I have been wondering whether I ought not to call up Scotland Yard, that splendid institution, and ask them to dispatch an officer to clear up this strange and possibly revolting mystery."

He paused impressively.

"I refer to the disappearance of Mr. George Ravini, a guest of Larmes Keep, who left this house at a quarter to five yesterday morning and was seen making his way into Siltbury."

"By whom?" asked Mr. Reeder.

"By an inhabitant of Siltbury, whose name for the moment I forget. Indeed, I never knew. I met him quite by chance walking down into the town."

He leaned forward over his desk and stared owlishly into Mr. Reeder's eyes.

"You have come about Ravini, have you not? Do not answer me: I see that you have! Naturally, one did not expect you to carry, so to speak, your heart on your sleeve. Am I right? I think I am."

Mr. Reeder did not confirm this conclusion. He seemed strangely unwilling to speak, and in ordinary circumstances Mr. Daver would not have resented this diffidence.

"Very naturally I do not wish a scandal to attach to this house," he said, "and I may rely upon your discretion. The only matter which touches me is that Ravini left without paying his bill: a small and unimportant aspect of what may possibly be a momentous case. You see my point of view? I am certain that you do."

He paused, and now Mr. Reeder spoke.

"At a quarter to five," he said thoughtfully, as though speaking to himself, "it was scarcely light, was it?"

"The dawn was possibly breaking o'er the sea," said Mr. Daver poetically.

"Going to Siltbury? Carrying his bag?"

Mr. Daver nodded.

"May I see his room?"

Daver came to his feet with a flourish.

"That is a request I expected, and it is a reasonable request. Will you follow me?"

Mr. Reeder followed him through the great hall, which was occupied solely by a military-looking gentleman, who cast a quick sidelong glance at him as he passed. Mr. Daver was leading the way to the wide stairs when Mr. Reeder stopped and pointed.

"How very interesting!" he said.

The most unlikely things interested Mr. Reeder. On this occasion the point of interest was a large safe—larger than any safe he had seen in a private establishment. It was six feet in height and half that in width, and it was fitted under the first flight of stairs.

"What is it?" asked Mr. Daver, and turned back, His face screwed up into a smile when he saw the object of the detective's attention.

"Ah! My safe! I have many rare and valuable documents which I keep here. It is a French model, you will observe—too large for my modest establishment, you will say? I agree. Sometimes, however, we have very rich people staying here—jewels and the like—it would take a very clever burglar to open that, and yet I, with a little key—"

He drew a chain from his pocket and fitted one of the keys at the end into a thin keyhole, turned a handle, and the heavy door swung open.

Mr. Reeder peeped in curiously. On the two steel shelves at the back of the safe were three small tin boxes—otherwise, the safe was empty. The doors were of an extraordinary thickness, and their inner face smooth except for a slab of steel the object of which apparently was to back and strengthen the lock. All this he saw at once, but he saw something else. The white enamelled floor of the safe was brighter in hue than the walls. Only a man of Mr. Reeder's powers of observation would have noticed this fact. And the steel slab at the back of the lock? Mr. Reeder knew quite a lot about safes.

"A treasure house—it almost makes me feel rich," chuckled Mr. Daver as he locked the door and led the way up the stairs. "The psychology of it will appeal to you, Mr. Reeder!"

At the head of the stairs they came to a broad corridor; Daver, stopping before the door of No. 7, inserted a key.

"This is also your room," he explained. "I had a feeling, which amounted almost to a certainty, that your visit was not wholly unconnected with this curious disappearance of Mr. Ravini, who left without paying his bill." He chuckled a little and apologized. "Excuse me for my insistence upon this point, but it touches me rather nearly."

Mr. Reeder followed his host into the big room. It was panelled from ceiling to floor and furnished with a luxury which surprised him. The articles of furniture were few, but there was not one which a connoisseur would not have noted with admiration. The four-poster bed was Jacobean; the square of carpet was genuine Teheran; a tallboy and dressing table with a settee before it were also of the Jacobean period.

"That was his bed, where the pajamas were found."

Mr. Daver pointed dramatically. But Mr. Reeder was looking at the casement windows, one of which was open.

He leaned out and looked down, and immediately began to take in the view. He could see Siltbury lying in the shadow of the downs, its lights just then beginning to twinkle; but the view of the Siltbury road was shut out by a belt of firs. To the left he had a glimpse of the hill road up which his cab had climbed.

Mr. Reeder came out from the room and cast his eyes up and down the corridor.

"This is a very beautiful house you have, Mr. Daver," he said.

"You like it? I was sure you would!" said Mr. Daver enthusiastically. "Yes, it is a delightful property. To you it may seem a sacrilege that I should use it as a boarding house, but perhaps our dear young friend Miss Belman has explained that it is a hobby of mine. I hate loneliness; I dislike intensely the exertion of making friends. My position is unique; I can pick and choose my guests."

Mr. Reeder was looking aimlessly toward the head of the stairs.

"Did you ever have a guest named Holden?" he asked.

Mr. Daver shook his head.

"Or a guest named Willington? Two friends of mine who may have come here about eight years ago?"

"No," said Mr. Daver promptly. "I never forget names. You may inspect our guest list for the past twelve years at any time you wish. Would they be likely to come for any reason"—Mr. Daver was amusingly embarrassed—"in other names than their own? No, I see they wouldn't."

As he was speaking, a door at the far end of the corridor opened and closed instantly. Mr. Reeder, who missed nothing, caught one glimpse of a figure before the door shut.

"Whose room is that?" he asked.

Mr. Daver was genuinely embarrassed this time.

"That," he said, with a nervous little cough, "is my suite. You saw Mrs. Burton, my housekeeper—a quiet, rather sad soul who has had a great deal of trouble in her life."

"Life," said Mr. Reeder tritely, "is full of trouble," and Mr. Daver agreed with a sorrowful shake of his head.

Now the eyesight of J.G. Reeder was peculiarly good, and though he had not as yet met the housekeeper, he was quite certain that the rather beautiful face he had glimpsed for a moment did not belong to any sad woman who had seen a lot of trouble. As he dressed leisurely for dinner, he wondered why Miss Olga Crewe had been so anxious that she should not be seen coming from the proprietor's suite. A natural and proper modesty, no doubt; and modesty was the quality in woman of which Mr. Reeder most heartily approved.

He was struggling with his tie when Daver, who seemed to have constituted himself a sort of personal attendant, knocked at the door and asked permission to come in. He was a little breathless and carried a number of press cuttings in his hand.

"You were talking about two gentlemen, Mr. Willington and Mr. Holden," he said. "The names seemed rather familiar. I had the irritating sense of knowing them without knowing them, if you understand, dear Mr. Reeder? And then I recalled the circumstances." He flourished the press cuttings. "I saw their names here."

Mr. Reeder, staring at his reflection in the glass, adjusted his tie nicely.

"Here?" he repeated mechanically, and looking round, accepted the printed slips which his host thrust upon him.

"I am, as you probably know, Mr. Reeder, a humble disciple of Lombroso and of those other great criminologists who have elevated the study of abnormality to a science. It was Miss Belman who quite unconsciously directed my thoughts to the Flack organization, and during the past day or two I have been getting a number of particulars concerning those miscreants. The names of Holden and Willington occur. They were two detectives who went out in search of Flack and never returned. I remember their disappearance very well, now the matter is recalled to my mind. There was also a third gentleman who disappeared."

Mr. Reeder nodded.

"Ah, you remember?" said Mr. Daver triumphantly. "Naturally you would. A lawyer named Biggerthorpe, who was called from his office one day on some excuse, and was never seen again. May I add"—he smiled good-humouredly—"that Mr. Biggerthorpe has never stayed here? Why should you imagine he had, Mr. Reeder?"

"I never did." Mr. Reeder gave blandness for blandness. "Biggerthorpe? I had forgotten him. He would have been an important witness against Flack if he'd ever been caught—hum!"

And then:

"You are a student of criminal practices, Mr. Daver?"

"A humble one," said Mr. Daver, and his humility was manifest in his attitude.

And then he suddenly dropped his voice to a hoarse whisper.

"Shall I tell you something, Mr. Reeder?"

"You may tell me," said Mr. Reeder, as he buttoned his waistcoat, "anything that pleases you. I am in the mood for stories. In this delightful atmosphere, amidst these beautiful surroundings, I should prefer—um—fairy stories—or shall we say ghost stories? Is Larmes Keep haunted, Mr. Daver? Ghosts are my specialty. I have probably seen and arrested more ghosts than any other living representative of the law. Sometime I intend writing a monumental work on the subject. 'Ghosts I Have Seen, or a Guide to the Spirit World,' in sixty-three volumes. You were about to say—?"

"I was about to say," said Mr. Daver, and his voice was curiously strained, "that in my opinion Flack himself once stayed here. I have not mentioned this fact to Miss Belman, but I am convinced in my mind that I am not in error. Seven years ago"—he was very impressive—"a gray-bearded, rather thin-faced man came here at ten o'clock at night and asked for a lodging. He had plenty of money, but this did not influence me. Ordinarily I should have asked him to make the usual application, but it was late, a bitterly cold and snowy night, and I hadn't the heart to turn one of his age away from my door."

"How long did he stay?" asked Mr. Reeder. "And why do you think he was Flack?"

"Because"—Daver's voice had sunk until it was an eerie moan—"he left just as Ravini left— early one morning, without paying his bill, and left his pajamas behind him!"

Very slowly Mr. Reeder turned his head and surveyed the host.

"That comes into the category of humorous stories, and I am too hungry to laugh," he said calmly. "What time do we dine?"

The gong sounded at that moment.

Margaret Belman usually dined at a table apart from the other guests. She went red and felt more than a little awkward when Mr. Reeder came across to her table, dragging a chair with him, and ordered another place to be set. The other three guests dined at separate tables.

"An unsociable lot of people," said Mr. Reeder as he shook out his napkin and glanced round the room.

"What do you think of Mr. Daver?"

J.G. Reeder smiled gently.

"He is a very amusing person," he said, and she laughed, but grew serious immediately.

"Have you found out anything about Ravini?"

Mr. Reeder shook his head.

"I had a talk with the hall porter; he seems a very honest and straightforward fellow. He told me that when he came down the morning after Ravini disappeared, the front door had been unbolted and unlocked. An observant fellow. Who is Mrs. Burton?" he asked abruptly.

"The housekeeper." Margaret smiled and shook her head. "She is rather a miserable lady who spends quite a lot of time hinting at the good times she should be having instead of being 'buried alive'—those are her words—at Siltbury."

Mr. Reeder put down his knife and fork.

"Dear me!" he said mildly. "Is she a lady who has seen better days?"

Margaret laughed softly.

"I should have thought she had never had such a time as she is having now," she said. "She's rather common and terribly illiterate. Her accounts that come up to me are fearful and wonderful things! But, seriously, I think she must have been in good circumstances. The first night I was here I went into her room to ask about an account. I did not understand—of course it was a waste of time, for books are mysteries to her—and she was sitting at a table admiring her hands."

"Hands?" he said.

She nodded.

"They were covered with the most beautiful rings you could possibly imagine," said Margaret, and was satisfied with the impression she made, for Mr. Reeder dropped knife and fork to his plate with a crash.

"Rings—?"

"Huge diamonds and emeralds. They took my breath away. The moment she saw me, she put her hands behind her, and the next morning she explained that they were presents given to her by a theatrical lady who had stayed here and that they had no value."

"Props, in fact," said Mr. Reeder.

"What is a prop?" she asked curiously, and Mr. Reeder waggled his head, and she had learnt that when he waggled his head in that fashion he was advertising his high spirits and good-humour.

After dinner he sent a waitress to find Mr. Daver, and when that gentleman arrived, Mr. Reeder had to tell him that he had a lot of work to do and request the loan of blotting pad and a special writing table for his room. Margaret wondered why he had not asked her, but she supposed that it was because he did not know that such things came into her province.

"You're a great writer, Mr. Reeder—he-he!" Daver was convulsed at his own little joke. "So am I! I am never happy without a pen in my hand. Tell me, as a matter of interest, do you do your best work in the morning or in the evening? Personally, it is a question that I have never decided to my own satisfaction."

"I shall now write steadily till two o'clock," said Mr. Reeder, glancing at his watch. "That is a habit of years. From nine to two are my writing hours, after which I smoke a cigarette, drink a glass of milk—would you be good enough to see that I have a glass of milk put in my room at once?—and from two I sleep steadily till nine."

Margaret Belman was an interested and somewhat startled audience of this personal confession. It was unusual in Mr. Reeder to speak of himself, unthinkable that he should discuss his work. In all her life she had not met an individual who was more reticent about his private affairs. Perhaps the holiday spirit was on him, she thought. He was certainly younger-looking that evening than she had ever known him.

She went out to find Mrs. Burton and convey the wishes of the guest. The woman accepted the order with a sniff.

"Milk? He looks the kind of person who drinks milk. He's nothing to be afraid of!"

"Why should he be afraid?" asked Margaret sharply, but the reproach was lost upon Mrs. Burton. "Nobody likes detectives nosing about a place—do they, Miss Belman? And he's not my idea of a detective."

"Who told you he was a detective?"

Mrs. Burton looked at her for a second from under her heavy lids, and then jerked her head in the direction of Daver's office.

"He did," she said. "Detectives! And me sitting here, slaving from morning till night, when I might be doing the grand in Paris or one of them places, with servants to wait on me instead of me waiting on people. It's sickening!"

Twice since she had been at Larmes Keep, Margaret had witnessed these little outbursts of fretfulness and irritation. She had an idea that the faded woman would like some excuse to make her a confidante, but the excuse was neither found nor sought. Margaret had nothing in common with this rather dull and terribly ordinary lady, and they could find no mutual interest which would lead to the breakdown of the barriers. Mrs. Burton was a weakling; tears were never far from her eyes or voice, nor the sense of her mysterious grievances against the world far from her mind.

"They treat me like dirt," she went on, her voice trembling with her feeble anger, "and she treats me worst of all. I asked her to come and have a cup of tea and a chat in my room the other day, and what do you think she said?"

"Whom are you talking about?" asked Margaret curiously. It did not occur to her that the "she" in question might be Olga Crewe. It would have required a very powerful effort of imagination to picture the cold and worldly Olga talking commonplaces with Mrs. Burton over a friendly cup of tea; yet it was of Olga that the woman spoke. But at the very suggestion that she was being questioned, her thin lips closed tight.

"Nobody in particular.—Milk, did you say? I'll take it up to him myself."

Mr. Reeder was struggling into a dressing jacket when she brought the milk to him. One of the servants had already placed pen, ink, and stationery on the table, and there were two fat manuscript books visible to any caller, and anticipating eloquently Mr. Reeder's literary activities.

He took the tray from the woman's hand and put it on the table.

"You have a nice house, Mrs. Burton," he said encouragingly. "A beautiful house. Have you been here long?"

"A few years," she answered.

She made as if to go, but lingered at the door. Mr. Reeder recognized the symptoms. Discreet she might be, a gossip she undoubtedly was, aching for human converse with any who could advance a programme of those trivialities which made up her conversational life.

"No, sir, we never get many visitors here. Mr. Daver likes to pick and choose."

"And very wise of Mr. Daver. By the way, which is his room?"

She walked through the doorway and pointed along the corridor.

"Oh, yes, I remember, he told me. A charming situation. I saw you coming out this evening."

"You have made a mistake—I never go into his room," said the woman sharply. "You may have seen—" She stopped, and added—"somebody else. Are you going to work late, sir?"

Mr. Reeder repeated in detail his plans for the evening.

"I should be glad if you would tell Mr. Daver that I do not wish to be interrupted. I am a very slow thinker, and the slightest disturbance to my train of thought is fatal to my—er—power of composition," he said, as he closed the door upon her, and, waiting until she had time to get down the stairs, locked it and pushed home the one bolt.

He drew the heavy curtains across the open windows, pushed the writing table against the curtains so that they could not blow back, and, opening the two exercise books, so placed them that they formed a shade that prevented the light from falling upon the bed. This done, he changed quickly into a lounge suit, and, lying on the bed, pulled the coverlet over him and was asleep in five minutes.

Margaret Belman had it in her mind to send up to his room after eleven, before she herself retired, to discover whether there was anything he wanted, but fortunately she changed her mind—fortunately, because Mr. Reeder had planned to snatch five solid hours' sleep before he began his unofficial inspection of the house, or alternatively before the period arrived when it would be necessary that he should be wide-awake.

* * * * *

At two o'clock to the second he woke and sat up on the edge of the bed, blinking at the light. Opening one of his trunks, he took out a small wooden box from which he drew a spirit stove and the paraphernalia of tea-making. He lit the little lamp, and while the tiny tin kettle was boiling, he went to the bathroom, undressed, and lowered his shivering body into a cold bath. He returned fully dressed to find the kettle boiling.

Mr. Reeder was a very methodical man; he was, moreover, a careful man. All his life he had had a suspicion of milk. He used to wander round the suburban streets in the early hours of the morning, watch the cans hanging on the knockers, the bottles deposited in corners of doorsteps, and ruminate upon the enormous possibilities for wholesale murder that this light-hearted custom of milk delivery presented to the criminally minded. He had calculated that a nimble homicide, working on systematic lines, could decimate London in a month.

He drank his tea without milk, munched a biscuit, and then, methodically clearing away the spirit stove and kettle, he took from his grip a pair of thick-soled felt slippers and drew them on his feet. In his trunk he found a short length of stiff rubber, which, in the hands of a skillful man, was as deadly a weapon as a knife. This he put in the inside pocket of his jacket. He put his hand into the trunk again and brought out something that looked like a thin rubber sponge bag, except that it was fitted with two squares of mica and a small metal nozzle. He hesitated about this, turning it over and over in his hand, and eventually this went back into the trunk. The stubby Browning pistol, which was his next find, Mr. Reeder regarded with disfavour, for the value of firearms, except in the most desperate circumstances, had always seemed to him to be problematical.

The last thing to be extracted was a hollow bamboo, which contained another, and was in truth the fishing rod for which he had once expressed a desire. At the end of the thinner one was a spring loop, and after he had screwed the two lengths together, he fitted upon this loop a small electric hand lamp and carefully threaded the thin wires through the eyelets of the rod, connecting them up with a tiny switch at the handle, near where the average fisherman has his grip. He tested the switch, found it satisfactory, and when this was done he gave a final look round the room before extinguishing the table lamp.

In the broad light of day he would have presented a somewhat comic figure, sitting cross-legged on his bed, his long fishing rod reaching out to the middle of the room and resting on the footboard; but at the moment Mr. J.G. Reeder had no sense of the ridiculous, and, moreover, there were no witnesses.

From time to time he swayed the rod left and right, like an angler making a fresh cast. He was very wide-awake, his ears tuned to differentiate between the normal noises of the night—the rustle of trees, the soft purr of the wind—and the sounds which could only come from human activity.

He sat for more than half an hour, his fishing rod moving to and fro, and then he was suddenly conscious of a cold draught blowing from the door. He had heard no sound—not so much as the clink of a lock; but he knew that the door was wide open.

Noiselessly he drew in the rod till it was clear of the posts of the bed, brought it round toward the door, paying out until it was a couple of yards from where he sat—with one foot on the floor now, ready to leap or drop, as events dictated.

The end of the rod met with no obstruction. Reeder held his breath—listening. The corridor outside was heavily carpeted.. He expected no sound of footsteps. But people must breathe, thought Mr. Reeder, and it is difficult to breathe noiselessly in a silent corridor in the dead of night. Conscious that he himself was a little too silent for a supposedly sleeping man, he emitted a lifelike snore and gurgle which might be expected from a middle-aged man in the first stages of slumber.

Something touched the end of the rod, pushing it aside. Mr. Reeder turned the switch and a blinding ray of light leapt from the lamp and focussed in a circle on the opposite wall of the corridor.

The door was open, but there was nothing human in sight.

And then, despite his wonderful nerve, his flesh began to go goosey, and a cold sensation tingled up his spine. Somebody was there—hiding—waiting for the man who carried the lamp, as they thought, to emerge.

Reaching out at a full arm's length, he thrust the end of the rod through the doorway into the corridor.

Swish!

Something struck the rod and snapped it. The lamp fell on the floor, lens uppermost, and flooded the ceiling of the corridor. In an instant Reeder was off the bed, moving swiftly, till he came to the cover afforded by the wide-open door. Through the crack he had a limited view of what might happen outside.

There was a deadly silence. In the hall downstairs a clock ticked solemnly, whirred, and struck the quarter to three. But there was no movement; nothing came within the range of the upturned lamp, until—

He had just a momentary flash of vision. The thin white face; the hairy lips parted in a grin; wild dirty white hair, and a bald crown; a short bristle of white beard; a claw-like hand reaching for the lamp—

Pistol or rubber? Mr. Reeder elected the rubber. As the hand closed over the lamp, he left the cover of the room and struck. He heard a snarl like that of a wild beast; then the lamp was extinguished as the apparition staggered back, snapping the thin wire.

The corridor was in darkness. He struck again and missed; the violence of the stroke was such that he overbalanced and fell on one knee, and the truncheon flew from his grasp. He threw out his hand, gripped an arm, and with a quick jerk brought his capture into the room and switched on the light.

A round, soft hand, covered with a silken sleeve—

As the lights leapt to life, he found himself looking into the pale face of Olga Crewe!

CHAPTER X

FOR a moment they stared at one another, she fearfully, he amazed. Olga Crewe!
Then he became conscious that he was still gripping her arm, and let it drop. The arm fascinated Mr. Reeder—he scarcely looked at anything else.

"I am very sorry," said Mr. Reeder. "Where did you come from?"

Her lips were quivering; she tried to speak, but no words came. Then she mastered her momentary paralysis and began to speak, slowly, laboriously:

"I—heard—a noise—in—the—corridor—and—came—out. A noise—I—was—frightened."

She was rubbing her arm mechanically; he saw a red welt where his hand had gripped. The wonder was that he had not broken her arm.

"Is—anything—wrong?"

Every word was created and articulated painfully. She seemed to be considering its formation before her tongue gave it sound.

"Where is the light switch in the hall?" asked Mr. Reeder. This was a more practical matter—he lost interest in her arm.

"Opposite my room."

"Turn it on," he said, and she obeyed meekly.

Only when the corridor was illuminated did he step out of his room, and even then in some doubt, if the Browning in his hand meant anything.

"Is anything wrong?" she asked again. By now she had taken command of herself. A little colour had come to her white face, but the live eyes were still beholding terrible visions.

"Did you see anything in the passage?" he answered.

She shook her head slowly.

"No, I saw nothing—nothing. I heard a noise and I came out."

She was lying—he did not trouble to doubt this. She had had time to pull on her slippers and find the flimsy wrap she wore, and the fight had not lasted more than two seconds. Moreover, he had not heard her door open; therefore it had been open all the time, and she had been spectator or audience of all that had happened.

He went down the corridor, retrieved his rubber truncheon, and came back to her. She was half standing, half leaning against the door post, rubbing her arm. She was staring past him so intently that he looked round, though there was nothing to be seen.

"You hurt me," she said simply.

"Did I? I'm sorry."

The mark on the white flesh had gone blue, and Mr. Reeder was naturally a sympathetic man. Yet, if the truth be told, there was nothing of sorrow in his mind at that moment. Regret, yes. But the regret had nothing to do with her hurt.

"I think you'd better go to your bed, young lady. My nightmare is ended. I hope yours will end as quickly, though I shall be surprised if it does. Mine is for the moment; yours, unless I am greatly mistaken, is for life!"

Her dark, inscrutable eyes did not leave his face as she spoke.

"I think it must have been a nightmare," she said. "It will last all my life? I think it will!"

With a nod she turned away, and presently he heard her door close and the lock fasten.

Mr. Reeder went back to the far side of his bed, pulled up a chair and sat down. He did not attempt to close the door. Whilst his room was in darkness, and the corridor lighted, he did not expect a repetition of his bad and substantial dream.

The rubber truncheon was a mistake, he admitted regretfully. He wished he had not such a repugnance to a noisier weapon. He laid the pistol on the cover of the bed within reach of his hand. If the bad dream came again—

Voices!

The murmur of a whispered colloquy and a fierce, hissing whisper that dominated the others. Not in the corridor, but in the hall below. He tiptoed to the door and listened.

Somebody laughed under his breath, a strange, blood-curdling little laugh; then he heard a key turn and a door open, and a voice demand:

"Who is there?"

It was Margaret. Her room faced the head of the stairs, he remembered. Slipping the pistol into his pocket, he ran round the end of the bed and into the corridor. She was standing by the banisters, looking down into the dark. The whispered voices had ceased. She saw him out of the corner of her eye and turned with a start.

"What is wrong, Mr. Reeder? Who put the corridor light on? I heard somebody speaking in the vestibule."

"It was only I."

His smile would in ordinary circumstances have been very reassuring, but now she was frightened, childishly frightened. She had an insane desire to cling to him and weep.

"Something has been happening here," she said. "I've been lying in bed listening and haven't had the courage to get up. I'm horribly scared, Mr. Reeder."

He beckoned her to him, and as she came, wondering, he slipped past her and took her place at the banisters. She saw him lean over and the light from a hand lamp sweep the space below.

"There's nobody there," he said airily.

She was whiter than he had ever seen her.

"There was somebody there," she insisted. "I heard footsteps on the tiled paving after you put on your flash lamp."

"Probably Mrs. Burton," he suggested. "I thought I heard her voice."

And now arrived a newcomer on the scene. Mr. Daver had appeared at the end of the corridor. He wore a flowered silk dressing gown buttoned up to his chin.

"Whatever is the matter, Miss Belman?" he asked. "Don't tell me that he tried to get into your window! I'm afraid you're going to tell me that! I hope you're not, but I'm afraid you will! Dear me, what an unpleasant thing to happen!"

"What has happened?" asked Mr. Reeder.

"I don't know, but I have an uncomfortable feeling that somebody has been trying to break into this house," said Mr. Daver.

He was genuinely agitated; the girl could almost hear his teeth chatter.

"I heard somebody trying the catch of my window and looked out, and I'll swear I saw—something! What a dreadful thing to happen! I have half a mind to telephone for the police."

"An excellent idea," murmured Mr. Reeder, suddenly his old deferential and agreeable self. "You were asleep, I suppose, when you heard the noise?"

Mr. Daver hesitated.

"Not exactly asleep," he said. "Between sleeping and waking. I was very restless to-night for some reason."

He put up his hand to his throat, his dressing gown had gaped for a second. He was not quite quick enough.

"You were probably restless," said Mr. Reeder softly, "because you omitted to take off your collar and tie. I know of nothing more disturbing."

Mr. Daver made a characteristic grimace.

"I dressed myself rather hurriedly—" he began.

"Better to undress yourself hurriedly," chided Mr. Reeder, almost playfully. "People who go to bed in stiff white collars occasionally choke themselves to death. And there is sorrow in the home of the cheated hangman. Your burglar probably saved your life."

Daver made as though to speak, suddenly retreated, and slammed the door.

Margaret was looking at Mr. Reeder apprehensively.

"What is the mystery—was there a burglar? Oh, please tell me the truth! I shall get hysterical if you don't!"

"The truth," said Mr. Reeder, his eyes twinkling, "is very nearly what that curious man told you—there was somebody in the house, somebody who had no right to be here, but I think he has gone, and you can go to bed without the slightest anxiety."

She looked at him oddly.

"Are you going to bed, too?"

"In a very few moments," said Mr. Reeder cheerfully.

She held out her hand with an impulsive gesture. He took it in both of his.

"You are my idea of a guardian angel," she smiled, though she was near to tears.

"I've never heard," said Mr. Reeder, "of guardian angels with side whiskers."

It was a mean advantage to take of her, yet he was ridiculously pleased as he repeated his little jeu d'esprit to himself in the seclusion of his room.

CHAPTER XI

MR. REEDER closed the door, put on the lights, and set himself to unravel the inexplicable mystery of its opening. Before he went to bed he had shot home the bolt, had turned the key in the lock, and the key was still on the inside. It struck him, as he turned it, that he had never heard a lock that moved so silently or a bolt that slipped so easily into its groove. Both lock and bolt had been recently oiled. He began a scrutiny of the inside face of the door, and provided a simple solution to the somewhat baffling incident of its opening.
The door consisted of eight panels, carved in small lozenge-shaped ornaments. The panel immediately above the lock moved slightly when he pressed it, but it was a long time before he found the tiny spring which held it in place. When that was found, the panel opened like a miniature door. He could thrust his hand through the aperture and slide back the bolt with the greatest ease.
There was nothing very unusual or sinister about this. He knew that many hotels and boarding houses had methods by which a door could be unlocked from the outside—a very necessary precaution in certain eventualities. Mr. Reeder wondered whether he would find a similar safety panel on the door of Margaret Belman's room.
By the time he had completed his inspection, it was daylight, and, pulling back the curtains, he drew a chair to the window and made a survey of as much of the grounds as lay within his line of vision.
There were two or three matters which were puzzling him. If Larmes Keep was the headquarters of the Flack gang, in what manner and for what reason had Olga Crewe been brought into the confederation? He judged her age at twenty-four; she had been a constant visitor, if not a resident, at Larmes Keep for at least ten years, and he knew enough of the ways of the underworld to realize that they did not employ children. Also she had been to a public school of some kind, and that would have absorbed at least four of the ten years. Mr. Reeder shook his head in doubt.
Nothing would happen now until dark, he decided, and, stretching himself upon the bed, he pulled the coverlet over him and slept till a tapping at the door announced the coming of the housemaid with his morning tea. She was a round-faced woman, just past her first youth, with a disagreeable cockney accent and the brusque and familiar manner of one who was an indispensable part of the establishment. Mr. Reeder remembered that the girl had waited on him at dinner.
"Why, sir, you haven't undressed!" she said.
"I seldom undress," said Mr. Reeder, sitting up and taking the tea from her. "It is such a waste of time. For no sooner are your clothes off than it is necessary to put them on again."
She looked at him hard, but he did not smile.
"You're a detective, ain't you? Everybody at the cottage knows that you are. What have you come down about?"
Now Mr. Reeder could afford to smile cryptically. There was a suppressed anxiety in the girl's voice.
"It is not for me, my dear young lady, to disclose your employer's business."
"He brought you down? Well, he's got a nerve!"
Mr. Reeder put his finger to his lips.

"About the candlesticks?"
He nodded.
"He still thinks somebody in the house took them?"
Her face was very red, her eyes snapped angrily. Here was exposed one of the minor scandals of the hotel.
It was not an uninteresting sidelight. For if ever guilt was written on a woman's face it was on hers. What these candlesticks were and how they disappeared, Mr. Reeder could guess. Petty larceny runs in well-defined channels.
"Well, you can tell him from me—" she began shrilly, and he raised a solemn hand.
"Keep the matter to yourself—regard me as your friend," he begged.
He was in his lighter moments a most mischievous man, a weakness that few suspected in Mr. J.G. Reeder. Moreover, he wanted badly some inside information about the household, and he had an idea that this infuriated girl who flounced out and slammed the door behind her would supply him with that information. In his most optimistic moments he could not dream that in her raw hands she held the secret of Larmes Keep.
As soon as he came down, Mr. Reeder decided to go to Daver's office; he was curious to learn the true story of the missing candlesticks. The sound of an angry voice reached him, and as his hand was raised to knock at the door, it was opened by somebody who was holding the handle on the inside, and he heard a woman's angry voice.
"You've treated me shabbily: that's all I can say to you, Mr. Daver! I've been working for you five years and I've never said a word about your business to anybody! And now you bring a detective down to spy on me! I won't be treated as if I was a thief or something! If you think that's behaving fair and square, after all I've done for you, and minding my own business.... Yes, I know I've been well paid, but I could get just as much money somewhere else. I've got my pride, Mr. Daver, the same as you have, and I think you've been very underhand, the way you've treated me. I'll go to-night, don't you worry!"
The door was flung open and a red-faced girl of twenty-five flounced out and dashed past the eavesdropper, scarcely noticing him in her fury. The door shut behind her; evidently Mr. Daver was in as bad a temper as the girl—a fortunate circumstance, as it proved, and Mr. Reeder decided it might be inadvisable to advertise that he had overheard the whole or part of the conversation.
When he strolled out into the sunlit grounds, of all the people who had been disturbed during the night he was the brightest and showed the least sign of fatigue. He met the Rev. Mr. Dean and the Colonel, who was carrying a golf bag, and they bade him a gruff good-morning. The Colonel, he thought, was a little haggard; Mr. Dean gave him a scowl as he passed.
Walking up and down the lawn, he examined the front of the house with a critical eye. The lines of the Keep were very definite: harsh and angular; not even the Tudor windows, which at some remote period had been introduced to its stony face, could disguise its ancient grimness.
Turning an angle of the house, he reached the strip of lawn that faced his own window. Behind the lawn was a mass of rhododendron bushes, which might serve a useful purpose, but which in certain circumstances might also be a danger point.
Immediately beneath his window was an angle of the drawing room, a circumstance that gave him cause for satisfaction. Mr. Reeder's experience favoured a bedroom that was above a public apartment.
He went back on his tracks and came to the other end of the lawn. Those three windows, brightly curtained, were evidently Mr. Daver's private suite. Beneath them, the wall was black, the actual

stone being obscured by a thick growth of ivy. He wondered what this lightless and doorless space contained.

As he returned to the front of the house he saw Margaret Belman. She was standing in front of the doorway, shading her eyes from the sun, evidently searching her limited landscape for somebody. Seeing him, she came quickly to meet him.

"Oh, there you are!" she said, with a sigh of relief. "I wondered what had happened to you—you didn't come down to breakfast."

She looked a little peaked, he thought. Evidently she had not rounded off the night as agreeably as he.

"I haven't slept since I saw you," she said, answering his unspoken question. "What happened, Mr. Reeder? Did somebody really try to get into the house—a burglar?"

"I think somebody tried, and I think succeeded," said Mr. Reeder carefully. "Burglaries happen even in—um—hotels, Miss—um—Margaret. Has Mr. Daver notified the police?"

She shook her head.

"I don't know. He has been telephoning all the morning—I went to his room just now and it was locked, but I heard his voice. And, Mr. Reeder, you didn't tell me the terrible thing that happened the night I left London. I saw it in the newspaper this morning."

"Terrible thing?"

J.G. Reeder was puzzled. Almost he had forgotten the adventure of the spring gun.

"Oh, you mean the little joke?"

"Joke!" she said, shocked.

"Criminals have a perverted sense of humour," said Mr. Reeder airily. "The whole thing was—um—an elaborate jest designed to frighten me. One expects such things. They are the examination papers which are set to test one's intelligence from time to time."

"But who did it?" she asked.

Mr. Reeder's gaze wandered absently over the placid countryside. She had a feeling that it bored him even to recall so trivial an incident in a busy life.

"Our young friend," he said suddenly, and, following the direction of his eyes, she saw Olga Crewe.

She was wearing a dark gray knitted suit and a big black hat that shaded her face, and there was nothing of embarrassment in the half smile with which she greeted her fellow guest.

"Good-morning, Mr. Reeder. I think we have met before this morning." She rubbed her arm good-humouredly.

Mr. Reeder was all apologies.

"I don't even know now what happened," she said, and Margaret Belman learned for the first time what had happened before she had made her appearance.

"I never thought you were so strong—look!" Olga Crewe pulled back her sleeve and showed a big blue-black patch on her forearm, cutting short his expression of remorse with a little laugh.

"Have you shown Mr. Reeder all the attractions of the estate?" she asked, a hint of sarcasm in her tone. "I almost expected to find you at the bathing pool this morning."

"I didn't even know there was a bathing pool," said Mr. Reeder. "In fact, after my terrible scare last night, this—um—beautiful house has assumed so sinister an aspect that I expect to bathe in nothing less dramatic than blood!"

She was not amused. He saw her eyes close quickly and she shivered a little.

"How gruesome you are! Come along, Miss Belman."

Inwardly Margaret resented the tone, which was almost a command, but she walked by their side. Clear of the house, Olga stopped and pointed.

"You must see the well. Are you interested in old things?" asked Olga, as she led the way to the shrubbery.

"I am more interested in new things, especially new experiences," said Mr. Reeder, quite gaily. "And new people fascinate me!"

Again that quick, frightened smile of hers.

"Then you should be having the time of your life, Mr. Reeder," she said, "for you're meeting people here whom you've never met before."

He screwed up his forehead in a frown.

"Yes, there are two people in this house I have never met before," he said, and she looked round at him quickly.

"Only two? You've never met me before!"

"I've seen you," said Mr. Reeder, "but I have never met you."

By this time they had arrived at the well, and he read the inscription slowly before he tested the board that covered the top of the well with his foot.

"It has been closed for years," said the girl. "I shouldn't touch it," she added hastily, as Reeder stooped and, catching the edge of the board, swung it back trap fashion, leaving an oblong cavity.

The trap did not squeak or creak as he turned it back; the hinges were oiled; there was no accumulation of dust between the two doors. Going on to his hands and knees, he looked down into the darkness.

"How many loads of rubble and rock were used to fill up this well?" he asked.

Margaret read from the little notice board.

"Hum!" said Mr. Reeder, groped in his pockets, took out a two-shilling piece, poised the silver coin carefully and let it drop.

For a long, long time he listened, and then a faint metallic tinkle came up to him.

"Nine seconds!" He looked up into Olga's face. "Deduct from the velocity of a falling object the speed at which sound travels, and tell me how deep this hole is."

He got to his feet, dusted the knees of his trousers, and carefully dropped the trap into position.

"Rock there may be," he said, "but there is no water. I must work out the number of loads requisite to fill this well entirely—it will be an interesting morning's occupation for one who in his youth was something of a mathematical genius."

Olga Crewe led the way back to the shrubbery in silence. When they came to the open: "I think you had better show Mr. Reeder the rest of the establishment," she said. "I'm rather tired." And with a nod, she turned away and walked toward the house.

Mr. Reeder gazed after her with something like admiration in his eyes.

"The rouge would, of course, make a tremendous difference," he said, half speaking to himself, "but it is very difficult to disguise voices—even the best of actors fail in this respect."

Margaret stared at him.

"Are you talking to me?"

"To myself," said Mr. Reeder humbly. "It is a bad habit of mine, peculiar to my age, I fear."

"But Miss Crewe never uses rouge."

"Who does—in the country?" asked Mr. Reeder, and pointed with his walking stick to the wall along the cliff. "Where does that lead? What is on the other side?"

"Sudden death," said Margaret, and laughed.

For a quarter of an hour they stood leaning on the parapet of the low wall, looking down at the strip of beach below. The small channel that led to the cave interested him. He asked her how deep it was. She thought that it was quite shallow, a conclusion with which he did not agree. "Underground caves sound romantic, and that channel is deeper than most. I think I must explore the cave. How does one get down?"

He looked left and right. The beach was enclosed in a deep little bay, circled on one side by sheer cliff, on the other by a high reef of rock that ran far out to sea. Mr. Reeder pointed to the horizon.

"Sixty miles from here is France."

He had a disconcerting habit of going off at a tangent.

"I think I will do a little exploring this afternoon. The walk should freshen me."

They were returning to the house when he remembered the bathing pool and asked to see it.

"I wonder Mr. Daver doesn't let it run dry," Margaret said. "It is an awful expense. I was going through the municipality's account yesterday, and they charge a fabulous sum for pumping up fresh water."

"How long has it been built?"

"That is the surprising thing," she said. "It was made twelve years ago, when private swimming pools were things unheard of in this country."

The pool was oblong in shape; one end of it was tiled and obviously artificially created. The farther end, however, had for its sides and bottom natural rock. A great dome-shaped mass served as a diving platform. Mr. Reeder walked all round, gazing into the limpid water. It was deepest at the rocky end, and here he stayed longest, and his inspection was most thorough. There seemed a space—how deep he could not tell—at the bottom of the bath, where the rock overhung.

"Very interesting," said Mr. Reeder at last. "I think I will go back to the house and get my bathing suit. Happily I brought one."

"I didn't know you were a swimmer," smiled the girl.

"I am the merest tyro in most things," said Mr. Reeder modestly.

He went up to his room, undressed and slipped into a bathing suit, over which he put his overcoat. Olga Crewe and Mr. Daver had gone down to Siltbury. To his satisfaction, he saw the hotel car descending the hill road cautiously in a cloud of dust.

When Mr. Reeder threw off his coat to make the plunge there was something comically ferocious in his appearance, for about his waist he had fastened a belt to which was fastened in a sheath a long-bladed hunting knife, and in addition there dangled a water-proof bag in which he had placed one of the many little hand lamps that he invariably carried about with him. He made the most human preparations: put his toes into the cold water, and shivered ecstatically before he made his plunge. Losing no time in preliminaries, he swam along the bottom to the slit in the rock which he had seen.

It was about two feet high and eight feet in length, and into this he pulled his way, gripping the roof to aid his progress. The roof ended abruptly; he found nothing but water above him, and he allowed himself to come to the surface, catching hold of a projecting ledge to keep himself afloat whilst he detached the waterproof bag from his belt, and, planting it upon the shelf, took out his flashlamp.

He was in a natural stone chamber, with a broad, vaulted roof. He was, in fact, inside the dome-shaped rock that formed one end of the pool. At the farthermost corner of the chamber was an opening about four feet in height and two feet in width. A rock passage that led downward, he saw. He followed this for about fifty yards and noted that, although nature had hewn or worn this queer corridor at some remote age—possibly it had been an underground waterway before some gigantic upheaval of nature had raised the land above water level—the passage owed something of its practicability to human agency. At one place there were marks of a chisel; at another, unmistakable signs of blasting. Mr. Reeder retraced his steps and came back to the water. He fastened and resealed his lamp, and, drawing a long breath, dived to the bottom and wormed his way through the aperture to the bath and to open air. He came to the surface to gaze into the horror-stricken face of Margaret Belman.

"Oh, Mr. Reeder!" she gasped. "You—you frightened me! I heard you jump in, but when I came here and found the bath empty I thought I must have been mistaken. Where have you been? You couldn't stay under water all that time."

"Will you hand me my overcoat?" said Mr. Reeder modestly, and when he had hastily buttoned this about his person: "I have been to see that the County Council's requirements are fully satisfied," he said solemnly.

She listened, dazed.

"In all theatres, as you probably know, my dear Miss—um—Margaret, it is essential that there should be certain exits in case of necessity. I have already inspected two this morning, but I rather imagine that the most important of all has so far escaped my observation. What a man! Surely madness is akin to genius!"

He lunched alone, and apparently no man was less interested in his fellow guests than Mr. J.G. Reeder. The two golfers had returned and were eating at the same table. Miss Crewe, who came in late and favoured him with a smile, sat at a little table facing him.

"She is uneasy," said Mr. Reeder to himself. "That is the second time she has dropped her fork. Presently she will get up, sit with her back to me—I wonder on what excuse?"

Apparently no excuse was necessary. The girl called a waitress toward her and had her glass and tableware shifted to the other side of the table. Mr. Reeder was rather pleased with himself. Daver minced into the dining room as Mr. Reeder was peeling an apple.

"Good-morning, Mr. Reeder. Have you got over your nightmare? I see that you have! A man of iron nerve. I admire that tremendously. Personally, I am the most dreadful coward, and the very hint of a burglar makes me shiver. You wouldn't believe it, but I had a quarrel with a servant this morning and she left me shaking! You are not affected that way? I see that you are not! Miss Belman tells me that you tried our swimming pool this morning. You enjoyed it? I am sure you did!"

"Won't you sit down and have coffee?" asked Mr. Reeder politely, but Daver declined the invitation with a flourish and a bow.

"No, no, I have my work. I cannot tell you how grateful I am to Miss Belman for putting me on the track of the most fascinating character of modern times. What a man!" said Mr. Daver, unconsciously repeating J.G. Reeder's tribute. "I've been trying to trace his early career—no, no, I'll stand: I must run away in a minute or two. Is anything known about his early life? Was he married?"

Mr. Reeder nodded. He had not the slightest idea that John Flack was married, but it seemed a moment to assert the universality of his knowledge. He was quite unprepared for the effect upon Daver. The jaw of the yellow-faced man dropped.

"Married?" he squeaked. "Who told you he was married? Where was he married?"

"That is a matter," said Mr. Reeder gravely, "which I cannot discuss."

"Married!" Daver rubbed his little round head irritably, but did not pursue the subject. He made some inane reference to the weather and bustled out of the room.

Mr. Reeder settled himself in what he called the banqueting hall with an illustrated paper, awaiting an opportunity which he knew must present itself sooner or later.

The servants he had passed under review. Girls were employed to wait at table, and these lived in a small cottage on the Siltbury side of the estate. The manservants, including the hall porter, seemed above suspicion. The porter was an old army man with a row of medals across his uniform jacket; his assistant was a chinless youth recruited from Siltbury. He apparently was the only member of the staff that did not live in one of the cottages. In the main, the women servants were an unpromising lot. The infuriated waitress was his only hope, although as likely as not she would talk of nothing but her grievances.

From where he sat he had a view of the lawn. At three o'clock the Colonel and the Rev. Mr. Dean and Olga Crewe passed out of the main gate, evidently bound for Siltbury. He rang the bell and, to his satisfaction, the aggrieved waitress came and took his order for tea.

"This is a nice place," said Mr. Reeder conversationally.

The girl's "Yes, sir" was snappy.

"I suppose," mused Mr. Reeder, looking out of the window, "that this is the sort of situation that a lot of girls would give their heads to get and break their hearts to lose?"

Evidently she did not agree.

"The upstairs work isn't so bad," she said, "and there's not much to do in the dining room. But it's too slow for me. I was at a big hotel before I came here. I'm going to a better job—and the sooner the better."

She admitted that the money was good, but she had a longing for that imponderable quantity which she described as "life." She also expressed a preference for man guests.

"Miss Crewe—so called—gives more trouble than all the rest of the people put together," she said. "I can't make her out. First she wants one room, then she wants another. Why she can't stay with her husband, I don't know."

"With her—?" Mr. Reeder looked at her in pained surprise. "Perhaps they don't get on well together?"

"They used to get on all right. If they weren't married, I could understand all the mystery they're making—pretending they're not, him in his room and she in hers, and meeting like strangers. When all that kind of deceit is going on, things are bound to get lost," she added inconsequently.

"How long has this been—er—going on?" asked Mr. Reeder.

"Only the last week or so," said the girl viciously. "I know they're married, because I've seen her marriage certificate—they've been married six years. She keeps it in her dressing case."

She looked at him with sudden suspicion.

"I oughtn't to have told you that. I don't want to make trouble for anybody, and I bear them no malice, though they've treated me worse'n a dog," she said. "Nobody else in the house but me knows. I was her maid for two years. But if people don't treat me right, I don't treat them right."

"Married six years? Dear me!" said Mr. Reeder.

And then he suddenly turned his head and faced her.

"Would you like fifty pounds?" he asked. "That is the immense sum I will give you for just one little peep at that marriage certificate."

The girl went red.

"You're trying to catch me," she said, hesitated, and then: "I don't want to get her into trouble."

"I am a detective," said Mr. Reeder, "but I am working on behalf of the Chief Registrar, and we have a doubt as to whether that marriage was legal. I could, of course, search the young lady's room and find the certificate for myself, but if you would care to help me, and fifty pounds has any attraction for you—"

She paused irresolutely and said she would see. Half an hour later she came into the hall with the news that she had been unsuccessful in her search. She had found the envelope in which the certificate had been kept, but the document itself was gone.

Mr. Reeder did not ask the name of the bridegroom, nor was he mentioned, for he was pretty certain that he knew that fortunate man. He put the question, and the girl answered as he had expected.

"There is one thing I would like to ask you: do you remember the name of the girl's father?"

"John Crewe, merchant," she said promptly. "The mother's name was Hannah. He made me swear on the Bible I'd never tell a soul that I knew they were married."

"Does anybody else know? You said 'nobody,' I think?"

The girl hesitated.

"Yes, Mrs. Burton knows. She knows everything."

"Thank you," said Mr. Reeder, and, opening his pocketbook, took out two five-pound notes.

"What was the husband's profession—do you remember that?"

The woman's lips curled.

"Secretary. Why call himself secretary, I don't know, and him an independent gentleman!"

"Thank you," said Mr. Reeder again.

He telephoned to Siltbury for a taxicab.

"Are you going out?" asked Margaret, finding him waiting under the portico.

"I am buying a few presents for friends in London," said Mr. Reeder glibly; "a butter dish or two, suitably inscribed, would, I feel sure, be very acceptable."

The taxi did not take him to Siltbury. Instead, he followed a road which ran parallel with the sea coast, and which eventually landed him in an impossible sandy track, from which the ancient taxi was extricated with some difficulty.

"I told you this led nowhere, sir," said the aggrieved driver.

"Then we have evidently reached our destination," replied Mr. Reeder, applying his weight to push the machine to a more solid foundation.

Siltbury was not greatly favoured by London visitors, the driver told him on the way back. The town had a pebbly beach and people preferred sand.

"There are some wonderful beaches about here," said the driver, "but you can't reach 'em."

They had taken the left-hand road, which would bring them eventually to the town, and had been driving for a quarter of an hour when Mr. Reeder, who sat by the driver, pointed to a large scar in the face of the downs on his right.

"Siltbury Quarries," explained the cabman. "They're not worked now; there are too many holes."

"Holes?"

"The downs are like a sponge," said the man. "You could lose yourself in the caves. Old Mr. Kimpon used to work the quarries many years ago, and it broke him. There's a big cave there you can drive a coach and four into! About twenty years ago, three fellows went in to explore the caves and never came out again."

"Who owns the quarry now?"

Mr. Reeder wasn't very interested, but when his mind was occupied with a pressing problem he had a trick of flogging along a conversation with appropriate questions, and if he was oblivious of the answers they produced, the sound of the human voice had a sedative effect.

"Mr. Daver owns it now. He bought it after the people were lost in the caves, and had the entrance boarded up. You'll see it in a minute."

They were climbing a gentle slope. As they came to the crest, he pointed down a tidy-looking roadway to where, about two hundred yards distant, Reeder saw an oblong gap in the white face of the quarry. Across this, and falling the cavity except for an irregular space at the top, was a heavy wooden gate.
"You can't see it from here," said the driver, "but the top hole is blocked with barbed wire."
"Is that a gate or a hoarding he has fixed across?"
"A gate, sir. Mr. Daver owns all the land from here to the sea. He used to farm about a hundred acres of the downs, but it's very poor land. In those days he kept his wagons inside the cave."
"When did he give up farming?" asked Mr. Reeder, interested.
"About six years ago," was the reply, and it was exactly the reply Mr. Reeder had expected. "I used to see a lot of Mr. Daver before then," said the driver. "In the old times I had a horse cab, and I was always driving him about. He used to work like a slave—on the farm in the morning, down in the town buying things in the afternoon. He was more like a servant than a master. He used to meet all the trains when visitors arrived—and they had a lot of visitors in those days, more than they have now. Sometimes he went up to London to bring them down. He always went to meet Miss Crewe when the young lady was at school."
"Do you know Miss Crewe?"
Apparently the driver had seen her frequently, but his acquaintance was very limited.
Reeder got down from the cab and climbed the barred gate on to the private roadway. The soil was chalky and the road had the appearance of having been recently overhauled. He mentioned this fact to the cabman and learned that Mr. Daver kept two old men constantly at work making up the road, though why he should do so he had no idea.
"Where would you like to go now, sir?"
"To a quiet place where I can telephone," said Mr. Reeder.
These were the facts that he carried with him, and vital facts they were. During the past six years, the life of Mr. Daver had undergone a considerable change. From being a harassed man of affairs, "more like a servant than a master," he had become a gentleman of leisure. The mystery of the Keep was a mystery no longer. He got Inspector Simpson on the telephone and conveyed to him the gist of his discovery.
"By the way," said Simpson at the finish, "the gold hasn't been sent to Australia yet. There has been trouble at the docks. You don't seriously anticipate a Flack 'operation,' do you?"
Mr. Reeder, who had forgotten all about the gold convoy, made a cautious and noncommittal reply.
By the time he returned to Larmes Keep, the other guests had returned. The hall porter said they were expecting a "party" on the morrow, but as he had volunteered that information on the previous evening Mr. Reeder did not take it very seriously. He gathered that the man spoke in good faith, without any wish to deceive, but he saw no signs of unusual activity; nor, indeed, was there accommodation at the Keep for more than a few more visitors.
He looked around for the aggrieved servant and missed her. A discreet inquiry revealed the fact that she had left that afternoon.
Mr. Reeder went to his room, locked the door, and busied himself in the examination of two great scrapbooks which he had brought down with him. They were the official records of Flack and his gang. Perhaps "gang" was hardly a proper description, for he seemed to use and change his associates as a theatrical manager uses and changes his cast. The police knew close on a score of men who from time to time had assisted John Flack in his nefarious transactions. Some had gone to prison, and had spent the hours of their recovered liberty in a vain endeavour to

reëstablish touch with so generous a paymaster. Some, known to be in his employ, had vanished, and were generally supposed to be living in luxury abroad.

Reeder went through the book, which was full of essential facts, and jotted down the amounts which this strange man had acquired in the course of twenty years' depredations. The total was a staggering one. Flack had worked feverishly, and though he had paid well he had spent little. Somewhere in England was an enormous reserve. And that somewhere, Mr. Reeder guessed, was very close to his hand.

For what had John Flack worked? To what end was this accumulation of money? Was the sheer greed of the miser behind his thefts? Was he working aimlessly, as a madman works, toward some visionary objective?

Flack's greed was proverbial. Nothing satisfied him. The robbery of the Leadenhall Bank had been followed a week later by an attack upon the London Trust Syndicate, carried out, the police discovered, by an entirely new confederation, gathered within a few days of the robbery and yet so perfectly rehearsed that the plan was carried through without a hitch.

Mr. Reeder locked away his books and went downstairs in search of Margaret Belman. The crisis was very near at hand, and it was necessary for his peace of mind that the girl should leave Larmes Keep without delay.

He was halfway down the stairs when he met Daver coming up, and at that moment he received an inspiration.

"You are the very gentleman I wished to meet," he said, "I wonder if you would do me a great favour?"

Daver's careworn face wreathed in smiles.

"My dear Mr. Reeder," he said enthusiastically, "do you a favour? Command me!"

"I have been thinking about last night and my extraordinary experience," said Mr. Reeder.

"You mean the burglar?" interrupted the other quickly.

"The burglar," agreed Mr. Reeder. "He was an alarming person, and I am not disposed to let the matter rest where it is. Fortunately for me, I have found a finger print on the panel of my door."

He saw Daver's face change.

"When I say I have found a finger print, I have found something which has the appearance of a finger print, and I can only be sure if I examine it by means of a dactyloscope. Unfortunately, I did not imagine that I should have need for such an instrument, and I am wondering if you could send somebody to London to bring it down for me?"

"With all the pleasure in life," said Daver, though his tone lacked heartiness. "One of the men—"

"I was thinking of Miss Belman," interrupted J.G. Reeder, "who is a friend of mine and would, moreover, take the greatest possible care of that delicate mechanism."

Daver was silent for a moment, turning this over in his mind.

"Would it not be better if a man—and the last train down—"

"She could come down by car; I can arrange that."

Mr. Reeder fumbled his chin.

"Perhaps it would be better if I brought down a couple of men from the Yard."

"No, no," said Daver quickly. "You can send Miss Belman. I haven't the slightest objection. I will tell her."

Mr. Reeder looked at his watch.

"The next train is at eight thirty-five, and that is the last train, I think. The young lady will be able to get her dinner before she starts."

It was he who brought the news to the astonished Margaret Belman.

"Of course I'll go up to town; but don't you think somebody else could get this instrument for you, Mr. Reeder? Couldn't you have it sent down—"

She saw the look in his eyes and stopped.

"What is it?" she asked, in a lower voice.

"Will you do this for—um—me, Miss—um—Margaret?" said Mr. Reeder, almost humbly.

He went to the lounge and scribbled a note, while Margaret telephoned for the cab. It was growing dark when the closed landau drew up before the hotel and J.G. Reeder, who accompanied her, opened the door.

"There's a man inside," he said, dropping his voice to a whisper. "Please don't scream: he's an officer of police and he's going with you to London."

"But—but—" she stammered.

"And you'll stay in London to-night," said Mr. Reeder. "I will join you in the morning—I hope."

CHAPTER XII

MR. REEDER was in his room, laying out his moderate toilet requirements on the dressing table, and meditating upon the waste of time involved in conforming to fashion—for he had dressed for dinner—when there came a tap at the door. He paused, a well-worn hairbrush in his hand, and looked around.
"Come in," he said, and added: "if you please."
The little head of Mr. Daver appeared around the opening of the door, anxiety and apology in every line of his peculiar face.
"Am I interrupting you?" he asked. "I am terribly sorry to bother you at all, but Miss Belman being away, you quite understand? I'm sure you do."
Mr. Reeder was courtesy itself.
"Come in, come in, sir," he said. "I was merely preparing for the night. I am a very tired man, and the sea air—"
He saw the face of the proprietor fall.
"Then, Mr. Reeder, I have come upon a useless errand. The truth is"—he slipped inside the door, closed it carefully behind him as though he had an important statement to make which he did not wish to be overheard—"my three guests are anxious to play bridge, and they deputed me to ask if you would care to join them?"
"With pleasure," said Mr. Reeder graciously. "I am an indifferent player, but if they will bear with me, I shall be down in a few minutes."
Mr. Daver withdrew, babbling his gratitude and apologies.
The door was hardly closed upon him before Mr. Reeder crossed the room and locked it. Stooping, he opened one of the trunks, took out a long, flexible rope ladder, and dropped it through the open window into the darkness below, fastening one end to the leg of the four-poster. Leaning out of the window, he said something in a low voice, and braced himself against the bed to support the weight of the man who came nimbly up the ladder into the room. This done, he replaced the rope ladder in his trunk, locked it, and, walking to a corner of the room, pulled at one of the solid panels. It hinged open and revealed the deep cupboard which Mr. Daver had shown him.
"That is as good a place as any, Brill," he said. "I'm sorry I must leave you for two hours, but I have an idea that nobody will disturb you there. I am leaving the lamp burning, which will give you enough light."
"Very good, sir," said the man from Scotland Yard, and took up his post.
Five minutes later, Mr. Reeder locked the door of his room and went downstairs to the waiting party.
They were in the big hall, a very silent and preoccupied trio, until his arrival galvanized them into something that might pass for light conversation. There was indeed a fourth present when he came in: a sallow-faced woman in black, who melted out of the hall at his approach, and he guessed her to be the melancholy Mrs. Burton. The two men rose at his approach, and after the usual self-deprecatory exchange which preceded the cutting for partners, Mr. Reeder found himself sitting opposite the military looking Colonel Hothling. On his left was the pale girl; on his right, the hard-faced Rev. Mr. Dean.
"What do we play for?" growled the Colonel, caressing his moustache, his steely blue eyes fixed

on Mr. Reeder.

"A modest stake, I hope," begged that gentleman. "I am such an indifferent player."

"I suggest sixpence a hundred," said the clergyman. "It is as much as a poor parson can afford."

"Or a poor pensioner either," grumbled the Colonel, and sixpence a hundred was agreed.

They played two games in comparative silence. Reeder was sensitive of a strained atmosphere but did nothing to relieve it. His partner was surprisingly nervous for one who, as he remarked casually, had spent his life in military service.

"A wonderful life," said Mr. Reeder in his affable way.

Once or twice he detected the girl's hand, as she held the cards, tremble never so slightly. Only the clergyman remained still and unmoved, and incidentally played without error.

It was after an atrocious revoke on the part of his partner, a revoke which gave his opponents the game and rubber, that Mr. Reeder pushed back his chair.

"What a strange world this is!" he remarked sententiously. "How like a game of cards!"

Those who were best acquainted with Mr. Reeder knew that he was most dangerous when he was most philosophical. The three people who sat about the table heard only a boring commonplace, in keeping with their conception of this somewhat dull-looking man.

"There are some people," mused Mr. Reeder, looking up at the lofty ceiling, "who are never happy unless they have all the aces. I, on the contrary, am most cheerful when I have in my hand all the knaves."

"You play a very good game, Mr. Reeder."

It was the girl who spoke, and her voice was husky, her tone hesitant, as though she was forcing herself to speak.

"I play one or two games rather well," said Mr. Reeder. "Partly, I think, because I have such an extraordinary memory—I never forget knaves."

There was a silence. This time the reference was too direct to be mistaken.

"There used to be in my younger days," Mr. Reeder went on, addressing nobody in particular, "a knave of hearts, who eventually became a knave of clubs, and drifted down into heaven knows what other welters of knavery! In plain words, he started his professional—um—life as a bigamist, continued his interesting and romantic career as a tout for gambling hells, and was concerned in a bank robbery in Denver. I have not seen him for years, but he is colloquially known to his associates as 'the Colonel': a military looking gentleman with a pleasing appearance and a glib tongue."

He was not looking at the Colonel as he spoke, so he did not see the man's face go pale.

"I have not met him since he grew a moustache, but I could recognize him anywhere by the peculiar colour of his eyes and by the fact that he has a scar at the back of his head, a souvenir of some unfortunate fracas in which he became engaged. They tell me that he became an expert user of knives—I gather he sojourned a while in Latin America—a knave of clubs and a knave of hearts—hum!"

The Colonel sat rigid, not a muscle of his face moving.

"One supposes," Mr. Reeder continued, looking at the girl thoughtfully, "that he has by this time acquired a competence which enables him to stay at the very best hotels without any fear of police supervision."

Her dark eyes were fixed unwaveringly on his. The full lips were closed, the jaws set.

"How very interesting you are, Mr. Reeder!" she drawled at last. "Mr. Daver tells me you are associated with the police force?"

"Remotely, only remotely," said Mr. Reeder.

"Are you acquainted with any other knaves, Mr. Reeder?"

It was the cool voice of the clergyman, and Mr. Reeder beamed around at him.

"With the knave of diamonds," he said softly. "What a singularly appropriate name for one who spent five years in the profitable pursuit of illicit diamond-buying in South Africa, and five unprofitable years on the breakwater in Capetown, becoming, as one might say, a knave of spades from the continual use of that necessary and agricultural implement, and a knave of pickaxes, too, one supposes. He was flogged, if I remember rightly, for an outrageous assault upon a warder, and on his release from prison was implicated in a robbery in Johannesburg. I am relying on my memory, and I cannot recall at the moment whether he reached Pretoria Central—which is the colloquial name for the Transvaal prison—or whether he escaped. I seem to remember that he was concerned in a banknote case which I once had in hand. Now, what was his name?"

He looked thoughtfully at the clergyman. "Gregory Dones! That is it—Mr. Gregory Dones! It is beginning to come back to me now. He had an angel tattooed on his left forearm, a piece of decoration which one would have imagined sufficient to keep him to the narrow paths of virtue, and even to bring him eventually within the fold of the church."

The Rev. Mr. Dean got up from the table, put his hand in his pocket and took out some money.

"You lost the rubber, but I think you win on points," he said. "What do I owe you, Mr. Reeder?"

"What you can never pay me," said Mr. Reeder, shaking his head. "Believe me, Gregory, your score and mine will never be wholly settled to your satisfaction!"

With a shrug of his shoulders and a smile, the hard-faced clergyman strolled away. Mr. Reeder watched him out of the corner of his eye and saw him disappear toward the vestibule.

"Are all your knaves masculine?" asked Olga Crewe.

Reeder nodded gravely.

"I hope so, Miss Crewe."

Her challenging eyes met his.

"In other words, you don't know me?" she said bluntly. And then, with sudden vehemence: "I wish to God you did! I wish you did!"

Turning abruptly, she almost ran from the hall.

Mr. Reeder stood where she had left him, his eyes roving left and right. In the shadowy entrance of the hall, made all the more obscure by the heavy dark curtains which covered it, he saw a dim figure standing. Only for a second, and then it disappeared. The woman Burton, he thought.

It was time to go to his room. He had taken only two steps from the table when all the lights in the hall went out. In such moments as these Mr. Reeder was a very nimble man. He spun round and made for the nearest wall, and stood waiting, his back to the panelling. And then he heard the plaintive voice of Mr. Daver.

"Who on earth has put the lights out? Where are you, Mr. Reeder?"

"Here!" said Mr. Reeder, in a loud voice, and dropped instantly to the ground. Only in time; he heard a whistle, a thud, and something struck the panel above his head.

Mr. Reeder emitted a deep groan and crawled rapidly and noiselessly across the floor. Again came Daver's voice.

"What on earth was that? Has anything happened, Mr. Reeder?"

The detective made no reply. Nearer and nearer he was crawling toward where Daver stood. And then, as unexpectedly as they had been extinguished, the lights went on. Daver was standing in front of the curtained doorway, and on the proprietor's face was a look of blank dismay, as Mr. Reeder rose at his feet.

Daver shrank back, his big white teeth set in a fearful grin, his round eyes wide open. He tried to speak and his mouth opened and closed, but no sound issued. From Reeder his eyes strayed to the panelled wall—but Reeder had already seen the knife buried in the wood.

"Let me think," he said gently. "Was that the Colonel or the highly intelligent representative of the Church?"

He went across to the wall and with an effort pulled out the knife. It was long and broad.

"A murderous weapon," said Mr. Reeder.

Daver found his voice.

"A murderous weapon," he echoed hollowly. "Was it—thrown at you, Mr. Reeder? How very terrible!"

Mr. Reeder was gazing at him sombrely.

"Your idea?" he asked, but by now Mr. Daver was incapable of replying.

Reeder left the shaken proprietor lying limply in one of the big armchairs and walked up the carpeted stairs to the corridor. And if against his black coat the automatic was not visible, it was nevertheless there.

He stopped before his door, unlocked it, and threw it wide open. The lamp by the side of the bed was still burning. Mr. Reeder switched on the wall light, peeped through the crack between the door and the wall before he ventured inside.

He shut the door, locked it, and walked over to the cupboard.

"You may come out, Brill," he said. "I presume nobody has been here?"

There was no answer, and he pulled open the cupboard door quickly.

It was empty!

"Well, well," said Mr. Reeder, and that meant that matters were everything but well.

There was no sign of a struggle; nothing in the world to suggest that Detective Brill had not walked out of his own free will and made his exit by the window, which was still open.

Mr. Reeder tiptoed back to the light-switch and turned it; stretched across the bed and extinguished the lamp; and then he sidled cautiously to the window and peeped round the stone framing. It was a very dark night, and he could distinguish no object below.

Events were moving only a little faster than he had anticipated; for this, however, he was responsible. He had forced the hands of the Flack confederation, and they were extremely able hands.

He was unlocking the trunk when he heard a faint sound of steel against steel. Somebody was fitting a key into the lock, and he waited, his automatic covering the door. Nothing further happened, and he went forward to investigate. His flash-lamp showed him what had happened. Somebody outside had inserted a key, turned it and left it in the lock, so that it was impossible for the door to be unlocked from the inside.

"I am rather glad," said Mr. Reeder, speaking his thoughts aloud, "that Miss—um—Margaret is on her way to London!"

He pursued his lips reflectively. Would he be glad if he also was at this moment en route for London? Mr. Reeder was not very certain about this.

On one point he was satisfied—the Flacks were going to give him a very small margin of time, and that margin must be used to the best advantage.

So far as he could tell, the trunks had not been opened. He pulled out the rope-ladder, groped down to the bottom, and presently withdrew his hand, holding a long white cardboard cylinder. Crawling under the window, he put up his hand and fixed an end of the cylinder in one of the china flower-pots that stood on the broad window-sill and which he had moved to allow the ingress of Brill. When this had been done to his satisfaction, he struck a match and, reaching up, set fire to a little touch-paper at the cylinder's free end. He brought his hand down just in time; something whizzed into the room and struck the panelling of the opposite wall with an angry smack. There was no sound of explosion. Whoever fired was using an air pistol. Again and again, in rapid succession, came the pellets, but by now the cylinder was burning and spluttering, and in another instant the grounds were brilliantly illuminated as the flare burst into a dazzling red flame that, he knew, could be seen for miles.

He heard a scampering of feet below, but dared not look out. By the time the first tender load of detectives had come flying up the drive, the grounds were deserted.

With the exception of the servants, there were only two persons at Larmes Keep when the police began their search. Mr. Daver and the faded Mrs. Burton alone remained. "Colonel Hothling" and "the Rev. Mr. Dean" had disappeared as though they had been whisked from the face of the earth.

Big Bill Gordon interviewed the proprietor.

"This is Flack's headquarters, and you know it. You'll be well advised to spill everything and save your own skin."

"But I don't know the man; I've never seen him!" wailed Mr. Daver. "This is the most terrible thing that has happened to me in my life! Can you make me responsible for the character of my guests? You're a reasonable man? I see you are! If these people are friends of Flack, I have never heard of them in that connection. You may search my house from cellar to garret, and if you find anything that in the least incriminates me, take me off to prison. I ask that as a favour. Is that the statement of an honest man? I see you are convinced!"

Neither he nor Mrs. Burton nor any of the servants who were questioned in the early hours of the morning could afford the slightest clue to the identity of the visitors. Miss Crewe had been in the habit of coming every year and of staying four and sometimes five months. Hothling was a newcomer, as also was the parson. Inquiries made by telephone of the chief of the Siltbury police confirmed Mr. Daver's statement that he had been the proprietor of Larmes Keep for twenty-five years, and that his past was blameless. He himself produced his title deeds. A search of his papers, made at his invitation, and of the three tin boxes in the safe, produced nothing but support for his protestations of innocence.

Big Bill interviewed Mr. Reeder in the hall over a cup of coffee at three o'clock in the morning. "There's no doubt at all that these people were members of the Flack crowd, probably engaged in advance against his escape, and how they got away the Lord knows! I have had six men on duty on the road since dark, and neither the woman nor the two men passed me."

"Did you see Brill?" asked Mr. Reeder, suddenly remembering the absent detective.

"Brill?" said the other in astonishment. "He's with you, isn't he? You told me to have him under your window—"

In a few words Mr. Reeder explained the situation, and together they went up to No. 7. There was nothing in the cupboard to afford the slightest clue to Brill's whereabout. The panels were sounded, but there was no evidence of secret doors—a romantic possibility which Mr. Reeder had not excluded, for this was the type of house where he might expect to find them.

Two men were sent to search the grounds for the missing detective, and Reeder and the police chief went back to finish their coffee.

"Your theory has turned out accurate so far, but there is nothing to connect Daver."

"Daver's in it," said Mr. Reeder. "He was not the knife-thrower; his job was to locate me on behalf of the Colonel. But Daver brought Miss Belman down here in preparation for Flack's escape."

Big Bill nodded.

"She was to be hostage for your good behaviour." He scratched his head irritably. "That's like one of Crazy John's schemes. But why did he try to shoot you up? Why wasn't he satisfied with her being at Larmes Keep?"

Mr. Reeder had no immediate explanation. He was dealing with a madman, a person of whims. Consistency was not to be expected from Mr. Flack.

He passed his fingers through his scanty hair.

"It is all rather puzzling and inexplicable," he said. "I think I'll go to bed."

He was dreaming sleeplessly, under the watchful eye of a Scotland Yard detective, when Big Bill came bursting into the room.

"Get up, Reeder!" he said roughly.

Mr. Reeder sat up in bed, instantly awake.

"What is wrong?" he asked.

"Wrong! That gold lorry left the Bank of England this morning at five o'clock on its way to Tilbury and hasn't been heard from since!"

CHAPTER XIII

AT the last moment the bank authorities had changed their minds, and overnight had sent £53,000 worth of gold for conveyance to the ship. They had borrowed for the purpose an army lorry from Woolwich, a service which is sometimes claimed by the national banking institution. The lorry had been accompanied by eight detectives, the military driver also being armed. Tilbury was reached at half-past eleven o'clock at night, and the lorry, a high-powered Lassavar, had returned to London at two o'clock in the morning. It had been again loaded in the bank courtyard under the eyes of the officer, sergeant, and two men of the guard that is on duty on the bank premises from sunset to sunrise. A new detachment of picked men from Scotland Yard, each carrying an automatic pistol, loaded the lorry for its second journey, the amount of gold this time being £73,000 worth. After the boxes had been put into the van, they had climbed up, and the lorry had driven away from the bank. Each of the eight men guarding this treasure was passed under review by a high officer of Scotland Yard who knew every one personally. The lorry was seen in Commercial Road by a detective inspector of the division, and its progress was noted also by a police cyclist patrol who was on duty at the junction of Ripple and Barking roads.

The main Tilbury road runs within a few hundred yards of the village of Rainham, and it was at this point, only a few miles distant from Tilbury, that the lorry disappeared. Two motor-cyclist policemen, who had gone out to meet the gold convoy and who had received a telephone message from the Ripple road to say that it had passed, grew uneasy and telephoned to Tilbury. It was an airless morning, with occasional banks of mist lying in the hollows, and part of the road, especially near the river, was covered with patches of white fog, which dispersed about eight o'clock in the morning under a southeasterly wind. The mist had almost disappeared when the search party from Tilbury pursued their investigations and came upon evidence of the tragedy which the morning was to reveal. This was an old Ford motor car that had evidently run from the read, miraculously missed a telegraph pole, and ditched itself. The machine had not overturned; there were no visible marks of injury; yet the man who sat at the wheel was stone dead when he was found. An immediate medical examination failed to discover an injury of any kind to the man, who was a small farmer of Rainham, and on the face of it it looked as though he had died of a heart attack whilst on his way to town.

Just beyond the place where he was found, the road dips steeply between high banks. It is known as Coles Hollow, and at its deepest part the cutting is crossed by a single-track bridge, which connects two portions of the farm through which the road runs. The dead farmer and his car had been removed when Reeder and Inspector Simpson of Scotland Yard, who had been put in charge of the case, arrived on the spot. No news of any kind had been received of the lorry; but the local police, who had been following its tracks, had made two discoveries. Apparently, in going through the cutting, the lorry had run almost head-on into the wall of the bank on the right, for there was a deep scoop in the clayey soil which the impact had hollowed out.

"It almost appears," said Simpson, "that the lorry swerved here to avoid the farmer's car. There are his wheel tracks, and you notice they were wobbling from side to side. Probably the man was already dying."

"Have you traced the lorry tracks from here?" asked Reeder.

Simpson nodded and called a sergeant of the Essex Constabulary, who had charted the tracks.

"They seem to have turned up north toward Becontree," he said. "As a matter of fact, a policeman at Becontree said he saw a large lorry come out of the mist and pass him, but that had a tilt on it and was going toward London. It was an army lorry, too, and was driven by a soldier."
Mr. Reeder had lit a cigarette and was holding the flaming match in his hand, staring at it solemnly.
"Dear me!" he said, and dropped the match and noticed that its flame was soon extinguished. And then he began what seemed to be a foolish search of the ground, striking match after match.
"Isn't there light enough for you, Mr. Reeder?" asked Simpson irritably.
The detective straightened his back and smiled. Only for a second was he amused, and then his long face went longer than ever.
"Poor fellow!" he said softly. "Poor fellow!"
"Whom are you talking about?" demanded Simpson, but Mr. Reeder did not reply. Instead, he pointed up to the bridge in the centre of which was an old and rusted water wagon, the type which certain English municipalities still use. He climbed up to the bank and examined the iron tank, opened the hatches and groped inside, lighting matches to aid his examination.
"Is it empty?" asked Simpson.
"I am afraid it is," said Mr. Reeder, and inspected the worn hose leading from its iron spindles. He descended the cutting more melancholy than ever.
"Have you thought how easy it is to disguise an ordinary army lorry?" he asked. "A tilt, I think the sergeant said, and on its way to London."
"Do you think that was the gold van?"
Mr. Reeder nodded.
"I'm certain," he said.
"Where was it attacked?"
Mr. Reeder pointed to the mark of the wheels on the side of the road.
"There," he said simply, and Simpson growled impatiently.
"Stuff! Nobody heard a shot fired, and you don't think our people would go down without a fight, do you? They could have held their own against five times their number, and no crowd has been seen on this road!"
Mr. Reeder nodded.
"Nevertheless, this is where the convoy was attacked and overcome," he said. "I think you ought to look for the lorry with the tilt, and get on to your Becontree man and get a closer description of the machine he saw."
In a quarter of an hour the police car brought them to the little Essex village, and the policeman who had seen the wagon was interviewed. It happened a few minutes before he went off duty, he said. There was a thick mist at the time, and he heard the rumble of the lorry wheels before it came into sight. He described it as a typical army wagon. So far as he could tell it was gray, and had a black tilt with "W.D." and a broad arrow painted on the side, "W.D." standing for War Department, the broad arrow being the sign of the Government. He saw one soldier driving and another sitting by his side. The back of the tilt was laced up and he could not see into the interior. The soldier, as he passed, had waved his hand in greeting, and the policeman had thought no more about the matter, until the robbery of the gold convoy was reported.
"Yes, sir," he said, in answer to Reeder's inquiry, "I think it was loaded. It went very heavily on the road. We often get these lorries coming up from Shoeburyness."
Simpson had put through a telephone inquiry to the Barking police, who had seen the military wagon. But army convoys were no unusual sight in the region of the docks. Either that or one

similar was seen entering the Blackwall Tunnel, but the Greenwich police, on the south side of the river, had failed to identify it, and from there on all trace of the lorry was lost.

"We're probably chasing a shadow anyway," said Simpson. "If your theory is right, Reeder—but it can't be right! They couldn't have caught these men of ours so unprepared that somebody didn't shoot, and there's no sign of shooting."

"There was no shooting," said Mr. Reeder, shaking his head.

"Then where are the men?" asked Simpson.

"Dead," said Mr. Reeder quietly.

It was Scotland Yard, in the presence of an incredulous and horrified commissioner, that Mr. J.G. Reeder reconstructed the crime.

"Flack is a chemist; I think I impressed it upon you. Did you notice, Simpson, on the bridge across the cutting an old water cart? I think you have since learned that it does not belong to the farmer who owns the land, and that he has never seen it before. It may be possible to discover where that was purchased. In all probability you will find that it was bought a few days ago at the sale of some municipal stores. I noticed in the Times there was an advertisement of such a sale. Do you realize how easy it would be not only to store under pressure, but to make, in that tank, large quantities of a deadly gas, one important element of which is carbon monoxide? Suppose this, or, as it may prove, a more deadly gas, has been so stored, do you realize how simple a matter it would be on a still, breathless morning to throw a big hose over the bridge and fill the hollow with the gas? That is, I am sure, what happened. Whatever else was used, there is still carbon monoxide in the cutting, for when I dropped a match it was immediately extinguished, and every match I struck near the ground went out. If the car had run right through and climbed the other slope of the cutting, the driver and the men inside the lorry might have escaped death. As it was, rendered momentarily unconscious, the driver turned his wheel and ran into the bank, stopping the lorry. They were probably dead before Flack and his associate, whoever it was, jumped down, wearing gas masks, lifted the driver back into the lorry and drove on."

"And the farmer—" began the commissioner.

"His death probably occurred some time after the lorry had passed. He also descended into that death hollow, but the speed at which his car was going carried him up nearer the cutting, though he must have been dead by the time he got out."

He rose and stretched himself wearily.

"Now I think I will go and interview Miss Belman and set her mind at rest," he said. "Did you send her to the hotel, as I asked you, Mr. Simpson?"

Simpson stared at him in blank astonishment.

"Miss Belman?" he said. "I haven't seen Miss Belman!"

CHAPTER XIV

HER head in a whirl, Margaret Belman had stepped into the cab that was waiting at the door of Larmes Keep. The door was immediately slammed behind her and the cab moved off. She saw her companion; he had shrunk into a corner of the landau, and greeted her with a little embarrassed grin. He did not speak until the cab was some distance from the house.
"My name's Gray," he said. "Mr. Reeder hadn't a chance to introduce me. Sergeant Gray, C.I.D."
"Mr. Gray, what does all this mean—this instrument I am to get?"
Gray coughed. He knew nothing about the instrument, he explained, but his instructions were to put her into a car that would be waiting at the foot of the hill road.
"Mr. Reeder wants you to go up by car. You didn't see Brill anywhere, did you?"
"Brill?" she frowned. "Who is Brill?"
He explained that there had been two officers inside the grounds, himself and the man he had mentioned.
"But what is happening? Is there anything wrong at Larmes Keep?" she asked.
She had no need to ask the question. That look in J.G. Reeder's eyes had told her that something indeed was very wrong.
"I don't know, miss," said Gray diplomatically. "All I know is that the Chief Inspector is down here with a dozen men and that looks like business. I suppose Mr. Reeder wanted to get you out of it."
She didn't "suppose," she knew, and her heart beat a little quicker.
What was the mystery of Larmes Keep? Had all this to do with the disappearance of Ravini? She tried hard to think calmly and logically, but her thoughts were out of control.
The landau stopped at the foot of the hill, and Gray jumped out. A little ahead of him she saw the tail light of a car drawn up by the side of the roadway.
"You've got the letter, miss? The car will take you straight to Scotland Yard, and Mr. Simpson will look after you."
He followed her to the car and held open the door for her, and stood in the roadway watching till the tail light disappeared round a bend of the road.
It was a big, cosy landaulette, and Margaret made herself comfortable in the corner, pulled the rug over her knees, and settled down to the two hours' journey. The air was a little close; she tried unsuccessfully to pull down one of the windows, then tried the other. Not only was there no glass to the windows, but the shutters were immovable. Something scratched her knuckle. She felt along the frame of the window—screws, recently inserted. It was a splinter of the raw wood which had cut her.
With growing uneasiness she felt for the inside handle of the door, but there was none. A search of the second door revealed a like state of affairs.
Her movements must have attracted the attention of the driver, for the glass panel was pushed back and a harsh voice greeted her.
"You can sit down and keep quiet! This isn't Reeder's car; I've sent it home."
The voice went into a chuckle that made her blood run cold.
"You're coming with me—to see life. Reeder's going to weep tears of blood. You know me, eh? Reeder knows me. I wanted to get him to-night. But you'll do, my dear."
Suddenly the glass panel was shut to. He turned off the main road and was following a

secondary, his object being, she guessed, to avoid the big towns and villages en route. She put out her hand and felt the wall of the car. It was an all-weather body with a leather back. If she had a knife she might cut—
She gasped as a thought struck her, and, reaching up, felt the metal fastening that kept the leather hood attached. Exerting all her strength, she thrust back the flat hook and, bracing her feet against the front of the machine, pulled at the leather hood. A rush of cold air came in as the hood began slowly to collapse. The closed car was now an open car. She could afford to lose no time. The car was making thirty miles an hour, but she must take the risk of injury. Scrambling over the back of the hood, she gripped tight at the edge, and let herself drop into the roadway. Although she turned a complete somersault, she escaped injury in some miraculous fashion, and, coming to her feet, cold with fear and trembling in every limb, she looked round for a way of escape. The hedge on her left was high and unpenetrable. On her right was a low wooden fence, and over this she climbed, as she heard the squeak of brakes and saw the car come to a standstill. Even as she fled, she was puzzled to know what kind of land she was on. It was not cultivated; it was more like common land, for there was springy down beneath her feet, and clumps of gorse bushes sent out their spiny fingers to clutch at her dress as she flew past. She thought she heard the man hailing her, but fled on in the darkness.
Somewhere near at hand was the sea. She could smell the fragrance of it. Once when she stopped to take breath she could hear the distant thunder of the waves as they rolled up some unseen beach. She listened, almost deafened by the beating of her own heart.
"Where are you? Come back, you fool—"
The voice was near at hand. Not a dozen yards away she saw a black figure moving, and had all she could do to stifle the scream that rose in her throat. She crouched down behind a bush and waited, and then to her horror she saw a beam of light spring from the darkness. Her pursuer had an electric lamp and was fanning it across the ground.
Detection was inevitable, and, springing to her feet, she ran, doubling from side to side in the hope of outwitting him. Now she found the ground sloping under her feet, and that gave her additional speed. She had need of it, for he saw her against the skyline, and came on after her, a babbling, shrieking fury of a man. And now capture seemed inevitable. She made one wild leap to escape his outstretched hands, and her feet suddenly trod on nothing. Before she could recover, she was falling, falling. She struck a bush, and the shock and pain of the impact almost made her faint. She was falling down a steep slope, and her wild hands clutched tree and sand and grass, and then just as she had given up all hope, she found herself rolling over and over on a level plateau, and came to rest with one leg hanging over a sheer drop of two hundred feet. Happily, it was dark.
Margaret Belman did not realize how near to death she had been till the dawn came up.
Below her was the sea and a stretch of yellow sand. She was looking into a little bay that held no sign of habitation so far as she could see. This was not astonishing, for the beach was only approachable from the water. Somewhere on the other side of the northern bluff, she guessed, was Siltbury. Beneath her a sheer fall over the chalky face of the cliff; above her, a terribly steep slope, which might be negotiated, she thought hopefully.
She had lost one shoe in her fall, and after a little search found this, so near to the edge of the cliff that she grew dizzy as she stooped to pick it up.
The plateau was about fifty yards long and was in the shape of a half moon, and almost entirely covered with gorse bushes. The fact that she found dozens of birds' nests was sufficient proof that this spot was not visited even by the most daring of cliff climbers. She understood now the

significance of the low rail on the side of the road, which evidently followed the sea coast westward for some miles. How far was she from Larmes Keep? she wondered—until the absurdity of considering such a matter occurred to her. How near was she to starvation and death was a more present problem.

Her task was to escape from the plateau. There was a chance that she might be observed from the sea, but it was a remote one. The few pleasure boats that went out from Siltbury did not go westward; the fishing fleet invariably tacked south. Lying face downward, she looked over the edge in the vain hope that she would find an easy descent, but none was visible. She was hungry, but, though she searched the nests, there were no eggs to be found.

There was nothing to be done but to make a complete exploration of the plateau. Westward it yielded nothing, but on the eastern side she discovered a scrub-covered slope which apparently led to yet another plateau, not so broad as the one she was on.

To slide down was an easy matter; to check herself so that she did not go beyond the plateau offered greater difficulty. With infinite labour, she broke off two stout branches of a thick furze bush, and using these as a skier uses his stick to check her progress, she began to slide down, feet first. She could move slowly enough when the face of the declivity was composed of sand or loam, or when there were friendly bushes to hold, but there were broad stretches of weatherworn rock to slide across, and on these the stick made no impression and her velocity increased at an alarming rate.

And then, to her horror, she discovered that she was not keeping direction; that, try as she would, she was slipping to the left of the plateau, and though she strove desperately to move farther to the right, she made no progress.

The bushes that littered the upper slope were more infrequent here. There was indication of a recent landslide, which might continue down to the sea level or might end abruptly and disastrously over the edge of some steep cliff. Slipping, sometimes on her back, sometimes sideways, sometimes on her face, she felt her momentum increase with every yard she covered. The ends of the furze sticks were frayed to feathery splinters, and already the desired plateau was above her. Turning her head, she saw the white face of it dropping to the unseen deeps.

Now she knew the worst. The slope twisted round a huge rock and dropped at an acute angle into the sea. Almost before she could realize the danger ahead, she was slipping faster and faster through the loam and sand, the centre of a new landslide she had created. Boulders of a terrifying size accompanied her—she escaped being crushed under one by a hair's breadth.

And then without warning she was shot into the air as from a catapult. She had a swift vision of tumbling green below, and in another second the water had closed over her and she was striking out with all her strength....

It seemed almost an eternity before she came to the surface. Fortunately, she was a good swimmer, and, looking round, she saw that the yellow beach was less than fifty yards away. But it was fifty yards against a falling tide, and she was utterly exhausted when she dragged herself ashore and fell on the sand.

She ached from head to foot; her hands and limbs were lacerated. She felt that her body was one huge bruise. As she lay recovering her breath she heard one comforting sound, the splash of falling water. Half-way down the cliff face was a spring, and, staggering across the beach, she drank eagerly from her cupped hands. She was parched; her throat was so dry that she could hardly articulate. Hunger she might bear, but thirst was unendurable. She might remain alive for days, supposing she were not discovered before that time.

There was now no need for her to make a long reconnaissance of the beach; the way of escape lay open to her. A water-hollowed tunnel led through the bluff and showed her yet another beach beyond. Siltbury was not in sight. She had no idea how far she was from that desirable habitation of human beings, and did not trouble to think. After she had satisfied her thirst, she took off her shoes and stockings and made for the tunnel.

The second bay was larger and the beach longer. There were, she found, small masses of rocks jutting far into the sea that had to be negotiated with bare feet. The beach was longer than she had thought, and, so far as she could see, there was no outlet, nor did the cliff diminish in height. She had expected to find a cliff path, and this hope was strengthened when she discovered the rotting hull of a boat drawn high and dry on the beach.

It was, she judged, about eight o'clock in the morning. She had started wet through, but the warm sun dried her rags—as rags they were. She had all the sensations of a shipwrecked mariner on a desert island, and after a while the loneliness and absence of all kinds of human society began to get on her nerves.

Before she reached the end of the beach she saw that the only way into the next bay was by swimming to where the rocky barrier was low enough to be climbed. She could with great comfort to herself have discarded what remained of her clothes, but beyond these rocks might lie civilization; so, tying her wet shoes and stockings together, she made fast her shoes, and, knotting the stockings about her waist, waded into the sea and swam steadily, looking for a likely place to land. This she found—a step-shaped pyramid of rocks that looked easier to negotiate than in fact they were. By dint of hard climbing, she came to the summit.

The beach here was shorter; the cliff considerably higher. Across the shoulder of rock running to the sea she saw the white houses of Siltbury, and the sight gave her courage. Descending from the rocky ridge was even more difficult than climbing, and she was grateful when at last she sat upon a flat ledge and dangled her bruised feet in the water.

Swimming back to the land taxed her strength to the full. It was nearly an hour before her feet touched firm sand and she staggered up the beach. Here she rested until the pangs of hunger drove her toward the last visible obstacle.

There was one which was not visible. After a quarter of an hour's walk, she found her way barred by a deep sea river which ran under the overhung cliff. She had seen this place before—where was it? And then she remembered, with an exclamation.

This was the cave that Olga had told her about, the cave that ran under Larmes Keep. Shading her eyes, she looked up. Yes, there was the little landslide part of the wall that had been carried away projected from a heap of rubble on the cliff side.

Suddenly Margaret saw something which made her breath come faster. On the edge of the deep channel which the water had cut in the sand was the print of a boot, a large, square-toed boot with a rubber heel. It had been recently made. She looked farther along the channel and saw another—it led to the mouth of the cave. On either side of the rugged entrance was a billow of firm sand left by the retreating waters, and again she saw the footprint. A visitor to the cave, perhaps, she thought. Presently he would come out and she would explain her plight, though her appearance left little need for explanation.

She waited, but there was no sign of the man. Stooping, she tried to peer into its dark depths. Perhaps, if she were inside out of the light, she could see better. She walked gingerly along the sand ledge, but as yet her eyes, unaccustomed to the darkness, revealed nothing.

She took another step, passed into the entrance of the cave; and then, from somewhere behind, a bare arm was flung round her shoulder, a big hand closed over her mouth. In terror, she struggled madly, but the man held her in a grip of iron. Then her senses left her and she sank limply into his arms.

CHAPTER XV

MR. REEDER was not an emotional man. For the first time in his life Inspector Simpson learned that behind the calm and imperturbable demeanour of the Public Prosecutor's chief detective lay an immense capacity for violent language. He fired a question at the officer, and Simpson nodded.
"Yes, the car returned. The driver said that he had orders to go back to London. I thought you had changed your plans. You're staying with this bullion robbery, Reeder?"
Mr. Reeder glared across the desk, and despite his hardihood Inspector Simpson winced.
"Staying with hell!" hissed Reeder.
Simpson was seeing the real and unsuspected J.G. Reeder and was staggered.
"I'm going back to interview that monkey-faced criminologist, and I'm going to introduce him to forms of persuasion which have been forgotten since the Inquisition!"
Before Simpson could reply, Mr. Reeder was out of the door and flying down the stairs.
It was the hour after lunch, and Daver was sitting at his desk, twiddling his thumbs, when the door was pushed open unceremoniously and Mr. Reeder came in. He did not recognize the detective, for a man who in a moment of savage humour slices off his side whiskers brings about an amazing change in his appearance. And with the banishing of those ornaments, there had been a remarkable transformation in Mr. Reeder's demeanour. Gone were his useless pince-nez which had fascinated a generation of law-breakers; gone the gentle, apologetic voice, the shyly diffident manner.
"I want you, Daver!"
"Mr. Reeder!" gasped the yellow-faced man, and turned a shade paler.
Reeder slammed the door to behind him, pulled up a chair with a crash, and sat down opposite the hotel proprietor.
"Where is Miss Belman?"
"Miss Belman?"
Astonishment was expressed in every feature. "Good gracious, Mr. Reeder, surely you know? She went up to get your dactyloscope—is that the word? I intended asking you to be good enough to let me see this—"
"Where—is—Miss—Belman? Spill it, Daver, and save yourself a lot of unhappiness."
"I swear to you, my dear Mr. Reeder—"
Reeder leaned across the table and rang the bell.
"Do—do you want anything?" stammered the manager.
"I want to speak to Mrs. Flack—you call her Mrs. Burton, but Mrs. Flack is good enough for me!"
Daver's face was ghastly now. He had become suddenly wizened and old.
"I'm one of the few people who happen to know that John Flack is married," said Reeder; "one of the few who knows he has a daughter. The question is, does John Flack know all that I know?" He glowered down at the shrinking man.
"Does he know that after he was sent to Broadmoor his sneaking worm of a secretary, his toady and parasite and slave, decided to carry on in the Flack tradition, and use his influence and his knowledge to compel the unfortunate daughter of mad John Flack to marry him?"
A frenzied, almost incoherent voice wailed:

"For God's sake—don't talk so loud."

But Mr. Reeder went on:

"Before Flack went to prison he entrusted to his daughter his famous encyclopædia of crime. She was the only person he trusted; his wife was a weak slave whom he had always despised. Mr. Daver, the secretary, got possession of those books a year after Flack was committed to Broadmoor. He organized his own little gang at Flack's old headquarters, which were nominally bought by you. Ever since you knew John Flack was planning an escape—an escape in which you had to assist him—you've been living in terror that he would discover how you had double-crossed him. Tell me I'm a liar and I'll beat your miserable little head off. Where is Margaret Belman?"

"I don't know," said the man sullenly. "Flack had a car waiting for her—that's all I know."

Something in his tone, something in the shifty slant of his eyes infuriated Reeder. He stretched out a long arm, gripped the man by the collar and jerked him savagely across the desk. As a feat of physical strength it was remarkable; as a piece of propaganda of the frightfulness that was to follow, it had a strange effect upon Daver. He lay limp for a second, and then, with a quick jerk of his collar, he wrenched himself from Reeder's grip and fled from the room, slamming the door behind him. By the time Reeder had kicked an overturned chair from his path, and opened the door, Daver had disappeared.

When Reeder reached the hall, it was empty. He met none of the servants (he learned later that the majority had been discharged that morning, paid a month's wages, and sent to town by the first train). He ran out of the main entrance on to the lawn, but the man he sought was not in sight. The other side of the house drew blank. One of the detectives on duty in the grounds, attracted by Mr. Reeder's hasty exit, came running into the vestibule as he reached the bottom of the stairs.

"Nobody came out, sir," he said, when Reeder explained the object of his search.

"How many men are there in the grounds?" asked Reeder shortly. "Four? Bring them into the house. Lock every door, and bring back a crowbar with you. I am going to do a little investigation that may cost me a lot of money. No sign of Brill?"

"No, sir," said the detective, shaking his head sadly. "Poor old Brill! I'm afraid they've done him. The young lady get to town all right, sir?"

Mr. Reeder scowled at him.

"The young lady—what do you know about her?" he asked sharply.

"I saw her to the car," said Detective Gray.

Reeder gripped him by the coat and led him into the vestibule.

"Now, tell me, and tell me quickly, what sort of car was it?"

"I don't know, Mr. Reeder," said the man in surprise. "An ordinary kind of car, except that the windows were shuttered, but I thought that was your idea."

"What sort of body had it?"

The man described the machine as accurately as possible; he had only made a superficial inspection. He thought, however, it was an all-weather body. The news was no more than Reeder had expected; neither added to nor diminished his anxiety. When Gray had returned with his three companions and the doors had been locked, Mr. Reeder, from the landing above, called them to the first floor. A very thorough search had already been made by the police that morning; but, so far, Daver's room had escaped anything but superficial attention. It was situated at the far end of the corridor, and was locked when the search party arrived. It took less than two minutes to force an entrance. Mr. Daver's suite consisted of a sitting room, a bedroom, and a handsomely fitted bathroom. There were a number of books in the former, a small empire table on which were neatly arranged a pile of accounts, but there was nothing in the way of documents to reveal his relationship with the Flack gang.

The bedroom was beautifully furnished. Here again, from Reeder's point of view, the search was unsatisfactory.

The suite formed one of the angles of the old Keep, and Reeder was leaving the room when his eyes, roving back for a last look around, were arrested by the curious position of a brown leather divan in one corner of the room. He went back and tried to pull it away from the wall, but apparently it was a fixture. He kicked at the draped side and it gave forth a hollow wooden sound.

"What has he got in that divan?" he asked.

After considerable search Gray found a hidden bolt, and, throwing this back, the top of the divan came up like the lid of a box. It was empty.

"The rum thing about this house, sir," said Gray as they went downstairs together, "is that one always seems on the point of making an important discovery and it always turns out to be a dud."

Reeder did not reply; he was too preoccupied with his growing distress. After a while, he spoke.

"There are many queer things about this house—" he began.

And then there came a sound which froze the marrow of his bones. It was a shrill shriek; the scream of a human soul in agony.

"Help! Help, Reeder!"

It came from the direction of the room he had left, and he recognized Daver's voice.

"Oh, God—!"

The sound of a door slamming. Reeder took the stairs three at a time, the detectives following him. Daver's door he had left ajar, but in the short time he had been downstairs it had been shut and bolted.

"The crowbar, quick!"

Gray had left it below and, flying down, returned in a few seconds.

No sound came from the room. Pushing the claw of the crowbar between architrave and door at the point where he had seen the bolt, Reeder levered it back, and the door flew open with a crash. One step into the apartment, and then he stood stock still, glaring at the bed, unable to believe his eyes.

On the silken counterpane, sprawled in an indescribable attitude, his round, sightless eyes staring at the ceiling, was Daver. Mr. Reeder knew that he was dead before he saw the terrible wound or the brown-hilted knife that stuck out from his side.

Reeder leaned down and listened for a heartbeat—felt the still warm wrist, but it was a waste of time, as he knew.

He made a quick search of the clothing. There was an inside pocket in the waistcoat, and here he found a thick pad of banknotes.

"All thousands," said Mr. Reeder, "and ninety-five of them. What's in that packet?"

It was a little cardboard folder and contained a steamship ticket from Southampton to New York, made out in the name of "Sturgeon," and in the coat pocket Reeder found a passport which was stamped by the American Consul and bore the same name.

"He was ready to jump—but he delayed it too long," he said. "Poor devil!"

"How did he get here, sir?" asked Gray. "They couldn't have carried him—"

"He was alive enough when we heard him," said Reeder curtly. "He was being killed when we heard him shriek. There is a way into this room we haven't discovered yet. What's that?"

It was the sound of a muffled thud, as if a heavy door had been closed. It seemed to come from somewhere in the room. Reeder took the crowbar from the detective's hand and attacked the panel behind the settee. Beneath was solid wall. He ripped down another strip, with no more enlightening result. Again he opened the divan. Its bottom was made of a thin layer of oak. This, too, was ripped off; beneath this again was the stone floor.

"Strip it," said Reeder, and when this was done he stepped inside the divan and seesawed gingerly from one end to the other.

"There's nothing here," he said. "Go downstairs and 'phone Mr. Simpson. Tell him what has happened."

When the man had gone, he resumed his examination of the body. Daver had carried, attached to one of the buttons of his trousers, a long gold chain. This was gone; he found it broken off close to the link, and the button itself hanging by a thread. It was while he was making his examination that his hand touched a bulky package in the dead man's hip pocket. It was a worn leather case, filled with scraps of memoranda, mostly indecipherable. They were written in a formless hand, generally with pencil, and the writing was large and irregular, while the paper used for these messages was of every variety. One was a scrawled chemical formula; another was a brief note which ran:

"House opposite Reeder to let. Engage or get key. Communicate usual place."

Some of these notes were understandable, some beyond Mr. Reeder's comprehension. But he came at last to a scrap which swept the colour from his cheeks. It was written in the same hand on the margin of a newspaper and was crumpled into a ball:

"Belman fell over cliff 6 miles west Larme. Send men to get body before police discover."

Mr. J.G. Reeder read and the room spun round.

CHAPTER XVI

WHEN Margaret Belman recovered consciousness, she was in the open air, lying in a little recess, effectively hidden from the mouth of the cave. A man in a torn shirt and ragged trousers was standing by her side, looking down at her. As she opened her eyes she saw him put his finger to his mouth, as though to signal silence. His hair was unkempt; streaks of dried blood zigzagged down his face, and the hair above, she saw, was matted. Yet there was a certain kindliness in his disfigured face which reassured her, as he knelt down and, making a funnel of his hands, whispered:
"Be quiet! I'm sorry to have frightened you, but I was scared you'd shout if you saw me. I suppose I look pretty awful."
His grin was very reassuring.
"Who are you?" she answered in the same tone.
"My name's Brill, C.I.D."
"How did you get here?" she asked.
"I'd like to be able to tell you," he answered grimly. "You're Miss Belman, aren't you?"
She nodded. He lifted his head, listening, and, flattening himself against the rock, craned out slowly and peeped round the edge of his hiding place. He did not move for about five minutes, and by this time she had risen to her feet. Her knees were dreadfully shaky; she felt physically sick; her mouth was dry and parched.
Apparently satisfied, he crept back to her side.
"I was left on duty in Reeder's room. I thought I heard him calling from the window—you can't distinguish voices when they whisper—asking me to come out quick as he wanted me. I'd hardly dropped to the ground before—gosh!" He touched his head gingerly and winced. "That's all I remember till I woke up and found myself drowning. I've been in the cave all the morning—naturally."
"Why naturally?" she whispered.
"Because the beach is covered with water at high tide and the cave's the only place. It is a little too densely populated for me just now."
She stared at him in amazement.
"Populated? What do you mean?"
"Whisper!" he warned her, for she had raised her voice.
Again he listened.
"I'd like to know how they get down—Daver and that old devil."
She felt herself going white.
"You mean—Flack?"
He nodded.
"Flack's only been here about an hour, and how he got down, God knows. I suppose our fellows are patrolling the house?"
"The police?" she asked in astonishment.
"Flack's headquarters—didn't you know it? I suppose you wouldn't. I thought Reeder—I mean Mr. Reeder—told you everything."
He was rather a talkative young man, more than a little exuberant at finding himself alive, and with good reason.

"I've been dodging in and out the cave all the morning. They've got a sentry on duty up there"—he nodded toward Siltbury. "It's a marvellous organization. They held up a gold convoy this morning and got away with it—I heard the old man telling his daughter. The strange thing is that, though he wasn't there to superintend the steal, his plan worked out like clockwork. It's a curious thing, any crook will work for old Flack. He's employed the cleverest people in the business, and Ravini is the only man that ever sold him."

"Do you know what has happened to Mr. Ravini?" she asked, and he shook his head.

"He's dead, I expect. There are a lot of things in the cave that I haven't seen, and some that I have. They've got a petrol boat inside as big as a church—the boat I mean— Hush!"

Again he shrank against the cliff. Voices were coming nearer and nearer. Perhaps it was the peculiar acoustics of the cave which gave him the illusion that the speakers were standing almost at their elbow. Brill recognized the thin, harsh voice of the old man and grinned again, but it was not a pleasant smile to see.

"There's something wrong, something damnably wrong. What is it, Olga?"

"Nothing, Father."

Margaret recognized the voice of Olga Crewe.

"You have been very good and very patient, my love, and I would not have planned to come out, but I wanted to see you settled in life. I am very ambitious for you, Olga."

A pause, and then:

"Yes, Father."

Olga Crewe's voice was a little dispirited, but apparently the old man did not notice this.

"You are to have the finest husband in the land, my dear. You shall have a house that any princess would envy. It shall be of white marble with golden cupolas—you shall be the richest woman in the land, Olga. I have planned this for you. Night after night as I lay in bed in that dreadful place I said to myself: 'I must go out and settle Olga's future.' That is why I came out—only for that reason. All my life I have worked for you."

"Mother says—-" began the girl.

"Pah!" Old John Flack almost spat the word. "An unimaginative commoner with the soul of a housekeeper! She has looked after you well? Good. All the better for her. I would never have forgiven her if she had neglected you. And Daver? He has been respectful? He has given you all the money you wanted?"

"Yes, Father."

Margaret thought she detected a catch in the girl's voice.

"Daver is a good servant. I will make his fortune. The scum of the gutter—but faithful. I told him to be your watchdog. I am pleased with him. Be patient a little while longer. I am going to see all my dreams come true."

The voice of the madman was tender, so transfigured by love and pride that it seemed to be a different man who was speaking. Then his voice changed again.

"The Colonel will be back to-night. He is a trustworthy man—Gregory also. They shall be paid like ambassadors. You must bear with me a little while longer, Olga. All these unpleasant matters will be cleared up. Reeder we shall dispose of. To-morrow at high tide we leave..."

The sound of the voices receded until they became an indistinguishable murmur. Brill looked round at the girl and smiled again.

"Can you beat him?" he whispered admiringly. "Crazy as a barn coot! But he has the cleverest brain in London—even Reeder says that. God! I'd give ten years' salary and all my chance of promotion for a gun!"

"What shall we do?" she asked after a long silence.

"Stay here till the tide turns, then we'll have to take our chance in the cave. We'd be smashed to pieces if we waited on the beach."

"There's no way up the cliff?"

He shook his head.

"There's a way out through the cave if we can only find it," he said. "One way? A dozen! I tell you that this cliff is like a honeycomb. One of these days it will collapse like froth on a glass of beer! I heard Daver say so, and the mad fellow agreed. Mad? I wish I had his brain! He's going to dispose of Reeder, is he? The cemeteries are full of people who've tried to dispose of Reeder!"

CHAPTER XVII

IT seemed an eternity before the tide turned and began slowly to make its noisy way up the beach. Most of the time Margaret was alone in the little recess, for Brill made periodical reconnaissances into the mouth of the cave. She would have accompanied him, but he explained the difficulties she would find.
"It is quite dark until the tide comes in, and then we get the reflected light from the water and you can see your way about quite easily."
"Is there anybody there?"
He nodded.
"Two chaps who are tinkering about with a boat. She's high and dry at present on the bed of the channel, but she floats out quite easily."
The first whirl of water was around them when he came out from the cave and beckoned her.
"Keep close to the wall," he whispered, "and hold fast to my sleeve."
She obeyed and followed him, and they slipped round to the left, following a fairly level path. Before they had come into the cave, he had warned her that under no circumstances must she speak, not even whisper, except through hollowed hands placed against his ear. The acoustics of the cave were such that the slightest sound was magnified.
They went a long way to the left, and she thought that they were following a passage; it was not until later that she discovered the huge dimensions of this water-hollowed cavern. After a while, he reached back and touched her right hand, as a signal that he was turning to the right.
Whilst they were waiting on the beach, he had drawn a rough plan in the sand, and assured her that the ledge on which they now walked offered no obstacle. He pressed her hand to warn her he was stopping, and, bending down, he groped at the rocky wall where he had left his shoes. Up and up they went; she began to see dimly now, though the cave remained in darkness and she was unable with any accuracy to pick out distant objects. His arm came back and she found herself guided into a deep niche, and he patted her shoulder to tell her she could sit down.
They had to wait another hour before a thin sheet of water showed at the mouth of the cave, and then, as if by magic, the interior was illuminated by a ghostly green light. The height of it was impossible to tell from where she sat, because just above them was a low and jagged roof. The farther side of the cave was distant some fifty yards, and here the rocky wall seemed to run straight down from the roof to the sandy bottom. It was under this that she saw the motor boat, a long gray craft, entirely devoid of any superstructure. It lay heeled over on its side, and she saw a figure walk along the canted deck and disappear down a hatchway. The farther the water came into the cave, the brighter grew the light. He circled his two hands about her ear and whispered:
"Shall we stay here or try to find a way out?" and she replied in like fashion:
"Let us try."
He nodded, and silently led the way. It was no longer necessary for her to hold on to him. The path they were following had undoubtedly been shaped by human hands. Every dozen yards was a rough-hewn block of stone put across the path step fashion. They were ascending, and now had the advantage of being screened by the cave from people on the boat, for on their right rose a jagged screen of rock.
They had not progressed a hundred yards before screen and wall joined, and beyond this point progress seemed impossible. The passage was in darkness. Apparently Brill had explored the

way, for, taking the girl by the arm, he moved to the right, feeling along the uneven wall. The path beneath was more difficult, and the rocky floor made walking a pain. She was near to exhaustion when she saw, ahead of her, an irregular patch of gray light. Apparently this curious gallery led back to the far end of the cave, but before they reached the opening, Brill signalled her to halt.

"You'd better sit down," he whispered. "We can put on our shoes."

The stockings that she had knotted about her waist were still wet, and her shoes two soggy masses, but she was glad to have some protection for her feet. Whilst she was putting them on, Brill crept forward to the opening and took observation.

The water which had now flooded the cave was some fifty feet below him, and a few paces would bring them to a broad ledge of rock which formed a natural landing for a flight of steps leading down from the misty darkness of the roof to water level. The steps were cut in the side of the bare rock; they were about two feet in breadth and were unprotected even by a makeshift handrail. It would be, he saw, a nerve-racking business for the girl to attempt the climb, and he was not even sure that it would be worth the attempt. That they led to one of the many exits from the cave, he knew, because he had seen people climbing up and down those steps and disappearing in the darkness at the top. Possibly the stairs broadened nearer the roof, but even so it was a very severe test for a half-starved girl who he guessed was on the verge of hysteria; he was not quite certain that he himself would not be attacked by vertigo if he made the attempt. There was a space behind the steps that brought him to the edge of the rock, part of the floor of the cave, and it was this way that he intended to guide Margaret. There was no sound; far away to his right the men on the launch were apparently absorbed in their work. Returning, he told the girl his plan, and she accompanied him to the foot of the steps. At the sight of that terrifying stairway, she shuddered.

"I couldn't possibly climb those," she whispered as he pointed upward into the gloom.

"I have an idea there is a sort of balcony running the width of the cave, and it was from there I was thrown," he said. "I have reason to know that there is a fairly deep pool at the foot of it. When the tide is up, the water reaches the back wall—that is where I found myself when I came to my senses."

"Is there any other way from the cave?" she asked.

He shook his head.

"I'm blessed if I know. I've only had a very hasty look round, but there seems to be a sort of tunnel at the far end. It's worth while exploring—nobody is about, and we are too far from the boat for them to see us."

They waited for a while, listening, and then, Brill walking ahead, they passed the foot of the stairs and followed a stony path which, to the girl's relief, broadened as they progressed. Margaret Belman never forgot that nightmare walk, with the towering rock face on her left, the straight drop to the floor of the cave on her right hand.

They had now reached the limit of the rocky chamber, and found themselves confronted with the choice of four openings. There was one immediately facing them; another—and this was also accessible—about forty feet to the right; and two others which apparently could not be reached. Leaving Margaret, Brill groped his way into the nearest. He was gone half an hour before he returned with a story of failure.

"The whole cliff is absolutely bored with rock passages," he said. "I gave it up because it is impossible to go far without a light."

The second opening promised better. The floor was even and it had this advantage, that it ran straight in line with the mouth of the cave, and there was light for a considerable distance. She followed him along this passage.

"It is worth trying," he said, and she nodded her agreement.

They had not gone far before he discovered something which he had overlooked on his first trip. At regular intervals there were niches in the wall. He had noticed these but had failed to observe their extraordinary regularity. The majority were blocked with loose stone, but he found one that had not been so guarded and felt his way round the wall. It was a square, cell-like chamber, so exactly proportioned that it must have been created by the hand of man. He came back to announce his intention of exploring the next of the closed cells.

"These walls haven't been built up for nothing," he told her, and there was a note of suppressed excitement in his voice.

The farther they progressed, the poorer and more inadequate was the light. They had to feel their way along the wall until the next recess was reached. Flat slabs of rock, laid one on the other, had been piled up in the entrance, and the work of removing the top layers was a painful one. Margaret could not help him. She sat with her back to the wall and fell into the uneasy sleep of exhaustion. She had almost ceased to be hungry, though her throat was parched with a maddening thirst. She woke heavily and found Brill shaking her shoulder.

"I've been inside." His voice was quavering with excitement. "Hold out your hands, both together!"

She obeyed mechanically and felt something cold drop into her palm, and, drooping her head, drank. The sting of wine took her breath away.

"Champagne," he whispered. "Don't drink too much or you'll get tight!"

She sipped again. Never had wine tasted so delicious.

"It's a storehouse; boxes of food, I think, and hundreds of bottles of wine. Hold your hand."

He poured out another portion of wine; most of it escaped through her fingers, but she drank eagerly the few drops that remained.

"Wait here."

She was very much awake now; she peered into the darkness toward the place where he had disappeared. Ten minutes, a quarter of an hour passed, and then, to her joy, there appeared from behind the stony barrier, revealing in silhouette the hole through which Brill had crawled, a white and steady light. She heard the creak and crash of a box being opened, saw the bulk of the detective as he appeared in the hole, and in a second he was by her side.

"Biscuits," he said. "Luckily the box was labelled."

"What was the light?" she asked, as she seized the crackers eagerly.

"A small battery lantern; I knocked it over as I was groping. The place is simply stocked with grub! Here's a drink for you."

He handed her a flat, round tin, guided her finger to the hole he had punched.

"Preserved milk—German, and good stuff," he said.

She drank thirstily, not taking her lips from the tin until it was empty.

"This seems to be the ship's store," he said, "but the great blessing is the lamp. I'm going in to see if I can find a box of refills; there isn't a great deal of juice left in the battery."

His search occupied a considerable time, and then she saw the light go out and her heart sank, until it flashed up again, this time more brilliant than ever. He scrambled out and dropped down the rugged wall and pushed something heavy into her hand.

"A spare lamp," he said. "There are half a dozen there and enough refills to last us a month."

He struck the stone wall with something that clanged.

"A case opener," he explained, "and a useful weapon. I wonder which of these storehouses holds the guns?"

The exploration of the passage could now be made in comparative comfort. There was need of the lamps, for a few yards farther on the tunnel turned abruptly to the right and the floor became more irregular. Brill turned on his light and showed the way. Now the passage turned to the left, and he pointed out how smooth were the walls.

"Water action," he said. "There must have been a subterranean river here at one time."

Twisting and turning, the gallery led now up, now down, now taking almost a hairpin turn, now sweeping round in an almost perfect curve, but leading apparently nowhere.

Brill was walking ahead, the beam of his lamp sweeping along the ground, when she saw him stop suddenly. Stooping, he picked something from the ground.

"How the dickens did this get here?"

On the palm of his hand lay a bright silver florin, a little battered at the edge, but unmistakably a two-shilling piece.

"Somebody has been here—" he began and then she uttered a cry.

"Oh!" gasped Margaret. "That was Mr. Reeder's!"

She told him of the incident at the well; how J.G. Reeder had dropped the coin to test the distance. Brill put the light of his lamp on the ceiling; it was solid rock. And then he sent the rays moving along, and presently the lamp focussed on a large round opening.

"Here is the well that never was a well," he said grimly and, flashing the light upward, looked open-mouthed at the steel rungs fitted every few inches in the side of the well.

"A ladder," he said slowly. "What do you know about that?"

He reached up, standing on tiptoe, but the nearest rung was at least a yard beyond his hand, and he looked round for some loose stones which he could pile up and from the top of which he could reach the lowest bar of the ladder. But none was in sight, except a few splinters of stone which were valueless for his purpose. And then he remembered the case-opener; it had a hook at the end. Holding this above his head, he leapt. The first time he missed; the second time the hook caught the steel rung and the handle slipped from his grip, leaving the case-opener dangling. He rubbed his hands on the dusty floor and sprang again. This time he caught and held, and with a superhuman effort pulled himself up until his hand gripped the lower rung. Another struggle, and he had drawn himself up hand over hand till his feet rested on the bar.

"Do you think if I pulled you up you have strength to climb?" he asked.

She shook her head.

"I'm afraid not. Go up alone; I will wait here."

"Keep clear of the bottom," he warned her. "I may not fall, but as likely as not I shall dislodge a few chunks of rock in my progress."

The warning was well justified, she found. There was a continuous shower of stone and earth as he progressed. From time to time, he stopped to rest. Once he shouted down something which she could not distinguish. It was probably a warning, for a few seconds later a mass of rock as large as a man's head crashed down and smashed on the floor, sending fragments flying in all directions.

Peeping up from time to time, she could see the glimmer of his lamp growing fainter; and now, left alone, she began to grow nervous, and for company switched on her light. She had hardly done so when she heard a sound which brought her heart to her mouth. It was the sound of footsteps; somebody was walking along the passage toward her.

She turned the switch of the lamp and listened. The old man's voice! Only his, and none other.

He was talking to himself, a babble of growling sound that was becoming more and more distinct. And then, far away, she saw the glow of a reflected light, for the passage swept around at this point and he would not be visible until he was upon her.

Slipping off her shoes, she sped along in the darkness, tumbling and sliding on the uneven pathway. After a while panic left her and she stopped and looked back. The light was no longer visible; there was neither sound nor sign of him; and, plucking up courage, after a few minutes she retraced her steps. She dared not put on the light, and must guess where the well opening was. In the darkness she passed it and she was soon a considerable distance beyond the place where Brill had left her.

Where had Flack gone? There were no side passages. She was standing by one of the recesses, her hand resting on the improvised stone screen, when to her horror she felt it moving away from her, and had just time to shrink back when she saw a crack of light appear on the opposite wall and broaden until there was outlined the shape of a doorway.

"... To-night, my dear, to-night ... I'm going up to see Daver. Daver is worrying me.... You are sure nothing has happened that might shake my confidence in him?"

"Nothing, Father. What could have happened?"

It was Olga Crewe's voice. She said something else which Margaret could not hear, and then she heard the chuckling laugh of the old man.

"Reeder? He's busy in London! But he'll be back to-night...."

Again a question which Margaret could not catch.

"The body hasn't been found. I didn't want to hurt the girl, but she was useful ... my best card.... I could have caught Reeder with her—had it all arranged."

Another question.

"I suppose so. The tide is very high. Anyway, I saw her fall...."

Margaret knew they were talking about her, but this interested her less than the possibility of discovery. She walked backward, step by step, hoping and praying that she would find a niche into which she could shrink. Presently she found what she wanted.

Flack had come out into the passage and was standing talking back into the room.

"All right, I'll leave the door open.... Imagination. There's plenty of air. The well supplies that. I'll be back this evening."

She dared not look, but after a while his footsteps became fainter. The door was still open, and she saw a shadow growing larger on the opposite wall as Olga approached the entrance.

Presently she heard a sigh; the shadow became small again and finally disappeared. Margaret crept forward, hardly daring to breathe, until she came up behind the open door.

It was, she guessed, made of stout oak, and the surface had been so cunningly camouflaged with splinters of rock that it differed in no respect from the walled recess into which Brill had broken. Curiosity is dominant in the most rational of individuals, and, despite her terrible danger, Margaret was curious to see the inside of that rocky home of the Flacks. With the utmost caution she peeped round. She was surprised at the size of the room and a little disappointed in its furnishing. She had pictured rich rugs and gorgeous furniture, the walls perhaps covered with silken hangings. Instead, she saw a plain deal table on which stood a lamp, a strip of threadbare carpet, two basket chairs and a camp bed. Olga was standing by the table, looking down at a newspaper; her back was toward the girl, and Margaret had time to make a more prolonged scrutiny.

Near the table were three or four suitcases, packed and strapped as though in preparation for a journey. A fur coat lay across the bed, and that was the only evidence of luxury in this grim apartment. There was a second person in the room. Margaret distinguished in the shadow the drooping figure of a woman—Mrs. Burton.

She took a step forward to see better, her feet slipped upon the smooth surface of the rock and she fell forward against the door, half closing it.

"Who is there? Is that you, Father?"

Margaret's heart nearly stopped beating, and for a moment she stood paralyzed, incapable of movement. Then, as Olga's footsteps sounded, she turned and fled along the passage, gripping tight her lantern. Olga's voice challenged her, but on and on she ran. The corridor was growing lighter, and with a gasp of horror she realized that, in the confusion of the moment, she had taken the wrong direction and she was running toward the great cave, possibly into the old madman's hands.

She heard the quick patter of footsteps behind her and flew on. And now she was in the almost bright light of the huge cavern. There was nobody in sight, and she followed the twisting ledge that ran under the wall of rock until she came to the foot of the long stairs. And then she heard a shout. Somebody on the boat had seen her. As she stood motionless with fear, mad John Flack appeared. He was coming toward her through the passage by which she and Brill had reached the interior of the cave. For a second he stared at her as though she were some ghastly apparition of his mad dreams, and then with a roar he leaped toward her.

She hesitated no longer. In a second, she was flying up that awful staircase, death on her right hand, but a more hideous fate behind. Higher and higher up those unrailed stairs—she dared not look, she dared not think; she could only keep looking steadfastly upward into the misty gloom where this interminable Jacob's ladder ended on some solid floor. Not for a fortune would she have looked behind, or vertigo would have seized her. Her breath was coming in long sobs; her heart beat as though it would burst. She dared pause for an infinitesimal time to recover breath before she continued her flight. He was an old man; she could outdistance him. But he was a madman, a thing of terrible and abnormal energy. Panic was leaving her; it exhausted too much of her strength. Upward and upward she climbed, until she was in gloom, and then, when it seemed that she could get no farther, she reached the head of the stairs. A broad, flat space, with a rocky roof which, for some reason, had been straightened with concrete pillars. There were dozens of these pillars ... once she had taken a fortnight's holiday in Spain; there was a cathedral in Cordoba of which this broad vault reminded her ... all sense of direction was lost now. She came with terrifying suddenness to a blank wall; ran along it until she came to a narrow opening where there were five steps and here she stopped to turn on her light. Facing her was a steel door with a great iron handle, and the steel door was ajar.

She pulled it toward her, ran through, pulled the door behind her; it fastened with a click. It had something attached to its inner side, a steel projection—as she shut the door a box fell with a crash. There was yet another door before her, and this was immovable. She was in a tiny white box of a room, three feet wide, little more in depth. She had no time to continue her observations. Someone was fumbling with the handle of the door through which she had come. She gripped in desperation at the iron shelf and felt it slide a little to the right. Though she did not know this, the back part of the shelf acted as a bolt. Again she heard the fumbling at the handle and the click of a key turning, but the steel door remained immovable, and Margaret Belman sank in a heap to the ground.

CHAPTER XVIII

J.G. REEDER came downstairs, and those who saw his face realized that it was not the tragedy he had almost witnessed which had made him so white and drawn.
He found Gray in Daver's office, waiting for his call to London. It came through as Reeder entered the room, and he took the instrument from his subordinate's hand. He dismissed the death of Daver in a few words, and went on:
"I want all the local policemen we can muster, Simpson, though I think it would be better if we could get soldiers. There's a garrison town five miles from here; the beaches have to be searched, and I want these caves explored. There is another thing: I think it would be advisable to get a destroyer or something to patrol the waters before Siltbury. I'm pretty sure that Flack has a motor boat—there's channel deep enough to take it, and apparently there is a cave that stretches right under the cliff.... Miss Belman? I don't know. That is what I want to find out."
Simpson told him that the lorry carrying the gold had been seen at Sevenoaks, and it required a real effort on Mr. Reeder's part to bring his mind to such a triviality.
"I think soldiers will be best. I'd like a strong party posted near the quarry. There's another cave there where Daver used to keep his wagons. I have an idea you might pick up the money tonight. That," he added, a little bitterly, "will induce the authorities to use the military!"
After the ambulance had come and the pitiable wreck of Daver had been removed, he returned to the man's suite with a party of masons he had brought up from Siltbury. Throwing open the lid of the divan, he pointed to the stone floor.
"That flag works on a pivot," he said, "but I think it is fastened with a bolt or a bar underneath. Break it down."
A quarter of an hour was sufficient to shatter the stone flooring, and then, as he had expected, he found a narrow flight of stairs leading to a square stone room which remained very much as it had been for six hundred years. A dusty, bare apartment which yielded its secret. There was a small open door and a very narrow passage, along which a stout man would walk with some difficulty, and which led to behind the panelling of Daver's private office. Mr. Reeder realized that anybody concealed here could hear every word that was spoken. And now he understood Daver's frantic plea that he should lower his voice when he spoke of the marriage. Crazy Jack had learned the secret of his daughter's degradation. From that moment Daver's death was inevitable.
How had the madman escaped? That required very little explanation. At some remote period, Larmes Keep had evidently been used as a show place. He found an ancient wooden inscription fixed to the wall, which told the curious that this was the torture chamber of the old Counts of Larme; it added the useful information that the dungeons were immediately beneath and approached through a stone trap. This the detectives found, and Mr. Reeder had his first view of the vaulted dungeons of Larmes Keep.
It was neither an impressive nor a thrilling exploration. All that was obvious was that there were three routes by which the murderer could escape, and that all three ways led back to the house, one exit being between the kitchen and the vestibule.
"There is another way out," said Reeder shortly, "and we haven't found it yet."
His nerves were on edge. He roamed from room to room, turning out boxes, breaking open cupboards, emptying trunks. One find he made: it was the marriage certificate, and it was

concealed in the lining of Olga Crewe's dressing case.

At seven o'clock, the first detachment of troops arrived by motor van. The local police had already reported that they had found no trace of Margaret Belman. They pointed out that the tide was falling when the girl left Larmes Keep, and that, unless she was lying on some invisible ledge, she must have reached the beach in safety. There was a very faint hope that she was alive. How faint J.G. Reeder would not admit.

A local cook had been brought in to prepare dinner for the detective, but Reeder contented himself with a cup of strong coffee—food, he felt, would have choked him.

He had posted a detachment in the quarry and, returning to the house, was sitting in the big hall, pondering the events of the day, when Gray came flying into the room.

"Brill!" he gasped.

J.G. Reeder sprang to his feet with a bound.

"Brill?" he repeated huskily. "Where is Brill?"

There was no need for Gray to point. A dishevelled and grimy figure, supported by a detective, staggered through the doorway.

"Where have you come from?" asked Reeder.

The man could not speak for a second. He pointed to the ground, and then, hoarsely:

"From the bottom of the well.... Miss Belman is down there now!"

Brill was in a state of collapse, and not until he had had a stiff dose of brandy was he able to articulate a coherent story. Reeder led a party to the shrubbery and the windlass was tested.

"It won't bear even the weight of a woman, and there's not sufficient rope," said Gray, who made the test.

One of the officers remembered that, in searching the kitchen, he had found two window-cleaners' belts, stout straps with a safety hook attached. He went in search of these while Mr. Reeder stripped his coat and vest.

"There's a gap of four feet halfway down," warned Brill. "The stone came away when I put my foot on it, and I nearly fell."

Reeder, his lamp swung around his neck, peered down into the hole.

"It's strange I didn't see this ladder when I saw the well before," he said, and then remembered that he had only opened one half of the hinged trap.

Gray, who was also equipped with a belt, descended first, as he was the lighter of the two. By this time half a company of soldiers were on the scene, and by the greatest of good fortune the unit that had been turned out to assist the police was a company of the Royal Engineers. While one party went in search of ropes, the other began to extemporize a hauling gear.

The two men worked their way down without a word. The lamps were fairly useless, for they could not show them the next rung, and after a while they began to move more cautiously. Gray found the gap and called a halt while he bridged it. The next rung was none too secure, Mr. Reader thought, as he lowered his weight upon it, but they passed the danger zone with no other mishap than that which was caused by big pebbles dropping on Reeder's head.

It seemed as though they would never reach the bottom, and the strain was already telling upon the older man when Gray whispered:

"This is the bottom, I think," and sent the light of his lamp downward. Immediately afterward, he dropped to the rocky floor of the passage, Mr. Reeder following.

"Margaret!" he called in a whisper.

There was no reply. He threw the light first one way and then the other, but Margaret was not in sight, and his heart sank.

"You go farther along the passage," he whispered to Gray. "I'll take the other direction."
With the light of his lamp on the ground, he half walked, half ran along the twisting gallery. Ahead of him he heard the sound of a movement not easily identified, and he stopped to extinguish the light. Moving cautiously forward, he turned an angle of the passage and saw at the far end indication of light. Sitting down, he looked along, and after a while he thought he saw a figure moving against this artificial skyline. Mr. Reeder crept forward, and this time he was not relying upon a rubber truncheon. He thumbed down the safety catch of his Browning and drew nearer and nearer to the figure. Most unexpectedly it spoke.
"Olga, where has your father gone?"
It was Mrs. Burton, and Reeder showed his teeth in an unamused grin.
He did not hear the reply; it came from some recessed place, and the sound was muffled.
"Have they found that girl?"
Mr. Reeder listened breathlessly, craning his neck forward. The "No" was very distinct.
Then Olga said something that he could not hear, and Mrs. Burton's voice took on her old whine of complaint.
"What's the use of hanging about? That's the way you've always treated me. Nobody would think I was your mother. I wonder I'm not dead, the trouble I've had. I wouldn't be surprised if he didn't murder me some day, you mark my words!"
There came an impatient protest from the hidden girl.
"If you're sick of it, what about me?" said Mrs. Burton shrilly. "Where's Daver? It's funny your father hasn't said anything about Daver. Do you think he's got into trouble?"
"Oh, damn Daver!"
Olga's voice was distinct now. The passion and weariness in it would have made Mr. Reeder sorry for her in any other circumstances. He was too busy being sorry for Margaret Belman to worry about this fateful young woman.
She did not know, at any rate, that she was a widow. Mr. Reeder derived a certain amount of gruesome satisfaction from the superiority of his intelligence.
"Where is he now? Your father, I mean?"
A pause, as she listened to a reply which was not intelligible to Mr. Reeder.
"On the boat? He'll never get across. I hate ships, but a tiny little boat like that— Why couldn't he let us go, when we got him out? I begged and prayed him to—we might have been in Venice or somewhere by now, doing the grand."
The girl interrupted her angrily, and then Mrs. Burton apparently melted into the wall.
There was no sound of a closing door, but Mr. Reeder guessed what had happened. He came forward stealthily till he saw the bar of light on the opposite wall, and, reaching the door, listened. The voices were clear enough now; clearer because Mrs. Burton did most of the talking.
"Do you think your father knows?" She sounded rather anxious. "About Daver, I mean? You can keep that dark, can't you? He'd kill me if he knew. He's got such high ideas about you—princes and dukes and such rubbish! If he hadn't been mad, he'd have cleared out of this game years ago, as I told him, but he'd never take much notice of me."
"Has anybody ever taken any notice of you?" asked the girl wearily. "I wanted the old man to let you go. I knew you would be useless in a crisis."
Mr. Reeder heard the sound of a sob. Mrs. Burton cried rather easily.
"He's only stopping to get Reeder," she whimpered. "What a fool trick! That silly old man! Why, I could have got him myself if I was wicked enough!"
From farther along the corridor came the sound of a quick step.

"There's your father," said Mrs. Burton, and Reeder pulled back the jacket of his Browning, sacrificing the cartridge that was already in the chamber in order that there should be no mistake. The footsteps stopped abruptly, and at the same time came a booming voice from the far end of the passage. It was asking a question. Evidently Flack turned back; his footsteps died away. Mr. Reeder decided that this was not his lucky day.

Lying full length on the ground, he could see John Flack clearly. A pressure of his finger, and the problem of this evil man would be settled eternally. It was a fond idea. Mr. Reeder's finger closed around the trigger, but all his instincts were against killing hi cold blood.

Somebody was coming from the other direction—Gray, he guessed. He must go back and warn him. Coming to his feet, he went gingerly along the passage. The thing he feared happened. Gray must have seen him, for he called out in stentorian tones:

"There's nothing at the other end of the passage, Mr. Reeder—"

"Hush, you fool!" snarled Reeder, but he guessed that the mischief was done.

He turned round, stooped again and looked. Old John Flack was standing at the entrance of the tunnel, his head bent. Somebody else had heard the detective's voice. With a squeak of fear, Mrs. Burton had bolted into the passage, followed by her daughter—an excursion which effectively prevented the use of the pistol, for the women completely masked the man whose destruction J.G. Reeder had privately sworn.

By the time he came to the end of the passage overlooking the great cave, the two women and Flack had disappeared.

Mr. Reeder's eyesight was of the keenest. He immediately located the boat, which was now floating on an even keel, and presently saw the three fugitives. They had descended to the water's edge by a continuance of the long stairway which led to the roof and were making for the rocky platform which served as a pier for the craft.

Something smacked against the rock above his head. There was a shower of stone and dust, and the echoes of the explosion which followed were deafening.

"Firing from the boat," said Mr. Reeder calmly. "You had better lie down, Gray—I should hate to see so noisy a man as you reduced to compulsory silence."

"I'm very sorry, Mr. Reeder," said the penitent detective. "I had no idea—'

"Ideas!" said Mr. Reeder accurately.

Smack smack!

One bullet struck to the left of him, the other passed exactly between him and Gray. He was lying down now, with a small projection of rock for cover.

Was Margaret on the boat? Even as the thought occurred to him, he remembered Mrs. Burton's inquiry. As he saw another flash from the deck of the launch, he threw forward his hand. There was a double explosion which reverberated back from the arched roof, and although he could not see the effect of his shots, he was satisfied that the bullets fell on the launch.

It was pushing off from the side. The three Flacks were aboard. And now he heard the crackle and crash of her engine as her nose swung round to face the cave opening. And then into his eyes from the darkening sea outside the cave flashed a bright light that illuminated the rocky shelf on which he lay and threw the motor boat into relief.

The destroyer!

"Thank God for that!" said Mr. Reeder fervently.

Those on the motor launch had seen the vessel and guessed its portent. The launch swung round until its nose pointed to where the two detectives lay, and from her deck came a roar louder than ever. So terrible was the noise in that confined space that for a second Mr. Reeder was too dazed even to realize that he was lying half buried in a heap of debris, until Gray pulled him back to the passage.

"They're using a gun—a quick-firer!" he gasped.

Mr. Reeder did not reply. He was gazing fascinated, at something that was happening in the middle of the cave, where the water was leaping at irregular intervals from some mysterious cause.

Then he realized what was taking place. Great rocks, disturbed by the concussion, were falling from the roof. He saw the motor boat heel over to the right, swing round again, and head for the open. It was less than a dozen yards from the cave entrance when, with a sound that was indescribable, so terrific, so terrifying that J.G. Reeder was rooted to the spot, the entrance to the cave disappeared!

CHAPTER XIX

IN an instant the air was filled with choking dust. Roar followed roar as the rocks continued to fall.

"The mouth of the cave has collapsed!" roared Reeder in the other's ear. "And the subsidence hasn't finished."

His first instinct was to fly along the passage to safety, but somewhere in that awful void were two women. He switched on his light and crept gingerly back to the bench whence he had seen the catastrophe. But the rays of the lamp could not penetrate into the fog of dust for more than a few yards.

Crawling forward to the edge of the platform, he strove to pierce the darkness. All about him, above, below, on either side, a terrible cracking and groaning was going on, as though the earth itself was in mortal pain. Rocks, large and small, were falling from the roof; he heard the splash of them as they struck the water. One fell on the edge of the platform with a terrific din and bounced into the pit below.

"For God's sake, don't stay here, Mr. Reeder. You will be killed."

It was Gray shouting at him, but J.G. Reeder was already feeling his way toward the steps which led down to where the boat had been moored, and to which he guessed it would drift. He had to hold the lamp almost at his feet. Breathing had become a pain. His face was covered with powder; his eyes smarted excruciatingly; dust was in his mouth, his nose; but still he went on—and was rewarded.

Out of the dust mist came groping the ghostly figure of a woman. It was Olga Crewe.

He gripped her by the arm as she swayed, and pushed her against the rocky wall.

"Where is your mother?" he shouted.

She shook her head and said something; he lowered his ear to her mouth.

"... boat ... great rock ... killed."

"Your mother?"

She nodded. Gripping her by the arm, he half led, half dragged her up the stairs. He found Gray waiting at the top. As easily as though she were a child, Mr. Reeder caught her up in his arms and staggered the distance that separated them from the mouth of the passage.

The pandemonium of splintering rock and crashing boulder was continuous. The air was thicker than ever. Gray's lamp went out, and Mr. Reeder's was almost useless. It seemed a thousand years before they pushed into the mouth of the tunnel. The air was filled with dust even here, but as they progressed it grew clearer, more breathable.

"Let me down—I can walk," said the husky voice of Olga Crewe, and Reeder lowered her gently to her feet.

She was very weak, but she could walk with the assistance that the two men afforded. They stopped at the entrance of the living room. Mr. Reeder wanted the lamp—wanted more the water which she suggested would be found in that apartment.

A cold draught of spring water worked wonders on the girl too.

"I don't know what happened," she said, "but when the cave opening fell in, I think we drifted toward the stage—we always called that place the stage. I was so frightened that I jumped immediately to safety, and I'd hardly reached the rock when I heard a most awful crash. I think a portion of the wall must have fallen on to the boat. I screamed, but hardly heard myself in the

noise. This is punishment! This is punishment! I knew it would come! I knew it! I knew it!"
She covered her grimy face with her hands, and her shoulders shook in the excess of her sorrow and grief.
"There's no sense in crying." Mr. Reeder's voice was sharp and stern. "Where is Miss Belman?"
She shook her head.
"Where did she go?"
"Up the stairway—Father said she escaped. Haven't you seen her?" she asked, raising her tearful face as she began slowly to realize the drift of his question.
He shook his head, his narrowed eyes surveying her steadily.
"Tell me the truth, Olga Flack. Did Margaret Belman escape, or did your father—?"
She was shaking her head before he had completed his sentence, and then, with a little moan, she drooped and would have fallen had not Gray supported her.
"We had better leave the questioning till later."
Mr. Reeder seized the lamp from the table and went out into the tunnel. He had hardly passed the door before there was a crash, and the infernal noises which had come from the cave were suddenly muffled. He looked backward, but could see nothing. He guessed what had happened.
"There is a general subsidence going on in this mass of earth," he said. "We shall be lucky if we get away."
He ran ahead to the opening of the well, and a glad sight met his eyes. On the floor lay a coil of new rope, to which was attached a body belt. He did not see the thin wire which came down from the mouth of the well, but presently he detected a tiny telephone receiver that the engineers had lowered. This he picked up, and his hail was immediately answered.
"Are you all right? Up here it feels as if there's an earthquake somewhere."
Gray was fastening the belt about the girl's waist, and after it was firmly buckled:
"You mustn't faint—do you understand, Miss Crewe? They will haul you up gently, but you must keep away from the side of the well."
She nodded, and Reeder gave the signal. The rope grew taut, and presently the girl was drawn up out of sight.
"Up you go," said Reeder.
Gray hesitated.
"What about you, sir?"
For answer Mr. Reeder pointed to the lowest rung, and, stooping, gripped the leg of the detective and, displaying an unsuspected strength, lifted him bodily so that he was able to grip the lower rung.
"Fix your belt to the rod, hold fast to the nearest rung, and I will climb up over you," said Mr. Reeder.
Never an acrobat moved with greater nimbleness than this man who so loved to pose as an ancient. There was need for hurry. The very iron to which he was clinging trembled and vibrated in his grasp. The fall of stone down the well was continuous and constituted a very real danger. Some of the rungs, displaced by the earth tremors, came away in their grasp. They were less than halfway up when the air was filled with a sighing and a hissing that brought Reeder's heart to his mouth.
Holding on to a rung of the ladder, he put out his hand. The opposite wall, which should have been well beyond his reach, was at less than arm's length away!
The well was bulging under unexpected and tremendous stresses.
"Why have you stopped?" asked Gray anxiously.

"To scratch my head," snarled Reeder. "Hurry!"

They climbed another forty or fifty feet, when from below came a rumble and a crash that set the whole well shivering.

They could see starlight now, and distant objects, which might be heads, that overhung the mouth of the well.

"Hurry!" breathed J.G. Reeder, and moved as rapidly as his younger companion.

Boom!

The sound of a great gun, followed by a thunderous rumbling, surged up the well.

J.G. Reeder set his teeth. Please God, Margaret Belman had escaped from that hell—or was mercifully dead!

Nearer and nearer to the mouth they climbed, and every step they took was accompanied by some new and awful noise from behind them. Gray's breath was coming in gasps.

"I can't go any farther!" croaked the detective. "My strength has gone!"

"Go on, you miserable—" yelled Reeder, and whether it was the shock of hearing such violent language from so mild a man, or the discovery that he was within a few feet of safety, Gray took hold of himself, climbed a few more rungs, and then felt hands grip his arm and drag him to safety.

Mr. Reeder staggered out into the night air and blinked at the ring of men who stood in the light of a naphtha flare.

Was it his imagination, or was the ground swaying beneath his feet?

"Nobody else to come up, Mr. Reeder?"

The officer in charge of the engineers asked the question, and Reeder shook his head.

"Then all you fellows clear!" said the officer sharply. "Move toward the house and take the road to Siltbury—the cliff is collapsing in sections."

The flare was put out, and the soldiers, abandoning their apparatus, broke into a steady run toward Larmes Keep.

"Where is the girl—Miss Crewe?" asked Reeder, suddenly remembering her.

"They've taken her to the house," said Big Bill Gordon, who had made a mysterious appearance from nowhere. "And, Reeder, we have captured the gold convoy! The two men in charge were a fellow who calls himself Hothling and another named Dean—I think you know their real names. Caught them just as the lorry was driving into the quarry cave. This means a big thing for you—"

"To h— with you and your big things!" stormed Reeder, in a fury. "What big things do I want, my man, but the big thing I have lost?"

Very wisely, Big Bill Gordon made no attempt to argue the matter.

They found the banqueting hall crowded with policemen, detectives, and soldiers. The girl had been taken into Daver's office, and here he found her in the hands of the three women servants who had been commandeered to run the establishment while the police were in occupation. The dust had been washed from her face, and she was conscious, but still in the half-stupefied condition in which Reeder had found her.

She stared at him for a long time as though she did not recognize him and was striving to recall that portion of her past in which he had figured. When she spoke, it was to ask a question.

"There is no news of—Father?"

"None," said Reeder, almost brutally. "I think it will be better for you, young lady, if he is dead."

She nodded.

"He is dead," she said with conviction. And then, rousing herself, she struggled to a sitting position and looked at the servants. Mr. Reeder interpreted that glance and sent the women away.

"I don't know what you are going to do with me," she said, "but I suppose I am to be arrested. I should be arrested, for I have known all that was happening, and I tried to lure you to your death."

"In Bennett Street, of course," said Mr. Reeder. "I recognized you the moment I saw you here—you were the lady with the rouged face."

She nodded and continued:

"Before you take me away, I wish you would let me have some papers that are in the safe," she said. "They have no value to anybody but myself."

He was curious enough to ask her what they were.

"They were letters—in the big, flat box that is locked. Even Daver did not dare open that. You see, Mr. Reeder"—her breath came more quickly—"before I met my—husband, I had a little romance—the sort of romance that a young girl has when she is innocent enough to dream and has enough faith in God to hope. Is my husband arrested?" she asked suddenly.

Mr. Reeder was silent for a moment. Sooner or later, she must know the truth, and he had an idea that this awful truth would not cause her very much distress.

"Your husband is dead," he said.

Her eyes opened wider.

"Did my father——"

"Your father killed him—I suppose so. I am afraid I was the cause. Coming back to find Margaret Belman, I told Daver all that I knew about your marriage. Your father must have been hiding behind the panelling and heard."

"I see," she said simply. "Of course it was Father who killed him—I knew that would happen as soon as he learned the truth. Would you think I was heartless if I said I am glad? I don't think I am really glad—I'm just relieved. Will you get the box for me?"

She put her hand down her blouse and pulled out a gold chain at the end of which were two keys. "The first of these is the key of the safe. If you want to see the—the letters, I will show them to you, but I would rather not."

At that moment he heard hurrying footsteps in the passage outside; the door was pulled open and a young officer of engineers appeared.

"Excuse me, sir," he said, "but Captain Merriman thinks we ought to abandon this house. I've got out all the servants, and we're rushing them down to Siltbury."

Reeder stooped down and drew the girl to her feet.

"Take this lady with you," he said, and, to Olga: "I will get your box, and I may not—I am not quite sure—ask you to open it for me."

He waited till the officer had gone, and added:

"Just now I am feeling rather—tender toward young lovers. That is a concession which an old lover may make to youth."

His voice had grown husky. There was something in his face that brought the tears to her eyes.

"Was it—not Margaret Belman?" she asked in a hushed voice, and she knew before he answered that she had guessed well.

Tragedy dignified this strange-looking man, so far past youth, yet holding the germ of youth in his heart. His hand fell gently on her shoulder.

"Go, my dear," he said. "I will do what I can for you—perhaps I can save you a great deal of unhappiness."

He waited until she had gone, then strolled into the deserted lounge. What an eternity had passed since he had sat there, munching his toast and drinking his cup of tea, with an illustrated newspaper on his knees!

The place in the half gloom seemed full of ancient ghosts. The House of Tears! These walls had held sorrows more poignant, more hopeless than his.

He went to the panelled wall and rubbed his finger down the little scar in the wood that a thrown knife had made and smiled at the comparative triviality of that offence.

He had reason to remember the circumstances without the dramatic reminder which nature gave. Suddenly the floor beneath him swayed, and the two lights went out. He guessed that the earth tremors were responsible for the snapping of wires, and he hurried into the vestibule and had passed from the house when he remembered Olga Crewe's request.

The lantern was still hanging about his neck. He switched it on and went back to the safe and inserted the key. As he did so, the house swayed backward and forward like a drunken man. The smashing of glass, the crash of overturned wardrobes startled him so that he almost fled with his mission unperformed. He even hesitated; but a promise was a promise to J.G. Reeder. He put the key in again, turned the lock, and pulled open one of the great doors—and Margaret Belman fell into his arms!

CHAPTER XX

HE stood, holding the half-swooning girl, peering into the face he could only see by the reflected light of his lantern, and then suddenly the safe fell back from him without warning, leaping a gaping cavern.

He lifted her in his arms, ran across the vestibule into the open air. Somebody shouted his name in the distance, and he ran blindly toward the voice. Once he stumbled over a great crack that had appeared in the earth, but managed to recover himself, though he was forced to release his grip of the girl.

She was alive—breathing—her breath fanned his cheek and gave him new strength.

The sound of falling walls behind him; immense, hideous roarings and groanings; thunder of sliding chalk and rock and earth—he heard only the breathing of his burden, felt only the faint beating of her heart against his breast.

"Here you are!"

Somebody lifted Margaret Belman from his arms. A big soldier pushed him into a wagon, where he sprawled at full length, breathless, more dead than alive, by the side of the woman he loved; and then, with a whirr of wheels, the ambulance sped down the hillside toward safety. Behind him, in the darkness, the House of Tears shivered and crackled, and the work of ancient masons vanished piecemeal, tumbling over new cliffs, to be everlastingly engulfed and hidden from the sight of man.

Dawn came and showed, to an interested party that had travelled by road and train to the scene of the great landslide, one gray wall, standing starkly on the edge of a precipice. A portion of the wrecked floor still adhered to the ruins, and on that floor the bloodstained bed where Old Man Flack had laid his murdered servant.

The story that Olga Flack told the police, which appears in the official records of the place, was not exactly the same as the story she told to Mr. Reeder that afternoon when, at his invitation, she came to the flat in Bennett Street. Mr. Reeder, minus his glasses and his general air of respectability which his vanished side whiskers had so enhanced, was at some disadvantage.

"Yes, I think Ravini was killed," she said, "but you are wrong in supposing that I brought him to my room at the request of my father. Ravini was a very quick-witted man and recognized me. He came to Larmes Keep because he"—she hesitated—"well, he was rather fond of Miss Belman. He told me this, and I was rather amused. At that time I did not know his name, although my husband did, and I certainly did not connect him with my father's arrest. He revealed his identity, and I suppose there was something in my attitude, or something I said, which recalled the schoolgirl he had met years before. The moment he recognized me as John Flack's daughter, he also recognized Larmes Keep as my father's headquarters.

"He began to ask me questions: whether I knew where the Flack million, as he called it, was hidden. And of course I was horrified, for I knew why Daver had allowed him to come.

"My father had recently escaped from Broadmoor, and I was worried sick for fear he knew the trick that Daver had played. I wasn't normal, I suppose, and I came near to betraying my father, for I told Ravini of his escape. Ravini did not take this as I had expected; he rather overrated his own power, and was very confident. Of course, he did not know that Father was practically in the house, that he came up from the cave every night—"

"The real entrance to the cave was through the safe in the vestibule?" said Mr. Reeder. "That was an ingenious idea. I must confess that the safe was the last place in the world I should have considered."

"My father had it put there twenty years ago," she said. "There always was an entrance from the centre of the Keep to the caves below, many of which were used as prisons or as burying places by the ancient owners of Larmes."

"Why did Ravini go to your room?" asked Mr. Reeder. "You will excuse the—um—indelicacy of the question, but I want—"

She nodded.

"It was a last desperate effort on my part to scare Ravini from the house. You mustn't forget that I was watched all the time; Daver or my mother were never far from me, and I dared not let them know, and through them my father, that Ravini was being warned. He had decided to stay on—until I made my request for an interview and told him that I wanted him to leave by the first train in the morning after he learned what I had to tell him."

"And what had you to tell him?" asked Mr. Reeder.

She did not answer immediately, and he repeated the question.

"That my father had decided to kill him."

Mr. Reeder's eyes almost closed.

"Are you telling me the truth, Olga?" he asked gently, and she went red and white.

"I am not a good liar, am I?" Her tone was almost defiant. "Now I'll tell you. I met Ravini when I was little more than a child. He meant ... a tremendous lot to me, but I don't think I meant very much to him. He used to come down to see me in the country where I was at school—"

"He's dead?"

She could only nod her head. Her lips were quivering.

"That is the truth," she said at last. "The horror of it was that he did not recognize me when he came to Larmes Keep. I had passed completely from his mind until I revealed myself in the garden that night."

"Is he dead?" asked Mr. Reeder for the second time.

"Yes," she said. "They struck him down outside my room—I don't know what they did with him. They put him through the safe, I think." She shuddered.

J.G. Reeder patted her hand.

"You have your memories, my child," he said to the weeping girl, "and your letters."

It occurred to him after Olga had gone that Ravini must have written rather interesting letters.

CHAPTER XXI

MISS MARGARET BELMAN decided to take a holiday in the only pleasure resort that seemed worth while or endurable. She conveyed this intention to Mr. Reeder by letter.

"There are only two places in the world where I can feel happy and safe [she wrote]. One place is London and the other New York, where a policeman is to be found at every street corner, and all the amusements of a country life are to be had in an intensified form. So, if you please, can you spare the time to come with me to the theatres I have written down on the back of this sheet, to the National Gallery, the British Museum, the Tower of London (no, on consideration I do not think I should like to include the Tower of London: it is too mediæval and ghostly), to Kensington Gardens, and similar centres of hectic gaiety. Seriously, dear J.G. (the familiarity will make you wince, but I have cast all shame outside), I want to be one of a large, sane mass—I am tired of being an isolated, hysterical woman."

There was much more in the same strain. Mr. Reeder took his engagement book and ran a blue pencil through all his appointments before he wrote, with some labour, a letter which, because of its caution and its somewhat pompous terminology, sent Margaret Belman into fits of silent laughter.
She had not mentioned Richmond Park, and with good reason, one might suppose, for Richmond Park in the late autumn, when chilly winds abound, and the deer have gone into winter quarters—if deer ever go into winter quarters—is picturesque without being comfortable, and only a pleasure to the æsthetic eyes of those whose bodies are suitably clothed in woollen underwear.
Yet, one drab afternoon, Mr. Reeder chartered a taxicab, sat solemnly by the side of Miss Margaret Belman, as the cab bumped and jerked down Clarence Lane, possibly the worst road in England, before it turned through the iron gates of the park.
They came at last to a stretch of grass land and bush, a place in early summer of flowering rhododendrons, and here Mr. Reeder stopped the cab and they both descended and walked aimlessly through a little wood. The ground sloped down to a little carpeted hollow. Mr. Reeder, with a glance of suspicion and some reference to rheumatism, seated himself by Miss Belman's side.
"But why Richmond Park?" asked Margaret.
Mr. Reeder coughed.
"I have—um—a romantic interest in Richmond Park," he said. "I remember the first arrest I ever made—"
"Don't be gruesome," she warned him. "There's nothing romantic about an arrest. Talk of something pretty."
"Let us, then, talk of you," said Mr. Reeder daringly; "and it is exactly because I want to talk of you, my dear Miss—um—Margaret—Margaret that I have asked you to come here."
He took her hand with great gentleness as though he were handling a rare objet d'art, and played with her fingers awkwardly.
"The truth is, my dear—"
"Don't say 'Miss,'" she begged.

"My dear Margaret"—this with an effort—"I have decided that life is too—um—short to delay any longer a step which I have very carefully considered—in fact"—here he floundered hopelessly into a succession of "um's" which were only relieved by occasional "er's."
He tried again.
"A man of my age and peculiar temperament should perhaps be considering matters more serious—in fact, you may consider it very absurd of me, but the truth is—"
Whatever the truth was could not be easily translated into words.
"The truth is," she said quietly, "that you think you're in love with somebody?"
First Mr. Reeder nodded, then he shook his head with equal vigour.
"I don't think—it has gone beyond the stage of hypothesis. I am no longer young—I am in fact a confirmed—no, not a confirmed, but—er—"
"You're a confirmed bachelor," she helped him out.
"Not confirmed," he insisted firmly.
She half turned and faced him, her hands on his shoulders, looking into his eyes.
"My dear," she said, "you think of being married and you want somebody to marry you. But you feel that you are too old to blight her young life."
He nodded dumbly.
"Is it my young life, my dear? Because, if it is—"
"It is." J.G. Reeder's voice was very husky.
And for the first time in his life Mr. J.G. Reeder, who had had so many experiences, mainly unpleasant, felt the soft lips of a woman against his.
"Dear me!" said Mr. Reeder breathlessly, a few seconds later. "That was rather nice."

Red Aces

First published in The Thriller magazine, February 9, 1929

I. — THE THREAT

WHEN a young man is very much in love with a most attractive girl he is apt to endow her with qualities and virtues which no human being has ever possessed. Yet at rare and painful intervals there enter into his soul certain wild suspicions, and in these moments he is inclined to consider the possibility that she may be guilty of the basest treachery and double dealing.

Everybody knew that Kenneth McKay was desperately in love. They knew it at the bank where he spent his days in counting other people's money, and a considerable amount of his lunch hour writing impassioned and ill-spelt letters to Margot Lynn. His taciturn father, brooding over his vanished fortune in his gaunt riverside house at Marlow, may have employed the few moments he gave to the consideration of other people's troubles in consideration of his son's new interest. Probably he did not, for George McKay was entirely self-centred and had little thought but for the folly which had dissipated the money he had accumulated with such care, and the development of fantastical schemes for its recovery.

Kenneth went over to Beaconsfield every morning on his noisy motorbike and came back every night, sometimes very late, because Margot lived in London; they dined together at the cheaper restaurants and sometimes saw a film. Kenneth was a member of an inexpensive London club which sheltered at least one sympathetic soul. Except for Rufus Machfield, the confidant in question, he had no friends.

'And let me advise you not to make any here,' said Rufus.

He was a military-looking man of forty-five, and most people found him rather a bore, for the views which he expressed so vehemently, on all subjects from politics to religion, which are the opposite ends of the ethical pole, he had acquired that morning from the leading article of his favourite daily. Yet he was a genial person—a likeable man.

He had a luxurious flat in Park Lane, a French valet, a Bentley and no useful occupation.

'The Leffingham Club is cheap.' he said, 'the food's not bad and it's near Piccadilly. Against that you have the fact that almost anybody who hasn't been to prison can become a member–'

'The fact that I'm a member—' began Ken.

'You're a gentleman and a public school man,' interrupted Mr Machfield sonorously. 'You're not rich, I admit—'

'Even I admit that,' said Ken, rubbing his untidy hair.

Kenneth was tall, athletic, as good-looking as a young man need be, or can be without losing his head about his face. He had called at the Leffingham that evening especially to see Rufus and confide his worries. And his worries were enormous. He looked haggard and ill: Mr Machfield thought it possible that he had not been sleeping very well. In this surmise he was right.

'About Margot—' began the young man. Mr Machfield smiled. He had met Margot, had entertained the young people to dinner at his flat, and twice had invited them to a theatre party. Kenneth took a letter from his pocket and passed it across to his friend, and Machfield opened and read it.

Dear Kenneth: I'm not seeing you any more. I'm broken hearted to tell you this. Please don't try to see me—please! M.

'When did this come?'

'Last night. Naturally, I went to her flat. She was out. I went to her office—she was out. I was late for the bank and got it hot and strong from the manager. To make matters worse, there's a fellow dunning me for two hundred pounds—everything comes at once. I borrowed the money from father. What with one thing and another I'm desperate.'

Mr Machfield rose from his chair.

'Come home and have a meal, he said. 'As for the money—'

'No, no, no!' Kenneth McKay was panic-stricken. 'I don't want to borrow from you.' For a moment he sat in silence, then: 'Do you know a man named Reeder—J.G. Reeder?'

Machfield shook his head.

'He's a detective,' explained Kenneth. 'He has a big bank practice. He was down at our place today—weird-looking devil. If he could be a detective anybody could be!'

Mr Machfield said he recalled the name.

'He was in that railway robbery, wasn't he? J.G. Reeder—yes. Pretty smart fellow—young?'

'He's as old as—well, he's pretty old. And rather old-fashioned.'

Rufus snapped his finger to the waiter and paid his bill.

'You'll have to take pot luck—but Lamontaine is a wonderful cook. He didn't know that he was until I made him try.'

So they went together to the little flat in Park Lane. and Lamontaine, the pallid, middle-aged valet who spoke English with no trace of a foreign accent, prepared a meal that justified the praise of his master. In the middle of the dinner the subject of Mr Reeder arose again.

'What brought him to Beaconsfield—is there anything wrong at your bank?'

Rufus saw the young man's face go red.

'Well—there has been money missing; not very large sums. I have my own opinion, but it isn't fair to—well, you know.'

He was rather incoherent, and Mr Machfield did not pursue the inquiry.

'I hate the bank anyway—I mean the work. But I had to do something, and when I left Uppingham my father put me there—in the bank, I mean. Poor chap, he lost his money at Monte Carlo or somewhere—enormous sums. You wouldn't dream that he was a gambler. I'm not complaining, but it's a little trying sometimes.'

Mr Machfield accompanied him to the door that night and shivered.

'Cold—shouldn't be surprised if we had snow,' he said.

In point of fact the snow did not come until a week later. It started as rain and became snow in the night, and in the morning people who lived in the country looked out upon a white world: trees that bore a new beauty and hedges that showed their heads above sloping drifts.

II. — MURDER!

THERE was a car coming from the direction of Beaconsfield. The man on the motorcycle in the centre of the snowy road watched the lights grow brighter and brighter. Presently, in the glare of the headlamps, the driver of the car saw the motor cyclist, realized it was a policeman, saw the lift of his gloved hand and stopped the car. It was not difficult to stop, for the wheels were racing on the surface of the road, which had frozen into the worst qualities of ice. And snow was falling on top of this.

'Anything wrong—'

The driver began to shout the question, and then saw the huddled figure on the ground. It lay limply like a fallen sack; seemed at first glimpse to have nothing of human shape or substance. The driver jumped out and went ploughing through the frozen snow.

'I just spotted him when I saw you,' said the policeman. 'Do you mind turning your car just a little to the right—I want more light on him.'

He dismounted, propped up his bike and went heavy-footed to where the man lay.

The second inmate of the car got to the wheel and turned the vehicle with some difficulty so that the light blazed on the dreadful thing.

Then he got out of the car, lingered nervously by the motor bike and finally joined the other two.

'It's old Wentford,' said the policeman.

'Wentford... good God!'

The first of the two motorists fell on his knees by the side of the body and peered down into the grinning face.

Old Benny Wentford!

'Good God!' he said again.

He was a middle-aged lawyer, unused to such a horror. Nothing more terrible had disturbed the smooth flow of his life than an occasional quarrel with the secretary of his golf club. Now here was death, violent and hideous—a dead man on a snowy road... a man who had telephoned to him two hours before, begging him to leave a party and come to him, though the snow had begun to fall all over again.

'You know Mr Wentford—he has told me about you.'

'Yes, I know him. I've often called at his house—in fact, I called there tonight but it was shut up. He made arrangements with the Chief Constable that I should call... h'm!'

The policeman stood over the body, his hands on his hips.

'You stay here—I'll go and phone the station,' he said.

He got on the motorbike and kicked it to life.

'Er... don't you think we'd better go?' Mr Enward, the lawyer, asked nervously. He had no desire to be left alone in the night with a battered corpse and a clerk whose trembling was almost audible.

'You couldn't turn your car,' said the policeman—which was true, for the lane was very narrow. They heard the sound of the engine and presently they heard it no more.

'Is he dead, Mr Enward?' The young man's voice was hollow.

'Yes... I think so... the policeman said so.'

'Oughtn't we to make sure? He may only be... injured?'

Mr Enward had seen the face in the shadow of an uplifted shoulder. He did not wish to see it again.

'Better leave him alone till a doctor comes... it is no use interfering in these things. Wentford... good God!'

'He's always been a little bit eccentric, hasn't he?' The clerk was young and, curiosity being the tonic of youth, he had recovered some of his courage. 'Living alone in that tiny cottage with all his money. I was cycling past it on Sunday—a concrete box: that's what my girl friend called it. With all his money—'

'He is dead, Henry,' said Mr Enward severely, 'and a dead person has no property. I don't think it quite—um—seemly to talk of him in—um—his presence.'

He felt the occasion called for an emotional display of some kind. He had never grown emotional over clients; least of all could this tetchy old man inspire such feeling. A few words of prayer perhaps would not be out of place. But Mr Enward was a churchwarden of a highly respectable church and for forty years had had his praying done for him. If he had been a dissenter... but he was not. He wished he had a prayer book.

'He's a long time gone.'

The policeman could not have got far, but it seemed a very long time since he had left.

'Has he any heirs?' asked the clerk professionally.

Mr Enward did not answer. Instead, he suggested that the lights of the car should be dimmed. They revealed this Thing too plainly. Henry went back and the lights. It became terribly dark when the lights were lowered, and eyesight played curious tricks: it seemed that the bundle moved. Mr Enward had a feeling that the grinning face was lifting to leer slyly at him over the humped shoulder.

'Put on the lights again, Henry,' the lawyer's voice quavered. 'I can't see what I am doing.'

He was doing nothing; on the other hand, he had a creepy feeling that the Thing was behaving oddly. Yet it lay very still, just as it had lain all the time.

'He must have been murdered. I wonder where they went to?' asked H hollowly, and a cold shiver vibrated down Mr Enward's spine.

Murdered! Of course he was murdered. There was blood on the snow, and the murderers were... He glanced backward nervously and almost screamed. A man stood in the shadowy space behind the car: the car lights reflected by the snow just revealed him.

'Who... who are you, please?' croaked the lawyer.

He added 'please' because there was no sense in being rough with a man who might be a murderer.

The figure moved into the light. He was slightly bent and even more middle-aged than Mr Enward. He wore a strange black hat, a long raincoat and large, shapeless gloves. About his neck was an enormous yellow scarf, and Mr Enward noticed, in a numb, mechanical way, that his shoes were large and square toed and that he carried a tightly furled umbrella on his arm though the snow was falling heavily.

'I'm afraid my car has broken down a mile up the road.' His voice was gentle and apologetic; obviously he had not seen the bundle. In his agitation Mr Enward had stepped into the light of the lamps and his black shadow sprawled across the deeper shadow.

'Am I wrong in thinking that you are in the same predicament?' asked the newcomer. 'I was unprepared for the—er—condition of the road. It is lamentable that one should have overlooked this possibility.'

'Did you pass the policeman?' asked Mr Enward. Whoever this stranger was, whatever might be his character and disposition, it was right and fair that he should know there was a policeman in the vicinity.

'Policeman?' The man was surprised. 'No, I passed no policeman. At my rate of progress it was very difficult to pass anything—'

'Going towards you... on a motorbike,' said Mr Enward rapidly. 'He said that he would be back soon. My name is Enward—solicitor—Enward, Caterham and Enward.'

He felt it was a moment for confidence.

'Delighted!' murmured the other. 'We've met before. My name—er—is Reeder—R, double E, D, E, R.'

Mr Enward took a step forward.

'Not the detective? I thought I'd seen you... look!' He stepped out of the light and the heap on the ground emerged from shadow. The lawyer made a dramatic gesture. Mr Reeder came forward slowly.

He stooped over the dead man, took a torch from his pocket and shone it steadily on the face. For a long time he looked and studied. His melancholy face showed no evidence that he was sickened or pained.

'H'm!' he said, and got up dusting the snow from his knee. He fumbled in the recesses of his overcoat, produced a pair of glasses, put them on awkwardly and surveyed the lawyer over their top.

'Very—um—extraordinary. I was on my way to see him.'

Enward stared.

'You were on your way? So was I! Did you know him?'

Mr Reeder considered this question.

'I—er—didn't—er—know him. No, I had never met him.'

The lawyer felt that his own presence needed some explanation.

'This is my clerk, Mr Henry Greene.'

Mr Reeder bowed slightly.

'What happened was this...'

He gave a very detailed and graphic description, which began with the recounting of what he had said when the telephone call came through to him at Beaconsfield, and how he was dressed and what his wife had said when she went to find his Wellington boots—her first husband had died through an ill-judged excursion into the night air on as foolish a journey—and how much trouble he had had starting the car, and how long he had had to wait for Henry.

Mr Reeder gave the impression that he was not listening. Once he walked out of the blinding light and peered back the way the policeman had gone; once he went over to the body and looked at it again; but most of the time he was wandering down the lane, searching the ground with his torch, with Mr Enward following at his heels lest any of his narrative be lost.

'Is he dead... I suppose so?' suggested the lawyer.

'I—er—have never seen anybody—er—deader,' said Mr Reeder gently. 'I should say, with all reverence and respect, that he was—er—extraordinarily dead.'

He looked at his watch.

'At nine-fifteen you met the policeman? He had just discovered the body? It is now nine thirty-five. How did you know that it was nine-fifteen?'

'I heard the church clock at Woburn Green strike the quarter.'

Mr Enward conveyed the impression that the clock struck exclusively for him. Henry halved the glory: he also had heard the clock.

'At Woburn Green—you heard the clock? H'm... nine-fifteen!'

The snow was falling thickly now. It fell on the heap and lay in the little folds and creases of his clothes. 'He must lived somewhere about here?' Mr Reeder asked the question with great deference.

'My directions were that his house lay off the main road you would hardly call this a main road... fifty yards beyond a noticeboard advertising land for sale—desirable building land.'

Mr Enward pointed to the darkness.

'Just there—the noticeboard. Curiously enough, I am the—er—solicitor for the vendor,'

His natural inclination was to emphasize the desirability of the land, but he thought it was hardly the moment. He returned to the question of Mr Wentford's house.

'I've only been inside the place once—two years ago, wasn't it, Henry?'

'A year and nine months,' said Henry exactly. His feet were cold, his spine chilled. He felt sick.

'You cannot see it from the lane,' Enward continued. 'Rather a small, one-storey cottage. He had it specially built for him apparently. It isn't exactly... a palace.'

'Dear me!' said Mr Reeder, as though this were the most striking news he had heard that evening. 'In a house he built himself! I suppose he has, or had, a telephone?'

'He telephoned to me,' said Mr Enward; 'therefore he must have a telephone.'

Mr Reeder frowned as though he were trying to pick holes in the logic of this statement.

'I'll go along and see if it is possible to get through to the police,' he suggested.

'The police have already been notified,' said the lawyer hastily. 'I think we all ought to stay here together till somebody arrives.'

The man in the black hat, now absurdly covered with snow, shook his head. He pointed.

'Woburn Green is there. Why not go and arouse the—um—local constabulary?'

That idea had not occurred to the lawyer. His instinct urged him to return the way he had come and regain touch with realities in his own prosaic parlour.

'But do you think...' he blinked down at the body. 'I mean, it's hardly an act of humanity to leave him—'

'He feels nothing. He is probably in heaven,' said Mr Reeder, and added. 'Probably. Anyway, the police will know exactly where they can find him.'

There was a sudden screech from Henry. He was holding out his hand in the light of the torch.

'Look—blood!' he screamed.

There was blood on his hand, certainly.

'Blood—I didn't touch him! You know that, Mr Enward—I ain't been near him!'

Alas for our excellent educational system; Henry was reverting. 'Not near him I ain't been—blood!'

'Don't squeak, please.' Mr Reeder was firm. 'What have you touched?'

'Nothing—I only touched myself.'

'Then you have touched nothing,' said Mr Reeder with unusual acidity. 'Let me look.'

The rays of his torch travelled over the shivering clerk.

'It is on your sleeve—h'm!'

Mr Enward stared. There was a red, moist patch of something on Henry's sleeve.

'You had better go on to the police station,' said Mr Reeder. 'I'll come and see you in the morning.'

III. — THE RED ACES

ENWARD sat himself gratefully in the driver's seat, keeping some distance between himself and his shivering clerk. The car was on a declivity and would start without trouble. He turned the wheels straight and took off the brake. The vehicle skidded and slithered forward, and presently Mr Reeder, following in its wake, heard the sound of the running engine.

His torch showed him the noticeboard in the field, and fifty yards beyond he came to a path so narrow that two men could not walk abreast. It ran off from the road at right angles, and up this he turned, progressing with great difficulty, for he had heavy nails in his shoes. At last he saw a small garden gate on his right, set between two unkempt hedges. The gate was open, and this methodical man stopped to examine it by the light of his torch.

He expected to find blood and found it; just a smear. No marks on the ground, but then the snow would have obliterated those. It had not obliterated the print of footmarks going up the winding path. They were rather small, and he thought they were recently made. He kept his light on them until they led him into view of the squat house with its narrow windows and doorways. As he turned he saw a light gleam between curtains. He had a feeling that somebody was looking out at him. In another moment the light had vanished. But there was somebody in the house.

The footsteps led up to the door. Here he paused and knocked. There was no answer, and he knocked again more loudly. The chill wind sent the snowflakes swirling about him. Mr Reeder, who had a secret sense of humour, smiled. In the remote days of his youth his favourite Christmas card was one which showed a sparkling Father Christmas knocking at the door of a wayside cottage. He pictured himself as a bowler-hatted Father Christmas, and the whimsical fancy slightly pleased him.

He knocked a third time and listened; then, when no answer came, he stepped back and walked to the room where he had seen the light and tried to peer between the curtains. He thought he heard a sound—a thud—but it was not in the house. It might have been the wind. He looked round and listened, but the thud was not repeated, and he returned to his ineffectual starings. There was no sign of a fire. He came back to knock for the fourth time, then tried the other side of the building, and here he made a discovery. A narrow casement window, deeply recessed and made of iron, was swaying to and fro in the wind, and beneath the window was a double set of footmarks, one coming and one going. They went away in the direction of the lane.

He came back to the door, and stood debating with himself what steps he should take. He had seen in the darkness two small white squares at the top of the door, and had thought they were little panes of toughened glass such as one sees in the tops of such doors. But, probably in a gust of wind, one of them became detached and fell at his feet. He stooped and picked it up: it was a playing card—the ace of diamonds. He put his torch on the second: it was the ace of hearts. They had both apparently been fastened side by side to the door with pins—black pins. Perhaps the owner of the house had put them there. Possibly they had some significance, fulfilled the function of mascots.

No answer came to his knocking, and Mr Reeder heaved a deep sigh. He hated climbing; he hated more squeezing through narrow windows into unknown places; more especially as there was probably somebody inside who would treat him rudely. Or they might have gone. The footprints, he found, were fresh; they were scarcely obliterated, though the snow was falling heavily. Perhaps the house was empty, and its inmate, whose light he had seen, had got away while he was knocking at the door. He would not have heard him jump from the window, the snow was too soft. Unless that thud he had heard—Mr Reeder gripped the sill and drew himself up, breathing heavily, though he was a man of considerable strength.

There were only two ways to go into the house: one was feet first, the other head first. He made a reconnaissance with his torch and saw that beneath the window was a small table, standing in a tiny room which had evidently been used as a cloakroom, for there were a number of coats hanging on hooks. It was safe to go in head first, so he wriggled down on to the table, feeling extraordinarily undignified.

He was on his feet in a moment, gripped the handle of the door gingerly and opened it. He was in a small hall, from which one door opened. He tried this: it was fast, and yet not fast. It was as though somebody was leaning against it on the other side. A quick jerk of his shoulder, and it flew open. Somebody tried to dash past him, but Mr Reeder was expecting that and worse. He gripped the fugitive.

'I'm extremely sorry,' he said in his gentle voice. 'It is a lady, isn't it?'

He heard her heavy breathing, a sob...

'Is there a light?'

He groped inside the lintel of the door, found a switch and turned it. Nothing happened for a moment, and then the lights came on suddenly. There was apparently a small generator at the back of the house which operated when any switch was turned on.

'Come in here, will you, please?'

He pressed her very gently into the room. Pretty, extraordinarily pretty. He did not remember ever having met a young lady who was quite as pretty as this particular young lady, though she was very white and her hair was in disorder, and on her feet were snow-boots the impression of which he had already seen in the snow.

'Will you sit down, please?'

He closed the door behind him.

'There's nothing to be afraid of. My name is Reeder.'

She had been terrified for that moment; now she looked up at him intensely.

'You're the detective?' she shivered. 'I'm so frightened. I'm so frightened!'

Mr Reeder looked round the room. It was pleasantly furnished—not luxuriously so but pleasantly. Evidently a sitting-room. Except that the mantelpiece had fallen or had been dragged on the floor, there was no sign of disorder. The hearth was littered with broken china ornaments and vases; the board itself was still held in position at one end. The fireplace and the blue hearthrug were curiously stained. And there were other little splodges of darkness on the surface of the carpet, and a flowerpot was knocked down near the door.

He saw a wastepaper basket and turned over its contents. Covers of little books apparently—there were five of them, but no contents. By the side of the fireplace was a dwarf bookcase. The books were dummies. He pulled one end of the case and it swung out, being hinged at the other end.

'H'm!' said Mr Reeder, and pushed the shelves back into their original position.

There was a cap on the floor by the table and he picked it up. It was wet. He examined it, thrust it into his pocket and turned his attention to the girl.

'How long have you been here, Miss—I think you'd better tell me your name.'

She was looking up at him.

'Half an hour. I don't know... it may be longer.'

'Miss—?' he asked again.

'Lynn—Margot Lynn.'

He pursed his lips thoughtfully.

'Margot Lynn. And you've been here half an hour. Who else has been here?'

'Nobody,' she said, springing to her feet. 'What has happened? Did he—did they fight?'

He put his hand on her shoulder gently and pressed her down into the chair.

'Did who fight whom?' asked Mr Reeder. His English was always very good on these occasions.
'Nobody has been here,' she said inconsequently.
Mr Reeder passed the question. 'You came from—?'
'I came from Bourne End station. I walked here. I often come that way. I'm Mr Wentford's secretary.'
'You walked here at nine o'clock because you're Mr Wentford's secretary? That was a very odd thing to do.'
She was searching his face fearfully. 'Has anything happened? Are you from the police? Has anything happened to Mr Wentford? Tell me, tell me!'
'He was expecting me: you knew that?'
She nodded. Her breath was coming quickly. He thought she found breathing a painful process. 'He told me—yes. I didn't know what it was about. He wanted his lawyer here too. I think he was in some kind of trouble.'
'When did you see him last?'
She hesitated. 'I spoke to him on the telephone—once, from London. I haven't seen him for two days.'
'And the person who was here?' asked Mr Reeder after a pause.
'There was nobody here! I swear there was nobody here!' She was frantic in her desire to convince him. 'I've been here half an hour—waiting for him. I let myself in—I have a key. There it is.'
She fumbled with trembling hands in her bag and produced a ring with two keys, one larger than the other.
'He wasn't here when I came in. I—I think he must have gone to London. He is very—peculiar.'
Mr J.G. Reeder put his hand in his pocket, took out two playing cards and laid them on the table.
'Why did he have those pinned to his door?'
She looked at him round-eyed.
'Pinned to his door?'
'The outer door,' said Mr Reeder, 'or, as he would call it, the street door.'
She shook her head.
'I've never seen them before. He's not the kind of man to put up things like that. He is very retiring and hates drawing attention to himself.'
'He was very retiring,' repeated Mr Reeder, 'and hated drawing attention to himself.'

IV. — J.G. REEDER'S THEORY

SOMETHING in his tone emphasized the tense he used. She shrank back.
'Was?' Her voice was a whisper. 'He's not dead... oh, my God! he's not dead?'
Mr Reeder smoothed his chin.
'Yes, I'm afraid—um—he is dead.'
She clutched the edge of the table for support. Mr Reeder had never seen such horror, such despair in a human face before,
'Was it... an accident—or—or—'
'You're trying to say "murder",' said Reeder gently. 'Yes, I'm very much afraid it was murder.'
He caught her in his arms as she fell and, laying her on the sofa, went in search of water. The taps were frozen, but he found some water in a kettle and, filling a glass with this, he returned to sprinkle it on her face, having a vague idea that something of the sort was necessary; but he found her sitting up, her face in her hands.
'Lie down, my dear, and keep quiet,' said Mr Reeder, and she obeyed meekly.
He looked round the room. The thing that struck him anew was the revolver which hung on the wall near the right-hand side of the fireplace just above the bookcase. It was placed to the hand of anybody who sat with his back to the window. Behind the armchair was a screen, and, tapping it, Mr Reeder discovered that it was of sheet iron.
He went outside to look at the door, turning on the hall light. It was a very thick door, and the inside was made of quarter-inch steel plate, screwed firmly to the wood. Leading from the kitchen was the bedroom, evidently Wentford's. The only light here was admitted from an oblong window near the ceiling. There was no other window, and about the narrow window was a stout steel cage. On the wall by the bed hung a second gun. He found a third weapon in the kitchen and behind a coat hanging in the hall, a fourth.
The cottage was a square box of concrete. The roof, as he afterwards learned, was tiled of sheet iron, and, except for the window through which he had squeezed, there was none by which ingress could be had.
He was puzzled why this man, who evidently feared attack, had left any window so large as that through which he had come. He afterwards found the broken wire which must have set an alarm bell ringing when the window was opened.
There was blood on the mat in the hall, blood in the tiny lobby. He came back to where the girl was lying and sniffed. There was no smell of cordite, and having seen the body, he was not surprised.
'Now my dear.'
She sat up again.
'I am not a police officer; I am a—er—a gentleman called in by your friend, Mr Wentford—your late friend,' he corrected himself, 'to do something—I know not what! He called me by phone; I gave him my—um—terms, but he offered me no reason why he was sending for me. You, as his secretary, may perhaps—'
She shook her head.
'I don't know. He'd never mentioned you before he spoke to me on the telephone.'
'I'm not a policeman,' said Mr Reeder again, and his voice was very gentle; 'therefore, my dear,

you need have few qualms about telling me the truth, because these gentlemen, when they come, these very active and intelligent men, will probably discover all that I have seen, even if I did not tell them. Who was the man who went out of this house when I knocked at the door?'

Her face was deathly pale, but she did not flinch. He wondered if she was as pretty when she was not so pale. Mr Reeder wondered all sorts of odd little things like that; his mind could never stagnate.

'There was nobody—in this house—since I have been here—'

Mr Reeder did not press her. He sighed, closed his eyes, shook his head, shrugged his shoulders. 'It's a great pity,' he said. 'Can you tell me anything about Mr Wentford?'

'No,' she said in a low voice. 'He was my uncle. I think you ought to know that. He didn't want anybody to know, but that must come out. He's been very good to us—he sent my mother abroad; she's an invalid. I conducted his business.' All this very jerkily.

'Have you been here often?'

She shook her head.

'Not often,' she said. 'We usually met somewhere by appointment, generally in a lonely place where one wouldn't be likely to meet anybody who knew us. He was very shy of strangers, and he didn't like anybody coming here.'

'Did he ever entertain friends here?'

'No.' She was very emphatic. 'I'm sure he didn't. The only person he ever saw was the police patrol on this beat. Uncle used to make him coffee every night. I think it was for the company—he told me he felt lonely at nights. The policeman kept an eye on him. There are two—Constable Steele and Constable Verity. My uncle always sent them a turkey at Christmas. Whoever was on duty used to come up here on his motorbike.'

The telephone was in the bedroom and Mr Reeder remembered he had promised to phone. He got through to a police station and asked a few questions. When he got back he found the girl by the window, looking between the curtains.

Somebody was coming up the path. They could hear voices and, looking through the curtain, he saw a string of torches and went out to meet a local sergeant and two men. Behind them was Mr Enward. Reeder wondered what had become of Henry. Possibly he had been lost in the snow; the thought interested him.

'This is Mr Reeder.' Enward's voice was shrill. 'Did you telephone?'

'Yes, I telephoned. We have a young lady here—Mr Wentford's niece.'

Enward repeated the words, surprised. 'His niece here? Really? I knew he had a niece. In fact—' He coughed. It was an indelicate moment to speak of legacies.

'She'll be able to throw some light on this business,' said the sergeant, more practical and less delicate.

'She could throw no light on any business,' said Mr Reeder, very firmly for him. 'She was not here when the crime was committed—in fact, she arrived some time after. She has a key which admitted her. Miss Lynn acts as her uncle's secretary, all of which facts, gentlemen, I think you should know.'

The sergeant was not quite sure about the propriety of noticing Mr Reeder. To him he was almost a civilian, a man without authority, and his presence was therefore irregular. Nevertheless, some distant echo of J.G. Reeder's fame had penetrated into Buckinghamshire. The police officer seemed to remember that Mr Reeder either occupied or was about to occupy a semi-official position remotely associated with police affairs. If he had been a little clearer on the subject he would also have been more definite in his attitude. Since he was not so sure, it was expedient, until Mr Reeder's position became established, to ignore his presence—a peculiarly difficult course to follow when an officially absent person is standing at your elbow, murmuring flat contradictions of your vital theories.

'Perhaps you'll tell me why you are here, sir?' said the sergeant with a certain truculence.

Mr Reeder felt in his pocket, took out a large leather case and laid it carefully on the table, first dusting the table with the side of his hand; then he unfolded the case and took out, with exasperating deliberation, a thick pad of telegrams. He fixed his glasses and examined the telegrams one by one, reading each through. At last he shook one clear and handed it to the officer. It ran:

'WISH TO CONSULT WITH YOU TONIGHT ON VERY IMPORTANT MATTER. CALL ME WOBURN GREEN 971. VERY URGENT. WENTFORD.'

'You're a private detective, Mr Reeder?'

'More intimate than private,' murmured that gentleman. 'In these days of publicity one has little more than the privacy of a goldfish in his crystal habitation.'

The sergeant saw something in the wastepaper basket and pulled it out. It was a small looseleafed book. There was another, indeed, many. He piled five on the table; but they were merely the covers and nothing more.

'Diaries,' said Mr Reeder gently. 'You will observe that each one is dingier than the other.'

'But how do you know they're diaries?' demanded the police officer testily.

'Because the word "diary" is printed on the inside covers,' said Mr Reeder, more gently than ever. This proved to be the case, though the printing had been overlooked. Mr Reeder had not overlooked it; he had not even overlooked the two scraps of burnt paper on the hearth, all that remained of those diaries.

'There is a safe let into the wall behind that bookcase.' He pointed. 'It may or may not be full of clues. I should imagine it is not. But I shouldn't touch it if I were you, Sergeant,' he said hastily, 'not without gloves. Those detestable fellows from Scotland Yard will be here eventually, and they'll be very rude if they photograph a fingerprint and find it's yours.'

Gaylor of the Yard came at half past two. He had been brought out of his bed through a blinding snowstorm and along a road that was thoroughly vile.

The girl had gone home. Mr Reeder was sitting meditatively before the fire which he had made up, smoking the cheapest kind of cigarette.

'Is the body here?'

Mr Reeder shook his head.

'Have they found that motor cycle policeman, Verity?'

Again Mr Reeder signalled a negative. 'They found his bike on the Beaconsfield road with bloodstains on the saddle.'

He was staring into the fire, the cigarette drooping limply from his mouth, on his face an air of unsettled melancholy; he did not even turn his head to address Inspector Gaylor.

'The young lady has gone home, as I said. The local constabulary gave you particulars of the lady, of course. She acted as secretary to the late Mr Wentford, and he appears to have been very fond of her, since he has left his fortune two-thirds to the young lady and one-third to his sister. There is no money in the house as far as can be ascertained, but he banks with the Great Central Bank, Beaconsfield branch.' Reeder fumbled in his pocket. 'Here are the two aces.'

'The two what?' asked the puzzled inspector.

'The two aces.' Mr Reeder passed the playing cards over his shoulder, his eyes still on the fire. 'The ace of diamonds, and I believe the ace of hearts—I am not very well acquainted with either.'
'Where did you get these?'
The other explained, and Gaylor examined the aces.
'Why are you so sure that these cards were put up after the murder — why shouldn't they have been put up before?'
J.G. groaned at his scepticism and, reaching out, took a pack of cards from a little table.
'You will find the two aces missing from this pack. You would have also found that two cards had been stuck together. Blood does that. No fingerprints. I should imagine the cards were sorted over after the untimely demise of Mr Wentford, and the two significant aces extracted and exhibited.'
The inspector made a very careful search of the bedroom and came back to find Mr Reeder nodding himself to sleep.
'What did they do to the girl—these local blokes?' asked Gaylor coarsely.
Reeder's right shoulder came up in a lazy shrug.
'They escorted her to the station and took a statement from her. The inspector was kind enough to furnish me with a copy—you'll find it on this table. They also examined her hands and her clothes, but it was quite unnecessary. There is corroborative evidence that she arrived at Bourne End station at twelve minutes past eight as she says she did—the murder was committed at forty minutes past seven, a few minutes before or after.'
'How on earth do you know that? Is there any proof?'
Mr Reeder shook his head. 'A romantic surmise.' He sighed heavily. 'You have to realize, my dear Gaylor, that I have a criminal mind. I see the worst in people and the worst in every human action. It is very tragic. There are moments when—' He sighed again. 'Forty minutes past seven,' he said simply. 'That is my romantic surmise. The doctor will probably confirm my view. The body lay here,' he pointed to the hearthrug, 'until—well, quite a considerable time.'
Gaylor was skimming two closely written sheets of foolscap. Suddenly he stopped.
'You're wrong,' he said. 'Listen to this statement made at the station by Miss Lynn. "I rang up my uncle from the station, telling him I might be late because of the snowy road. He answered 'Come as soon as you can.' He spoke in a very low tone; I thought he sounded agitated!" That knocks your theory about the time a bit skew-whiff, eh?'
Mr Reeder looked round and blinked open his eyes.
'Yes, doesn't it? It must have been terribly embarrassing.'
'What was embarrassing?' asked the puzzled police officer.
'Everything,' mumbled Mr Reeder, his chin falling on his chest.

V. — THE MISSING POLICEMAN

'THE trouble about Reeder,' said Gaylor to the superintendent in the course of a long telephone conversation, 'is that you feel he does know something which he shouldn't know. I've never seen him in a case where he hasn't given me the impression that he was the guilty party—he knew so much about the crime.'

'Humour him,' said the superintendent. 'He'll be in the Public Prosecutor's Department one of these days. He never was in a case that he didn't make himself an accessory by pinching half the clues.'

At five o'clock the detective shook the sleeper awake.

'You'd better go home, old man,' he said. 'We'll leave an officer in charge here.'

Mr Reeder rose with a groan, splashed some soda-water from a syphon into a glass and drank it.

'I must stay, I'm afraid, unless you've any very great objection.'

'What's the idea of waiting?' asked Gaylor in surprise.

Mr Reeder looked from side to side as though he were seeking an answer.

'I have a theory—an absurd one, of course—but I believe the murderers will come back. And honestly I don't think your policeman would be of much use, unless you were inclined to give the poor fellow the lethal weapon necessary to defend himself.'

Gaylor sat down squarely before him, his large gloved hands on his knees.

'Tell papa,' he said.

Mr Reeder looked at him pathetically.

'There is nothing to tell, my dear Mr Gaylor; merely suspicion, bred, as I said, in my peculiarly morbid mind, having perhaps no foundation in fact. Those two cards, for example—that was a stupid piece of bravado. But it has happened before. You remember the Teignmouth case, and the Lavender Hill case, with the man with the slashed chest?'

Gaylor took the cards from his pocket and examined them.

'A bit of tomfoolery,' was his verdict.

Mr Reeder sighed and shook his head at the fire.

'Murderers as a rule have no sense of humour. They are excitable people, frightened people, but they are never comic people.'

He walked to the door and pulled it open. Snow had ceased to fall. He came back.

'Where is the policeman you propose leaving on duty?' he asked.

'I'll find one,' said Gaylor. 'There are half a dozen within call. A whistle will bring one along.'

Mr Reeder looked at him thoughtfully.

'I don't think I should. Let's wait until daylight—or perhaps you wish to go? I don't think anybody would harm you. I rather fancy they would be glad to see the back of you.'

'Harm me?' said Gaylor indignantly, but Reeder took no notice of the interruption.

'My own idea is that I should brew a dish of tea, and possibly fry a few eggs. I'm rather hungry.'

Gaylor walked to the door and frowned out into the darkness. He had worked with Reeder before, and was too wise a man to reject the advice summarily. Besides, if Reeder was entering or had entered the Public Prosecutor's Department, he would occupy a rank equivalent to superintendent.

'I'm all for eggs,' said Gaylor, and bolted the outer door.

The older man disappeared into the kitchen and came back with a kettle, which he placed on the fire, went out again and returned with a frying-pan.

'Do you ever take your hat off?' asked Gaylor curiously.

Mr Reeder did not turn his head, but shook the pan gently to ensure an even distribution of the boiling fat.

'Very rarely,' he said. 'On Christmas Days sometimes.'

And then Gaylor asked a fatuous question; at least, it sounded fatuous to him, and yet subconsciously he felt that the other might supply an immediate answer.

'Who killed Wentford?'

'Two men, possibly three,' said Mr Reeder instantly; 'but I rather think two. Neither was a professional burglar. One at any rate thought more of the killing than of any profit he might have got out of it. Neither found anything worth taking, and even if they had opened the safe they would have discovered nothing of value. The young lady, Miss Margot Lynn, could, I think, have saved them a lot of trouble in their search for treasure—I may be mistaken here, but I rarely fall into error. Miss Margot is—'

He stopped, looked round quickly.

'What is it?' asked Gaylor, but Reeder put his finger to his lips.

He rose, moving across the room to the door which led to the tiny lobby through which he had made his entrance. He stood with one hand on the knob, and Gaylor saw that in the other was a Browning. Slowly he turned the handle. The door was locked from the inside.

In two strides Reeder was at the front door, turned the key and pulled it open. Then, to the inspector's amazement, he saw his companion take one step and fall sprawling on his face in the snow. He ran to his assistance. Something caught him by the ankle and flung him forward. Reeder was on his feet and assisted the other to rise.

'A little wire fastened between the door posts,' he explained. A bright beam shot out from his torch as he turned the corner of the house. There was nobody in sight, but the window, which he had fastened, was open and there were new footprints in the snow leading away into the darkness.

'Well, I'm damned!' said Gaylor.

J.G. Reeder said nothing. He was smiling when he came back into the room, having stopped to break the wire with a kick.

'Do you think somebody was in the lobby?'

'I know somebody was in the lobby,' he said. 'Dear me! How foolish of us not to have had a policeman posted outside the door! You notice that a pane of glass has been cut? Our friend must have been listening there.'

'Was there only one?'

'Only one,' said Mr Reeder gravely. 'But was he the one who came that way before—I don't think so.'

He took the frying-pan from the hearth where he had put it and resumed his frying of eggs, served them on two plates and brewed the tea. It was just as though death had not lurked in that lobby a few minutes before.

'No, they won't come back; there is no longer a reason for our staying. There were two, but only one came into the house. They may have a long way to travel, and they would not risk being anywhere near at daybreak. At six o'clock the agricultural labourer of whom the poet Gray wrote so charmingly will be on his way to work, and they won't risk meeting him either.'

They had a solemn breakfast, Gaylor plying the other with questions, which in the main he did not answer.

'You think that Miss Lynn is in this—in the murder, I mean?'

Reeder shook his head.

'No, no,' he said. 'I'm afraid it isn't as easy as that.'

Daylight had come greyly when, having installed a cold policeman in the house, they plodded down the lane. Reeder's car had been retrieved in the night, and a more powerful vehicle, fitted with wheel chains, was waiting to take them to Beaconsfield. They did not reach that place for two hours, for on their way they came upon a little knot of policemen and farm labourers looking sombrely at the body of Constable Verity. He lay under some bushes a few yards from the road, and he was dead.

'Shot,' said a police officer. 'The divisional surgeon has just seen him.'

Stiff and cold, with his booted legs stretched wide, his overcoat turned up and his snow-covered cap drawn over his eyes, was the officer who had ridden out from the station courtyard so unsuspectingly the night before. His bike had already been found; the bloodstains that had puzzled and alarmed the police were now accounted for.

Gaylor and Reeder drove on into Beaconsfield. Gaylor was a depressed and silent man; Mr Reeder was silent but not depressed.

As they came out into the main road he turned to his companion, and asked:

'I wonder why they didn't bring their own aces?'

VI. — THE VEILED WOMAN

MR KINGFETHER, manager of the Beaconsfield branch of the Great Central Bank, was at work very early that morning, for he had a letter to write, and his managerial office gave him the privacy he required. He was a serious man, with serious-looking glasses on a pale, plump face. He had a little black moustache and his cheeks and chin were invariably blue, for he had what barbers call a 'strong beard.'

The newspapers arrived as he was writing. They were pushed under the closed outer door of the bank and, being at the moment stuck for the alternative to an often reiterated term of endearment, he rose and brought them into the office and sat down to glance through them. There were two papers, one financial and one human.

He read the latter first, and there was the murder in detail, though it had only occurred the night before. The discovery of the constable's body was not described, because it had not been discovered when the paper went to press.

He read and re-read, his mind in a whirl, and then he took the telephone and called Mr Enward. 'Good morning, Kingfether... Yes, yes, it's true... I was practically a witness—they've found the poor policeman dead... yes, murdered... yes, shot... I was the last person to speak to him. Dreadful, dreadful, dreadful! That such horrors can be—I say that such horrors can be... I said that such... What's the matter with your phone? He banks with you? Really? Really? I'll come over and talk with you...'

Mr Kingfether hung up the telephone and wiped his face with his handkerchief. It was a face that became moist on the least provocation. Presently he folded the newspaper and looked at his unfinished letter. He was on the eighth page and the last words he had written were:

'... can hardly live the day through without seeing your darling face, my own...'

It was obvious that he was not writing to his general manager, or to a client who had overdrawn his account.

He added 'beloved' mechanically, though he had used the word a dozen times before. Then he unfolded the paper and read of the murder again.

A knock at the side door: he went out to admit Enward. The lawyer was more important than usual. Participation in public affairs has this effect. And a news agency had telephoned to ask whether they could send a photographer, and Mr Enward, shivering at the telephone in his pyjamas, had said 'Yes' and had been photographed at his breakfast table at 7.30 am, poising a cup of tea and looking excessively grave. He would presently appear in one hundred and fifty newspapers above the caption 'Lawyer Who Discovered His Own Client Murdered'.

'It's a terrible business,' said Enward, throwing off his coat. 'He banked with you? I'm in charge of his affairs, Kingfether, though heaven knows I'm ignorant about 'em! I don't know how he stands... what's his credit here?'

Mr Kingfether considered. 'I'll get the ledger from the safe,' he said.

He locked the centre drawer of his desk, because his letter to Ava Burslem was there and other documents, but Enward saw nothing offensive in the act of caution; rather was it commendable.

'Here's his account.' Kingfether laid the big ledger on the desk and opened it where his thumb marked a page. 'Credit three thousand four hundred pounds.'

Enward fixed his glasses and looked.

'Has he anything on deposit? Securities—no? Did he come often to the bank?'
'Never,' said Kingfether. 'He used the account to pay bills. When he wanted ready money he posted a bearer cheque and I posted back the money. He has, of course, sent people here to cash cheques.'
'That six hundred pounds withdrawn five days ago.' Enward pointed to the item.
'It's strange that you should point that out—it was paid over the counter four days ago. I didn't see the person who called for it—I was out. My clerk McKay cashed the cheque. Who's that?'
There was a gentle rapping at the door. Mr Kingfether went out of the room and came back with the caller.
'How fortunate to find you here!' said J.G. Reeder. He was spruce and lively. A barber had shaved him, somebody had cleaned his shoes. 'The account of the late Mr Wentford?' He nodded to the book.
It was generally known that J.G. Reeder acted for the Great Central Bank, and the manager did not question his title to ask questions. Mr Enward was not so sure.
'This is rather a serious matter, Mr Reeder,' he said, consciously grave. 'I am not so sure that we can take you into our confidence—'
'Hadn't you better see the police and ask them if they are prepared to take you into their confidence?' asked Mr Reeder, with a sudden ferocity which made the lawyer recoil.
Once more the manager explained the account.
'Six hundred pounds—h'm!' Mr Reeder frowned. 'A large sum—who was the drawer?'
'My clerk McKay said it was a lady—but she wore a thick veil.'
Reeder stared at him.
'Your clerk McKay? Of course—a fair young man. How stupid of me! Kenneth—or is it Karl—Kenneth, is it? H'm! A heavily veiled lady. Have you the number of the notes?'
Kingfether was taken aback by the question. He searched for a book that held the information, and Mr Reeder copied them down, an easy task since the tens and the fives ran consecutively.
'When does your clerk arrive?'
Kenneth was supposed to arrive at nine. As a rule he was late. He was late that morning.
Mr Reeder saw the young man through a window in the manager's office and thought that he did not look well. His eyes were tired; he had shaved himself carelessly, for his chin bore a strip of sticking plaster. Perhaps that accounted for the spots on the soiled cuff of his shirt, thought Mr Reeder, when he confronted the young man.
'No, I will see him alone,' said Reeder.
'He's rather an insolent pup,' warned Mr Kingfether.
'I have tamed lions,' said Mr Reeder.
When Kenneth came in:
'Close the door, please, and sit down. You know me, my boy?'
'Yes, sir,' said Kenneth.
'That is blood on your shirt cuff, isn't it?... cut your chin, did you? You haven't been home all night?'
Kenneth did not answer at once.
'No sir. I haven't changed my shirt, if that's what you mean.'
Mr Reeder smiled. 'Exactly.'
He fixed the young man with a long, searching glare. 'Why did you go to the house of the late Mr Wentford last night between the hours of eight-thirty and nine-thirty?'
He saw the youth go deathly white.

'I didn't know he was dead—I didn't even know his name until this morning. I went there because... well, I was low enough to spy on somebody... follow them from London and sneak into the house—'

'The young lady, Margot Lynn. You're in love with her? Engaged to her, perhaps?'

'I'm in love with her—I'm not engaged to her. We are no longer... friends,' said Kenneth in a low voice. 'She told you I'd been there, I suppose?' and then, as a light broke on him: 'Or did you find my cap? It had my name in it.'

Mr Reeder nodded. 'You came down on the same train as Miss Lynn? Good. Then you will be able to prove that you left Bourne End station—'

'No, I shan't,' said Kenneth. 'I slipped out of the train on to the line. Naturally I didn't want her to see me. I got out through the level crossing. There was nobody about—it was snowing heavily.'

'Very awkward.' Mr Reeder pursed his lips. 'You thought there was some sort of friendship between Mr Wentford and the young lady?'

Kenneth made a gesture of despair. 'I don't know what I thought—I was just a jealous fool.'

There was a long silence.

'You paid out six hundred pounds the other day to a lady on Mr Wentford's cheque?'

'I didn't know that Wentford was—' began Ken, but Mr Reeder brushed aside that aspect of the situation. 'Yes, a veiled lady. She came by car. It was a large sum of money, but the day before Mr Kingfether had told me to honour any cheque of Mr Wentford's no matter to whom the money was paid.'

J.G. Reeder asked very little more. He was, it seemed, the easiest man in the world to satisfy. Before he left he saw the manager alone.

'Did you tell Mr McKay that he was to honour any cheque of Mr Wentford's, no matter to whom the money was paid?'

The answer came instantly.

'Of course not! Naturally I should expect him to be sure that the person who presented a cheque had authority. And another curious thing which I have not mentioned. I lunch at the inn opposite and I usually have a seat in the window, where I can see these premises, but I have no recollection of any car drawing up to the bank.'

'H'm!' was all that Mr Reeder said.

He made a few inquiries in Beaconsfield and the neighbourhood and went on to Wentford's house, where Gaylor had arranged to meet him. The inspector was pacing up and down the snowy terrace in front of the house and he was in very good spirits.

'I think I've got the man,' he said. 'Do you know anybody named McKay?'

Mr Reeder looked at him slyly.

'I know a dozen,' he said.

'Come inside and I'll show you something.'

Reeder followed him into the room. The carpet had been taken up, the furniture moved. Evidently a very thorough search had been in progress. Gaylor swung back the bookcase: the safe door was ajar.

'We got the keys from the maker—quick work! They were down here by eight-thirty.'

He stooped down and pulled out three bundles. The first was made up of bills, the second of used cheques, the third was a thick bundle of French banknotes, each to the value of 1000 francs.

'That is surprise No. 1,' began the detective, flourishing the money. 'French money—'

'I'm afraid it doesn't surprise me,' said Mr Reeder apologetically. 'You see, I've been examining the gentleman's bank book. By the way, here are the numbers of notes drawn from Mr

Wentford's account.' He handed over a slip of paper.

'Six hundred pounds is a lot of money,' said Gaylor. 'I'll phone these through. Well, what else did you find in the bank book?'

'I observed,' said Mr Reeder, 'though I will not emphasize the fact, that all the money he paid was in banknotes. Number 2 is—?'

The inspector extracted a sheet of headed paper from one heap. Written in pencil was what was evidently a memorandum from somebody who signed himself 'D. H. Hartford.'

'I have found that the man who is employing a detective to find you is George McKay of Sennet House, Marlow. I don't know what his intentions are, but they're not pleasant. There is nothing to worry about, he is employing one of the most incompetent private detectives in the business.'

'Extraordinary!' said Mr Reeder, and coughed.

'The first thing to do is to find Hartford—' began Gaylor.

'He's in Australia,' Mr Reeder interrupted. 'At the time that letter was written his office address was 327, Lambs Buildings. He became bankrupt and left the country hurriedly.'

'How do you know?' asked Gaylor, astonished.

'Because I—um—was the incompetent private detective engaged to find Mr Lynn or, as he called himself, Mr Wentford. And I didn't find him,' said Mr Reeder.

'Why did McKay want to find this man?'

'He owed him money. I know no more than that. The search fell off because—um—Mr McKay owed me money. One has to live.'

'Then you knew about Wentford?'

Mr Reeder took counsel with himself.

'Um—yes. I recognized him last night—I once had a photograph of him. I thought it was very odd. I also—er—drove over to Marlow and made inquiries. Mr McKay—Mr George McKay did not leave his house last night, and at the moment the murder was committed was entertaining the—um—vicar to dinner.'

'You're a killjoy,' Gaylor said, and Mr Reeder sighed heavily. Gaylor got up and stood squarely before him. 'What do you know about these murders, Reeder?' he challenged.

Mr Reeder spread his hands wide. His glasses, set askew, slipped a little further down his nose. He was not a very imposing figure.

'I am a strange man, Mr Gaylor; I am cursed, as you are aware, with a peculiarly evil mind. I am also intensely curious—I have always been. I am curious about criminals and chickens—I have perhaps the finest Rhode Island Reds in London, but that is by the way. It would be cruel to give you my theories. The blood on the policeman's motorcycle: that is interesting. And Henry—I suppose Mr Enward's clerk has another name—the blood on his coat, though he did not go near the body of the late Mr Wentford, that is interesting. Poor Henry is suffering from a severe chill and is in bed, but his mother, an admirable and hardworking woman, permitted me to see him. Then the two aces pinned to the door, all very, very, very interesting indeed! Mr Gaylor, if you will permit me to interview old George McKay I will undertake to tell you who committed these murders.'

'The girl told you something—the girl Lynn?'

'The girl has told me nothing. She also may be very informative. I propose spending a night or two in her flat—um—not, I hope, without a chaperone.'

Gaylor looked at him, amazed. Mr Reeder was blushing.

VII. — WHO KILLED WENTFORD?

THE last page of the letter which Eric Kingfether had begun with such ease in the early part of the morning was extremely difficult to compose. It had become necessary to say certain things; it was vital that he should not put his communication into writing.

In desperation he decided to make a break with practice. He would go to London. It was impossible to leave before the bank closed, but he could go immediately afterwards, though there was urgent work which should have kept him on the bank premises until six, and some private work of serious importance that should have occupied him until midnight. When the bank closed he handed over the key of the safe to Kenneth.

'I've been called to town. Balance up the books and put them in the safe. I'll be back by six; I'd like you to wait for me.'

Kenneth McKay did not receive the suggestion favourably. He also wished to get away.

'Well, you can't!' said the other sharply. 'The bank inspector will be in tomorrow to check the Wentford account. It will probably be required as evidence.'

Mr Kingfether got out his car and drove to London. He parked in a Bloomsbury square and made his way on foot to a big mansion block behind Gower Street. The elevator man who took him up grinned a welcome.

'The young lady's in, sir,' he said.

The 'young lady' herself opened the door to his ring. 'Look who's here!' she said in surprise, and stood aside to let him in.

She was wearing an old dressing gown and did not look as attractive as usual.

'In another half hour I'd have been out,' she said. 'I didn't get up till after lunch. These late nights are surely hell!'

She led the way to a sitting-room which was hazy with cigarette smoke. It was a large room, its floor covered with a soft carpet that had once cost a lot of money but was now mottled with stains. In front of the fire was a big divan, and on this she had been reclining. The furnishing and appointments of the room were of that style which is believed to be oriental by quite a large number of people. The whole room was half way to blowsiness. It had a stale, sweet scent.

'Well, my dear, what brings you up to town? I told you to snatch a few hours sleep—round about one you looked like a boiled owl, and that's not the state to be in when you're chasing money.'

She was dark and good-looking by certain standards. Her figure was robust, and nature had given generously to the amplification of her visible charms.

For a very long time they talked, head to head. She was an excellent listener; her sympathy had a sincere note. At half past five:

'Now off you pop and don't worry. The governor will be seeing you tonight—talk it over with him. I think you'd better, in case anything turns up... you know what I mean.'

He took a letter out of his pocket and gave it to her with an air of embarrassment.

'I wrote it, or rather started it, this morning... I couldn't finish it. I mean every word I say.'

She kissed him loudly.

'You're a darling!' she said.

Mr Kingfether came back to his office to find only a junior in charge. McKay, despite instructions to the contrary, had gone, and the manager sat down to a rough examination of important books in no condition to do justice to his task. He possessed one of those slow-starting tempers that gathers momentum from its own weight. A little grievance and a long brooding

brought him to a condition of senseless and unrestrainable fury.
He was in this state when Kenneth McKay returned.
'I asked you to stay in, didn't I?' He glowered at his subordinate.
'Did you? Well, I stayed in until I finished my work. Then the bank inspector came.'
Mr Kingfether's face went white. 'What did he want? Redman didn't tell me he called.'
'Well, he did.' Kenneth passed into the outer office.
Kingfether sat scribbling oddly on his blotting-pad for a moment, and then for the first time saw the letter that had been placed on the mantelpiece. It was marked 'Urgent, confidential. Deliver by hand,' and was from head office.
He took it up with a shaking hand and, after a long hesitation, tore the seal. There was a small mirror on the wall above the fireplace, and he caught sight of his face and could hardly believe that that ghost of a man was himself.
There was no need to read the letter twice through. Already he knew every word, every comma. He stood blinking at his reflection, and then went into the outer office. He found Kenneth collecting some personal belongings from his desk.
'I suppose the inspector came about the Wentford cheque?' he said.
The young man looked round at him.
'Wentford cheque? I don't know what you're talking about. You don't mean the cheque I cashed for the woman?'
It required an effort on the manager's part to affirm this.
'What was wrong with it?'
'It was forged, that's all.'
'Forged?' Kenneth frowned at him.
'Yes... didn't the inspector say anything? He left a letter for me, didn't he?'
Kenneth shook his head.
'No. He was surprised to find that you weren't here. I told him you had gone up to head office. I'm getting a bit sick of lying about you. What's the yarn about this cheque?'
Again it required a painful effort on the manager's part to speak.
'It was forged. You've to report to head office tomorrow morning... some of the banknotes have been traced to you... the cheque was out of your office book.'
It was out, yet he felt no relief.
McKay was looking at him open-mouthed.
'You mean the cheque that was changed by that woman?'
The word 'woman' irritated Mr Kingfether.
'A lady was supposed to have called, a veiled lady—'
'What do you mean by "supposed"?' demanded Kenneth. 'You say that the notes were traced to me—I issued them: is that what you mean?'
'You have them—some of them—in your private possession;—that's all.'
Incredulity showed in Kenneth's face. 'Me? You mean that I stole them?'
Kingfether had reached the limit of endurance. 'How the hell do I know what you did?' he almost shouted. 'Head office have written to say that some of the notes you paid over the counter have been traced through a moneylender named Stuart to you.'
The young man's face changed suddenly.
'Stuart... Oh?' was all that he said. A moment later he went blundering out of the side door, leaving Mr Kingfether to continue his aimless scribblings on his blotting-pad.
Kenneth reached Marlow just before the dinner hour, and he came into the study where old

George McKay was usually to be found, working out his eternal combinations. To Kenneth's amazement, his father greeted him with a smile. Instead of the cards, his table was covered with packages of documents and the paraphernalia of correspondence.

'Hullo, son—we've had a stroke of luck. The arbitrators have decided in my favour. I knew jolly well I hadn't parted with my rights to the dyeing process when I sold out, and the company has to pay close on a hundred thousand back royalties.'

Kenneth knew of this wrangle between his father and his late company that had gone on through the years, but he had never paid very much attention to it.

'That means a steady income for years, and this time I'm going to look after things—here!'

He pointed to the grate. The fireplace was filled with half-burnt playing cards.

'They've asked me to rejoin the board as chairman. What's the matter, Kenny?'

Kenneth was sitting on the opposite side of the table, and his father had seen his face.

Briefly he told his story, and George McKay listened without comment until he had finished.

'Wentford, eh? He's going to be a curse to me to the end of my days.'

Kenneth gasped his amazement. 'Did you know him?'

Old George nodded. 'I knew him all right!' he said grimly. 'Reeder was here this morning—'

'About me?' asked the other quickly.

'About me,' said his father. 'I rather gathered that he suspected me of the murder.'

Kenneth came to his feet, horrified. 'You? But he's mad! Why should you—'

Mr McKay smiled dourly. 'There was quite a good reason why I should murder him,' he said calmly; 'such a good reason that I have been expecting the police all the afternoon.'

Then abruptly he changed the subject.

'Tell me about these banknotes. Of course I knew that you had borrowed the money from Stuart, my boy. I was a selfish old man to let you do it—how did the money come to you?'

Kenneth's story was a surprising one. 'I had it a couple of days ago,' he said. 'I came down to breakfast and found a letter. It wasn't registered and the address was hand printed, I opened it, without any idea of what it contained. Just then I was terribly upset about Stuart—I thought head office might get to know about my borrowing money. And when I found inside the letter twenty ten-pound notes you could have knocked me out.'

'Was there any letter?'

'None. Not even "from a friend."'

'Who knew about you being in debt?'

One name came instantly to Kenneth's mind.

'You told your Margot, did you... Wentford's niece? His real name was Lynn, by the way. Could she have sent it?'

'It wasn't her who drew the money, I'll swear! I should have known her. And though she wore a veil, I could recognize her again if I met her. Kingfether's line is that no woman came; he's suggesting that the cheque was cashed by me. He even says that the cheque was out of a book which I keep in my drawer for the use of customers who come to the bank without their cheque books.'

George McKay fingered his chin, his keen eyes on his son.

'If you were in any kind of trouble you'd tell me the truth, my boy, wouldn't you? All this worry has come through me. You're telling me the truth now, aren't you?'

'Yes, father.'

The older man smiled.

'Fathers have the privilege of asking "Are you a thief?" without having their heads punched! And most young people do stupid things—and most old people too! Lord! I once carried a quarter of a million bank at baccarat! Nobody would believe that, but it's true. Come and eat, then go along and see your Margot.'

'Father, who killed that man Wentford?'

There was a twinkle in McKay's eyes when he answered: 'J.G. Reeder, I should think. He knows more about it than any honest man should know!'

VIII. — REEDER—THE DEVIL

WHEN her visitor was gone, Ava opened the letter he had left with her, read a few lines of it, then threw letter and envelope into the fire. Funny, the sameness of men... they all wrote the same sort of stuff... raw stuff dressed up poetically... yet they thought they were being different from all other men. She did not resent these stereotypes of passion, nor did she feel sorry for those who used them. They were just normal experiences. She sat clasping her knees, her eyes on the fire. Then she got up dressed quickly and, going into Gower Street, found a cab.
She was set down at a house in an exclusive Mayfair street, and a liveried footman admitted her and told her there was company. There usually was in the early evening. She found twenty men and women sitting round a green table, watching a croupier with a large green shade over his eyes. He was turning up cards in two rows, and big monies, staked in compartments marked on the green table, went into the croupier's well or was pushed, with additions, to the fortunate winner.
The usual crowd, she noted. A pretty girl looked up and smiled then turned her eyes quickly and significantly to the young man by her side.
Ava found the governor in his room. He was smoking alone and reading the evening newspaper when she came in.
'Shut the door,' he ordered. 'What's wrong?'
'Nothing much. Only Feathers is bit worried.' She told him why.
Rufus Machfield smiled.
'Don't you worry, my pet,' he said kindly. 'There's been a murder down his way—did he tell you anything about that? I've just been reading about it. I should be surprised if old Reeder didn't get to the bottom of it—clever fellow, Reeder.'
He picked up his newspaper from the floor and his cigar from the ashtray where he had laid it. 'Rather a coincidence, wasn't it, Ava? Feathers pickin' on that account... Wentford's?'
She looked at him thoughtfully.
'Was it a coincidence?' she asked. 'That's what's worrying me. Did he pick on this poor man's account because he knew that he was going to be dead in a few days? I got a horrible creepy feeling when he was sitting beside me. I kept looking at his hands and wondering if there was blood on them!'
'Shuh!' said Machfield contemptuously. 'That rabbit!'
He opened a panel in the wall—it was nothing more romantic than a serving hatch when it was built—and glanced at the gamesters.
'They're playing for marbles!' he said in fine scorn. 'But they never do play high in the afternoon. Look at Lamontaine: he's bored sick.'
And certainly the croupier did not look happy. He closed the panel.
'I suppose you'll be raided one of these days?' she said.
'Sure!' he answered easily. 'But I've got another couple of houses ready for starting.'
'What do you think about Feathers? Will he squeal when they find him out?'
'Like a stuck pig,' said Machfield. 'He'll go down for nine months and get religion. That's the kind of fellow who gives the prison chaplain an interest in life. Ava, I've got a little job for you.'
She was alert, suspicious.

'Nothing much. I'll tell you all about it. Shall I open a bottle?'

'Yes, if it's milk,' she said. 'What's the little job and how much does it carry?'

'Would you faint if I said a thousand?' he asked, and opened the hatch again, looking through and closing it.

'Who are you expecting?' she asked. '... all right, don't be rude. No thousands never make me faint. Especially when they're talked about—'

'Now listen.'

Machfield was too good a talker to be brief. He led from a preamble to sections, into subsections...

'One minute.'

He interrupted his explanation to lift the hatch. She saw him bringing it down; then unexpectedly he raised it again. Was it the effect of odd lighting, or had his face changed colour? He dropped the hatch softly and gaped round at her.

'Who let him in? That doorman has "shopped" me—'

'Who is it?' she asked.

He beckoned her to his side, lifting the panel an inch.

'Stoop!' he hissed. 'Look... that fellow with the side-whiskers.'

'Oh—is he anybody?' She did not recognize the visitor. Possibly he was a bailiff; he looked hopelessly suburban, like the people who serve writs. They always wear ready-made ties and coloured handkerchiefs that stick out of their breast pockets.

'Reeder... J.G. Reeder!'

She wanted to raise the hatch and look, but he would not allow this.

'Go out and see what you can do... wait a bit.'

He lifted a house telephone and pressed a knob.

'Who was that fellow... the old fellow with side-whiskers? Got a card... what name... Reeder?'

He put down the phone unsteadily. Mr Machfield gave his membership cards to the right people. They were issued with the greatest care and after elaborate inquiries had been made as to the antecedents of the man or woman so honoured.

'Go and get acquainted... he doesn't know you. Go round through the buffet room and pretend you've just come in.'

When she reached the gaming room, Ava found Mr Reeder was sitting opposite the croupier. How he got that favoured chair was a mystery. His umbrella was between his knees. In front of him was a pile of banknotes. He was 'punting' gravely, seemingly absorbed in the game.

'Faîtes vos jeux, messieurs et mesdames,' said the croupier mechanically.

'What does he mean by that?' asked Mr Reeder of his nearest neighbour.

'He means "Make your bet",' said the girl, who had drawn up a chair by his side.

Mr Reeder made ten coups and won six pounds. With this he got up from the table and recovered his hat from beneath his chair.

'I always think that the time to—um—stop playing cards is when you're winning.' He imparted this truth to the young lady, who had withdrawn from the table at the same time.

'What a marvellous mind you have!' she said enthusiastically.

Mr Reeder winced.

'I'm afraid I have,' he said.

She shepherded him into the buffet room; he seemed quite willing to be refreshed at the expense of the house.

'A cup of tea, thank you, and a little seed cake.'

Ava was puzzled. Had the whole breed of busies undergone this shattering deterioration?

'I prefer seed to fruit cake,' he was saying. 'Curiously enough chickens are the same. I had a hen once—we called her Curly Toes—who could eat fruit and preferred it...'

She listened—she was a good listener. He offered to see her home.

'No—if you could drop me at the corner of Bruton Street and Berkeley Square—I don't live far from there,' she said modestly.

'Dear me!' said Mr Reeder, as he signalled a cab. 'Do you live in a mews too? So many people do.'

This was disconcerting.

'Perhaps you will come and see me one day—I am Mrs Coleforth-Ebling, and my phone number—do write this down—'

'My memory is very excellent,' murmured Mr Reeder.

The cab drove up at that moment and he opened the door.

'Ava Burslem—I will remember that—907, Gower Mansions.' He waved his hand in farewell as he got into the cab.

'I'll be seeing you again, my dear—toodle-oo!'

Mr Reeder could on occasions be outrageously frivolous. 'Toodle-oo!' was the high-water mark of his frivolity It was not remarkable that Ava was both alarmed and puzzled. Brighter intellects than hers had been shaken in a vain effort to reconcile Mr Reeder's appearance and manner with Mr Reeder's reputation.

She went back into the house and told Rufus Machfield what had happened.

'That man's clever,' said Machfield admiringly. 'If I were the man who had killed Wentworth or whatever his name is, I'd be shaking in my shoes. I'll walk round to the Leffingham and see if I can pick up a young game-fish. And you'd better dine with me, Ava—I'll give you the rest of the dope on that business I was discussing.'

The Leffingham Club was quite useful to Mr Machfield. It was a kind of potting shed where likely young shoots could be nurtured before being bedded out in the gardens of chance. Even Kenneth McKay had had his uses.

When Mr Reeder reached Scotland Yard, where they had arranged to meet, he found Inspector Gaylor charged with news.

'We've had a bit of luck!' he said. 'Do you remember those banknotes? You took their numbers... you remember? They were paid out on Wentford's account!'

'Oh, yes, yes, yes,' said Mr Reeder. 'To the veiled lady—'

'Veiled grandmother!' said Gaylor. 'We've traced two hundred pounds' worth to a moneylender. They were paid by Kenneth McKay, the bank clerk who cashed the cheque—and here's the cheque!'

He took it from a folder on his desk.

'The signature is a bad forgery; the cheque itself was not torn from Wentford cheque-book but from a book kept at the bank under McKay's charge!'

'Astounding!' said Mr. Reeder.

'Isn't it?' Mr Gaylor was smiling. 'So simple! I had the whole theory of the murders given me tonight. McKay forged and uttered the note, and to cover up his crime killed Wentford.'

'And you instantly arrested him?'

'Am I a child in arms?' asked Gaylor reproachfully. 'No, I questioned the lad. He doesn't deny that he paid the money lender, but says that the money came to him from some anonymous source. It arrived at his house by registered post. Poor young devil, he's terribly worried. What are we waiting for now?'

'A Gentleman Who Wants to Open a Box,' said Mr Reeder mysteriously.

'Reeder releases his mysteries as a miser pays his dentist,' said Gaylor to the superintendent. 'He knows I know all about the case—I admit he is very good and passes on most of the information he gets, but the old devil will keep back the connecting links!'

'Humour him,' said the superintendent.

IX. — TRAPPED!

MARGOT LYNN had spent a wretched and a weary day. The little city office which she occupied, and where she had conducted most of her uncle's business, had become a place of bad dreams.

She had never been very fond of her tyrannical relative who, if he had paid her well, had extracted the last ounce of service from her. He was an inveterate speculator, and had made considerable monies from his operations on the Stock Exchange. It was she who had bought and sold on his telephoned instructions, she who put his money into a London bank. Over her head all the time he had held one weapon: she had an invalid mother in Italy dependent on his charity. All day long, people had been calling at the office. A detective had been there for two hours, taking a new statement; reporters had called in battalions, but these she had not seen. Mr Reeder had supplied her with an outer guard, a hard-faced woman who held the Pressmen at bay. But the police now knew everything there was to know about 'Wentford's' private affairs—except one thing. She was keeping faith with the dead in this respect, though every time she thought of her reservation her heart sank.

She finished her work and went home, leaving the building by a back door to avoid the patient reporters. They were waiting for her at her flat, but the hard-faced Mrs Grible swept them away. Once safely in the flat, a difficulty arose. How could she tactfully and delicately dismiss the guard which Mr Reeder had provided? She offered the woman tea, and Mrs Grible, who said very little, embarrassed her by making it.

'I'm greatly obliged to you and Mr Reeder,' she said after the little meal. 'I don't think I ought to take up any more of your time—'

'I'm staying until Mr Reeder comes,' said the lady.

Very meekly the girl accepted the situation.

Mr Reeder did not come until ten o'clock. Margot was half dead with weariness, and would have given her legacy to have undressed and gone to bed.

For his part, he was in the liveliest mood, an astounding circumstance remembering that he had had practically no sleep for thirty-six hours. In an indefinable way he communicated to her some of his own vitality. She found herself suddenly very wide awake.

'You have seen the police, of course?' Mr Reeder sat on a chair facing her, leaning on the handle of his umbrella, his hat carefully deposited on the floor by his side. 'And you have told them everything? It is very wise. The key, now—did you tell them about the key?'

She went very red. She was—thought Mr Reeder—almost as pretty when she was red as when she was white.

'The key?' She could fence, a little desperately, with the question, although she knew just what he meant.

'At the cottage last night you showed me two keys—one the key of the house, the other, from shape and make, the key of a safe deposit.'

Margot nodded.

'Yes. I suppose I should have told them that. But Mr Wentford—'

'Asked you never to tell. That is why he had two keys, one for you and one for himself.'

'He hated paying taxes—' she began.

'Did he ever come up to London?'

'Only on very wet and foggy days. I've never been to the safe deposit, Mr Reeder. Anything that is there he placed himself. I only had the key in case of accidents.'

'What was he afraid of—did he ever tell you?'

She shook her head.

'He was terribly afraid of something. He did all his own housework and cooking—he would never have anybody in. A gardener used to come every few days and look after the electric light plant, and Mr Wentford used to pay him through the window. He was afraid of bombs—you've seen the cage round the window in his bedroom? He had that put there for fear somebody should throw in a bomb while he was asleep. I can't tell you what precautions he took. Except myself and the policeman, and once Mr Enward the lawyer, nobody has ever entered that house. His laundry was put outside the door every week and left at the door. He had an apparatus for testing milk and he analysed every drop that was left at the door before he drank it—he practically lived on milk. It wasn't so bad when I first went to him —I was sixteen then—but it got worse and worse as the years went on.'

'He had two telephones in the house,' said Mr Reeder. 'That was rather extravagant.'

'He was afraid of being cut off. The second one was connected by underground wires—it cost him an awful lot of money.' She heaved a deep, relieved sigh. 'Now I've told everything, and my conscience is clear. Shall I get the keys?'

'They are for Mr Gaylor,' said Mr Reeder hastily. 'I think you had better keep them and give them to nobody else. Not even to the person who calls tonight.'

'Who is calling tonight?' she asked.

Mr Reeder avoided the question. He looked at Mrs Grible, grim and silent.

'Would you mind—er—waiting outside?'

The obedient woman melted from the room.

'There is one point we ought to clear up, my dear young friend,' said Mr Reeder in a hushed voice. 'How long had you been in your uncle's house when Mr Kenneth McKay appeared?'

If he had struck her she could not have wilted as she did. Her face went the colour of chalk, and she dropped into a chair.

'He came through the window into the little lobby? I know all about that—but how long after you arrived?'

She tried to speak twice before she succeeded.

'A few minutes,' she said, not raising her eyes.

Then suddenly, she sprang up.

'He knew nothing about the murder—he was stupidly jealous and followed me... and then I explained to him, and he believed me... I looked through the window and saw you and told him to go... that is the truth, I swear it is!'

He patted her gently on the shoulder.

'I know it is the truth, my dear—be calm, I beg of you. That is all I wanted to know.'

He called Mrs Grible by name. As she came in, they heard the bell of the front door ring. It was followed by a gentle rat-tat.

'Who would that be?' asked Margot. She was still trembling.

'It may be a reporter—it may not be.' Mr Reeder rose. 'If it is some stranger to see you on urgent business, perhaps you would be kind enough to mention the fact that you are quite alone.'

He looked helplessly round.

'That—' He pointed to a door.

'Is the kitchen,' she said, hardly noticing his embarrassment.

'Very excellent.' He was relieved. Opening the door, he waved Mrs Grible to precede him. 'If it should be reporters we will deal with them,' he said, and closed the door behind him.

There was a second ring of the bell as Margot hurried to the door. Standing outside was a girl. She was elegantly dressed, was a little older than Margot, and pretty.

'Can I see you, Miss Lynn? It's rather important.' Margot hesitated.

'Come in, please,' she said at last. The girl followed her into the sitting-room. 'All alone?' she said lightly. Margot nodded.

'You're a great pal of Kenneth's, aren't you?' She saw the colour come into Margot's face, and laughed.

'Of course you are—and you've had an awful row?'

'I've had no awful row,' said Margot quietly.

'Well, he's a darling boy, and he's in terrible trouble.'

'Trouble—what kind of trouble?' asked Margot quickly.

'Police trouble—'

The girl swayed and caught at the back of a chair.

'Don't get upset!' Ava was enjoying her part. 'He'll be able to explain everything—'

'But he said he believed me...' She was on the point of betraying the presence of the hidden Mr Reeder, but checked herself in time.

'Who said so?' asked Ava curiously. 'A copper—policeman, I mean? Don't take any notice of that kind of trash. They'd lie to save a car fare! We know that Kenneth didn't forge the cheque—'

Margot's eyes opened wide in amazement.

'Forge a cheque—what do you mean? I don't understand what you're talking about.'

For a moment Ava was nonplussed. If this girl did not know about the forgery, what was agitating her? The solution of this minor mystery came in a flash. It was the murder! Kenneth was in it! She went cold at the thought.

'Oh, my God! I didn't think of that!' she gasped.

'Tell me about this forgery—' began Margot, and her visitor remembered her errand.

'I want you to come along and see Kenneth. He's waiting for you at my flat—naturally he can't come here. He'll tell you everything.'

Margot was bewildered.

'Of course I'll come, but—'

'Don't "but," my dear—just slip into your things and come along. Kenneth told me to ask you to bring all the keys you have—he said they can prove his innocence—'

'Dear, dear, dear!' said a gentle voice, and Ava flung round, to face the man who had come into the room.

She was trapped and knew it. That old devil!

'The key of the larder now, would that be of any use to you?' asked Mr Reeder in his jocular mood. 'Or the key of Wormwood Scrubs?'

'Hullo, Reeder!' The girl was coolness itself. 'I thought you were alone, Miss Lynn. I didn't know you were entertaining Mr and Mrs Reeder.'

Such an outrageous statement made Mr Reeder blush, but it did not confuse him. Nor did Mrs Grible seem particularly distressed.

'This lady is Mrs Grible, of my department,' he said gravely.

'She must have some use,' said Ava. She picked up her coat which she had taken off. 'I'll phone you later, Miss Lynn.'

'The cells at Bow Street police station are hygienically equipped, but they have no telephones,' said Mr Reeder, and for the first time in many years Ava lost her nerve.

'What's the idea—cells?' she demanded loudly. 'You've got nothing on me—'

'We shall see—will you step this way?' He opened the door of the kitchen. 'I should like to have a few words with you.'

He heard a knock at the outer door and looked at Margot.

'I shall be on hand,' he said.

She went to the door—and stepped back at the sight of her visitor. It was Kenneth McKay. He looked at her gravely, and without a word took her into his arms and kissed her. He had never kissed her that way before.

'Can I see you?'

She nodded and took him back to her room. The other three had disappeared.

'It is only right that you should know, darling, that I'm in terrible trouble. I've just come from home, and I suppose the police are after me. They may be after my father, too. He knew Wentford—hated him. I didn't dream that—'

'Ken—what about you? Why do the police want you?'

He looked at her steadily.

'It's about a forged cheque. Some of the money has been traced to me. Darling, I've come to ask you something, and I want you to tell me the truth. Kingfether as good as told me I was a liar when I said I'd cashed it for a veiled woman. I don't mind really what he says—he's a crook, that fellow! Money has been missing from the bank—they sent old Reeder down weeks ago—'

'How did they trace money to you?' she interrupted. 'And what do you want me to tell you?'

'You knew that I owed money—I told you.' She nodded. 'And how worried I was about it. I can't remember whether I told you how much I owed—'

She shook her head.

'You didn't,' she said, and he drew a long breath.

'Then it wasn't you,' he said.

He described the arrival of the letter containing the bank notes.

'Two hundred pounds, and of course I wanted the money badly.'

'Who else knew that you were short of money?' she asked.

'Oh, everybody.' He was in despair. 'I talked about it—Kingfether said that he never ordered me to cash any cheque that came, and that the story of a veiled woman arriving by car from London when he was out at lunch was all moonshine—hullo!'

He saw the door of the kitchen opening and gasped at the sight of Mr Reeder.

'It wasn't moonshine, my young friend,' said Mr Reeder. 'In fact, I—er—have interviewed a garage keeper who filled up the tank of the lady's car, and incidentally saw the lady.'

He turned to the room and beckoned Ava. Kenneth stared at her.

'Well?' she said defiantly. 'Do you think you'll know me again?'

'I know you now!' he said huskily. 'You're the woman who cashed the cheque!'

'That's a damned lie!' she screamed.

'S-sh!' said Mr Reeder, shocked.

'I've never seen him before!' she added, and Margot gasped.

'But you told me—'

'I've never seen him before,' insisted the woman.

'You'll see him again,' said Mr Reeder gently. 'You on one side—the wrong side—of the witness box, and he on the other!'

Then she lost her head.

'If there was a swindle, he was in it!' she said, speaking rapidly. 'You don't suppose any clerk would pay out six hundred pounds to somebody he'd never seen before unless he had his instructions and got his corner! How did I know the cheque was forged? It seemed all right to me.'

'May it continue to seem all right,' said Mr Reeder piously. 'May you be consoled through the long period of your incarceration with the—er—comfort of a good conscience. I think you'll get three years—but if your previous convictions influence the judge, I fancy you'll get five!'

Ava collapsed.

'You can't charge me,' she whimpered. 'I didn't forge anything.'

'There is a crime called "uttering",' said Mr Reeder. '"Uttering—knowing to be forged." Will you take the young lady's arm, Mrs Grible? I will take the other—probably we shall meet a policeman en route. And did I say anything about "conspiracy"? That is also an offence. Mind that mat, Mrs Grible.'

X. — THE RAID

THERE was some rather heavy play at Mr Machfield's private establishment—heavier than usual, and this gave the proprietor of the house cause for uneasiness. If Mr Reeder had reported his visit that afternoon to the police, and they thought the moment expedient, there would be a raid tonight, and in preparation for this all doors leading to the mews at the back were unfastened, and a very powerful car was waiting. Machfield might or might not use that method of escape. On the other hand, he could follow his invariable practice, which was to appear among those present as a guest: a fairly simple matter, because he was not registered as the proprietor of the house; indeed the premises were unlicensed, which was the cause of his fear.
Certainly the car would have its uses, if everything went right and there was no untoward incident. Just lately, however, there had been one or two little hitches in the smooth running of his affairs and, being superstitious, he expected more.
He looked at his watch; his appointment with Ava was at midnight, but she had promised to phone through before then. At a quarter to nine, as he stood watching the players there came a newcomer at the tail of three others. He was wearing a dinner jacket, as were the majority of people round the board, and he looked strangely out of place in those surroundings, though his blue chin was newly shaved and his black hair was glossy.
Mr Machfield watched him wander aimlessly around the table, and then caught his eye and indicated that he wished to see him. Soon afterwards he walked out of the room and Mr Kingfether followed.
'You're rather silly to come tonight, K,' said Mr Machfield. 'There's just a chance of a raid—Reeder was here this afternoon.'
The manager's jaw dropped.
'Is he here now?' he asked, and Mr Machfield smiled at the foolishness of the question.
'No, and he won't be coming tonight, unless he arrives with a flying squad. We'll keep that bird out at any rate'
'Where's Ava?' asked Kingfether.
'She'll be in later,' lied Machfield. 'She had a bit of a headache, and I advised her not to come.'
The bank manager helped himself to a whisky from a decanter on the sideboard.
'I'm very fond of that girl,' said Kingfether.
'Who isn't?' asked the other.
'To me'—there was a tremor in the younger man's voice—'she is something outside of all my experience. Do you think she's fond of me, Machfield?'
'I'm sure she is,' said the other heartily; 'but she's a woman of the world, you know, my boy, and women of the world don't carry their hearts on their sleeves.'
He might have added that, in the case of Ava, she carried the business equivalent of that organ up her sleeve, ready for exhibition to any susceptible man, young or old.
'Do you think she'd marry me, Machfield?'
Machfield did not laugh. He had played cards a great deal and had learned to school his countenance. Ava had two husbands, and had not gone through the formality of freeing herself from either. Both were officially abroad, the foreign country being that stretch of desolate moorland which lies between Ashburton and Tavistock. Here, in the gaunt convict establishment

of Princetown, they laboured for the good of their souls, but with little profit to the taxpayers who supported them, and even supplied them with tobacco.

'Why shouldn't she? But mind, she's an expensive kind of girl, K,' said Machfield very seriously. 'She costs a lot of money to dress, and you'd have to find it from somewhere—fifteen hundred a year doesn't go far with a girl who buys her clothes in Paris.'

Kingfether strode up and down the apartment, his hands in his pockets, his head on his chest, a look of gloom on a face that was never touched with brightness.

'I realize that,' he said, 'but if she loved me she'd help to make both ends meet. I've got to cut out this business of the bank; I've had a fright, and I can't take the risk again. In fact, I thought of leaving the bank and setting up a general agency in London.'

Machfield knew what a general agency was when it was run by an inexperienced man. An office to which nobody came except bill collectors. He didn't, however, wish to discourage his client; for the matter of that, Kingfether gave him little opportunity for comment.

'There's going to be hell's own trouble about that cheque,' he said. 'I had a letter from head office—I have to report to the general manager in the morning and take McKay with me. That's the usual course.'

Such details were distasteful to Mr Machfield. He needed all the spare room in his mind for other matters much more weighty than the routine of the Great Central Bank, but he was more than interested in the fate of McKay.

Kingfether came back to Ava, because Ava filled his horizon.

'The first time I ever met her,' he said, 'I knew she was the one woman in the world for me. I know she's had a rough time and that she's had a battle to live. But who am I to judge?'

'Who, indeed?' murmured Mr Machfield, with considerable truth. And then, pursuing his thought, 'What will happen to Mr Kenneth McKay?'

Only for a moment did the manager look uncomfortable.

'He is not my concern,' he said loudly. 'There's no doubt at all that the signature on the cheque—'

'Oh, yes, yes,' said the other impatiently. 'We don't want to discuss that, do we? I mean, not between friends. You paid me the money you owed me, and there was an end to it so far as I am concerned. I took a bit of a risk myself, sending Ava down—I mean, letting Ava go,' he corrected, when he saw the look on the other's face. 'What about young McKay?'

The manager shrugged his shoulders.

'I don't know and I really don't care. When I got back to the bank this afternoon he'd gone, though I'd left instructions that he was to stay until I returned. Of course, I can't report it, because I did wrong to go away myself, and it was rather awkward that one of our bank inspectors called when I was out. I shall have to work all night to make up arrears. McKay might have helped me. In fact, I told him—'

'Oh, he came back, did he?'

'For five minutes, just before six o'clock. He just looked in and went out again. That's how I knew the inspector had called. I had to tell this pup about the cheque and the banknotes. By the way, that's a mystery to me how the notes came into his hands at all—I suppose there's no mistake about them? If he was in the habit of coming here he might have got them from the table. He doesn't come here, does he?'

'Not often.' Machfield might have added that nobody came to that place unless they had a certain amount of surplus wealth, or the means by which easy money could be acquired.

There were quite a number of his clients who were in almost exactly the same position as Mr Kingfether—people in positions of trust, men who had the handling of other people's money. It was no business of Machfield's how that money was obtained, so long as it was judiciously spent. It was his boast that his game was straight; as indeed it was—up to a point. He had allowed himself throughout life a certain margin of dishonesty, which covered both bad luck and bad investments. Twice in his life he had gone out for big coups. Once he had failed, the other time he had succeeded but had made no money.

He was not persona grata in all the countries of the world. If he had arrived at Monte Carlo he would have left by very nearly the next train, or else the obliging police would have placed a car at his disposal to take him across to Nice, a resort which isn't so particular about the character of her temporary visitors.

'I'm sorry for McKay in a way, but it's a case of his life or mine, Machfield. Either he goes down or I go down—and I'm not going down.'

Nothing wearied Machfield worse than heroics. And yet he should have been hardened to them, for he had lived in an atmosphere of hectic drama, and once had seen a victim of his lying dead by his own hand across the green board of his gaming table. But it was years ago.

'You'd better slide back to the room,' he said. 'I'll come in a little later. Don't play high: I've still got some of your papers, dear boy.'

When he returned to the room, the manager had found a seat at the table and was punting modestly and with some success. The croupier asked a question with a flick of his eyelids, and almost imperceptibly Machfield shook his head, which meant that that night, at any rate, Kingfether would pay for his losses in cash, that neither his IOUs nor cheques would be accepted.

From time to time the players got up from the tables, strolled into the buffet, had a drink and departed. But there was always a steady stream of newcomers to take their places. Mr Machfield went back to his study, for he was expecting a telephone message. It came at a quarter past ten. A woman's voice said: 'Ava says everything is OK.'

He replaced the telephone with a smile. Ava was a safe bet: you could always trust that girl, and he did not question her ability to keep her visitor occupied for at least two hours. After that he would do a little questioning himself. But it must be he, and not that other fool.

Kingfether was winning; there was a big pile of pound and five-pound notes before him. He looked animated, and for once in his life pleased. The bank was winning too; there was a big box recessed into the table, and this was full of paper money and every few minutes the pile was augmented.

A dull evening! Mr Machfield would be glad when the time came to put on his record of the National Anthem. He always closed down on this patriotic note; it left the most unlucky of players with the comforting sense that at least they had their country left to them.

He was looking at the long folding door of the room as it opened slowly. It was second nature in him to watch that opening door, and until this moment he had never been shocked or startled by what it revealed. Now, however, he stood dumbfounded, for there was Mr Reeder, without his hat, and even without his umbrella.

Nobody noticed him except the proprietor, and he was frozen to the spot. With an apologetic smile Mr Reeder came tiptoeing across to him.

'Do you very much mind?' he asked in an urgent whisper. 'I find time hanging rather heavily on my hands.'

Machfield licked his dry lips.

'Come here, will you?'

He went back to his study, Reeder behind him.

'Now, Mr Reeder, what's the idea of your coming here? How did you get in? I gave strict instructions to the man on the door—'

'I told him a lie,' said Mr Reeder in a hushed tone, as though the enormity of his offence had temporarily overcome him. 'I said that you had particularly asked me to come to night. That was very wrong, and I am sorry. The truth is, Mr Machfield, even the most illustrious of men have their little weaknesses; even the cleverest and most law-abiding their criminal instincts, and although I am neither illustrious nor clever, I have the frailties of my—er—humanity. Not, I would add, that it is criminal to play cards for money—far from it. I, as you probably know, or you may have heard, have a curiously distorted mind. I find my secret pleasures in such places as these.'

Mr Machfield was relieved, immensely relieved. He knew detectives who gambled, but somehow he had never associated Mr J.G. Reeder with this peculiar weakness.

'Why, certainly, we're glad to see you, Mr Reeder,' he said heartily.

He was so glad indeed that he would have been happy to have given this odd-looking man the money wherewith to play.

'You'll have a drink on the house—not,' he added quickly, 'that I am in any position to offer you a drink. I am a guest the same as yourself, but I know the proprietor would be annoyed if you came and went without having one.'

'I never drink. A little barley water perhaps?'

There was, unfortunately, no barley water in the establishment, but this, as Machfield explained, would be remedied in the future—even now if he wished. Mr Reeder, however, would not hear of putting 'the house' to trouble. He was anxious to join the company, and again by some extraordinary quality of good luck, he managed to insinuate himself so that he sat opposite the croupier. Somebody rose from their chair as he approached, and Mr Reeder took the vacant seat. He might have taken a chair on the opposite side of the table, for at the sight of him a pallid Kingfether had whipped out his handkerchief and covered the lower part of his face as though he were suffering from a bad cold.

Stealthily he rose from his seat and melted into the fringe of people standing behind the players.

'Don't let me drive you away, Mr Kingfether,' said Reeder—and everybody heard him.

The manager dropped back till he stood against the wall, a limp helpless figure, and there he remained through the scene that followed.

Mr Reeder had produced a bundle of banknotes which he counted with great care. It was not a big bundle. Mr Machfield, watching, guessed he was in the ten-pound line of business, and certainly there was no more than that on the table.

One by one those little notes of Reeder's disappeared, until there was nothing left, and then a surprising thing happened. Mr. Reeder put his hand in his pocket, groped painfully and produced something which he covered with his hand. The croupier had raised his cards ready to deal—the game was trente-et-quarante—when the interruption came.

'Excuse me.' J.G. Reeder's voice was gentle but everybody it the table heard it. 'You can't play with that pack: there are two cards missing.'

The croupier raised his head. The green-shade strapped to his glossy head threw a shadow which hid the top half of his face.

He stared blandly at the interrupter—the dispassionate and detached stare which only a professional croupier can give.

'Pardon?' he said, puzzled. 'I do not understand, m'sieur. The pack is complete. It is never questioned—'

'There are two cards without which I understand you cannot play your game,' said Mr Reeder, and suddenly lifted his hand.

On the table before him were two playing cards, the ace of diamonds and the ace of hearts. The croupier looked down at them, and then, with an oath, pushed back his chair and dropped his hand to his hip.

'Don't move—I beg of you.'

There was an automatic in Mr Reeder's hand, and its muzzle was directed towards the croupier's white waistcoat. 'Ladies and gentlemen, there is nothing to be alarmed about. Stand back from the table against the wall, and do not come between me and Monsieur Lamontaine!'

He himself stepped backward.

'Over there!' he signalled to Machfield.

'Look here, Reeder—'

'Over there!' snarled J.G. Reeder. 'Stand up by your friend. Ladies and gentlemen,'—he addressed the company again without taking his eyes from the croupier—' this establishment is not licensed. Your names and addresses will be taken, but I will use my best endeavours to avoid police court proceedings, because we are after something much more important than that.'

And then the guests saw strange men standing in the doorway. They came from all directions—from Machfield's study, from the hall below, from the roof above. They handcuffed Lamontaine and took away the two guns he carried, one in each hip pocket—Machfield was unarmed.

'What will the charge be?'

'Mr Gaylor will tell you that at the police station. But I think the question is unnecessary. Honestly, don't you, Mr Machfield?'

Machfield said nothing.

XI. — DEDUCTION

MR REEDER kept what he called a casebook, in which he inscribed passionless accounts of all the cases in which he was engaged. Some of these cases had no value except to the technician, and would not interest anyone except perhaps the psychopathologist. Under the heading 'Two Aces' appeared this account, written in his own handwriting.

Ten years ago,—wrote Mr Reeder—there arrived at the Hotel Majestic in Nice a man who described himself in the hotel register as Rufus Machfield. He had a number of other names, but it is only necessary that Machfield should be used to identify this particular character. The man had a reputation as a cardsharp and, in the pursuit of his nefarious calling, had 'worked' the ships plying between England and New York. He had also been convicted on two occasions as a professional gambler in Germany.

He was of Danish origin, but at the time was a naturalized Englishman, with a permanent address in Colvin Gardens, Bayswater. At the Majestic Hotel he had met with Charles or Walter Lynn, an adventurer who had also 'operated' the ships on the North Atlantic. On one of these trips Lynn had become acquainted with Mr George McKay, a prosperous woollen merchant of Bradford. There is no evidence that they ever played cards together, and Mr McKay does not recall that they did. But the friendship was of value to Lynn because Mr McKay was in the habit of coming to Nice every year, and was in residence at the time Lynn and Machfield met. McKay was known as a resolute and successful gambler, and before now had figured in sensational play.

The two men, Lynn and Machfield, conferred together and decided on a scheme to rob McKay at the tables. Gambling in Nice is not confined to the recognized establishments. There was at the time a number of Cercles Privés where play was even higher than at the public rooms, and the most reputable of these was 'Le Signe' which, if it was not recognized, was winked at by the French authorities.

In order to swindle McKay, a patron of this club, it was necessary to secure the co-operation and help of an official. Lynn's choice fell on a young croupier named Lamontaine, and he in turn was to suborn two other croupiers, both of whom it was intended should receive a very generous share of the money.

Lamontaine proved to be a singularly pliable tool. He had married a young wife and had got into debt, and he was fearful that this should come to the ears of the club authorities. An interview was arranged in Lyons; the scheme was put before the croupier by Lynn, and he agreed to come in, taking a half share for himself and his two fellow croupiers, the other half being equally divided between Lynn and Machfield. Lynn apparently demurred at the division, but Machfield was satisfied with his quarter share; the more so as he knew McKay had been winning very heavily, and providing he had the right kind of betting, there would be a big killing.

The game to be played was baccarat, for McKay could never resist the temptation of taking a bank, especially a big bank. It was very necessary that arrangements should be hurried on before the merchant left the South of France, and a fortnight after the preliminaries, Lamontaine reported that everything was in trim, that he had secured the co-operation of his comrades, and it was decided that the coup should be brought off on the Friday night.

It was arranged that Lynn should be the player, and that after play was finished the conspirators should meet again at Lyons, when the loot was to be divided. The cards were to be stacked so that the bank won every third coup. It was arranged that the signal for the conspirators to begin their betting was to be the dealing of two aces, the ace of diamonds and the ace of hearts. Somebody would draw a six to these, and the banker would have a 'natural'—which means, I understand, that he would win.

Thereafter the betting was to be done by Lynn, and the first was a banco call—which meant, as the card lay, that the bank would be swept into their pockets. They knew McKay would bid for the bank, but they would bid higher, and Lynn then took the bank with a capital of a million francs. Fourteen times the bank won, and had now reached enormous proportions, so much so that every other table in the room was deserted, and the table where this high play was going on was surrounded by curious watchers.

There were fourteen winning coups for the bank, and the amount gathered up at the finish by Lynn was something in the neighbourhood of £400,000. Lamontaine states that it was more, but Machfield is satisfied that it was in that region. The money was taken to the hotel, and the following night Lynn left for Lyons. He was to be joined the next day by Machfield, and on the Sunday they were to meet the croupier in Paris and pay him his share.

The night that Lynn left, however, one of the officials of the rooms made a statement to his chief. He had lost his nerve and he betrayed his comrades. Lamontaine, with the other croupier, was arrested on a charge of conspiracy, and Machfield only got away from the South of France by the skin of his teeth. He journeyed on to Lyons and arrived there in the early hours of the following afternoon. He hoped that no news of the arrests would have got into the papers and scared his partner; and certainly he did not wire warning Lynn. When he got to the hotel he asked for his friend, but was told that he had not arrived, nor had he made a reservation of the rooms which had been agreed upon.

From that moment he disappeared from human ken, and neither Machfield nor any of his friends were able to trace him. It was no accident: it was a deliberate double-cross.

Machfield played the game as far as he was able, and when he was released from prison and came to Paris, a broken man, for his young wife had died while he was in gaol, he helped the croupier as well as he could, and together they came to England to establish gaming-houses, but primarily to find Lynn and force him to disgorge.

There was another person on the track of Lynn. McKay, who had been robbed, as he knew after the French court proceedings, employed me to trace him, but for certain reasons I was unable to justify his confidence.

I do not know in what year or month Lamontaine and Machfield located their man. It is certain that 'Mr Wentford,' as he called himself, lived in increasing fear of their vengeance. When they did locate him he proved to be an impossible man to reach. I have no doubt that the house was carefully reconnoitred, his habits studied, and that attempts were made to get at him. But those attempts failed. It is highly probable, though no proof of this exists, that he was well informed as to his enemy's movements, for so far as can be gathered from the statement of his niece and checked by the admissions of Machfield, Lynn never left his house except on the days when Machfield and Lamontaine were in Paris—they frequently went to that city over the week-end. It was Lamontaine who formed the diabolical plan which was eventually to lead to Wentford's death. He knew that the only man admitted to the house was the policeman who patrolled that part of the country, so he studied police methods, even got information as to the times on which the beat was patrolled, and on the night of the murder, soon after it was dark, he travelled down to Beaconsfield by car through the storm, accompanied by Machfield.

Lamontaine at some time or other had been on the French stage—he spoke perfect English—and I have no doubt was in a position to make himself up sufficiently well to deceive Wentford into opening the door. At seven o'clock Constable Verity left the station and proceeded on his patrol. At seven-thirty he was ruthlessly murdered by a man who stepped out of hiding and shot him point-blank through the heart.

The body was taken into a field and laid out, the two murderers hoping that the snow would cover it. Lamontaine was already wearing the uniform of a police constable and, mounting the motorbike, he rode on to Wentford's house. The old man saw him through the window, and, suspecting nothing, got down and opened the door.

He may not have realized that anything was wrong until he was back in his parlour, for it was there that he was struck down. The two men intended leaving him in the cottage, but a complication arose while they were searching the place, or endeavouring to open the safe behind the bookcase. The telephone rang, one of them answered in a disguised voice and heard Margot Lynn say that she was coming on but was delayed.

The thing to do now was to remove the body. Lifting it out, they laid it over the motorcycle and, guiding the machine down to the road, pushed it towards Beaconsfield. Here a second complication arose: the lights of Mr Enward's car were seen coming toward them. The body was dropped by the side of the road, and the constable took his place on the bike. The seat was smothered with the blood of the murdered man, and Mr Enward's clerk must have quite innocently rubbed his sleeve against it, for it was afterwards discovered that his coat was stained. That gave me my first clue, and I was able, owing to my peculiar mind, to reconstruct the crime as it had been committed.

The two men joined one another again in the vicinity of the cottage. They were not able to make any further attempt that night. One of them, however, heard that the girl knew where the money was cached. I am afraid I was responsible for this, and it was intended that she should be taken away, with the key of the safe deposit...

Machfield had already become acquainted with the straightened circumstances of young McKay, the son of his victim, and probably to hit at his father, who he must have known was still hunting for him, used an opportunity which was offered by chance, to ruin him, as he believed.

Two hundred pounds, representing a portion of the money obtained from the bank by a fraudulent manager (3 years Prison; Central Criminal Court) through the instrumentality of his woman friend (5 years: CCC) was sent anonymously to the younger McKay by Machfield, and was traced to the young man.

After this came a note, also in Mr Reeder's hand:

'Rufus John Machfield and Antonio Lamontaine (sentence: death, CCC) executed at Wandsworth Prison, April 17th. Executioner Ellis.'

Mr Reeder was a stickler for facts.

Kennedy the Con Man

First published in The Thriller, Feb 23, 1929

THE man who stood with such an air of ease in the dock of the North-West London Police Court bore himself with a certain insolent dignity. There was a smile which was half contemptuous, half amused, on his bearded face.

If, from time to time, his long white fingers thrust through the mass of golden-brown hair that was brushed back from his high and narrow forehead, the gesture revealed neither nervousness nor embarrassment. Rather was this a trick of habit.

Though he wore no collar or tie, and his clothes and shoes were daubed with last night's mud, the clothes were new and well cut; the diamond ring which he wore, and which now sparkled offensively in the early morning light, hinted most certainly at an affluence which might be temporary or permanent.

He had in his possession when arrested—quote the exact itemization of the constable who had given evidence on the matter—the sum of eighty-seven pounds ten shillings in notes, fifteen shillings in silver coinage, a gold and platinum cigarette case, a small but expensive bottle of perfume—unopened—and a few keys.

His name was Vladimir Litnoff; he was a Russian subject and his profession was that of an actor. He had appeared in Russian plays, and spoke English with the faintest trace of an accent. Apparently, when he was in wine, as he had been on the previous evening, he spoke little but Russian, so that the two policemen who supported the charge of being drunk, and guilty of insulting and disorderly behaviour, could adduce no other than the language of offensive gesture to support their accusation.

The magistrate took off his glasses and leaned back in his chair wearily.

'While you are living in this country you must behave yourself,' he said conventionally. 'This is the second time you have been charged with disorderly conduct, and you will pay two pounds.'

Mr Litnoff smiled, bowed gracefully and stepped lightly from the dock.

Chief Inspector Gaylor, who was waiting in the corridor to give evidence on a much more serious charge, saw him pass and returned his smile good-humouredly. The policeman who had 'picked up' the Russian followed from the court.

'Who is that man?' asked Gaylor.

'A Russian, sir. He was properly soused—drunk, in the Brompton Road. He was quiet enough but wouldn't go away. Him and his brooches!'

'His whatses?' asked the Inspector.

'That's what he said when I took him—about the only English thing he did say: "You shall have my beautiful brooch—worth ten thousand!" I don't know what he was talking about. Another thing he said was that he'd got property in Monro—he shouted this out to the crowd as me and PC Leigh was taking him away.'

'Monro—that's in Scotland somewhere.'

Just then Gaylor was called into court.

Later in the evening, as he glanced through his evening newspaper, he read an account of the police court proceedings. It was headed:

DRUNKEN MAN'S BRIBE OFFER TO POLICE.
TEN THOUSAND POUND BROOCH THAT WAS DECLINED.

PC Smith stated that the prisoner had offered him a ten thousand pound brooch to let him go.
The Magistrate: Did he have this brooch in his possession?
Witness: No, your Worship. In his imagination.
(Laughter).

'Now Reeder would see something very peculiar about that,' said Gaylor to his young wife, and she smiled.
She liked Mr J.G. Reeder and, quite mistakenly, was sorry for him. He seemed so pathetically inefficient and helpless compared with the strong, capable men of Scotland Yard. Many people were sorry for Mr Reeder—but there were quite a number who weren't.
Jake Alsby, for example, was sorry for nobody but himself. He used to sit in his cell during the long winter evenings on Dartmoor and think of Mr Reeder in any but a sympathetic mood. It was a nice, large, comfortable cell with a vaulted roof. It had a bed, with gaily coloured blankets, and was warm on the coldest day. He had the portrait of his wife and family on a shelf. The family ranged from a hideous little boy of ten to an open-mouthed baby of six months. Jake had never seen the baby in the flesh. He did not mind whether he saw his lady wife or family again, but the picture served as a stimulant to his flagging animosities. It reminded Jake that the barefaced perjury of Mr J.G. Reeder had torn him from his family and cast him into a cold dungeon. A poetical fancy, but none the less pleasing to a man who had never met the truth face to face without bedecking the reality with ribbons of fiction.
It was true that Jake forged Bank of England notes, had been caught with the goods and his factory traced; it was true that he had been previously convicted for the same offence, but it was not true—as Mr Reeder had sworn—that he had been seen near Marble Arch on the Monday before his arrest. It was Tuesday. Therefore Mr Reeder had committed perjury.
To Jake came a letter from one who had been recently discharged from the hospitality of HM Prison at Princetown. It contained a few items of news, one of which was:

saw your old pal reeder yesterday he was in that machfield case him that done in the old boy at born end reeder don't look a day older he asked me how you was and I said fine and he said what a pity he only got seven he oughter got ten and I said...

What his literary friend said did not interest the enraged man. There and then he began to think up new torments for the man who had perjured an innocent man—it was Tuesday, not Monday—into what has been picturesquely described as a 'living hell.'
Three months after the arrival of this letter Jake Alsby was released, a portion of his sentence having been remitted for good conduct: that is to say, he had never once been detected in a breach of prison regulations. The day he was released, Jake went to London to find his family in the care of the local authority, his wife having fled to Canada with a better man. Almost any man was better than Jake.
'This is Reeder's little joke!' he said.
He fortified himself with hot spirits and went forth to find his man.
He did not follow a direct path to Mr Reeder's office, because he had calls to make, certain acquaintances to renew. In one of these, a most reputable hostelry, he came upon a bearded man who spoke alternately in English and in a strange elusive language. He wore no collar or tie—when Vladimir reached his fourth whisky he invariably discarded these—and he spoke loudly of a diamond clasp of fabulous value. Jake lingered, fascinated. He drank with the man, whose

language might be Russian but whose money was undoubtedly English, as was his language occasionally.

'You ask me, my frien', what profession am I? An actor, yes! But it pays nothing. This, that, the other impresario rob—all rob. But my best work? I am ill! That is good work! Delirium—what-you-call-it? Swoons? Yes, swoons—voice 'usky, eh?'

'I know a graft like that,' said Jake, nodding wisely. 'You chews soap.'

'Ah—nasty—no... ty durak!'[* You fool]

Jake did not know that he was being called a fool, would not have been very upset if he had known. He was sure of one thing, that he was hooked up with a generous spender of money—a prince of fellows, seen in the golden haze of alcohol. He had not yet reached the stage where he wanted to kick anybody. He was in that condition when he felt an inward urge to tell his most precious secrets.

'Ever 'eard feller call' Reeder?' he asked profoundly. 'Reg'lar old 'ound—goin' to get him!'

'Ach!' said his new-found friend.

'Gonna get 'im!' said Jake gravely.

The bearded man tilted up his glass until no dreg remained in the bottom. He seized Jake's arm in a fierce friendliness and led him from the bar. The cold air made Jake sag at the knees.

'Le's go 'n bump 'um,' he said thickly.

'My frien'—why kill, eh?' They were walking unsteadily along arm in arm. Once Jake was pushed into the gutter by an unanticipated lurch. 'Live—drink! See my beautiful brooch my farm... vineyards... mountains... I'll tell you, my frien'—somebody must know.'

This street through which they were passing was very dark and made up of small shops. Jake was conscious that he had passed a dairy when he became aware that a man was standing squarely in their path.

'Hub!... You want me... gotta brooch?'

It was Vladimir who spoke; he also was very drunk. The stranger did not speak.

The crash of the explosion made Jake Alsby reel. He had never heard a gun fired at close quarters. He saw the Russian swaying on his feet, his head bent as though he were listening... he was fumbling at his waistcoat with both hands. 'Here... what's the game?' Jake was sober now.

The man came nearer, brushed past him, thrusting his shoulder forward as he passed. Jake staggered under the impact. When he looked round, the shooter had melted into the thick darkness—there was a narrow opening of a mews hereabouts.

'Hurt, mate?'

The Russian had gone down to his knees, still gripping at his waistcoat. Then he pitched forward and hit the pavement horribly.

Jake himself went white... he looked round, and, turning, fled. He wanted to be out of this—murder! That's what it was, murder.

He raced round the corner of the street and into the arms of a policeman. Whistles were blowing. Even as he fought to escape, he knew the impossibility of such a hope: policemen were running from everywhere.

'All right—I done nothin'... there's a guy shot round the corner... some feller did it.'

Two officers took him to the station, and as a precautionary measure he was searched.

In the right hand pocket of his overcoat was found an automatic that had been recently fired.

Mr J.G. Reeder rang his bell and sighed. He sighed because it was the fourth time he had rung the bell without anything happening.

There were moments when he saw himself walking into the next room and addressing Miss

Gillette in firm but fatherly tones. He would point out to her the impossible situation which was created when a secretary ignored the summons of her employer; he would insist that she did not bring into the office, or, if she brought, should not in business hours read the tender or exciting fiction which she favoured; he would say, in the same firm and fatherly way, that perhaps it would be better for everybody concerned if she found a new occupation, or a similar occupation in the service of somebody who had less exacting views on the question of duty. But always, when he rose from his chair after ringing four times, determined to settle the matter there and then, he sat down again and rang a fifth time.

'Dear, dear!' said Mr Reeder; 'This is very trying.'

At that moment Miss Gillette came into the room. She was pretty and slight and small. She had a tip-tilted nose and a faultless complexion, and her dully golden hair was a little untidy.

'I'm sorry,' she said. 'Did you ring?'

Between her fingers she held a long, jade-green cigarette holder. Mr Reeder had once asked her not to come into his office smoking: she invariably carried her cigarette in her hand nowadays, and he accepted the compromise.

'I think I did,' he said gently.

'I thought you did.'

Mr Reeder winced as she put her cigarette holder on the mantelpiece and, pulling a chair forward, sat down at his desk. She carried a book under her arm, and this she opened and laid on the table.

'Shoot,' she said, and Mr Reeder winced again.

The trouble about Miss Gillette was her competence. If she had made mistakes, put letters in the wrong envelopes or forgotten appointments, Mr Reeder would have gone away to some foreign land, such as Eastbourne or Brighton, and would have written to her a sad letter of farewell, enclosing a month's salary in lieu of notice. But she was devastatingly competent: she had built up a structure of indispensability; she had, in the shortest space of time, developed herself into a habit and a fixture.

'You mean that I am to proceed?' he asked gravely.

Another woman would have wilted under the reproof; there was something very wiltless about Miss Gillette. She just closed her eyes wearily.

'Let's go,' she said, and it was Mr Reeder who was reproved. 'This is a report on the Wimburg Case,' he said, and began his hesitant dictation.

As he grew into his subject, he spoke with greater and greater rapidity. Never once did Miss Gillette interrupt with a question, to gain time for her lagging pencil. There was a ceaseless snap as the pages of her notebook turned.

'That is all,' he said breathlessly. 'I trust that I did not go too fast for you?'

'I hardly noticed that you were moving,' she said, wetted her fingers and flicked back the pages. 'You used the word "unsubstantial" three times: once you meant "inadequate" and once "unreal." I would suggest that we alter those.'

Mr Reeder moved uncomfortably in his chair. 'Are you sure?' he asked feebly.

She was always sure, because she was always right.

It was not true to say that Mr Reeder had ever engaged a secretary. It was Miss Gillette who engaged him. By one of those odd coincidences which are unacceptable to the lovers of fiction but which occur in everyday life, she arrived at Mr Reeder's office on the day and at the hour he was expecting a temporary typist from an agency. For some reason the agency lady did not arrive or, if she did, was interviewed by Miss Gillette who, fulfilling the practice of the young queen bee, destroyed her rival—in the nicest possible sense. And when Mr Reeder, having concluded the work for which he had engaged her, would have dismissed her with a ten-shilling note, shyly tendered and brazenly accepted, he learned that she was a fixture. He lay awake for an hour on the following Friday night, debating with himself whether he should deduct the ten shillings from her salary.

'Are there any appointments?' he asked.

There were none. Mr Reeder knew there were none before he asked. It was at this point that daily embarrassment was invariably overcome.

'Nothing in the papers, I suppose?'

'Nothing except the Pimlico murder case. The funny thing is that the man who was killed—'

'Nothing funny about—um—that, my dear lady,' murmured Mr Reeder. 'Funny? Dear, dear!'

'When I said "funny," I didn't mean "amusing" but "odd,"' she said. 'And if you are getting back for "unsubstantial," you will be pleased to know that you have got. He was Vladimir Litnoff—you remember, the man who was drunk and said that he had a brooch.'

Mr Reeder nodded calmly. Apparently Litnoff's death was not startling news.

'It is my—um—mind, my dear young friend. I see evil things where other people see innocent things. And yet, in the question of human relationships, I take the kindliest and most charitable views. H'm! The young man who was with you at the Regal Cinema, for example—'

'Was the young man I'm going to marry when we earn enough to support one another,' she said promptly. 'But how the devil did you see us?'

'S'sh!' said Mr Reeder, shocked. 'Strong—um—language is—um—most...'

She was looking at him frowningly.

'Sit down,' she said, and Mr Reeder, who knew little of the rights of secretaries, but was quite sure that ordering their employers to sit down in their own offices was outside the table of privileges, sat down.

'I like you, John or Jonas or whatever the "J" stands for,' she said, with outrageous coolness. 'I didn't realize that you were a detective when I came to you. I've worked for successions of tired businessmen, who bucked up sufficiently towards evening to ask me out to supper, but never a detective. And you're different from all the men I've ever met. You've never tried to hold my hand—'

'I should hope not!' said Mr Reeder, going very red. 'I'm old enough to be your father!'

'There isn't such an age,' she said. And then, very seriously: 'Would you speak to Tommy Anton if I brought him here?'

'Tommy—you mean your—um—'

'My "um"—that describes him,' she nodded. 'He's a wonderful fellow—terribly awkward and shy, and he'll probably make a bad impression, as you do, but he's a really nice man.'

Now Mr Reeder had been many things, but he had never acted in loco parentis, and the prospect was, a trifle terrifying.

'You wish me to ask him—er—what his intentions are?'

She smiled at this, and she had a dazzling and beautiful smile.

'My dear, I know what his intentions are, all right. You don't meet a man day after day for over a year without finding out something about his private ideas. No—it's something else.'

Mr Reeder waited.

'If you were an ordinary employer,' she went on, 'you'd take me by the scruff of the neck and fire me.' Mr Reeder disclaimed such a ferocious quality with a feeble shake of his head. 'But you're not.'

She got up and walked to the window and looked out. What was she going to say? A most ghastly thought occurred to Mr Reeder, one that made a cold shiver down his spine. But it was not that, for she turned suddenly.

'Tommy has been robbed of twenty-three thousand pounds,' she said.

He stared at her owlishly.

'Robbed?'

She nodded.

'When?'

'More than a year ago—before I met him. That isn't why he's selling cars on commission. He tries to sell them, but he isn't very successful. His partner robbed him. Tommy and this man Seafield were at Oxford together, and when they came down they started a car business. Tommy went to Germany to negotiate for an agency. When he came back Seafield had gone. He didn't even leave a note—he just drew the money from the bank and went away.'

She saw a new light in Mr Reeder's eyes and could not but marvel that what to him was so small a matter should be of such immediate interest.

'And no message with his wife?... Unmarried, eh? H'm! He lived... ?'

'At an hotel—he was a bachelor. No, he didn't tell anybody there—just said he was going away for a day or two.'

'Left his clothes behind and didn't even pay his bill,' murmured Mr Reeder.

Miss Gillette was surprised.

'You know all about it, then?'

'My strange mind,' he said simply.

There was a tap at the outer door.

'You'd better see who that is,' said Mr Reeder.

She went to the door and opened it. Standing on the mat outside was a clergyman, wearing a long black overcoat. He looked at her dubiously.

'Is this Mr Reeder's office—the detective?' he asked.

She nodded, regarding the unexpected visitor with interest. He was a man of fifty, with greying hair. A mild, rather pallid man, who seemed to be ill at ease, for the fingers that gripped his umbrella, which he held about its middle as though he were all ready to signal a cab, clasped and unclasped in his agitation.

He looked at Mr Reeder helplessly. Mr Reeder, for his part, twiddled his thumbs and gazed at the visitor solemnly. It almost seemed that he was smitten dumb by the uniform of his visitor's rectitude.

'Won't you sit down, please?' There was something, of the churchwarden in Mr Reeder's benevolent gesture.

'The matter I wish to speak about—well, I hardly know how to begin,' said .the clergyman.

Here Mr Reeder could not help him. It was on his tongue to offer the conventional suggestion that the best way to begin any story was to tell the unvarnished truth. Somehow this hardly seemed a delicate thing to say to a man of the cloth, so he said nothing.

'It concerns a man named Ralph—the merest acquaintance of mine... hardly that. I had corresponded with him on certain matters pertaining to the higher criticism. But I can hardly remember what points he raised or how I dealt with them. I never keep correspondence, not because I am unbusinesslike, but because letters have a trick of accumulating, and a filing system is a tyranny to which I will never submit.'

Mr Reeder's heart could have warmed to this frank man. He loathed old letters and filing was an abominable occupation.

'This morning I had a call from Mr Ralph's daughter. She lives with her father at Bishop's Stortford in Essex. Apparently she came upon my name written on an envelope which she found in a wastepaper basket in her father's office—he had a small office in Lower Regent Street, where he attended to whatever business he had.'

'And your name is...?'

'Ingham. Dr Ingham.'

'What was his business?' asked Mr Reeder.

'Actually he had none. He was a retired provision merchant who had made a fortune in the City. He may have had, and probably has, one or two minor interests to occupy his spare time. He came up to London last Thursday—curiously enough, I had a telephone call from him at my hotel when I was out. Since that day he has not been seen.'

'Dear me!' said Mr Reeder. 'What a coincidence!'

Dr Ingham looked a painful inquiry.

'That you should have thought of me,' said Mr Reeder. 'It is very odd that people who lose people always come to me. And the young lady—she told you all this?'

Dr Ingham nodded.

'Yes. She is naturally worried. It appears that she had a friend, a young man, who did exactly the same thing. Just walked out of his hotel and disappeared. There may be explanations, but it is very difficult to tell a young lady—'

'Very,' Mr Reeder coughed discreetly, and said "very" again.

'She suggested that you should come to me?'

The clergyman nodded. He appeared to be embarrassed by the nature of his mission.

'To be exact, she wished to come herself—I thought it was a friendly thing to interview you on her behalf. I am not a poor man, Mr Reeder; I am, in fact, rather a rich man, and I feel that I should render whatever assistance is possible to this poor young lady. My dear wife would, I am sure, heartily endorse my action—I have been married many years, and I have never found myself in disagreement with the partner of my joys and sorrows. You, as a married man—'

'Single,' said Mr Reeder, not without a certain amount of satisfaction. 'Alas! Yes, I am—um—single.'

He looked at his new client glumly.

'The young lady is staying—'

'In London, yes,' nodded the other. 'At Haymarket Central Hotel. You'll take this case?'

Mr Reeder pulled at his nose and fingered his close-clipped side-whiskers. He put his glasses on and took them off again.

'Which case?' he asked.

Dr Ingham was pained.

'The case I have outlined.' He groped beneath his clerical coat and produced a card. 'I've written Mr Lance Ralph's office address on the back of my card—'

J.G. took the card and read its written inscription; turned it over and read the printed inscription. This gentleman was a doctor of divinity, and lived at Grayne Hall, near St Margaret's Bay, in the County of Kent.

'There isn't a case,' said Mr Reeder with the tenderness of one who is breaking bad news. 'People are entitled to—um—disappear. Quite a number of people, my dear Dr Ingham, refuse to exercise that right, I am sorry to say. They disappear to Brighton, to Paris, but reappear at later intervals. It is a common phenomenon.'

The cleric looked at him anxiously, and passed his umbrella from one hand to the other. 'Perhaps I haven't told you everything that should have been told,' he said. 'Miss Ralph had a fiancé—a young man in a prosperous business, as she tells me, who also vanished, leaving his partner—'

'You are referring to Mr Seafield?' But to his surprise, and perhaps to his annoyance, the clergyman showed no sign of surprise.

'Joan had a great friend in your office. Am I right in surmising it is the young lady who opened the door to me? This is how your name came up. We were discussing whether she should go to the police, when she mentioned your name. I thought you were the least unpleasant alternative, if you don't mind that description.'

Mr Reeder bowed graciously. He did not mind. There followed an uncomfortable lacuna of silence, which neither of the men seemed inclined to fill. Mr Reeder ushered his visitor to the door and went back to his desk, and for five minutes scribbled aimlessly on his blotting pad. He had a weakness for making grotesque drawings, and was putting an extra long nose on the elongated head of one of his fanciful sketches when Miss Gillette came in unannounced.

'Well, what do you think of that?' she asked.

Mr Reeder stared at her.

'What do I think of what, Miss Gillette?' he demanded.

'Poor Joan, and she's such a darling. We've kept our friendship all through the Seafield business—'

'But how did you know about it?'

Mr Reeder was very seldom bewildered, but he was frankly bewildered now.

'I was listening at the door,' said Miss Gillette shamelessly. 'Well, not exactly listening, but I left my door open and he talks very loudly; parsons get that way, don't they?'

J.G. Reeder's face wore an expression that was only comparable to that of a wounded fawn.

'It is very—um—wrong to listen,' he began, but she dismissed all questions of propriety with an airy wave of her hand.

'It doesn't matter whether it's right or wrong. Where is Joan staying?'

This was a moment when Mr J.G. Reeder should have risen with dignity, opened the door, pressed a fortnight's wages into her hand, and dismissed her to the outer darkness, but he allowed the opportunity to pass.

'Can I bring Tommy to see you?'

She leant on the table, resting her palms on the edge. Her enthusiasm was almost infectious.

'Tommy doesn't look clever, but he really is, and he's always had a theory about Seafield's bolting. Tommy says that Frank Seafield would never have bought a letter of credit—'

'Did he have a letter of credit? I thought you told me that he drew the money out of the bank?'

Miss Gillette nodded.

'It was a letter of credit,' she said emphatically, 'for £6300. That's how we knew he'd gone abroad. The letter was cashed in Berlin and Vienna.'

For a long time Mr J.G. Reeder looked out of the window. 'I should like to talk with Tommy,' he said gravely, and when he looked round Miss Gillette had gone.

For a quarter of an hour he sat with his hands folded on his lap, his pale eyes fixed vacantly on the chimney-pot of a house on the opposite side of the street, and then he heard a knock on the outer door. Rising slowly, he went out and opened it. The last person he expected to see was Inspector Gaylor.

'The Litnoff murder—are you interested?'

Mr Reeder was interested in all murders, but not especially in the Litnoff case.

'Do you know that Jake Alsby was on his way to see you?'

Jake Alsby—Mr Reeder frowned; he knew the name and, going over the file of his mind, could place him.

'So far as my own opinion goes, Jake is a dead man,' said Gaylor. 'He'd been drinking with the Russian, who had quite a lot of money in his possession. A few minutes after they left the bar Litnoff was shot and Jake, bolting for his life, was found in possession of a loaded gun. Men have been hanged on less evidence than that.'

'I—um—doubt it. Not the fact that men have been—er—hanged on insufficient evidence, but that our poor friend was the guilty person. Jake is a "regular," and regulars do not carry guns—not in this country.'

Gaylor smiled significantly.

'He was searching for you,' he said. 'He admits as much, and that makes his present attitude a little odd. For now he wants you to get him out of his trouble!'

'Dear me!' said Mr Reeder, faintly amused.

'He thinks if he could see you for a few minutes and tell you what happened, you would walk out of Brixton Prison and lay your hand upon the man who committed the murder. There's a compliment for you!'

'Seriously?' J.G. Reeder was frowning again.

Gaylor nodded.

'It's funny, isn't it? The fellow was undoubtedly on his way to give you hell and yet the first thing he does when he gets into trouble is to squeak to you for help! Anyway, the Public Prosecutor says he'd like you to see him. Brixton has been notified. They know you there, and if you feel like listening to a few more or less fantastic lies, you ought to have an interesting evening.'

He had in his pocket-book two press cuttings which fairly covered the Litnoff shooting. Mr Reeder accepted them with every evidence of gratitude, although he had very complete particulars of the case in the drawer of his writing table.

Gaylor had one quality which Mr Reeder admired—he was no 'lingerer.' There were many interesting people in the world who did not know where their interest ended: men who outstayed the excuse for their presence and dawdled from subject to subject. Gaylor was blessed with a sense of drama and could make his abrupt exit upon an effective line. He made such an exit now.

'You needn't ask him to tell you about the diamond clasp,' he said. 'He'll tell you that! But don't forget that the last time Litnoff was charged that bizarre note came into the evidence.'

When he had gone, Mr Reeder fixed his glasses and read the cuttings which the detective had left. He found nothing that he did not already know. Jake Alsby was, as he had said, a "regular," an habitual criminal with a working knowledge of the common law in so far as it affected himself. No old lag carries firearms. Judges are most unsympathetic in their attitude towards armed criminals, and Jake and his fellows knew too well the penalties of illicit armament to take the dreadful risk of being found in possession of an automatic.

J.G. had a criminal mind. He knew exactly what he would have done had he been Jake Alsby and shot his companion. He would have thrown away the gun before he bolted. That Jake had not done so was proof to him that he was unaware that the gun was in his pocket.

He was musing on this matter when he heard the door of the outer office open and the sound of low voices. A moment later Miss Gillette came in, a little out of breath. She closed the door behind her.

'I've brought them both,' she said rapidly. 'I phoned to Joan—she was just going out... Can I ask them to come in?'

He felt that it was almost an act of humility that she should ask his permission, and bowed his head.

Tommy Anton was a tall young man; the sort that perhaps two women in the course of the years would regard as good-looking, but the rest would scarcely notice. Joan Ralph, on the other hand, was distinctly pretty and unusual. She was dark and clear-skinned, and had one of those supple figures that gave Mr Reeder the impression that its owner did not wear sufficient clothes for warmth or safety.

'This is Tommy, and this is Joan.' Miss Gillette introduced them unnecessarily, for Mr Reeder could hardly have mistaken one for the other.

The moment he saw them, he knew they would have nothing new to tell him if they were left to tell their own stories. He listened with great patience to the repetition of all he knew.

Tommy Anton gave a graphic description of his own amazement, consternation and emotions when he had discovered that his partner had vanished. He paid a loyal tribute to the character and qualities of the missing man—'Did Mr Seafield ever talk to you about a diamond brooch?' interrupted Mr Reeder.

Tommy stared at him.

'No—we were in the car trade. He seldom discussed his private affairs. Of course, I knew about Joan—'

'Did your father ever speak of a diamond brooch clasp?' Mr Reeder addressed the girl, and she shook her head.

'Never... he never spoke about jewellery except—it was years ago when I first met Frank—Father put some money into the Pizarro expedition and so did Frank; they were awfully enthusiastic about it.'

Mr Reeder looked up at the ceiling and went rapidly over the folders of his memory. When she was on the point of explaining, he stopped her with a gesture.

'Pizarro expedition... to recover the buried treasure of the Incas. It was organized by Antonio Pizarro, who claimed to be a descendant of the conqueror of Peru... his real name was Bendini—a New York Italian with three convictions for high-class swindles... the company was registered in London, and all the people who put money into the scheme lost it—isn't that right?'

He beamed at her triumphantly and she smiled.

'I don't know as much about it as you. Father put five hundred pounds into it and Frank put a hundred—he was at Oxford then. I know they lost their money. Frank didn't mind very much, but Father was annoyed, because he was sure there were great treasure houses in Peru that had yet to be discovered.'

'And was there a talk of diamond brooches?' asked Mr Reeder.

She hesitated.

'Jewels—I don't remember that there was anything said about brooches.'

J.G. wrote down three words, one of which, she saw, was 'Pizarro.' The second seemed to bear some resemblance to 'Murphy.' She thought the association of the two names was a little incongruous. He questioned her shortly about her own situation. She had a small private income and there was no immediate urgency so far as money was concerned.

And then she asked if she could see him alone. Mr Reeder had a happy feeling that Miss Gillette entirely disapproved of the request. She could do no less than withdraw, taking her Tommy with her. He found himself being sorry for that dumb ordinary and young man—so ordinary indeed that Mr Reeder for the first time became conscious of his mental superiority to his secretary.

He had even the courage to open the door and look out. The murmur of voices from Miss Gillette's room assured him that they were safe from the eavesdropping propensities of that curious young lady.

'Mr Reeder,' he realized from her tone that Joan Ralph was finding some difficulty in fitting her thoughts into words, 'I suppose it has occurred to you that my father may have gone off with—somebody. I am not stupid about these things and I know that men of his age do have—well, affairs. But I am perfectly sure that Father had none. Dr Ingham hinted tactfully that this might be the situation; he was awfully sweet about it, but I know that he's wrong. Father had no friends. I used to open all his letters and there was never one that he objected to my seeing.'

'The letters that came to the office too?' he asked.

She smiled at the question.

'Naturally I didn't see those—those were very few, and there's nothing furtive about Father. I did know that he was corresponding with Dr Ingham; my father was what is known as a High Churchman and wrote letters to the Church papers. That's practically the only friend he had outside our little circle at Bishop's Stortford.'

Mr Reeder looked at her thoughtfully.

'Did you think Frank Seafield had—um—a lady friend?' he asked.

She was emphatic on this point. He would have been surprised if she had not been.

He guided her to Miss Gillette's room and presently he heard the three go out. That Miss Gillette should have left the office without asking permission was not remarkable.

With great care he composed three telegrams, and, calling at the Post Office, handed them in. One was certainly addressed to Murphy.

A bus deposited him within walking distance of Brixton Prison, where men under remand are segregated.

Mr Reeder was not unknown at Brixton, though his visits were rare, and within a few minutes of his arrival he was taken to a bare waiting-room where he was joined by Jake Alsby.

The man was shaken. The rather defiant impertinent criminal Mr Reeder had known had disappeared, and in his place was a man terror-stricken by the fate which had overcome him.

'You know me, Mr Reeder.' His manner was a little wild, and the hand that emphasized almost every sentence was trembling. 'I never had a gun in my life, and I'd no more think of shooting a man than I would of cutting my own throat. I bashed a fellow or two—'

'And there are one or two that you intended bashing,' said Mr Reeder, pleasantly.

'It was drink, Mr Reeder,' pleaded Jake. 'I suppose Gaylor told you that I was coming to see you. That dirty dog would say anything to put me wrong. Besides, Mr Reeder, I didn't know this Russian—why should I want to shoot him?'

Mr Reeder shook his head.

'People sometimes shoot the merest acquaintances,' he said brightly. 'Now tell me all about it, Alsby, with fewer lies than usual. Maybe I can help you, I don't say that I can, but it may be possible.'

Alsby told his story as coherently as he could. Occasionally Mr Reeder had to bring him back from rambling side issues but, on the whole, the tale he had to tell was convincing. He forgot, however, one important detail.

'When that man was charged with being drunk some days ago,' said Mr Reeder, 'he talked to the police in his—um—intoxication, of a diamond clasp—'

'That's right, sir,' interrupted the man eagerly. 'He mentioned it to me, too. I'd forgotten all about that. He told me I could see it. I thought it was just being soused that made him speak that way and, to tell you the truth, I'd forgotten all about it.' And then a new note of anxiety came into his tone: 'Has that been lost? I swear I never saw it.'

J.G. Reeder looked at him long and fixedly. A gentle glow of satisfaction came to him. He had spoken of the clasp to Joan Ralph for no other reason than his recollection of the police court proceedings against Litnoff. That reference to the diamond brooch had intrigued him at the time he had read it. Litnoff had no history as a receiver—that fact had been brought out in court.

'Try to remember, Alsby, what other things he said.'

Alsby knitted his forehead in an agony of recollection.

'I can't remember anything, Mr Reeder. I wasn't with him long after we left the boozer—the public house. He was going home; he lived in Bloomsbury—Lammington Buildings. That was a funny thing: I'd known of Lammington Buildings through a pal of mine, who got five years for slush printing. He had a friend who lived there.'

Mr Reeder was interested mainly because the only address which the police knew in connection with Litnoff was his lodging in Pimlico.

'How did all this come out, that he was living in Lammington Buildings?' he asked.

'He wanted to take a taxi. I told him I was living in Holborn. He said "You can drop me at Lammington Buildings." After that he sort of corrected himself, but I knew he'd let his address slip out. You're going to do something for me, ain't you, Mr Reeder? You've always been fair to me.'

'That is not my recollection of your expressed opinion,' said Mr Reeder acidly.

Going back to town he pondered on the possibility that Litnoff also might have had a 'friend' in this block of flats.

It was raining heavily when his bus dropped him at the corner of Southampton Row; but it had been raining more or less all day, and since he wore his shabby raincoat he did not think it necessary to unfurl the umbrella which he carried on his arm, summer and winter, although it was never known to be opened.

He found Lammington Buildings without much trouble. It was situated in a side turning off Gower Street.

Mr Reeder opened his inquiries with the hall porter. The name of Litnoff was unknown; but the hall porter was a reader of newspapers and had seen a portrait of the murdered man. Almost before Mr Reeder could put a question, the porter blurted out his suspicion.

'I bet that's Schmidt. If it isn't, it's his twin brother. In fact, I was just writing a letter to the Daily Megaphone. I always thought that Schmidt was a queer customer. He only slept here once or twice a month. I was talking to Mrs Adderly this afternoon about him. As a matter of fact, she's in his flat now, though she's one of those kind of women who wouldn't talk. You can't get a word out of her. I says to her "Suppose the police come here and want to know?" "Let 'em come," she says. What can you do with a woman like that?'

Mr Reeder could supply no reply to this pertinent question, and then, surprisingly, the hall porter said:

'I know you, Mr Reeder, the moment I put my eyes on you. You were in the Orderley Street affair. I was the porter at the hotel, if you'll remember, who saw the man getting out of the window...'

He went, with surprising accuracy, into the particulars of a case in which the detective had figured many years before.

Mr Reeder was a good listener. He had discovered at the very early stages of his career that the art of listening was the art of detection, and he allowed the porter to continue his reminiscences before he asked: 'Is Mrs Adderly in the flat now?'

The porter pointed dramatically to a door that led to the front of the vestibule.

'Do you want to see her?'

'I should like to,' said Mr Reeder.

The porter rang and knocked. After a considerable time the door was opened a little way, and the space was filled by a suspicious looking and bare-armed lady, who wore a soiled apron and had a face which was equally in need of hot water and soap.

'This is Mr Reeder,' said the porter, with such satisfaction that it was evident he had no deep affection for the untidy charwoman. 'The well-known detective,' he added.

Mrs Adderly wilted at the word.

'Everything can be explained,' she said, a little incoherently, and as Mr Reeder followed her into the hall, she slammed the door in the face of the outraged porter, who at least expected to participate in the portion of the confidences which hitherto she had withheld from him.

'Will you come in, sir?'

She led the way into a barely furnished little room which obviously had served as a sitting-room. There was a table, a sideboard, a small square carpet on the floor, and a couple of chairs. On one wall was a map printed, as Mr Reeder discovered, in Switzerland. It showed a section of the Canton of Vaud, and there was an irregular patch outlined in red ink; from the contours, it evidently stood at some considerable height upon the lake. Its significance Mr Reeder did not grasp till much later.

'I don't know what to say or what to do next,' said Mrs Adderly. She spoke very rapidly, without full stops, commas, or any other form of punctuation. 'The money was honestly come by and I put it in the Post Office bank except the rent which I paid and I have a receipt with the stamp on it and I have done what Mr Schmidt told me to do as I can prove by his letter. I am a widow with five mouths to fill...'

She went on to explain that they were the property of her five legitimate offspring, that she 'did' for respectable families, and that she had never been in trouble, or accepted 'assistance' even in her most difficult times.

'What money is this?' interrupted Mr Reeder when he thought she had gone far enough.

The money that had come to her on Wednesday. She had found it on the table in the dining-room with a letter. Beneath her skirt she had a pocket. Mr Reeder looked discreetly away while she explored this receptacle, and presently brought out an envelope from which she took a single sheet of notepaper.

'Please pay the rent with the enclosed. I am going away to France, and shall not be back for three months. You may take double-wages while I am gone, and I do not wish you to discuss my business.'

The letter was written in a neat clerkly hand.

'You found this on the table, you say?'

'On Wednesday morning; I put the money into the Post Office savings bank,' she went on even more rapidly. 'I paid the rent and I've got a printed receipt with a stamp on it—'

'Nobody doubts that,' said Mr Reeder soothingly.

'If you're in the police—'

'I am not,' said Mr Reeder. 'I really am not a policeman at all, I am—um—an investigator.'

She knew very little about her employer. Three days a week she used to come to tidy the flat. For this purpose she was entrusted with a key. She had very strict orders that, if the door did not yield when she turned the key and was obviously bolted on the inside, she was to go away. This had happened three times in the course of the past year. Mr Schmidt, though a very healthy-looking gentleman, was an invalid. Sometimes he had very bad spells, and she had come to find the atmosphere of his bedroom sickly with the smell of drugs. He never spoke about his business, and when he spoke at all, it was with a very strong foreign accent. She had an idea he was an actor, because she had once seen a box containing wigs and moustaches and theatrical make-up, and she had seen a photograph of him in some theatrical role.

Although it was a ground floor flat, it only consisted of three rooms and a kitchenette, and one room was entirely bare.

The bedroom contained a wooden bedstead with a mattress, comparatively new, a small dressing chest, a mirror, a little table and two chairs. The bed was not made, but the blankets were neatly folded at the foot of the bare mattress and covered with a sheet. On the wall was a lithographed portrait of a man in a foreign uniform. Mr Reeder guessed it was Russian. Over the bed was hung a shelf which contained four or five Russian books, and here he made a discovery, for on the flyleaf of one was a long inscription in French:

Presented to me by the Grand Duke Alexander on the occasion of my performance in 'Revisor.'

Beneath this was a single letter 'L.'

The main interest for Mr Reeder lay in the fact that the handwriting was not the same as that in the letter.

In the small cupboard he found two medicine bottles half filled. He sniffed one and discovered the unmistakable smell of chloroform. He was hardly as much impressed by the contents as by the labels, which were those of a Bloomsbury chemist. He left Mrs Adderly and went in search of the disgruntled hall porter.

'Mr Schmidt' had had visitors, but apparently they came after 11 o'clock at night, at which hour the porters went off duty; the lift, being an automatic one, was operated by the tenants themselves. He would not have known of this, but for the fact that one of the other tenants in the building had seen people going into or coming from the flat in the middle of the night. They were invariably men.

A chemist's shop on the corner of the block was Mr Reeder's next objective. The chemist was a suspicious man, not inclined to answer readily to the detective's questions. Mr Reeder, however, carried authority in the shape of a small warrant card, for he had definite association with the Public Prosecutor's Department.

Both the chemist and his assistant had seen Mr Schmidt. He had called to have medicines made up and to purchase surgical supplies.

'Surgical supplies?' Mr Reeder was almost excited. 'Dear me, how excellently that fits my theory! Pardon me, my dear sir... I—um—was rather carried away. Now, could you describe Mr Schmidt?'

They could describe him quite graphically, and Mr Schmidt was undoubtedly the dead Litnoff. Mr Reeder went home to his house in the Brockley Road, feeling rather satisfied with his discoveries. He had no illusion about his 'luck.' In a few days the police would discover Litnoff's home in Lammington Buildings—they found it the next day through the medium of a laundry mark as a matter of fact—and at best he was only those few days ahead of the 'regulars.' There were no letters for him, and he had his tea and toast reading the evening newspapers the while; at nine o'clock he was in the act of writing up his diary when he heard the tinkle of the street door bell.

The housekeeper left the two visitors in the hall, and announced them to Mr Reeder with bated breath.

'Two young ladies,' she said primly. 'I told them you never saw Visitors, but one of them said she was going to see you if she had to wait all night.'

If Mr Reeder had harmonized with the tone of sharp disapproval, he would have ordered them immediately to be thrown into the street. 'Show them up, please,' he said.

One, at least, was Miss Gillette. He guessed the other, and guessed correctly, for Joan Ralph came into the room behind his trying secretary.

'I would have telephoned you, but I didn't think it was safe,' said Miss Gillette almost before she was in the room. 'You remember you asked Joan about a diamond clasp, or brooch, or something?'

Mr Reeder offered her a chair.

'Have you seen it?'

A foolish question, he felt, when he saw Miss Gillette's visible scorn.

'Of course we haven't seen it. Joan and I went to dine tonight at the Corner House. Then a red-haired young man came up and asked Joan if she ever wore plus-fours.'

Mr Reeder leant back in his chair.

'If she wore plus-fours?' he repeated somewhat scandalized.

Miss Gillette nodded energetically.

'He was terribly nervous,' said Miss Gillette. 'I've never known a red-haired man to be nervous before; they are usually rather, well, you know, the other way about, but he started talking a lot of stuff about his father being a jeweller and being ill, and then he mentioned a diamond brooch. He said he'd under-valued it. I thought he was drunk. Joan didn't.'

'What was his name?'

Joan Ralph shook her head.

'It was extraordinary, because I was once photographed in plus-fours. I dressed up in my uncle's for a play, I was rather amused and took a picture, and said it was the best photograph that he ever had of me.'

Mr Reeder ran his fingers through his scanty hair.

'What did he say about the brooch?'

Miss Gillette was not sure that he said anything that was intelligent. It was not until after she had threatened to call for the manager, and the red-haired young man had retired abashed—' It was only then,' said Miss Gillette, 'that we felt that we oughtn't to have been so stupid and we should have asked him his name and address.'

Mr Reeder nodded his agreement.

'He was a jeweller, his father was ill, he had under-valued a brooch, and he has seen a portrait of my young friend in plus-fours. That's very remarkable. It's a great pity; you will very likely never see him again—'

'But we have,' interrupted Miss Gillette. 'He was on the bus and he followed us right down here, in fact—he's outside the house at this minute.'

Mr Reeder stared at her.

'Did you speak to him?'

'Of course we didn't speak to him,' said Miss Gillette scornfully. 'He didn't speak to us either, and he just sat in the corner of the bus and kept looking at us behind his newspaper.'

Mr Reeder walked to the window, pulled aside the curtain gently, and peered out. Standing under a lamp post, and barely visible, was a figure of a man, and even as Mr Reeder looked, as though

aware of the scrutiny, he turned rapidly in the direction of Lewisham High Road.
In a moment Mr Reeder was out of the room, flying down stairs, but when he came to the street it was absolutely empty of pedestrians. A bus was moving towards London. He saw a slim figure of a young man leap on the footboard. By the time he reached the corner of the road, the vehicle was beyond pursuit. Mr Reeder looked round for a taxi, but there was none in sight, and with great reluctance and conscious that he was bare-headed and that a drizzling rain was falling and, in consequence, he must look a little ridiculous, he made his way back to the house.
And yet for all his failure, there was a curious sense of elation in J.G. Reeder's heart, for the mystery of certain strange disappearances was almost solved.
To Miss Gillette he was a great disappointment, for he seemed no longer interested in red-haired young men, or brooches, or even young ladies in plus-fours, and she went back to London, with her friend, her faith shaken in her employer.
With great care Mr Reeder composed an agony column advertisement which he telephoned to four newspapers:
'Red-haired young man, please communicate with plus-four girl.'
The address that followed was that of his own office.
Miss Gillette arrived an hour late, which was not very remarkable. She had not seen the advertisements, so Mr Reeder had nothing to explain. Her interest in his affairs had apparently waned completely.
At 12 o'clock she came into his room and announced that she had a lunch engagement, and might not be back until three. He was not very sorry. He rather wished she would not come back till three o'clock on some date to be named by himself, and he wished that he had the courage to tell her so.
There was no response to his advertisement, and he regretted that his telephone number had not been included in his address.
Miss Gillette had hardly left before the first of Mr Reeder's visitors came. Inspector Gaylor was curious to know what had been the result of the visit to Brixton Prison.
'I am inclined to agree with you,' he said, when Reeder had sketched the conversation he had had with the prisoner. 'At any rate, there is no evidence on which we could get a conviction. The gun was of foreign make, and we've been able to trace one important fact—that when it was sold in Belgium, Alsby was still in prison. It might, of course, have been resold to him, but that's unlikely.'
'Have you ever heard of the Pizarro Syndicate?' asked Mr Reeder unexpectedly.
Gaylor had an excellent memory, possibly the better because he had been on that particular case.
'The Treasure Hunters,' he smiled. 'It's strange you should mention Pizarro. I was trying to trace a man named Gelpin, who was one of the biggest shareholders and one of the biggest dupes. I wanted him, to get particulars of a former clerk of his, but I just couldn't find him, which is strange, since he was a fairly rich man.'
'Dead,' suggested Mr Reeder.
Gaylor shook his head. 'No, he's abroad somewhere, I think, anyway he left the Midlands two years ago.'
Mr Reeder pursed his lips and looked at the detective tragically.
'Left the Midlands two years ago,' he repeated mechanically. 'Dear me... Went abroad with a letter of credit, I am sure. How many people were in the Pizarro Syndicate?'
Gaylor was looking at him suspiciously.
'What's the idea? Has any other member of the Syndicate gone to live abroad?'

'Two, to my knowledge.' Then there was a dead silence which Mr Reeder broke. 'One was a young man called Seafield.'
Gaylor nodded.
'I remember that name, yes?'
'The other's name was Ralph,' said Mr Reeder slowly.
He took from his drawer a written précis that he had prepared that morning and passed it silently to the inspector. Gaylor read very slowly, and naturally so, since J.G.'s writing was not the most legible.
When he had finished, he reached for the telephone.
'I happen to know that Gelpin's bank was the Scottish and Midland in Birmingham. Do you mind if I call them?'
Within five minutes he was talking to the bank. Mr Reeder only heard the questions and the monosyllabic rejoinders.
Presently Gaylor hung up the receiver.
'Letter of credit,' he said shortly, 'cashed in Paris, Budapest and Madrid. Since then the bank has had three cheques for considerable amounts. They've been cashed in foreign cities, and were accompanied by letters from Mr Gelpin. The bank manager says that Gelpin is a man who loves travel, so that he's not at all alarmed about it, and he's got a pretty good balance. He said one thing which may, or may not, have some bearing: that when Gelpin left, he announced his intention of going to Montreux.'
Mr Reeder remembered instantly the little map on the wall of Litnoff's room with the red irregular triangle.
Mr Reeder rose at that moment to go to the door of the outer office to take in a cablegram from a Western Union messenger. He walked to the window, opened it and read the page of typescript. It was signed 'Murphy' and was from the head of the New York Detective Department.
'Pizarro gang has not operated for past ten years. Pizarro in Sing-Sing serving life sentence. His right-hand man Kennedy was last heard of in California twelve years ago, believed to be reformed character. Nothing here of new Pizarro enterprise.'
Gaylor read the telegram and handed it back to Reeder.
'Do you think this is a Pizarro stunt?'
'My unpleasant mind leads me to that conclusion,' said Mr Reeder.
The Rev Dr Ingham came at two o'clock, at the moment when Mr Reeder was eating one of the two large buns which he invariably purchased on his way to the office, and which as invariably served him for lunch.
He could almost sense the excited condition in which the cleric came by the rapidity and nervousness of his knock.
'My dear fellow the most amazing thing has happened... Mr Ralph has been found!'
J.G. Reeder should have been overjoyed by the intelligence; instead he looked a little grieved.
'This is very pleasant news,' he said, 'very pleasant indeed.'
The clergyman fished inside his clerical coat and produced a telegram.
'I happened to call on Miss Ralph this morning and while I was in the hotel this telegram came. Naturally the young lady is beside herself with relief—I confess that I also am feeling happier.'
Mr Reeder took the telegram. It was handed in at Berlin West and was addressed to Joan Ralph, Haymarket Hotel.

SHALL BE IN GERMANY FOR A MONTH. WRITE TO ME HOTEL MARIENBAD

MUNICH. MARK LETTER 'AWAIT ARRIVAL.' LOVE FATHER.

'Remarkable,' said Mr Reeder.
'I thought so. I asked the young lady to let me have the cable to show you.'
'Remarkable,' said Mr Reeder again.
'It is remarkable,' agreed Dr Ingham. 'And yet it isn't. He may have been called away to Germany and had no time to communicate with his daughter—'
'I wasn't referring to that,' said Mr Reeder. 'When I said it was remarkable, I was thinking that it was both odd and remarkable that he should have cabled her at an hotel where she has never stayed before.'
Dr Ingham's jaw dropped.
'Good heavens!' he gasped. His face had gone pale; it was though there had come to him a sudden realization of just what this telegram might signify. 'That did not occur to me... She had never stayed there before—are you sure?'
Mr Reeder nodded.
'She mentioned it casually last night just before she was leaving—I presume she told you she called on me? No, usually she stays at the hotel her father patronizes. She stayed at the Haymarket because it was close to Mr Ralph's office. At any rate, he would have cabled to Bishop's Stortford.'
'It is strange,' said the clergyman after a pause.
'It is strange,' said Mr Reeder. 'It has assumed the appearance of—um—a case. Distinctly a case.'
For a long time he seemed totally absorbed in the rivulets of rain which trickled down the panes of his window.
'It's certainly bewildering,' said Dr Ingham at last. 'I confess I am becoming alarmed. This red-haired young man, for example—'
'Miss Ralph told you that?'
'Miss Gillette—your charming secretary. She arrived at the hotel with her brother—'
'Her young man,' corrected Mr Reeder, and coughed.
'Really? She didn't introduce him.'
'She never does anything that she should do,' said Mr Reeder bitterly.
He swung round in his swivel chair as though forcing himself from the hypnotic attractions of wriggling rain drops.
'The red-haired young man is also remarkable. I am rather worried about him. He stands as it were on the threshold of—um—life. In a few years' time he may be in the happy enjoyment of a red-haired wife and—um—red-haired children. To be cut off in his prime, and just because his father was ill and he under-valued a diamond brooch or clasp, would be grossly unfair.'
The clergyman stared at him blankly.
'I don't quite know what you mean. To be cut off... You don't mean that this young man is in danger?'
'I wonder!' said Mr Reeder.
For a long while they sat gloomily surveying each other.
'I am bewildered,' sighed Dr Ingham at last. 'I feel as if I had strayed into some terrible land of unreality. Mr Reeder'—he leant forward—'I have been discussing this matter with my wife—a woman of remarkable acumen. She has a theory which, I must confess, I regard as entirely fantastic. I should not have mentioned it to you, but for the doubts you have concerning this Berlin telegram, which, I imagined, cleared up the mystery. I said to her only last night, "My

dear, if you told Mr Reeder your theory, he would think you had been reading detective literature!" She is an invalid—very seldom leaves the house. I feel that it would be asking you a great deal if I suggested you should spend a week-end with us.'

Mr Reeder hesitated.

'I seldom go out,' he said, 'but what is your good lady's theory?'

The doctor smiled.

'I feel I ought to apologize for even advancing such a suggestion. Years ago when I was in America I was swindled. The sum was insignificant, but it was a lesson to me. Here was I, an independent man, thanks to my dear father's beneficence, and yet the cupidity which is latent in all of us overcame my scruples and I invested in a ridiculous get-rich-quick scheme—a sort of treasure hunt, organized by a rascal called Pizarro!'

Mr Reeder nodded, but offered no comment.

'My dear wife has an idea that behind Mr Ralph's disappearance is some diabolical plot—'

Mr Reeder raised a long forefinger; it might have been a gesture of warning. It was in truth an indication that he wished to speak.

'On Saturday afternoon I have nothing particular to do,' he said. 'May I trespass on your hospitality? May I say with respect that your wife is a very intelligent lady, and I should like to meet her.'

Dr Ingham would send his car to meet the Dover Express. The plan was agreeable to Mr Reeder, but—'I must return at night, I—um—never sleep in any bed but my own.'

Dr Ingham understood this prejudice against strange beds. He had an alternative suggestion, namely that Mr Reeder should make the whole journey by car.

'It will take a little longer, but it's a very good road, and I could have you picked up at your place in Brockley which is on the way.'

Here again he found J.G. Reeder agreeable.

For the remainder of the day Mr Reeder waited in vain for some communication from the red-haired youth, but none had come when Miss Gillette returned to the office, which was somewhere in the region of five o'clock. He was not exactly idle; an assistant whom he sometimes employed came to see him at his urgent request, and spent a profitable afternoon searching certain records at Somerset House.

By the time Miss Gillette returned he had a complete list of English subscribers of the Pizarro Syndicate, and, with three exceptions, he had sent telegrams to their known addresses. He did not send to Mr Ralph, the missing Seafield, or yet to Mr Gelpin.

Miss Gillette brought one item of news: she had spent the afternoon in committee with her fiancé and Joan Ralph, and they had come to the conclusion that something was wrong. It hardly seemed worth a committee meeting, thought Mr Reeder, but he avoided trouble by refraining from making such provocative comment.

He left the office at six o'clock and wandered off to Scotland Yard and went immediately to Gaylor's room.

'I could have saved you the trouble,' said Gaylor, when Reeder told him about the telegrams he had sent. 'We've already been in touch with the local police and they're making inquiries. We've found two subscribers, but they are very poor people and not likely to be affected. I also had a look at that map in Schmidt's flat, and I've been on the telephone to the Montreux police. They say that the area marked out in red ink is a derelict farm, the property of a Russian. The police chief was very decent; he sent a couple of men climbing about Glion to investigate, and they report there is nobody there, the place is in a state of ruin, and it hasn't been occupied for a number of years. There used to be a caretaker, but he was withdrawn. The Russian was of course Litnoff. Apparently he was there only once or twice in his life, and never lived at the farm. It's a puzzling business.'

'To me it is as clear as the running water in the mountain stream,' said Mr Reeder poetically, 'but that, of course, is because I have a criminal mind.'

He returned to his office at nine that evening, after a frugal dinner. No telegrams had arrived. The only letter awaiting him was one from a former client, enclosing a cheque.

The drizzle had turned to rain. It pelted down on Mr Reeder's mackintosh and flowed in spasmodic splashes from the brim of his disreputable hat, as he trudged towards the nearest bus that would take him home.

It was not the sort of night when people would be abroad. Again he found the lounger in a yellow oilskin coat standing at the corner of Brockley Road, and another idler pacing leisurely up and down. This man turned at the sound of his steps and came towards him.

'Have you got a match, governor?' His voice was harsh and common, and did not somehow go with his respectable attire, for he had a blue trench coat buttoned up to his chin and belted about his waist. The point of Mr Reeder's umbrella came up until it pointed just above that belt.

'I haven't a match. If I had, I would not be so foolish as to put my hands in my pocket so as to give it to you,' he said haranguingly. 'Now, if you will kindly stand out of my way, you will save yourself a lot of trouble.'

'I asked you civilly, didn't I?' growled the man.

'Your civility doesn't amuse me,' said Mr Reeder, and then suddenly his hand shot out and he got the man by the shoulder, exhibiting a strength which none would have suspected in him, and sent him flying towards the road.

He passed through a little iron gate, slammed it behind him. 'And you can tell Kennedy from me he's wasting his time.'

'I don't know what you're talking about,' snarled the man.

Mr Reeder did not parley with him. He mounted the steps, fitted the key in the lock and entered. He stopped long enough to hang his wet raincoat in the hall, remove his galoshes, and then went up to his room. He was in darkness. He did not switch on the light, and crossing the room, he pulled aside the heavy curtains and looked out.

The man in the blue trench coat was still standing in front of the house, but now he had been joined by the loiterer in the yellow oilskin coat, and they were talking together.

Mr Reeder was cursed with a sense of humour which was peculiar to himself. He went into his bedroom, and from a shelf in the cupboard he took a small air pistol, and 'breaking it,' inserted a pellet. At the distance which separated him from his two watchers an air pistol would not be dangerous, but it should be very painful. Gently lifting the sash, he took aim and pressed the trigger. He heard the man in the yellow oilskin yell and saw him leap into the air.

'What's biting you?' demanded blue trench coat.

'Somep'n bit me.'

He was clasping his neck and rolling his head backwards and forwards in pain.

Mr Reeder broke the pistol again, put another pellet in the breech and took even more accurate aim.

'Say listen,' said the man in the trench coat. He said no more. His hat went flying, and looking up in his bewilderment, he saw Mr Reeder leaning out of the window.

'Go away,' said Mr Reeder gently.

He did not hear the reply because he closed the window quickly. He objected to profanity on

principle. But when a few minutes later he looked out again the two men had disappeared.
It was 11 o'clock when he went to bed. He was by no means a light sleeper, or he would have heard the first pebble that struck his window. The second woke him, and for a good reason: the stone was heavier and the pane smashed.
He got out of bed quickly and very cautiously went to the edge of the window and looked out. There was nobody in sight. Pushing open the casement he made a more careful survey: the street was empty. He could see no living soul; and then, as his eyes became accustomed to the gloom, he saw a figure moving in the shadow of the one laurel bush which decorated the front garden of his house.
This time Mr Reeder did not take an air pistol, but a very businesslike Browning in the pocket of his dressing-gown. He went noiselessly down the stairs, unbolted the door, opened it and flashed a concentrated beam of a powerful spotlight into the garden. It was neither trench coat nor oilskin, but a bedraggled youth, hatless, whose wet clothes seemed skin tight.
From the darkness came a beseeching voice:
'Is that Mr Reeder... For God's sake take the light off me.'
'Oh, it's you, is it?' said J.G. gently, and a little incongruously it sounded, even to himself. 'Did you see my advertisement?'
The young man made a dart through the door into the hall. Mr Reeder followed him, closed and bolted the door. He could almost hear his visitor trembling.
'Which way do I go?' he whimpered.
J.G. led the way up the stairs into the study, and switched on the light.
The red-haired youth was a pitiable sight: his face streaked with blood, the knuckles of his hands were bleeding. He had neither collar nor tie, and as he stood, his soaked clothes formed an ever-growing pool on Mr Reeder's shabby carpet.
'I didn't intend coming here, but after they tried to kill me—'
'I think you'd better have a hot bath,' interrupted Mr Reeder.
Fortunately the bathroom was on the first floor, and by some miracle the water was really hot. He left the trembling youth to divest himself of his sodden clothes, and going upstairs, selected a few articles of wearing apparel.
In his study he had coffee-making equipment and in the cupboard a large seed cake. He was partial to seed cake.
The coffee was brewed and the young man came into the room. He was not an attractive young man. He was very pale, he had a very large nose and a long bony chin. He was very thin, and Mr Reeder's clothes did not so much fit as cover him.
He drank the coffee eagerly, looked at the seed cake, shuddered, but betook of it, while Reeder built up the dying fire.
'Now, Mr—'
'Edelsheim, Benny Edelsheim,' said the young man. 'I live in Pepys Road, New Cross. Did the girls tell you about me? I wish I hadn't run away that night you chased me. She's a stunning looking girl, isn't she? I don't mean the blonde—the other one.'
'Have you wakened me up in the middle of the night to discuss the attractions of brunettes?' demanded Mr Reeder gently. 'Who hit you?'
The young man felt his head gingerly. He had tied about it a large handkerchief which Mr Reeder had supplied.
'I don't know, I think it was the fellow in the yellow coat... There were two of them. I was just going into my house—my father's house, when a man asked me if I had a match. I didn't like the

look of him, but I was feeling for the match when he hit me. There was a car halfway down the hill—it used to be called Red Hill once...'

'The topography is familiar to me,' said Mr Reeder. 'What did you do when he hit you?'

'I ran,' said the other simply. 'I tried to shout, but I couldn't, and then the other fellow, who was standing by the car, tripped me up.'

He looked at his knuckles. 'That's where I got that. I think there were three of them. A chauffeur was standing by the car and he made a dive at me, but I dodged and doubled up the hill—with the fellow in the yellow coat behind me.'

'What time was this?' asked Mr Reeder.

'About nine. I was coming to see you, in fact I had made up my mind to. I knew where you lived, but I thought I'd go home first and talk to the old man—my father. We've got a jeweller's shop in the Clerkenwell Road, but he's been ill for nearly a year, and I've been running the business.'

'And you got away?' said Mr Reeder, hastening the narrative.

'In a sense I did,' said Edelsheim. 'I got over the top of the hill. I couldn't see a policeman anywhere. It's disgraceful the rates we pay and no policemen! My God, it was awful. I didn't see them for a bit, and I thought I'd slipped them, and then I saw the lights of the car coming. If I'd had any sense I'd have knocked at the nearest house and gone in. And no policeman, Mr Reeder!' His voice was thin and hysterical. 'That's what we pay rates and taxes for, and no so-and-so policemen in sight!'

He did not say 'so-and-so,' but Mr Reeder thought his profanity was excusable.

'As I saw the car, I got over the rails of a recreation ground or something. They must have seen me, because the car stopped right opposite the place where I'd jumped. I didn't see the man following, but I sort of felt him. Then I found I was in a cemetery. My God, it was awful dodging in and out of the crosses and things! I climbed the wall and got out, and then I did meet a policeman. He thought I was drunk, so I bolted again.'

'Did you see the man in the yellow coat?'

'Not till I got here. It was nearer twelve than eleven. I was just thinking of calling you and of what you would say to me, when I saw them both. They were coming up from the Lewisham High Road, walking together. I dived into your front garden and hid behind the bush. One of them walked up the steps and tried the door. He had a torch. I nearly died of fright. They were messing about here for an hour.'

'And you were afraid to ring for fear that they saw you?'

'That's right. I waited until they'd gone and I started chucking stones. I've broken two or three windows in this room, too.'

Mr Reeder poured out another cup of coffee, and from the warming effect of the fire and the hot drink Mr Benny Edelsheim grew a little more confident.

'Is she here?' he asked. 'The dark-haired one?'

'She is not here,' said Mr Reeder severely.

Then suddenly the young man became plaintive again. 'What's it all about?' he demanded. 'I saw your advertisement this evening. I didn't see how it could be anything to do with that, and yet when I was dodging in and out of the cemetery, the idea came to me that these fellows were after me because of that advertisement, the clasp and everything, and what I said to the girl. Have I done anything wrong? I'm sorry. I don't, as a rule, talk to girls without an introduction. If I've offended her relations—you're not her father, are you?'

'I am not a father,' said Mr Reeder emphatically.

'I didn't think you were,' said Edelsheim, 'because I knew about you. You're a detective. My old man—my father says you're the most wonderful detective of the age. I wanted to come and explain to you that I didn't mean any harm.'

Mr Reeder pushed forward the plate of seed cake.

'You, my dear young friend,' he said, 'are no more, as it were, than a cog in a wheel of a very complicated machine. I can quite understand how you had embarrassed the employers of those two ferocious men. Now let us get to the really important point—just tell me what you said, why you addressed those young ladies in the restaurant.'

Benny munched the seed cake with an agonized expression; it was obvious he did not like seed cake, but his hunger had compelled him to overcome his scruples.

'I recognized her the moment I saw her. She's in my thoughts night and day, Mr Reeder. There are some faces that hit you right in the eye, so to speak, that sort of make an impression on you—she's not married, is she?' he asked anxiously.

'Practically,' said Mr Reeder.

The young man's face assumed an expression of acute pain.

'She is engaged,' explained Mr Reeder, in haste to remove any wrong impression he might have created.

'I shall never see another face like that,' said Benny dismally. 'I'm romantic, Mr Reeder, I don't mind admitting it. I fell in love with her the moment I saw her photograph. She was wearing plus-fours. You've no idea what I felt like when I saw that picture. I thought here's the woman for me, and I only saw it for a second. He opened his pocketbook on the counter, the gentleman who called at the shop, and he took out the photograph, because the clasp was in the same compartment, wrapped up in tissue paper, so I had a good look at the picture, and I said to myself—'

'Yes, yes,' said Mr Reeder with a certain testiness. 'Please don't bother about your emotions at the moment, Mr Edelsheim. Tell me something about the clasp.'

'The clasp, oh, yes. You want to know about that? It was a very pretty thing, half a buckle of diamonds and emeralds. I know a lot about stones. I was in Hatton Garden for eighteen months. My old man—my father believed in starting me at the bottom of the ladder—'

'Did he want to sell the clasp?'

Benny shook his head.

'No, he wanted it valued. We do a lot of valuation work, and I'm supposed to be pretty good at it. We've got a very big business, half a dozen assistants, and we have a branch at Bristol.'

'You valued it?' said Mr Reeder.

'I valued it at £2500, but I made a mistake. Even the best of us make mistakes. I remember once—'

'You've under-valued it by £250?'

'That's right. I told the young lady so when I met her. I thought she'd tell her friend—'

'Her father,' corrected Mr Reeder.

'Oh, was that her father?' Benny was more interested in the parentage of his ideal than in the sordid question of a diamond and emerald clasp. 'Yes, I under-valued it by £250. What he really wanted to know was whether the stones were genuine and, of course, I could tell him that. I don't think he'd have worried about the wrong valuation, and I shouldn't have spoken about it, but I wanted a sort of introduction to the young lady—you're a man of the world, Mr Reeder—'

'What time did he come into the shop?'

Benny, his mouth full of seed cake, looked thoughtful.

'About five o'clock in the evening.'

'And when you valued the clasp, what happened?'
'He wrapped it up and took it away with him. I asked him if he wanted to sell it, and he said no.'
'You never saw him again?'
Benny shook his head.
'That was last Wednesday week?'
'Tuesday,' said Benny promptly. 'I happen to know that, because I had a date—an engagement to take a certain party to the pictures, and I was anxious to shut up the shop and get away.'
Mr Reeder jotted down a few notes on his blotting-pad.
'Have you ever valued that clasp before?'
Benny Edelsheim looked at him with an open mouth.
'It's curious that you should ask that, Mr Reeder. I haven't, but my father has. I was describing the piece to him, and he said he was certain he'd valued the same piece six months ago Of course, he may have made a mistake, but he's got a marvellous memory.' He enlarged upon the memory of his parent, but Mr Reeder was not listening.
'Why Clerkenwell?' murmured Mr Reeder. 'Do you advertise?'
'We're the best advertised valuers in London,' said Benny proudly. 'That's our speciality. I can't tell you how upset my father was when I made a mistake. It sort of reflects on the firm. Oh, yes, we carry big ads, in all papers. Valuation of jewellery. You must have seen our name.'
Mr Reeder nodded.
'That accounts for it,' he said.
He looked at the clock. The minute hand pointed to half past two. Picking up the telephone, he called the nearest cab rank and gave his address.
'I'm going to take you home,' he said. 'You'd better make a bundle of your wet clothes while I dress.'
By the time the taxi arrived, Mr Reeder, feeling very much awake, was ready. He went out first, but there was no need of his caution, less need for the automatic that he held in his pocket.
The journey to Pepys Road was uneventful. He waited until the young man had entered his house, then he drove to the nearest police station and had a consultation with the night officer. When Benny Edelsheim looked out of his window the next morning he found a uniformed policeman standing stolidly before the house, and felt for the first time his rates and taxes were justified.
The morning brought a surprise to Mr Reeder. When he arrived at his office he found Miss Gillette already on duty. That in itself was a notable event. She was entertaining in her room a very early caller in Dr Ingham, and from the solicitude in her tone it almost seemed that she was mothering him. Miss Gillette was one of those uncomfortable people whose maternal instinct was highly developed.
As Mr Reeder paused at the half-opened door, he heard her speaking.
'I shouldn't worry about it, Dr Ingham. Reeder will put a stop to any of that sort of nonsense. He's much cleverer than he looks.'
Her maligned employer passed softly into his room and rang the bell.
'I didn't hear you come in—you scare the life out of me sometimes,' she complained, and added: 'Mr Ingham is here.'
'Dr Ingham,' said Mr Reeder reproachfully. 'You are—um—a little careless about—um—prefixes.'
'He's been attacked—somebody tried to break into his house last night,' said Miss Gillette. 'Poor soul, he has a terrible face!'

'Let me see it, please,' said J.G.

The clergyman had evidently passed a strenuous night. The bridge of his handsome nose bore a strip of sticking plaster. One eye, at the moment concealed behind a shade, was blue and swollen, and his lower lip was badly cut.

'I'm afraid I look rather ghastly,' he said, as he shook hands with the detective.

The undamaged portion of his face was white and drawn, and when he said he had had no sleep that night Mr Reeder was not surprised.

He had gone back to St Margaret's on the previous night, and had driven himself from Dover, arriving at his house at ten o'clock.

'Grayne Hall is built on the site of an old castle,' he said. 'There wasn't enough of the original structure to restore, so I had the walls pulled down and erected a modern residence. Naturally it's very isolated, but there's some very excellent timber, and I've made a good garden. I returned before midnight, but I'd hardly got to bed before my wife said that she heard a noise below. I went down, unarmed, of course, for I do not own so much as a shot-gun. I'd reached the hall and was feeling for the light switch, when somebody struck me. I had a fearful blow on the face, but I managed to find an old battle-axe which hung on the wall—luckily for me. With this I defended myself. My wife, who'd heard the fracas in the hall, screamed, and I heard one of my assailants say: "Run for it, Kennedy!" Immediately after, the hall door was thrown open, and I saw two, or it may have been three, people run into the garden and vanish.'

'Dear me,' said Mr Reeder. 'One of them said: "Run for it, Kennedy!" You're sure it was that?'

'I could swear that was the name. Afterwards I remembered, or rather my dear wife remembered, that a man named Kennedy had been a member of the Pizarro gang.'

Mr Reeder was examining the clergyman's injuries thoughtfully.

'No weapon was used?'

Dr Ingham smiled painfully.

'That's a poor consolation!' he said with some acerbity. 'No, I rather think that I was struck by a fist that was holding a weapon. In the darkness this rascal must have struck wildly.'

He had not sent for the police. Apparently he had no exalted opinion of the Kentish constabulary, and he admitted a horror of figuring in newspapers. Mr Reeder could understand this: he also had a horror of publicity.

'Whether these people were plain burglars who were disturbed at their work, or whether revenge for some fancied injury was at the bottom of their dastardly action, I cannot make up my mind. With Mrs Ingham the Pizarro case is an obsession. She is, by the way, looking forward with great eagerness to meeting you. Now tell me, Mr Reeder, what am I to do? I will be guided entirely by your advice. To go to the police now seems to be a fairly useless proceeding. I cannot describe the men—except for a second when they were silhouetted in the open doorway, I never saw them. My butler and my gardener made inquiries this morning, but nobody else seems to have seen them. Not even the coastguard who has a cottage quite close.'

Mr Reeder sat with half-closed eyes, his large hands folded on his lap.

'It is very odd,' he murmured at last. 'Kennedy, Casius Kennedy. A bad—um—egg. He inherited it from his mother, a lady with a very—um—unpleasant history.'

He pursed his under lip, his eyes had dropped a little lower.

'It is odd, extremely odd.'

Dr Ingham drew a long breath.

'What am I to do?' he demanded.

'Ask for police protection,' said Mr Reeder. 'Have an officer sleeping in the house and another

stationed on the grounds. I hope to see you on Saturday.'
He rose with startling abruptness and jerked out his hand.
'Till Saturday,' he said, and Dr Ingham went out, a very dissatisfied man.
Mr Reeder was no angel that morning. He was in a mood the like of which Miss Gillette could not remember. She discovered this very soon.
'What did you tell the doctor?' she asked.
'When I want you, I will ring for you, young lady,' he snapped.
She went out, a little dazed by his mutiny. She heard the key turn in his lock and when she got through to him by telephone, he was most unpleasant.
'I think I will go home, Mr Reeder,' she said.
'I will send your wages by post,' said he.
She went out of the office, slamming the door behind her, which—apart from the slam—was exactly what he intended she should do.
The door to the corridor he locked in the same fashion before he rang up Inspector Gaylor.
'I want a couple of men,' he said. 'I'm nervous, or, shall I say, apprehensive.'
'I wondered when you'd start getting that way,' said Gaylor. 'I'm having young Edelsheim shadowed. Thanks for your letter. Is there any other development?'
Mr Reeder told him of the doctor's unpleasant adventure.
'Oh!' said Gaylor, and then after a silence. 'That will keep.'
'So I thought,' said Mr Reeder. 'Do you mind if I use your name rather freely today?'
'So long as you don't try to borrow money on it!' said Gaylor, who had a painful sense of humour.
REEDER spent a long time after that searching a trade telephone directory and ringing up various yachting agencies. He had become suddenly interested in pleasure cruisers. He drew a blank for the first nine inquiries, but the tenth rewarded him. It was not difficult to secure the answers he wanted, but when he called a sticky and uncommunicative agent he used the name of Gaylor with great freedom and invariably secured the information he required.
The tenth call needed this incentive, but the result was beyond expectations. Mr Reeder spent a happy hour with his notes and a nautical almanac. By this time the two Scotland Yard men had arrived, and when soon after lunch a district messenger brought a square and heavy parcel, having the label of a West End bookseller, they were very useful, for one of them had been for a year in the Explosives Department at Scotland Yard and had a sensitive ear for the faint ticking that came from within the parcel.
'It's a time bomb, but it may also have a make and break attachment.'
They watched it sink heavily into a pail of water, and when, after half an hour, the Yard man took it out again, the ticking had ceased.
'They've been getting ready for this racket for a long time,' said the detective. 'That bomb wasn't made in a hurry—'
The telephone bell rang at that moment and Mr Reeder answered it.
'Is that you, Reeder?' It was Gaylor's voice and he was speaking very quickly. 'I'm coming round to pick you up. We've found Gelpin.'
'Eh?' said Mr Reeder.
'Dead—shot through the heart. A ranger found his body in Epping Forest. Be ready.'
The telephone clicked, but Mr Reeder still stood with the receiver in his hand, a terrifying frown on his face.
'Anything wrong, sir?' asked the detective.

J.G. nodded.

'I'm wrong: if I had the brain of a—um—great man, I should have expected this.'

What 'this' was he did not elucidate. A few minutes later he was one of a party of five packed in a police tender and was heading for Epping.

It was nearly dark when the car pulled up by the side of a forest by-road. A ranger led them to the spot where the body lay.

It was that of a man above medium height, and more than ordinarily broad of shoulder.

Though George Gelpin was between fifty and sixty, he had been in life a model of a man. He had been rider to hounds, a keen cricketer, something of an athlete.

'Nothing in his pockets—no identification marks of any kind. If we hadn't got his photograph and his description—they arrived this morning from Birmingham—we should have had the devil's job in tracing him.'

One of the group they had found standing about the body was a doctor. He supplied certain data which confirmed Mr Reeder in his opinion. But the chief confirmation came when he examined the outspread hands of the silent figure.

There was no mark of car wheels, and the bushes behind which the man was found showed no evidence of crushing. It might have been an ordinary case of suicide, and the doctor ventured this opinion.

A revolver had been found near the body. He must have been shot with the muzzle almost touching his coat, for it was burnt.

'We haven't got the number of the revolver, but we're making inquiries about it. I don't think they're necessary. It will be a day or two before we can trace it. Did you get that gun?'

One of the waiting detectives took it out of his pocket. It was a small six-chambered Colt.

One of the detectives who had been on guard over the body when they arrived offered a piece of information.

'There is an initial scratched on the back plate of the butt,' he said. 'F.S.'

He took the weapon from his pocket and passed it across to Gaylor.

'F. S.,' frowned the inspector. 'That's a pretty common initial.'

'Frank Seafield, for example,' said Mr Reeder, and Gaylor gaped at him.

'Why should it be Seafield? That's wildly improbable, Reeder.'

However, when they returned to London and Mr Reeder contacted Seafield's late partner, Gaylor found that the surmise was not so wild. Tommy Anton called at Scotland Yard and saw and identified the weapon.

'That's Frank's,' he said immediately. 'He always carried a revolver. He had no reason to, so far as I know, but he was rather on the theatrical side.'

Joan Ralph had gone back to Bishop's Stortford. They reached her by telephone. She too had seen the revolver and described it accurately.

'That beats me,' said Gaylor.

Mr Reeder put down the phone. They were sitting in the inspector's room at Scotland Yard, where a meal had been brought to them from a neighbouring restaurant.

'It doesn't beat me, possibly because I am over sanguine,' said Mr Reeder, 'possibly because my peculiar mentality leads me astray.'

'But suppose it is suicide—' began Gaylor, and stopped.

'You were thinking that it is quite usual that a suicide tries to remove all marks of his identification?' said Mr Reeder. 'That is perfectly true. Will you tell me this: why is the suit he was wearing so old a stained and shabby, and why was he wearing slippers?'

'Boots,' Gaylor broke in. 'Elastic-sided boots.'

'Slippers,' insisted Mr Reeder. 'And why was there no mud on them? And why was the front of him wet and the back on which he lay almost dry? It rained all last night and he couldn't have walked through the forest without getting soaked to the skin.'

Gaylor pinched his long upper lip, looked moodily at the remains of his dinner. 'Tennant tells me that they tried to bomb you this afternoon. It's the Pizarro gang, of course. Kennedy?'

'His very self,' said Mr Reeder, flippantly and ungrammatically. 'And I shouldn't be surprised if almost anything happened. I told my housekeeper to go home to her mother. Most housekeepers have mothers to go home to. I shall stay up here tonight.'

'Where?' asked Gaylor curiously.

'That's my secret,' said Mr Reeder gravely.

They went out of the Yard together, when Gaylor had an idea.

'If you want to get out of the way, I should go down to St Margaret's Bay. I think you'll be safe there.'

'An excellent idea,' said Mr Reeder. 'A very excellent idea, but unfortunately the doctor is still in London.'

He went to his office, accompanied by one of the two detectives who had been appointed to watch over him. The other was still in Miss Gillette's room—Mr Reeder suspected that he was asleep, for it was some time before he opened the door to him.

'There's a telegram for you,' he said, and handed it to Mr Reeder. It was from Dr Ingham. Would he (Mr Reeder) come down as soon as he could? There had been remarkable developments at Grayne.

The telegram had been dispatched from Dover. Mr Reeder sent his reply over the telephone. He would arrive on the following afternoon at three o'clock. Then, strangely enough, contrary to all his expressed intentions, he went home to his housekeeperless establishment in the Brockley Road and slept alone in his silent home. And more strangely still, he slept most peacefully.

If he had not gone home he would have missed the letter which came by the morning post. It was from Miss Gillette. She was leaving him. Mr Reeder sighed happily.

'I think I ought to help Tommy,' she wrote. 'The Rev Dr Ingham has promised to help him start a new business. Dr Ingham has been most kind and I shall never be sufficiently grateful to you for having been unconsciously instrumental in bringing Tommy into touch with him. He wrote before he left London yesterday, suggesting that I might help in creating the new business, and I think you would like to see his postscript so I have torn it off.'

She remained ever his sincerely.

The slip of paper which accompanied the letter was in the doctor's handwriting.

'P.S. I shall never forgive myself if I have robbed Mr Reeder of his secretary. He is a man for whom I have the highest regard.'

'H'm,' said Mr Reeder, 'how very nice... how extraordinarily kind!' He spoke aloud to his coffee machine and his electric toaster, but he was never so loquacious as when he was addressing an inanimate audience.

His housekeeper returned during the morning and she packed his battered suitcase under his personal supervision. He went to his office before lunch, met Gaylor by appointment and handed to him the batch of telegrams which had arrived during the morning. Gaylor examined them casually.

'I know all about these,' he said. 'Nine of the seventeen English subscribers to Pizarro's scheme are missing. I can tell you more—with 'em went the best part of eighty thousand pounds. By the way, I'm offering no further evidence against Jake Alsby. I've got him inside for his own safety, but he'll be discharged next week.'

Gaylor came to the station to see him off.

'Have a good time. If the Pizarro crowd chase you to Dover, send me a postcard.'

Inspector Gaylor, as has already been stated, had a perverted sense of humour.

Throughout the journey Mr Reeder read a book which was entitled The Thousand Funniest After-Dinner Stories. He read them all, the whole thousand, and never smiled once.

He had a trick of moving his lips as he read. The military-looking man who sat opposite him had never seen Mr Reeder at close quarters before and was silently amused. Once he tried to start a conversation, but Mr Reeder was not a great conversationalist on a railway journey and the attempted affability faded to silence.

At Dover station, Mr Reeder got out and his companion followed. Three men lounged up to Mr Reeder's fellow-passenger, and with a nod he indicated the detective, who was passing through the barrier.

'That's your man,' he said, 'keep close to him.'

The car which was waiting for Mr Reeder had scarcely left the station yard, when the four entered a black saloon and followed.

The drive from Dover to St Margaret's Bay was not a comfortable one. Heavy gusts of wind-borne rain drove across the downs. Below, as the car mounted the cliff road, he could see breakers creaming the yellow-green waters of the Straits, and out at sea a little coasting tramp was taking water over her bows in alarming quantities.

Grayne Hall was not in the residential area of St Margaret's Bay. It stood aloof in a fold of the downs and within a very short distance of the cliff's edge. A red brick building, with squat chimneys that were not at all in harmony with the Elizabethan architecture of the house.

'We used to have high twisted chimneys, but the wind blew them down. You've no idea what the wind is like here,' explained Dr Ingham before dinner.

The car passed through a pair of ornamental iron gates and up a broad drive to the portico before the door. The doctor was waiting and with him a tall slight woman, who looked very young until she was seen closer at hand. Even then she might deceive any but the most critical, for her brown hair had a glint of gold in it, and the beauty of her face had not entirely faded.

'Welcome!' Dr Ingham had a bandage over one eye and his injured nose was still covered with plaster. But he was in a pleasantly jovial mood. Perhaps he was relieved at the sight of his visitor, for he subsequently admitted that he had been expecting a telegram from Mr Reeder, regretting his inability to put in an appearance.

'I want you to persuade Mrs Ingham that this is not the most forsaken spot on the face of the earth, my dear Reeder. And if you can allay her fears about a repetition of the attack on me I shall be completely grateful.'

Mrs Ingham's red lips curled in a smile. She was, Mr Reeder discovered, a well-read, knowledgeable woman. As she showed him round the lovely grounds—the spring flowers were a joy to the eye—she gave him every opportunity to study her. He himself said little—she gave him no chance, for she never stopped talking. Her voice was low but monotonous. She had definite views on almost every subject. She told him that she was a graduate of a famous New

England university—she was obviously proud of this and repeated the information twice. She was pretty, probably nearer forty than thirty. She had deep dark brown eyes, the most delicate of features, and jet black eyebrows which contrasted attractively with the colour of her hair.

'...I remember the Pizarro case—I had just left college and naturally I was thrilled because he came from our home town. And, Mr Reeder, I'm sure that all these disappearances have something to do with the Pizarro outfit. I've been racking my brains all day trying to think how my husband has offended them. Maybe he preached against them. I've a kind of recollection that he had a threatening letter when we were in Boston soon after we married. Not that my husband would worry about threatening letters...'

There was much more to see in the grounds: here and there a crumbling ruin of a wall to remind the observer of the dead glories of Grayne Castle. One interesting feature Mr Reeder discovered was a flight of steps leading down the face of the cliff. It was guarded by an iron hand rail and gave the occupants of Grayne Hall, a private way to the beach.

'If anybody wants to bathe on pebbles,' said Mrs Ingham.

The room allotted to Mr Reeder's use gave him a beautiful view of the sea and the flower garden in front of the house. It was furnished with rare taste—he saw in the decorations Mrs Ingham's hand. A pleasant retreat, but in many, many ways a dangerous one. He went up to his room after tea and found his clothes had been unpacked by his host's valet. Later came the individual to assist Mr Reeder. A bathroom opened from the bedroom and Mr Reeder was under the shower when the valet knocked. He came out, to find the man folding the discarded day clothes and hanging them neatly in the wardrobe.

The contents of his pockets were placed neatly on the dressing table.

'Thank you,' murmured Mr Reeder. 'I—um—shall not require you any more. I will ring if I do.'

He closed the door on the retiring valet, turned the key and began to dress at his leisure. Mr Reeder liked the routine of well run country houses and Grayne Hall was extraordinarily well run. He came down to find himself alone in the drawing-room. A fine aromatic cedar log burnt on the open grate, above which was a picture which might have been a Rembrandt.

The soft hangings of the room, the austere furnishings, the pastel coloured walls, were very soothing. Dr Ingham came into warm his hands before the fire.

'I suppose Elsa gave you the full benefit of her theories? There may be something in them. I've been trying to think how I might have offended these birds. A sermon maybe. I used to be a powerful preacher—took current events as my text. Come into my study and have a drink. Elsa won't be down for hours.' He conducted Mr Reeder across the panelled hall, through a deeply recessed door into as comfortable a room as the heart of man could desire.

Deep armchairs, a low divan before the fire, walls covered with bookshelves, and a big empire desk were the main features of the room.

'Comfort, comfort, comfort!' said the cleric as he opened a walnut cabinet and took out a silver tray laden with glasses. To these he added a square decanter and a syphon. 'Say when.'

He splashed the soda into the brown whisky and Mr Reeder sipped daintily.

'Elsa wants me to keep firearms in the house. Now you, as a detective, I suppose would think nothing of that. To me it is an abhorrent practice. I may not be a great preacher, but I am, I hope, a good Christian, and the idea of taking life—I presume you carry a gun?'

Mr Reeder shook his head.

'On occasions that dreadful necessity has been forced upon me,' he said. 'I dislike the practice. I have—er—two such weapons, but I have never had to use them. One is at my office and one at my private residence.'

The doctor looked serious.

'You disappoint me, Mr Reeder. I am not a nervous man, but in view of what happened the other night'—he touched his injured face—' I should have felt a little safer. Hello, sweetness.'

Sweetness wore a perfectly cut gown of deep crimson velvet. Mr Reeder thought that she looked twenty-four and not a day over, and had he the courage of a lady's man—a quality he much envied—he would have said as much.

'What were you talking about?' she asked.

'We were talking of guns,' said Mr Reeder loudly, 'um—revolvers.'

She smiled at this.

'And my husband was giving his well-known views of the sanctity of human life,' she said scornfully.

Mr Reeder smiled.

'My dear,' said her husband, 'all this arose from a question I asked Mr Reeder: whether he carried weapons. He doesn't.'

'I expect poor Thomas was terribly disappointed,' said Mrs Ingham. 'When he unpacked your bag he had expected to find it full of guns and handcuffs.'

She took them back to the drawing-room, but either she thought it was a painful subject, or she wanted to postpone the discussion till after dinner, for she made no reference, to her husband's experience.

It was Mr Reeder who brought up that matter. They were passing through the hail on their way to the dining-room.

They had passed the broad stairs on which the battle between Dr Ingham and his midnight intruders had been fought, and Mr Reeder tried to visualize the scene. But there were occasions when his imagination failed, and this was one.

The dining-room had been fashioned like an Elizabethan banqueting hall in miniature. There was a big Tudor fireplace, a minstrel gallery, and he noticed with surprise that the floor was of flag stones.

'That is the original floor of the old castle,' said Mrs Ingham proudly. 'The builders unearthed it while they prepared the foundation, and my husband insisted that it should remain. Of course we had it levelled, and in some cases the flags had to be replaced. But it was in a marvellous state of preservation. It used to belong to the deBoisy family—'

Mr Reeder nodded.

'De Tonsin,' he said gently. 'The deBoisys were related by marriage, and only one deBoisy occupied the castle in 1453.'

She was a little taken aback by his knowledge.

'Yes, I have made a study of this place,' Mr Reeder went on. 'I am something of a student of archaeology.' He beamed up and down the room approvingly. 'Dirty work.'

Mrs Ingham lifted her eyebrows.

'I don't get you?'

'On this floor,' said Mr Reeder almost jovially, 'wicked old barons were slicing off their enemies' heads and were dropping them into the deepest dungeon beneath the—um.' No, he had never heard of a moat. It could not well be that, could it?

As the footman placed a cup of soup before him, and the tall butler poured him out a glass of wine, Mr Reeder looked at the glass, held it up to the light.

'That's good stuff. I can quite imagine,' he said reminiscently, 'that dramatic scene when Geoffrey deBoisy induced his old rival to come to dinner. How he must have smiled as his varlets ended—

um—the unfortunate gentleman with wine from a poisoned flagon.'
He finished the scrutiny of the wine and put it down untasted.
Mrs Ingham was amused.
'You have a mediaeval mind, Mr Reeder.'
'A criminal mind,' said the gentleman.
He did not drink throughout the meal, and Dr Ingham remembered that he had merely sipped his whisky in the study.
'Yes, I am a teetotaller in a sense,' said Mr Reeder, 'but I find life so completely exciting that I require no other stimulant.'
He had observed that the man who had valeted him was also the footman. He waited till the two servants were at the other end of the room, and then: 'Your man is looking rather ill. Has he also been injured in the fight?'
'Thomas? No, he didn't appear on the scene until it was all over,' said Dr Ingham, in surprise. 'Why?'
'I thought I saw a bandage round his throat.'
'I haven't noticed it,' said the host.
'Which axe was it you used?' Mr Reeder asked.
The panelled walls were entirely innocent of armour or battle axes.
'We've had them moved,' said Mrs Ingham. 'It occurred to me afterwards that these dreadful people might have used the battle axe instead of my husband.'
The conversation flagged. The coffee was served on the table, and Mr Reeder helped himself liberally to sugar. He refused a cigar and, apologizing for his bad manners, took one of his own cigarettes.
'Matches, Thomas,' said Dr Ingham, but before the footman could obey, Mr Reeder had taken a box from his pocket and struck a match.
It was no ordinary match: the light of it blazed blindingly white so that he had to screw up his eyes to avoid the glare. Only for a moment, then it died down, leaving the party blinking.
'What was that?' asked Ingham.
Mr Reeder stared hopelessly at the box.
'Somebody has been playing a joke on me,' he said. 'I am terribly sorry.'
They were very ordinary looking matches. He passed the box across to his host, who struck one, but produced nothing more startling than a mild yellow flame.
'I've never seen anything so extraordinary,' said the beautiful lady who sat on his left. 'It was almost like a magnesium flare.'
The incident of the match passed. It was the doctor who led the conversation to the Pizarros and Mrs Ingham who elaborated her theory. J.G. Reeder sat listening, apparently absorbed.
'I don't think he was a really bad man,' Mrs Ingham was saying when he interrupted.
'Pizarro was a blackguard,' said Mr Reeder. 'But he had the kind of nature one would have expected in a half-bred Dago.'
If he saw Mrs Ingham stiffen, he gave no sign.
'Kennedy, his confederate,' he went on, 'was, as I said this afternoon, a man to be pitied. His mother was a moral leper, a woman of no worth, the merest chattel.'
Dr Ingham's face had gone white and tense, his eyes glowed like red coals, but J.G. Reeder, sitting there with his hands thrust into his trouser pockets, his cigarette hanging limply from his lower lip, continued as though he had the fullest approval of the company.
'Kennedy was really the brain of the gang, if you can call it a brain, the confidence man with

some sort of college education. He married Pizarro's daughter, who was not a nice young lady. He was, I think, her fourth lover before he married her—if they were married at all...'

'Take that back, you damned liar!'

The woman was on her feet, glowering down at him, her shrill voice almost a scream.

'You liar, you beast!'

'Shut up!'

It was Dr Ingham's voice—harsh, commanding. But the injunction came too late. One of Mr Reeder's hands had come out from his pocket and it held an automatic of heavy calibre. He came to his feet so quickly that they were unprepared for the manoeuvre.

Mr Reeder pushed the chair behind, and leant back against the wall. Thomas, the footman, had come in running, but stopped now at the sight of the gun. Mr Reeder addressed him: 'I'm afraid I hurt you on Thursday night,' he said, pleasantly. 'A pellet from an air pistol can be very painful. I owe you an apology—I intended it to be for your friend.'

He nodded towards the butler.

'It was very stupid of you, Dr Ingham, to allow your two men to come to London, and it led to very unpleasant consequences. I saw the dead man today. Rather a powerful looking fellow named Gelpin. The knuckles of his hand were bruised. I presume that, in an unguarded moment you went too near him without your bodyguard.'

He reached one of the long windows, and with a quick movement of his hand he drew the curtain aside. The window was open. The military-looking man who had accompanied him from London climbed through. Then followed the three who had followed Mr Reeder to the house. Dr Ingham stood paralysed to inaction.

Suddenly he turned and darted towards the small door in a corner of the room. Mr Reeder's gun exploded and the panel of the door split noisily. Ingham stood stock still—a pitiable, panic-stricken thing, and he came staggering back.

'It wasn't my idea, Reeder,' he said. 'I'll tell you everything. I can prove I had nothing to do with it. They are all safe, all of them.'

Stooping, almost beneath his feet he turned back the heavy carpet, and Reeder saw a large stone flag in which was inserted a heavy metal ring.

'They're all alive... every one of them. I shot Gelpin in self defence. He'd have killed me if I hadn't killed him.'

'And Litnoff?' asked Mr Reeder, almost good-humouredly.

Dr Ingham was silent.

Mr Reeder wrote in his casebook:

Dr Ingham's real name was Casius Kennedy. He was born in England, convicted at the age of seventeen for obtaining money under false pretences. He afterwards became a reformed character and addressed many revival meetings, and he was known as a boy preacher. He was again convicted; on a charge of obtaining money by fraud, sentenced to nine months' imprisonment, and on his discharge emigrated to America, where he fell in with Pizarro and assisted him in most of his swindles.

He was very useful to Pizarro, gaining, as he did, the confidence of his victims by his appeals in various pulpits. He either acquired, or assumed, the title of doctor of divinity.

After the biggest of the Pizarro swindles he escaped to California and in some way, which is not known, acquired a very considerable fortune, most of which he lost in speculation subsequent to his arrival in England.

In his statement to me he was emphatic on this one point: that after he had built Grayne Hall on the foundations of the old castle, and he discovered the commodious dungeons which, I can testify, were in a remarkable state of preservation beneath the house, he had no intention of making illicit use of them until his heavy losses compelled him to look around for a method of replenishing his exchequer.

Five years ago he met a Russian actor named Litnoff, a drunkard who was on the point of being arrested for debt, and who was afraid that he might be deported to his own country, where he was wanted for a number of political offences.

Kennedy and his wife, with the approval and assistance of Litnoff, evolved a scheme whereby big money could be made. Litnoff took a small flat in London mansions, which was cheaply furnished, and it was here that the swindle was worked. Very carefully and with all his old cleverness, Kennedy got in touch with the likely victims, and naturally he chose the credulous people who would subscribe money to the Pizarro Syndicate. One by one the 'doctor' made their acquaintance. He studied their habits, their methods of life, found out at what hotels they stayed when they were in London, their hobbies and their weaknesses. In some cases it took three months to establish confidence, and when this was done, Kennedy mentioned casually the story of the dying Russian who had escaped from Petrograd with a chest full of jewellery looted from the palaces of the nobility.

Mr Ralph's statement may be taken as typical of them all:

'I met Dr Ingham, or Kennedy, after some correspondence, He was very charming and obviously wealthy. He was staying at the best hotel in London, and I dined with him twice—on one occasion with his wife.

'He told me he was engaged in voluntary mission work, in the course of which he had attended a dying Russian, who put up a most extraordinary proposition, namely: that he should buy a small farm in Switzerland, the property of Litnoff, on which he had buried half a million pounds' worth of jewellery. The story, though seemingly far-fetched, could be confirmed. His brother was living on the farm. Both men had been chased and watched until life had become unendurable.

'"There is something in this story," said the clergyman. "This fellow, Litnoff, has in his possession a piece of jewellery which must be worth at least two thousand pounds. He keeps it under his pillow."

'I was intrigued by the story, and when the doctor asked me if I would like to see the man, I agreed to meet him one night, promising not to mention to a soul the Russian's secret.

'Dr Ingham called for me at midnight. We drove to a place in Bloomsbury and I was admitted to a very poorly furnished flat. In one of the rooms was a very sick-looking man, who spoke with difficulty in broken English. He told me of all the espionage to which he and his brother were subjected. He was in fear of his life, he said. He dared not offer the jewels for fear that the agents of the Russian government traced him. His scheme seemed, from my point of view, to be beyond risk to myself. It was that I should go out to Montreux, see his brother, inspect the jewels and buy the farm, the purchase money to include the contents of the chest. If I was not satisfied, or if I thought there was any trick, I needn't pay my money until I was sure that the deal was genuine.

'He showed me a diamond clasp, told me to take it away with me and have it valued.

'This conversation took a very long time: he spoke with great difficulty, sometimes we had to wait for ten minutes while he recovered his breath. I took the clasp with me and had it valued, returning it to Dr Ingham the same night.

'It was he who suggested that my safest plan was to carry no money at all, but buy a letter of credit. He was most anxious, he said, that I should take no risk.

'I was much impressed by the seeming genuineness of the scheme and by the fact that the risk was apparently negligible. He asked me to respect the Russian's urgent plea that I should not speak a word to a soul either about my intentions or my plans. I bought the letter of credit, and it was arranged that I should travel to Dr Ingham's house by car, spend the night there and go on by the mid-day boat to Calais and Switzerland.

'I arrived at Grayne Hall at about six o'clock in the evening, and I was impressed by the luxury of the place. I hadn't the slightest suspicion that anything was wrong.

'At half past seven I joined Dr Ingham and his wife at dinner. I didn't drink anything until the port came round, but after that I have no recollection of what happened until I woke and found myself in a small stone chamber. There was a candle fixed to a stone niche, with half a dozen other candles and a box of matches to supply the light, the only light I saw until I was rescued. There was an iron bed, a patch of carpet on the floor, and a washstand, but no other furniture. Twice in the twenty-four hours the two men, who are known as Thomas and Leonard, and whom I remember having seen acting as servants, took me out for exercise up and down a long stone corridor which ran the length of the house. I did not see any other prisoner but I knew they were there because I had heard one shouting. My letter of credit had been taken from me. I only saw the man Kennedy once, when he came down and asked me to write a letter on the notepaper of a foreign hotel, addressed to my daughter, and telling her I was well and that she was not to worry about me.'

It was clear that the success of the scheme depended on the discretion of Litnoff. The man was a drunkard, but so long as he gave no hint of where his money came from, there was no danger to the gang. It was when he began to talk about the diamond clasp that the Kennedys decided that, for their own safety, they must silence him. They knew the game was up and made preparations for a getaway, but to the end they hoped they might avoid this. I discovered by inquiry that a small yacht had been chartered provisionally a week before their arrest. It was at the time in Dover Harbour, and if their plans were carried out, they were leaving a few days after my arrival at Grayne Hail.

A new complication arose when Kennedy went down to carry food to the prisoners on the night of Gelpin's death. The two servants were away in London. They had been commissioned to stop Edelsheim from seeing me. It is possible that Kennedy over-rated his strength, or placed too much reliance on the revolver which he carried—one which he had taken from another prisoner—Frank Seafield.

Kennedy states that Gelpin, who was a very strong man, attacked him without provocation; as to this we shall never know the truth, but he was killed in the corridor, because the other prisoners heard the shot.

In the early hours of the morn the two servants returned, and the body was driven straight away to London and deposited in Epping Forest.

I cannot exactly state when my own suspicions concerning Dr Ingham were aroused. I rather think it was on the occasion of his first visit to me. His obvious anxiety to anticipate the arrival of Joan Ralph, Alsby's statement, my talk with the chemist, and Edelsheim's narrative all pointed to one conclusion; obviously here was a confidence trick on a large scale and, after I had seen the survey map of the district in which Grayne Hall is situated, and made a few inquiries about the old castle, the possibility that this was a case of wholesale kidnapping became a certainty.

I had to be sure that 'Dr Ingham' was Kennedy, and on the last occasion we met in my office, I was compelled, I regret to say, to slander his mother. Though he was livid with rage, he kept control of himself, but he showed me enough to satisfy me that my suspicions were correct.

I tried the same trick at Grayne Hall, but I only did it after lighting a magnesium match, which was a signal agreed upon between myself and the police who, I knew, were outside the house, that it was time for them to make a move.

Underneath he wrote:

Casius Kennedy, convicted of murder at the CCC. Executed at Pentonville Prison. (Elford—executioner.)
Elsa Kennedy, convicted at CCC. Life.
Thomas J. Pentafard, convicted at CCC. Criminal conspiracy and accessory to murder. Life.
Leonard Polenski, convicted at CCC. Criminal conspiracy and accessory to murder. Life.

The Crook in Crimson

First published as "The Crook in Crimson" in The Thriller, Mar 23, 1929

Chapter I: Hope!

IN the dusk of the evening the waterman brought his skiff under the overhanging hull of the Baltic steamer and rested on his oars, the little boat rising and falling gently in the swell of the river. A grimy, unshaven, second officer looked down from the open porthole and spat thoughtfully into the water. Apparently he did not see the swarthy-faced waterman with the tuft of grey beard, and as apparently the waterman was oblivious of his appearance. Presently the unshaven man with the faded gold band on the wrist of his shabby jacket drew in his head and shoulders and disappeared.

A few seconds later a square wooden case was heaved through the porthole and fell with a splash in the water. For a moment one sharp corner was in sight, then it sank slowly beneath the yellow flood. A small black buoy bobbed up, and the waterman watched it with interest. To the buoy was attached a stout cord, and the cord was fastened to the case. He waited, moving his oars slowly, until the buoy was on the point of being sucked out of sight; then, with a turn of his wrist, he hooked an oar under the cord—literally hooked, for at the end of the short blade was a little steel crook.

Pushing the boat forward, he reached for the buoy and drew this into the stern sheets, fastened the cord round a wooden pin, and, lifting his oars, allowed the tide to carry him under the steamer's stern. Anchored in midstream was a dingy-looking barge and towards this he guided the skiff.

A heavily-built young man came from the aft deck of the barge, and, reaching down a boathook, drew the skiff alongside. The swarthy man held on to the side of the barge, whilst the boathook was transferred to the taut line astern. The younger man did no more than fasten the soaking cord to a small bight. By this time the occupant of the skiff was on board.

'Nobody about, Ligsey?' he asked gruffly.

'Nobody, cap'n,' said the younger man.

The captain said nothing more, but walked to the deck-house astern and disappeared down the companion-way, pulling the hatch close after him. There he stayed till the estuary was a black void punctured with dim ships' lights.

Ligsey went forward to where his youthful assistant sat on an overturned bucket, softly playing a mouth-organ. He stopped being musical long enough to remark that the tide was turning.

'We going up to-night?' he asked.

Ligsey nodded. He had already heard the chuff-chuff of the motor in the stern of the barge, where the skipper was starting it.

'What we hangin' around here for?' asked the youth curiously. 'We've missed one tide—we could have been up to Greenwich by now. Why don't Captain Attymar—'

'Mind your own business!' growled the mate.

He heard the swarthy man calling him and went aft.

'We'll get that case in and stow it.' he said in a low voice. 'I left a place in the bricks.'

Together they pulled gingerly at the cord and brought the square, soaked packing-case to sight. Ligsey leaned over and gripped it with an instrument like a pair of huge ice-tongs, and the dripping case was brought to the narrow deck and stowed expeditiously in the well of the barge.

The Alloluna invariably carried bricks between a little yard on the Essex coast and Tenny's

Wharf. Everybody on the river knew her for an erratic and a dangerous-steering craft. The loud chuffing of her engine was an offence. Even nippy tug.boats gave her yawing bows a wide berth. The boy was called aft to take charge of the engine, and Ligsey took the tiller. It was five o'clock on a spring morning when she came to Tenny's Wharf, which is at Rotherhithe.

As a wharfage it had few qualities attractive to the least fastidious of bargees. It consisted of a confined space with room for two builders' lorries to be backed side by side (though it required some manoeuvring to bring them into position), and the shabby little house where Joe Attymar lived. Through the weather-beaten gate, which opened at intervals to admit the builders' carts, was Shadwick Lane. It had none of the picturesque character of the slum it used to be, when its houses were of wood and water-butts stood in every back-yard. Nowadays it consists of four walls, two on either side of the street. Bridging each pair is an inverted 'V' of slate, called a roof, and at frequent intervals there are four red chimney-pots set on a small, square, brick tower. These denote roughly where lateral walls divide one hutch from another. Each partition is called a 'house,' for which people pay rent when they can afford it. The walls which face the street have three windows and a doorway to each division.

Joe Attymar's house did not properly stand in the lane at all, and Shadwick Lane was only remotely interested in the barge-master, for the curious reason that he could reach his house and yard by Shadwick Passage, a tortuous alley that threaded a way between innumerable back-yards, and under the shadow of a high warehouse, to Tooley Street. Year after year the swarthy man with the little iron-grey beard and the shaggy eyebrows brought his barge up the river, always with a cargo of bricks. And invariably the barge went down empty and without his presence; for, for some reason, there was neither passenger nor skipper on the down-river trip. This fact was unknown to the people of Shadwick Lane. They were even unaware that Joe Attymar did not sleep in his house more than one night every month. They knew, of course, from the muddy old motor-car that he drove through the wide gates occasionally, that he went abroad, but guessed that he was engaged in the legitimate business of lighterman.

THERE are gaming houses which harass the police, strange little clubs and other establishments less easy to write about, but Mr Attymar was not associated with one of these. Such problems are, in one shape or another, perennial! Occasionally they grow acute and just at that moment the question of systematic smuggling was worrying Scotland Yard considerably.

Chief Constable Mason sent for Inspector Gaylor.

'They've pulled in a fellow who was peddling dope in Lisle Street last night,' he said, 'You might see him after his remand. I have an idea he'll squeak.'

But the man in question was no squeaker, though he had certainly given that impression when he was taken red-handed. He said enough, however, to the patient detective to suggest that he might say more.

'All that I could find out,' said Gaylor, 'is that this selling organization is nearly foolproof. The gang that we rushed last year isn't handling the output, but I'm satisfied that it still has the same governor.'

'Get him,' said the Chief, who was in the habit of asking for miracles in the same tone as he asked for his afternoon tea. And then a thought struck him. 'Go along and see Reeder. The Public Prosecutor was telling me today that Reeder is available for any extra work. He may be able to help, anyway.'

Mr Reeder heard the request, sighed and shook his head. 'I'm afraid it is rather—um—outside my line of business. Dope? There used to be a man named Moodle. It may not have been his name, but he had associations with these wretched people—'

'Moodle, whose name was Sam Oschkilinski, has been dead nearly a year,' said Gaylor.
'Dear me!' said Mr Reeder, in a hushed voice appropriate to one who has lost a dear friend. 'Of what did he die?'
'Loss of breath,' said Gaylor vulgarly.
Mr Reeder knew nothing more that he could recall about dope merchants.
'Haven't you some record on your files?' suggested Gaylor.
'I never keep files, except—um—nail files,' said Mr Reeder.
'Perhaps,' suggested Gaylor, 'one of your peculiar friends—'
'I have no friends,' said Mr Reeder
But here he did not speak the exact truth.
Mr Reeder was an authority on poultry and his acquaintance with Johnny Southers began in a fowl-house. Johnny lived three doors from Mr Reeder. He was rather a nice young man, fair-haired and good-looking. He had in Mr Reeder's eyes the overwhelming advantage of being a very poor conversationalist.
Anna Welford lived in the house opposite, so that it may be said that the scene was set, for the curious tragedy of Joe Attymar, on a very small stage.
It was through the unromantic question of a disease which attacked Johnny Southers' prize hens that Mr Reeder met Anna. She happened to be in the Southers' back garden when Mr Reeder was engaged in his diagnosis. She was a slim girl, rather dark, with amazing brown eyes.
Johnny did not fall in love with her at first sight. He had known her since she was so high: when he was a boy she was endurable to him. As a young man he thought her views on life were sound. He discovered he was in love with her as he discovered he was taller than his father. It was a subject for surprise.
It was brought home to him when Clive Desboyne called in his new car to take Anna to a dinner-dance. He resented Mr Desboyne's easy assurance, the proprietorial way he handed Anna into the car. Thereafter Johnny found himself opening and examining packing-cases and casks and barrels at the Customs House with a sense of inferiority and the hopelessness of his future.
In such a mood he consulted his authority on poultry, and Mr Reeder listened with all the interest of one who was hearing a perfectly new and original story which had never been told before by or to any human being.
'I know so very little—um—about love,' said Mr Reeder awkwardly. 'In fact—er—nothing. I would like to advise you to—um—let matters take their course.'
Very excellent, if vague, advice. But matters took the wrong course, as it happened.

Chapter II: Reeder's Investigation

ON the following Saturday night, as Mr Reeder was returning home, he saw two men fighting in Brockley Road. He had what is called in Portuguese a repugnancio to fighting men. When the hour was midnight and the day was Saturday, there was a considerable weight of supposition in favour of the combat being between two gentlemen who were the worse for intoxicating drink, and it was invariably Mr Reeder's practice to cross, like the Philistine, to the other side of the road.

But the two young men who were engaged in such a short silent and bitter contest were obviously no hooligans of lower Deptford. Nevertheless, Mr Reeder hardly felt it was the occasion to act either as mediator or timekeeper.

He would have passed them by, and did in fact come level with them, when one walked across the road, leaving his companion—though that hardly seems the term to apply to one who had been so bruised and exhausted that he was hanging on to the railings—to recover as best he could. It was then that Mr Reeder saw that one of the contestants was John Southers. He was husky and apologetic.

'I'm terribly sorry to have made a fuss like this,' he said. 'I hope my father didn't hear me. This fellow is intolerable.'

The intolerable man on the other side of the street was moving slowly towards where a car was parked by the pavement. They watched him in silence as he got in and, turning the car violently, went off towards the Lewisham High Road and, from the direction he took, central London.

'I've been to a dance,' said the young man, a little inconsequently.

'I hope,' said Mr Reeder with the greatest gentleness, 'that you enjoyed yourself.'

Mr Southers did not seem disposed at the moment to offer a fuller explanation. As they neared Reeder's gate he said:

'Thank God, Anna was inside before it started! He's been insulting to me all the evening. As a matter of fact, she asked me to call and take her home, otherwise I shouldn't have met him.'

There had been a dance somewhere in the City, at a livery hall. Anna had gone with Clive Desboyne, but the circumstances under which Johnny called for her were only vaguely detailed. Nor did Mr Reeder hear what was the immediate cause of the quarrel which had set two respectable young men at fisticuffs in the reputable suburban thoroughfare.

To say that he was uninterested would not be true. The matter, however, was hardly pressing. He hoped that both parties to the little fracas might have forgotten the cause of their quarrel by the following morning.

He did not see Johnny again for the remainder of the week. Mr Reeder went about his business, and it is doubtful whether Johnny occupied as much as five minutes of his thoughts, until the case of Joe Attymar came into his purview.

He was again called to Scotland Yard on a consultation. He found Gaylor and the Chief Constable together, and they were examining a very dingy-looking letter which had come to the Yard in the course of the day.

'Sit down, Reeder,' said the chief. 'Do you know a man called Attymar?'

Mr Reeder shook his head. He had never heard of Joe Attymar.

'This is a thing we could do ourselves without any bother at all,' interrupted the Chief, 'but there are all sorts of complications which I won't bother you with. We believe there's a member of the staff of one of the Legations in this business, and naturally we want this fact to come out accidentally, and not as the result of any direct investigation by the police.'

Mr Reeder then learned about Joe Attymar, the barge-master, of the little wharf at the end of Shadwick Lane, of the small house nearby, and the barge Allanuna that went up and down the Thames year in and year out and brought bricks. He did not hear at that moment, or subsequently, what part the Legation played, or which Legation it was, or if there was any Legation at all. In justice to his acumen it must be said that he doubted this part of the story from the first, and the theory at which he eventually arrived, and which was probably correct, was that the part he was called upon to play was to stampede Attymar and his associates into betrayal of their iniquity. For this was at a period when Mr Reeder's name and appearance were known from one end of the river to the other, when there was hardly a bargee or tug-hand who could not have drawn, and did not draw, a passable caricature of that worthy man who had been instrumental in breaking up one of the best-organized gangs of river thieves that had ever amalgamated for an improper purpose.

Mr Reeder scratched his nose and his lips drooped dolefully. 'I was hoping—um—that I should not see that interesting stream for a very long time.'

He sat down and listened patiently to a string of uninteresting facts. Joe Attymar brought bricks up the river—had been bringing them for many years—at a price slightly lower than his competitors. He carried for four builders, and apparently did a steady, if not too prosperous, trade. He was believed locally to be rolling in money, but that is a reputation which Shadwick Lane applied to any man or woman who was not forced at frequent intervals to make a call at the local pawn shop. He kept himself to himself, was unmarried, and had no apparent interests outside of his brick lighterage.

'Fascinating,' murmured Mr Reeder. 'It sounds almost like a novel, doesn't it?'

After he had gone...

'I don't see what's fascinating about it,' said Mason, who did not know Mr Reeder very well.

'That's his idea of being funny,' said Gaylor.

It was a week later, and the Allanuna lay at anchor off Queensborough, when a small boat towed by a local boatman, carrying a solitary passenger, came slowly out, under the watchful and suspicious eye of Ligsey, the mate. The boat rowed alongside the barge, and Ligsey had a view of a man with a square hat and lopsided glasses, who sat in the stern of the boat, an umbrella between his legs, apparently making a meal of the big handle! And, seeing him, Ligsey, who knew a great deal about the river and its scandals, started up from his seat with an exclamation. He was blinking stupidly at the occupant of the boat when Mr Reeder came up to him.

'Good morning,' said Mr Reeder.

Ligsey said nothing.

'I suppose I should say "afternoon,"' continued the punctilious Mr Reeder. 'Is the captain aboard?'

Ligsey cleared his throat.

'No, sir, he ain't.'

'I suppose you wouldn't object if I came aboard?'

Mr Reeder did not wait for the answer, but, with surprising agility, drew himself up on to the narrow deck of the barge. He looked round with mild interest. The hatches were off, and he had a good view of the cargo.

'Bricks are very interesting things,' he said pleasantly. 'Without bricks we should have no houses;

without straw we should have no bricks. It seems therefore a very intelligent act to pack bricks in straw, to remind them, as it were, of what they owe to this humble—um—vegetable.'

Ligsey did not speak, but he swallowed.

'What I want to know,' Mr Reeder went on, and his eyes were never still, 'is this. Would it be possible to hire this barge?'

'You'll have to ask the captain about that,' said Ligsey huskily.

His none too clean face was a shade paler. The stories of Reeder that had come down the river had gained in the telling. He was credited with supernatural powers of divination; his knowledge and perspicuity were unbounded. For the first time in years Ligsey found himself confronted with slowly-moving machinery of the law; it was a little terrifying and his emotions were not at all what he had anticipated. He used to tell Joe Attymar: '... If they ever come to me I'll give 'em a saucy answer.' And here 'they' had come to him, but no saucy answer hovered on his lips. He felt totally inadequate.

'When are you expecting the captain?' asked Mr Reeder, in his blandest manner.

'Tonight or tomorrow—I don't know,' stammered Ligsey. 'He'll pick us up, I suppose.'

'Gone ashore for dispatches?' asked Mr Reeder pleasantly. 'Or possibly to wire to the owners? No, no, it couldn't be that: he is the owner. How interesting! He'll be coming off in a few moments with sealed orders under his arm. Will you tell me'—he pointed to the hold—'why you leave that square aperture in the bricks? Is that one of the secrets of packing, or shall I say stowage?'

Ligsey went whiter.

'We always leave it like that,' he said, and did not recognize the sound of his own voice.

Mr Reeder would have descended to the cabin, but the hatch was padlocked. He did invite himself down to the little cubby hole, in the bow of the boat, where Ligsey and the boy slept; and, strangely enough, Mr Reeder carried in his pocket, although it was broad daylight, a very powerful torch which revealed every corner of Ligsey's living place as it had never been revealed before.

'Rather squalid, isn't it?' asked Mr Reeder, 'A terrible thing to have to live in these circumstances and conditions. But of course one can live in a much worse place.'

He made this little speech after his return to the fresh air of the deck, and he was fanning himself with the brim of his high-crowned hat.

'One can live for example,' he went on, surveying the picturesque shore of Queensborough vacantly, 'in a nice clean prison. I know plenty of men who would rather live in prison than at—um—Buckingham Palace—though, of course, I have no knowledge that they've ever been invited to Buckingham Palace. But not respectable men, men with wives and families.'

Ligsey's face was a blank.

'With girls and mothers.'

Ligsey winced.

'They would prefer to remain outside. And, of course, they can remain outside if they're only sufficiently sensible to make a statement to the police.'

He took from his pocket-book a card and handed it almost timorously to Ligsey.

'I live there,' said Mr Reeder, 'and I'll be glad to see you any time you're passing—are you interested in poultry?'

Ligsey was interested in nothing.

Mr Reeder signalled to the boatman, who pulled the skiff alongside, and he stepped down into the boat and was rowed back to the shore.

There was one who had seen him come and who watched him leave by train. When night fell, Joe Attymar rowed out to the barge and found a very perturbed lieutenant.

'Old Reeder's been here,' blurted Ligsey, but Joe stopped him with a gesture.

'Want to tell the world about it?' he snarled. 'Come aft.'

The thickset young man followed his commander.

'I know Reeder's been here: I've seen him. What did he want?'

Briefly Ligsey told him quite a number of unimportant details about the visit. It was not remarkable that he did not make any reference to the card or to Mr Reeder's invitation.

'That's done it,' said Ligsey when he had finished. 'Old Reeder's got a nose like a hawk. Asked me why we left that hole in the bricks. I've never had to deal with a detective before—'

'You haven't, eh?' sneered the other. 'Who was that water man who came aboard off Gravesend the other night? And why did I drop half-hundredweight of good stuff overboard, eh? You fool! We've had half a dozen of these fellows on board, all of 'em cleverer than Reeder. Did he ask you to tell him anything?'

'No,' said Ligsey instantly.

Joe Attymar thought for a little time, and then: 'We'll get up the anchor. I'm not waiting for the Dutch boat,' he said.

Ligsey's sigh of relief was audible at the other end of the barge.

Chapter III: Death

THIS visit of Reeder was the culmination of a series of inquiries he had conducted in the course of a few days. He turned in a short report to Scotland Yard, and went home to Brockley Road, overtaking Johnny Southers as he turned from Lewisham High Road. Johnny was not alone. 'Anna and I were discussing you,' he said, as they slackened their steps to match the more leisurely pace of Mr Reeder. 'Is it possible for us to see you for five minutes?'
It was possible. Mr Reeder ushered them up to his big, old fashioned sitting-room, inwardly hoping that the consultation would have no reference to the mysterious workings of the young and human heart.
They were going to get married.
'Anna's father knows, and he's been awfully decent about it,' said Johnny, 'and I'd like you to know too, Mr Reeder.'
Mr Reeder murmured something congratulatory. That matter of love and loving was at any rate shelved.
'And Desboyne has been awfully decent—I told Anna all about that rather unpleasant little scene you witnessed—he never told her a word. He wrote apologizing to Anna, and wrote an apology to me. He has offered me a very good position in Singapore if I care to take it—he's terribly rich, and it sounds very good.'
'It doesn't sound good to me.' Anna's voice was decisive. 'I appreciate Clive's generosity, but I don't think Johnny ought to give up his Civil Service work except for something better in England. I want you to persuade him, Mr Reeder.'
Mr Reeder looked from one to the other dismally. The idea of persuading anybody to do anything in which he himself was not greatly absorbed filled him with dismay. As a mentor to the young he recognized his limitations. He liked Johnny Southers as he liked any decent young fellow. He thought Anna Welford was extraordinarily pretty; but even these two facts in conjunction could not arouse him to enthusiasm.
'I don't want much persuading,' said Johnny, to his relief. 'I've got something else up my sleeve—a pretty big thing. I'm not at liberty to talk about it; in fact, I've been asked not to. If that comes off, the Singapore job will be refused. It isn't so very difficult now. The point is this, Mr Reeder: if you were offered a partnership in a thriving concern, that could be made into something very big if one put one's heart and soul into it, would you accept?'
Mr Reeder looked at the ceiling and sighed. 'Hypotheses always worry me, Mr Southers. Perhaps, when the moment comes, if you could tell me all about the business, I may be able to advise you, although I confess I have never been regarded as a man whose advice was worth two—um—hoots.'
'That's what I wanted to see you about, Mr Reeder.' Anna nodded slowly. 'I'm so terribly afraid of Johnny leaving the service for an uncertainty, and I do want him to talk the matter over with you. I don't want to know his secrets'—there was the ghost of a smile in her eyes—'I think I know most of the important ones.'
Mr Reeder looked round miserably. He felt himself caught and entangled in a network of dull domesticity. He was, if the truth be told, immensely bored and, had he been more temperamental, he might have screamed. He wished he had not overtaken these loitering lovers, or that they

would apply to one of those periodicals which maintain a department devoted to advising the young and the sentimental in the choice of their careers. It was with the greatest happiness that he closed the door on their small mystery and devoted himself to the serious business of high tea. Mr Reeder had many anxieties to occupy his mind in the next few days, and the fact that he had added Joe Attymar to his list of his enemies, even if he were aware of the fact, was not one of these.

In the gaols of a dozen countries were men who actively disliked him. Meister of Hamburg, who used to sell United States bills by the hundredweight, Lefere, the clever wholesale engraver of lire notes, Monsatta, who specialized in English flyers, Madame Pensa of Pisa, who for many years was the chief distributor of forged money in Eastern and Southern Europe, Al Selinski, the paper maker, Don Leishmer, who printed French milles by the thousand, they all knew Mr Reeder, at least by name, and none of them had a good word for him, except Monsatta, who was large-minded and could detach himself from his personal misfortunes.

Letters came to Mr Reeder from many peculiar sources. It was a curious fact that a very large number of Mr Reeder's correspondents were women. A sensible number of the letters which came to him were of a most embarrassing character.

His name had been mentioned in many cases that had been heard at the Old Bailey. He himself had, from time to time, stood up in the witness stand, a lugubrious and unhappy figure, and had given evidence in his hesitant and deferential way against all manner of wrong-doers, but mostly forgers.

He was variously described as 'an expert,' as 'a private detective,' as 'a bank official.' In a sense he was all these, yet none of them entirely. Judges and certain barristers knew that he was at the call of the Public Prosecutor's Department. It was said that privately he enjoyed a status equivalent in rank to a superintendent of police. He certainly had a handsome retaining fee from the Bankers' Association, and probably drew pay from the Government, but nobody knew his business. He banked at Torquay and the manager of the bank was his personal friend.

But the net result of his fugitive appearances in court was that quite intelligent women were seized with the idea that he was the man who should be employed to watch their husbands and to procure the evidence necessary for their divorces. Business men wrote to him asking him to investigate the private lives of their partners; quite a few commissions were offered by important commercial concerns, but none of these appealed to Mr Reeder, and with his own hand he would write long and carefully punctuated letters explaining that he was not a private detective in the real sense of the word.

He was not surprised, therefore when, some four days after his talk with Johnny Southers, he received a letter addressed from a Park Lane flat, requesting his services. He turned first to the signature and with some difficulty deciphered it as 'Clive Desboyne.' For a moment the name, while it had a certain familiarity, was difficult to attach, and then he remembered the quarrel he had witnessed, and realized that this was the other party to that unhappy conflict.

The letter was typewritten and ran:

'Dear Sir, I happen to know your private address because Miss Welford pointed it out to me one evening when I was visiting her. I am in rather a delicate position, and I am wondering whether I could employ your services professionally to extricate myself? Since the matter affects Southers, whom I think you know (I have learned since that you were a witness of a certain disgraceful episode, for which I was probably more to blame than he), I thought you might be willing to see me. I want you to undertake this task on a professional basis and charge me your usual fees. I

shall be away until Friday night, but there is no immediate urgency. If I could call some time after ten on Friday I should be eternally grateful.
Yours, etc.'

Mr Reeder's first inclination was to take out a sheet of paper and write a firm but polite refusal to see Mr Desboyne, however stringent might be his predicament. He had written the first three words when one of those curious impulses which came to him at times, and which so often urged him to the right course, stayed his hand. Instead he sent a laconic telegram agreeing to the young man's suggestion.

The day of the appointment was a busy one for Mr Reeder. Scotland Yard had made two important discoveries—a small garage in the north of London, which contained nearly 400 lbs. of marijuana, had been raided in the early hours of the morning, and this was followed up by a second raid in a West End mansion flat, where large quantities of heroin and cocaine were unearthed by the police.

'It looks as though we've found one of the principal distributing agents,' said Gaylor. 'We've got the barge under observation, and we're taking the chance of arresting Attymar as soon as he steps on board.'

'Where is it?'

'Off Greenwich,' said Gaylor.

Mr Reeder dived down into his pocket and produced an envelope. The paper was grimy, the address was a scrawl. He took from this as dingy a letter and laid it on the table before Gaylor.

'Dear Sir, I can give you informacion. I will call at your howse on Sunnday morning. From a Friend.'

Gaylor inspected the envelope. The date-stamp was 'Greenwich.'

'He had some doubt about sending it at all: the flap has been opened and closed again—I presume this is Ligsey; his real name is William Liggs. He's had no convictions, but he hasn't been above suspicion. You'll see him?'

'If he comes,' said Mr Reeder. 'So many of these gentlemen who undertake to supply information think better of it at the last moment.'

'It may be too late,' said Gaylor.

It was at the end of a very heavy and tiring day that Mr Reeder went back to his house, forgetting the appointment he had so rashly made. He had hardly got into the house before the bell rang, and it was then that he realized, with bitter regret, that he had robbed himself of an hour's sleep which was badly needed.

Mr Desboyne explained that he had driven down from his club, where he had bathed and changed after his long journey from the West of England.

'I feel very ashamed to bother you at this hour of the night, Mr Reeder,' he said with an apologetic smile, 'but I feel rather like the villain of the piece, and my vanity has made me put matters right.'

Mr Reeder looked round helplessly for a chair, found one and pointed to it, and Desboyne drew it up to the table where the detective was sitting.

He was a man of thirty-three or thirty-five, good-looking, with a very pleasant, open face and a pair of grey eyes that twinkled good-humouredly.

'You saw the fight?... Lord! that fellow could punch! I thoroughly deserved what I got, which certainly wasn't very much. I was very rude to him. But then, like a fool, I went to the other extreme, and I've got him a job in Singapore—of course he'll take it—and I'm most anxious to get out of my offer.'

Mr Reeder looked at him in surprise, and the young man laughed ruefully.

'I suppose you think that's odd? Well, I'm rather impetuous and I've got myself into a bit of a hole. And it's a bigger hole than I knew, because I'm terribly fond of Anna Welford, and she's terribly unfond of me! Southers is rather in the position of a successful rival, so that everything I say or do must be suspect. That's the awful thing about it!'

'Why do you wish to cancel the appointment?' asked Mr Reeder.

He could have added that, so far as he could recall, the appointment had already been cancelled. Clive Desboyne hesitated.

'Well, it's a difficult story to tell.'

He rose from his seat and paced up and down the room, his hands thrust into his pockets, a frown on his face.

'Do you remember the night of the fight? I don't suppose that's graven on your memory. It arose out of something I said to our friend as we left the City hall. Apparently—I only discovered this afterwards—there was a man out there waiting to see Southers, but in the excitement of our little fracas—which began in the City, by the way—Southers didn't see the man, who either followed him to Lewisham or came on ahead of him. He must have been present in the street when the fight took place. When I got home that night the hall-porter asked me if I would see a very seedy-looking individual and, as I wasn't in the mood to see anybody, I refused. A few days later I was stopped in Piccadilly by a man who I thought was a beggar—a healthy-looking beggar, but most beggars are that way. He started by telling me he'd seen the fight, and said he could tell me something about Southers. I wasn't feeling as savage then as I had been, and I'd have hoofed him off, but he was so insistent, and in the end I told him to call at my flat. He came that night and told me the most extraordinary story. He said his name was'—Clive Desboyne frowned—'the name's slipped me for the moment, but it will come back. He was a mate or assistant on a barge run by a man named Attymar—'

'Ligsey?' suggested Mr Reeder, and the other nodded.

'That's the name—Ligsey. I'm cutting the story short because it took a tremendous long time to tell, and I don't want it to bore you as it bored me. They've been running some kind of contraband up the river on the barge, for apparently Attymar is a smuggler on a large scale. That was a yarn I didn't believe at first, though, from the things he told me, it seemed very likely that he spoke the truth. Certain articles were smuggled up the river on the barge, and others were passed through the Customs by Southers.'

Mr Reeder opened his mouth very wide.

'Now I'll tell you the truth.' Clive Desboyne's voice was very earnest. 'I wanted to believe that story. In my heart of hearts I dislike John Southers—I'd be inhuman if I didn't. At the same time I wanted to play the game. I told this fellow he was a liar but he swore it was true. He thinks the police are going to arrest Attymar, and when they do, Attymar will spill the beans, to use his own expression. In the meantime I have recommended Southers to a very important and responsible job in Singapore, and naturally, if this story comes out, I'm going to look pretty foolish. I don't mind that,' he added quietly, 'but I do mind Anna Welford marrying this man.'

Mr Reeder plucked at his lower lip. 'Do you know Attymar?'

The young man shook his head.

'I can't even say that I know Ligsey, but if he keeps his promise I shall know Attymar tomorrow morning.'

'What was his promise?' asked Mr Reeder.

'He says Attymar has documentary proof—he didn't use that expression but that is what he meant—and that he was going to Attymar's house tonight to get it.'

Again Mr Reeder thought, staring into vacancy.

'When did you see him last?'

'The morning I wrote to you, or rather the morning you received the letter.' He made a little gesture of despair. 'Whatever happens, Anna's going to think I'm the most awful—'

The telephone bell rang sharply. Mr Reeder, with a murmured apology, picked up the receiver and listened with a face that did not move. He only asked 'What time?' and, after a long pause, said 'Yes.' As he was replacing the receiver, Desboyne went on:

'What I should like to do is to see Attymar—'

Mr Reeder shook his head. 'I'm afraid you won't see Attymar. He was murdered between nine and ten tonight.'

Chapter IV: The Arrest

IT was half past twelve when Mr Reeder's taxi brought him into Shadwick Lane, which was alive with people. A police cordon was drawn across the gate, but Gaylor, who was waiting for him, conducted him into the yard.
'We're dragging the river for the body,' he explained.
'Where was it committed?' asked Mr Reeder.
'Come inside,' said the other grimly, 'and then you will ask no questions.'
It was not a pleasant sight that met Mr Reeder's eyes, though he was a man not easily sickened. The little sitting-room was a confusion of smashed furniture, the walls splashed with red. A corner table, however, had been left untouched. Here were two glasses of whisky, one full, the other half empty. A half-smoked cigar was carefully laid on a piece of paper by the side of these.
'The murder was committed here and the body was dragged to the edge of the wharf and thrown into the water,' said Gaylor. 'There's plenty of evidence of that.
'We've taken possession of a lot of papers, and we found a letter on the mantelpiece from a man named Southers—John Southers. No address, but evidently from the handwriting a person of some education. At nine twenty-five tonight Attymar had a visitor, a young man who was admitted through the wicket gate, and who was seen to leave at twenty five minutes to ten, about ten minutes after he arrived.'
Gaylor opened an attaché case and took out a battered, cheap silver watch; which had evidently been under somebody's heel. The glass was smashed, the case was bent out of shape. The hands stood at nine-thirty.
'One of the people here recognized this as Ligsey's—a woman who lives in the street who had pawned it for him on one occasion. It's important, because it probably gives us the hour of the murder, if you allow the watch to be a little fast or slow. It's hardly likely to be accurate. We've sent a description round of Southers; although it isn't a very good one, it'll probably be sufficient. I'm having a facsimile of the writing—'
'I can save you the trouble; here is the young man's address.'
Mr Reeder took a notebook from his pocket, scribbled a few lines and handed it to the detective. He looked glumly at the bloodstained room and the evidence of tragedy, followed the detective in silence, while Gaylor, with the aid of a powerful light, showed the telltale stains leading from the wharf, and...
'Very interesting,' said Mr Reeder. 'When you recover the bodies I should like to see them.'
He stared out over the river, which was covered by a faint mist—not sufficient to impede navigation, but enough to shroud and make indistinct objects thirty or forty yards away.
'The barge is at Greenwich, I think,' he said, after a long silence. 'Could I borrow a police launch?'
One of the launches was brought in to the crazy wharf and Mr Reeder lowered himself gingerly, never losing grip of the umbrella which no man had seen unfurled. It was a chilly night, an easterly wind blowing up the river, but he sat in the bow of the launch motionless, sphinxlike, staring ahead as the boat streaked eastwards towards Greenwich.
It drew up by the side of the barge, which was moored close to the Surrey shore, and a quavering voice hailed them.
'That you, Ligsey?'
Mr Reeder pulled himself on board before he replied. 'No, my boy,' he said gently, 'it is not

Ligsey. Were you expecting him?'

The youth held up his lantern, surveyed Mr Reeder and visibly quailed.

'You're a copper, ain't yer?' he asked tremulously. 'Have you pinched Ligsey?'

'I have not pinched Ligsey,' said Mr Reeder, patting the boy gently on the back. 'How long has he been gone?'

'He went about eight, soon after it was dark; the guv'nor come down for him.'

'The guv'nor come down for him,' repeated Mr Reeder in a murmur. 'Did you see the governor?'

'No, sir; he shouted for me to go below. Ligsey always makes me go below when him and the guv'nor have a talk.'

Mr Reeder drew from his pocket a yellow carton of cigarettes and lit one before he pursued his inquiries.

'Then what happened?'

'Ligsey come down and packed his ditty box, and told me I was to hang on all night, but that I could go to sleep. I was frightened about being left alone on the barge—'

Mr Reeder was already making his way down the companion to Ligsey's quarters. Evidently all the man's kit had been removed; even the sheets on his bed must have been folded and taken away, for the bunk was tumbled.

On a little swing table, which was a four-foot plank suspended from the deck above, was a letter. It was not fastened, and Mr Reeder made no secret in opening and reading its contents. It was in the handprint which, he had been informed, was the only kind of writing Attymar knew.

'Dear Mr Southers, If you come aboard the stuff is in the engine-room. I have got to be very careful because the police are watching.'

When he questioned the boy, whose name was Hobbs, he learned that Ligsey had come down and left the letter. Mr Reeder went aft and found the hatchway over the little engine-room unfastened, and descended into the strong-smelling depths where the engine was housed. It was here, evidently, that Attymar remained during his short voyages. There was a signal bell above his head, and a comfortable armchair had been fixed within reach of the levers.

His search here was a short one. Inside an open locker he found a small, square package, wrapped in oiled paper, and a glance at the label told him its contents, even though he did not read Dutch.

Returning to the boy, he questioned him closely. It was no unusual thing for Attymar to pick up his mate from the barge. The boy had once seen the launch, and described it as a very small tender. He knew nothing of Mr Southers, had never seen him on board the ship, though occasionally people did come, on which occasions he was sent below.

At his request, Mr Reeder was put ashore at Greenwich and got on the telephone to Gaylor. It was now two o'clock in the morning, and much had happened.

'We arrested that man Southers; found his trousers covered with blood. He admits he was at Attymar's house tonight, and tells a cock-and-bull story of what he did subsequently. He didn't get home till nearly twelve.'

'Extraordinary,' said Mr Reeder, and the mildness of the comment evidently irritated Inspector Gaylor.

'That's one way of putting it, but I think we've made a pretty good capture,' he said. 'We've got enough evidence to hang him. Attymar's left all sorts of notes on his invoices.'

'Amazing,' said Mr Reeder, and gathered from the abruptness with which he was cut off that, for some mysterious reason, he had annoyed the man at Scotland Yard.

He sent back a short report with the documents and the drugs to Scotland Yard, and drove home by taxi. It was three o'clock by the time he reached Brockley Road, and he was not surprised to find his housekeeper up and to hear that Anna Welford was waiting for him.

She was very white and her manner was calm.

'You've heard about Johnny being arrested—' she began. Mr Reeder nodded.

'Yes, I gave them the necessary information as to where he was to be found,' he said, and he saw the colour come and go in her face.

'I—I suppose you—you had to do your duty?' she said haltingly. 'But you know it's not true, Mr Reeder. You know Johnny... he couldn't...' Her voice choked.

Mr Reeder shook his head.

'I don't know Johnny really,' he said apologetically. 'He is—um—the merest acquaintance, Miss Welford. I am not saying that in disparagement of him, because quite a number of people who aren't my friends are respectable citizens. Did you see him before he was arrested?'

She nodded.

'Immediately before?'

'Half an hour before. He was terribly disappointed; he had gone to see about this partnership but he had a feeling that he'd been tricked, for nothing came of it. He'd arranged to see me, and I waited up for him... he was crossing the road to his own house when he was arrested.'

'Did he wear a blue suit or a grey suit?'

'A blue suit,' she said quickly.

Mr Reeder looked at the ceiling.

'Of course he wore a blue suit; otherwise—um...' He scratched his chin irritably. 'It was a cold night, too. I can't understand until I have seen his—um—trousers.'

She looked at him in bewilderment, a little fearfully. And then suddenly Mr Reeder gave one of his rare smiles and dropped a gentle hand on her shoulder.

'I shouldn't be too worried if I were you,' he said with a kindly look in his eyes. 'You've quite a number of good friends, and you will find Mr Desboyne will do a lot to help your Johnny.'

She shook her head.

'Clive doesn't like Johnny,' she said.

'That I can well believe,' said Mr Reeder good-humouredly. 'Nevertheless, unless I'm a bad prophet, you will find Mr Desboyne the one person who can clear up this—um—unpleasantness.'

'But who was the man who was killed? It's all so terribly unreal to me. Attymar was his name, wasn't it? Johnny didn't know anybody named Attymar. At least, he didn't tell me so. I'm absolutely stunned by this news, Mr Reeder. I can't realize its gravity. It seems just a stupid joke that somebody's played on us. Johnny couldn't do harm to any man.'

'I'm sure he couldn't,' said Mr Reeder soothingly, but that meant nothing.

Chapter V: The Red Stains

MR REEDER's housekeeper had, since his arrival, behaved with a certain secretiveness which could only mean that she had something important to communicate. It was after he had seen the girl to her house that he learned what the mystery was all about.

'The young gentleman who came to see you last night,' she said in a low voice. 'I've put him in the waiting-room.'

'Mr Desboyne?'

'That's the name,' she nodded. 'He said he wouldn't go until he'd seen you.'

In a few seconds Clive Desboyne was shown in.

'I've only just heard about Southers' arrest—it's monstrous! And the things I said about him tonight. Mr Reeder, I'll spend all the money you want to get this young man out of his trouble. My God, it's awful for Anna!'

Mr Reeder pulled at his long nose and said he thought it was rather unpleasant. 'And,' he added, 'for everybody.'

'They say this man Ligsey is dead too. If I'd had any sense I'd have brought over the note I had of our conversation.'

'I could call for it in the morning,' said Mr Reeder, and his voice was surprisingly brisk.

Mr Desboyne gazed at him in startled astonishment. It was as though this weary man with the drooping lips and tired eyes had suddenly received a great mental tonic.

'You made notes? Not one man in ten would have thought of that,' said Mr Reeder. 'I thought I was the only person who did it.'

Clive Desboyne laughed.

'I've given you the impression that I'm terribly methodical,' he said, 'and that isn't quite exact.' He looked at the watch on his wrist. 'It's too late to ask you to breakfast.'

'Breakfast is my favourite meal,' said Mr Reeder gaily.

Late as was the hour, he was standing in front of the polished mahogany door of 974, Memorial Mansions, Park Lane, at nine o'clock next morning. Mr Desboyne was not so early a riser, and indeed had doubted whether the detective would keep his promise. Mr Reeder was left standing in the hall while the valet went to inquire exactly how this strangely appearing gentleman should be disposed of.

There was plenty to occupy Mr Reeder's attention during his absence, for the wide hall was hung with photographs which gave some indication of Desboyne's wide sporting and theatrical interests. There was one interesting photograph, evidently an enlargement of a snapshot showing the House of Commons in the background, which held Mr Reeder's attention, the more so as the photograph also showed the corner of Westminster Bridge across which buses were moving. He was looking at this when Clive Desboyne joined him.

'Here is a piece of detective work,' said Mr Reeder triumphantly, pointing to the photograph. 'I can tell you almost to the week that picture was taken. Do you see those two omnibuses bearing the names of two plays? I happen to know there was only one week in the year when they were both running together.'

'Indeed,' said Desboyne, apparently not as impressed by this piece of deduction as Mr Reeder had expected.

He led the way to the dining-room, and Reeder found by the side of his plate three foolscap sheets covered with writing.

'I don't know whether you'll be able to read it,' said Desboyne, 'but you'll notice there are one or two things that I forgot to tell you at the interview. I think on the whole they favour Southers, and I'm glad I made a note of them. For example, he said he had never seen Southers and only knew him by name. That in itself is rather curious.'

'Very,' said Mr Reeder. 'Regarding that photograph in the hall—it must have been in May last year. I remember some years ago, by a lucky chance, I was able to establish the date on which a cheque was passed, as distinct from the date on which it was drawn, by the fact that the drawer had forgotten to sign one of his initials.'

It was surprising how much Mr Reeder, who was not as a rule a loquacious man, talked in the course of that meal. Mostly he talked about nothing. When Clive Desboyne led him to the murder Mr Reeder skilfully edged away to less unpleasant topics.

'It doesn't interest me very much, I confess,' he said. 'I am not a member of the—um—Criminal Investigation Department; I was merely called in to deal with this man's smuggling—and he seems to have smuggled pretty extensively. It is distressing that young Southers is implicated. He seems a nice lad, and has rather a sane view of the care of chickens. For example, he was telling me that he had an incubator...'

At the end of the meal he asked permission to take away the notes for study, and this favour was granted.

He was at the house in Shadwick Lane half an hour later. Gaylor, who had arranged to meet him there, had not arrived, and Mr Reeder had two men who had had semi-permanent jobs on the wharf. It was the duty of one to open and close the gates and pilot the lorries to their positions. He had also, as had his companion, to assist at the loading.

They had not seen much of Attymar all the years they had been there. He usually came in on one of the night or early morning tides. Ligsey paid them their wages.

'There was never any change,' said one mournfully. 'We ain't had the gates painted since I've bin here—we've had the same little anvil to keep the gate open—'

He looked round first one side and then the other. The same little anvil was not there.

'Funny,' he said.

Mr Reeder agreed. Who would steal a rusty little anvil? He saw the place where it had lain; the impression of it still stood in the dusty earth.

Later came Gaylor, in a hurry to show him over the other rooms of the house. There was a kitchen, a rather spacious cellar, which was closed by a heavy door, and one bedroom that had been divided into two unequal parts by a wooden partition. The bedroom was simply but cleanly furnished. There was a bed and bedstead, a dressing-table with a large mirror, and a chest of drawers, which was empty. Indeed, there was no article of Attymar's visible, except an old razor, a stubbly shaving brush and six worn shirts that had been washed until they were threadbare.

From the centre of the ceiling hung an electric light with an opalescent shade; another light hung over a small oak desk, in which, Gaylor informed him, most of the documents in the case had been found. But Mr Reeder's chief interest was in the mirror, and in the greasy smear which ran from the top left hand corner almost along the top of the mirror. The glass itself was supported by two little mahogany pillars, and to the top of each of these was attached a piece of string.

'Most amusing,' said Reeder, speaking his thoughts aloud.

'Remind me to laugh,' said Mr Gaylor heavily. 'What is amusing?'

For answer Mr Reeder put up his hand and ran the tip of his finger along the smear. Then he began to prowl around the apartment obviously looking for something, and as obviously disappointed that it could not be found.

'No, nothing has been taken out of here,' said Gaylor in answer to his question, 'except the papers. Here's something that may amuse you more.'

He opened a door leading to the bedroom. Here was a cupboard—it was little bigger. The walls and floor were covered with white tiles, as also was the back of the door. From the ceiling projected a large nozzle, and in one of the walls were two taps.

'How's that for luxury? Shower bath—hot and cold water. Doesn't that make you laugh?'

'Nothing makes me laugh except the detectives in pictures,' said Mr Reeder calmly. 'Do you ever go to the cinema, Gaylor?'

The inspector admitted that occasionally he did.

'I like to see detectives in funny films, because they always carry large magnifying glasses. Do they make you laugh?'

'They do,' admitted Mr Gaylor, with a contemptuous and reminiscent smile.

'Then get ready to howl,' said Mr Reeder, and from his pocket took the largest reading glass that Gaylor had ever seen.

Under the astonished eyes of the detective Reeder went down on his knees in the approved fashion, and began carefully to scrutinize the floor. Inch by inch he covered, stopping now and again to pick up something invisible to the Scotland Yard man, and placed it in an envelope which he had also taken from his pocket.

'Cigar ash?' asked Gaylor sardonically.

'Almost,' said Mr Reeder.

He went on with his search, then suddenly he sat back on his heels, his eyes ablaze, and held up a tiny piece of silver paper, less than a quarter of an inch square. Gaylor looked down more closely.

'Oh, it's a cigarette you're looking for?'

But Mr Reeder was oblivious to all sarcasm. Inside the silver paper was a scrap of transparent paper, so thin that it seemed part of the tinsel. Very carefully, however, he separated the one from the other, touched its surface and examined his finger-tips.

'Where's the fireplace?' he asked suddenly.

'There's a fireplace in the kitchen—that's the only one.' Mr Reeder hurried downstairs and examined this small apartment. There were ashes in the grate, but it was impossible to tell what had been burnt.

'I should like to say,' said Gaylor, 'that your efforts are wasted, for we've got enough in the diary to hang Southers twice over. Only I suspect you when you do things unnecessarily.'

'The diary?' Mr Reeder looked up.

'Yes, Attymar's.'

'So he kept a diary, did he?' Mr Reeder was quite amused. 'I should have thought he would, If I had thought about it at all.'

Then he frowned.

'Not an ordinary diary, of course? Just an exercise book. It begins—let me see—shall we say two weeks ago, or three weeks?'

Gaylor gazed at him in amazement. 'Mason told you?'

'No, he didn't tell me anything, partly because he hasn't spoken to me. But, of course, it would be in a sort of exercise book. An ordinary printed diary that began on the first of January would be unthinkable. This case is getting so fascinating that I can hardly stop laughing!'

He was not laughing; he was very serious indeed, as he stood in the untidy yard in front of the little house and looked across its littered surface.

'There is no sign of the tender that brought Ligsey here? The little boy on the barge was much more informative than he imagined! I'll tell you what to look for, shall I? A black, canoe-shaped motor boat which might hold three people at a pinch. Remember that—a canoe-shaped boat, say ten feet long.'

'Where shall I find it?' asked the fascinated Gaylor.

'At the bottom of the river,' said Mr Reeder calmly, 'and in or near it you will find a little anvil which used to keep the gate open!'

Mr Reeder had a very large acquaintance with criminals, larger perhaps than the average police officer, whose opportunities are circumscribed by the area to which he is attached; and he knew that the business of detection would be at a standstill if there were such a thing in the world as a really clever criminal. By the just workings of providence, men who gain their living by the evasion of the law are deprived of the eighth sense which, properly functioning, would keep them out of the hands of the police.

He made yet another survey of the house before he left, pointed out to Gaylor something which that officer had already noticed, namely, the bloodstains on the floor and the wall of a small lobby which connected the main living-room with the yard.

'Naturally I saw it,' said Gaylor, who was inclined to be a little complacent. 'My theory is that the fight started in the sitting-room; they struggled out into the passage—'

'That would be impossible,' murmured Mr Reeder.

Chapter VI: Mystery

John Southers made a brief appearance at the Tower of London Police Court—a dazed, bewildered young man, so overwhelmed by his position that he could do no more than answer the questions put to him by the magistrate's clerk.

Gaylor had seen him earlier in the morning.

'He said nothing except that he went to Attymar's house—oh, yes, he admits that—by appointment. He says Attymar kept him waiting for some time before he opened the door, and then only allowed him to come into the lobby. He tells some rambling story about Attymar sending him to meet a man at Highgate. In fact, it's the usual Man story.'

Mr Reeder nodded. He was not unacquainted with that mysterious man who figures in the narratives of all arrested persons. Sometimes it was a man who gave the prisoner the stolen goods in the possession of which he had been found; sometimes it was the man who asked another to cash a forged cheque; but always it was a vague Somebody who could never be traced. Half the work of investigation which occupied the attention of the detective force consisted of a patient search for men who had no existence except in the imaginations of prisoners under remand.

'Did he see him?' asked Mr Reeder.

Gaylor laughed. 'My dear chap, what a question!'

Mr Reeder fondled his bony chin. 'Is it possible to—um—have a little chat with our friend Southers?'

Gaylor was dubious, and had reason for his doubt. Chief Constable Mason and the high men at Headquarters were at the moment writhing under a periodical wave of criticism which sweeps across Scotland Yard at regular intervals; and their latest delinquency was the cross-examination of a man under suspicion of a serious crime. There had been questions in Parliament, almost a Royal Commission.

'I doubt it,' said Gaylor. 'The Chief is feeling rather sick about this Hanny business, and as the kick has come down from your department it isn't likely that they'll make an exception. I'll ask Mason and let you know.'

Mr Reeder was home that afternoon when Anna Welford called. She was most amazingly calm. Mr Reeder, who had shown some hesitation about receiving her, was visibly relieved.

'Have you seen Johnny?' was the first question she asked.

Mr Reeder shook his head, and explained to her that in the strictest sense he was not in the case, and that the police were very jealous of interference.

'Clive has been to see me,' she said when he had finished, 'and he has told me everything—he's terribly upset.'

'Told you everything?' repeated Mr Reeder.

She nodded.

'About Ligsey, and the story that Clive told you. I understood—in a way. He is doing everything he can for Johnny; he has engaged a lawyer and briefed counsel.'

For the second time Mr Reeder motioned her to a chair and, when she was seated, continued his own restless pacing.

'If there was any truth in that story, your Johnny should be rather well off,' he said. 'The wages of sin are rather—um—high. Yet his father told me this morning—I had a brief interview with him—that young Mr Southers' bank balance is not an excessive one.'

He saw her lower her eyes and heard the quick little sigh. 'They've found the money—I thought you knew that,' she said in a low voice.

Mr Reeder halted in his stride and peered down at her.

'They've found the money?'

She nodded.

'The police came and made a search about an hour ago, and they found a box in the toolshed with hundreds of pounds in it, all in notes.'

Mr Reeder did not often whistle, but he whistled now.

'Does Mr Desboyne know this?' he asked.

She shook her head.

'Clive doesn't know. It happened after he'd left. He's been terribly nice—he's made one confession that isn't very flattering to me.'

Reeder's eyes twinkled.

'That he is—um—engaged to somebody else?' he suggested, and she stared at him in amazement. 'Do you know?'

'One has heard of such things,' said Mr Reeder bravely.

'I was very glad,' she went on. 'It removed the'—she hesitated—'personal bias. He really is sorry for all he has said and done. Johnny's trouble has shaken him terribly. Clive thinks that the murder was committed by this man Ligsey,'

'Oh!' said Mr Reeder. 'That is interesting.'

He stared down at her, pursing his lips thoughtfully. 'The—um—police rather fancy that Mr Ligsey is dead,' he said, and there was a note of irritation in his voice as though he resented the police holding any theory at all. 'Quite dead—um—murdered, in fact.'

There was a long pause here. He knew instinctively that she had come to make some request, but it was not until she rose to go that she spoke her thoughts.

'Clive wanted to see you himself to make a proposition. He said that he didn't think you were engaged on the—official side of the case. He's got a tremendous opinion of your cleverness, Mr Reeder, and so of course have I. Is it humanly possible for you to take up this case... Johnny's side, I mean? Perhaps I'm being silly, but just now I'm clutching at straws.'

Mr Reeder was looking out of the window, his head moving from side to side.

'I'm afraid not,' he said. 'I really am afraid not! The people on your—um—friend's side are the police. If he is innocent, I am naturally on his side, with them. Don't you see, young lady, that when we prove a man's guilt we also prove everybody else's innocence?'

It was a long speech for Mr Reeder, and he had not quite finished. He stood with his hands deep in his pockets, his eyes half closed, his body swaying to and fro.

'Let me see now... if Ligsey were alive?... A very dense and stupid young man, quite incapable, I should have thought, of—um—so many things that have happened during the last twenty-four hours.'

After Anna had left, he went to Southers' house and interviewed Johnny's father. The old man was bearing his sorrow remarkably well. Indeed, his principal emotion was a loud fury against the people who dared accuse his son.

He led the way to the toolshed in the yard and showed the detective just where the box had been hidden.

'Personally, I never go into the shed. It's Johnny's. He's fond of gardening and, like you, Mr

Reeder, he has a fancy for poultry.'

'Is the shed kept locked?'

'No, I've never seen it locked,' said old Southers.

The place from which the box had been extricated was at the far end of the shed. It had been concealed behind a bag of chicken seed.

Mr Reeder took a brief survey of the garden: it was an oblong strip of ground, measuring about a hundred yards by twenty. At the further end of the garden was a wall which marked the boundary of the garden which backed on to it. The garden could be approached either from the door leading to a small glass conservatory, or along a narrow gravel strip which ran down one side of the house. Ingress, however, was barred by a small door stretched across the narrow path.

'But it's seldom locked,' said Southers. 'We leave it open for the milkman; he goes round to the kitchen that way in the morning.'

Mr Reeder went back to the garden and walked slowly along the gravel path which ran between two large flower-beds. At the farther end was a wired-in chicken run. Mr Reeder surveyed the flower-beds meditatively.

'Nobody has dug up the garden?' he asked, and, when the other replied in the negative: 'Then I should do a bit of digging myself if I were you, Mr Southers,' he said gently; 'and whether you tell the police what you find, or do not tell the police, is entirely a matter for your own conscience.'

He looked up at the sky for a long time as though he were expecting to see something unusual, and then:

'If it is consistent with your—um—conscience to say nothing about your discovery, and if you removed it or them to a safe place where it or they would not be found, it might be to the advantage of your son in the not too distant future.'

Mr Southers was a little agitated, more than a little bewildered, when his visitor left.

Mr Reeder was to learn that the ban on his activities in regard to the Attymar murder had been strengthened rather than relaxed, and he experienced a gentle but malignant pleasure in the thought that in one respect he had made their task a little more difficult.

It was Gaylor who brought the news.

'I spoke to the Chief about your seeing Southers in Brixton, but he thought it was best if you kept out of the case until the witnesses are tested.'

Mr Reeder's duties in the Public Prosecutor's Department were to examine witnesses prior to their appearance in court, to test the strength or the weakness of their testimony, and he had been employed in this capacity before his official connection with the department was made definite.

'At the same time,' Gaylor went on, 'if you can pick up anything we'll be glad to have it.'

'Naturally,' murmured Mr Reeder.

'I mean, you may by accident hear things—you know these people: they live in the same street: and I think you know the young lady Southers is engaged to?'

Mr Reeder inclined his head.

'There's another thing, Mr Reeder,' Gaylor evidently felt he was treading on delicate ground, having summarily declined and rejected the assistance of his companion. 'If you should hear from Ligsey—'

'A voice from the grave,' interrupted Mr Reeder.

'Well, there's a rumour about that he's not dead. In fact, the boy on the barge, Hobbs, says that Ligsey came alongside last night in a skiff and told him to keep his mouth shut about what he'd seen and heard. My own opinion is that the boy was dreaming, but one of Ligsey's pals said he'd also seen him or heard him—I don't know which. That's a line of investigation you might take on for your own amusement—'

'Investigation doesn't amuse me,' said Mr Reeder calmly; 'it bores me. It wearies me. It brings me in a certain—um—income, but doesn't amuse me.'

'Well,' said the detective awkwardly, 'if it interests you, that's a line you might take up.'

'I shall not dream of taking up any line at all. It means work, and I do not like work.'

Here, however, he was permitting himself to romance.

That afternoon he spent in the neighbourhood which Ligsey knew best. He talked with lorry drivers and van boys, little old women who kept tiny and unremunerative shops, and the consequence of all his oblique questionings was that he made a call in Little Calais Street, where lived an unprepossessing young lady who had gained certain social recognition—her portrait would appear in the next morning's newspapers—because she had been engaged to the missing man. She had, in fact, walked out with him, among others, for the greater part of a year.

Miss Rosie Loop did not suggest romance; she was short, rather stout, had bad teeth and a red face; for the moment she was important, and might not have seen Mr Reeder but for the mistaken belief that he was associated with the Press.

'Who shall I say it is?' asked her blowsy mother, who answered the door.

'The editor of The Times,' said Mr Reeder without hesitation.

In the stuffy little kitchen where the bereaved fiancée was eating bread and jam, Mr Reeder was given a clean Windsor chair, and sat down to hear the exciting happening of the previous night.

'I haven't told the Press yet,' said Rosie, who had a surprisingly shrill voice for one so equipped by nature for the deeper tones. 'He come last night. I sleep upstairs with mother, and whenever he used to anchor off the crik he used to come ashore, no matter what time it was, and throw up a couple of stones to let me know he was here. About 'arf past two it was last night, and lord! it gave me a start.'

'He threw up the stones to let you know he was there?' suggested Mr Reeder.

She nodded violently.

'And was it Mr Ligsey?'

'It was him!' she said dramatically. 'I wouldn't go to the window for a long time, but mother said "Don't be such a fool, a ghost carn't hurt yer," and then I pulled up the sash and there he was in his old oilskin coat. I asked him where he'd bin, but he was in a 'urry. Told me not to get worried about him as he was all right.'

'How did he look?' asked Mr Reeder.

She rolled her head impatiently.

'Didn't I tell yer it was the middle of the night. But that's what he said—"Don't get worried about anything"—and then he popped off.'

'And you popped in?' said Mr Reeder pleasantly. 'He didn't have a cold or anything, did he?'

Her mouth opened.

'You've seen him? Where is he?'

'I haven't seen him, but he had a cold?'

'Yes, he had,' she admitted, 'and so would you 'ave if you 'ad to go up and down that river all day and night. It's a horrible life. I hope he's going to give it up. He's bound to get some money if he comes forward and tells the police the truth. It was very funny, me thinkin' he was dead. We'd bin to buy our black—hadn't we, mother?'

Mother offered a hoarse confirmation.

'And all the papers sayin' he was dead, an' dragging the river for him, an' that Captain Attymar.

He used to treat Ligsey like a dog.'

'He hasn't written to you?'

She shook her head.

'He was never a one for writing.'

'What time was this?'

She could tell him exactly, because she had heard Greenwich church striking the half-hour.

Mr Reeder might be bored with investigation, but he found some satisfaction in boredom. The Allanuna still lay off Greenwich, and he hired a boat to take him to the barge. The disconsolate Master Hobbs was still on board, and even the fact that he was now commander did not compensate him for his loneliness, though apparently the police had supplied him with food and had arranged to relieve him that evening.

He was very emphatic about the visitation of Ligsey. He had rowed alongside and whistled to the boy—the whistle had wakened him. From under the companion steps he had looked over and seen him sitting in the boat, a big white bandage round his head. Miss Rosie had said nothing about the white bandage but, calling there on his way home, Reeder had confirmation.

'Yes, I forgot to tell you about that,' said Rosie. 'I see it under 'is 'at. I said "What's that white round your head?" Fancy me forgettin' to tell you that!'

As a matter of form, Mr Reeder, when he got home that night, jotted down certain sequences. At some time after eight on the night of the murder, Attymar had come in a launch, had collected Ligsey and taken him towards London. At nine-thirty Johnny Southers had called at Attymar's house and, according to his story, had been sent on a fool's errand to Highgate. At some time about eleven o'clock the murder had been discovered—Mr Reeder put down his pen and frowned.

'I'm getting old and stupid,' he said, reached for the telephone and called a number to which he knew Gaylor would certainly be attached at that hour.

It was Gaylor's clerk who answered him and, after about four minutes' wait, Gaylor himself spoke.

'Have you found anything, Mr Reeder?'

'I find I am suffering from a slight softening of the brain,' said Mr Reeder pleasantly. 'Do you realize I never asked how the murder was discovered?'

He heard Gaylor laugh.

'Didn't I tell you? It was very simple. A policeman on his beat found the wicket door open, saw the lantern on the ground and the other lantern burning in the lobby of the house—what's the matter?'

Mr Reeder was laughing.

'Pardon me,' he said at last. 'Are you sure there wasn't an alarm bell ringing?'

'I didn't hear of any alarm bell—in fact, I don't know that there is one.'

Mr Reeder exchanged a few commonplaces, denied that he was making any inquiries about Ligsey and, replacing the receiver, sat back in his chair, his hands clasped about his middle and real amusement in his eyes.

Later he had a call from the solicitor engaged to defend young Southers. He also suggested that Mr Reeder should place his services at the call of the defence; but again he refused.

Opening the telephone directory, he found the number of Mr Clive Desboyne, and it was that gentleman who answered his call.

'That's odd, I was just going to ring you up,' said Desboyne. 'Have you taken up the case?'

'I am wavering,' replied Reeder. 'Before I reach a decision I'd like to have another talk with you.

Could I call at your flat tonight about—nine?'
There was a pause.
'Certainly. I was going out, but I'll wait in for you.'
At the conclusion of this call Mr Reeder again leaned back in his chair, but this time he was not smiling; he was rather puzzled. Perhaps he was thinking of Ligsey; possibly he was impressed by the generosity of this man who was ready to spend a considerable part of his fortune to prove the innocence of a man he disliked.
Whatever trains of thoughts started and slowed, switched into side tracks or ran off into tributary lines, they all arrived at one mysterious destination...
'It will be spring-cleaning,' said Mr Reeder, as he got up from his chair.

Chapter VII: The Revolver Clue

REEDER spent the rest of the afternoon in the West End of London, calling upon a succession of theatrical agents. Some were very important personages who received him in walnut-panelled salons; a few were in dingy offices on third floors; one, and the most important of these, he interviewed in the bar of a public-house in St. Martin's Lane—a fat and seedy man, with a fur collar and frayed cuffs, a half-stupid tippler with no business but many reminiscences; and, as he proudly claimed, the best collection of old theatrical programmes in London.
Mr. Reeder, who was a good listener and very patient, heard all about the agent's former grandeur, the amount of commission out of which eminent artistes had swindled him, and at last he accompanied his bibulous companion to his lodgings off the Waterloo Road, and from seven till eight was engrossed in masses of dog-eared literature.
Mr. Reeder had a meal in a Strand restaurant and drove to Park Lane. As the lift carried him to the floor on which Desboyne's flat was situated—
'I'm sure its spring cleaning,'? murmured Mr. Reeder to himself.
He rang the bell of the flat and waited. Presently he heard the sound of footsteps echoing hollowly in the hall. Clive Desboyne opened the door with an apologetic smile.
'I hope you don't mind the place being in confusion?' he said. 'We've started our spring cleaning. The truth is, I'd arranged to go away today if this wretched business hadn't turned up.'
The carpet had been taken up from the floor of the hall, the walls had been stripped, and the crystal pendant which lit the hall showed through a gauze covering. Clive Desboyne's own study had, however, been left untouched by the decorators. 'I'm going to clear out to an hotel tomorrow. It'll probably be the Ritz-Carlton, but if you want me urgently my solicitors will be able to put us in touch. Now, Mr. Reeder, you're going to do this for Anna and me?'
Mr. Reeder shook his head feebly.
'You've got to do it,' insisted the other energetically. 'You're the only detective in London in whom I've any confidence. I know you're attached to the Public Prosecutor's Department, but I've been making a few inquiries too,' he said with a little smile, 'and I hear that you take outside commissions.'
'Banks,' said Mr. Reeder reverently. 'Banks—not private work.'

'I shall insist!' Clive was very earnest. 'I've told Anna everything—about the way I behaved over young Southers. Honestly, I still think that Ligsey's story was true and that Southers was making something on the side. A lot of decent people, otherwise perfectly honest, do that sort of thing, and I'm not condemning him. In fact, when I expressed my—what's the word for being shocked?'
'Horror, amazement?' suggested Mr. Reeder.
'Well, whatever it was—I was being a hypocrite. I myself haven't always been rich. I've known what it is to be devilishly poor. If I hadn't made good speculations when I was quite a kid, I should probably be worse off than Southers.'
'You're rather fond of the young lady?' said Mr. Reeder after an interregnum of silence.
Again Desboyne laughed.
'Of course I am! The fact that a man is engaged to another girl—and the sweetest girl in the world—doesn't prevent him philandering. Of course, it's got me into quite a lot of trouble, but the fact remains, I'm terribly fond of Anna. I won't say I love her like a brother, because I'm tired of being a hypocrite. I'm going to try to get Southers out of the mess he's in; and that doesn't mean I love him like a brother, either! Now, Mr Reeder, what do you want to see me about, if it isn't to tell me that you're taking up this case?'
All that Mr. Reeder wanted to see Clive Desboyne about was spring cleaning, but he could not say this. He had, however, a good excuse for calling: Ligsey was apparently alive, he explained. Clive Desboyne was not impressed.
'I didn't worry whether he was alive or dead,' he said frankly. 'Naturally, I don't know what theory the police have, but I understood from the newspapers that they were concentrating on the murder of Attymar—that is the charge against John Southers. If Ligsey is alive I'm hardly likely to meet him, unless, of course, he feels, as so many of these crooks do, that once one has given them money they're entitled to a pension! If I hear from him I'll let you know.'
As they came out into the hall Mr. Reeder's eyes wandered up and down the bare walls.
'You will have this repainted, Mr. Desboyne?' he asked. 'At present it is rather a delicate cream. If I were you I should have it painted green. Green is a very restful colour, but possibly my views are—um—suburban.'
'I think they are,' said the other good-humouredly.

Mr. Reeder had made an appointment to see the bibulous agent at ten o'clock. The agent knew where certain photographs were to be obtained, and had promised to be waiting at the corner of St. Martin's Lane at that hour. Mr. Reeder arrived as St. Martin's Church clock was striking, but there was no sign of Billy Gurther. He had not appeared at half-past ten, and Mr. Reeder decided to go to his house, for he was very anxious to complete his dossier.
The landlady at Mr. Gurther'a lodgings had a surprising and disconcerting story to tell. Mr. Reeder had hardly left (she had witnessed his departure) before a messenger came, and Billy had gone out. He had returned in half an hour, very voluble and excited. He had been given a commission to collect cabaret turns in Spain. He had to leave London some time after nine, travel all night, and catch the Sud Express in the morning. He was plentifully supplied with

money.

'He was so excited, he was nearly sober,' said the uncharitable landlady. The sudden departure of an obscure music-hall agent, of whose existence he had been unaware until that afternoon, did not at all distress Mr. Reeder. It was the circumstances which attended his leaving, its rapidity, and, most important of all, the knowledge that was behind tint sudden move, which made him alert and watchful.

He might not be persona grata at Scotland Yard, but little things like that did not trouble Mr. Reeder and later that night he drove to the big building on the Thames Embankment and sought, nay, demanded, an interview with the Chief Constable, who should have been at home and in bed, but was in fact in consultation with his five chiefs when the detective arrived.

The first message sent to Mr. Reeder was cold and unpromising. Would he call in the morning? It was Gaylor who was detached from the conference to carry this message.

'Go back to your chief, Mr. Gaylor,' said Reeder acidly, 'and tell him I wish to see him this evening, at once. If I see him tomorrow it will be at the Home Office.'

This was a threat: nobody knew it better than Gaylor. The exact extent and volume of Reeder's power was not known. One thing was certain: he could be extremely unpleasant, and the consequences of his displeasure might even affect a man's career. Gaylor returned instantly and summoned him to the conference, and there Mr. Reeder sat down and, quite uninvited, expounded a theory, and supported his fantastic ideas with a considerable amount of grimy literature.

'We can stop Gurther at Southampton,' suggested Gaylor, but Reeder shook his head.

'I think not. Let him soak into the Continent, and then we may pick him up without any trouble. Send a man to Southampton, and let him shadow him to Paris. In Paris he can blanket him.'

Mason nodded.

'If your theory is correct, there must be a method of proving it,' he said; 'not a simple one perhaps—'

'On the contrary, a very simple one,' said Mr. Reeder.

He turned to Gaylor.

'You remember the bedroom above the one where the murder took place, or where we think it was committed? You probably took a photograph.'

'I'll get it right away,' said Gaylor, and left the room. He was back with a sheaf of photographic enlargements which he laid on the table.

'There it is,' said Reeder, and pointed.

'The clock? Yes, I noticed that.'

'Naturally,' said Reeder.

'But most people who go to sea, or even bargees, have it put there.'

The little clock was fastened to the ceiling, immediately over the bedstead, so that anybody lying in bed could look up and tell the time. It had luminous hands, Reeder had noticed.

'I want you to have that clock removed and the ceiling plastered. I want you to take away the bed and put a table and chair there. In two days I think I will make the further prosecution of young

Southers unnecessary.'

'You can do as you like,' said Mason. 'You're well in the case now, Mr Reeder. I've put out a special call to get Ligsey, and the river police are searching all the reaches.'

'The river police are more likely to get Mr. Ligsey than any other section of the Metropolitan Police Force,' replied Reeder.

Big Ben was striking eleven as he mounted a bus that carried him from Westminster Bridge to the end of his road. In the days, and particularly the nights, when Mr. Reeder was heavily engaged in his hazardous occupation his housekeeper remained on duty until he was ready to go to bed. She met him at the door now with a telephone message.

'Mr. Gaylor called up, sir. He says he's sending you a lacquered box which he wishes you to examine, and will you be careful not to touch it with your fingers because of the prince? He didn't say which prince it was.'

'I think I know His Highness,' said Mr. Reeder, who was a little ruffled that Gaylor should find it necessary to warn him against oversmearing fingerprints. 'Has the box arrived?'

'Ten minutes ago, sir.'

'When did Mr. Gaylor telephone?'

She was rather vague as to this; thought it might have been half an hour before. In that case, thought Reeder, it must have been immediately after he left the Yard, and the box must have come on by cyclist messenger.

He found it on his table in a service envelope, and took it out: a heavy, oblong box about six inches long and three inches square. Pen-printed on the lid, which was tacked down, were the words: 'Mr. Reeder to see and return. Room 75, New Scotland Yard.' Reeder weighed the package in his hand.

Some people remember by smell, some trust to their eyesight, and the recollections of vision. Mr. Reeder had a remarkable sense of weight—and he remembered something that weighed just as heavy as this. He put the package carefully on the table and rang through to Scotland Yard. Gaylor had gone. He tried him at his house, but he had not arrived.

'Tell him to phone the moment he comes in,' he said, and went to his desk to examine for the third time that day, the old music-hall programmes and playbills, photographs, cuttings from the Era and the Stage, the data which he had collected in the course of the day.

At one o'clock his housekeeper came in and asked if anything more would be required.

'Nothing at all,' said Mr. Reeder. And then a thought struck him. 'Where do you sleep?'

'In the room above, sir.'

'Above this?' said Mr. Reeder hastily. 'No, no, I think you'd better stay in the kitchen until I hear from Mr. Gaylor. If you could make yourself comfortable there, in fact if you could sleep there, I should be very much obliged. There is nothing to be alarmed about,' he said, when he saw consternation dawning in her face. 'It is merely that I may want to—um—send a detective upstairs to—um—overhear a conversation.'

It was a lame excuse. Mr. Reeder was a poor liar; but his housekeeper was a very simple soul and, except that she insisted on going up to make the room tidy, agreed to retire to the basement.

She had hardly gone when Gaylor came through, and for five minutes he and Reeder spoke together. After this the detective settled down to await his coming, and Inspector Gaylor did not arrive alone, but brought with him two expert officials from the Explosives Department. One of them had a delicate spring-balance, and with this the package was weighed.

'Allow an ounce and a quarter for the wood,' said the expert, 'and that's the exact weight of a Mills bomb. I'm sure you're right, Mr. Reeder.'

He held the package to his ear and shook it gently.

'No, nothing more complicated.'

He took a case of instruments from his pocket and removed a slither of wood from the lid.

'Yes, there's the lever, and the pin's out,' he said after examining it under a strong light.

He cut away the side, and revealed a black, segmented egg shape, grinning as he recognized an old friend.

'You see that?' He pointed to a little hole at the end of the box. 'The fellow who brought this was taking no risks: he kept an emergency pin through until it was delivered. I'll have this out in a jiff.'

It was no idle promise. Mr. Reeder watched with interest as the skilful fingers of the man removed the lid, catching the lever at the same time and holding it firm against the swelling side. From his pocket he took a steel pin and thrust it home, and the bomb became innocuous.

'You've kept every scrap of paper, of course?' said Gaylor. 'There was no other packing but this?'

Every piece of paper was carefully folded and put in an envelope, and the two explosive experts went down to pack away Mr. Reeder's dangerous gift.

'There was a lot you didn't tell the chief,' said Gaylor at parting. 'That's the trouble with you, you old devil!'

Mr. Reeder looked pained.

'That is not a very pleasant expression,' he said.

'But it is,' insisted Gaylor. 'You always keep back some juicy bit to spring on us at the last moment. It's either your sense of drama or your sense of humour.'

For a moment Reeder's eyes twinkled, and then his face became a mask again.

'I have no—um—sense of humour,' he said.

He had at any rate a sense of vanity, and he was irritated that his little idiosyncrasy had been so cruelly exposed to description.

He was up at six the next morning, and by half past seven was on his way to the Thames Valley. On the previous day he had telephoned to eight separate boathouses between Windsor and Henley, and he was satisfied that he had found what he wanted in the neighbourhood of Bourne End. He had telephoned to the boatbuilder on whom he was calling, and he found that industrious man at work in his yard.

'You're the gentleman who wanted to know about the Zaira? I was going to send one of my boys up to see if she was still tied up, but I haven't been able to spare him this morning.'

'I'm rather glad you haven't,' said Mr. Reeder.

'It was a funny thing you telephoning to me when did,' said the builder. 'She'd just gone past on her way to Marlow. No, I've never seen her before, but I caught the name; in fact, it was because she was new in this part of the river that I noticed her. She's a forty-foot cruiser, nearly new, and I should think she's got pretty powerful engines. As it was, she made a bit of a wash.'

He explained that after Mr. Reeder's inquiry he had telephoned through to Marlow, had learned that the boat had not passed, and had sent one of his assistants up the towpath to locate her.

'She's lying at a private quay that runs in from the river to a big red house which has been empty for years. There's nobody on board her, and I suppose the owner's had permission from the agents. Are you thinking of buying her?'

That view had never presented itself to Mr. Reeder. He thought for a long time, and gave the boatbuilder the impression that it was only a question of price that prevented him from ownership.

'Yes, it's quite usual for people to tie up and leave their boats for months at a time, especially at a private quay like that. It's not safe: you get a craft full of rats, especially in the winter months. These big boats cost a lot to keep up, and you couldn't afford to have a caretaker on board.'

Mr. Reeder made a very leisurely way along the towpath, stopping now and again to admire the lovely reach. Although he had explicit instructions, he might have passed the narrow canal which runs in from the river, in spite of the brick bridge across, for the stream was choked with weeds, and ran apparently into a tangle of trees and undergrowth. With some difficulty Mr. Reeder reached its bank. He then saw that the canal was brick-lined. Nevertheless, though he had this indication of its edge, he walked gingerly.

It opened to a larger pool, a sort of backwater. Passing a clump of bushes, he came suddenly upon the boat. The bow lay almost within reach of his hand. It was tied up fore and aft and had a deserted appearance. Across the forepart of the boat was drawn a canvas cover, but he was prepared for this by the description of the boatbuilder. Mr. Reeder slipped his hand in his pocket and went cautiously along the length of the boat. He noted that all the portholes were not only closed but made opaque with brown paper.

'Is anybody there?' he called loudly.

There was no answer. In midstream a moorhen was paddling aimlessly; the sound of his voice sent it scurrying to cover.

The foremost part of the ship was evidently the engine-room, and possibly accommodation for a small crew. The living saloon was aft. It was these that had their portholes covered. Both cabins were approached from the well deck amidships, and he saw here a canvas-covered wheel. The doors were padlocked on the outside.

Mr. Reeder looked around, and stepped on to the boat down a short ladder to the well. He tried the padlock on the saloon door. It was fast; but it was a simple padlock, and if fortune favoured him, and the boat he sought was really discovered, he had prepared for such an emergency as this.

He tried three of the keys which he took from his pocket before the lock snapped back. He unfastened the hasp, turned the handle and pulled open the door. He could see nothing for a moment, then he switched on a torch and sent its rays into the interior.

The saloon was empty. The floor of it lay possibly eighteen inches below the level of the deck on which he was standing. And then—
Lying in the middle of the floor, and glittering in the light of his lamp, was a white-handled, silver-plated revolver.

'Very interesting,' said Mr. Reeder, and went down into the saloon.

He reached the bottom of the steps and turned, walking backwards with his face to the door through which he had come, the muzzle of his Browning covering the opening. Presently his heel kicked the pistol. He took another step back and stooped to pick it up.

CHAPTER VIII: RED ROBE

MR REEDER was conscious of a headache and that the light shining in his eyes was painful. It was a tiny globe which burned in the roof of the cabin. Somebody was talking very distressedly; the falsetto voices Mr. Reeder loathed. His senses came back gradually.

He was shocked to find himself one of the figures in a most fantastical scene; something which did not belong to the great world of reality in which he lived and had his being. He was part of an episode, torn bodily from a most imaginative and impossible work of fiction.

The man who sat in one corner of the lounge, clasping his knees, was— Mr. Reeder puzzled for a word. Theatrical, of course. That red silk robe, Mephistophelian cap, and a long black mask with a lace fringe that even hid the speaker's chin. His hands were covered with jewelled rings which scintillated in the feeble light overhead.

Mr. Reeder could not very well move; he was handcuffed, his legs were strapped painfully together, and in his mouth was a piece of wood lightly tied behind his ears. It was not painful, but it could be, he realized. At any rate he was spared the necessity of replying to the exultant man who sat at the other end of the settee.

'Did you hear what I said, my master of mystery?'

He spoke with a slightly foreign accent, this man in the red robe.

'You are so clever, and yet I am more clever, eh? All of it I planned out of my mind. The glittering silver pistol on the floor—that was the only way I could get you to stoop and bring your head into the gas. It was a very heavy gas which does not easily escape, but I was afraid you might have dropped a cigarette, and that would have betrayed everything. If you had waited a little time the gas would have rolled out of the open door; but no, you must have the pistol, so you stooped and picked it up, and voilà!'

His hands glittered dazzlingly.

'You are used to criminals of the stupid kind,' he went on. 'For the first time, my Reeder, you meet one who has planned everything step by step. Pardon me.'

He stepped down to the floor, leaned forward and untied the gag.

'I find it difficult if conversation is one-sided,' he said pleasantly. 'If you make a fuss I shall shoot you and that will be the end. At present I desire that you should know everything. You know me?'

'I'm afraid I haven't that pleasure,' said Mr. Reeder, and the man chuckled.

'If you had lived, I would have been your chief case, your chef d'oeuvre, the one man of your acquaintance who could plan murder and—what is the expression?—get away with it! Do you know where you are?'

'I'm on the Zaira,' said Mr. Reeder.

'Do you know who is her owner?'

'She is owned by Mr. Clive Desboyne.'

The man chuckled at this.

'Poor fellow! The lovesick one, eh? For him this boat is—where do you think?—at Twickenham, for its spring repairs. He told you perhaps he had been mad enough to let it for two months? No, he did not tell you? Ah, that is interesting. Perhaps he forgot.'

Mr. Reeder nodded slowly.

'Now tell me, my friend—my time is very short and I cannot waste it here with you—do you know who killed Attymar?'

'You are Attymar,' said Mr. Reeder, and was rewarded by a shrill chuckle of delighted laughter.

'So clever, after all! It is a good thing I have you, eh? Otherwise'—he shrugged his shoulders lightly. 'That is the very best joke—I am Attymar! Do I speak like him, yes? Possibly—who knows?'

He slipped from his seat and came stealthily towards Reeder and fixed the gag a little tighter.

'Where shall you be this night, do you think, with a big, heavy chain fastened around you? I know all the deepest holes in this river, and years and years will pass before they find your body. To think that this great London shall lose its Mr. Reeder! So many people have tried to kill you, my friend, but they have failed because they are criminals—just stupid fellows who cannot plan like a general.'

Mr. Reeder said nothing; he could not raise his hand far enough to relieve the pressure on his mouth, for attached to the centre link of the handcuffs was a cord fastened to the strap about his ankles.

The man in the red cloak bent over him, his eyes glaring through the holes in the mask.

'Last night I tried you. I say to myself, "Is this man stupid or is he clever?"' He spoke quickly and in a low voice. 'So I send you the little bomb. I would have sent it also to Desboyne—he also will die tonight, and our friend Mr. Southers will be hanged, and there will be the end of you all! And I will go sailing to the southern seas, and no man will raise his hand against me, because I am clever.'

Mr. Reeder thought he was a little monotonous. In spite of his terrible position, he was intensely bored. The man in the red cloak must have heard something, for he went quickly to the door and listened more intently, then, mounting the stairs, slammed the door behind him and put on the padlock.

Presently Mr. Reeder heard him mount the side of the boat and guessed he had stepped ashore to meet whatever interruption was threatened. It was, in truth, the boatbuilder, who had come to make inquiries, and the grey-haired man with the stoop and the white moustache and twisted face was able to assure him that Mr. Reeder had made an offer for the boat, but it had been rejected, and that the detective had gone on to Marlow.

The prisoner had a quarter of an hour to consider his unfortunate position and to supply a remedy. Mr. Reeder satisfied himself that it was a simple matter to free his hands from the steel cuffs. He had peculiarly thin wrists and his large, bony hands were very deceptive. He freed one, adjusted the gag to a less uncomfortable tension, and brought himself to a sitting position. He swayed and would have fallen to the floor but for a stroke of luck. The effort showed him how dangerous it would be to make an attempt to escape before he recovered strength. His gun had been taken from him; the silver-handled revolver had also been removed. He resumed his handcuffs and had not apparently moved when his captor opened the door, only to look in.

'I'm afraid you will have to do without food today—does it matter?'

Now Mr. Reeder saw that on the inside of the saloon door was a steel door. It was painted the same colour as the woodwork, and it was on this discovery that he based his hope of life. For some reason, which he never understood, his enemy switched on two lights from the outside, and this afforded him an opportunity of taking stock of his surroundings.

The portholes were impossible—he understood now why they had been made airtight with brown paper. It would be as much as he could do to get his arms through them. Having decided upon his plan of campaign, Mr. Reeder acted with his customary energy. He could not allow his life to depend on the caprice of this man. Evidently the intention was to take him out late at night, loaded with chains, and drop him overboard; but he might have cause to change his mind. And that, Mr. Reeder thought, would be very unfortunate.

His worst forebodings were in a fair way to being realized, did he but know. The man who stood in his shirt sleeves, prodding at the centre of the backwater, had suddenly realized the danger which might follow the arrival of a curious-minded policeman. The boatbuilder would certainly gossip. Reeder had something of an international reputation, and the local police would be only too anxious to make his acquaintance.

Gossip runs up and down a river with a peculiar facility. He went into the engine cabin, where he had stowed his fantastic robe and hat, and dragged out a little steel cylinder. Unfasten that nozzle, leave it on the floor near where the helpless man lay, and in a quarter of an hour perhaps...

He cold-bloodedly pulled out two links of heavy chain and dropped them with a crash on the deck. Mr. Reeder heard the sound; he wrenched one hand free of the cuff, not without pain, broke the gag and, drawing himself up into a sitting position, unfastened the first of the two straps. His head was splitting from the effect of the gas. As his feet touched the floor he reeled. The second cuff he removed at his leisure. He was so close to the door now that he could drop the bar. It stuck for a little while, but presently he drew it down. It fell with a clatter into the pocket.

The man on the deck heard, ran to the door and tugged, drew off the padlock and tried to force his way in.

'I'm afraid you're rather late,' said Mr. Reeder politely.

He could almost feel the vibration of the man's fury. His vanity had been hurt; he had been proved a bungler by the one man in the world he wished to impress, whilst life held any impressions for him.

Then the man on the bridge heard a smash and saw some splinters of glass fly from one of the ports. There were five tiny airholes in one of the doors, but four of these had been plugged with clay. Taking the cylinder, he smashed the nozzle end through the obstruction. A wild, desperate idea came to the harassed man. Reeder heard the starting wheel turn, and presently the low hum of machinery. He heard the patter of feet across the deck and peered through the porthole, but it was below the level of the bank.

He looked round for a weapon but could find none. Of one thing he was certain: Mr. Red Robe would not dare to run for the river. There was quite enough traffic there for him to attract attention. He could not afford to wait for darkness to fall; his position was as desperate as Reeder's own had been—

Bang!

It was the sound of a shot, followed by another. Reeder heard somebody shout, then the sound of a man crashing through the bushes. Then he heard the deep voice of Clive Desboyne.

'Reeder... are you there? How are you?'

Mr. Reeder, a slave to politeness, put his mouth up to the broken porthole.

It was some time before Desboyne could knock off the padlock. Presently the door was opened and Mr. Reeder came out.

'Thank God, you're safe!' said the other breathlessly. 'Who was the old bird who shot at me?' He pointed towards the place where the backwater turned.

'Is there a house there or a road or something? That's the way he went. What's happened?'

Mr. Reeder was sitting on a deck chair, his throbbing head between his hands. After a while he raised his face.

'I have met the greatest criminal in the world,' he said solemnly. 'He's so clever that he's alive. His name is Attymar!'

Clive Desboyne opened his mouth in amazement.

'Attymar? But he's dead!'

'I hope so,' said Mr. Reeder viciously, 'but I have reason to know that he isn't. No, no, young man, I won't tell you what happened. I'm rather ashamed of myself. Anyway, I am not particularly proud of being caught by this'—he paused—'amateur. Why did you come?'

'It was only by luck. I don't know why I came. I happened to phone through to Twickenham about some repairs to the boat—by the way, you must have seen a picture of it hanging in my hall. In fact, it was in that picture where you were clever enough to tell the date. I lend the Zaira at times; I lent it a few months ago to an Italian, but he so ill-used it that I sent a message that it was to be sent back to the yard. They telephoned along the river for news of it, and that's when I learnt you were down here—you look rotten.'

'I feel rotten,' said Mr. Reeder. 'And you came—'

'I drove down. I had a sort of feeling in my mind that something was wrong. Then I met a man who'd seen the builder, and he told me about the little old fellow. Until then I didn't know that he was in the boat, and I came along to make inquiries. For some reason, which I can't understand, he no sooner saw me than he pulled a gun and let fly at me; then he turned and went like mad through those bushes.'

'Have you a gun?' asked Mr. Reeder.

Desboyne smiled.

'No, I don't carry such things.'

'In that case it would be foolish to pursue my ancient enemy. Let one of the Buckingham Constabulary carry on the good work. Is your car anywhere handy?'

There was a road apparently within fifty yards.

'Good Lord!' said Desboyne suddenly. 'I left it outside the gates of an empty house. I wonder whether that's the place where the old boy went— and whether my car is still there?'

It was there, in the drive of a deserted house: the new car which had so excited the disgust of poor Johnny Southers. With some difficulty Clive started it up, and the action recalled something to him.

'Did we leave the engines of the boat running?' he asked suddenly. 'If you don't mind I'll go back and turn them off; then I'll notify the police, and I'll send a man to bring the Zaira into Maidenhead.'

He was gone ten minutes. Mr. Reeder had an opportunity of walking round the car and admiring it.

Rain had fallen in the night: he made this interesting discovery before Desboyne returned.

'We'll run up to Marlow and I'll get a man to go down and collect the boat,' he said as he climbed in. 'I've never heard anything more amazing. Tell me exactly what happened to you.'

Mr. Reeder smiled sadly.

'You will pardon me if I do not?' he asked gently. 'The truth is, I have been asked by a popular newspaper to write my reminiscences, and I want to save every personal experience for that important volume.'

He would talk about other subjects, however; for example, of the fortunate circumstance that Desboyne's car was still there though it was within reach of the enemy.

'I've never met him before. I hope I'll never meet him again,' said Desboyne. 'But I think he can be traced. Naturally, I don't want to go into court against him. I think it's the most ridiculous experience, to be shot at without replying.'

'Why bother?' asked Mr. Reeder. 'I personally never go into court to gratify a private vendetta, though there is a possibility that in the immediate future I may break the habit of years!'

He got down at the boathouse and was a silent listener while Clive Desboyne rang up a Twickenham number and described the exact location of the boat.

'They'll collect it,' he said as he hung up. 'Now, Mr. Reeder, what am I to do about the police?'

Mr. Reeder shook his head.

'I shouldn't report it,' he said. 'They'd never understand.' On the way back to London he grew more friendly to Clive Desboyne than he had ever been before, and certainly he was more communicative than he had been regarding the Attymar murder.

'You've never seen a murder case at first hand—'

'And I'm not very anxious to,' interrupted the other.

'I applaud that sentiment. Young people are much too morbid,' said Mr. Reeder. 'But this is a crime particularly interesting, because it was obviously planned by one who has studied the art of murder and the methods of the average criminal. He had studied it to such good purpose that he was satisfied that if a crime of this character were committed by a man of intelligence and acumen, he would—um—escape the consequence of his deed.'

'And will he?' asked the other, interested.

'No,' said Mr. Reeder, rubbing his nose. He thought for a long time. 'I don't think so. I think he will hang; I am pretty certain he will hang.'

Another long pause.

'And yet in a sense he was very clever. For example, he had to attract the attention of the policeman on the beat and establish the fact that a murder had been committed. He left open the wicket gate on the—um—wharf, and placed a lantern on the ground and another within the open door of his little house, so that the policeman, even if he had been entirely devoid of curiosity, could not fail to investigate.'

Clive Desboyne frowned.

'Upon my life I don't know who is murdered! It can't be Attymar, because you saw him today; and it can't possibly be Ligsey, because, according to your statement, he's alive. Why did Johnny Southers go there?'

'Because he'd been offered a job, a partnership with Attymar. Attymar had two or three barges, and with vigorous management it looked as if his business might grow into a more important concern. Southers didn't even know that this man Attymar was the type of creature he was. An appointment was made on the telephone; Southers attended; he interviewed Attymar or somebody in the dark, during which time I gather he was sprinkled with blood—whose blood, we shall discover. There was a similar case in France in eighteen-forty-seven. Madame Puyères...'

He gave the history of the Puyères case at length.

'That was our friend's cleverness, the blood-sprinkling, and the lantern- placing: but he made one supreme error. You know the house—no, of course, you've never been there.'

'Which house?' asked Clive curiously.

'Attymar's house. It's little more than a weighing shed. You haven't been there? No, I see you haven't. If you would like a little lecture, or a little demonstration of criminal error, I would like to show you at first- hand.'

'Will it save Johnny Southers—this mistake?' asked Desboyne curiously.

Mr. Reeder nodded.

'Nothing is more certain. How amazing are the—um—vagaries of the human mind! How peculiar are the paths into which—um—vanity leads us!'

He closed his eyes and seemed to be communing with himself all the way through Shepherd's Bush. Desboyne put him down at Scotland Yard, and they arranged to meet at the end of Shadwick Lane that same afternoon.

'There is no further news of Ligsey,' said Gaylor when Reeder came into his office.

'I should have been surprised if there had been,' said Mr. Reeder cheerfully, 'partly because he's dead, and partly because—well, I didn't expect any communication from him.'

'You know he telephoned the Chief last night?'

'I shouldn't be surprised at that,' said Mr. Reeder, almost flippantly.

They talked about Johnny Southers and the case against him, and of the disappointing results of a careful search of the garden. They had dug up every bed and had done incalculable damage to Mr. Southers' herbaceous borders.

'Our information was that he had a couple of thousand pounds cached there in real money, but we found nothing.'

'How much was there in the box you discovered in the tool shed?'

'Oh, only a hundred pounds or so,' said Gaylor. 'The big money was hidden in the garden, according to what we were told. We didn't find a penny.'

'Too bad,' said Mr. Reeder sympathetically. Then, remembering: 'Do you mind if I take a young—um—friend of mine over Attymar's house this afternoon? He's not exactly interested in the crime of wilful murder, but as he is providing for the defence of young Mr. Southers—'

'I don't mind,' said Gaylor, 'but you'd better ask the Chief.'

The Chief Constable was out, and the opportunity of meeting him was rendered more remote when Clive Desboyne rang him up, as he said, on the off-chance of getting him at Scotland Yard, and invited him out to lunch.

'Anna Welford is coming. I've told her you think that Johnny's innocence can be established, and she's most anxious to meet you.'

Mr. Reeder was in something of a predicament but, as usual, he rose to the occasion. He instantly cancelled two important engagements, and at lunchtime he sat between a delighted girl and a rather exhilarated benefactor. The one difficulty he had anticipated did not, however, arise. She had some shopping to do that afternoon, so he went alone with Clive Desboyne to what the latter described as 'the most gruesome after-lunch entertainment' he had ever experienced.

CHAPTER IX: THE SECOND TRAP

A CAR dropped them at the end of Shadwick Lane, which had already settled down to normality and had grown accustomed to the notoriety which the murder had brought to it.
There was a constable on duty on the wharf, but he was inside the gate. Mr. Reeder opened the wicket and Olive Desboyne stepped in. He looked round the littered yard with disgust visible on his face.
'How terribly sordid!' he said. 'I'm not too fastidious, but I can't imagine anything more grim and miserable than this.'
It was grimmer for the—um—gentleman who was killed,' said Mr. Reeder.
He went into the house ahead of his companion, pointed out the room where the murder was committed, 'as I feel perfectly sure,' he added; and then led the way up the narrow stairs into what had been Captain Attymar's sitting-room. 'If you sit at that table you'll see the plan of the house, and I may show you one or two very interesting things.'
Mr. Reeder switched on a handlamp on the table and Clive Desboyne sat down, and followed, apparently entranced, the recital of J.G. Reeder's theory.
'If you have time—what is the time?'
Clive Desboyne looked up at the ceiling, stared at it for a while.
'Let me guess,' he said slowly. 'Four o'clock.'
'Marvellous,' murmured Mr. Reeder. 'It is within one minute. How curious you should look up at the ceiling! There used to be a clock there.'
'In the ceiling?' asked the other incredulously.
He rose, walked to the window and stared out on to the wharf. From where he stood he could see the policeman on duty at the gate. There was nobody watching at a little door in the ragged fence which led to Shadwick Passage. Suddenly Clive Desboyne pointed to the wharf.
'That is where the murder was committed,' he said quietly. Mr. Reeder took a step towards the window and cautiously craned his neck forward. He did not feel the impact of the rubber truncheon that crashed against the base of his skull, but went down in a heap.
Clive Desboyne looked round, walked to the door and listened, then stepped out, locked the door, came down the stairs and on to the wharf. The policeman eyed him suspiciously, but Mr. Desboyne turned and carried on a conversation with the invisible Reeder.
He strolled round to the front of the house. Nobody saw him open the little gate into the passage. The end of Shadwick Lane was barred, but Gaylor did not remember the passage until too late. It was he who found Reeder and brought him back to consciousness.
'I deserve that,' said Mr. Reeder when he became articulate. 'Twice in one day! I'm getting too old for this work.'

CHAPTER X: THE FINAL PLUNGE

ONE of those amazing things which so rarely happen, that fifty-thousand-to-one-against chance, had materialized, and the high chiefs of Scotland Yard grew apoplectic as they asked the why and the wherefore. A man wanted by the police on a charge of murder had walked through a most elaborate cordon. River police had shut off the waterway; detectives and uniform men had formed a circle through which it was impossible to escape; yet the wanted man had, by the oddest chance, passed between two detectives who had mistaken him for somebody they knew. While Reeder was waiting at Scotland Yard he explained in greater detail the genesis of his suspicion.

'The inquiries I made showed me that Attymar was never seen in daylight, except by his crew, and then only in the fading light. He had established buying agencies in a dozen continental cities, and for years he has been engaged in scientific smuggling. But he could only do that if he undertook the hardships incidental to a bargemaster's life. He certainly reduced those hardships to a minimum for, except to collect the contraband which was dumped near his barge, and bring it up to the wharf he had first hired and then bought in the early stages of his activity, he spent few nights out of his comfortable bed.

'I was puzzled to account for many curious happenings. If Clive Desboyne had not taken the trouble to appear in Brockley at almost the hour at which the crime would be discovered—he knew the time the policeman came down Shadwick Lane—my suspicions might not have been aroused. It was a blunder on his part, even in his clever assumption of frankness, to come along and tell me the story of what Ligsey had told him; for as soon as the crime was discovered and I examined the place, I was absolutely certain that Ligsey was dead, or Clive would never have dared to invent the story.

'Desboyne prides himself on being a clever criminal. Like all criminals who have that illusion, he made one or two stupid blunders. When I called at his flat I found the walls covered with photographs, some of which showed him in costume. It was the first intimation I had that he had been on the stage. There was also a photograph of the Zaira when it was going upstream, with the House of Commons in the background. Attached by the painter at the stern was a small canoe-shaped tender, which had been faithfully described to me that day by the boy Hobbs. Desboyne knew he had blundered, but hoped I saw no significance in those two photographs, especially the photograph of him dressed up as a coster, with the identical make-up that Attymar wore.

'I started inquiries, and discovered that there was a Clive Desboyne who worked in music-halls, giving imitations of popular characters and making remarkably quick changes on the stage. I met people who remembered him, some who gave me the most intimate details about his beginnings. For ten years he had masqueraded as Attymar, sunk all his savings in a barge, rented the wharf and house, and eventually purchased it. He is an extraordinary organizer, and there is no doubt that in the ten years he's been working he's accumulated a pretty large fortune. Nobody, of course, associated the bargemaster with this elegant young man who lived in Park Lane.

'What Ligsey knew about him I don't know. Personally, I believe that Ligsey knew very little, and could have told us very little. Attymar discovered that Ligsey was communicating with me. Do you remember the letter he sent to me? I told you the envelope had been opened—and so it had, probably by "Attymar." From that moment Ligsey was doomed. Clive's vanity was such that he thought he could plan a remarkable crime, throw the suspicion on the man he hated, and at the same time remove Ligsey, the one danger, from his path. I should think that he had been planning Johnny Southers' end for about three weeks before the murder. The money that was found in the tool house was planted there on the actual night of the murder, while the money in the garden—'

'Money in what garden?' asked Mason. 'The garden was searched but none was found.'

Mr. Reeder coughed. 'At any rate, the money in the tool house was put there to support the suspicion. It was clumsily done. The message, the piece of paper, the old invoices, as well as the story that Desboyne told me with such charming effect were designed with two objects. One was to cover the disappearance of Attymar and the other to ruin Southers.

'But perhaps his cleverest and most audacious trick was the one he performed this morning. He had me in his boat; he had been waiting for me; probably had watched me from the moment I arrived at Bourne End. Then, wearing his fantastic get-up, and jealous to the very last that I should suspect him, he planned his scheme for my—um—unpleasant exit. I give him credit for his resourcefulness. As a quick change artist he has probably few equals. He could go on to the bank and deceive the boatbuilder from Bourne End. Who could believe that he was a little old man with a humped shoulder? He could equally come to my rescue when there was no other way of throwing suspicion from himself. Unfortunately for him, I saw not only that the car had been in the grounds all night, and that his story of having driven down from town was a lie, but—um—certain other things.'

The telephone rang, and Mason lifted the receiver.

'She went out a quarter of an hour ago—you don't know where?... It was Desboyne, was it? She didn't say where she was meeting him?'

Reeder sighed and rose wearily.

'Do I understand that Miss Anna Welford has been allowed to leave her house?' There was a quality of exasperation in his tone, and Mason could not but agree that it was justified. For the first request that Reeder had made, and that by telephone from Rotherhithe, was that a special guard should be put over Anna Welford. Certain of Mason's local subordinates, however, thought that the least likely thing that could happen would be that Desboyne would come into the neighbourhood, and here they were right. Matters had been further complicated by the fact that the girl had gone out that day, and was still out when the police officers called. She had rung up, however, a moment before Desboyne had telephoned, and had given her number, which was transferred to him. Later, when she was called up at the address she had given, it was discovered that she had gone out to meet him; nobody knew where.

'So really,' said Gaylor, 'nobody is to blame.'

'Nobody ever is!' snapped Mr. Reeder.

It was Clive Desboyne's conceit that he should arrange to meet the girl at the corner of the Thames Embankment, within fifty yards of Scotland Yard. When she arrived in some hurry, she saw nothing that would suggest that anything unusual had happened, except the good news he had passed to her over the telephone.

'Where's Johnny?' she asked, almost before she was within talking distance, and he was amused. 'I really ought to be very jealous.'

He called a taxi as he spoke, and ordered the man to drive him to an address in Chiswick.

'Reeder hasn't been on to you, of course? I'm glad—I wanted to be the first to tell you.'

'Is he released?' she asked, a little impatiently.

'He will be released this evening. I think that is best. The authorities are very chary of demonstrations, and Scotland Yard have particularly asked that he should give no newspaper interviews, but should spend the night, if possible, out of town. I've arranged with my cousin that he shall stay at his place till tomorrow.'

It all seemed very feasible, and when of his own accord he stopped the cab and, getting out to telephone, returned to tell her that he had phoned her father that she would not be back before eight, the thought of his disinterestedness aroused a warm glow of friendship towards him.

'I've been besieged by reporters myself, and I'm rather anxious to avoid them. These damned papers will do anything for a sensation.'

The swift express van of one of these offending newspapers passed the taxi at that moment. On its back doors was pasted a placard.

ALLEGED MURDERER'S DARING ESCAPE

Later the girl saw another newspaper poster.

POLICE OF METROPOLIS SEARCHING FOR MURDERER

The taxi drove up a side street and, as he tapped on the window, stopped. There was a garage a little further along and, leaving Anna, he went inside and came out in a few moments with a small car.

'I keep this here in case of emergency,' he explained to her. 'One never knows when one might need a spare car.'

Exactly why he should need a spare car in Chiswick he did not attempt to explain.

Avoiding the Great West Road, he took the longer route through Brentford. Rain was falling heavily by the time they reached Hounslow.

She was so grateful to him for all he had done that she did not resist his suggestion that they should go on to Oxford. She wondered why until they were on the outskirts of the town, and then he explained with a smile that Johnny had been transferred to Oxford Gaol that morning.

'I kept this as a surprise for you,' he said. 'Only about three people in London know, and I was most anxious that you shouldn't tell.'

They went into a café on the other side of the city, and she was puzzled why he should prefer this rather poverty-stricken little place to an hotel, but thought it was an act of consideration on his part—part of the general scheme for avoiding reporters. They lingered over tea until she grew a little restless.

'We'll go to the prison and make inquiries,' he told her.

Actually they did go to the prison, and he descended and rang the bell. When he came back he was grinning ruefully.

'He was released half an hour ago. My cousin's car picked him up. We can go on.'

It was getting dark now and the rain continued to fail steadily. They took another route towards London, passed through a little town which she thought she recognized as Marlow, turned abruptly from the main road, and as abruptly again up a dark and neglected carriage drive. She had a glimpse of the sheen of a stagnant backwater on her left, and then the car drew up before a forbidding looking door and, stepping down, Clive Desboyne opened the door with his key.

'Here we are,' he said pleasantly and, before she realized what had happened, she was in a gloomy hall smelling of damp and decay.

The door thundered close behind her.

'Where are we? this isn't the place,' she said tremulously, and at that moment all her old suspicions, all her old fears of the man returned.

'It is quite the place,' he said.

From the pocket of his raincoat he took a torch and switched it on. The house was furnished, if rotting carpets and dust-covered chairs meant anything. He held her firmly by the arm, walked her along the passage then, opening a door, pushed her inside. She thought there was no window, but found afterwards that it was shuttered.

The room was fairly clean; there was a bed, a table and a small oil stove. On a sideboard were a number of packets of foodstuffs.

'Keep quiet and don't make a fuss,' he said.

Striking a match, he lit a paraffin lamp that stood on the table.

What does this mean?' she asked. Her face was white and haggard.

He did not answer immediately, and then: 'I'm very fond of you—that's what it means. I shall probably be hanged in about six weeks' time, and there's a wise old saying that you might as well be hanged for a sheep as for a lamb. You for the moment are the lamb.'

The bright, shining eyes were fixed on hers. She almost fainted with horror.

'That doesn't mean I'm going to murder you or cut your throat or do any of the things I tried to do to Mr. Reeder this morning—oh, yes, I was the fantastical gentleman on the Zaira. The whole thing happened a few yards away from where you're standing. Now, Anna, you're going to be very sensible, my sweet—there's nobody within five miles of here who is at all concerned—'

The hinges of the door were rusty: they squeaked when it was moved. They squeaked now. Clive Desboyne turned in a flash, fumbling under mackintosh and coat.

'Don't move,' said Mr. Reeder gently. It was his conventional admonition. 'And put up your hands. I shall certainly shoot if you do not. You're a murderer—I could forgive you that. You're a liar—that, to a man of my high moral code, is unpardonable.' The dozen detectives who had been waiting for three hours in this dank house came crowding into the room, and snapped irons on the wrists of the white-faced man.

'See that they fit,' said Mr. Reeder pleasantly. 'I had a pair this morning which were grossly oversize.'

The Guv'nor

Chapter I: HATRED

THE affair of Mary Keen was never forgotten by Robert Karl Kressholm. He was a good hater, as Mr. J.G. Reeder was to say of him one day.
Yet it was an odd circumstance that Mary, dead and buried in Westbury Churchyard, should remain as a raw place in the mind of a man who was, to all appearance and certainly by protestation, madly in love with a child— she was little more—who was twenty years his junior. But Bob Kressholm was like that. He was vain, had complete and absolute confidence in his own excellences. He might congratulate himself that he was young at thirty-seven and looked younger; that he was good-looking in an instantly impressing way and looked little older than at eighteen, when Mary had chosen Red Joe Brady in preference to himself.
Mary was dead of a broken heart—she passed three days after Joe had been released from a short-term sentence in Dartmoor. If Bob could have found her he would have offered consolation of sorts, but Joe had very carefully hidden her and his boy.
Kressholm never went to prison. He was too clever for that. Banks and jewellers' stores might become impoverished in a night, but "the Guv'nor" could not be associated with the happening. He was, he believed with reason, the greatest organiser in what is picturesquely described as "The Underworld." Nobody had ever brought a mind like his to the business of burglary. He had his own office and plant in Antwerp for the reconstruction of stolen goods. In Vienna a respectable broker handled such bonds and negotiable stock as came his way. He could boast to such intimates as Red Joe that he was "squawk-proof" and was justified in the claim. He came down to Exeter, where Haddin's Amusement Park was operating, partly to see and partly to dazzle Joe out of his dull but respectable mode of living. A big Rolls limousine was an advertisement of his own prosperity.
He did not see the balloon ascent, but the parachute dropped square in the road before his car, and the chauffeur had just time to pull up on the very edge of a tangled mass of cord, silk envelope and laughing girlhood.
"Where the devil did you come from?"
"Out of the everywhere," she mocked him.
She wore a boy's trousers, a blue silk shirt and a beret—an unusual head-dress in those days— and she' was lovely: golden-haired, fair-skinned and supple.
This was Wenna, daughter of Lew Haddin.
He drove her to the fair and delivered her to her father. Having come for the day, he stayed for the week; Red Joe had a bed put for him in his own caravan. Joe had a second van—a motor caravan, but this was not in the fair-ground. It was garaged in the town. His guest heard about this and drew his own conclusions—at the moment he was not interested in Red Joe's dangerous hobby.
And every day he grew more and more fascinated by the girl. He brought flowers to her, which she accepted, a jewelled bracelet, which she refused. Fat Lew Haddin offered lame apologies, for he was a good-natured man who gave things away rather readily and would have married off his

daughter to almost anybody rather than worry.

Red Joe added to his unpopularity and stirred up all the smouldering embers of hatred by speaking very plainly to his guest.

"She's only a kid, Bob, and what have you and I to give any woman? The certainty of getting her a pass on visiting day and the privilege of writing her a letter once a month."

Kressholm answered coldly:

"Personally I've never been in stir, and I don't know what the regulations are about wives visiting husbands, and that sort of thing. Are you after her?"

"She's about the same age as my boy," said Joe wrathfully.

"Oh, you want her for the family, eh? You think you've got a call on all the women in the world. You're getting bourgeois, Red, since you've become a monkey dealer."

Red Joe wasn't quite sure what "bourgeois" meant, but he guessed it was applied offensively.

Bob lived mostly in Paris and spoke two or three languages rather well. He was more than a little proud of his education, which was the basis of his superiority complex. Wenna, who had been a woman at twelve, had no doubts about Mr. Kressholm.

"What am I to do with this feller, Joe? The old man is no protection for an innocent maiden; he wanted me to go riding with his lordship yesterday, and saw nothing wrong in the idea that I should go up to London for a week and stay with Kressholm's friends. Fathers are not what they used to be."

Joe did not want to quarrel with his former associate; there were very special reasons why he should not. But before he could discuss the matter with Bob Kressholm, the girl had settled the affair.

There were two slaves of hers in the circus—Swedish gymnasts, who would have strangled Bob Kressholm and sat up all night to bury him, but she did not ask for outside help.

It happened in a little wood near the grounds on the last evening of the fair. She gave nobody the details of the encounter, not even Red Joe. All he knew was that Kressholm had left Exeter very hurriedly just as soon as the knife wound on his shoulder was dressed and cauterised by a local surgeon.

Wenna had learned quite a lot about knife play from one of her Swedish gymnasts, who had left his country as a result of his dexterity in this direction.

Thereafter Bob Kressholm had another grievance to nourish. A few months after he returned to Paris he learned that Mr. J.G. Reeder was interesting himself in a new issue of "slush" which, in the argot of the initiated, means forged money. And then he remembered the locked motor caravan which was Joe Brady's, but which he never slept in, or even brought to the fair ground. He returned to London on the very day Mr. Reeder had reached a certain conclusion.

Chapter II: MR. REEDER

"BRADY'S work," said J.G. Reeder.

He had fixed the bank-note against a lighted glass-screen and was examining it through a magnifying glass.

It was the fourteenth five-pound note he had inspected that week. Mr. Reeder knew all that there was to be known about forged bank-notes; he was the greatest authority in the world on the subject of forgery, and could, as a rule, detect a "wrong 'un" by feeling a corner of it. But these notes, which had been put into circulation in the year 1921, were not ordinary notes. They were so extraordinary that it required a microscopic examination to discover their spurious nature. He looked gloomily at the chief inspector (it was Ben Peary in those days) and sighed.

"Mr. Joseph Brady," he repeated; "but Mr. Joseph Brady is now an honest man. He is following a—um—peaceable and—er— picturesque profession."

"What profession?" asked Peary.

"Circus," replied Reeder soberly. "He was born in a circus—he has returned to his—um— interesting and precarious element."

When Red Joe Brady had finished a comparatively light sentence for forgery, he had announced his intention of going straight. It is a laudable but not unusual decision that has been made by many men on their release from prison. He told the governor of the gaol and the chief warder, and, of course, the chaplain (who hoped much, but was confident of little) that he had had enough of the crooked game and that henceforth...

He told Mr. Reeder this, taking a special journey to Brockley for the purpose.

Mr. Reeder expressed his praise at such an admirable resolution, but did not believe him.

It was pretty well known that Joe had money—stacks of it, said his envious competitors—for he was a careful man. He was not the kind that squandered his illicit gains and he had made big money. For example; what happened to the hundred thousand pounds bank robbery which was never satisfactorily explained: Kressholm had his cut, of course, but it was only a quarter. Bob used to brood on this; it was his illusion that there wasn't a cleverer man at the game than he. Anyway, the red-haired athlete, who had once been billed as Rufus Baldini, the Master of the High Trapeze, and was known in the police circles as Red Joe, had a very considerable nest-egg, maintained his boy at a first-class boarding school and, generally speaking, was rich.

He came out of prison to take farewell of a dying wife at a moment of crisis for Lew Haddin, of Haddin's Grand Travelling Amusement Park. That fat and illiterate man had employed a secretary to manage his private and business affairs, and the secretary had vanished with eighteen thousand pounds which he had drawn from Lew's London bank. And at the time Lew was wading through a deep and sticky patch of bad trading.

Joe was an excellent business man and, outside of his anti-social activities, an honest man. The death of his wife and the consciousness of new responsibilities had sobered him. He arrived at the psychological moment, had in an accountant to expose the tangle at its worst, and bought a half- interest in the amusement park, which for two years enjoyed exceptional prosperity.

The underworld also has its artists who work for the joy of working. There was no reason why Joe should fall again into temptation, but his draughtsmanship was little short of perfection, and he found himself drawing again. He might have confined himself to sketches of currency for his own amusement if there had not fallen into his hands the "right paper."

Now, the "right paper," is very hard to come by. As a rule, it does not require such an expert as Mr. Reeder to detect the difference between the paper on which English bank-notes are printed and the paper which is made for the special use of forgers. You can buy in Germany passable imitations which have the texture and the weight, and, to the inexpert finger, the feel of a bank-note. It is very seldom that paper is produced which defies detection.

Eight thousand sheets came to Joe from some well-intentioned confederate of other days, and his first inclination was to make a bonfire of them; but then the possibilities began to open up before his reluctant eyes... There was sufficient electric power at his disposal from the many dynamos they had in their outfit, and there were privacy and freedom from observation...

Mr. Reeder located Joe and put him under observation. A surreptitious search of his caravan revealed nothing. One morning Mr. Reeder packed his bag and went north.

There was a great crowd of people in the Sanbay Fair Ground when Mr. Reeder descended from the station fly which brought him to the outskirts of the town; he had not come direct from the station. He and his companion had made a very careful search of a caravan in a lock-up garage at the Red Lion.

Haddin's Imperial Circus and Tropical Menagerie occupied the centre of the ground. The tower of Haddin's Royal Razzy Glide showed above the enormous tent, and Haddin's various side-shows filled all the vacant sites. The municipality did not wholly approve of Haddin's, his band wagons, his lions and tigers, his fat ladies and giants, but the municipality made a small charge for admission to the ground, "for the relief of rates."

Mr. Reeder paid a humble coin, stoutly ignored the blandishments of dark- eyed ladies who offered him opportunities for shooting at the celluloid balls which dipped and jumped on the top of a water jet, was oblivious to the attractions of ring boards and other ingenious methods.

He had come too late for the only free attractions: the balloon ascent and the parachute jump by "the Queen of the Air." She was at the moment of Mr. Reeder's arrival resting in the big and comfortable caravan which was Mr. Haddin's home and centre.

But it was to see the "Queen of the Air" that Mr. Reeder had taken this long and troublesome journey. He sought out and found Red Joe Brady, whose caravan was a picture of all that was neat and cosy. Brady opened the door, saw Reeder at the foot of the steps, and for a moment said nothing; then:

"Come up, will you?"

He had seen behind Mr. Reeder three men whose carriage and dress said "detectives" loudly.

"What's the idea, Mr. Reeder?"

Mr. Reeder shook his head sadly.

"All this is very unpleasant, Joe; and very unnecessary. I have searched that caravan of yours at the garage. Need I say any more?"

Joe reached his hat and overcoat from the peg. "I'm ready when you are," he said.

Joe was like that. He never made trouble where trouble was futile, nor excuses where they were vain.

Wenna heard the news after he had been taken away, and wept, not so much for Joe as for Danny, the boy who had spent his holidays with the circus and who had found his way into her susceptible heart.

Mr. Reeder was in the vestibule of the Old Bailey one day, and was conscious that somebody was looking at him, and turned to meet the glare of two eyes of burning blue fixed on him with an expression of malignity which momentarily startled him. She was very lovely and very young, and he was wondering in what circumstances he had deprived her of her father's care, when she came across to him.

"You're Reeder?" Her voice was quivering with fury.

"That's my name," he said in his mild way. "To whom have I the honour—"

"You don't know me, but you will! I've heard about you. You're the man who took Joe—took away Danny's father! You wicked old devil! You— you—"

Mr. Reeder was more embarrassed to see her weep than to hear her recriminations. He did not see her again for a very long time, and then in circumstances which were even less pleasant. Generally speaking, Red Joe Brady was lucky to get away with ten years. Men had had lifers dished out to them for half that Joe had done.

Chapter III: A CROOK'S REQUEST

AFTER his sentence Joe asked if he could see Mr. J.G. Reeder, and Mr. Reeder, who had no qualms whatever about meeting men for whose arrest and conviction he was responsible, went down to the cells under the court and found Red Joe handcuffed in readiness for his departure by taxi-cab to Wormwood Scrubbs.

Such occasions as these can be very painful, and it was not unusual for a prisoner to express his frankest opinions about the man who had brought him to ruin. But Joe was neither offensive nor reproachful. He was a spare man of medium height, and was in the late thirties or the early forties. His neatly brushed hair was flaming red—hence his nickname.

He met the detective with a little smile and asked him to sit down.

"I've no complaints, Mr. Reeder—you gave me a square deal and told no lies about me, and now I want to ask you a favour. I've got a boy at a good school; he doesn't know anything about me and I don't want him to know. I had the sense to put a bit of money aside and tie up the interest so that the bank will pay his fees, and give him all the pocket money he wants while I'm away. And a good friend of mine is going to keep an eye on him. The police don't know anything about the boy or his school. They're fair, I admit it, but they might go nosing around and find out that he's my son. They're fair, but they're clumsy, and it might happen that they'd give away the fact that his father was in stir."

"It's very unlikely, Joe," said Reeder, and the prisoner nodded.

"It's unlikely but it happens," he said. "If it does I want you to step in and look after the boy's interests. You can stop them going too far."

"Who is your 'good friend'?" asked Reeder, and the man hesitated.

"I can't tell you who he is—for reasons," he said.

There was something of uneasiness in his tone; only for the briefest moment did he reveal his doubt.

"I've known him years; in fact, he and I courted the same lady—my poor little wife, who's dead and gone. But he's a good scout and he's got over all that."

"Is he straight?" asked Mr. Reeder.

Joe was silent, pondering this question.

"With me, yes. Bob Kressholm—well, you know him, but he's never been 'inside.'"

Mr. Reeder said nothing.

"He's clever too. One of the wisest men in this country."

Reeder turned his grave eyes upon the man.

"I'd like to help you, Joe; but you'd be wise to give me the name of the school. I might do a little bit of overlooking myself."

Joe shook his head.

"I can't do that—I've asked Bob, and it would look as if I didn't trust him. All I want to ask you to do is to cover up the kid if anything comes out. I want that boy never to know what a crooked thing is."

The detective nodded, and they rose together. The taxi-cab was waiting and two warders stood by the open door. Joe changed the subject and considered his own and immediate misfortune.

"I can't understand how you got me," he said. "I thought I was well away with that second caravan. I hand it to you, you're smart."

Mr. Reeder offered him no enlightenment, nor did he ask the name of the boy. He knew that to the wild-eyed girl Red Joe was just "Danny's father." The next day he went in search of Bob Kressholm.

He found Bob sipping an absinthe frappé in a café near Piccadilly Circus. He was a lithe, dark man, who, in his confidence, surveyed the approach of the detective without apprehension; but when Mr. Reeder sat down by his side with a weary little sigh, Kressholm edged away from him.

"I saw a friend of yours yesterday, Mr.—um—Kressholm."

"Red Joe—yuh! I saw he'd gone down."

"Looking after his son, eh? Guardian of innocent childhood, H'm?"

Kressholm moved uneasily.

"Why not? Joe's a pal of mine. Grand feller, Joe. We only quarrelled twice—about women both times."

"You're a good hater," said Mr. Reeder gently.

He knew nothing then about Wenna Haddin and her ready knife. Nor what she had said to him about Danny.

He saw the man's face twitch.

"I've forgotten all about it—women do not interest me really."

Mr. Reeder sat, his umbrella between his knees, his bony hands gripping the crooked handle.

"H'm," he said, "a good hater. Joe wanted to know how he was caught. I didn't tell him that somebody called me up on the 'phone and told me all about the second caravan."

Kressholm turned his scowling face to the other.

"Who called you up?" he demanded truculently.

"You did," said Mr. Reeder softly. "You were under observation at the time—you didn't know that, but you were. I knew you were a friend of Brady's. I believe you were in the graft but I could never prove it. And you were seen to telephone to me from a public booth in the Piccadilly Tube at eleven twenty-seven one night—that was the hour at which the information came to him. Be careful what you do with that boy, Mr. Kressholm. That is all."

He got up, stood for a moment staring down at the uneasy man, and made his leisurely way from the restaurant.

Kressholm left London a week later, and very rarely returned; in the years that followed he proved himself an excellent organiser.

Danny Brady went out to him in less than a year.

In some mysterious way the story of his father's antecedents had reached the head master of his select school, and his guardian was asked to remove him. The boy came to see Wenna Haddin when the fair was at Nottingham. She was less depressed by his expulsion (for it was no less) than exhilarated by the prospect of his going to Paris.

A tall stripling, with dark auburn hair, he had grown since the girl had seen him last. She listened gravely to the recital of his plans, and her heart ached a little. If she did not like Mr. Reeder she hated Bob Kressholm.

"He's a queer man, Danny. I hope you'll be all right."

"Stuff! Of course I'll be all right," he scoffed. "Bob's a grand man—he wants me to call him Bob. Besides, he's a great friend of my father's."

She did not reply to this. Wenna was older than her years, knew men instinctively, and bitterly regretted all she had said about Danny that day in the wood, when she put into words the fantastical marriage plan of Danny's father.

So Danny went out; he came back a year later, a man, a careless, worldly young man, who had plenty of money to spend and had odd ideas about men and women, and the rights of property. She used to correspond with him. Sometimes he answered her letters, sometimes months went past before he wrote to her.

Years went on, and Wenna seemed not a day older to him when he came back under a strange name. The old troth was re-plighted. He had had some experience in love-making. She felt curiously a stranger.

Two days after he left she heard of a big jewel robbery in Hatton Garden, and, for no reason at all, knew that he was the "tall, slight man" who had been seen to leave the office of a diamond merchant before his unconscious figure was found huddled up behind his desk. For by now Danny was an able lieutenant of the Governor.

Chapter IV: THE GOV'NOR

ALMOST everybody associating with the criminal world had heard of "the Guv'nor." Scotland Yard referred to him jestingly. Inspector Gaylor did not believe in governors, except the "guv'nors" who ran the whizzing gangs, and he was acquainted with them because he had met and testified against these minor bosses, and had had the satisfaction, which only a policeman feels, in seeing them removed in the black van which runs regularly between the Old Bailey and Pentonville Prison.

But the real Governor, the big man, was a myth, a mariner's tale. Even when the jewel robberies began to assume serious proportions, nobody dared suggest that this visionary character had any connection with the crimes.

But to hundreds of lawless men, who spent the greater part of their lives in the cells of convict prisons, the Governor was a holy reality. He was immensely wealthy, he paid large sums to poor guys for their work and spent fortunes to keep them out of prison. At the very suggestion that a newcomer to Dartmoor was a highly paid lieutenant of the Governor, he was treated with respect which amounted to reverence.

This shining and radiant figure was, alas, unreachable. Nobody knew his identity. There was no channel by which a poor and bungling burglar might approach his divinity. They told stories about him—half-true, half- imaginary. He was a titled gentleman, who lived in a great house in the country and had his own motor cars and horses. He was a publican who kept a saloon in Islington. He was a trusted member of the C.I.D., who misused his position to his great advantage.

Certainly he chose discreet men to serve him, for never had any crime been brought home to him through the failure or loquacity of an assistant.

"The Governor!" said Inspector Gaylor scornfully, when there was first suggested to him the authorship of the Hatton Garden robbery. "You've been reading detective stories. That's Harry Dyall's work."

But when they pulled in Harry Dyall, his alibi was police-proof, and the more closely the crime was examined the more satisfied were the police that the robbery had been carried out by a master—which Harry was not.

"That's no corporal's job—it's a general's. If Bob Kressholm was in England I should say it was his," said Gaylor, who was called in by the city police.

It is very difficult for the police to believe in organised systems of crime carried out under the direction of one man.

"They meet in a dark cellar, I suppose," he sneered at the subordinate to whom the Governor was becoming a reality. "Wear masks and whatnots. Get that idea out of your mind, Simpson. Those things only happen in books."

The Governor and his general staff did not meet in dark cellars, nor did they wear masks. There is a big hotel near the Place de l'Opera in Paris which is rather noisy and rather expensive. The noisiest of all the rooms is the big saloon situated in one corner of the block. Here the incessant pip-squeak of taxi-cabs, the deep boom of motor horns, the thunder and ramble of cumbersome omnibuses are caught and amplified.

Four men played bridge; a fifth, and the younger, looked on impatiently.

The eldest of the four helped himself to a whisky and soda from a little table at his side, and threw down a card. The others followed suit mechanically. Nobody worried about the game. The cards might be convenient if some unexpected visitor arrived, though it was very unlikely that any such interruption would come.

"They called in Reeder over that Hauptman job of ours—you know that, Tommy?"

The man he addressed nodded.

"Reeder?" asked the young watcher. "Isn't he the fellow who pinched my father?"

Bob Kressholm nodded.

"Reeder is hot, but he doesn't as a rule touch anything but forgery. You needn't worry about him, Danny. Yes, he pinched your father. You owe him one for that."

The young man smiled.

"I remember—Wenna loathes him" he said. "Funny how women hold on to their prejudices. I was talking to her last week—"

Bob Kressholm's eyelids snapped.

"Talking to her—was she in Paris?"

For a moment Danny was embarrassed.

"Yes; she came over with her father to see a turn at the Hippique."

Kressholm was about to say something, but changed his mind.

"Anyway, Reeder's working with the police—he is in the Public Prosecutor's office now. You're not known in London, are you, Peter?"

Peter Hertz grunted something uncomplimentary about South Africa, a country where he was known, and Kressholm chuckled.

"Fine! But they don't send their prints over to Scotland Yard, so you're safe. Now listen, I've got a job for you boys..."

They listened for half an hour, and under his direction drew little plans on the backs of bridge markers. At eleven they separated. Danny Brady would have gone too, but the other asked him to wait behind.

"Stay on—I want to talk to you, kid." Kressholm was greyer than he had been when Red Joe went down for his ten.

"Why didn't you tell me Wenna was over?" he asked.

Danny looked uncomfortable.

"I didn't think you'd be interested, Bob," he said. Kressholm forced a smile.

"Always interested in Wenna—she doesn't like me. I saw her a couple of months ago and she treated me like a dog! God, she's lovely!"

That came out involuntarily. Danny's discomfort increased.

"She said nothing about me?" The young man lied with a head shake. "You and she are good friends, eh?"

"Why, yes. As a matter of fact, I gave her a ring—"

Kressholm nodded slowly; his blazing eyes were fixed on the carpet lest they betrayed him.

"Is that so? Gave her a ring? That's fine. I suppose you'll be thinking of throwing in your hand after this and settling down, eh? There's circus blood in you too."

Danny's face went red.

"I'm not going back on you," he said loudly. "I owe a lot to you, Bob—"

"I don't know that you do," said the other.

Here he did an injustice to himself as a tutor. For five years he had revealed wrong as an amusing kind of right, and black as an artistic variant of white. Crime had no shabby background in the golden flood-light of romance; its shabby rags, in the glamour with which he had invested them, became delightful vestments.

"You're doing the job—you're the Big Shot in the game, Danny. I wouldn't trust anybody but you. And talking of big shots—"

He went into his bedroom and came back with something in his hand that glittered in the lights of the chandelier.

"That's the first time I've trusted you with a gun. Don't be afraid to use it—you're not to get caught. There will be three cars planted for you with the engines running. I'll give you the plan. I'll have an aeroplane just outside of London. If you're pinched, don't worry: the Governor will get you out."

"That's the first time I've trusted you with a gun. Don't be afraid to use it."

The young man examined the revolver, fascinated. His hand trembled; he had a moment of exaltation, such as the young knight must have felt when the golden spurs were fastened to his heel.

"You can trust me, Governor," he breathed; "and if there's no get-out, send me the Life of Napoleon."

The Life of Napoleon had a special interest for the Governor's friends.

He stayed on for an hour whilst Bob talked about West End jewellers, their peculiarities and weaknesses...

Chapter V: MURDER!

MR. J.G. REEDER began to take a solicitous interest in West End jewellers' shops soon after the Hauptmann affair. For the Hauptmann affair was serious; that a shop manager should be bludgeoned in broad daylight and three emerald necklaces snatched from a show-case was bad enough; that the two thieves should escape with their booty was a very black mark against police administration.

Questions were being asked in Parliament, an under-secretary interviewed a police chief and made pointed comments on efficiency. Then it was that Mr. Reeder was asked to "collaborate." He was a member of the Public Prosecutor's staff, and for some strange reason was persona grata at Scotland Yard—which is odd, remembering how extremely unpopular non-service detectives are at that institution.

So it came to be that Mr. Reeder spent quite a lot of time wandering about the West End of London, his frock-coat buttoned tightly, his square-topped bowler hat at the back of his head, a disconsolate figure of a man. Jewellers came to know him; they were rather amused by his helplessness and ignorance of the trade.

One of them spoke to Inspector Gaylor.

"What use would he be in a raid? He must be a hundred years old!"

"A hundred and seven," said Gaylor soberly. "At the same time I wouldn't advise you to stand in his way if he's in a hurry."

Griddens was robbed that night, the contents of the strong room taken; the night watchman was never seen again. Then the Western Jewellers Trust had a visit which cost the underwriter twelve thousand pounds. Mortimer Simms, the court jewellers, was robbed in daylight.

Mr. Reeder was in bed when two of these robberies occurred. When he appeared after the Mortimer Simms affair he was subjected to a certain amount of derision.

But Mr. Reeder was not distressed. He continued his studies and delved into the mysteries of precious stones. He handled diamonds which were not diamonds but white sapphires, to the top of which a slither of diamond was attached. He examined samples of the faker's art which were entirely new to the detective. He learned of Antwerp agencies which were exclusively run for the disposal of stolen gems, and of other matters of criminal ingenuity which, he confessed in a tone of mingled admiration and shocked surprise, he had never dreamed about.

After the Mortimer Simms robbery he seldom left the West End; actually lived in a small hotel near Jermyn Street, and applied himself more closely to the study of jewels and their illicit collectors.

There was a long and blameless interval during which the Governor's men did not operate. Then one day a typewritten letter came to Mr. Reeder. It ran:

"Keep your eyes skinned. The Seven Sisters are going—and how! Conduit Street will be getting lively soon."

There was no signature. The paper on which the letter was written had a soft, matt surface such as you may find in the racks of any French hotel, and the "e" in "eyes" had been inadvertently typed "é." A week passed and nothing happened.

Then, on a dreary afternoon...

The Seven Sisters lay glittering in their blue velvet case for all who cared to stop and admire. They had been written about and photographed, and usually there was a sprinkling of people before Donnyburne's plate-glass window, doing homage to these seven perfectly matched diamonds which had once adorned a royal crown.

To-day, because it was raining and a gusty wind was blowing, people hurried down Conduit Street without pausing before the big jeweller's store to pay homage.

A big two-seater car drew slowly to the side of the kerb, passed in front of a stationary taxi-cab and came to a halt twenty yards west of Donnyburne's. A young man, wearing a long trench coat, got out at his leisure, examined one of the front tyres carefully, and walked slowly to the back of the car. A taxi driver, who stood on the edge of the kerb, smoking a short clay pipe, looked at the young man curiously, though there was little reason for curiosity, for there was nothing extraordinary about him. He was rather good-looking; his skin was a deep olive; on his upper lip was a small reddish moustache. The hair under the soft hat was red too, but nobody observed him very closely at the moment.

He walked back to Donnyburne's and stood before the window, examining the Seven Sisters. Then, without haste, he seemed to be drawing a circle with his finger. There was a curious squeaking sound, and when he pushed at the window the circle of glass fell inward. He lifted the case, snapped down the lid and walked back to where his car was waiting. The taxi driver had his back towards him, and saw him pass and jump into the car, which stood with its engines running. Then:

"Stop that man!"

Danny pushed inwards the circle of glass and snatched up the case of diamonds

Somebody screamed the words from the doorway of the jeweller's. It was unfortunate that a policeman turned the corner and came into sight at that moment. He saw the gesticulating shop assistant, and as the car moved he leaped upon the running-board and caught the left arm of the driver. For a second the young man jerked backward, but he could not loose the hold. His knees gripped the steering column as the car gathered speed; his right hand fell into his side pocket. "That's yours," he said very calmly, and as cold-bloodedly as a butcher might destroy a beast, he shot the policeman through the face.

It was done in a second. He dropped the gun to his side, gripped the wheel and spun round the corner.

He had not seen the elderly man with the side whiskers and the queer top hat, a man who, in spite of the rain, did not wear an overcoat nor was his umbrella unfurled. If he had seen him he might not have considered Mr. Reeder a serious obstacle to his plans. Indeed, he gasped his amazement when, just as the car took a turn, he jumped to the running-board.

"Stop, please!"

The driver dropped his hand to his side. Before he could raise it something sprayed into his face, something that took the breath from his body and left him fighting for air.

Mr. Reeder switched off the engine, guided the car to the kerb, and allowed it to crash itself violently to a standstill against a stationary lorry. It had hardly stopped before he gripped the young man and dragged him on to the sidewalk.

Police whistles were blowing; he saw two policemen running, and handed over his prisoner.

"Search him before you take him to the station," he said gently. "It is quite permissible in the case of a man who is carrying dangerous firearms."

He picked up the pistol from the seat of the car, examined it carefully and dropped it into his pocket. The young man had recovered from the shock of the ammonia fumes that had been vaporised into his face, and by this time he was handcuffed. A cab drew up to the edge of the kerb, and the policeman signalled him.

"No, no." Mr. Reeder was very insistent. "There is too little room in a cab. Perhaps that gentleman would help us."

He nodded to a stout man in a big limousine which had pulled up to give its occupant an opportunity of satisfying his curiosity.

The stout man went pale at the suggestion that his car should be used for the conveyance of a murderer, but eventually he took his seat by the driver. It was to Marlborough Street that the prisoner was taken, and whilst the inspector was telephoning to Scotland Yard Mr. Reeder offered intelligent advice.

"Take every stitch of his clothing from him and give him new clothes, even if you have to buy them," he said. "I'm afraid I have a—um— rather—um—criminal mind, and I am just putting myself in this—er—unfortunate young man's place, and wondering exactly what I should do."

The clothing was removed; an old suit was discovered, and, by the time Chief Inspector Gaylor arrived from Scotland Yard, Mr. Reeder was making a very careful examination, not of the pockets, but of the lining of the murderer's discarded waistcoat. Between the lining and the shaped cloth of the breast he found a thin white paper which contained as much reddish powder as could be put upon the little finger-tip. In the lining of the coat he found its fellow. In the heel of the right boot, running the length of the sole, was a double-edged knife, thin and very flexible and keen.

"Pretty well equipped, Mr. Reeder." Gaylor viewed the discoveries with interest. "It almost supports your view."

"It quite supports my view, Mr. Gaylor, if you will allow me to say so." Mr. Reeder was apologetic. "As a rule I do not believe in—um— organised crime. The story of Napoleon Fagins at the heads of large bodies of men banded together for—um—illegal purposes is one at which—well, frankly, I have smiled hitherto."

"He got away with the Seven Sisters, eh?" Mr. Gaylor looked around. "Where are they?" Mr. Reeder shook his head.

"I'm afraid they're not here. That is one of the mysteries—indeed, the only mystery—of the raid. The assistant saw him from the moment he committed the crime till the moment he got into his car. When we arrested him we found neither the diamonds nor the case. The car is in the yard, being scientifically dissected, if I may employ so gruesome an illustration. I picked up the machine as it came round the corner, and there was no chance of his getting rid of the diamonds whilst he was under my eye.

"I searched his pockets the moment the police came up. And that—um—is that."

It was no coincidence that he had been in the region of Donnyburne's that afternoon. Mr. Reeder did not as a rule pay very much attention to anonymous "squawks," but he had been impressed by the paper, and the "e" with the acute accent. Such an afternoon was climatically most favourable for such a raid, and it was only by a fluke that he was not an actual witness of the murder. He had heard the shot and almost instantly the murderer's car had come into sight.

"He has given the name of John Smith, which is highly unimaginative. There are no papers to identify him. The car was hired from the Golston Garage—hired by the week, and a substantial deposit paid. John Smith has been seen in the West End of London, but nothing is known against him, and for the moment it is impossible to trace his address. I should imagine that he was living at a good hotel somewhere in the West End of London. He has lived in Paris, I should think; his shoes, his shirt and his necktie are French made. He probably arrived in London a week ago."

There was nothing to be gained by questioning John Smith. He seemed to feel the disgrace of wearing block-made clothes more acutely than the brand of murderer, and when the inspector questioned him he was indifferent and unrepentant.

"There's one thing I'd like to ask you—was that old bird who gassed me J.G. Reeder? I'd like to have him alone for a few minutes."

"You with a gun, I suppose?" said Gaylor savagely.

He was no philosopher where a comrade had been killed in the execution of his duty. People who kill policemen receive no consideration from such of the police as happen to be alive.

"With your hands, eh? He'd beat the life out of you, you dirty murderer!"

John Smith was amused.

"I shan't hang, don't worry," he said, almost airily. "Don't ask me who my confederates are, because I wouldn't dream of telling you. Besides, the new police regulations prevent your asking me questions, don't they?"

He showed two rows of even white teeth in a smile.

Chapter VI: THE BLOODSTAINED CAB

HE was as confident the next morning, the more so since his hotel address had been discovered and he was allowed to wear his own clothes, after they had been carefully searched.
The proceedings at the police court were formal. An indubitable murderer was in custody, and for the moment the police were concentrating on their search for the missing diamonds. Whither they had gone was a mystery. The taximan whose cab was near Donnyburne's said he had seen the murderer carrying a blue velvet case in his hand; that was the first thing that aroused his suspicion. He had not seen the murder committed; he had been looking round at the moment for his fare, a middle-aged lady whom he had picked up at Victoria and who had kept him waiting an hour, and eventually had not returned.
"It's the first time I've been bilked for ten years," he said. He had this little trouble of his own. He had heard the shot, had seen the car go round the corner, leaving a dead man lying half in the road and half on the sidewalk, and had run to his assistance. A woman who was walking on the other side of the road, who also had heard the shot and had seen the machine pass on, was emphatic that nothing had been thrown from the car, nor did it seem likely to Mr. Reeder that the robber should attempt to throw away the gems he had won so dearly.
The car, as he had said, had been inspected, the lining removed, and had been stripped to its chassis and the inner panelling unscrewed. But there was no sign of the seven diamonds.
Not for the first time in his life, Mr. J.G. Reeder was up against the unbelievable. He had scoffed at gangs all his life; and here undoubtedly, and in the heart of London, was operating no mere confederacy of two or three men, whose acts were dictated by opportunity and expediency, but a body directed by a master mind (Mr. Reeder shuddered at the discovery that he was accepting such a bogey as a master criminal), operating on pre-determined plans and embodying not one branch of the criminal profession but several.
After the police court proceedings he went, as usual, by tramcar, a sad-looking figure, sitting in a corner seat, resting his hands upon the handle of his umbrella and expressing his gloom on his face.
The long journey was all too short for him, for he was resolving many things in his mind.
It was dark when he came to Brockley Road. As he alighted from the car and cautiously crossed that motor-infected thoroughfare he was amazed to see a familiar figure standing on the corner of the street. Gaylor did not often honour him by visiting the neighbourhood.
"You are here, are you?" Inspector Gaylor was obviously relieved.
Another man had alighted from the tramcar at the same time as Mr. Reeder, but he had hardly noticed him.
"It's all right, Jackson." Gaylor addressed him familiarly. "You'll find Benson up the road. Stay outside Mr. Reeder's house. I will give you fresh instructions when I come out."
They passed into Mr. Reeder's modest domicile together.

"You've got a housekeeper, haven't you, Mr. Reeder? I'd like to talk to her."

Mr. Reeder looked at him, pained.

"Aren't you being a little mysterious, my friend? You may think it odd, but I detest mysteries."

He was saved the trouble of ringing for his housekeeper, for that amiable lady came from some lower region to meet her employer.

"Has anybody been here?" asked Gaylor.

Mr. Reeder sighed, but did not protest.

"Yes, sir, a gentleman came with a letter. He said it was very urgent."

"Nothing else?" asked Gaylor. "He didn't leave a parcel?"

"No, sir," said the housekeeper, surprised.

Gaylor nodded.

The two men went to Mr. Reeder's study. The curtains were drawn, a little fire burned in the grate. It was one of those high-ceilinged rooms, and had an atmosphere of snug comfort. Gaylor closed the door.

"There's the letter." He pointed to the desk.

It was typewritten, addressed to "J.G. Reeder, Esq." and marked "Very Urgent."

"Do you mind seeing what it says?"

Mr. Reeder opened the letter. It was a closely typed sheet of manuscript, which had neither preamble nor signature. It ran:

"Re John Smith. I am asking you what may seem at first to be an impossible favour. You are one of those who saw the shooting of Constable Burnett, and your evidence will be of the greatest importance in the forthcoming trial. I do not hope to save him if he comes into court. If you will help him to escape by such methods as I will outline to you, I will place to your credit the sum of fifty thousand pounds. If you refuse, I will kill you. I am putting the matter very clearly, so that there can be no mistake on either side. It is not necessary to tell you that fifty thousand pounds will provide you with comfort for the rest of your life and place you in a position of independence. I promise you that your name will not be connected with the escape. John Smith must not hang. I will stop at nothing to prevent this. Nothing is more certain than that you will meet your death if you refuse to help. If you are interested, and you agree, insert an advertisement in the agony column of The Times next Tuesday, in the following terms:

'JOHNNY,—meet me at the usual place.—JAMES.'

and we will go further into this matter."

Reeder put down the letter and stared incredulously at his companion.

"Well?" said Gaylor.

"Dear me, how stupid!" murmured Mr. Reeder. He looked up at the ceiling. "That makes forty-one, or is it forty-two?"

"Forty-two what?" asked Gaylor curiously.

"Forty-two people have threatened to take my life if I didn't do something or other, or because I have done something—or is it forty-three?"

"I have had a similar letter," said Gaylor. "I found it at my house when I got home to-night.

Reeder, this is one of the biggest things we have ever struck. It is certainly the biggest thing I have ever known in my experience as a police officer. It is something more than an ordinary gang. These people have money and probably influence, and for some reason or other we have hurt them pretty badly when we took this young man. What are you going to do?"

Mr. Reeder pursed his lips as if his immediate intention was to whistle.

"Naturally, I shall not put in the advertisement as our friend suggests," he said. "Why next Tuesday? Why not to-morrow? What is the reason for the delay? The letter was urgently delivered; it is sure to call for an urgent reply. It is a little too obvious."

Gaylor nodded.

"That is what I thought. In other words, nothing will happen to you until next Tuesday. My impression is that we are in for a troublesome time almost immediately; that is why I telephoned to the Yard to have one of my men pick you up and shadow you down here. These people will move like lightning. Do you remember what this fellow said this morning in court? The whole story was a fabrication and a case of mistaken identity. That is a pretty conventional excuse, Reeder, but it was very well timed. Who are the witnesses against this man? You are one of the principals; I am, in a way, another. The shop assistant is a third. The two policemen who arrested him hardly count. Huggins, the taxi-driver, one of the most important, disappeared at six o'clock this evening."

Mr. Reeder nodded at him thoughtfully. "I foresaw that possibility," he said.

"His taxi-cab was found in a side street off the Edgware Road," Gaylor went on. "There was blood on the seat and on the window of the cab. He lives over the mews very near the place where it was found. He hasn't been home, and I don't suppose he'll come home," he added grimly. "I have got two men looking after the shop assistant, who lives at Anerley. He also has had a warning not to go to court. Does that strike you as interesting?"

The fatal cab was found by a policeman... There was blood on the seat and over the wind-screen. Mr. Reeder did not answer. He loosened his frock coat, put his hat carefully on a side table and sat down at his desk. He stared absently at Gaylor for some time before he spoke, then, opening a drawer, he took out a folder and extracted two sheets of foolscap.

"It is very bad to have preconceived ideas, Mr. Gaylor," he said. "I did not believe in gangs. I thought they were a figment—if you will excuse the expression—of the novelist's imagination, and here I am discussing them as seriously as though they were a normal condition of life. By the way, I knew the cabman had disappeared. It was silly of us not to have arrested him—in fact, I went to arrest him, and then I heard of the—um—accident."

Gaylor gaped at him.

"Arrest him?" incredulously. "Why on earth?"

"He had the Seven Sisters—the diamonds. Obviously nobody else could have had them. They were tossed into the cab by Smith—whose name, I think, is Danny Brady—as he passed. In fact, the cab was planted there for the purpose. Huggins—an interesting name— was one of the gang. The blood-stained cab is picturesque, but unconvincing. I should have the Channel ports very carefully watched and circulate a description of the—um—deceased."

Chapter VII: BLUE FUNK

MR. REEDER'S theory had a rapid confirmation. "Huggins" was picked up the next night, not at a Channel port, but at Harwich, and he took his place in the dock as an accessory to the murder. Friday came and passed. There was no evidence of reprisal. Gaylor would have placed detectives on guard before and in Mr. Reeder's house, but that gentleman grew so unusually testy at the suggestion that the inspector decided to let his colleague die any way he wished.

"Die be—um—blowed!" said Mr. Reeder, and apologised for his vulgarity. "That letter was what is called in America a—um—'front.' In other words, it was a show-off and meant nothing. I suspect friend Kressholm is establishing an alibi."

"A little late for an alibi," said Gaylor.

"Not so late as you think," was Reeder's cryptic reply.

It was during the trial of Daniel Brady that Kressholm came to London. There was no reason why he should not. He held a British passport, and there was not a scrap of evidence to connect him with the crime.

He had not been at his hotel five minutes when they telephoned from the inquiry office to ask him if he would see a lady. Before they told him Wenna's name he knew who it was.

Sorrow had refined, as it had aged, her. He never realised how much older than Danny she was till he saw that pale, haggard face.

"I've seen Danny," she said breathlessly. "He told me that he was coming to London. I've called here three times this afternoon. He believes in you—"

"What did he tell you?" His voice was sharp.

The two men seized their victim and dragged him from the interior of the van.

Danny's confidence in him did not outweigh his alarm. That he should be even remotely associated with this crime...

She shook her head impatiently.

"You needn't worry, Kressholm; I know you are in this. No, no, he didn't tell me, but I know. What can we do? You've got to save him."

He was staring at her hungrily, and, distressed as she was, she did not realise that even in this tragic moment his interest was for her and not for the man who stood in the shadow of the scaffold.

"I don't know what we can do. I'm getting the best lawyers. Only Reeder's tied him up pretty completely."

"Reeder" she gasped. "That old man! Has he done this?"

Bob Kressholm nodded.

"He's always been down on the Bradys," he said glibly. "That old bird will rather die than let up on Danny. He was waiting for him—in fact, he arrested him."

She sat down heavily in a chair and buried her face in her hands. He stood looking at the slim, bent back. That must be the ring that Danny gave her —the glittering sapphire on her finger. He went angrily hot at the thought.

It must be ten years since that disagreeable episode in the wood. She had forgotten all that perhaps... he had been a little raw. At any rate, she had forgiven him or she would not be here.

"I hate to see you like this, Wenna," he said. "I'll fix Reeder for you one of these days."

She sprang to her feet, her eyes blazing.

"One of these days—you? Don't worry, Kressholm, I'll fix him. If anything happens to Danny—" Her voice broke.

He soothed her with the clumsiness which was part of his insincerity.

She would have attended the trial, but he dissuaded her; she would upset Danny, he said. In truth he was anxious that she should not meet Reeder, that astute man who had a disconcerting habit of telling unpleasant truths, and he was glad that the girl had taken his advice when, on the opening day of the trial, Reeder approached him outside the Old Bailey.

"You're giving evidence, of course, Mr. Kressholm?"

The other man turned his suspicious eye upon his questioner.

"What do I know about it? I know Danny, of course, but I've been out of the crooked game so long that he wouldn't have told me he was going to do a fool thing like shooting a copper."

"Indeed?" Mr. Reeder inclined his head graciously. "I suppose that governors do not take risks—"

"Governors!" said the man scornfully. "Where did you get that word? You've been listening to those penny-dreadful flatties at the Yard! No, I tried to keep the boy straight he's the son of my pal, and that's why he is having all the legal assistance that money can buy."

"And Mr. Huggins—who, by the way, was identified this morning by a South African police officer, who happened to be in London, as Peter Hertz —is his father a friend of yours?"

For a second Bob Kressholm was embarrassed.

"Naturally I shall look after him," he said at last. "I don't know the bird, but they say that he is a friend of Danny's. I don't even know the gang."

Mr. Reeder looked down at the pavement for a long time.

"Is there anything wrong with my boots?" asked Kressholm facetiously.

Mr. Reeder shook his head.

"No—only I shouldn't like to be standing in them," he said. "Red Joe Brady is due for release in a month's time."

He left the master-man with this unpleasant reminder.

The trial ran its inevitable course. On the second day the jury retired and returned with a verdict of guilty against Brady and Hertz. Danny was sentenced to death and Hertz to fourteen years' penal servitude.

Mr. Reeder was not in court. It was not his business to be there, so he did not hear the commendations of the judge, or see Danny's frosty smile as the sentence of death was passed and there came to him the realisation that the all-powerful Governor was for once impotent. He had listened to Reeder's evidence closely, and only once did he appear startled; that was when the

detective told of the warning he had had that the Seven Sisters were threatened.
Mr. Reeder read the account in the late editions of the newspapers and sighed drearily. Kressholm was not in court at the last, and had asked for an interview with the young man, a request which was refused.

It was nearly midnight and Mr. Reeder was preparing to go to bed, when he heard the front bell ring. He had had installed a small house telephone on to the street. It saved him a lot of trouble when his housekeeper had gone to bed. He pressed the knob which lit a small red lamp in the lintel of the street door and incidentally showed the concealed receiver of the 'phone, and asked: "Who is there?"

To his surprise, "Kressholm" was the reply.

Kressholm was the last man in the world he expected to see that night. He went downstairs slowly, switched on the light in the hall and opened the door. The man was alone.

"I'm sorry to disturb you—" he began.

"I'll take your apologies in my office," said Reeder. "Do you mind walking ahead of me?"

He followed the visitor into the big room which was office and living-room, and, closing the door, pointed to a chair.

"I'll stand," said Kressholm shortly.

He was nervous. His restless hands moved from one button of his overcoat to the other. He put down his hat in one place, took it up and put it down in another.

"I want you to understand, Reeder," he began.

"Mister Reeder," said that gentleman gently. "If ever I put you in the dock you can call me what you like; for the moment I would rather be called 'mister' which means 'master,' and I will be your master sooner or later, or my name is Smith!"

Kressholm was taken aback by the correction. He scowled a little and then laughed nervously.

"Sorry, Mr. Reeder, but this case has rattled me. You see, the boy was in my charge. His father and I were old friends."

Mr. Reeder had sat down at his writing-table. He leaned back now and sighed.

"Is all this necessary?" he asked. "It is not conscience that has brought you here; it is blue funk, isn't it?"

Kressholm went an angry red.

"I am afraid of nobody in the world." He raised his voice. "Not you —, and not that damned—"

"S-sh!" J.G. Reeder was apparently shocked. "I do not like strong language. You are afraid of nobody but Red Joe. I wonder, too, if you are afraid of that little circus girl who has paid several visits to your hotel? Miss Haddin, isn't it?"

Bob Kressholm stared but said nothing. He found a difficulty in speaking.

"She was—um—engaged to the young man. A fiery young woman; I remember her—yes. If she knew what I know—"

"I don't know what you mean," said Kressholm huskily.

"Then let me tell you why you have called on me," said Mr. Reeder.

He folded his arms on the table and fixed the other with a steely eye.

"When I see his father, you want me to tell him that I and Mr. Gaylor were offered fifty thousand pounds to secure his escape. We were also threatened with death if we did not agree."

Kressholm's face was ludicrous in its blank amazement.

"That is just what you wished to ask me," Mr. Reeder went on; "but you don't exactly know how to broach the subject. Well, it is difficult to convey to a police officer the fact that you have both tried to bribe and threaten him without involving yourself in a lot of trouble. I will save you a little trouble, anyway. You were establishing your defence. You trained this boy the way he has gone, and it is going to take the whole Metropolitan Police Force to save your life. If you are wise you will go back to France and let Red Joe give the French police the bother of arresting him for your murder."

"If you think I am afraid of Red Joe—"

Mr. Reeder nodded.

"You are terrified, and I think you have very good reason."

Reeder walked to the door and opened it.

"I don't want to talk to you any more, Kressholm." He glanced down. "I see you are wearing shoes this evening. Well, I should not like to be in those, either."

Kressholm gave no further explanation. None of his gang, seeing him now, would have recognised the ruthless Governor they knew.

Chapter VIII: A PRISON TRAGEDY

DANNY BRADY was a foolish young man, but he had quite enough intelligence to know that his appeal, which he would make automatically, was doomed to failure. He was completely satisfied on the subject when the governor, making his morning visit to the condemned cell, told him that a parcel of books had arrived for him.

He showed Danny the list and told him he could have one volume at a time. Danny chose The Life of Napoleon. He spent the greater part of the day writing a letter to the girl he would never see again, and took The Life of Napoleon to bed with him. About eleven o'clock he put the book on the floor.

"Leave it there," he said to one of the watchers. "I don't think I am going to sleep very well to-night."

Now, a condemned prisoner may not sleep with his face covered. When Danny drew the coarse sheet over his head one of the watching warders admonished him.

"Turn down that sheet!" he said.

Just at that moment the sheet began to go red very rapidly, for Danny had cut his throat with a safety razor blade which had been carefully bound into the cover of the book.

All the available doctors could not save Danny's life; he died before twelve. The prison governor and four warders sat up all night long taking evidence from the warders concerned.

Mr. Reeder went down and saw the book. Afterwards he called at a London hotel where he knew Kressholm was staying. The man had recovered something of his old poise. He expressed his deep sorrow at the death of his young friend, but could give no information about that fatal Life of Napoleon. He admitted that in his youth he had been a bookbinder—that fact was registered on his documents at Scotland Yard, for Bob Kressholm had been twice in the hands of the police.

"I know nothing about it," he said. "I only put 'bookbinder' because I thought I'd get an easy job in prison. I don't see how the razor blade could be put into the binding—"

"It is a very simple matter," said Mr. Reeder patiently. "The boy had only to tear off the inside paper, and it was easy, because it was stuck with gum that had not even been set."

He and Gaylor made a search of the man's baggage, but found nothing in the nature of a bookbinding outfit. There was not sufficient evidence to have justified an arrest, but Kressholm spent that night in Scotland Yard answering interminable questions, and was a weary man when they had finished with him.

The sensation came into the afternoon papers in the shape of a short paragraph issued by Scotland Yard.

"Daniel Brady, lying under sentence of death, succeeded in committing suicide last night at eleven o'clock. The weapon was a safety razor blade which had been smuggled into the prisoner, bound in the cover of a book, by some person or persons unknown."

It was the next day that the inquest provided the full story of the tragedy. Mr. Reeder read it from start to finish, though he had heard the evidence of every witness before the case came to court. He was reading the newspaper in the room where he had interviewed Kressholm, and had put it down by his side, when there was a tap at his door and his housekeeper came in.

"Will you see a man named Joseph Brady?" she asked.

Mr. Reeder drew a long breath. He looked from the woman to the newspaper, then picked up the paper, carefully folded it and put it into his wastepaper basket.

"Yes, I will see Joseph Brady," he said softly.

Joe had not changed, save that his hair, which had been red, was almost white, and the smooth face that Reeder had known was drawn and haggard.

Reeder pushed up a chair for the stricken man, and he dropped into it. For fully five minutes neither spoke, then Joe lifted his head, and said:

"Thank God he went that way!"

Reeder nodded.

"I read about the case in prison." Brady's voice was even and steady. "I thought I'd get to London in time to see him, but I got there the morning after it happened. I could have seen him then, but it would have meant going to the inquiry and giving evidence, and telling a lot of things that I want to keep to myself."

There was another long interregnum of silence. The man sat, head bent, his arms folded on his breast. He showed no other evidence of his emotion. After a while he looked up.

"You're as straight a man as I've ever met, Reeder. I've heard other lags say they look upon you more as a pal than an enemy, but that isn't why I've come to see you. I've come to talk about"—there was a pause— "Kressholm—Bob Kressholm."

"Why bother with him?" asked Mr. Reeder, and knew he was saying something very inane.

A quick smile came and left the man's face.

"I thought I'd tell you something. I know all that Kressholm's done to my boy, and I know why he did it—about this kid Wenna, I mean. No, I haven't seen her, I won't see her yet. I've been talking with the boys, you know—the underworld, you call it—"

"I don't, but quite a lot of people do. And what did they tell you?"

"They say Danny was caught on a squeal—that somebody planted you to get him. The same man, I guess, who told you about my printing plant in the caravan." He paused expectantly, and when Mr. Reeder said nothing he laughed harshly. "I thought so! I've got money—stacks of it. I'm one of the few crooks who have ever made a fortune and kept it. I'm going to spend that money wisely. I'm going to use it to kill Kressholm."

Mr. Reeder murmured something admonitory, but the man shook his head.

"I'm telling you that I'm going to kill him. That's going to be my little joke. But I shan't be caught, and I shan't be punished. I'm going to hang him, Reeder—hang him by the neck till he's dead. That's the sentence I've passed on him! And neither you nor any other man will know it. That's the thought that's keeping me sane."

"You're mad, you fool," said Mr. Reeder, with unusual roughness. "No murderer ever gets away with it in this country. I'm not taking too much notice of what you say—I feel terribly sorry for you. If I were not an—um—officer of the law I should say he deserved almost anything that's coming to him. Get out of the country—go to the Cape or somewhere. I'll help you at Scotland Yard—"

Red Joe shook his head.

"I stay here. I'm not leaving this country even if Kressholm leaves. He'll come back—there's nothing more certain than that—and I'll kill him, Reeder! I came to tell you that, and to tell Scotland Yard that."

He picked up his hat and walked to the door. For once in his life Mr. Reeder found himself entirely devoid of speech. He walked to the window and looked out: a taxi-cab was waiting; he saw the man enter and drive off, and, going back to the telephone, he called Gaylor.

The inspector was out and was not reachable. Mr. Reeder contented himself with writing the gist of the interview and sending it by express post to Scotland Yard.

It occurred to him afterwards that it was his duty to arrest the man summarily; he was a convict on licence, and had uttered threats to murder, which in itself was a felony. But somehow that solution never occurred to Mr. Reeder. And it must be admitted, although he was on the side of the law, that it took him a long time to energise himself into ringing up the hotel where he knew Kressholm was staying. He did not expect to find that good hater, and was surprised when, after a short delay, Kressholm's voice replied to his.

The man listened and laughed scornfully. Evidently something had happened which had removed his fear of Red Joe, and what that something was Mr. Reeder was curious to know, but was not satisfied. It was Bob Kressholm who pointed out the strict path of duty, and Mr. Reeder was pardonably annoyed.

"If he threatened me why didn't you pinch him?" demanded Kressholm. "You'd look silly if he did me in—but he won't."

"Why are you so sure, my dear friend?" asked Mr. Reeder gently.

"Because, my dear friend," mocked Kressholm's voice, "I am a pretty difficult man to reach."

Chapter IX: THE CARAVAN SECRET

MR. REEDER was well aware of the fact; Kressholm never moved without his escort of gunmen. He had seen them hovering in the background that day at the Old Bailey. Not for nothing was he called "the Governor"; the very title presupposed a following. He had doubled his escort since he heard that Red Joe was out of prison. His men slept in the rooms on either side of his. He had a guard outside the hotel.

Kressholm would have gone to Paris—he knew the bolt holes better there, and had a certain pull with important officials, and, but for Wenna, he would have left England on the day of the inquest. But Wenna was unusually humble and pathetically helpless. Old Lew Haddin came down to London to bring her back to the show. He was not so much concerned by the tragedy which had broken her as by the loss of an attraction.

"I'll come when I'm ready," she said.

Lew complained sadly to Kressholm that girls were quite different from what they had been in the days of his mother.

"No respect for God or man—or fathers," he quavered. "She's afraid of nothing. She was making lions jump through hoops when she was ten, and she thinks no more of dropping two thousand feet on a parachute than you and me would think of walking downstairs."

He complained, but left her alone.

She had so far forgotten her old detestation of Bob Kressholm that she used to go to dinner with him in his suite. If she contributed nothing to his happiness—for she would sit for hours, hardly speaking a word, staring past him—she added zest and determination to this man who was in her thrall. He saw a grand culmination to these years of disappointment and rebuff. Red Joe he did not fear—he would be "taken care of." If he were uneasy at all it was because Joe made no direct attempt to see him, did not communicate by word or letter.

Though he professed to be without fear, he heaved a sigh of relief when he heard, from the man whom he had set to shadow him, that Brady had left one afternoon for the Continent. For one moment he had an idea of ringing up Scotland Yard and reporting this irregularity. A convict is not allowed to leave the district to which he is assigned, and a breach of this law might bring about his return to prison to complete his sentence.

Only once he spoke to Wenna Haddin about Joe. She answered his question with a shake of the head.

"No, I haven't seen him—poor man; I expect he's too heartbroken to see anybody. I think if anybody loved Danny as much as I did it was his father."

She thought for a long time, then she said: "I'd like to see him. Perhaps he'd help."

"With Reeder?" And, when she nodded: "Don't be silly! Joe thinks Reeder is the best chap in the world! That surprises you, doesn't it? But then, you see, Joe doesn't know what Reeder's done for him. That old man is as artful as the devil. If you told Joe he'd laugh at you."

She was eyeing him steadily.

"Why? If you can convince me you could convince him."

He was rather taken aback.

"I didn't convince you, I merely told you the truth," he said.

She did not answer this, and he reached out and laid his hand on hers. She made no attempt to withdraw it.

"Poor Red Joe!" Her voice softened.

He never knew how simple or complex she was; whether she was either, or just a humdrum medium made radiant through the eyes of his passion. Old Lew Haddin, white-haired and obese, could talk for hours in his monotonous, sleep-making voice and always the subject was Wenna and her peculiar values. Red Joe once said she had the brains of a general, but, by accounts, some generals are rather stupid.

"Why poor Joe?" he asked, and suddenly tightened his grip on her hand.

"We have kept his caravan just as he left it," she said. "Nobody uses it, of course; I tidy it every week. Lew grumbles at the cost of haulage" (she invariably referred to her parent in this familiar way) "and deducts it from Joe's share; he owns half the park." As she spoke she looked at him oddly. "You are a friend of Joe's?"

"Yes."

She nodded.

"Then I can ask you something. He was charged with forging bank-notes, wasn't he? Could they imprison him again supposing they found something else against him?"

Kressholm became suddenly very attentive. "Like what?" he asked.

"Bonds and letters of credit. I found the plates in the wall lining of the caravan. He had a sort of secret panel there. Nobody knew it."

Bob Kressholm's heart leapt.

"Are they there still?" he asked. He tried to give a note of carelessness to his inquiry.

She nodded.

"Yes, the plates, and the papers, and everything. Could the law punish him for that?"

He considered this.

"I shouldn't think so," he said.

He had hazy notions about the English law, but here he saw the making of a second charge, which might easily dispose of a serious menace. She told him that Joe had had an assistant, a man who still worked with the circus, and who was the only person beside herself who had access to the van.

When he left her that night Kressholm had made up his mind. He tried to get in touch with the detective, but J.G. Reeder was out of town. He was working on a case in the South of England. What that case was Kressholm learned from the newspapers, and his hopes rose higher.

Chapter X: THE LIAR

MR. REEDER was very heavily engaged, but found time to call at Kressholm's hotel.
"I'd have come to you—" began Bob.
"I'd rather you didn't." J.G. could be offensive on occasions. "I have already a—um—bad name in Brockley."
Kressholm swallowed this with a grin.
"I noticed in the newspapers that you were working on a case, and I wondered if I could help you," he said. "I'd like to do you a turn if I could."
"I'm so sure of that," murmured Mr. Reeder. "It is a great joy to know that one's efforts are appreciated by the—um—unconvicted classes."
Without further preliminary Kressholm told him of what he had learnt from the girl, and J.G. Reeder listened without apparent interest. Yet, if this story were true, here was a big link in the chain he was piecing together with such difficulty.
"Are you sure that this story isn't suggested by the foolish paragraph you read in the newspapers?" he asked.
"If I die this minute—" began Kressholm.
"You would go straight to hell," said Mr. Reeder gravely. He was one of those old-fashioned people who believed in hell.
"No, this is straight, Mr. Reeder," protested Kressholm. "I thought that you ought to know this. I'm not telling you this because I am scared of Joe, so that I want to get him out of the way. I am telling you—well, because I feel that you ought to know."
Mr. Reeder nodded slowly.
"In the interest of justice, of course," he said. "Very—um— commendable. Where is this—er—entertainment park at the present moment?"
"They will be near Barnet next Monday," said Kressholm; then, anxiously: "What is the law on the subject, Mr. Reeder?"
J.G. pursed his lips thoughtfully.
"I'm not a lawyer," he said. "But, of course, it is very, very wrong to —um—be in possession of the instruments of forgery. And this assistant, you say, is still carrying on the—er—bad work?"
"So she—so I understand," Kressholm corrected himself hastily.
He offered a suggestion which was received without comment: Joe's caravan was invariably parked on the outside edge of the camp, and could be approached without observation. The night watchman who patrolled the fair-ground rarely went as far.
"I will undertake to get you the key of the van. As a matter of fact, I am staying the night on Monday. I suppose you could get a search warrant and that sort of thing; but I am asking you as a personal favour to make sure I'm right before you get a warrant. I do not want to be brought into this."

"You don't want to be brought into anything, Mr. Kressholm," said Reeder unpleasantly. "Hitherto you have been very successful. Is the young lady a friend of yours now?"
If he had stopped to think Bob Kressholm would have realised that no young lady's name had been mentioned.
"We have always been good friends," he said, and then realised his mistake. "I suppose you mean Miss Haddin I don't know what she's got to do with it."
"A nice young lady, but rather—impetuous," said Mr. Reeder. "She thought I was responsible for Joe's arrest, when really it was you. She probably thinks I was responsible for Danny Brady's death, when it was —um—you know, I think, who it was. It is all very interesting."
Mr. Reeder had something to think about. Nobody credited so staid and matter-of-fact a man with such an insatiable sense of curiosity as he possessed. All that night until he retired to his chaste bedroom he pondered the information Bob Kressholm had offered. His acquaintance with the law told him that the re-arrest of Red Joe would be followed by an acquittal. The man had served imprisonment for an act of forgery and if some other act, which had occurred concurrently, was revealed, the law would take a lenient view.
The mysterious assistant was another matter. Mr. Reeder had not heard of an assistant, but then there was quite a number of happenings about which he knew nothing.
It was a coincidence that he had been occupied for two or three days with the matter of forged letters of credit. There was no secret about this. The fact that the forged letters had been cashed and that Mr. J.G. Reeder, "the well-known forgery expert," had been in consultation with certain bank managers in Brighton had been published in the morning newspaper, and had been read by Kressholm. The man who was passing the letters had also negotiated some bearer bonds of a spurious character. That fact, too, was public property.
And yet all the evidence he had accumulated pointed to a certain hochstapler in Berlin, about whom the Berlin Criminal Police were pursuing close inquiries. There was a German end to it beyond any doubt, but that did not mean that the letters had not been forged in England. A search warrant would be easy to secure, and as easy to execute. Yet he hesitated to make the necessary application. If the truth be told, Mr. Reeder had a sneaking sympathy with Red Joe.
The police thought they had removed every kind of plate and press from the van. It was quite possible that the press had been renewed and was being employed to print from the plates which only Joe could have made. He consulted Gaylor on the subject, but the inspector was not enthusiastic. It was one of those frequently recurring periods when the police were unpopular because they had failed to secure two important convictions, and the usual questions were being asked in the House of Commons.
"It's the German crowd, I should think. Where did you get the information from? I'm sorry."
That was a question that police officers did not ask Mr. Reeder; he either volunteered the source or refused it, for he was very jealous about betraying the confidence of the least worthy of men. There was reason in this, because such revelations frequently compromised other and more important "squeaks."
Reviewing all the possibilities, J.G. Reeder decided not to pay a nocturnal visit to the Haddin

menage, and when Mr. Kressholm rang him up at his home, he cut short the elaboration of that gentleman's instructions.

It was a disappointed man who travelled to Barnet on the Monday afternoon, though his discomfort was short lived.

He had re-established contact with Wenna Haddin—an amazing accomplishment, all the more remarkable because he had recovered all the old fascination she had exercised. Ten years is a very long time; men and women change in that period, especially women.

But time had stood still for Wenna; the slim beauty of her went to his head like wine, and when she gave him a cold welcome at the door of the big caravan which old Lew had built for her, he could have shut his eyes and believed that it was only yesterday that their acquaintance had ended dramatically in that little plantation near the Exeter fair ground.

"Lew is away," she said. "He has gone to Liverpool to see a shipment of wild beasts that have arrived from Africa. You will sleep in his van."

He glanced at her sleeping bunk, covered now with a gaily coloured cloth. Above the head of the bed was a framed photograph of Danny Brady—the only picture in the van.

"Poor old Dan!" he said. "I feel responsible." She looked at him steadily.

"Why?" she asked.

Kressholm shrugged his shoulders.

"I should have given him a better training. Honestly, I tried to keep him out of the crooked game, Wenna."

She smiled faintly.

"He was too useful for you to keep him out," she said. "Let us be sincere with one another as far as we can be."

She had the disconcerting habit of directness—nobody made Bob Kressholm feel so foolish as she did.

"You're 'the Governor,' aren't you? I've heard about you, of course," she went on. "We have all sorts of queer people working for us—old gaol birds and people who should be if they had everything that was coming to them. Were you in London when Danny was arrested?"

He shook his head.

"I rarely leave Paris." And then, feeling that the occasion called for a little frankness: "I'll tell you the truth, Wenna. I knew that Danny was doing this job. He was one of my best men. He was impetuous and undisciplined. The last thing I said to him before he left Paris was 'For God's sake don't carry a gun.' He promised me he wouldn't."

She was looking past him out of the curtained window, and she sighed.

"Reeder, of course, knew as much about the business as I did—I'll hand it to that old bird; he's got the best information bureau in the world."

She looked round at him.

"And yet he's never caught you," she said. "That's queer, isn't it?"

Bob Kressholm chuckled.

"The man who catches me has got to be up very early in the morning," he said complacently.

Chapter XI: At 4 a.m.

WENNA changed the subject abruptly, told him the news of the camp. They had had to shoot an elephant the previous week; he had got out of hand and attacked his keeper. Four new turns were coming from Germany, they were acrobats; and a new woman rider.

He learned from another source, when he was wandering about the grounds, watching the men renovating the vans, that Wenna had had a narrow escape from death when the fair was at Nottingham. The old balloon in which she made her spectacular ascent had burst in mid-air, and she had only just time to release herself. Even then, the parachute did not open until she was less than a hundred feet from the ground. Fortunately, she had fallen on the top of a straw rick, uninjured.

He talked to her about this over the meal she had served in her van.

"It was nothing," she said carelessly. "I was hoping the parachute wouldn't open—I'm glad it did now. There's something I want to do very badly. Lew's got a new balloon; it's the one you saw being filled in the grounds."

"You've got to cut this parachute jumping, Wenna," he said.

"Why?" she asked. She did not raise her eyes from her plate.

"You're going to cut the circus business altogether." His voice shook a little. "This morning you said I was the Governor—I am. I've made a fortune, Wenna, and I'm cutting my little circus too. I've bought a villa at Como, where I'm going to live half the year, and I'm going to travel the other half. I'm going to call it the Villa Wenna."

"Why?" she asked again, and when he spoke his voice was husky.

"I've wanted you all these years, and now more than ever. I've only loved two women in my life, Wenna, and you make me forget the other one."

She pushed the plate away from her and looked up at him suddenly.

"Is this a marriage proposal or are you suggesting one of those attachments that are so popular in circuses?" she asked coolly.

Her self-possession took his breath away.

"Why, of course—marriage," he blurted. "You're thinking of what happened that time at Exeter? I've hated myself ever since. Wenna, I'm crazy about you."

He reached out for her hand, but this time she drew it away.

"I'll think about it," she said brusquely, and at that moment the big Swede who was her servant came in with a huge pot of coffee.

He was a big man, hideously ugly, and lame in one leg, the result of a bad fall; he and his brother had been Wenna's bodyguard as long as she could remember. They were both past the age for active work in the ring, but Kressholm had always thought, and had no reason to change his opinion now, that he would prefer the hug of a bear to a rough and tumble with these broad-shouldered giants.

"Stephan wears well," he said, when the man had gone, and added jocularly: "I believe if you told him to cut my throat he'd do it."

She seemed disinclined to discuss Stephan, and when the table was cleared she found a pack of cards and they played piquet together. Throughout the game she seldom spoke, and he had the impression that her mind was far away from the cards, though she played with all her old skill. But in other respects she was vague, distraite, and when she spoke at all, which was rarely, she gave him the impression that she was making a conscious effort.

At the end she threw down her hand and leaned back in her folding chair with a sigh.

"So you're going to marry me, are you, and take me away out of all this? Como?" She shivered, and her face hardened. "That's where we were going, to Como—Danny and I," she said, very evenly. And then she changed the subject with that odd abruptness which he had observed of late. "Have you seen Reeder?"

The question startled him out of his self-possession. "Reeder?" he stammered. "No; why should I see Reeder? You've got that man on your mind."

She nodded.

"Yes, very much on my mind. You haven't seen him?" Her eyes were searching his face.

Kressholm laughed. He realised how artificial that laugh was. Wenna turned to a cupboard set in the wall by the bed head, and, opening it, took out a key.

"You asked me if you could look over Joe's van—here is the key of it. You won't find the plates, and you're not to make any attempt. I'm trying to get in touch with Joe. I want him to take the things away."

She was going to say something, but checked herself, walked to the door and opened it. "Good-night," she said.

He tried to take her hand, intending no more than to kiss it, but she snatched it away from him and slammed the door before he was half-way down the steps.

He found the Swede waiting to show him to his van.

"You want to see Joe's van, don't you?" He had a hoarse, deep voice which was hardly human.

"Sure," said Kressholm. "You might show me where it is. I don't think I'll look at it to-night; I'll wait till the morning."

The Swede led the way in silence past shrouded wagons and traction engines, stopping before a van the contour of which, despite the darkness, Kressholm recognised. He only wanted to locate it, in case Reeder changed his mind. Then he followed the Swede back to his own sleeping place, bade him good-night, and went inside, bolting the door.

Wenna puzzled him. He had the sense that she was expecting some tremendous happening—her mind was certainly not upon her visitor.

By the aid of a travelling lamp which the Swede had lit for him, Kressholm sat down to finish some important work that he had begun before he had left London. It was true that he was surrendering the title of which he was so proud, and the chieftainship of the group of gangs which he had directed so skilfully. There was reason more or less; his jewellery factory at Antwerp had been visited by the police, and from the fact that they were accompanied by an

English detective Bob Kressholm guessed that this search was a direct consequence of the Seven Sisters raid.

The French police were working too. He had received news that a "club" of his had been raided; worse still, his own private apartments on the Etoile had been visited by detectives and searched. Unless he had fallen into some error, it was impossible that he could be associated either with the gang or with the Antwerp establishment. His connection with questionable enterprises was hidden four deep, and the police would be clever to connect him with any of the big jewel robberies which had exercised European police circles during the past five years.

Now was a good time to finish, with Joe on his track, and Reeder knowing considerably more about him than he had guessed.

He was totalling up his investments and bank balances in various parts of Europe, and the sum of them was most satisfactory.

He undressed, put out the light and went to bed. He did not sleep well, though the bed was comfortable enough. Somewhere in the fair-ground a lion was roaring hungrily throughout the night. He dozed, only to wake to a sound which, even in his sleep, had got on his nerves.

He looked at his watch; it had stopped, and, heaving out of bed, he went to the door, drew aside the curtains and looked out.

He uttered an exclamation under his breath.

A man moved out of the shadow of a covered wagon a dozen yards away; and then, to his amazement, he saw a girl's figure go to meet the unknown watcher. A distant church bell boomed four o'clock.

A man moved out of the shadow of a covered wagon.

The man and the girl had disappeared. Presently they came into view again —it was Wenna. There was no other figure like hers in the world; he could not be mistaken.

She stood for a little time, talking in whispers to the Swedish giant, then stole away as softly as she had come.

He was puzzled, a little alarmed. What were they doing there at that hour of the morning? He resolved to ask the girl at the first opportunity. Though he had advertised his fearlessness, he shot a second bolt on the door and went to bed. It was daylight when he woke to the hammering on the door. The Swede was wearing his Sunday best suit and a collar that fitted awkwardly round his muscular throat.

"If you want any breakfast you'd better have it," he growled. "Hans and I are going away for the day."

He brought in a tray and put it on the bed whilst he fixed the table folded against the wall of the caravan. When Kressholm had dressed and shaved he went to the girl's van and found her sitting on the steps, a cigarette between her white fingers. There was no evidence that she had been up all night; she was as fresh and rested as though she had slept the clock round.

"How did you sleep?" she asked, without looking at him.

"Badly. You ought to give those lions something to eat. Wenna, what were you doing near my caravan at four this morning?"

He expected her to deny this, but to his surprise she did not attempt to conceal her presence at that hour.

"Somebody left open a door of the monkey cage and a couple of them got out," she said. "They usually obey me—we found them. Did I disturb you, or was it the lions? They're old, and angry because they can never get enough to eat. I want Lew to shoot them and get another pair. Sims, the trainer, is afraid of them, which is bad—Lew will have to fire that man. When a trainer is scared of the animals he's taming, he ought to quit."

"I'll do a little taming," he said good-humouredly.

"You!" was all she said, but it annoyed him.

Before he could express his annoyance she went on.

"There was only one man who could deal with lions, and that was Joe. They'd stand on their heads for him, though he was never a trainer. Give me that key."

He had forgotten all about the key.

"I thought of looking round Joe's van," he said. "I've changed my mind."

She was waiting on the step to take the key from him.

Something was wrong; how badly wrong he could not guess. He did not know that she had been waiting all that night for the advent of Mr. Reeder, and that she had counted on his treachery to bring the detective into her hands. Her hatred of the man who had brought her lover to his death was an overwhelming obsession. Reeder did not know this; it was unguessed even by Kressholm. He was to make a discovery before the night was out.

Chapter XII: THE CONVICT'S REVENGE

MR. REEDER had had a heavy day. He had been successful in isolating, if not in capturing, the authors of the letter of credit. They were, as he suspected, a German gang operating in Leipzig. That afternoon he spent the greater part of an hour on the telephone, speaking to the German police, and, though weary in mind and body, he had the satisfaction of an accomplishment as he made his way home.

He left Scotland Yard just before dark, and reached home without any mishap. His housekeeper came to him and reeled off the names of callers and the gist of telephone messages. She had an unusual memory and rarely committed telephone messages or even names and addresses to paper. He listened with closed eyes, stirring his tea, as she went through her record.

"A man called a quarter of an hour before you came in; a very tall man—a foreigner, I think. He wanted to see you. He said his name was Jones."

"A very foreign name," murmured Mr. Reeder, in a facetious mood. "One of the Joneses of Constantinople."

The housekeeper, who had no sense of humour at all, said she wasn't sure about that.

"What did he want—just to see me?"

"That's all, sir. I thought he acted a bit odd." Mr. Reeder smiled benevolently.

"All people act odd according to you, my dear lady. I'm afraid you have a mystery complex. You read too many—um—detective stories. Did anybody else call and act odd?"

She couldn't recall anybody who was not absolutely normal. Strange people did come to this modest house in Brockley Road, and they had names that were stranger than Jones. Mr. Reeder did not regard the personality or business of this particular visitor worth considering, and settled himself down to spend a peaceful evening preparatory to an early retirement. He had hardly finished his toast when his housekeeper came bustling in.

"He's called again—Jones. He says he's got a message from Mr. Brady—Mr. Joseph Brady."

Reeder nodded.

"Show him up."

He had never before seen the big man who came awkwardly into the room; he could not have forgotten a face like Stephan's.

"I come from Mr. Brady." He spoke very slowly, in the sing-sing tone of a Scandinavian, and he was obviously ill at ease.

"What is the message?" asked Reeder. The man cleared his throat.

"He asked me to say you come to him because he is ill, and he dare not come out because of all these talks about credit letters."

Mr. Reeder frowned. So far as he knew, Joe Brady was abroad.

"Where is he now?"

"He is out of bed, got up," said the man, "and now he himself is downstairs in the car."

"Tell him to come here."

The man shook his head.

"He will not come, that he says. If you will speak with him a little while, he shall be very pleased. I was with him working at the circus, the assistant of him."

Mr. Reeder remembered the mysterious assistant whom for a short space of time he had suspected.

"All right; go down and wait. I will be with you very shortly."

It was not extraordinary for him to have these furtive interviews with men who, wisely or wrongly, refused to come to his rooms, and although it was not what he expected of Red Joe, there might be a very special reason, and there was no harm in learning what it was.

When he got downstairs and closed the front door behind him he saw the man waiting on the pavement. A spatter of rain was falling; the beginnings of a north-west gale swept the deserted street. Near to the kerb was what Reeder thought was a tradesman's small delivery van. He did not give it a great deal of attention until the man pointed to the curtained back of the vehicle.

"He is there. Because of his sickness we have to carry him on a bed."

J.G. Reeder was half-way to the van when he smelt the trap.

It was too late: an arm like a steel bar closed round his throat, a huge hand covered his mouth. But it was no feeble old gentleman that the Swede was throttling. Reeder wrenched round and, freeing his arm, struck a blow which would have paralysed any man of ordinary strength.

"Hans!"

A second man leaped through the opening at the back of the van. Mr. Reeder did not feel the stick that struck him. When he recovered he was lying full length on a mattress. The car was apparently moving along a main thoroughfare, for he could hear the clang of tramcar bells. His hands and his legs were tied together, but they had not attempted to gag him.

When Mr. Reeder came to he was lying bound and helpless on the floor of the van.

"If you make a noise I hit you with this iron bar," said a threatening voice.

Stephan was squatting by his side.

Mr. Reeder's head ached a little, but not very much. He had, he boasted, the thickest skull of any man associated with the police force. But he would have dearly loved to have his hands free, and suggested this course in a weak voice which advertised his feebleness to the hearers. But they were adamant.

Where were they taking him? He tried to catch a glimpse of the road they were following, but the tarpaulin covers at the back of the van had been laced tight. They were still on the tram lines, and after a while he guessed by the fall in temperature that they were crossing the river.

He was resigned to anything which might happen and was ready to justify whatever disaster might overtake him. His stupidity had been unbelievable. To be caught by a trick which would not deceive the most junior detective that ever patrolled a London street! For that he deserved everything that happened.

But why—why? He had no active enemies; none certainly who could contrive so theatrical a vengeance. There were many who disliked him intensely, and prayed nightly for something unpleasant to happen to him; but they were first-year men, languishing in Dartmoor and Parkhurst, and no scheme of reprisals survives the first twelve months of prison. They would meet him when they were discharged with a self-conscious smile, and apologise to him for all the things they had promised when they were sentenced.

Kressholm's gang? It was hardly likely. Kressholm had nothing to gain ...

Mr. Reeder then remembered the story of the caravan, the obvious step that had been made to bring him to the amusement park. Kressholm couldn't get him there one way, so he was trying another. And yet Kressholm had no reason for taking a step which might jeopardise his own safety.

The girl!

The solution came like a flash. Kressholm had been the dupe. Of course, it was the girl who had told him all this fanciful story about forged plates, and Kressholm had fallen for it. She knew he was a traitor, then? That was some satisfaction, though little comfort. Mr. Reeder began to take a serious view of the position. Men he knew, and he could foretell to an nth what steps they would take in certain eventualities; but a woman was a mystery to Mr. Reeder, and had always remained so. If this fiery young woman had any reason for avenging the death of Danny Brady there might be some unhappy consequences to this ride.

The journey seemed interminable, but after something that was over an hour and seemed just within the limits of eternity, the car turned from the road and jolted over a rough track. Mr. Reeder's hearing was very good, though there were times when he pretended to be slightly deaf. He heard strange sounds which could only have one significance. He was being taken to a circus, and the mental prediction he had made was fulfilled.

There had been a scheme to get him here, but he was perfectly certain that Kressholm was not in it.

As the car stopped, Stephan leaned over, and folded a silk handkerchief over his prisoner's mouth, knotting it tightly behind. He and the other man, who descended from the driver's seat, lifted the detective and carried him across the field.

Rain was falling more heavily now, and the wind was so strong that the men staggered under their burden. Their progress took them past a monstrous, pear-shaped object which swayed and rolled so far that it touched one of his bearers.

This was the balloon on the trapeze of which Wenna swung to the awe of rustic crowds. Presently he felt himself being lifted into a caravan, and a few seconds later was lying on the dusty floor. Red Joe's caravan—he recognised it, and well he might, for he had once searched it most thoroughly. Stephan dragged him partly to a sitting position and propped him against the wall before he unfastened the handkerchief about the prisoner's mouth.

The only light came from a tiny oil lamp hanging on the wall, and by this he saw that the windows of the caravan were shattered, as also was the glass upper half of the door. Hans went out, but Stephan waited.

"I hope you won't have to wake the young lady from her beauty sleep," said Mr. Reeder politely.

"You shut up!" growled the Swede. "You'll be sorry when she comes!"

"I shan't be sorry when you go," said Mr. Reeder frankly. "You have certainly the most unpleasant face I have ever seen. I hate to hurt your feelings, but—ugh!"

Before the Swede could answer him the door was pulled open, and Wenna Haddin came in. She wore no hat or coat; her blouse was spotted with rain, her hair wildly dishevelled. She looked what she was, the very spirit of fury.

"You know me?" she breathed.

He looked at her critically.

"Yes, I think so..."

"Danny's girl—you know that! You trapped Danny... I've always hated you. You caught him, and then, when you knew he would appeal..."

She stopped. The words would not come.

"I found another means of killing him?" said Mr. Reeder. "Did Kressholm tell you that too?"

"You know what I'm going to do to you, don't you?" she went on breathlessly. "I'm going to put you in the lions' cage, and if anybody wants to know how it happened we'll tell them about a man who was prowling in the night—a sneaking, prying old detective!"

She turned quickly. Somebody was turning the handle. Before she could shoot the bolt Kressholm was in the caravan, looking from one to the other.

"What's the idea?... What are you doing?"

"What I tried to do last night," she said. Her voice was like steel. "I've got Reeder to the camp, where I wanted him! I thought you'd bring him— you told him all that I told you? Well, that was a lie—there are no plates here. I read in the newspaper that he was looking for forged letters of credit—and I passed this yarn on to you because I was sure you'd squeal. Joe always said you were a squealer!"

"And Joe," said Mr. Reeder, "was right."

There was a certain flippancy in his tone, though there was little excuse for light-heartedness.

"What are you going to do with him?"

Kressholm looked from the prisoner to the girl. The Governor governed nobody now; he was ludicrously impotent.

The girl stood over the bound figure of Mr. Reeder.

"He's going into the lions' cage—that's where! Into the lions' cage—and if you interfere I'll put you there too!"

She was half-hysterical. The actualities were more ugly than the plans of vengeance she had dreamt of. She was stricken with horror at the thing she planned to do.

The three of them stood looking down at where Reeder sat. Their backs to the door, none saw it open, until a rush of cold air made the girl turn.

"Hallo! Giving a party?" said the newcomer.

And then he saw Reeder and his mouth opened wide.

"The man who murdered your son, Joe! Reeder—he sent you to prison..."

Her voice was shrill, unnatural. Watching her closely, Mr. Reeder saw that she was on the verge of collapse. He saw something else: the white-faced Kressholm edged back along the side of the big caravan, but he did not pass Red Joe, whose hand shot out and gripped him.

"Is that so?" Red Joe's voice was a drawl. "Untie that gentleman. Hi, you Swede, I'm talking to you!"

There was an automatic pistol in his other hand. The giant was glaring at the intruder; at a signal from the girl he would have leaped to his death, but she put out a shaking hand.

"Untie him. You don't know what you're doing, Joe."

"I guess I do," said Red Joe.

Mr. Reeder rose and stretched himself. By the time he had recovered the circulation of his numbed hands he was alone in the locked caravan. He thumped at the door, but without success. There was nothing to do but to sit and wait.

Two hours passed, and then a key grated in the lock; the door swung open. It was Red Joe. He came in, closing the door behind him, his hands thrust deep into his pockets.

"There's a car waiting for you to take you home, Mr. Reeder," he said. "I'm sorry this happened. This girl was mad. I guess she's always been a little bit that way. She knows now—Kressholm told her the truth."

"Where is he?"

Joe's shoulders rose in a shrug.

"I've killed him," he said calmly. "She doesn't know; the two Swedes don't know. I sent them to their caravan. But I killed him as I said I'd kill him. I was going to shoot him, but then the other idea came to me. It gave me a chance of keeping my promise—to kill him so as you'd never find his body. I'm telling you this—we're alone together. If you can catch me I'm willing to be caught."

"You're under arrest," said Reeder.

All that night the police searched the fair-ground but there was no vestige of Kressholm. The night watchman had heard nothing; but then, he had been busy pegging down flapping canvas, and an hour before dawn the balloon had broken from its moorings and sailed away. The only people who ever saw that balloon again were officers on a homeward-bound Cape boat. They saw the big, sagging bag falling into the sea; there was no car attached to it, but something was swaying to and fro in the gale.

"Almost looks like a man hanging from that balloon," said the chief officer. He did not check the speed of the boat; the balloon had fallen five miles away and a heavy sea was running.

This conversation was not repeated to Mr. Reeder for years afterwards. Even then it was quite superfluous. He had already decided to his own satisfaction the way Bob Kressholm went.

THE MAN WHO PASSED

First published as "The Man from Sing-Sing" in The Thriller, Feb 7, 1931

CHAPTER I

MR. MANNERING was called "the Captain" in the village of Woodern Green, which is on the southern edge of Buckingham. Possibly because of his military appearance and the frigidity of his manner; though why captains are supposed to be frigid nobody knows.

He lived at Hexleigh Manor, which was a small house in a large park, and by all accounts he was a gentleman who had no great store of money. The Manor was something of a derelict when he rented it at a ridiculously low sum. The repairs upon which previous would-be tenants had insisted were apparently executed by the new tenant without the assistance of local builders, according to their account.

The captain had a staff of three, two of whom lived in the house and the third in a cottage within the grounds. They were three hard-faced men, who never came to the village, and it was believed that they were old soldiers who had served with the captain during the war.

It was to the cottage that all the provisions were delivered by local tradesmen—none of them was invited to go farther. The bills were paid weekly by cheque on a London bank.

One curious circumstance: no letters, save the inevitable appeals by secretaries of local working men's cricket, football or other clubs, were ever addressed to Captain or Mr. Mannering. He seemed to have no friends.

He had been there a year when he blossomed forth into something grander than an impecunious military gentleman. Vans arrived from London filled with expensive furniture; the dour man at the cottage engaged three gardeners; a local builder was called in to decorate the house, and an era of prosperity set in.

Mr. Reeder, of the Public Prosecutor's Department, became acquainted with Hexleigh Manor in a peculiar way. His hobby, as all the world knows, was chickens. He had a big poultry farm in Kent, and raised the choicest and the rarest birds in the kingdom. The stocking of the Hexleigh Manor poultry farm—a new branch of Captain Mannering's activities—brought down Mr. Reeder in his capacity of poultry expert.

Captain Mannering was in town—he drove to London almost every day in his closed sedan car—and the caller saw only the new poultry man, who was talkative. When the business was at an end Mr. Reeder climbed up into the seat of the little van which had brought him and his birds from London, and drove down the drive. His profit on the transaction was microscopic, but the satisfaction he had as a poultry fancier was of infinitely greater importance.

They passed the cottage, outside which the surly servant of the establishment was smoking. He looked up and Mr. Reeder saw him. He did not notice the angular man who sat beside the driver. "Dear me!" said Mr. Reeder, mildly surprised, for he had seen the cottager before.

He had a motto, which was that one should live honestly and let others live honestly, which is not quite the same as the less elaborate adage. But he was also very curious, and curiosity can be a nuisance to all sorts of people.

At Scotland Yard they called him "lucky," and pointed out amazing coincidences that had helped him to the solution of important mysteries; but Mr. Reeder used to suggest that he was responsible for all the coincidences that helped him.

In his spare time he came to Woodern Green and made a few inquiries, not because he expected that the results would be of any service to him, but because he wished to know. Knowledge was his working capital, and he would go to great trouble in its gathering. He hoarded facts as some women hoard scraps of silk, or mechanics hoard nuts and screws and odd nails and useless scraps of machine parts, not because they were of any immediate use, but because, some day...

His chief asked about his visit to Bucks, and Mr. Reeder sighed.

"Unfortunately I have—um—a very bad mind. I see—er—the worst, as it were, in everybody and the most—um— sinister meanings in the most innocent things—in fact, I have the mind of a criminal. Had I the courage, which of course I have not, I should have made—um—an interesting lawbreaker."

His superior smiled.

"Good. Go down and see that pompous gentleman at Mabberleys to-morrow and expound what your criminal instincts suggest for the better protection of his business."

So Mr. Reeder, in his mild way, quarrelled with a great man and later was by premeditation offensive to one who was not so great. The great man was Sir Wilfred Heinhall, K.B.E., and the rest of it. He was director of seventeen corporations and chairman of eight of these. He knew everything about business and economics, and trade balances and world conditions, but he didn't know much about men.

Mr. Reeder went down to the city, representing the Public Prosecutor, and in the course of a conversation which had as its subject the prosecution of an unfaithful servant, suggested that the methods of this particular corporation were rather antiquated.

"If I—er—may be permitted to offer the view—um —your checking system leaves—er—much to be desired."

"Stuff and nonsense!" said Sir Wilfred. "Are you telling me how to conduct my business? Did the Public Prosecutor send you down here to lecture ME on Filing Systems? Good heavens!"

He said a lot more, and Mr. Reeder said nothing much. There were few opportunities. He went meekly forth into the city street and boarded a bus that deposited him near to the Home Office.

It was in the afternoon, when he was leaving Whitehall, that he had occasion to stop a gentleman in the street. The gentleman did not wish to stop, but Mr. Reeder hooked his arm with the crook of his umbrella and pulled him back. It was a shockingly undignified action on the part of a reputable man, but Mr. Reeder did it with all the aplomb of a music-hall performer.

"What are you doing in town, Mr. Higson?" he asked.

The good-looking man of forty, brought to a standstill so unceremoniously, looked murder and smiled.

"Hallo, Reeder—"

"Mister Reeder," murmured the detective. "What is the game—snide or just ordinary thieving?"

Higson was well dressed, but that was part of his graft. Nobody could remember seeing Hymie Higson looking anything but in the bandbox class. He had a gold cigarette box in his pocket, and his watch-guard looked platinum and probably was.

"I'll tell you." Hymie's tone was neither respectful nor humble. "When you put me in with your damned perjury I had a snug bit of money put away. That breaks your so-and-so heart, you dirty old something-or-other! Fifteen thousand quid! I've done my time and you can't touch it. I'm going straight because I can afford to go straight—if I couldn't afford to, I'd be selling snide fivers and making a good living, and this time you wouldn't catch me, you old—"

Mr. Reeder tapped him on the ear with the heavy handle of his umbrella. It wasn't a heavy tap, but it was painful, and Hymie's hand went up with a cry.

"Don't be rude," said Mr. Reeder mildly, "or I'll trip you on to your back and push the ferrule of my umbrella into your right eye—or left eye, whichever is most convenient."

There was in Mr. Reeder something cold-bloodedly ferocious which Hymie suddenly remembered. He blinked at the detective, still holding his ear, and then abruptly turned and hurried away.

"Very curious," said Mr. Reeder.

But it was not so curious as the incident of the parlourmaid.

Few people would have given a thought to the parlourmaid. Certainly there was nothing in her appearance or manner to stimulate an interest in her relations. She was plain, long-faced and anaemic; her legs were broomsticks, her feet grotesquely large. Mr. Reeder was conscious of her long before she was completely conscious of Mr. Reeder.

She dusted his room with amazing caution, broke nothing that was valuable, made no attempt to tidy up his desk, was never in the way. She thought of him as "elderly," wondered why he was so old-fashioned as to wear square-topped felt hats and square-toed boots, and why he didn't shave his side-whiskers. All this in a vague way. She was never really interested in Mr. Reeder until his housekeeper told her he was a detective.

"Him?" incredulously.

"Mr. Reeder," said the housekeeper, more correctly.

"A copper?" definitely sceptical.

"Not a policeman, though he goes to Scotland Yard a lot—he's in the government."

"Good Gawd!" said the housemaid.

Her name was Elizabeth, and she was of the class that shortens that stately name to Lizzie. She pondered on Mr. Reeder after that, surveyed him furtively, craned her head out of upstairs windows to see him "come from business," dangling his closely furled umbrella and playing with his eye-glasses.

The question of Ena very naturally came into close association with Mr. Reeder. Ena's Ernie was Lizzie's absorbing problem. Ena was lovely, with a skin like ivory and teeth like white porcelain. She had the figure of a sylph and legs that people used to turn in the street to look at again. She was Lizzie's sister—nobody quite understood how this came about. Ena had worked in the city, where she had earned some fifty shillings a week for typing letters all of which began: "In reply to yours of even date." Now she didn't work anywhere; lived at home in a room which she had had specially furnished; drove hither and thither in taxi-cabs, and once or twice had come home in a beautiful car. On her fingers were two all too lovely diamond rings. She had three evening dresses, and withal was respectable. For Ena was engaged to be married to a young gentleman of fortune named Ernie Molyneux. He lived in the country, and came to town or to Brighton only for week-ends.

There was nothing odd about this engagement. Mr. Molyneux was a young and pallid man of twenty-six, slightly chinless but otherwise goodish looking. He was madly in love with Ena, whom he had met at a cinema and had brought home by train, calling upon her parents and being asked into the parlour and asked his views about the weather and the state of trade. And since he had given satisfactory replies to these questions, and had passed the test which mother always applied and had answered that he did not go much to church nowadays, but that he had sung in the choir, he was accepted. This was before his uncle in Australia died and left him all his money, and consequently before the taxi-cabs and the diamond rings.

There was nothing about this which worried Lizzie Panton. It was the advent of the gentleman from the West End which had disturbed the Panton household. He was a gentleman wearing evening dress and a heavy black moustache and dark-rimmed eye-glasses. He had come to Friendly Street, where the Pantons lived, at twelve o'clock one Saturday night. The Pantons were all in bed except Lizzie. She was washing out some stockings and things— being a "daily" she had little chance of doing her own work—and she it was who answered the knock.

"I'm sorry to bother you," said the stranger in a deep, aristocratic voice (the description is Lizzie's); "but is this Mr. Panton's house?"

"Yes," said Lizzie.

"Is that Ena?"

The stranger took a step into the passage and peered at her.

"No—Lizzie."

"Oh!"

A pause.

"You're the slav—the servant girl?"

Lizzie knew that he had been on the point of saying "slavey" and bridled.

"I'm parlourmaid at Mr. Reeder's," she said. After a longer pause he made her repeat that. "At Mr. Reeder's—which Mr. Reeder?"

"In Brockley Road."

She heard the quick intake of his breath. "Really! Is Ena at home?"

"She's just gone to bed. Is anything wrong with Ernie?"

The stranger hesitated.

"No; you're her sister, aren't you?" And, when Lizzie admitted the fact: "Ernest and she wrote out a paper to-night—a sort of advertisement. That must not appear."

Ena had come home early that night and the advertisement had been very completely discussed. As a matter of fact, it was Lizzie's idea originally to announce the engagement. "It will tie him down," she had said. And it had been "agreed," as the lawyers say, in this form:

"A marriage has been arranged and will shortly take place between Mr. Ernest Jakes Molyneux of Overdean, Birmingham, and Miss Ena Panton of Brockley."

Now, Friendly Street is distinctly in Deptford, but Ena thought Brockley was more respectable. "Has it been posted?"

"No, it hasn't," said Lizzie. "Wait a bit, I'll see Ena—won't you come in?"

No, he wouldn't come in. He preferred the unlighted passage way. Presently Ena came down in her new dressing-gown. She was a little peevish, for Ernie had been rather trying that night—shilly-shallying about the notice.

"Who are you, anyway?" she demanded. "I am Ernie's guardian," said the stranger.

It was evident to the shrewd Lizzie that he was controlling his impatience with an effort.

"I think the announcement is absolutely unnecessary, and it may spoil his chances with his other uncle, who doesn't want him to marry."

Ena was impressed. Her young man had not mentioned any other uncle, but uncles are an unlimited commodity.

"All right, I'll tear it up," she said reluctantly. "I was putting it in the Kentish Mercury, but if you don't think it's right—"

"May I have the paper that Ernest wrote?"

She had it upstairs, and, going up, brought it to him. Lizzie watched him walk back to the end of the street, where a taxi-cab was waiting for him, and then came in and shut the door.

"It's very funny," she said.

"It is funny," agreed her sister. "Ouch!" She gave a little scream.

"What's the matter?"

"I put my foot on a mouse or something!" panted the pretty sister, who was bare-footed. "Stuff! Mouse!"

Lizzie reached up and lit the gas. It was not a mouse—it was a furry something of familiar shape. Stooping down, she picked it up.

"A false moustache—why, that was what he was wearing!" she gasped.

The two girls looked at one another in amazement.

"That's funny," said Lizzie again.

Ena sat up half the night, writing to her boy. She often wrote, but he never replied by letter except once when she had had a note posted in mid-week in Birmingham. Her letters were invariably addressed to a place off the Haymarket which she discovered was a block of service flats. The "funniest" thing of all was that that same week came a letter from Ernie, saying that everything was a mistake, and that, though he loved her, it was best for everybody if they parted. He told her to keep all the presents he had given to her.

Ena wept, of course. She made a personal call at West End Mansions, to learn that Mr. Molyneux had given up his flat and had left no instructions as to where his letters were to be sent.

To Lizzie the crux of the mystery was that false moustache, until it was superseded by the second mystery. It was a letter addressed to Ena—a wild, more or less incoherent, adoring letter. It was from Ernie and bore the postmark, Birmingham Central, and no address. It was written on scraps of paper evidently torn from larger sheets.

"I love you more than anything... can't stop thinking about you... You alone could save my soul from the tyrant who is sucking my blood... If I could only see you and explain everything—but no, he stands behind me and it's all oil, oil, oil... Sometimes I wake up and say to myself suppose it's a lie. How can you tell if you're not on the ground? You can't see oil. I've read up the Encyclopaedia and it doesn't say anything like that. Only eight weeks to the thirty-first—what horrible thoughts possess me! It is the Inspector's fault. If he had done his duty the first time he would have seen through it, instead of which he was in a hurry to catch his train."

"I can't make head or tail of it," sniffed Ena.

"Except that he loves you," said her homely sister.

"I knew that," said Ena.

No further letter came from Ernie. One day Lizzie took her courage in both hands and carried the letter and the moustache to Mr. Reeder.

She chose an occasion which was favourable. It happened to be an evening off, and Mr. Reeder was dozing before the fire. She began an introduction which was full of "I hope you will excuse me, sir's" and "I don't know whatever you will think of me's."

Mr. Reeder blinked himself awake.

"Dear me, what is all this about?" he asked benevolently.

He then observed the parlourmaid for the first time.

"It's about my sister, sir," said Lizzie breathlessly. Mr. Reeder straightened himself, drew up to his desk and put on his glasses.

"About your sister—yes?"

He had a very extensive knowledge of Lizzie's class, and realised that, though it might be a very small matter, it was tremendous for her. A very conventional tragedy, perhaps, the sort of thing that breaks hearts daily in small and unimportant houses.

"It's her young man," began Lizzie, and told her disconnected story, reserving till the last the grand denouement of the false moustache.

Mr. Reeder listened, forgot nothing, filled in gaps, and could have recited the whole history of Ena's love affair without flaw, and much more accurately than could her breathless sister.

"May I see the letter and the moustache?" he asked.

She produced these articles from her apron pocket and laid them on the table.

"I haven't told Ena about the letter—I mean, taking it away —but I knew she kept it in the top left-hand drawer..."

There were some things which surprised Mr. Reeder in the story; there were some which did not surprise him at all. The paper the letter was written on, for example. He would have been surprised if it had been any other kind of paper. The moustache set him frowning. It was very well made, something better than one can buy in shops, the product of an expert theatrical wig-maker. There was gum on the upper edge of it, unevenly applied, and not the spirit gum which should have been applied.

He asked her many questions, few of which she could answer. In fact, he never seemed to stop asking questions, about all sorts of odd matters which had no bearing upon Ena's lover and the false moustache. Had Ernie given the girl money? Had Ena ever met the man with the moustache in Ernie's company, or anybody who might be he? Did Ernie ever talk about going abroad, to America, perhaps?

Mr. Reeder was amazingly interested, much more than she had ever expected him to be, in the love affair of her sister. Ernie was a nice chap, she explained.

"Is that his writing?"

He tapped the letter.

"Are you sure it's his writing?"

Lizzie was absolutely sure; she had seen his writing before. No, Ena had never received letters from him, but once he had written something in Ena's autograph book.

"Did you see him write it?" asked Mr. Reeder eagerly.

She nodded.

"How did he hold his pen like this?" Mr. Reeder seized a pen-holder.

"And before he wrote did he make one or two flourishes like this?"

He sent the point of the pen twirling round before it dropped to the paper, and Lizzie gaped at him.

"That's just what he did do!" she said. "I said to Ma at the time, by way of a joke, 'He doesn't know what to write, so he's sort of marking time —'"

Mr. Reeder nodded.

"That's what he was doing, marking time."

"Do you want to know what he wrote in the autograph book?"

Mr. Reeder hesitated for a fraction of a second. "Well—er— yes," he said.

It was quite unimportant, but he would be interested to know.

Ernie had written a little bit of poetry about the advantage of a young lady being good rather than clever, and doing noble things not thinking about them.

"Very—um—admirable," said Mr. Reeder,

CHAPTER II

TO say that he was interested was to understate Mr. Reeder's emotions. There was no mystery here except the mystery of Ernie's identity. And the greater mystery, more difficult to probe, who was the man with the aristocratic voice and the moustache who came down to Deptford, knocking up respectable people at twelve o'clock at night in order to prevent the insertion of an advertisement? Had she a copy of this? Lizzie could claim triumphantly that she had written it down word for word in an old memorandum book, and had it at home.

"What I think is this, sir," she said. "This young man is trying to give our Ena the go-by. When I say 'him' I mean perhaps his father or his mother —especially his mother. You know what these people are—they think their sons are marrying beneath them, when really they're marrying a heart of gold. I always say there's more happy marriages amongst the lower classes than amongst the upper classes. Look at the divorce courts—"

"Yes, yes," said Mr. Reeder absently. "I am sure. Though personally I —um—never look at divorce courts at all. But I am certain you're right."

He rose from his chair and began to stride up and down the room slowly, his hands in his pockets, his shoulders down, a frown on his classic face.

"Another thing," Lizzie went on, conscious of the impression she had made. "Suppose they stopped his allowance, they've got enough to live on in a quiet way for years—I mean, Ena's jewellery. It's worth two or three hundred pounds—"

"Could I see Ena? I suppose she knows you've come?" interrupted Mr. Reeder.

Lizzie felt and looked guilty.

"Well, to tell you the truth," she said awkwardly, "she doesn't. What she'll say when I tell her I've been to a detective I can't abear to think."

He nodded.

"Tell her," he said gently, "and bring her to see me to-morrow evening about this time. And ask her—um—to bring any other letters she may have. I—er—shall read them with the greatest sympathy and understanding."

He wanted to keep the letters which Lizzie already had, but she was firm on the point, and carried them off with her.

She spent the greater part of the night sitting up in bed, persuading her sister to see Mr. Reeder. Ena had been shocked, rather shrilly reproachful, had accused Lizzie of being underhand and sly, finally had wept and surrendered.

The next night she came to see Mr. Reeder's house with greater willingness because in the course of the day a further communication, even more mysterious, had been received from Ernie. It was a registered letter, containing three notes each for a hundred pounds, and a very short letter.

"When you get a wire from me giving a certain address say nothing to anybody, burn the wire and come straight to me. I cannot live without you. Go to Cook's and get a passport at once. Don't tell mother or Liz, but the clouds are breaking."

On the back of the letter was scrawled in pencil a long column of figures, evidently written in haste. They totalled to 310,740.

Mr. Reeder was not the kind of man that Ena had expected to meet. In truth, he was not the kind of man that anybody expected to meet; and he had long since classified new acquaintances as those who were disappointed when they first met him, and those who were relieved. Ena was in the relieved class.

He was very kindly and gentle, and not at all the hectoring, bullying detective she had expected. He asked her a lot of questions, very delicately put; questions which she did not realise were questions at all until afterwards; and she told him much more than she had ever imagined she could tell anybody. She was very fond of Ernie; she liked him ever so much; he had always been the gentleman, and, except that she had once heard certain reports, had never displayed the least inclination to fastness.

"He only had to tell me he didn't want me, and I would have understood," she said.

"But he does want you," said Mr. Reeder gently; "although I am afraid —" He shook his head.

"You don't think he means that?" asked the girl anxiously. "I mean, about going out there to him, and the passport?"

"Yes, I think he means that," said Mr. Reeder slowly. "I was thinking of something else. Um."

"I don't know really why I should be making a fuss at all," said Ena, jerking up her pretty chin. "It seems awful to tell all these things to strangers. I suppose his parents are against the match. But after all we've got to live our own lives, haven't we, Mr. Reeder? I mean, I believe in honouring your father and mother, but you can carry that sort of thing too far."

J.G. Reeder neither agreed nor disagreed.

"Did he ever tell you he was taking you abroad?" he asked.

Ena shook her head.

"Or tell you any place where you were likely to spend your—um—honeymoon?"

Ena had to admit that they had never discussed honeymoons. She said vaguely that she had kept him off the subject.

Mr. Reeder rubbed his nose, a little embarrassed. "So you can't tell me anything about any foreign towns you were likely to visit?"

She shook her head, and was within measurable distance of losing patience with him; for it seemed to her that the question of a suitable spot for a honeymoon was a little superfluous in view of the fact that she might not be having a honeymoon at all.

She had all the propriety of her class.

"Naturally I couldn't go out to him unless mother came with me," she said.

"Naturally," murmured Mr. Reeder.

She knew nothing about Ernie except that he was a gentleman. He had never spoken to her about work; that he was wealthy, two hundred pounds' worth of bank-notes testified. He stayed in Birmingham because he "had something to do with works." But what those works were, or where he had his private residence, she could offer no explanation.

"The point is this," said Ena hotly; "I don't allow any man to make a fool of me. If Ernie's given me up because I'm not good enough for his mother and father, there's as good fish—"

"In the sea as ever came out," suggested Mr. Reeder. "I think you're perfectly right."

He took up the little moustache and fingered it, asked her a number of questions about the height, the voice and the dress of the visitor. He was in evening dress, she thought. She had never seen him before or since.

As she walked home with her sister she discussed, not without acerbity, the waste of her time.

"I must say he's not my idea of a detective," she said, "with his hums and his haws and his ridiculous questions. He never once so much as looked at my rings to see if they were genuine."

"You know they're genuine," retorted Lizzie tartly.

Her sister was rather inclined to agree that Mr. Reeder had been a disappointment. He had hardly looked at the false moustache, which she had hoped would have struck him all of a heap, and had said practically nothing about it except that it was well made.

"And he's got a nerve to keep my letters!" fumed Ena, her sense of grievance growing.

"It's only one letter, and I can get it in the morning by asking for it," said Lizzie.

"Did I get it to-night by asking for it?" stormed the pretty little virago. "If that's the kind of man you're working for, I should change my job."

Lizzie said nothing. Already there was moving in her mind a very uneasy suspicion, and it was not directed to her employer.

Mr. Reeder went to his office the next morning with quite a lot to think about. It was very rarely that he hadn't. All the way up to town—he invariably travelled by tramcar—he turned over and over in his mind the problem of the parlourmaid's sister and her eccentric lover. Though he could not place his finger at the moment upon Ernie, he knew all about him, and just what that letter meant.

He was at some pains to explain the situation to the Assistant Public Prosecutor, who listened with interest to the theories he expounded. When Mr. Reeder had finished he shook his head.

"One could initiate inquiries, of course, but I doubt if that's our job. You might pass a note over to the chief constable, who may care to pursue the matter, but it is certainly not for us. The question will come to this department quite soon enough."

Mr. Reeder agreed, but he did not send any particulars to Scotland Yard, not even when he was called in for consultation on a matter which was that day, and for many weeks, to be the top-liner in every newspaper which loved a good mystery.

In reality it was a group of mysteries, each having no association with the other. The first was the affair of the Eton master. Mr. Friston was a Master of Arts, a man who was known to hold very strong and definite views on most subjects, particularly on the question of trade with Russia. He had spoken on this subject at important meetings in London, and his views had become so pronounced, so uncompromising, that he had been requested by his college authorities to limit his oratorical activities.

The master was a man of forty-eight, strong, active, and in one sense eccentric. It was his habit to rise at an unconscionably early hour. It was his boast that the maximum amount of sleep he required was five hours a day, and since it was his practice to go to bed at about nine o'clock every night, he was usually to be found working in his study at three o'clock in the morning, after a brisk walk through the deserted streets of Windsor. The Windsor police knew his habits, and when he came swinging past them, with a cheery "Good-morning," at an hour when modern folks were calling upon a dance band for an encore, they offered him only the polite attention which they were prepared to afford to Windsor Castle itself.

On this particular morning there was a light ground mist, but Mr. Friston was recognised by a policeman who stood under the shadow of the castle wall as he swung down the hill towards Eton. He turned to the left, and was not seen again until the policeman who had originally seen him was patrolling towards the college. By this time the mist had changed into a slight drizzle of rain. It was a quarter-past three when the slowly patrolling policeman, smoking a surreptitious cigarette, saw, lying half on the sidewalk and half in the road, the figure of a man. He hurried forward and flashed his light on its face. To his horror, he recognised the master.

Summoning assistance and an ambulance, the unconscious man was rushed to the hospital, where he was found to be suffering from concussion.

Searching the roadway, the police made a sensational discovery. This was no less than a bloodstained spanner—a long, narrow tool, peculiarly suitable to the purpose for which it had evidently been employed. It lay within a yard of where the unconscious man had been found. It was immediately packed in tissue paper and reserved for examination.

The Chief Constable of Berkshire, who had been communicated with, called in Scotland Yard; and this precaution was justified, for Mr. Friston died at noon without ever regaining consciousness or giving the slightest clue as to his assailant.

Mr. Reeder went down to Windsor with a small party of C.I.D. men, saw the body and the weapon. There was no question whatever that the spanner had been the instrument employed. Considerable violence must have been used, judging by the injuries.

"This is the weapon all right," said the inspector in charge. "There's blood and hair on the end of it, and the doctor says that one end of the spanner exactly fits the wound."

Mr. Reeder examined the gruesome relic and put it down without a word.

He was puzzled, much more puzzled than any of the officers who were with him. Obviously this spanner had caused the injuries from which the unhappy master had died, but there were certain peculiar features of the case which made him reject immediately the theories which were put forward as to motive.

"It couldn't have been robbery," said the chief inspector. "He had about ten pounds in his pocket when he was found. No, he's got on the wrong side of somebody in the political world, and they've waited for him. He has been threatened several times. This case might turn into a very big political sensation. Don't you agree, Mr. Reeder?"

Reeder shook his head.

"I—um—am afraid I don't," he said gently. "A sensation, yes, but not a political sensation. It is a peculiar case."

"I thought you might think that," said the inspector sarcastically. "I've had a feeling it was something like that ever since I came into it."

"It's a peculiar case," Mr. Reeder went on. "When Mr. Friston was found, his soft felt hat was still on his head, badly cut and battered, but still on his head. His servant, whom I took the liberty of interviewing, said that that was an eccentricity of his master, to wear his hat pulled tightly down almost over his ears—it was so tightly wedged that it did not fall off when he fell."

"It was cut through," said the inspector.

Mr. Reeder nodded.

"Certainly. Part of the hat was embedded in the wound, and, as you say, considerable violence must have been used."

He looked from one to the other pathetically.

"I—er—hate interfering with your work, inspector, or even to advance my own humble theories. I admit I'm puzzled."

"We're all that," said the inspector good-humouredly; "but isn't that a feature of every case, Mr. Reeder; you're puzzled at first, but after a bit of hard work the whole thing becomes as clear as daylight. The man who did it—"

"That isn't puzzling me so much," said Mr. Reeder. "The question which is rather distressing me is this—who was the other man who was killed?"

The inspector stared at him.

"The other man? Only one body was found." J.G. Reeder inclined his head.

"Yes, but there was another person killed by that spanner. For example, there is blood on it and hair."

"Well?" said Inspector Laymen. "You'd expect to find blood and hair after a murder like this."

"I don't think so," said Mr. Reeder gently; "not when—um— the actual weapon did not come into contact with the wound, and when the unfortunate gentleman is—um—bald."

Laymen gaped at him, ran his fingers through his hair.

"That's right," he said slowly, "there was practically no blood, and, as you say, he was bald!"

He unwrapped the spanner to make sure.

"It is all very disconcerting," Mr. Reeder went on. "Whoever killed the respected gentleman had already destroyed somebody else with the same weapon; or if he had not killed him, had injured him very severely."

Acting on this theory, the inspector ordered an extensive search of the neighbourhood, and the river bank for two miles was scrutinised carefully, without, however, discovering anything that might elucidate the second mystery.

Mr. Reeder spent the greater part of his day pursuing solitary inquiries; he did not rejoin the inspector and his party, but journeyed to London by train. At Paddington he bought all the evening newspapers and read the account of the tragedy with the greatest care, for newspaper men have sometimes a trick of picking up an odd and important clue which has escaped the official eye. There was nothing here, however, that helped toward a solution, and, after boarding his tram at Westminster Bridge, Mr. Reeder settled down to read the remainder of the news. He was a careful and systematic reader of newspapers; no item escaped his attention. He read even the advertisements carefully, and had been seen secretly marking the cross-word puzzles with a stub of pencil.

The tram had passed the ganglion of the Elephant and Castle when he saw a headline: "Dollars in Hayrick. Farm Labourer's Surprising Discovery."

"A farm labourer named Ward, in the employ of Mr. John Carter, a farmer, of Farnham, made a remarkable discovery this morning. He had occasion to go to the top of a hayrick, the thatching of which had been blown off in last week's gale. He was about to begin work when he noticed a flat packet lying on the top of the hay. Picking it up, he carried it to his employer, being unable to read, and Mr. Carter found the packet to contain twenty-five thousand dollars. They were fastened together with a rubber band, and, except that a few notes were sodden by the rain, they were undamaged. He immediately communicated with the Farnham police, who have taken charge of the notes and have instituted inquiries. There have been many burglaries in the neighbourhood during the past three months, and it is believed that this package was part of the proceeds, since several wealthy Americans were in residence here during the summer. Mr. Carter and his labourers made an exhaustive search of the hayrick, but no other valuables have been found."

Mr. Reeder kept a mental file of all important crimes, and though it was perfectly certain that there could have been burglaries in that neighbourhood, he could remember nothing of importance, nor could he recall the fact that any very important loss had been reported to the police.

He turned to the stop press and found two brief references; the first was to the hayrick discovery, and was headed:

DOLLARS IN HAYRICK (See page 1)

"A further packet containing twenty-five thousand dollars was discovered in a dry ditch within a mile of the first discovery."

"Humph!" murmured Mr. Reeder, and devoted his attention to the second item:

"MYSTERY OF BURNT CAR (See page 6)

"The car was bought by a man who gave the name of Stevenson at the Brickfield Garage, Waterloo Road."

He turned back to page 6, a little annoyed with himself that he had overlooked a news item so important that it called for further reference in the stop press. It was not a very exciting piece of news. A car had been found by the side of the road between Shrewton and Tilshead in Wiltshire. It was completely burnt out, and its owner or driver had disappeared. Neither the Shrewton nor the Tilshead police had had any report of the occurrence.

"Humph!" said Mr. Reeder again.

Half his success as an investigator came from his ability to build up stories from the flimsiest foundations. The truest and probably the cleverest thing that had been said about him was that he had an instinct for accurate association—accurate or not, he could join up disconnected incidents to make the most incredible stories. They were not only incredible but often fantastical, and more often than not had no other value than to afford him the interest and amusement which only the inventor finds in his creations.

All the way home J.G. Reeder made up stories, which brought in a burnt car, two packets of American bank-notes and an eminent master of Eton College struck down in the middle of the night by an unknown assailant.

Mr. Reeder never pursued these dream stories of his, unless there came to him that queer sense of conviction which belongs rather to instinct than to reason. They served to fill an idle hour, to serve as mental gymnastics to amuse him.

He had reached Brockley and was munching his evening muffins when he began his second story, and he was half-way through the preliminaries when he had that eerie sense that he was telling himself something which was true. He put down an unfinished muffin on the plate, gulped the remainder of his tea, and, wiping his buttery fingers on a serviette, rang the bell. The housekeeper came.

"Clear all this away," said Mr. Reeder. "I'm going to work."

His idea of work was peculiar; for two hours he sat at his desk, his hands clasped on his waistcoat, staring fixedly at his blotting-pad. Only at long intervals did he pick up the pencil and scribble a note on a sheet of paper or strike out some memorandum that he had previously written down.

At half-past ten he went to his room and changed into evening dress. It was an unusual outburst of gaiety on the part of Mr. Reeder. His housekeeper was almost shocked.

CHAPTER III

IT was a quarter to twelve when Mr. Reeder strolled into the Ragbag Club, which is situated in Wardour Street and is only heard of by the general public when it is periodically raided. In spite of the fact that he was a very rare visitor, he was recognised, and the head waiter found a corner table for him, and produced his inevitable bottle of Vichy and the as inevitable fried egg and bacon.

"Nobody here, Adolph?"

"Not yet, Mr. Reeder. They start coming in after the theatre."

The head waiter was a little nervous.

"Anything doing, sir?" he asked.

Mr. Reeder took a yellow carton of cigarettes from his trousers pocket, and lit one carefully before he replied.

"If you mean by that, Adolph, are the police raiding this speakeasy, I am unable to afford you any information. I should imagine, however, that you will be safe for to-night."

The head waiter looked his relief. Such a speculation on the part of his visitor was tantamount to a guarantee, and, indeed, Mr. Reeder had, before his arrival, notified Scotland Yard where he was spending the evening.

"Are you expecting anybody?"

The head waiter shook his head.

"Nobody you know, Mr. Reeder."

This was a mechanical assurance; Reeder had had it before.

He picked daintily at his bacon.

"Mr. Higson, now?" he suggested. "Mr. Hymie Higson?"

The head waiter looked uncomfortable.

"He hasn't been here since—"

"Let's have the truth," said Mr. Reeder softly. "If I deal fairly with a man I expect him to deal fairly with me. About a year ago"—he was devoting himself entirely to his supper, and apparently the story he now related was something to make conversation—"about a year ago there was considerable trouble, I believe, with a man whose name I forget for the moment, but whose offence was the passing of forged money. The money was traced here, to this delightful club, and to its very nice, polite head waiter, who is also the proprietor. I investigated the matter on behalf of the—um—authorities, and I discovered that you were perfectly innocent in the matter. I could, of course, have made matters very unpleasant for you, but, being a perfectly honest man and having no desire to inconvenience the general public, I—um—did not bring you into court as witness."

The head waiter cleared his throat.

"That's true, Mr. Reeder. I told you then that if I could ever do anything for you—"

"Well?" Mr. Reeder looked up, and this time the head waiter was not uncomfortable.

"Hymie hasn't been here since last Sunday night," he said; "but I'm expecting him to-night. In fact, he telephoned to me and asked me to have a hot supper ready for him in the private room. But the private room has been booked, so he's got to take it in the restaurant. I'm expecting him every minute now."

"When did he telephone?"

The waiter thought.

"This evening. He said he was very anxious to have the private room."

"Is he bringing somebody?"

The man shook his head.

"No, sir, he said nothing about that. He's only ordered supper for one."

"I'll wait," said Mr. Reeder.

The head waiter looked at him, troubled.

"There's nothing wrong, is there? I mean, if you have to make any kind of pinch, I wish you'd do it outside the club, Mr. Reeder. We've got such a bad name lately with the police—"

"I'm not going to pinch anybody," said J.G. cheerfully. "I merely want to renew an old and unpleasant acquaintance."

His opportunity came five minutes later, when Hymie Higson came in. He was wearing a long overcoat, which he slipped off and handed to the waiter at the door. Evidently the occasion was not a festive one, for he was not dressed for any party. He glanced round the room and then his eyes fell upon Mr. Reeder. He was all for pretending that he had not seen his bête noire, and was turning away when Mr. Reeder beckoned him.

The room was still sparsely tenanted, and there was no excuse whatever for the newly arrived visitor to make a hurried exit, and reluctantly he came across to where the detective was sitting.

"All alone?" asked Mr. Reeder pleasantly. "Sit down."

"I'm expecting some friends." Hymie was very cool and watchful. He stood at the table, ignoring the invitation.

"I think you'd better sit down," said Mr. Reeder amiably.

With great reluctance Hymie sat. He was a wiry man, with a keen, dark face and abnormally long, thin hands.

"Well, get it over." His tone was offensive. "It doesn't do me any good being seen speaking to a copper."

"It doesn't do me any good or any harm," rejoined Mr. Reeder. "Anybody who knows you and me will imagine that I am questioning a second-class crook, and an amateur at that. A buyer and passer of snide notes, a forger of acceptances, a card-sharper who robbed his young brother officers and was expelled from the service which he never adorned, a born confidence man, possibly a murderer, certainly a wholly undesirable citizen."

He said this with the greatest blandness, and with every accusation Hymie's eyes grew harder.

"You'll be able to write the story of my life," he said.

"I shall be able to contribute many interesting items," said Mr. Reeder suavely. And then, without a pause: "You had very bad luck with the money."

Master as he was of his emotions, Hymie blinked quickly twice.

"I don't get that."

"Fifty thousand dollars." Mr. Reeder did not look up. "Ten thousand pounds. An awful lot of money to leave behind you in ditches and hayricks."

"Ditches and hayricks?" Hymie spoke slowly. "Is this a new joke or a new puzzle or what? I don't understand you." And then he chuckled. "Good Lord! You mean the stuff in the evening papers about the fellow in Kent who found some American money on the top of a haystack? That's funny—one of the funniest things I've heard. Why should I know anything about it?"

"It wasn't in Kent," said Mr. Reeder carefully; "it was a place called Farnham."

"I've never been there in my life," smiled Hymie, "and that you can take as gospel truth, Reeder. I've never been there in my life. If I had been there I should hardly have been chucking bundles of thousand dollar-bills into hayricks. And if that's all you've got to talk to me about, you're wasting your own time and mine."

He rose abruptly, but Reeder's hand caught his arm.

"Sit down," he said. "There are one or two other questions I want to ask you."

"Ask 'em by letter, or better still go read an article I read the other day about the truth machine. You strap it on a man and when he lies you get a reaction. They tried it on a bird who'd murdered—"

He stopped suddenly. Reeder saw his face go suddenly hard and pinched.

"Who'd murdered?" he suggested.

Hymie laughed.

"I haven't come here to tell you granny stories," he said.

Hymie shook off the detaining hand and stalked away. He would have gone with less comfort if he had known that J.G. Reeder had also read that article on the truth machine which had appeared in an American magazine.

Hymie's meal was a frugal one, Mr. Reeder noticed. He was not in the restaurant long before he paid his bill and departed.

J.G. Reeder had a number of other inquiries to make, but none of these proved very satisfactory. He visited clubs less reputable than the Ragbag, dingy places where his evening dress excited guffaws of amusement; little upstairs rooms, clouded with smoke, where he was recognised and a deadly silence fell on his appearance. He buttonholed the most unlikely people and plied them with mysterious questions. He was a tired man when he got back to Brockley. The clock was striking three as he slipped into bed and pulled the coverlet over his shoulder, but he could not have closed his eyes before he heard the bell of the front door ringing. It rang incessantly, and, rising, he opened the window still further and looked out.

He saw an indistinct figure standing on the step. "Who's that?" he asked.

"It's Lizzie, sir. Can I see you? An awful thing has happened!"

"Wait a moment."

He closed the window, switched on his light, and, dressing hastily, went downstairs and admitted the sobbing parlourmaid. It was a long time before she became coherent, though he learned the object of her visit before she could relate the circumstances.

"Ena's gone... been took away... Oh, I'm sure something's happened to her, Mr. Reeder..."

He gave her some water, and after a while she became calmer and told her story. She had gone to bed at eleven o'clock. She and her sister slept in the front room, looking on to the street. They had talked for an hour on the inevitable subject of Ernie and his peculiar behaviour, and they must have fallen asleep somewhere about midnight.

At one o'clock Lizzie, who was a heavy sleeper, was awakened by voices. Stupid with sleep as she was, she sat up in bed and found Ena in her dressing-gown going out through the door. She had asked what was the trouble, and Ena had whispered: "It's Ernie. He's outside. He wants to see me for a minute."

Still half-asleep, Lizzie lay and waited. She heard no sound of voices, and presently she became wide awake. She heard the noise of a car driving off, and, getting out of bed, went to the door and listened. There was no sound. The narrow hall below was in darkness, and, lighting a candle, she went down the stairs in search of her sister. The front door was wide open, but her sister was nowhere visible.

Lizzie ran into the street and looked up and down. The thoroughfare was deserted. In the passage she found one of Ena's slippers, and, in alarm, she went upstairs and woke her mother. Ena had vanished. She had gone to the interview in a dressing-gown over her night-dress, had not even put on her stockings. The night was chilly, with a slight fog, not the kind of night that Ena would choose for a stroll, even if she were fully dressed.

"Have you notified the police?" asked Mr. Reeder quickly.

The woebegone Lizzie shook her head.

"Mother didn't want the disgrace of bringing in the police—" she began.

Mr. Reeder forced the disgrace upon this family by reaching for the telephone and calling the nearest police station. He had the good fortune to find the divisional inspector, and arranged to meet him at the house in Friendly Street.

As they walked together down Tanner's Hill Lizzie told him of her last talk with her sister.

"No, she said nothing unusual, but, naturally, the American money coming was a great surprise to us all."

Mr. Reeder stopped in his stride.

"The American money?" he said quickly. "What American money was this?"

"Dollars," said the girl; "foreign money—American—twenty-five notes for a thousand dollars, and a thousand dollars is worth more than two hundred pounds... Ena was surprised, and so was I. We had never seen so much money in our lives. Five thousand pounds, Mr. Reeder."

"Tell me about this," he said as they walked on slowly.

"It came by express post, not registered or anything, yesterday morning by the first post. Ena didn't tell mother anything about it, because Ernie said, 'Don't mention this to a soul.' She only told me because it got on her mind."

"He wrote a letter with it, did he?"

"Not a letter, just a scrap of paper fastened inside the band that went round the bank-notes. Just that—'Don't tell a soul about this, not even Lizzie.' Those were the very words. I'll show them to you."

"What did she do with the money?"

The girl considered this.

"I don't know. Oh, yes, I do," she said suddenly. "She put it under her pillow just before she went to sleep. I'd forgotten all about it."

"Where was it posted?"

"In London," said Lizzie. "I specially noticed this—London, W.1. It was posted the night before. Ena said, 'It's funny, Ernie being in London and not coming to see me'—that's what we were talking about last night."

She was certain that there was nothing more than this admonition, written on a scrap of paper fastened to the notes by a rubber band.

"But you'll see for yourself," she said, "and the envelope. Ena kept the money in the envelope. She's a very careful girl, is Ena—poor darling!"

She began to weep softly, and Mr. Reeder was uncomfortable.

When they reached the house they found that the divisional inspector and one of his men had already arrived, and were interviewing the tearful mother. Reeder went straight upstairs to the bedroom, and his first act was to turn back the pillow, still bearing the impression of Ena's pretty head. There was nothing beneath the pillow, neither letter nor notes. He pulled over the mattress, but the money was not there; nor was it in the locked drawer where she kept her treasures.

"She didn't put it in the drawer," insisted Lizzie. "I actually saw her put it under the pillow just before she went to bed. She had a little joke about having money to fall back upon."

Mr. Reeder pursed his lips.

"Did you see her when she was leaving the room? Did she have anything in her hand?"

Lizzie was uncertain. The room was dark, the blind drawn. The only thing she was sure about was that Ena was in the doorway and had spoken to her. She was so sleepy that she could not even remember the girl's exact words.

"I'm such a heavy sleeper," she confessed, "that Ena might have been having a long talk through the window. It was open; in fact, it was the cold air that woke me up."

One thing was clear to Reeder: whoever had called, and whatever was the whispered conversation they had held between window and pavement, the caller had asked her to bring with her the American bank-notes.

For whom would she go down in the middle of the night? He questioned Lizzie on this, but her memory was vague. It could not have been anybody who bore the slightest resemblance to the man with the false moustache, but, against this, Ena had not seen him.

The constable on the beat was found, and he was able to give a few vital details. He had seen a car drawn up at the end of the street, and had thought it belonged to a doctor. The only machines of importance that came into Friendly Street in the night were usually associated with births or deaths. He had spoken to the chauffeur, but, having no curiosity as to the ownership of the car, had asked him no questions. He had had the impression that there was somebody sitting inside the car, but he wasn't very sure about this, and when he had returned on his second visit, which was a quarter of an hour after Ena had disappeared, the "doctor's" car had gone.

A rough examination of the street by flashlight produced another clue—the second of Ena's slippers. It lay in the gutter, and had been run over, evidently by the car, for on the silken uppers was the mark of a diamond tyre tread. The slipper was found at a point midway between where the car had been seen waiting and the girl's home. The divisional inspector brought it into the house and examined it carefully, but it afforded them no assistance, the only suggestion it offered being that the slipper was kicked off between the house and the car by Ena in the course of a struggle.

The divisional inspector had a ready-made solution to the mystery, which was more flattering to Ena's enterprise than to her modesty, but this Reeder rejected.

"She didn't go willingly—of that I'm certain," he said, and here he was right.

CHAPTER IV

ENA PANTON did not fall asleep immediately her head touched the pillow. Her mind was excited. She was baffled by the amazing conduct of a young man towards whom she had pleasant feelings, though she could not, in the strictest sense of the term, regard herself as being in love with him.

Ernie was one of those indistinct and eager courtiers who impress not so much by their personality as by their sincerity. He had been in love, very much in love, and after the manner of her sex the girl had played on his emotions without finding them communicated to herself. She liked him; she was flattered by him. When he became munificent she was a little impressed by him. But she had never loved this chinless young man, with his sleek hair and his tiny moustache. Now he was a factor in life that gave her tremendous importance. Under her head reposed a fortune. She put her hand beneath the pillow and touched the envelope to make sure she was not dreaming.

She heard the clock strike hour by hour, and she was wide awake when the first pebble struck the window pane. She got out of bed, pulled up the blind gently so that she should not disturb her sister, and looked out. She saw a motor car standing by the kerb a little way along the street, and beneath the window a man muffled to the chin by the collar of his overcoat. Foreshortened as he was, and in the darkness—the house stood midway between two street lamps—she could not distinguish him. But it might be Ernie. She raised the window carefully and looked out.

"Is that you, Ena?" said a voice.

"Who is it?" she asked in the same tone. "Jack—Ernie's brother."

She had never known till then that Ernie had a brother.

"What's the matter?" she asked.

"Ernie wants to see you; he's in the car. Can you come down for a second?"

She hesitated, looked towards her sister, who, if the truth be told, was snoring.

"I don't know if I can," she said. "Can't you tell me?"

"It's about the money," whispered the voice urgently. "Bring it down with you and I'll explain. The police are after Ernie, and they may be after you."

This was a terrific shock to the respectable Ena, and threw her off her balance. A greater shock, since she had had some doubt as to whether any person in the world could possess so vast a sum as five thousand pounds without having acquired it dishonestly.

"I'll be down," she said, put on her slippers and her dressing-gown and, taking the money from under her pillow, opened the door.

It was at this point that Lizzie woke.

"It's all right. It's a man who wants to see me about Ernie," whispered the girl, and went pattering down the stairs.

She took off the chain, unlocked the door and opened it.

"I can't ask you in—" she began.

Nevertheless, he took a step into the passage and before she realised what had happened, a strong arm closed round her, a hand covered her mouth and nose.

"If you make a noise I'll kill you!" breathed an unpleasant voice in her ear.

Momentarily she was paralysed with fear, allowed herself to be led out into the cold street, and was only conscious that she had lost a slipper when her bare foot touched the pavement. This brought her back to sanity. The hands were still over her mouth, and with a jerk she tried to free herself. For a moment there was a breathless struggle, until he lifted her bodily and ran with her to the car. The chauffeur had opened the door, and the man got in, dragging her after him and flung her on the seat by his side.

"If you make a fuss I'll kill you," he said again. "I mean that. I could break that little neck of yours as easy as breaking a stick."

She subsided into the corner, sick and trembling, and, stooping, he picked up a rug and flung it over her, pulled down the blinds and settled himself by her side.

She could not see where the car was going. She felt it breast a hill, and guessed they were going into Lewisham. She began to cry and wail, and this her captor tolerated. Then suddenly she remembered.

"What have you done with the money, you thief? You're not Ernie's brother Jack... He has no brother."

The man laughed.

"What do you know about Ernie or his brothers or sisters or aunts or cousins?" he asked flippantly. "But you're quite right about the money; I've got it, in my pocket. I've lost too much through that damned fool's stupidity."

"Where is Ernie?" she asked.

He made no reply to this.

"What are you going to do with me?" she demanded after a long silence.

"It's not what I'm going to do, it's what you're going to do," he said. "You're going to write a letter to your mother or sister or your friend Mr. Reeder, and tell them that you've gone abroad with Ernie, and that you're perfectly happy, and that you'll be coming back in a year— and—"

"I'm not going abroad with you or Ernie," she stormed. "You'll be locked up for this—taking me out of the house—"

"You must be very pretty," said her captor cynically. "I haven't had a good look at you, but you must be very pretty. You're so damned unintelligent that there must be some points about you that would attract even a nit-wit like that copper-hearted bird."

The mention of Mr. Reeder gave her an idea.

"Mr. Reeder will find me," she said. "You'll not get away with it. He knows everything about Ernie. I showed him the letters that Ernie sent—"

"What letters?" asked the man quickly, and she realised she had made a mistake.

"One letter, anyway. The letter he sent from Birmingham."

She heard him gasp.

"Did he write to you from Birmingham? Was—was there any address on the letter?"

She hesitated, and she heard his sigh of relief.

"There wasn't," he said. "Reeder's got the letter, has he?"

She did not reply, and leaning over, he caught her by the shoulders and shook her roughly.

"When I speak to you, answer," he said. "Now, tell me all that Reeder knows."

She began to cry softly.

"If you snivel I shall be sorry for you, and if I'm sorry for you I shall kiss you," he said, and she sat bolt upright, stiff with fear.

There was nothing subtle about Ena. She had not even a native cunning.

"Lizzie took the letters to him, and he asked her a lot of questions as to how Ernie wrote, whether he made—you know—little circles in the air before he started to put his pen on the paper."

She heard the man whistle.

"He asked that, did he—the old devil!"

She realised she had to propitiate him, and it was not difficult for Ena to propitiate men, even men met under the present distressing circumstances.

"It was awful of you to take me away like this," she said. "You'll get into ever such trouble—"

"Never mind about that," he said curtly. "Go on telling me what Reeder said."

There was very little she could tell him, he realised after she had been talking for a little while.

"Does he know about the money—the money that was sent to you this morning—yesterday morning?" he corrected himself.

"No, but Lizzie will tell him."

"Was she awake when you left?" he asked quickly.

"Yes, she was—and I'll bet she took the number of this car, so the best thing you can do is to say it's a joke and take me back."

"That is not my idea of a joke," he said.

They did not speak again for the greater part of an hour. The car was flying through the country. Twice it passed over a long bridge. She asked where they were going. It was the third time she had put that question.

"You're going to a nice, quiet, country spot," said the man. "You'll have a little suite of your own, and if you've any brains you will sit down and amuse yourself with knitting. I'll get you some clothes to-morrow and if you don't make any attempt to escape you'll be treated decently. If you do try to get away—" He did not finish the sentence.

She fell asleep in the last half-hour of the journey, and was awakened when the car stopped. He took a large silk handkerchief and bound her eyes before he assisted her into a house which smelt close and musty, and guided her feet up the stairs which were so broad that, reaching out her hand, she could feel no balustrade.

He kept her waiting for about a quarter of an hour in a small, unfurnished room, and here she sat shivering on a chair, with a rug round her shoulders, until he came for her, and showed her into a bigger room that had evidently been hastily furnished with a bed. The windows were covered with wooden shutters. The room had been newly papered, and had the luxury of a small bathroom which led from the apartment, a bathroom which was apparently entirely without windows.

"I'll get you some food, and to-morrow I'll bring you books and anything you need."

He stood revealed now in the light he had switched on; a tall man, lithe, keen, good-looking. It was the first time Hymie Higson had seen the girl, and he could admire and approve Ernie's choice.

"You're a good-looker but dumb," he said good-humouredly.

"I can talk if I want—" she began.

"I don't mean that kind of dumbness." He tapped his head. "Maybe we'll improve your mind down here; and in the meantime I'll give you my word for what it is worth, that you won't be molested unless you attempt to escape. There's a man on guard below your window; there will always be somebody up in the house, and your chance of getting away is practically nil. What is more important, you'll be very sorry if you attempt to make your escape. I'm telling you."

He went away and came back with some hot tea and sandwiches, which he put on a table.

"You're a sensible girl, and you don't need me to tell you that if I'd go to the trouble of abducting you, which carries a sentence of ten years penal servitude, there's very little I'd stop short at. When I told you I'd break that little neck of yours I meant it. It would be harder to do now I've had a good look at you—but I'd do it! Will you please regard me as a sleeping dog and let me lie! And don't kick me!"

There was a certain refinement in his tone. She thought it was rather "aristocratic," and then in a flash remembered the man who had come in the false moustache, and promptly charged him with that visit. He nodded.

"That's true. I was trying to do you a turn. You didn't know it, but I was. If your sister hadn't gone to that"—he checked himself— "that man Reeder, if she hadn't spilt the beans to him, you wouldn't be in this mess. I wouldn't have minded the money the treacherous little dog sent you—after all, you're probably entitled to your cut."

Since she did not realise the significance of this innuendo it passed unchallenged.

He left her, and after some hesitation she drank the tea and finished the sandwiches, in some trepidation.

It was not until the first streaks of dawn showed through the cracks in the shutters that weariness overcame her, and, lying down on the bed, she pulled a rug over her and went to sleep. She must have slept throughout the day, for it was dusk when she woke up and, switching on the light, pushed the bell which Hymie had shown her.

It was some time before an answer came, in the shape of Hymie himself, carrying a tray.

"I'm sorry to keep you waiting," he said with mock humility; "but as I'm head cook and warder of this establishment, and I've no lady's maid to wait upon you, you'll have to be satisfied with the best I can give you."

The best was boiled eggs and new bread, and delicious butter. Being young and healthy, and with a young and healthy person's appetite, she was more concerned in the satisfaction of her hunger than in her immediate danger.

He went out of the room and came back with a bundle of clothes, which he threw on the bed.

"They're all new, and they've all been collected with considerable trouble from a dozen London stores. I guess old man Reeder has been circulating warnings to outfitters. If they had all been purchased at the same place, some copper-hearted chicken would have blown the works."

"What do you mean by 'copper-hearted'?" she asked curiously, and he was pleased to explain that a copper-hearted was one who had an affection for policemen and was predisposed to supply information to these indispensable servants of civilisation.

"That's all there is to it, baby."

"Are you American?" she asked, and he smiled, showing his white teeth.

"English by birth, American by education. I had the honour of spending my eighteenth birthday in an American college called Sing-Sing—you may have heard of the establishment."

"It's a prison, isn't it?" she said, and he chuckled.

"This growth of education on the part of the lower orders can be traced to the movies. Yes, my child, the college was Sing-Sing, and the actual form I was in was located in the death house, from which a well-directed 'life- boat'" (Footnote: i.e., Pardon.) "rescued me in time to serve with distinction in the Great War."

He waved his hand to the clothing.

"There's everything there that a lady requires," he said. "Not that you're a lady, but no doubt you dress like one. If I have omitted something, I hope you'll be immodest enough to tell me."

He went away after this and she bolted the door on him and dressed. Beyond the fact that the shoes were a size too large, the clothing fitted her, and she felt more at her ease. It was when he came back that he discovered that the door had a bolt.

"I overlooked that," he said when he was admitted.

He went to the door and called a name. Presently a man came in, who, without so much as looking at her, proceeded to remove the bolt.

"It isn't necessary if you play square," said Hymie, "and if you didn't play square that bolt would be no more use to you than post-cards in hell!"

CHAPTER V

MR. REEDER'S views on the deplorable state of his mind were familiar to most people, but he was never quite so much a criminal as he was in the twelve hours which followed the disappearance of Ena Panton.

He had suspicions amounting almost to certainty. But Scotland Yard is a very cautious machine, not easily set in motion. "Maybe's" and "Very likely's" do not send the wheels grinding. More important, it is very careful to hide from those on whom suspicion falls that they are suspect, and this care often arrests too close inquiries. But Mr. Reeder was not at Scotland Yard. He was an extraneous force that moved sometimes independently of, and sometimes in conjunction with, that establishment, but he was not entirely bound by the methods and formula of Scotland Yard. He interviewed the Assistant Director of Public Prosecutions, and this gentleman said all that Mr. Reeder expected him to say, which was that he should pass any exact information he had to the Criminal Investigation Department.

Between conjecture and exact information yawns a deep, wide gulf. Mr. Reeder might suppose all manner of things, but the only fact he had to go on was that a little typist, living in the poorest part of London, had left her house, scantily attired, in the middle of the night and had disappeared. There was not even definite information upon which the police could act that she was in possession of five thousand pounds in dollar currency. They had only the evidence of her sister, who admittedly knew little or nothing about foreign currency, and, in addition, there was a peculiar want of title to the money, supposing it had been under the girl's pillow as Lizzie had stated.

All that he could say in his minute to the C.I.D. was that the girl had disappeared, and all that Scotland Yard could reply politely, yet with a hint of flippancy, was that young ladies had heretofore walked out of their houses in the middle of the night, and even in the middle of the day, and flown to mysterious love nests which were of a quite innocuous character.

Inspector Grayson, who came over to consult with Mr. Reeder, put the matter from his point of view.

"There may be something very big behind it. On the other hand, you know how these people romance. For all you can tell the girl may have been fully dressed and waiting for the arrival of this young man. The fact that her old clothes were found in the room may mean nothing more than that she had something better to wear. This is disappearance six hundred and seventy-three, and against that you've got to balance four or five hundred that have turned up, very sorry for themselves, and hoping that everything will be forgotten and forgiven. The money part of it is a bit of a puzzle, but I think I've found the explanation of that."

He took out his pocket-book and produced some newspaper cuttings. They dealt with the finding of the two packets of bank-notes near Farnham.

"That is what started this yarn. She has read this in the paper and has probably invented the rest. You know what liars these people are— they'll do anything to get themselves into the limelight."

Mr. Reeder sighed. He always sighed when anybody else took a low view of human nature. It had been a bluff on his part to connect Hymie Higson with the discovery of the money on the hayrick, part of one of his fantastical stories, which had once seemed real and now had gone back to its old perspective. He rather wished he could see Higson again, because there was something about the man...

Was it Higson? Was Higson the abductor? He asked why he should be, and found no satisfactory answer.

Mr. Reeder sat down at his desk and fell to storytelling all over again, imagining the worst of everybody, imputing motives far from commendable to every man and woman associated in his mind with the case.

Ena might turn up again and make them all look foolish. He had only the evidence of a sleepy girl, not too intelligent, possibly not too truthful; a young lady whose passion for sensationalism had been stimulated by her devotion to the pictures.

On one point, however, he was certain; when the blow fell, as he knew it must inevitably fall, he was prepared for an event which shocked ten millionaire directors to their core, if indeed they possessed such a moral stiffening.

He was sent for the next day as soon as he reached the office. The Assistant Director was very perturbed.

"I want you to go down to the city and see Sir Wilfred Heinhall. It's very important, Reeder, so please don't go by bus—take a taxi."

"Certainly," said Mr. Reeder. "I will go the quickest way."

Actually he went by tube.

They were waiting for him in the stately anteroom to Sir Wilfred's palatial boardroom; two managers and a managing clerk escorted him into the gilded room with its crystal chandeliers and priceless paintings.

"Mr. Reeder, Sir Wilfred," they announced in hushed voices, and left him.

Sir Wilfred was pacing up and down a large and expensive Persian rug. His hands were thrust into his pockets, his whitish, sandy hair was disarrayed in a picturesque and alarming manner. He looked like a man who had not slept for a month.

"Sit down, Mr. Reeder," he said in a hollow voice. "Sit down! A most dreadful thing has happened, and I cannot help but recall your fateful words —yes, I think I could describe them as 'fateful'—the last time we met. I refer to our business system, with which I was all too satisfied—all too satisfied!"

He made a gesture of despair. Mr. Reeder sat down on the edge of the chair, his umbrella between his legs, his hands grasping the knob, and waited.

"When you told me, Mr. Reeder, that the system on which the Central and Southern Bank is run was archaic and out of date, I admit I scoffed. I have a distinct recollection of scoffing. I may have been rude to you."

"You were," murmured Mr. Reeder.

"I am sorry! I can say nothing more than that—I am sorry. A terrible thing has happened—the most terrible thing in the history of the bank. Mr. Reeder, we have been robbed of a fortune. Not here in London, Mr. Reeder, but—" He paused dramatically.

"In Birmingham?" said Mr. Reeder, and Sir Wilfred opened his mouth wide.

"In Birmingham? I have not told a soul where it was. I did not even tell the Public Prosecutor. I have not mentioned it even to my managing director—it was Birmingham, yes."

Mr. Reeder nodded slowly.

"By a clerk. I don't know what his surname was, but I imagine his Christian name was Ernest." Sir Wilfred sat down heavily.

"You knew?" He almost squeaked the words. "You knew that we were being robbed? His name is Ernest Graddle—an awful name, one which of itself should have sown suspicion in the mind of any careful manager. Ernest Graddle! A clerk earning a few pounds a week, who has been robbing the bank systematically for the past twelve months, beginning, it seems, with small sums, and gradually increasing until his last act was to convert a sum of eighty-five thousand pounds to his own use! Eighty-five thousand pounds!"

Mr. Reeder was not impressed.

"I thought it would be a pretty big sum. What is the total?"

"Three hundred and ten thousand pounds," said Sir Wilfred huskily. "An enormous sum. And we have been robbed by the simplest of tricks. One of our customers, a retired steelmaster, is something of an eccentric. He is also unfortunately something of a recluse. Instead of his money being invested he maintains a large current account; his balances sometimes are as much as half a million. Although banks are not supposed to pay interest on current accounts, we do allow him a small percentage—three per cent. It is on this account mainly that the money has been drawn. Our client, as I say, lives a retired life. He is extremely religious. I almost said that he was a religious maniac. He may not be a religious maniac, he may be just simply a maniac. No man would keep such an enormous sum on a current account. The bank manager has expostulated with him, but has received no reply to his expostulations. We have, I might say, taken every precaution, and yet this"—he tried to describe the absent Ernest, but failed—"this wretched fellow, scarcely more than a boy, has managed to take the money under the very eyes of our inspectors, under the eyes of our managers, under the eyes of the district manager! It is the most appalling thing that has happened in the history of banking."

Mr. Reeder knew better. More appalling things had happened in the history of banking, but he made a certain number of allowances for Sir Wilfred's natural indignation.

"I presume it will not affect the credit of the bank?" he asked, and Sir Wilfred swelled indignantly.

"Affect the credit of the bank, my dear sir? Stuff and nonsense!" He was quite his old self. "We have ten millions of reserve. The sum involved is, so to speak, a fleabite—in a sense. In another sense it is a colossal loss."

He would have enlarged upon the stability and security of the bank, but Mr. Reeder turned the conversation to a more practical direction.

"When was all this found out?" he asked.

It had been discovered two days before, explained Sir Wilfred. The clerk in question, Ernest Graddle, had not turned up to work. The manager, thinking he was ill, sent a message to where he was lodging, and then heard for the first time that Mr. Graddle, though he maintained the address, was very seldom in the habit of sleeping at home. He had left for London the previous night, taking with him all the possessions he kept at his lodgings. He had paid his landlord and had gone away about eight o'clock in a small, black motor car which he himself drove. The manager became suspicious, sent for an inspector.

"We had the auditors in, and of course, the moment these incompetent jackasses got down to the situation, they discovered what had happened. Graddle handled the account from which the money was stolen, and two or three hours' work on the books showed us just what had happened. Naturally, I have notified the police, who are now searching for him, and I have sent for you, Mr. Reeder, to take complete control of the case on behalf of the bank."

Mr. Reeder smiled.

"I'm afraid you can't do that," he said quietly. "I shall probably take a limited control of the case on behalf of the Public Prosecutor."

He could excuse Sir Wilfred's error, for he had spent many years of his life in the service of the Bankers Trust, and in the course of that association had saved them so many millions that when he retired from his position he was presented with a piece of plate which must have cost nearly twenty pounds.

He explained just where he could help, and Sir Wilfred for once took an intelligent view of the situation.

The manager, accountant and bookkeeper of the Birmingham branch were within call, and these J.G. Reeder took into the sub-manager's office, one by one, and questioned. The manager was quaking. The hour of an honourable retirement was near at hand. It looked to him as though the whole of his career with the bank must go for nothing, for Sir Wilfred had hinted to him that the handsome gratuity which the Central and Southern Bank paid to their managers on retirement might be withheld.

"I know nothing whatever about it. I am responsible, of course, for the account, but Graddle was immensely capable, and I don't know anybody I would have trusted sooner than him. The truth is, Mr. Reeder, our system is wrong. I've pointed this out to Sir Wilfred a dozen times. By the present method it is quite easy for a young clerk, especially if he has a confederate, to wipe out the entire branch balance!"

"Had Graddle any vices?"

The manager thought not. He was a quiet young man, a member of a debating society, and there was no breath of scandal against his name.

"Did he bet?"

Here the manager was emphatic. Graddle abominated gambling, and at local societies had twice given lectures on the evil effects of sweepstakes. There was no woman in the case; Graddle did not drink, nor had he any other objectionable habits.

"He was very ambitious, and often told me that if he were a very rich man he would play on the

Stock Exchange as a man plays on a piano. He said that fortunes could easily be acquired, and it was only the lack of capital which kept any man poor."

"That is probably true," said Mr. Reeder gravely, and the manager hastened to explain. Graddle was keenly interested in the oil market, though there was no evidence to prove that he had ever speculated a shilling on that or any other mart. His interest, however, was such that he had attended technical evening classes on oil engineering, was something of an authority on oil lands, or, if he was not, pretended to be.

It was his practice to spend his week-ends in London, and most of his spare cash went in this luxury. In his desk at the bank they had discovered a number of letters from people who had advertised interests in oil properties. Apparently he never passed an offer of oil lands without writing to the advertisers to discover the strength of it, though again there was no evidence that he had invested money.

Armed with this information, Mr. Reeder made the rounds of the city, and after a while he came to the London offices of an American bank, and discovered where the last eighty-five thousand pounds had been exchanged for American currency. Some four hundred and twenty odd thousand dollars had been paid to a young man, who had brought a covering letter from the Central and Southern Bank, and who had paid for his purchase in English notes. The bank had been warned days in advance that a customer was requiring a large sum in American money, so they were prepared. The description of the youth who made the exchange corresponded with the description furnished of Ernie.

Boiled down, it was a vulgar, commonplace bank theft, an "inside job" readily engineered, because of loose clerical systems, by an employee. It had its hundreds of parallels, and differed in only one respect from a score of similar cases.

In that one respect, however, the difference was marked. Ernie had no vices. He did not bet, he did not speculate. Mr. Reeder, however, knew differently. He interpreted that reference to oil in his letter to Ena, and it was not so difficult to see how the clerk had fallen into the toils. A large number of oil properties are advertised in the agony columns of the leading daily newspapers in the course of the year, and not all of these are genuine. A sensible proportion are inserted by sharks who are quite happy if they touch the little money of the hazardous speculator. Who was the shark?

Later in the day all the documents which had been collected from Ernie's desk were sent by train to London, and Mr. Reeder examined them very carefully. He had already sent a clerk to search the files of the leading dailies for advertisements extolling the potentialities of undeveloped oil-fields. Happily, he had English newspapers to deal with; had this happened in New York a few years before, not a clerk, but an army of clerks would have been required to check up these flattering offers.

Ernie's interest in oil had begun less than twelve months before, if he could judge by the letters, and had probably started with his reading of books on the world's oil production. A copy of one of these was found in his lodgings, well thumbed and annotated—he had left it behind when he had made his hurried flight. Mr. Reeder had therefore been fairly accurate in putting a year as the period to be covered by the searcher after alluring newspapers.

It made a formidable and voluminous collection of documents when it came into Mr. Reeder's hands that night. By the morning these would be checked up and the advertisers traced, if they were traceable.

Descriptions of the wanted man had been circulated by telegraph especially to motor-hire companies and to garage proprietors. At eight o'clock that evening Mr. Reeder was called on the telephone by the Chief Constable of Scotland Yard.

"We've traced that boy, Mr. Reeder. Do you remember the case of a motor car being found on the side of the Shrewton road, burnt out?"

Mr. Reeder almost jumped out of his chair. One of his stories was coming true!

"Yes."

"Well, that was his! He gave the name of Stevenson. The garage proprietor recognised the photograph."

CHAPTER VI

J.G. WAITED up till three in the morning to hear the report of the officer who had been sent specially down to examine the car and to gather fuller particulars. The car had been deliberately set on fire. That had been the police theory from the moment they found two empty petrol tins thrown into a near-by ditch. The number-plate had been broken off, and the machine had been identified by the chassis number. The newest discovery that the police made was that the car had been set on fire by a delayed fuse, and probably did not burst into flame until nearly half an hour after the man had deserted it.

Stevenson had also been identified by the proprietor of an inn at Andover. The boy had arrived late at night, driving the car which was afterwards found burnt, and had ordered supper, which was served to him in the coffee room. He carried with him a small suit-case, was very pale and agitated, and one of the waiters had remarked to the manager of the inn that he thought the visitor had been crying! He was certainly in a state bordering upon hysteria.

After he had finished and paid for his supper, saying that he was going on to Bournemouth, something went wrong with his car. He could not start it, and he behaved like a lunatic, screaming and raving at the motor mechanic who tried to put the matter right. The car required very little treatment; Mr. "Stevenson" had forgotten to switch on the ignition.

All the time he was at the inn he did not let go of his suit-case, and when he drove off it was between the steering column and his left knee.

At first the burnt-out car had not been connected in the mind of the motor mechanic with the Stevenson car. It was not until he saw it in a police station yard that he recognised it and reported his suspicions to the local inspector.

Now, to make Mr. Reeder's story true, this young man had to be hysterical! If he was calm and collected and in full possession of his senses, what had happened that fatal night was impossible. Certainly no packets of bank-notes would have been discovered on the tops of hayricks and in ditches; no eminent master of Eton would have been struck down and destroyed without warning.

Mr. Reeder could claim, though he never made such a claim, that he had known from the very beginning that Ernie was a bank clerk. He had an extensive knowledge of business papers; he knew the paper of the Central and Southern Bank, because the lower right-hand corner was invariably cut off as bank-notes are cut; and he knew that Ernie was a clerk, because bank clerks have a trick of making flourishes with their pens before they write, the reason being the necessity for making absolutely sure of the statement or figures they are copying, the flourish giving them just that amount of time to check up.

But bank clerks are not necessarily thieves because they possess money and give expensive presents to girls. Mr. Reeder was certain that if the explosive Sir Wilfred had been aware that he was in possession of these facts he would have regarded him as an accessory; but Sir Wilfred did not know, and Mr. Reeder's conscience was clear. That was one of the peculiar qualities of Mr.

Reeder's conscience, that nothing clouded it.

He secured a powerful car from the police, and went alone on a voyage of discovery, the area of his search being Buckinghamshire. A search of the records of a certain ministry had told him practically nothing. Mr. Mannering, who was also Mr. Hymie Higson, might have a real name—it was certainly neither Mannering nor Higson.

Reeder made many calls. If he had a weakness it was for working alone; and if he had a vice it was that he was uncommunicative. There were Scotland Yard officers who complained bitterly that he worked for "solo glory." But to do him the barest justice, Mr. Reeder never bothered about glory, any more than a man who plays a difficult game of patience takes any comfort from the thought that his success will win the plaudits of the crowd.

That was his system, to play patience in a closed room for the satisfaction of his own curiosity. If he failed, as he sometimes failed, he published his discredit; if he succeeded, he often hugged his triumph to himself, and none knew how great it was.

So that when he went down into Buckinghamshire he told nobody, and at the end of the day, after he had been deposited in Whitehall and the car dismissed, he stopped only long enough to eat muffins at a near-by restaurant before he strolled away to Paddington and travelled by train to Maidenhead. Here he chartered a cab, and in the darkness of the night was deposited near the home of Mr. or Captain Mannering.

The iron gates were closed; the wall in their vicinity was formidable. A quarter of a mile along a side road the ground was more vulnerable. In the dark of night Mr. Reeder found himself trudging through dead bracken to his objective.

* * * * *

Ena Panton might, as her keeper said, be "dumb," but she had the power of shrewd observation. One of the first things she observed, after she had settled down to her captivity, was that her prison had been most carefully prepared for her. It was as though her gaoler had planned her abduction weeks before he carried her away. The windows were shuttered, and the shutters were screwed into place so that they could not be opened. A ventilator grating had been recently placed in a wall high up out of reach, and a certain number of books had been provided for her entertainment. They were not books in which she herself was greatly interested, being mainly elementary works of science, two or three books about oil and oil-fields, and an amount of other literature equally dry and equally unappealing.

A day after her arrival a new set of books made their appearance, more to her liking. With them came magazines, fashion papers and the more interesting of the illustrated weeklies.

She challenged Hymie, with whom she was now on almost friendly terms.

"You've been planning to get somebody here for a long time."

"How did you know that?"

"Look at all the preparations you've made," she indicated, and he smiled.

"True, O dumbell!" he said. "Fancy you noticing that! Yes, I've been looking forward to the pleasure for a month."

She shook her head.

"No, you haven't. You had this place prepared for somebody else— for Ernie."
He stared at her.
"What makes you think that?" he asked.
She shook her head.
"I don't know. I've got a feeling. Where is Ernie?"
"He's gone abroad."
"Why?" she asked, and he sighed wearily.
"How many times have I told you not to ask questions?"
He went to the end of the room, pulled aside a curtain that hid a heavy door, and unlocked it.
"Come along for your little walk," he said. "Put your coat on—it's cold."
She struggled into the coat he had bought for her, and together they passed through the door on to a landing and down an outside staircase into the dark grounds. At first she had refused to go out with him, and he had not insisted.
"If you want to keep well you've got to take some exercise," he said. "If you prefer to live inside you can—the only thing I can tell you is that you're not going out by yourself."
She saw the wisdom of the arrangement, and the second night when he invited her she went with him meekly. She could see nothing except trees, and far away a dull red glow in the sky. She asked him where this was, and he refused to tell her.
"London?" she suggested.
"Very likely," was the answer.
On this, the fourth night, he took her out and she was feeling at her friendliest, was curious rather than frightened, questioned him as to what he intended doing with her and how eventually she was to be disposed of. He would have liked to supply a practical answer, for he was already feeling the embarrassment of her presence.
They were returning after a longer walk than usual. She had reached the foot of the stairs, when suddenly, without the least warning, he picked her up in his arms and kissed her. She fought back at him like a tiger cat, battling with wild rage. He said nothing, followed her when she went up the stairs and locked the door upon her. When he brought in her supper she retreated to a corner of the room, watching him.
"It's all right, you fool," he growled. "I lost my head, that's all —too much moonlight in my system."
If she could only get the key of that door! He carried it in his side pocket, making no attempt to hide the fact. She practised picking pockets, hung a woollen jacket over the back of a chair and filched from the pocket nuts that she had saved over from her meal. In a few hours she felt herself an adept, but he never gave her another opportunity, kept away from her, and she dared not risk a closer approach.
That night she went to bed with a sense of apprehension, fastened a chair under the knob of the main door leading to the building. It was nine o'clock when she retired. She woke two hours later suddenly and instantly. She had heard a sound, the stealthy movement of a key in a lock, and it came from the direction of the door that led down into the grounds.

In an instant she was out of the bed, switched on the light and slipped into her dressing-gown. She was white and shaking; her knees all but gave way under her as she moved stealthily across the room in the direction whence the sound had come.

There it was, a queer, tinkling noise, the fumbling of steel against steel.

"Go away!" she called shrilly. "If you come in I'll kill you. I have a knife."

The noise ceased. She waited tensely, listening. There was no other sound, but when she put her ear to the door she thought she heard feet moving.

There came another sound that sent her spinning round. A key had been thrust in the main door at the other end of the room, the lock snapped back, and Hymie came in, glowering.

"What are you trying to do—make a getaway? Go back to bed."

"Wasn't it you... trying to get through that door?" She pointed.

"That door?"

His voice changed. Crossing the room swiftly, and taking a key out of his pocket as he came, he unlocked the door and pulled it open. Nobody stood on the landing outside, nor was any person visible on the narrow stairs.

"Is this a fairy story or are you—"

He saw something, and, stooping, touched the landing. It was a wet footmark; his fingers, when he examined it, were muddy. Somebody had been there recently.

Locking the door, he hurried from the room and was gone a few minutes. When he returned he was wearing an overcoat and carrying a hand-lamp, and with this he examined the landing and the stairs. He tried the door at the foot of these; it was unlocked, and he was certain that he had locked it behind him when he had come in. It was raining; the ground under his feet was wet.

Hurrying back the way he came, he passed through the girl's room, and along a passage down the wide stairs to the hall. A man was sitting there, reading by the shaded light of a lamp. It was the thick-set man who had torn off the bolt in Ena's room.

"Wake up the boys," said Hymie. "Get Janny up from the cottage."

"What's wrong?" asked the man, putting down his newspaper.

"Somebody tried to get into the house through the outside staircase."

The man grinned.

"Burglars?" he asked sardonically, and Hymie showed his teeth to him.

"Do as you're told, will you!" he snarled.

Mr. Reeder's visit to the neighbourhood had not passed unnoticed. It had been disconcerting, but there was no immediate cause for alarm. He did not doubt for a moment that Reeder knew he was living here under the name of Captain Mannering; but Reeder would not suspect that the girl was here, and Hymie's greatest secret of all was hidden beyond fear of discovery.

Hymie was no ordinary criminal; he maintained an intelligence staff in unsuspected places. No search warrant could be applied for and issued without his knowledge—he banked upon this. The very hint that such a warrant was on its way would be sufficient to start him moving. But he had questioned his informant only that night over the telephone, and had been completely assured that Scotland Yard was not taking the step he most dreaded.

Reeder was different. Hymie knew the detective by repute. He did things which officialdom would never sanction, and a search warrant, for J.G. Reeder, was an absurd superfluity. It was Reeder; nobody but Reeder would dare... Reeder had probably watched him as he had come from the stairway.

When he had got his men together Hymie explained his plan.

"I'm taking this girl to France to-night," he said.

"She ought to have gone there first. I'll arrange to have her looked after and be back by to-morrow night. Have a car ready, and 'phone the hangar."

Hymie had served in the Air Force during the war, and he owned a powerful little two-seater 'plane that had been very useful to him. He housed this in a field behind Wycombe, but, as Mr. Reeder had suspected, the flying licence he held was issued neither to Mr. Higson nor Captain Mannering.

"I'll bet you that's what he's been looking for," said one of the men, and Hymie turned on him sharply.

"Who do you mean—Reeder?"

"He hasn't been snooping around the country for nothing," the man went on. "Didn't you say that when you met him at the club he was asking you why you left bundles of bank-notes lying around?"

"That was a guess," said Hymie hastily.

The man shook his head. It was the gardener who lived at the cottage, and he had excellent reason for knowing Reeder.

"He came here the day we got those damned chickens in," he said, "and I was sitting at the door of the cottage when his van passed. He couldn't help recognising me—he had me for a snide job four years ago, and that fellow is camera-eyed! If he knows you, he knows your record. He knows you're an airman, and that's why he's been down here—looking for the hangar. And if he's down here to-night, he's looking for the girl. If you take my advice, guv'nor, you'll have all the cars round and beat it."

Hymie considered this proposition, and it seemed reasonable. He had been a fool ever to hamper himself with this brainless little typist. On the face of it, this dangerous adventure had the appearance of a supreme act of folly. It is possible that Hymie thought there might be a pleasant solution, for he was not without his attractions.

"Get the cars ready. I'll go up and tell her," he said.

He ran up the stairs, along the passage, and, unlocking the door, flung it open. The room was in darkness.

"Get up and dress," he commanded. "We're going a little trip."

There was no answer.

He took a step to the left, felt for the light switch and turned it.

"Don't move," said Mr. Reeder's amiable voice.

He was sitting at the table, his square hat on the back of his head, his woollen muffler untidily disposed about his neck, and in his mittened hand was a long-barrelled automatic.

CHAPTER VII

FOR a second Hymie stared at him, dazed, shattered. He was paralysed to inaction for just the time it takes a man to count twenty.

"The young lady is waiting for me outside the other door—" began Mr. Reeder.

Hymie moved swiftly. With one hand he knocked up the light switch and the room was in darkness. In another second he was flying along the corridor and down the stairs. There was nobody in the hall. Hymie jumped for the front door, and, flinging it open, flew out into the night. He wore thin slippers and a dressing-gown. He scarcely noticed the gravel under his feet as he tore down the drive just as the first of the cars backed out of the garage behind the cottage.

"Get the gate open!" he roared

One of the men flew to the gate, turned the key and pulled, but the iron barrier moved only a few inches and then stuck. Somebody had slipped a handcuff around two bars, that effectively held it.

"Get an axe," breathed Hymie; "quick!"

One of the men ran into the garage and came back with a crowbar. It would seem a simple matter to smash one steel link, but it was nearly three minutes before the connecting handcuff was broken and the gate swung open.

"Your tyres are flat," said a hateful voice from the darkness. "I— um—took the liberty of deflating them. And even if I hadn't—"

As he spoke there came a whirr of wheels. A big car drew up with a jerk opposite the gate and across the path, barring all escape. Hymie turned and fled across the little park. He saw a dark figure standing by the side of the drive and fired from his hip. It was all that was necessary for Mr. Reeder, for he was a law-abiding man and could not bring himself to shoot unless he were shot at. Two sharp reports followed; Hymie felt the sting of a bullet in his thigh; one leg gave under him and he went crashing to the ground.

* * * * *

"Oh, yes," said Mr. Reeder apologetically, "I am afraid I did go down into Buckinghamshire without notifying Scotland Yard. But being, as I have always insisted, a—um—timid man, I did take the precaution of telephoning to the Buckinghamshire police, telling them what I was doing, and asking them to send a squad car to pick me up in an hour's time.

"I have always known that this pleasant country retreat was occupied by at least two crooks. The prosperity of Mr. Hymie Higson was such that I should have been foolish to the point of recklessness if I had not detailed one of my assistants to trail him; and once he was trailed, there was no difficulty at all in establishing the fact that Captain Mannering and Hymie were one and the same person.

"I was puzzled as to why Hymie should purchase a country estate, even though that estate was purchased very cheaply, until I made an examination of his American record, and found that his favourite pose was that of country gentleman, in which role he had fleeced quite a number of distinguished but unintelligent young men of the jeunesse dorée—a foreign expression meaning,

I believe, the golden youth.

"Whether Hymie originally intended to try that method of earning a livelihood in England on his release from prison, or whether it was forced upon him by the circumstances of finding the mug—if you will pardon the expression—I have not yet discovered. It is certain that he was in the habit of advertising oil properties for sale, and that he was by this means enabled to secure quite a considerable sum of money from various dupes. When first he heard from the unfortunate Ernest Graddle, he may not have realised the extent of his good fortune. Later, when they met, and Graddle handed to him a sum which he knew no bank clerk could have obtained honestly, it is possible that, under the threat of exposure, he learned the system by which Graddle had been robbing the bank of small sums for many years.

"Once he knew this, the rest was easy. Graddle made a systematic attack upon the account of a rich man who entrusted his money to the bank, and by a method so simple that a child of ten could have defeated it, was able to go on deceiving his manager, hoodwinking the inspectors—the reference in his letter was obviously to a bank inspector—and extracting huge sums, which he, like all people engaged in embezzlement, imagined he would be able to return when fortune smiled upon him, and delivering instantly the bulk of these monies to Mr. Hymie Higson.

"They were never seen together in London after their first meeting. Hymie was too clever to associate himself physically with a thief who, sooner or later, would be found out. They had certain rendezvous where they met; a flat in the Haymarket, a Maidenhead pleasure garden, and one or two other places which I have not yet been able to trace.

"On one of his excursions to London Ernest Graddle met a girl with whom he fell violently in love. She was undoubtedly pretty, and although she was poor, that fact would not weigh heavily with this young man who, if he had lived on his salary, would have been in her class. He bought her presents, gave her sums of money, and when the strain of his deception began to grow on him, made arrangements to marry her.

"The girl had social instincts, and asked that the engagement might be announced. Ernest agreed, I imagine, with some reluctance, and must subsequently have told Hymie, who would be furious. Such an announcement might attract attention to the girl, and indirectly to the young man. Immediately he obtained the offending advertisement, and in the course of his visit to Deptford learned that Ena's sister was in my employ. That, I— um—flatter myself, must have been a shock to Mr. Higson. I may be taking an immodest view of the—um—terror of my name, but I think I am right in saying that he was shocked.

"Naturally, he disguised himself when he came. In no circumstances must he be identified as having the least connection with Ernest Graddle. I imagine —though he will not confess this much—that he insisted upon the young man making one big steal and bolting. Then it was that Ernest was obstinate, insisted that he could not live without Ena Panton, though it was probably not until the night before he bolted that he confessed that he had broken his promise, and had again communicated with Ena and had sent her a portion of the stolen money, which he had changed into American currency.

"When Hymie learned that he had sent a package of bills to the girl he must have been beside himself with fury. The bills could be traced and the inevitable exposure precipitated. He must also have been having a very trying time with Ernest Graddle, who was love-sick, mad with fear and remorse, and in a state bordering upon dementia.

"The only evidence we have is the evidence given by the motor mechanic at Andover, and his description of Ernest is, I should imagine, a fairly faithful one.

"Hymie's plan was as follows. He would fly in the afternoon to Salisbury Plain, land in the dark—he is one of the cleverest night fliers that ever was thrown out of the Air Force—and Ernest was to go by road and pick him up at an agreed spot which was a quarter of a mile beyond Stonehenge. Hymie seems to have landed on the plain without attracting any attention. There is a big aerodrome within a few miles, and the appearance of a plane, even late at night, would not be regarded as remarkable.

"He must have told Ernest that he was taking him out of the country, probably to the South of France. In reality he had other plans. Ernest was too dangerous a man to be left at large in France where, when the robbery was known, his description would be circulated, and where most certainly he would be free to telegraph the girl to join him.

"A room had been prepared, a prison room, at Hymie's country house, and after the car had arrived, the baggage transferred to the plane, and the car saturated, and left with a delayed action firer, the machine took off without mishap. They could not have gone far before Ernest made the discovery that the 'plane was going in the wrong direction, and then Hymie must have told him the truth—that it was too dangerous for him to go abroad, and that he was taking him to a safe hiding place.

"What happened after this one can only conjecture. The boy was hysterical, mad with fear and fury. He may have suspected Hymie and threatened that none of the money in the suit-case should be his. He certainly opened it, with the intention of flinging its contents over the side of the 'plane. Two packets, and probably more, were actually jettisoned, before Hymie turned upon the demented young man and struck him with an iron spanner which lay to his hand. There was probably a struggle, in the course of which the spanner fell over the side of the aeroplane—with tragic results, as we know, for it struck an unoffending Eton master and killed him.

"If you take a map of the south of England and you draw a more or less straight line from the place where Hymie picked up his passenger to the hangar, you will see that it crosses Farnham, Windsor and Cookham, the slight deviation in those tracks being caused by a heavy ground mist which lay over a portion of Wiltshire, and which the airman was at some pains to avoid.

"I don't know how many times Ernest was struck. He was undoubtedly dead when the 'plane came to earth at the flying field which Hymie had first rented and subsequently bought.

"What was done immediately with the body it is impossible at the moment to say. It may have been left all day in the hangar. The evidence I have is that the shed was locked throughout that day, and that a man sat outside or wandered about it, not attempting to seek shelter, though the day was very wet and gusty.

"Higson's danger was not yet over. There remained the girl, and that ill-fated package of twenty-five thousand dollars, which was all the more significant since the mysterious discovery of similar packages on a Hampshire farm. It might be that he was even more concerned with the possibility that the young man had written very fully to his sweetheart, giving particulars of his crime, or, what was as bad, naming a rendezvous where they could meet. If I may be allowed the immodesty, the situation was further complicated by the fact that I was already in the case, and had seen both Ena and her sister. When I met Hymie at the club he was on his way to perform this bold stroke.

"The need for silencing the girl was an urgent one. This young lady tells me that he threatened to kill her, and I have not the slightest doubt that if she had been less attractive he would have put his threat into execution. As it was, she has taken no harm, and has something to talk about for the rest of her life, besides figuring—and this will give her the greatest pleasure—in an interesting murder trial. The moment her portrait is published in the newspapers she will receive hundreds of offers of marriage from that half-witted section of the population which exists for no other purpose than to offer marriage to notorious persons. So that, generally speaking, I do not think we need waste our sympathy on this young lady, and I am especially asking the bank, in view of the information she was able to give to me, to refrain from demanding the jewels which were donated to her by her unhappy lover. Oh, yes, she knows he is dead, and she has paid him the tribute of her—um—lamentations.

"Hymie went down to Deptford and carried out his plan as arranged. It was easier than he had imagined, and, as he had a hiding-place already prepared for her lover, there was no insuperable difficulty about finding some place where she could be hidden. Exactly what he intended doing eventually, I do not care to think.

"That gentleman is the solution of many minor mysteries, and, incidentally, releases from suspicion the three violent socialists who on a certain occasion had threatened Mr. Friston, and are, I believe, at this moment under police observation."

Mr. Reeder had an audience consisting of the heads of Scotland Yard, the chiefs of the Berkshire police and the Assistant Public Prosecutor. There was also an official stenographer.

"That's all righ, Mr. Reeder," said Grayson. "A very interesting story, and I have no doubt we shall be able to check up every point. You've done marvellously, though I've always had in my mind the possibility that the discovery of the money at Farnham had something to do with the murder of the Eton gentleman—"

Mr. Reeder murmured something; whether derisive or not, nobody could quite gather.

"I think, sir"—Grayson addressed the Assistant Public Prosecutor —"the matter may be left now in our hands."

"Where is the body?" asked Mr. Reeder. There was a little glint in his eyes, as though he were enjoying a secret joke.

"We'll find that—I had a talk to Hymie in the cells this morning, and of course he denied everything, and said exactly what you're saying: 'Find the body. You can't prosecute a man for murder without a body. I think that's the law.' But we'll find it—with the assistance of our friends from Berkshire," he added politely.

Mr. Reeder scratched his chin.

"You won't want my assistance in that respect? I have made a few inquiries—"
"No, no, no, you can leave it to us, Mr. Reeder."
There is nothing malicious about a Scotland Yard officer, very little petty jealousy, but since an official of that institution depends for his very living and his promotion upon discoveries for which he himself can take credit, he was not unnaturally desirous of coming in at the end. The Chief Constable said as much to the Assistant Public Prosecutor as they were walking along Whitehall to lunch.
"We'll have to come back to old Reeder. He's a sly old dog, and if Grayson hadn't been so cocky we should have known all the facts by now," he said, and here he was right.
Mr. Grayson had undertaken the most difficult problem of the case. An army of detectives searched house and grounds, dug up foundations, overturned hearth-stones, dragged the river, made examinations of garage floors, but the body of the murdered man was not discovered. It was the one secret which J.G. Reeder had not revealed.
He was an assiduous reader of American magazines and especially those lurid representatives of the magazine press which dealt with crime. And had not Hymie Higson once most incautiously mentioned the truth machine? And had not Mr. Reeder read the very article?
"There is only one place to hide a body," he said, when the Assistant Public Prosecutor hinted that for his own private information he would like to know his assistant's theory. "Have you ever heard of an elderly tramp named Peters? The name is unfamiliar to you, sir? It was unfamiliar to me. I never met the man in my life, partly because I do not associate with tramps, and partly because I did not know tramps had names. But there was such a person—Peters the tramp."
"You're being mysterious," smiled his chief.
Mr. Reeder shook his head. He was a little indignant that such a charge should be brought against him.
"There's no mystery except the peculiar workings of my mind. I have heard of the man Peters and of Hymie's great generosity to him—perhaps if you mention this to Scotland Yard, sir, they will immediately leap at the solution. As it is, I fear it is going to be difficult to bring home to Mr. Higson, or Mannering, or Brates—that is the name in which his aeroplane licence was issued—the responsibility for the death of this unfortunate young man."
Hymie held the same view. His confidence grew with the remands which were ordered of his case. Neither the wheedling, the threatening nor the bluff of police officers shook him.
Eventually Mr. Reeder was sent for— Scotland Yard had capitulated.
"We can't get this bird to talk, and all our efforts to find the body have come to nothing," said Grayson irritably.
Mr. Reeder produced from his overcoat pocket a magazine with an horrific cover.
"You may not have read this publication," he said; "but I subscribe to it, and so apparently does Mr. Higson or Mannering or Brates. Indeed, I learned some years ago that with the big shots of American crime this is the most favoured publication. It tells of past murders and of interesting developments in criminal detection. Not the least interesting of these is an article on the truth machine, the invention of a young Chicago scientist. A band is placed round the chest, another

round the arm, and a cardiograph is taken. A man so treated is asked a question, and if he tells the truth the little pointer on the ribbon shows no visible sign of agitation. If he lies, the pointer swings left and right, and the farther it swings the bigger is the lie. If you peruse this article you will read the story of a young motor salesman who disappeared, and was suspected of being murdered. The man so suspected was arrested and put under examination. The inquiry was never completed, because the criminal, realising his danger, secured an injunction from a Supreme Court judge to stop the experiment. But before it was arrested he had revealed several interesting facts. First, that he had killed the man he was supposed to have killed; secondly, that he had buried him in a certain section of space; thirdly, that the place he had chosen for burial was —a cemetery!"

Grayson gasped.

"A cemetery?"

Mr. Reeder nodded.

"I can imagine no more suitable place," he said. "It is certainly the last place you would disturb in your search. On the day following the murder of the young clerk, a tramp named Peters who had died in the neighbourhood was to have been buried in a common grave. Some unknown benefactor bought the plot, so that he should rest alone. That same night the grave was re-opened, and the body of Ernest Graddle was also interred."

* * * * *

About three months after Hymie Higson was effectively disposed of by the officers of the law, Lizzie the parlourmaid asked Mr. Reeder for a day off.

"Ena's getting married," she said, "to such a nice boy! She's ever so fond of him, and after all the poor girl's been through, it's a blessing! And do you know, Mr. Reeder, that the police won't give her back all those bank-notes that were taken away from her? They say the money belongs to the bank, although Ernie gave it to her, and if they took away the notes why didn't they take away her rings?"

Mr. Reeder was too weary to discuss a matter of ethics.

"Take your day off, Elizabeth," he said, "and be so kind as to bring me some muffins."

THE SHADOW MAN

First published in The Thriller, Jan 30, 1932

CHAPTER I

WHEN Mr. Reeder went to New York in connection with the Gessler Bank fraud he was treated as though he were a popular member of a royal family. New York policemen, who are more accustomed to seeing humanity in all sorts of odd shapes and appearances, and with that innate politeness and hospitality which is theirs, saw nothing amusing in the old-fashioned coat, which he kept tightly buttoned, in his square hat, or even his side whiskers. They offered him the respect which was due to a very great detective. They were less deceived by his seeming timidity and his preference for everybody's opinion but his own than were their English colleagues.
His stay was a comparatively short one, yet, in the time at his disposal, he glided through the police headquarters of four great American cities, saw Atlanta prison, and, two days before he sailed, travelled by train to Ossning, passed through the steel gates of Sing-Sing and inspected that very interesting building under the guidance of the Deputy Warden, from card index to death house.
"There's one man I'd have liked you to see," said the Deputy Warden just before they parted. "He's an Englishman—he's called Redsack. Have you ever heard of him?"
Mr. Reeder shook his head.
"There are so many people I've never heard of," he murmured apologetically, "and Mr. Redsack is one of them. Is he staying here— er—for a long time?"
"Life," said the other laconically, "and he's lucky to escape the chair. He's broken three prisons, but he won't break Sing-Sing—the most dangerous man we have in this institution."
Mr. Reeder rubbed his chin thoughtfully. "I—um—would like to have seen him," he said. The Deputy Warden smiled.
"Just now he's not visible, but he'll be out tomorrow," he said. "We had to put him in a punishment cell for trying to escape. I thought you might know him. He's had four convictions in the United States, and he's probably guilty of more murders than any prisoner inside these walls; he certainly has the biggest brain I've met with since I first dealt with criminals."
Mr. Reeder smiled sadly and shook his head.
"I have never yet met—um—anything that resembled a brain in the criminal world," he said, with a deep melancholy. "Redsack? What a pity his crimes were not committed in England."
"Why?" asked the Deputy Warden, in surprise.
"He would be dead by now," said Mr. Reeder, and heaved a deep sigh.
The departure of Mr. Reeder's ship was delayed twenty-four hours, and he filled in the time very profitably be gluing himself to the record department at Police Headquarters, New York, and making himself acquainted with Mr. Redsack.
Redsack was a consistently elusive person. There was no photograph of him that had not been cleverly distorted by his own facial manoeuvres. It was not true to say that he was an Englishman; he had been born in Vancouver and had been educated in London; and at thirty had a record that would have made him respected in any criminal circle and nowhere else. Almost

Mr. Reeder, albeit reluctantly, agreed with the Deputy Warden that this man showed evidence of genius. He was clever, he was ruthless. In the bare police records, and even without the assistance of an explanatory dossier, the investigator noticed three samples of the operation of a brilliant mind.

Mr. Reeder sailed at midnight on the following day. As, clad in his gay pyjamas, he climbed into his bed, he could have no idea that, five decks below him, working in the galley, was the man he had left in the punishment cell at Sing-Sing and, oddly enough, there was nothing in the newspapers about this astonishing fact.

When the Deputy Warden had said again at parting, a little regretfully:

"Pity you can't see Redsack. He'll be out tomorrow," he was unconsciously a prophet.

It was the most daring and the most sensational escape that Sing-Sing had known. It happened on a dull, wintry afternoon, when a dozen prisoners were at their exercises in the big yard of the old prison. They were watching, with some curiosity and interest, the manoeuvres of a balloon which, caught in a half-gale, was tacking over the Hudson in a vain effort to get back on its course. Ballooning was an unusual sport. Suddenly, without warning, something seemed to go wrong, and the big gas-bag, sagging in the middle, began to make a rapid and oblique descent. Its trail rope came over the wall of the prison yard, dragging along the ground and the nearest man to it seized it. As he did so, a heavy quantity of ballast was released from the gondola beneath the bag, and the balloon shot up, carrying with it a Mr. Redsack.

The guards saw their charge carried over their heads, and could neither fire at him nor do anything but watch helplessly.

The airship drifted across the Hudson into New Jersey, came low again.

Mr. Redsack dropped. It was near a small village. Conveniently close at hand, standing unattended by the side of the road, was a dilapidated car and on the back seat a suitcase. Nobody seemed to have witnessed his surprising descent but he drove for twenty minutes before stopping the car and changing into the clothes from the suitcase. He put the prison uniform in the empty case and left it in a convenient wood.

Near the outskirts of Jersey City, he abandoned the car, walked towards the city and boarded a bus. He came by ferry to New York and eventually to the quay where the outward mail was waiting. After that everything was very simple for Mr. Redsack.

Galley hands were scarce and money is an eloquent letter of recommendation. He had been assigned his watch, and was peeling potatoes with the greatest industry before the ship pulled out of New York harbour.

If you had told Mr. Reeder it was a coincidence that he should at this stage have been brought into contact with one of the most remarkable criminals of our time, he would have shaken his head half-heartedly and in the most apologetic terms have differed from you.

"It is no coincidence—um—that any detective should meet, or nearly meet, any criminal, any more than it is a coincidence that the glass of water you are—er—drinking should at some time or other have been part of the Atlantic Ocean."

When the people in Scotland Yard speculate upon this peculiar happening they always begin with the word "if". "If" Redsack had not been in the punishment cell; "if" Mr. Reeder had only seen him... Quite a lot of trouble might have been saved, and the L. and O. Bank was by no means the beginning or the end of it.

That Mr. Reeder forgot about Redsack is unlikely. When he reached England and went through the files the man's name was familiar. It was inevitable that his record should go down in an abbreviated form in his case-book, for Mr. Reeder despised the story of no criminal, and held the view that crime, like art, knew no frontiers.

But, strangely enough, the name of Redsack did not occur to the man from Whitehall in connection with the L. and O. Bank affair.

CHAPTER II

Mr Reeder very seldom went to the theatre. When he did he preferred the strong and romantic drama to the more subtle problem plays which are so popular with the leisured classes.
He went to see Killing Time, and was a little disappointed, for he detected "the man who did it" in the first act, and thereafter the play ceased to have any great interest for him.
The unpleasant happening of the evening occurred between the first and second acts, when Mr. Reeder was pacing the vestibule, smoking one of his cheap cigarettes, and speculating upon the advisability of recovering his coat and hat from the cloakroom and escaping after the interval bell had rung and the audience had gone back into the auditorium.
There approached him a resplendent man. He was stout, rather tall, very florid. He wore a perpetual smile, which was made up of nine-tenths of amused contempt. His stubby nails were manicured and polished; Mr. Reeder suspected that they were faintly tinted. His clothes fitted him all too perfectly, and when he smiled his way up to Mr. Reeder that gentleman had a feeling that he would like to go back and see the second act after all.
"You're Mr. Reeder, aren't you?" he said in a tone which challenged denial. "My name is Hallaty, Gunnersbury branch of the L. and O. Bank. You came down to see me one day about a fellow who'd been passing dud cheques."
Mr. Reeder fixed his glasses on the end of his nose and looked over them at his new acquaintance.
"Yes, I—um—remember there was a branch of the bank at Gunnersbury," he said. "Very interesting how these branches are spreading."
"It's rather funny to see you here at a theatre," smiled Mr. Hallaty.
"I—um—suppose it is," said Mr. Reeder.
"It's a funny thing," the loquacious man went on, "I was talking to a friend of mine, Lord Lintil—you may have met him. I know him personally; in fact, we're quite pals."
Mr. Reeder was impressed.
"Really?" he said respectfully. "I haven't seen Lord Lintil since his third bankruptcy. Quite an interesting man."
Mr. Hallaty was jarred but not shaken.
"Misfortune comes to everybody, even to the landed gentry," he said, a little sternly.
"You were talking to him about me?"
Mr. Reeder spared himself the admonition which was coming.
"And—um—what did you say about me?"
For a moment the Manager of the Gunnersbury branch did not seem inclined to pursue his aristocratic reminiscences.
"I was saying how clever you were."
Mr. Reeder wriggled unhappily.
"We were talking about these bank frauds that are going on, and how impossible it is to bring

the—what do you call 'ems— perpetrators to justice, eh? That's what we want to do, Mr. Reeder— bring 'em to justice."

His pale eyes never left Mr. Reeder's.

"A most admirable idea," agreed the detective.

He wondered if any helpful advice was likely to be forthcoming.

"I suppose there must be a system by which you can stop this sort of thing going on."

"I'm sure there must be," said Mr. Reeder.

He looked at his watch and shook his head.

"I am quite anxious to see the second act," he said untruthfully.

"Personally," Mr. Hallaty went on with the greatest complacency, "I'd like to be put in charge of one of these cases, on the basis of the old and well-known saying of which you've no doubt heard."

Mr. Reeder when he was most innocent was most malignant. He was innocent now.

"Set a thief to catch a thief? But surely not, Mr.—I didn't quite catch your name."

The man went purple.

"What I meant was Quis custodiet ipsos custodes?—a Latin proverb," he said loudly,

Fortunately the bell rang at that moment and Mr. Reeder made his escape. But it was only temporary. When he got outside the theatre that night, after the conclusion of the third and tamest act of the play, he found his banking friend waiting.

"I wondered if you'd like to come up to my club and have a drink?"

Mr. Reeder shook his head.

"It is delightful of you, Mr.—um—"

Mr. Hallaty told him his name for the third time. "But I never go to clubs and I do not drink anything stronger than barley water."

"Can I drop you anywhere?" asked Mr. Hallaty.

Mr. Reeder said he was walking and therefore could not be dropped.

"But I thought you lived at Brockley?"

"I walk there," said Mr. Reeder. "I find it so good for my complexion."

He was not unduly surprised at the persistence of this very self-satisfied man. Quite a number of people did their best to scrape acquaintance with the country's greatest authority on crime against banks; some out of morbid curiosity, some for more personal reasons, some who gave him an importance which perhaps he did not deserve, and desired to share it even to the smallest extent. Mr. Hallaty was a type, self-important, pompous, self-sufficient and quite self-satisfied. To Mr. Reeder's annoyance a few days later, when he was eating his bun and drinking his glass of milk at a teashop, the smiling man appeared before him and sat down at the same table. Mr. Reeder's bun was hardly nibbled, his milk remained untouched. There was no escape. He sat in silence, listening to Mr. Hallaty's views on crime, the detection of crime, banking methods and their inadequacy, but mainly about Mr. Hallaty's extraordinary genius, prescience and shrewdness.

"They'd be very clever to get past me, whether they're crooks or whether they're straight," said Mr. Hallaty.

He lit a small and disagreeable cigar. Mr. Reeder looked significantly at a sign which said "No Smoking.
"You don't mind, do you?" asked Hallaty.
"Very much," said Mr. Reeder, and the other man laughed as though it were the best joke in the world, and went on smoking.
"Personally," he said, "I think professional crooks are not clever. They think they are, but when they're matched against the intelligence of the average business man, or a man a little above the average, they're finished."
He chatted on in this vein until Mr. Reeder put down his bun, glared solemnly over his half-glass of milk, and said, with startling distinctness:
"Will you please go away? I want to have my lunch."
Thick-skinned as the man was, he was taken aback; went very red, apologised incoherently, and swaggered out of the shop without paying the bill for his cup of tea. Mr. Reeder paid it gratefully.
Recalling those two conversations, Mr. Reeder remembered later that most of the inquiries which the Bank Manager made had to do with systems of search for missing delinquents. When he got home that night he very carefully marked down the name of Mr. Hallaty in a little book the cover of which was inscribed with a big question mark.
Yet it seemed impossible to believe that a man who was so aggressive could be anything but an honest man. Men engaged in the tiresome trade of roguery are suave men, polite men. They soothe and please—it is part of their stock in trade. Only the twenty shillings to the pound and look-the-whole-world-in-the-face man could afford to be boorish. And Mr. Hallaty was undoubtedly boorish.
He was, as he claimed, the Manager of the Gunnersbury branch of the London and Orient Bank, and was a man of style and importance. He had a flat in Albemarle Street, drove his own car, had a chauffeur, a valet and quite a nice circle of reliable friends. He had also a very humble flat in Hammersmith, and this was his official address.
The Gunnersbury branch of the L. and O. was in its way rather important. It carried the accounts of half a dozen big plants on the Great West Road, The Kelson Gas Works, and the Brite-Lites Manufacturing Corporation, and was therefore responsible for very heavy pay-rolls.
About a month after the teashop talk Mr. Hallaty called at the London office of the Ninth Avenue Bank on Lombard Street, and said that he had had a request from the most important of his customers for a large supply of American currency. The customer in question was an Anglo-American concern, and in order to celebrate some new amalgamation the directors had decided to pay a big bonus in dollars. Could the Ninth Avenue Bank supply the necessary greenbacks—fifty-seven thousand dollars, no less?
The American bank, after the way of American banks, was obliging. It undertook to sell dollars to the required amount, and on the Friday afternoon at two o'clock Hallaty called and exchanged English currency for American.
At the headquarters of the L. and O. Bank there was rather an urgent conference of general and

assistant-general managers that afternoon.

"I'm worried about this man Hallaty," said the chief. "One of our secret service people has discovered that he is living at the rate of ten thousand a year."

"What is his salary?" somebody asked.

"Two thousand five hundred."

There was a little silence.

"He is a very careful man," said one. "He may have some very good investments." The question became instantly urgent, for at that moment came an official with a telephone message from yet another American bank— the Dyers Bank of New York. Mr. Hallaty had just purchased a hundred thousand dollars' worth of American currency. He had negotiated the purchase in the morning, giving as a reason the requirements of the Brite-Lite Corporation. The Dyers Bank had certain misgivings after the departure of Mr. Hallaty with a thousand notes for one hundred dollars tucked away in a brief case, and those misgivings were caused by a glimpse which one of the commissionaires had of the contents of the brief case—already half-full of American notes. The bank detectives sped to Gunnersbury—Mr. Hallaty was not there. He had the key of the vault, but the detectives had taken with them a duplicate key from the safe at the head office. There should have been, in preparation for the next day's pay-out, some 72,000 pounds in the vaults. In point of fact, there were a few odd bundles of ten-shilling and pound notes.

Mr. Hallaty was not at the flat where he was supposed to live, nor at the flat in Albemarle Street, where he actually lived. His valet was there, and his chauffeur.

The Axford airport had a clue to give. Mr. Hallaty had arrived that afternoon, seemingly with the intention of flying the small aeroplane which he kept there. He was well known as an amateur flyer and was a skilled pilot. When the aeroplane was removed from the hangar it was discovered that the wings had been slashed and other damage done which made the machine unusable. How it had happened was a mystery which nobody could explain.

Mr. Hallaty, on seeing the damage, had turned deathly pale and had re-entered his car and driven away, carrying with him his two suit-cases.

From that moment Mr. Hallaty was not seen. He vanished into London and was lost.

If the losses to the bank had been 72,000 pounds only, it would have been serious enough. Unfortunately, Hallaty was a very ingenious man, with a very complete knowledge of the English banking system. When accounts came in and were checked, when the clearing-house made its quick report and certain northern and midland banking branches presented their claims, it was found that considerably over a quarter of a million of money had vanished.

There was much to admire here in the way of perfect training and clever expedient, but the L. and O. directors were not sufficiently broad-minded to offer any testimonial to their missing Manager.

Three days after he had vanished, Mr. Reeder came upon the scene. He was in his most apologetic mood. He apologised for being called in three days after he should have been called in; he apologised to the gloomy Chairman for the offence of his unfaithful servant; he apologised for being wet (he carried a furled umbrella on his arm) and by inference regretted his side-whiskers, his hat and his tightly-fitting coat.

The Chairman, by some odd process of mind, felt that a considerable amount of responsibility had been lifted from his shoulders.

"Now, Mr. Reeder, you see exactly what has happened, and the bank is leaving everything in your hands. Perhaps it would have been wiser if we'd called you in before."

Mr. Reeder plucked up spirit to say that he thought it might have been.

"Here are the reports," said the General Manager, pushing a folder full of large, imposing manuscript sheets. "The police have not the slightest idea where he's gone to, and I confess that I never expect to see Hallaty or the money again."

Mr. Reeder scratched his chin.

"It would be improper in me if I said that I hope I never do," he sighed. "It's the Tynedale case all over again, and the Manchester and Oldham Bank case, and the South Devon Bank case—in fact—um—there is here the evidence of a system, sir, if I may venture to suggest such a thing."

The General Manager frowned.

"A system? You mean all these offences against the banks you have mentioned are organised?"

Mr. Reeder nodded.

"I think so, sir," he said gently. "If you will compare one with the other you will discover, I think, that in every case the Manager has, on one pretext or another, converted large sums of English currency into francs or dollars, that his last operation has been in London, and that he has vanished when the discovery of his defalcations has been made."

The General Manager shivered, for Reeder was presenting to him the ogre of the banking world—the organised conspirator. Only those who understand banking know just what this means.

"I hadn't noticed that," he said; "but undoubtedly it is a fact."

CHAPTER III

Other people had observed these sinister happenings. A bankers' association summoned an urgent meeting, and Mr. Reeder, an authority upon bank crimes, was called into consultation. In such moments as these Reeder was very practical, not at all vague. Rather was he definite—and when Mr. Reeder was definite he was blood-curdling. He came to a sensational point after a very diffident beginning.

"There are some things—er—gentlemen, to which I am loath to give the authority of my support. Theories which—um—belong to the more sensational press and certainly to no scientific system. Yet I must tell you, gentlemen, that in my opinion we are for the first time face to face with an organised attempt to rob the banks on the grand scale."

The president of the association looked at him incredulously.

"You don't mean to suggest, Mr. Reeder, that there is a definite co-ordination between these various frauds?"

Mr. Reeder nodded solemnly.

"They have that appearance. I would not care to give a definite opinion one way or the other, but I certainly would not rule that out."

One member of the association shook his white head.

"There are such things as crimes of imitation, Mr. Reeder. When some man steals money in a peculiar way, other weak-minded individuals follow suit."

Mr. Reeder smiled broadly.

"I'm afraid that won't do, sir," he said with the greatest kindness. "You speak as though the details of the fraud had been published. In three cases out of five the general public know nothing about these crimes. In no case have the particulars been published or have they been available even to the managers of branch banks. And yet in every case the crime has followed along exactly similar lines. In every case there has been a man, holding a responsible position in the bank, who, through gambling on the Stock Exchange or for some other reason or from habits of extravagance, has—I will not say been compelled to rob the bank, because a man is quite—um—a free agent in such matters, but has certainly succeeded in relieving your—er—various institutions of very considerable sums of money. These are the points I make."

He ticked them off on his fingers.

"First of all, a manager or assistant manager in straitened circumstances. Secondly, a very carefully organised plan to draw, upon one given day, the maxi-mum sum of money which can be drawn from headquarters, the changing over of the money into foreign currency, and the complete disappearance of the bank manager, all within twenty-four hours. It is an unusual kind of fraud, for it does not involve of itself any false book-keeping. In several cases we have found that a petty fraud, in comparison with the greater offence, has been going on for some time and has been obviously the cause of the greater crime. Gentlemen"—Mr. Reeder's voice was serious—"there is something very big in the way of criminal activity in London, and an organisation is in existence which is not only directing these frauds and profiting by them, but is offering to the men who commit them asylum during their stay here and facilities for getting out of the country without detection. I'm going to deal with the situation from this angle, and my only chance of putting a stop to it is if I am able to catch one of the minor criminals immediately before he brings off the big coup. I want from every bank a list of all their suspected staff, and I want this list before the bank inspectors go in to examine the books, and certainly before anything like an arrest is made."

Instructions to this effect were immediately issued, and the very next morning Mr. Reeder had before him in his bureau at the Public Prosecutor's office a list of bank officials against whom there was a question mark. It was a very small list, representing a microscopic percentage of the enormous staffs employed in the business of banking. One man had been betting heavily, and attached to his name was a list of his bookmakers and what, to Mr. Reeder, was more important, exact details as to the period of time his betting operations covered.

Reeder's pencil went slowly down the list until it stopped before the name of L. G. H. Reigate. Mr. Reigate was twenty-eight, and an assistant branch manager, and his "offence" was that he had been engaged in real estate speculation, had bought on a rising market, and for some time past had vainly endeavoured to get rid of his holdings. His salary was 1,500 pounds a year; he lived with a half-sister in a small flat at Hampstead. He had apparently no other vices, spent most of his evenings at home, did not drink and was a light smoker.

The reports were very thorough. There was not a detail which Mr. Reeder did not examine with the greatest care, for on these minor details often hang great issues.

He went through the remaining list and came back to Mr. Reigate. Evidently here there was a case which might repay his private and personal investigation. He jotted down the address on a scrap of paper and made a few inquiries in the City. They were entirely satisfactory, for on the third probe he found a Canadian bank which had been asked if it could supply Canadian dollars in exchange for sterling, and if the maximum amount could be so supplied on any average day. The inquiry had come not from this branch, but from a client of the branch. Reeder spread his feelers a little wider, and stumbled on a second inquiry from the same client. He went to the general manager of the head office. Mr. Reigate was known as a very conscientious young man and, except for the fact that he had been engaged in real estate speculation, the exact extent of which was unknown, there were no marks, black or red, against him.

"Who is the Branch Manager?" asked Mr. Reeder, and was told.

The gentleman in question was a very reliable man, though inclined to be impetuous.

"He is a most excellent fellow, but loses his head at times. As he always loses it on the side of the bank we have no serious complaints against him."

The name of the manager was Wallat, and that week a strange thing happened to him. He received a letter from a man whose name he did not remember, but who had apparently been an old customer of the bank.

"I wonder if you would care to take a fortnight's trip to the fjords on a luxury ship? A client of ours has booked two passages but is unable to go, and has asked me to present the passages to any friend of mine who may wish to make the trip. As you were so good to me in the past—I don't suppose you remember the circumstances or even recall my name—I should be glad to pass them on to you."

Now, the curious thing was that only a week before the Manager had spoken enviously of a friend of his who was making that very trip. He had always wanted to see Norway and the beauties of Scandinavia, and here out of the blue came an unrivalled opportunity.

His vacation was due; he immediately put in a request to headquarters for leave. The request went before the Assistant-General Manager and was granted. The boat was due to leave on the Thursday night, but on the Tuesday the Manager, in a burst of zeal, decided to make a rough examination of certain books.

What he found there put all ideas of holiday out of his mind. On the Wednesday morning he called before him Mr. Reigate, and the pale-faced young man listened with growing terror to a recital of the irregularities which had been discovered. At this sign of his guilt the Manager, true to his tradition, lost his head, threatened a prosecution and, in a moment of hysteria, sent for a policeman. It was an irregular act, for prosecutions are initiated by the directors.

Panic engendered panic; Reigate put on his hat, walked from the bank, and was immediately pursued by a bare-headed Manager. The young man, in blind terror, leapt on the back of an ambulance which happened to be passing, and was immediately dragged off by a policeman who had joined in the pursuit. If the Manager had only kept his head the matter could have been corrected. As it was, he charged his assistant with the defalcations. Reigate admitted them and was put into a cell.

Bank headquarters was furious. They had been committed to a prosecution, and, as a sequel, the possibility of an action for damages. Mr. Reeder was called in at once, and went into consultation with the bank's solicitors. He interviewed the young man, and found him incoherent with terror and quite incapable of giving any information. The next morning he was brought before a magistrate and remanded.

Apparently the magistrate took a serious view, for although Reigate, who was now a little calmer, asked for bail, that bail was put at a prohibitive sum. The young man was taken to prison. That afternoon, however, there appeared before the magistrate Sir George Polkley, who offered himself as surety. The name apparently was a famous one. Sir George was a well-known north country shipbuilder. He was accompanied at the police court by a gentleman who gave the name of an eminent firm of Newcastle solicitors. The surety was accepted, and Reigate was released from Brixton prison that afternoon.

At seven o'clock that night Scotland Yard rang up Mr. Reeder.

"You know Reigate was bailed out this afternoon?"

"Yes, I saw it in the newspapers," said Mr. Reeder. "Sir George Polkley stood surety—how on earth did he know Sir George?"

"We've just had a wire from Polkley's solicitors in Newcastle. They know nothing whatever about it. Sir George is in the south of France, and his solicitors have sent nobody to London to represent them. What is more, they have never heard of Reigate."

Mr. Reeder, lounging in his chair, sat bolt upright.

"Then the bail was a fake? Where is Reigate?"

"He can't be found. He drove away from Brixton in a taxi, accompanied by the alleged solicitor, and he has not been seen since."

Here was a problem for Mr. Reeder, and one after his own heart. Who had gone to all that trouble to get Reigate released—and why? His frauds, if they were provable, did not involve more than three or four hundred pounds. Who wanted him released on bail—immediately released? There was no question at all that, high as the bail was, the necessary sureties would have been forthcoming in twenty-four hours. But somebody was very anxious to get Reigate out of prison with the least possible delay.

Mr. Reeder interviewed the Public Prosecutor. "It's all very, very odd," he said, running his fingers through his thin hair. "I suppose it is susceptible of a very simple explanation, but unfortunately I've got the mind of a criminal."

The Public Prosecutor smiled.

"And how does your criminal mind interpret this happening?" he asked.

Mr. Reeder shook his head.

"Rather badly, I'm afraid. I—um—should not like to be Mr. Reigate!"

He had sent for the cowed and agitated Manager. He was a pompous little man, rotund of figure and round of face, and he perspired very easily.

For half an hour he sat on the edge of a chair, facing Mr. Reeder, and he spent most of that half-hour mopping his brow and his neck with a large white handkerchief.

"Headquarters have been most unkind to me, Mr. Reeder," he quavered. "After all the years of faithful service... The worst they can say about me is that I was misled through my zeal for the bank. I suppose it was wrong of me to have this young man arrested, but I was so shocked, so—if I may use the expression—devastated.

"Yes, I'm sure," murmured Mr. Reeder. "You were going on vacation, you tell me? That is news to me." It was now that he learned for the first time about the two passages for the fjords.

Fortunately the Manager had the letter with him. Mr. Reeder read it quickly, reached for his telephone and put through an inquiry.

"I seem to remember the address," he said as he hung up the 'phone. It has a familiar sound to it. I think you will find it is an accommodation address, and the gentleman who wrote to you has in fact no existence."

"But he sent the tickets! They're made out in my name," said the Manager triumphantly, and then his face fell. "I shan't be able to go now, of course."

Mr. Reeder looked at him, and in his eyes there was pained reproach.

"I'm afraid you won't be able to go now, and I'm quite satisfied in my mind that you would have been very sorry if you had gone! Those tickets were intended to serve one purpose—to get you out of the bank and out of England, and to give young Mr. Reigate an opportunity of bringing home the beans—if you'll excuse that vulgarity."

Mr. Reeder was both puzzled and enlightened. Here was another typical bank case, planned on exactly the same lines as the others, and revealing, beyond any question of doubt, the operation of a master mind.

As soon as he got rid of the Bank Manager he took a cab and drove to Hampstead. Miss Jean Reigate had just returned from work when he arrived. She had read of her brother's misfortune in the evening newspaper on her way back from her office, and it struck Mr. Reeder that she was not as agitated by the news as the world would expect her to be. She was a pretty girl, a slim brunette, and looked much younger than her twenty-four years.

"I haven't heard from my brother," she said. "He's really my half- brother, but we've been very great friends all our lives, and I'm terribly upset about all this."

She crossed to the window and looked out.

Reeder thought that she was not a young lady who very readily showed her feelings. She was obviously exercising great self-control now. Her lips were pressed closely together; her eyes were filled with unshed tears, and he sensed rather than observed the tension she was enduring. Suddenly she turned. "I'll tell you, Mr. Reeder."

She saw his eyebrows go up and smiled faintly.

"Oh, yes, I realise you haven't told me your name, but I know you. You're quite famous in the City."

Mr. Reeder was covered in genuine confusion, but came instantly to business when she hesitated. "Well, what are you going to tell me?" he asked gently.

"I'm almost relieved. That is what I was going to say: I've been expecting something to happen for a long time. Johnny hasn't been himself; he's been terribly worried over his land deals, and I know he's been short of cash —in fact, I lent him a hundred pounds last month. But I thought he'd got over the worst because he returned the money the following week— in fact much more than the money; five hundred dollars is worth nearly two hundred pounds."

"Dollars?" said Mr. Reeder sharply. "Did he repay you in dollars?"

She nodded.

"In dollar bills?"

"Yes, five bills of a hundred dollars. I put them in my bank."

Mr. Reeder was now very alert. "Where did he get them?" he asked.

She shook her head.

"I don't know. He had quite a lot of money in dollars, a big roll."

Reeder scratched his chin thoughtfully, but made no comment, and the girl went on.

"I thought maybe there was something wrong at the bank, and I had an idea that he'd borrowed this money and was putting things right. And yet he wasn't very happy about it. He told me that he might have to go out of the country for a few months, and that if he did I wasn't to worry."

"Was he a cheerful sort of fellow?"

"Very," she said emphatically, "until the past year, when property went down. He used to do quite a lot of buying and selling, and I think he made a lot of money before the slump came."

"Had he any friends in London?"

She shook her head.

"None you know? You've not met any?" he insisted.

"No," she said. "There used to be a man who called here, but he was not a friend," She hesitated. "I don't know whether I'm doing him any harm by telling you all this, but Johnny is really a very good man, a man of the highest principles. Something has gone wrong with him in the past few months, but I haven't the slightest idea what it was. He has been having terrible fits of depression, and one night he told me that it was much better that his conscience should be at rest than that he should tide over his difficulties. He wrote a long statement, which I knew was intended for the bank. He sat up half one night writing, and then he must have changed his mind because in the morning, while we were at breakfast, he took it out of his pocket, re-read it and put it in the fire. I have a feeling, Mr. Reeder, that he was not acting entirely on his own; that there was somebody behind him directing him."

Reeder nodded.

"That is the feeling I have, Miss Reigate," he said, and if your brother is as you describe him, I think we shall learn a lot from him."

"He has been under somebody's influence," said the girl, "and I am sure I know who that somebody was."

She would say no more than this, though he pressed her.

"Can I send him food in prison?" she asked, and learned now for the first time about the bail and Reigate's mysterious disappearance. She did not know Polkley, and so far as she was aware her brother had no association with Newcastle.

"But he knows you, Mr. Reeder," she said surprisingly. "He's mentioned you twice and once he told me that he thought of having a talk with you."

"Dear me!" said Mr. Reeder. "I don't think he kept his promise. He has never been to my office—"

She shook her head.

"He wouldn't have come to your office. He knows your address in Brockley Road." She gave the number, to his amazement. "In fact, one night he went to your house, because afterwards he said that at the last moment his courage had failed him."

"When was this?" asked Reeder.

"About a month ago," she answered.

CHAPTER IV

Mr. Reeder went back to Brockley that night in a discontented frame of mind. Give him the end of the thread, and he would follow it through all its complicated entanglements. He would sit patiently, untying knots, for days, for weeks, for months, even for years. But now he had not even the end of his thread. He had two isolated cases, distinct from one another, except that they were linked together by a similarity of method but, looking in all directions, he saw no daylight. The quietude of Brockley Road was very soothing to him. From near at hand came the gentle whirr of traffic passing up and down the Lewisham High Road, the rumble of lorries and the shrill voices of boys calling the final editions of the evening newspapers.

In the serenity of his home Mr. Reeder recuperated his dissipated energies. Here he could sit sometimes throughout the night, ambling through the dreams out of which his theories were constructed. Here he could put in order the vital little facts which so often meant the destruction of those enemies of society against whom he waged a ceaseless war.

He had very few visitors and practically no friends. In Brockley Road opinion was divided on his occupation. There was one school of thought that believed he was "retired", and this was by far the largest section of public opinion, for everything about him suggested retirement from bygone and respectable activities.

No neighbour dropped in on him for a quiet smoke and a chat. He had been invited to sedate family parties during the festive season, but had declined. And the method of his refusal was responsible for the legend that he had once been in love and had suffered; for invariably his letter contained references to a painful anniversary which he wished to keep alone. It didn't matter what date was chosen for the party, Mr. Reeder had invariably a painful anniversary which he wished to celebrate in solitude.

He sat at his large desk with a huge cup of tea and a large dish full of hot and succulent muffins before him, and went over and over every phase of these bank cases without securing a single inspiration which would lead him to that unknown force which was not only co-ordinating and organising a series of future frauds and robberies but had already robbed the banks of close on a million pounds.

Lewisham High Road at that hour was a busy thoroughfare, and nobody saw the extraordinary apparition, until a taxi driver, swerving violently, missed him. It was the figure of a man in a dressing-gown and pyjamas, darting from one side of the road to the other. His feet and his head were bare, and he ran with incredible speed up the hill and darted into Brockley Road. Nobody saw where he came from. A policeman made a grab at him as he passed, and missed him. In another second he was speeding along Brockley Road,

He hesitated before Mr. Reeder's house, looked up at the lighted window of his study, then, dragging open the gate, flew up the stone steps. Mr. Reeder heard the shouts, went to the window and looked out. He saw somebody run up the flagged pathway to the door, and immediately afterwards a motor-cyclist speeding up the road ahead of a small crowd. The motor-cyclist slowed before the door, and stopped for a second. At first Mr. Reeder thought that the explosions he heard were the backfire of the machine. Then he saw the flame of the third and fourth shots. They came from the driver's hand, and instantly the motor-cycle moved on, gathering speed, and went roaring out of his line of vision.

Reeder ran down the stairs and pulled open the door as a policeman came through the gate. A man was lying on the top step. He wore a red silk dressing-gown and pyjamas.

They bore him into the passage, and Mr. Reeder switched on all the lights. One glance at the white face told him the staggering story.

The policeman pushed back the crowd, shut the door and went down on his knees by the side of the prostrate figure.

"I'm afraid he's dead," said Mr. Reeder, as he unbuttoned the pyjama jacket with deft fingers and saw the ugliness of a violent dissolution.

"I think he was shot by the motor-cyclist."

"I saw him," said the policeman breathlessly. "He fired four shots."

Reeder made another and more careful examination of the man. He judged his age to be about thirty. His hair was dark, almost raven black; he was clean-shaven, and a peculiar feature which Reeder noticed was that he had no eyebrows.

The policeman looked and frowned, put his hand in his pocket and took out his notebook. He examined something that was written inside and shook his head.

"I thought he might be that fellow they're looking for tonight."

"Reigate?" asked Mr. Reeder.

"No, it can't be him," said the policeman. "He was a fair man with bushy eyebrows."

The dressing-gown was new, the pyjamas were of the finest silk. They made a quick examination of the pockets and the policeman produced a sealed envelope.

"I think I ought to hand this to the inspector, sir—" he began.

Without a word Mr. Reeder took it from his hand, and, to the constable's horror, broke the seal and took out the contents. They were fifty bills each for a hundred dollars.

"H'm!" said Mr. Reeder.

Where had he come from? How had he appeared suddenly in the heart of the traffic? The next hour Mr. Reeder spent making personal inquiries, without, however, finding a solution to the mystery.

A newsboy had seen him running on the sidewalk, and thought he had come out of Malpas Road, a thoroughfare which runs parallel with Brockley Road. A point-duty constable had seen him run along the middle of the road, dodging the traffic, and the driver of a delivery van was equally certain he had seen him on the opposite side of the road to that where he had been observed by the newspaper boy, running not up the hill but down. The motor-cyclist seemed to have escaped observation altogether.

At ten o'clock that night the chief officers of Scotland Yard met in Reeder's room. The dead man's finger-prints had been sent to the Yard for inspection, but had not been identified. The only distinguishing feature of the body was a small strawberry mark below the left elbow.

The Chief Constable scratched his head in bewilderment.

"I've never had a case like this before. The local police have called at every house in the neighbourhood where this fellow might have come from, and nobody is missing. What do you make of it, Mr. Reeder? You've had another look at the body, haven't you?"

Mr. Reeder nodded. He had had that gruesome experience and had made a much more thorough examination than had been possible in the passage.

"And what do you think?"

Mr. Reeder hesitated.

"I have sent a car for the young lady."

"Which young lady?"

"Miss—er—Reigate, the sister of our young friend."

He heard the ring of the bell and himself went down to open the door. It was the girl he had sent for. He took her into a small room on the ground floor.

"I'm going to ask you a question, Miss Reigate, which I'll be glad if you can answer. Had your brother any distinguishing marks on his body that you would be able to recognise?"

She nodded without hesitation.

"Yes," she said, a little breathlessly. "He had a small strawberry mark on his forearm, just below the elbow."

"The left forearm?" asked Mr. Reeder quickly.

"Yes, the left forearm. Why? Has he been found?"

"I'm afraid he has," said Mr. Reeder gently.

He told her his suspicion and left her with his housekeeper whilst he went up to explain to the men from the Yard just what he had discovered.

"It was very clear to me," he said, "that the hair had been dyed and the eyebrows shaved."

"Reigate?" said the Chief Constable incredulously, "If that's Reigate I'm a Dutchman. I've got a photograph of him. He's fair, almost a light blonde."

"The hair is dyed, very cleverly and by an expert."

Reeder pointed to the dollar bills lying on the table.

"The money was part of the system, the disguise was part of the system. Did you notice anything about the clothes?"

"I noticed they smelt strongly of camphor," said one of the detectives. "I've just been remarking to the Chief Constable that it almost seems as if the pyjamas and dressing-gown had been kept packed away from moths. My theory is that he must have had an outfit stowed away all ready for his getaway."

Mr. Reeder shook his head. "Not exactly that," he said; "but the camphor smell is a very important clue. I can't tell you why, gentlemen, because I am naturally secretive."

The body was identified beyond any question by the distressed and weeping girl. It was that of Jonathan Reigate, sometime Assistant Manager of the Wembley branch of the London and Northern Banking Corporation. He had been killed by four shots fired from a .38 automatic pistol, and any three of the four shots would have been fatal. As for the motor-cyclist, there was no one who could identify him or give the least clue.

At nine o'clock the next morning Reeder, accompanied by a detective-sergeant, made a minute search of the Reigate flat. It was a small, comfortably furnished apartment consisting of four rooms, a kitchen and a bathroom.

Reigate had occupied the larger of the two bedrooms, and in one corner was a small roll-top writing-desk which was locked when they arrived.

The dead man was evidently very methodical. The pigeon-holes were crammed with methodical memoranda, mainly dealing with the properties he had bought and sold. These the two men inspected item by item before they made a search of the drawers.

In the last drawer they found a small steel box which, after very considerable difficulty, they succeeded in opening. Inside were two insurance policies, a small memorandum book, in which apparently Reigate had kept a very full record of his family accounts and, in a small pay envelope, sealed down, they discovered two Yale keys. They were quite new and were fastened together by a flat steel ring. An inspection of these showed Reeder that they were intended for different locks, one being slightly larger than the other. There was no name on them and no indication whatever as to their purpose.

He examined the keys under a powerful magnifying glass, and the conclusion he reached was that probably they had never been used. At the bottom of the box, and almost overlooked because it lay under a black card that covered the bottom, he found a sheet of paper torn from a small notebook. Its contents were in a copperplate hand; certain words were underlined in red ink, carefully ruled. It consisted of a column of street names, and against each was a time. Mr. Reeder observed that the times ranged from ten in the morning till four o'clock in the afternoon, and that the streets (he knew London very well) were side streets adjacent to main thoroughfares. Against certain of the times and places a colour was indicated: red, yellow, white, pink; but these had been struck out in pencil, and in the same medium the word "yellow" had been written against all of them.

"What do you make of those, Mr. Reeder?"

Reeder looked through the list again carefully.

"I rather imagine," he said, "that it's a list of rendezvous. At this place and at this time there was a car ready to pick him up. Originally it was intended to have four cars, but for some reason or other this was impracticable. I take it that the colour means a flower or a badge of some kind by which Reigate could distinguish the car that was picking him up."

Later at Scotland Yard he elaborated his theory to an interested circle.

"What is clear now, if it wasn't clear before," he said, "is that there is an organisation working in England against the banks. It is more dangerous than I imagined, for obviously the man or men behind it will stop at nothing to save themselves if matters ever come to a pinch. They killed Reigate because they thought—and rightly—that he was coming to betray them."

CHAPTER V

Mr Reeder claimed that he had a criminal mind. That night, in his spacious study at Brockley, he became a criminal. He organised bank robberies; he worked out systems of defalcations; he visualised all the difficulties that the brain of such an organisation would have to contend against. The principal problem was to get out of England men who were known and whose descriptions had been circulated as being wanted by the police. Every port and every airport was watched; there was a detective staff at every aerodrome; Ostend, Calais, Boulogne, Flushing, the Hook of Holland, Havre and Dieppe were staffed by keen observers. No Atlantic liner sailed but it carried an officer whose business it was to identify questionable passengers.

For hours Mr. Reeder wallowed in his wickedness. Scheme succeeded scheme; possibility and probability were rubbed against one another and cancelled themselves out.

What was the organiser's chief difficulty? To avoid a close inspection of his protegees, and to keep them in a place where they would not be recognised.

The case of Reigate was a simple one. He was a man with a conscience, and though apparently he was heading for safety, that still, small voice of his had grown louder and he had decided to make a clean breast of everything. Having reached this decision, he had escaped from wherever he was confined and had made his way to Reeder's house—his sister had told the detective that the young man knew his address.

At midnight Mr. Reeder rose from his desk, lit his thirtieth cigarette, and stood for a long time with his back to the fireplace, the cigarette drooping limply from his mouth, his head on one side like a cockatoo, and cogitated upon his criminal past.

He went to bed that night with a sense that he was groping through a fog towards a certain door, and that when that door was opened the extraordinary happenings of the past few months would be susceptible of a very simple explanation.

On the following morning Mr. Reeder was in his office, and those who are not acquainted with his methods would have been amazed to find that he was engaged in reading a fairy story. He read it furtively, hiding it away in the drawer of his desk whenever there was the slightest suggestion of somebody entering. He loved fairy stories about wonderful little ladies who appeared mysteriously out of nowhere, and rendered marvellous assistance to poor but beautiful daughters of woodcutters, transforming them with a wave of their wands into no less lovely princesses, and by a similar wave turned wicked men and women into trees and rabbits and black cats. There were so many men and women in the world whom he would have turned into trees and rabbits and black cats.

He was reading the latest of his finds (Fairy Twinklefeet and the Twelve Genii) when he heard a heavy cough outside his door and the confident rap of the commissionaire's knuckles. He put away the book, closed the drawer, and said:

"Come in."

"Dr. Carl Jansen, sir."

Mr. Reeder leaned back in his chair.

"Show him in, please," he said.

Dr. Jansen was tall, rather stout, very genial. He spoke with the slightest of foreign accents.

"May I sit, please?" He beamed and drew his chair up to the desk almost before Mr. Reeder had murmured his invitation. "It was in my mind to see you, Mr. Reeder, to ask you to undertake a small commission for me, but I understand you are no longer private detective but official, eh?"

Reeder bowed. His finger-tips were together. He was looking at the newcomer from under his shaggy brows.

"I am in a very peculiar position," said Dr. Jansen. "I conduct here a small clinic for diseases of the 'eart, for various things. I am a generous man; I cannot 'elp it." He waved an extravagant hand. "I give, I lend, I do not ask for security, and I am—what is the word?—swindled. Now a great misfortune has come to me. I loaned a man a thousand pounds." He leaned confidentially across the table. "He has got into trouble—you have seen the case in the papers—Mr. Hallaty, the banker."

He waved his agitated hands again.

"He has gone out of the country without saying a word, without paying a penny, and now he writes to me to ask me for a prescription for the 'eart."

Mr. Reeder leaned back in his chair.

"He's written from where?" he asked.

From 'Olland. I come from 'Olland; it is my 'ome."

"Have you got the letter?"

The man fished out a pocket-book and from this extracted a sheet of notepaper. The moment Reeder saw it he recognised Hallaty's handwriting. It was very brief.

"Dear Doctor,—I must have the prescription for my heart. I have lost it. I cannot give you my address. Will you please advertise it in the agony column of The Times?"

It was signed "H."

If Dr. Jansen could have looked under those shaggy eyebrows he would have seen Mr. Reeder's eyes light up.

"May I keep this letter?" he asked.

The big man shrugged.

"Why, surely. I am glad that you should, because this gentleman seems to be in trouble with the police, and I do not want to be mixed up in it, except that I would like to get my thousand pounds. The prescription I will advertise because it is humanity."

Dr. Jansen took his departure after giving his address, which was a small flat in Pimlico. He was hardly out of the building before Mr. Reeder had verified his name and his qualifications from a work of reference. The letter he carried to Scotland Yard and to the Chief Constable.

"Smell it," he said.

The Chief sniffed.

"Camphor—and not exactly camphor. It's the same as we found in young Reigate's dressing-gown. I've sent it down to the laboratory; they say it's camphor-lactine, a very powerful disinfectant and antiseptic, sometimes used in cases of infectious diseases."

He heard a smack as Mr. Reeder's hands came together, and looked up in astonishment.

"Dear, dear me!" said Mr. Reeder.

He almost purred the words.

When he got back to his office in Whitehall the commissionaire told him that a lady was waiting to see him. Mr. Reeder frowned.

"All right, show her in," he said.

He pushed up the most comfortable chair for her.

"Mr. Reeder"—she spoke quickly and nervously—"I have found a note-book of my brother's and the full amounts that he took—"

"I have those," said Reeder. "It is not a very large amount, certainly not such an amount as would have justified the trouble and pains they took to get him out on bail."

"And in the note-book was this." She put a little cutting on the table.

Mr. Reeder adjusted his glasses and read:

"In your dire necessity write to the Brothers of Benevolence, 297 Lincoln's Inn Fields. Professional men who are short of money, and in urgent need of it will receive help without usury. Repayment spread over years. No security but our faith in you."

Mr. Reeder read it three times, his lips spelling the words; then he put the cutting down on the table.

"That is quite new to me," he said, with a suggestion of shamefacedness which made the girl want to laugh. "I'll have a search made of the newspapers and see how often this has appeared," he said. "Do you know when your brother applied for a loan?"

She shook her head.

"I remember the morning he cut it out. That was months ago. And then one night, when he had a friend here, I brought him in some coffee and I heard Mr. Hallaty say something about his brotherhood—"

"Mr. Hallaty?" Reeder almost squeaked the words. "Did your brother know Hallaty?" She hesitated. "Ye-es, he knew him. I told you there was a man who I thought had a bad influence on Johnny."

He saw a faint flush come to her face, and realised how pretty a girl she was.

"I was introduced to him at the dance of the United Banks, but he was rather a difficult man to—to get rid of."

Reeder's eyes twinkled.

"Did you ever tell him to go away? It's a very rude but simple process!"

She smiled.

"Yes, I did once. He came home one night when my brother wasn't in, and he was so objectionable that I asked him not to come again. I don't know how he met my brother, but he often came to the flat, and the curious thing was that after the time I spoke of—"

"When he was unpleasant to you?"

She nodded.

"—He made no attempt to see me, apparently he was no longer interested."

"Did you know Hallaty had disappeared after robbing the bank of a quarter of a million?"

She nodded.

"It very much upset Johnny; he couldn't talk about anything else. He was so nervous and worried, and I know he didn't sleep—I could hear him walking up and down in his room all night. He bought every edition of the papers to find out what had happened to Mr. Hallaty."

Mr. Reeder sat for a long time, pinching his upper lip.

"Does anybody know you found this book and this cutting?"

To his surprise she answered in the affirmative.

"It was the caretaker of the flat. He was helping me to turn out one of the cupboards and he found it," she said. "In fact he brought it to me. I think it must have fallen out of one of my brother's pockets. He used to hang some of his clothes there."

It was late in the afternoon when Mr. Reeder turned into Lincoln's Inn Fields, found No. 297, and climbed to the fourth floor, where a small board affixed to the wall indicated the office of this most benevolent institution.

He knocked, and a voice asked who was there. It was a husky, foreign voice. Presently the door was unlocked and opened a few inches.

Reeder saw a man of sixty, his face blotched and swollen, his white hair spread untidily over his forehead. He was meanly dressed and not too clean.

"What you want?" he asked, in a thick, guttural voice.

"I've come to inquire about the Brotherhood—"

"You write, please."

He tried to shut the door, but Mr. Reeder's square-toed shoe was inside. He pushed the door open and went in. It was a disorderly little office, grimy and cheerless. Though the day was warm, a small gas fire burnt on the hearth. The dingy windows looked as if they had never been opened.

"Where do you keep all your vast wealth?" asked Mr. Reeder pleasantly.

The old man blinked at him.

Reeder had evidence, apart from a bottle on the table, that this gentleman took a kindly interest in raw spirits. There was more than a suggestion that he slept in this foul room, for an old couch had the appearance of considerable use.

"You write here—we are agents. We are not to see callers."

"May I ask whom I have the pleasure of addressing?"

The old man glowered at him. "My name is Jones," he said. "That is for you sufficient."

There were one or two objects in the room which interested Reeder. On the window-sill was a small wooden stand containing three test tubes, and nearby half a dozen bottles of various sizes.

"You do a lot of writing?" said Reeder.

The little desk was covered with manuscript, and the man's grimy hands were smothered with ink stains.

"Yes, I do writing," said Mr. Jones sourly. "We do much correspondence; we never see people who call. We are agents only."

"For whom?" asked Reeder.

"For the Brotherhood. They live in France—in the south of France."

He spoke quickly and glibly.

"They do not desire that their benevolence shall be publicised. All letters are answered secretly. They are very rich men. That is all I can tell you, mister."

As he went down the stairs Mr. Reeder was whistling softly to himself —and that was a practice in which he did not often indulge— although all his questions and all his cajoling had not produced the address of these Brothers of Benevolence, who lived in the south of France and did good by stealth.

It was too late for afternoon tea and too early to go home. Mr. Reeder called a cab and drove back to Whitehall. He was crossing Trafalgar Square when he saw a car pass his, and had a glimpse of its occupant.

Dr. Jansen was looking the other way, his attention distracted by an accident which had overtaken a cyclist. Mr. Reeder slid back the partition.

"Follow that car," he said to the taxi driver, "and keep it in sight. I will see that the police do not stop you."

The car went leisurely through the Mall, up Birdcage Walk and, circling the war memorial, turned left into Belgravia. Reeder saw it stop before a pretentious-looking building, and told the cabman to drive on. Through the rear window he saw Dr. Jansen alight and, when he was out of sight, stopped the cab, paid him off and walked slowly back.

He met a policeman, who recognised and saluted him.

"That building, sir? Oh, that's the Strangers Club. It used to be the Banbury Club, for hunting people, but it didn't pay, and then a foreign gentleman opened it as a club of some kind. I don't know what they are, but they have scientific lectures every week—they've got a wonderful hall downstairs, and I believe the cooking's very good."

Now the Strangers Club was a stranger to Mr. Reeder, and he was not unnaturally interested. He did not attempt to go in, but passed with a sidelong glance and saw a plate-glass door and behind it a man in livery. The Strangers Club formed part of an island site. At the back some enterprising builder had erected a number of high buildings, tall, unlovely, their only claim to beauty being their simplicity. One of these was occupied by a dressmaking establishment. The second building had a more sedate appearance. Mr. Reeder noted the chaste inscription on the little silver plate affixed to a plain door, and went on finally to circumnavigate the island, coming back to where he had started.

Jansen's car had disappeared. When he came again abreast with the club, the man in the hall was not in sight. He crossed the road and took a long and interested survey of the building, and when this was done, he again went round to the back. There was a pair of big gates in that building, which was indicated by a silver plate. He found a chauffeur cleaning his car, made a few inquiries, and went to his office not entirely satisfied, but with a pleasant feeling that he was on his way to making a great discovery.

CHAPTER VI

Mr. Reeder was a source of irritation to the staff of the Public Prosecutor's office. He kept irregular hours, he compelled attendants to remain on duty and very often held up the work of the cleaners.

What troubled him at the moment was the thought that in some way he had taken a wrong turning in the course of investigation, and that it might be straying into no man's land. For his own encouragement he had dispatched cables to various parts of the world, and sat down in his office to wait for replies.

He had hardly dipped again in his book of fairy tales, when the telephone rang.

"A very urgent message, Mr. Reeder," said the operator's precise voice. "You are through to New Scotland Yard."

There was a click. It was the Chief Constable speaking.

"We found Hallaty. Will you come over?"

In three minutes Mr. Reeder was at Scotland Yard, and in the Chief Constable's office.

"Alive?" was the first question he asked.

The Chief Constable shook his head.

"No, dead."

Mr. Reeder heaved a long sigh.

"I was afraid of that. The trouble was that Hallaty was too clever. He wasn't in pyjamas, of course?" The Chief Constable stared at him.

"That's curious you should say that. No, he was in a sort of uniform, looking like an elevator attendant."

Late that afternoon a man riding a powerful motor-cycle had passed at full speed in the direction between Colchester and Clacton. He had stopped to ask the way to Harwich, for apparently he had missed the road. After he had gone on a light van had followed, taking the same direction as the motor-cyclist. A labourer, working in the field, had heard a staccato rattle of shots, and had fallen into the same error as Mr. Reeder had done on a previous occasion. He thought it was the sound of the motor-cycle. He saw the van stop for a short time, and then move on. He thought no more of the matter until he made his way back to the road on his way home. It was then he saw lying half in the ditch and half on the verge the body of a stout man in a dark-blue uniform. He was quite dead, and had been shot through the back. There was no sign of the motor-cycle, though the wheel tracks were visible on the road, and had swayed off onto the verge. Thereafter they were lost.

Detectives, who were on the spot from Colchester within half an hour, searched the road and discovered pieces of broken glass, obviously portions of a smashed lamp. They found also a small satchel, evidently carried by the man; it was empty.

Hallaty's head had been completely shaved. The examination of the clothes showed neither the maker's name nor any clue by which they could be identified, but when the clothes were stripped, it was found that underneath he wore a suit of silk pyjamas, similar in texture to that which was worn by the unfortunate Reigate.

Mr. Reeder made a rapid journey through Essex to the scene of the murder. He inspected the body and came back to London at midnight.

Again the Big Five sat in conference and Mr. Reeder offered his views.

"Hallaty was too clever. They all suspected that he had a plan for double-crossing them. You will remember that he was a pilot and had a plane at the Axford Airport. When he went to take it out he found that it had been damaged and was unflyable. That was their precaution. Hallaty had to go either their way, or no way. Even in this eleventh hour he hoped to fool them. That empty case was probably full of loot. Harwich? Of course he went to Harwich. He had a trunk packed there and a passport. He had another at Brighton. You know you can get from Brighton to Boulogne on a day trip."

"Did you know this?" asked the staggered Chief. Mr. Reeder looked guilty.

"I had an idea it might happen," he said. "The truth is, I have a criminal mind, Chief Constable. I put myself in their places and, having satisfied myself as to their class of mentality, I do just what they would do, and usually I am right. There isn't a cloakroom at any sea or air port in England that my agents have not very carefully searched, and Mr. Hallaty's cases have been in my care for a fortnight."

He was a very tired man, and welcomed the offer of the police squad car, which was to take him home. Tired as he was, however, he took greater precautions that night than he had taken for many years. With a detective he searched his house from basement to garret. He inspected the strip of back garden which was his very own, and even descended to the coal cellar, for he realised that he had made one false move that day—and that was to call at Lincoln's Inn Fields and interview the dirty little old man who had test tubes in his office.

He was sleeping heavily at six o'clock the next morning, when the telephone by the side of his bed woke him. He got up and to his surprise he heard and recognised the voice of Jean Reigate. It was weak and tremulous.

"Can I see you, Mr. Reeder?... Soon... Something terrible has happened."

Mr. Reeder was now wide awake. At his request the squad car had been held for him all night. It had remained parked outside his house not, as he explained, because he was afraid of dying, but because it would have been considerably inconvenient for everybody concerned if he did die that night.

He sat by the weary driver as the car sped through the empty streets and explained his system to a wholly uncomprehending and, if the truth be told, bored police officer.

"I think my weakness is a sense of the dramatic," he said. "I like to keep all my secrets to the very last, and then reveal them as though it were with —um—a bang. You may think that weakness is contemptible in a police officer, or one who has the honour to associate in the most amateur fashion with police officers, but there it is. It's my method, and it pleases me."

The driver felt it was necessary for him to offer some comment, and said:

"That was a very queer case." And Mr. Reeder, realising that his confidence if not rejected had

been at least slighted, relapsed into silence for the remainder of the journey.
The caretaker had opened the main doors when Reeder arrived and was a little scandalised at this early morning call.
"I don't think the young lady is up yet, sir."
"I assure you she is not only up, but dressed," said Mr. Reeder.
As he was being taken up in the lift, he remembered something.
"Are you the man who found the small book belonging to the late Mr. Reigate?"
"Yes, sir," said the man. "Rather remarkable finding it. He had some press cutting about some brothers. I didn't rightly understand it."
"Have you told anybody about finding the book?" The man considered.
"Yes, sir, I did. A reporter from a paper came up here and asked me if there was any news. He was a very nice fellow. As a matter of fact, he gave me a pound."
Mr. Reeder shook his head.
"My friend, you have no knowledge of papers. If you had, you'd know that a reporter never gives you money for anything. And you told him about the book, I suppose?" "As a matter of fact, I did, sir."
"And the newspaper cutting?"
The janitor pleaded guilty to that also.
Jean Reigate opened the door to him. She was white and shaking, and even now she was trembling from head to foot. The previous night she had arrived home at eleven o'clock. She had been to see some relations of her stepmother and they had kept her too late. She opened the door with her key, went inside the flat and was reaching for the light switch, when somebody came out of the hall cupboard behind her. Before she could scream a hand was placed over her mouth and she was forcibly held. Somebody whispered to her that if she did not scream no harm would come to her, and almost on the point of collapse she allowed the men—there were two apparently—to blindfold her, and, when this was done, she heard the light turned on.
She was led into her sitting-room and sat upon a chair. It was then that she became aware that a third man was in the flat. He was a foreigner and spoke with a harsh accent. Even though he whispered she noticed this, for there was an argument between two of the men.
Presently she felt somebody hold her by the arm and pull up the sleeve of her blouse, and immediately afterwards she felt a sharp pain in the forearm.
"This won't hurt you," said the voice that had first spoken to her, and then somebody else said: "Turn out the light."
The man was still holding her arm and apparently sitting by her side.
"Keep quiet and don't get excited," said the first man. "Nobody is going to hurt you."
She remembered very little after that. When she woke up she was lying on her bed, still fully dressed, and she was alone. The curtains and the blinds had been drawn up and she had a dim idea that as she woke she heard the door close softly. It was then about five o'clock. Her head was swimming, but not aching. She had a strange taste in her mouth and when she dragged herself to her feet, her legs gave way, and she had to support herself with a chair.

"Did you send for the police?"

"No," she said. "The first person I thought of was you. What have they done, Mr. Reeder?"

He examined her arm. There were three separate punctures. Then he went in and looked at the bedroom. Two chairs had been drawn up by the side of the bed. The atmosphere was still thick with cigarette and cigar smoke. There were butts of a dozen smoked cigarettes on the hearth. But what interested Mr. Reeder most was something the intruders had left behind. It was a fountain pen, and it had been overlooked, probably because the pen was the same colour as the table. He handled it gingerly, using a piece of paper, and carried it to the light. The pen was of a very popular make, but it offered a wonderful surface for finger-prints.

When he came back to the girl Mr. Reeder's face was very grave.

"They've done you no harm at all. I don't think they had any intention to hurt you. I was the gentleman they were out for."

"But how?" asked the bewildered girl.

Mr. Reeder did not reply immediately. He got on the telephone and called up a doctor he knew. "I don't think you will have any after-effects."

"What did they give me?" she asked.

"Scapolamin. It's main effect was to make you speak the truth. Not," said Mr. Reeder hastily, "that you ever speak anything but the truth, but rather it was to remove certain inhibitions. The questions they asked you were, I imagine, mainly about myself; what did you tell me, how much I knew. And I'm afraid"—he shook his head—"I am very much afraid that you told them much more than is good for me."

She looked at him with wide, disbelieving eyes.

"But who were they?"

Mr. Reeder smiled.

"I know two of them. The third may, of course, be the most dangerous of the trio, but I really don't think he matters."

That morning there was a swift raid on the premises at 297 Lincoln's Inn Fields, but the raiders arrived too late. They had to break open the door —the room was empty. Apparently there had been a considerable amount of destruction going on, for the gas fire had been dragged out of the hearth, and the original grate behind it was full of black paper. The test tubes had gone, and so had the manuscript which Mr. Reeder had seen on the desk. Inquiries made on the premises produced very little in the way of information. Mr. Jones had occupied his office for four years. He was believed to be a Swede, and he gave no trouble to anybody. Very few callers came. He paid his rent and his rates regularly and the only adverse criticism that was offered was that occasionally he used to sing in a strange language and in a stranger voice to the annoyance of the solicitor's clerks who occupied an office immediately below him.

Undoubtedly he drank. They found ten empty gin bottles in one cupboard and fourteen earthenware bottles in another.

After the raid Mr. Reeder took counsel with himself, and examined his motives in the most candid of lights. He had, he realised, sufficient evidence to produce most of the effects which were desirable. He sent for a file dealing with the bank crimes that had been recorded in the past two years, and very carefully he went over the names of the men who had vanished, and with them considerable sums of money.

From his pocket he took the two keys which he had found in Reigate's pocket. If he could find the lock for these, the matter would be developed to its end. Mr. Reeder was very anxious that he himself should fit these keys to the right locks, the more so since he had seen, as he thought, a very likely lock in the shop building immediately behind the Strangers Club.

He fought with himself for a long time. Starkly he arraigned his dramatic instincts before the bar of sane judgement, and in the end he condemned himself and sought an interview with the Chief Constable to detail his theories.

The Chief Constable had eaten something which had not agreed with him. It was a prosaic explanation for a fall of a great man, but he was at home, in the doctor's hands, and the Deputy Chief Constable occupied his chair.

It was unfortunate that Mr. Reeder and the Deputy Chief Constable had never seen eye to eye, and that there was between them an antagonism which can only be understood by those fortunate people who have worked in or watched the work of a great government department.

The Deputy Chief was due for retirement. He had a grievance against the world, and every Superintendent and Chief Inspector at Scotland Yard had a grievance against him.

He was a little man, very bald, thin of face, and thinner of mind, and it was his boast that he belonged to the old school. It was so old that it had fallen down—if the truth be told.

When Mr. Reeder had detailed his theories,

"My dear fellow," said the Deputy Chief Constable, "up to a point I am with you. But I will not accept—I never have accepted—the master criminal theory in any case with which I have been associated. There is a great temptation to fall for that romantic idea, but it doesn't work out. In the first place, there's no loyalty between criminals and therefore there can be no discipline, as we understand discipline. If the man is what you think, he could not command implicit obedience, and certainly in this country he could not find people to carry out his instructions without regard to their own safety. The other idea is, of course, fantastical. I happen to know all about the Strangers Club. It is extraordinarily well conducted and every Thursday there is a series of lectures in the basement lecture hall; they have been given by some of the greatest scientists in this country. Dr. Jansen has an international reputation—"

Mr. Reeder was staring at him owlishly. In his soul there was a fierce, malignant joy.

"There can be no question or doubt that there is quite a lot in your theory," the Deputy Chief Constable went on; "but I could not advise action being taken until we have made very careful observations and there's no chance of our making a mistake. Personally, the fact that two men who were defaulting cashiers have been killed, suggests to me that there was a little gang operating in each case, and that somebody has tried to double-cross them."

"And the silk pyjamas?" murmured Mr. Reeder.

The Deputy Chief was not prepared to explain the silk pyjamas.

It seemed to Mr. Reeder that the two Chief Inspectors, who were present at this interview, were not so completely happy about the matter as was their superior.

"As it is," that gentleman went on (he was the type of man who always had an afterthought, and insisted upon expressing it), "we may have got into very serious trouble in raiding the office of Mr. Jones. I've been inquiring into the Benevolent Brotherhood, and they are most highly recommended by bishops and other important persons of the church. No, Mr. Reeder, I don't think I can go any further in this matter in the lamentable absence of the Chief Constable and, anyhow, a day or two more or less isn't going to make any difference."

"Does it occur to you," asked Mr. Reeder gently, "that two men have been killed, there is quite a possibility of another seven going the way of all flesh?"

The Deputy smiled. That was all—he just smiled.

Outside, in the corridor, one of the Chief Inspectors overtook Mr. Reeder.

"Of course he's all wrong," he said, "and I'm going to take the responsibility of covering whatever work you do."

Mr. Reeder made an appointment for the Chief Inspector to meet him after dinner, and alone he went back to the Strangers Club, carefully avoiding the front. There was nobody in sight and he moved carefully along the wall, until he came to a small door, inserted first one key and then the other. At the twist of the second the door opened noiselessly.

Mr. Reeder drooped his head and listened. There was no sound. He had expected at least to hear a bell. Taking a torch from his trousers pocket, he sent a beam into the dark corridor. It was a little wider than he had expected and terminated, so far as he could see, with a flight of stairs which led up round a bend out of sight. On the left-hand side there was a wide door in the wall. He shone the torch upwards and saw a powerful light fixed to the ceiling, but there was no sign of a switch; presumably the light was operated from upstairs. He closed the door carefully, tried the second key on the bigger door, but this time without success.

At the appointed time he met Chief Inspector Dance and told him what he had discovered. They sat for over an hour in Mr. Reeder's room, discussing plans. At nine o'clock the Inspector left, and Mr. Reeder opened the safe in the office, took out a heavy Browning and loaded it with the greatest care. He pushed every cartridge into the chamber and out again, added a touch of oil here and there and finally, slipping a spare magazine into his waistcoat pocket, he pressed up the safety catch of the Browning and pushed the pistol behind the lapel of his tightly fitting coat.

The night commissionaire saw him go out, wearing one big yellow glove on his left hand and carrying the other. His hat was set at a jaunty angle and there was about him that liveliness which was only discernable in this very quiet man when trouble was in the offing. To his left wrist he had strapped a large watch, and as the hands pointed to twenty minutes to ten he walked almost jauntily up the steps of the Strangers Club, passed through the swing door and smiled genially at the porter.

That functionary was tall and broad-shouldered; he had a large round head and a wooden expression. "Whom do you want?" he asked curtly.

Evidently the servants at the Strangers Club, though they might be hand-picked for some qualities, were not chosen either for their good manners or their finesse.

"I would like to see Dr. Jansen. He did me the honour to call at my office —my name is Reeder."

CHAPTER VII

For a perceptible moment of time he saw a light dawn and die in the dull eyes of the hall porter.
"Why, surely!" he said. "I think the doctor is dining here tonight, Mr. Reeder, and he'll be glad to see you."
He went to a telephone and pressed a knob.
"It's Mr. Reeder, doctor... Yeh? He just dropped in to see you."
What the man at the other end of the 'phone said—and he said it at some length—it was impossible to overhear, but Reeder saw the man step back a little so that he could look through the glass doors into the street outside.
"No, that's all right, doctor," he said. "Mr. Reeder is by himself. You haven't got a friend, Mr. Reeder? Maybe you'd like to invite him in?"
Mr. Reeder shook his head.
"I have no friend," he said sadly. "It's one of the tragedies of my life that I have never been able to make friends."
The man was puzzled. Obviously he had heard a great deal of this redoubtable gentleman from the Public Prosecutor's office, and he was not quite sure of his ground. He gave Mr. Reeder a long, scrutinising glance, in which any antagonism there might have been was swamped by genuine curiosity. It was almost as though he doubted the evidence of his eyes.
Evidently somebody called him urgently at the other end of the wire, for he turned suddenly.
"That's all right, doctor. I'll bring him right up. Will you leave your coat here?"
Mr. Reeder regarded him with a pained expression.
"Thank you," he said. "I fear I might be cold."
At the far end of the hall there was a door. The janitor opened it, switched on the light and disclosed a comfortable little elevator. Mr. Reeder stepped in and turned so quickly that he might have gone in backwards. He had expected the porter to follow. Instead the man closed the door. There was a click and a gentle whirr and the lift shot upwards. It went up two storeys and then stopped, and the doors opened automatically—and there was Dr. Jansen, very genial, very prosperous-looking in his evening dress and his heavy gold watch guard, with an outstretched hand like a leg of mutton.
"I am most pleased to meet you again, Mr. Reeder. It is a great honour. You will follow me, sir?"
He went ahead, down a narrow passage, then, turning to the right, descended two flights of stairs, which, so far as Reeder could judge, brought him to the first floor. It was obvious that from the first floor which the elevator had passed there was no communication with this part of the building. It was almost unnecessary for the doctor to explain this.
He opened a door and disclosed a beautifully furnished room. It was long and narrow. A heavy pile carpet was laid over a rubber foundation, and the visitor had the sensation that he was walking on springs.
"My little sanctum," said Dr. Jansen. "What do you drink, Mr. Reeder?"

Mr. Reeder looked round helplessly.

"Milk?" he suggested, and not a muscle of the big man's face moved.

"Why, yes, we can give you that even."

Raising his voice:

"Send a glass of milk for Mr. Reeder," he said. "I have a microphonic telephone in my room. It saves much trouble," he added. "But you would maybe like me to shut it off?"

He turned a switch near the big Empire desk which stood in an alcove.

"Now you can talk and say just what you like, and nobody is going to listen to you. You will take your glove off, Mr. Reeder?"

"I'm only staying a few minutes," said Mr. Reeder gravely. "I wanted to see you about certain statements that have been made and which in some way suggest that this club is associated with a benevolent society run by an old gentleman called Jones."

Jansen chuckled. Whatever else he was, he was a good actor.

"Why, 'ow strange!" he said. "I know this Jones. In fact, I 'ave kept the old man alive, Is crazy, that benevolent society! But you know, Mr. Reeder, it is quite genuine. Some people get a lot of money out of those poor men who live in the south of France."

Mr. Reeder inclined his head gravely.

"It has that appearance. In fact, I was speaking with the Chief Constable tonight. We were discussing whether there was anything sinister—if I may use that expression—about the society, and he took the view that it was quite genuine. I am perfectly satisfied in my own mind that the brotherhood is responsible for giving quite a lot of money to people who felt an urgent need for it."

Jansen was watching him, projecting his mind into Reeder's, taking his point of view—Mr. Reeder knew it.

"The whole thing arose out of a discovery of an unfortunate young man named Reigate," Mr. Reeder continued. "He was shot at my door and after his death there was found in a notebook an advertisement of this brotherhood. That, and one or two other curious circumstances... Oh, yes, I remember, two keys we found in his desk, gave the case a rather mysterious aspect."

Mr. Reeder was suffering under a great disadvantage. By a curious trick of mind he had entirely forgotten the excuse on which Jansen had called at the Public Prosecutor's office. Such a thing had happened once before, and he was as a man who was walking over a bridge from which one plank was missing.

"This man Hallaty now," began Jansen, and in a flash the reason for the call was revealed. "You remember, Mr. Reeder, the man who owes me money, and who is in Holland."

"He returned," said Mr. Reeder gravely. "He was found shot in Essex. Probably he had come back from the Hook of Holland to Harwich, and now—"

There was a tinkle of a bell and Dr. Jansen opened a panel in the wall which hid a small service lift, and took out a glass of milk.

Mr. Reeder sipped at it gently. He had a palate of extraordinary keenness, and would have detected instantly the presence in that harmless fluid of any quantity which was not so harmless, but the milk tasted like milk. He took a longer sip and put it down, and he thought he saw in the face of Dr. Jansen just a hint of relief.

"And now, doctor, I am going to ask you a great favour. I am going to ask you to show me round your club, about which I have heard so much."

The smile left the doctor's face.

"That I'm afraid I cannot do. In the first place, it is not my club, and in the second, it is one of the rules of this establishment, Mr. Reeder, that there should be no intrusion on the privacy of members."

"Of whom you have how many?"

"Six hundred and three."

Mr. Reeder nodded.

"I have seen the list," he said. "They are mainly honorary members who are admitted to the ground floor for your lectures. I've yet to have the satisfaction of seeing a list—um—of your members."

Jansen looked at him thoughtfully.

"Why then," he said, "come along and meet them."

He walked past Mr. Reeder, opened the door and stood aside for his guest to pass.

"Maybe you would like me to go first?" he said, with a smile, and Reeder knew that war had been declared, and followed him up the stairs. Again they were in the long corridor, and presently the doctor stood by the door of the lift, and pressed a bell. When the lift came up it was to all appearances the same elevator that he had seen before. It had the same black and white tiled floor, and yet Mr. Reeder had a feeling that it was a little newer, a little cleaner than when he had seen it last.

As his foot touched the floor, he felt it give under him. Throwing the full weight upon his right leg, he sprang backwards. He heard something swish past his head. There was a crash where the short leaden club struck, and, recovering his balance, Reeder lashed out with his gloved hand. Dr. Jansen went down like a log, no remarkable circumstance—for under Mr. Reeder's glove was a knuckleduster.

For a moment he stood, automatic in hand, looking down at the dazed man at his feet. Jansen blinked up at him, and made a movement to rise.

"You can get up," said Reeder; "but you'll keep your hands away."

Then all the lights went out.

The detective stepped back quickly, so quickly that he collided with somebody, who was behind him. Again he struck out, but this time missed. He was deafened by the bang of an explosion. He was so close to the pistol that the powder stung his cheek. Twice he fired in the direction of the flash and then he suddenly lost consciousness. He did not feel the blow that hit him, but went painlessly down into oblivion.

"Put on the lights now, Jansen. Has he hit anybody?"

The lights went up suddenly. The bullet-headed porter was looking stupidly at a wrist and arm that were red with blood.

A shorter edition of the porter came into view round the angle of the corridor, and looked at the senseless detective.

"Help me get him into the cubby, Jansen."

Jansen only stopped to inspect the wound of the hall porter.

"There's nothing to it," he said. "Bind it up with your handkerchief. It's just a scratch. Gee, you're lucky, Fred!"

He turned his attention to the senseless man. There was neither malice nor anger, but rather admiration in his glance.

"Help me get him into the cubby," he said.

In reality he needed no help. He was a man of extraordinary strength. Stooping, he lifted the unconscious Reeder, dragged him through the passage into a little room, and dropped him into a chair.

"He's O.K.," he said.

The little man, who had come from the passage, looked at the detective with an expression of amazement.

"Is that the bull?" he said incredulously.

Jansen nodded.

"That's the bull," he said grimly. "And don't laugh, Baldy. That guy's got more men in stir than any other fellow that ever broke from the pen."

"He looks nuts to me," grunted Baldy.

He had a shock of fair hair. Mr. Reeder, who was listening intently, found himself wondering, in his inconsequent way, how he had earned his name.

"Feed him some water. Here, give it to me."

Jansen took a glass from the man's hand and threw it into the face of the drooping figure. Mr. Reeder opened his eyes and stared round. His glove had been pulled off. The knuckleduster had disappeared.

"I hand it to you, Reeder," said Jansen amiably. "If I'd not been all kinds of a sap, I'd have known you had that duster in your glove."

He felt his jaw and grinned. "Have a drink?"

He turned the leaves of a table and a nest of decanters rose.

"Brandy will do you no harm."

He poured out a large portion and handed it to the detective; Mr. Reeder sipped it.

Putting his hand to his head he felt a large egg-sized bump, but no abrasion.

"All right, Baldy. I'll ring for you." Jansen dismissed his assistant. When he had gone: "Let's get right down to cases. You're Reeder. Who am I?"

"Your name is Redsack," said Reeder without hesitation. "You are what I would describe as a fugitive from justice."

Jansen nodded amiably.

"You're right first time," he said. "That Dutch accent wasn't bad though? Now how far have you got, Reeder? You and me are old-timers and hard boiled. We'll talk it right out, just as we feel, and we're not going to get sour with each other. You went out for a prize and got a blank. There's only one way of treating blanks, Reeder—and that's the way you're going to be treated. Have some more brandy?"

"Thank you, I've had enough."

"Maybe you'd like a cup of tea?"

Jansen was genuinely solicitous. He was not acting. He had pronounced the sentence of death upon the man who had come seeking his life, but he was entirely without animosity. Death was the natural and proper sequel to failure, because dead men cannot take the stand and testify to one's undoing.

"I think I would like a cup of tea."

Jansen turned the switch and bellowed an order. Then switched it off again.

"You can't say you haven't met Jansen." He grinned again.

Mr. Reeder nodded and winced.

"No, I met him in Lincoln's Inn Fields—a very unpleasant old gentleman."

"A clever old guy," interrupted Redsack. "In his way as clever as you. I picked him up when I came to England. He was doping then, and sleeping on the old Thames Embankment. He'd been so long away from home and he had no friends in England, I thought Jansen might be as good a name for me as for him, and he didn't care anyway. It's been a grand racket, Reeder; if I clear up tonight we'll go on for a year or two.

"I came to this country with ten thousand dollars. Part of it I brought on the boat, and part of it I snitched from a passenger's cabin. It was so long since I'd been in England that I didn't know how easy it was. You're all so damn law-abiding here that any big racket, if it looks good, would surely get past."

He settled himself comfortably in his chair, but rose almost immediately to open the panel, and take out a cup of tea.

"You can drink that. If you like, I'll drink half of it. Say, these poisoners make me sick. You know what I got the dungeon for in Sing-Sing? It was for beating up a guy who'd poisoned his wife and mother-in-law. I just hated to see him around. He told them I was trying to escape and that he wouldn't stand by me. But that's ancient history, Mr. Reeder. Drink your tea."

Mr. Reeder drank and put down the cup carefully.

"I wasn't a month in this country before I found a young bank clerk who'd been playing the races and snitching money from the bank. He got tight and told me all about it, and I saw how easy it was to make big money; so I just organised him, and he got away with a hundred thousand dollars."

He leaned forward and raised a warning finger.

"Don't say I didn't play fair with him, because I did. We shared fifty-fifty. The great thing was to hide him up for a month, and the next big thing was to get him away, and that was hard. I never realised before that England was surrounded by water, and that's where Jansen came in useful. I set him up in some rooms in Harley Street, but he was never entirely satisfactory, because we couldn't keep him sober. We had one or two narrow escapes with the invalids he was escorting across the Channel. He chuckled as though it were a pleasant memory, and then with a deprecating smile: You know what it is, Reeder, when you and me have to depend on second-class people and not on ourselves. We're so near being sunk that a life-belt doesn't mean a damned thing."

"When did you start the nursing home for infectious diseases?"

Mr. Redsack laughed uproariously and smacked his knee.

"Say, I wasn't sure whether you knew about that. You're clever. You got it, did you? Why, that happened after one or two of these birds had tried to double-cross us. You see, what we did was to put this advertisement in every paper once a week. Naturally we had thousands of letters, but we waited till we got a man who could hand in the dough. You've got no idea how bank clerks don't know how to look after money! If he was just an ordinary five-cent man, we passed him on. But you'd be surprised at the number of big fellows— I once had an Assistant General Manager, who was so old that he couldn't be dishonest. But we got a good few real smarties; as soon as we picked on them, we'd tell them that, as a very special honour and on the recommendation of the Lord knows who, they'd been elected members of the Strangers Club. We got a whole range of private rooms. But naturally we didn't want any member to meet another member. We gave 'em good food, free tickets for the theatre. Just made them feel they were staying with Uncle John. How the hell they thought we did it on ten dollars a year I don't know. But I dare say you find, Reeder, that thieves are mean cusses.

"Once we got them here the benevolent brothers started their operations. I was the agent, and I had to make sure they were men you could trust. I'm not going to give you the long of it, but it was not easy to get the smarties to fall for this grand idea. Most men are thieves at heart, but the thing that scares them is: how am I going to get away without a lagging? They can get the stuff all right, but where is it going to be put? Where will they hide? How will they leave the country? We did everything for them; passports, transportation. Why, we even chartered a tug to get that guy who pulled down half a million from the Liverpool bank, from England to Belgium, and he didn't leave from Dover either. He went from London by water to Zeebrugge, and was carried aboard and ashore on a stretcher with so many bandages on his face that half the people who saw him land were crying before the ambulance took him on to Brussels. We made more than half a million bucks out of that, and he is living like a prince in Austrak.

"We give service, Reeder. That's the keynote of our organisation— service. We took 'em out of London in ambulances marked 'infectious diseases only'. Can you see any policeman with children of his own stopping them and inspecting the patients? Why, you could smell that camphor dope before you saw the ambulance.

"You guessed right when you took an inspection of our nursing home at the back, and you guessed right when, after you had opened the door, you decided you wouldn't go in. We keep all our run-aways snug in that home for a month. Sometimes two months, and no harm comes to them. They are out of the country as per contract. Service!"

He shook his head, and used the word lovingly.

"We picked 'em up from the bank, we brought 'em to London, we hid them and we got 'em out of the country, and never had a failure. Hallaty was yellow. In the first place, he didn't bring all the stuff to us; he cached nearly half of it at a small public house on the Essex road. Then he tried to get away and we naturally had to go after him. That kid Reigate, he got religious. We thought we had everything set, but he jumped out of the ambulance on his way to Gravesend, and naturally Baldy, his escort, had to stop him talking.

"I'm glad you didn't come in when you used that key. I shouldn't have had the pleasure of talking to you. We had a machine gun on you, and Baldy was all ready with his motor-cycle to cover up the sound. But you didn't come in and, honestly, Reeder, I'm glad."

He was very earnest. "You're the kind of guy I wanted to meet."

He shook his head, genuinely sad.

"I wish I could think of some other way out for you, but you're tied up to your graft, the same as I am to mine."

Mr. Reeder smiled with his eyes, and that was very rare in him.

"May I say not—um—as a matter of politeness, but in all sincerity, that if I have to go out at the hands of a desperado—if you'll forgive me using the word—I would prefer that it should be the best kind of desperado and an—um—artist." He paused.

"May I ask whether you plan to let the matter end in this interesting and complicated building, or have you a more spectacular method in your mind?"

Mr. Redsack smiled.

"You're a classy talker, Reeder, and I could listen to you for hours. Naturally you would think that I'd be thinking of something bad for a fellow who's given me the worst sock in the jaw I've ever had in my life." He touched his swollen cheek tenderly. But I've got no malice in me. I guess we'll try the grand old-time American operation. We'll take you for a ride. If you've got any particular place you'd prefer, why, I'm willing to oblige you, Mr. Reeder, so long as it gives me a chance of getting back before daylight."

Mr. Reeder thought for a minute.

"I naturally would prefer Brockley, which has been, as it were, and to use an expression which will be familiar to you, Mr. Redsack, my home town, but I realise that this highly populated suburb is not suitable for your purpose, and I suggest, respectfully, that one of the arterial roads out of London would suit both of us admirably."

Redsack switched on his loudspeaker and gave an order.

He took from the belt under his waistcoat a large-sized automatic and examined it as carefully as Mr. Reeder earlier in the evening had inspected his own lethal weapon.

"Let's go," he said.

He led the way, opened the door again, and Mr. Reeder passed through into the passage.

"Turn right!"

Mr. Reeder followed his directions, and came to the blank end of the passage.

"There's a door there that'll open in a minute," said Redsack encouragingly.

They waited a few seconds. Nothing happened. Pushing past him, Redsack rapped on the wall and a narrow crack appeared in one corner. It opened wider and wider, and the door swung open.

"Say what's the idea?" said Redsack loudly, and even as he spoke he whipped out his gun and fired twice.

It was a lucky day for Chief Inspector Dance. One bullet whipped off his hat; the second passed between his arm and his coat.

He fired back, but by this time Redsack was flying along the passage and had turned the corridor. When they came up, halting gingerly to feel their way, there was nobody in sight. They heard the whirr of the lift, but whether it was going up or down they could not tell.

Then again the lights went out from some central control.

"Back to where we came," said Dance.

They fled along the passage, through the door, down the steep flight of stairs. These turned sharply, and Mr. Reeder saw what it was. They were out in the mews, but not quickly enough; as Dance fumbled with the lock, they heard two gates open with a crash, the pulsation of an engine and the roar of it as it shot past. By the time they were out in the mews the Strangers Club had lost its proprietor, janitor and chief attendant.

"Both keys worked," Dance reported hastily. "I gathered he'd got you and I advanced the time five minutes."

He saw Mr. Reeder rub his head.

"Hurt?" he asked anxiously.

"Only in my feelings," said Mr. Reeder.

They made a quick search of the garage and found the battered motor-cycle on which Hallaty had tried to make his escape, and the big ambulance with its warning sign, which had assisted Redsack so vitally in his ingenious scheme.

"If the Deputy Chief had given me the sanction to raid this place, I'd have had enough men here to catch 'em," growled Dance. "Where is this nursing home, and which is the way in?"

It took a long time before they finally reached the secret suites where three panic-stricken 'patients' were waiting their discharge to that life of comfort which their depredations had earned for them.

CHAPTER VIII

Back at Scotland Yard, a chastened Deputy Chief Constable was anxious to do all that was possible to correct his error, for he had been on the 'phone to his sick chief, and what passed between them is not on record.

In the middle of the night a more careful search was made of the garage. Mr. Reeder had seen a door which, he had imagined, led to a store. When the lights were turned on, the thickness of the doors revealed the character of this store. It was a steel-lined safe—it was empty. The accumulations of five years' hard work had gone. A barrage, immediately laid down about London, was established too late, and at five o'clock in the morning a tug left Greenwich and proceeded leisurely down the river, made its signal to Gravesend and passed out into the open sea.

The thing that came between Mr. Redsack and his future appeared in the form of a smoky cloud in the horizon, and a grey hull. From one tiny mast broke a string of little flags, The Master of the tug reported to his chief passenger and charter party.

"A destroyer, sir," he said.

"What does he say?" asked Redsack, interested in the nautical drama.

The Master consulted his signal book.

"Heave to, I am searching you'," he read.

Redsack considered this.

"Suppose we don't?" he suggested.

"He'll sink us," said the alarmed Master. "Why shouldn't we let him come aboard?"

"That's O.K. with me," said Redsack.

He turned to the tall janitor, yellow-faced and shivering in spite of his heavy overcoat. "If I was sure they'd take me back to Sing-Sing, why, I wouldn't mind," he said. "Sing-Sing's kind of a lucky prison to me. But now I'm so damned English that it's Dartmoor or nothing, I guess. Or maybe they don't hang people at Dartmoor."

He considered the problem as the destroyer came nearer and nearer, and then he went down to the little cabin and scribbled a note.

"Dear Mr. Reeder,—I said last night it was you or me, and I guess it's me."

He signed his name with a flourish, sat down on the hard sofa, took out a cigar. He heard the bump of a boat as it came alongside and an authoritative voice demanding particulars of the passengers.

Mr. Redsack placed his cigar carefully into a little polished stove and shot himself.

THE TREASURE HOUSE

Published as "The Prisoner of Sevenways" in The Thriller, Feb 14, 1931

CHAPTER I

Mr. J.G. Reeder did odd things. And he did oddly kind things. There was once a drug addict, whom he first prosecuted and then befriended; but there was nothing unusual in that. He did the same with a young man many years later, and as a result earned for himself the high commendation of his superiors.

But helping this drug addict led apparently nowhere. It involved a great deal of trouble, and it was an unsavoury case, and in the end Mr. Reeder achieved nothing, for the man he tried to assist died in hospital without friends and without money.

It is true that the man in the next bed knew him, and communicated a great deal of information to a ferret-faced chauffeur, who subsequently made certain inquiries.

A more satisfactory adventure in the field of loving kindness was Mr. Reeder's association with a certain well-educated young burglar. That led to much that was pleasant to think about and remember.

The story of the treasure house really begins with a man who had no faith in the stability of stock markets, and believed in burying his talents in the ground. He was not singular in this respect, for the miser in man is a very common quality, and though Mr. Lane Leonard was no miser in the strictest sense of the word, being in fact rather generous of disposition, he was wedded to the reality of wealth, and there is nothing quite so real as gold. And gold he accumulated in startling quantities at a period when gold was hard to come by. Gold in buried chests would not satisfy him; he must have gold visible and reachable—but mainly visible. That is why he hoarded his wealth in large boxes made of toughened glass, having these containers further enclosed in steel wire baskets; for gold is very heavy and the toughest of glass is brittle.

They said on the New York Stock Exchange that John Lane Leonard was a lucky man, but he never regarded himself that way. He was not a member of the house, and had begun as a dabbler in the kerb market, buying on margins and accumulating a very modest fortune, which became colossal overnight, through no pre-science of his own, but rather because of a lucky accident. He was as near to being ruined as made no difference. Three partners, who had pooled their shares with him, became panic stricken at a bear raid and left him to hold the baby; and whilst he was holding this very helplessly, not quite sure whether he should drop it and run, powerful financial interests, of whose existence he was quite unaware, struck so savagely at the bears that they were caught short. The sensational rise in prices placed Mr. Lane Leonard rich in excess of his own imagination.

He was not a millionaire then, but he had not long to wait before another piece of luck brought him into the seven-figure class. If he had had a sense of humour, he would have recognised just how much he owed to the spin of somebody else's coin; but, being devoid of this quality, he gave large credit to his own acumen and foresight. There were any number of people who fostered the illusion that he had the mind and vision of a great financier. His brother-in-law, Digby Olbude, was one of his most vehement and voluble sycophants.

Lane Leonard was English, and had married an English wife; a dull lady, who hated New York and was home-sick for Hampstead, a pleasant suburb it was never designed she should see again. She died, more or less of inanition, three years after her husband had acquired both his riches and a sneaking desire for American citizenship.

By this time John Lane Leonard was an authority on all matters pertaining to finance. He wrote articles for the London Economist which were never published, because in some way they did not fit in with the views of the editor or, indeed, with the views of anybody who had an elementary knowledge of economics. Whatever Digby thought about them, he said they were great. He used to drink in those days and dabble in margins and when he lost, as he so frequently did, John Lane Leonard paid.

They parted at last over a matter of a hundred thousand dollars, and although this sum also had to be found by the millionaire, it was in his heart to forgive his erratic relative by marriage, for he never forgot that Digby completely approved of and admired him, and had helped him considerably in his preparation of a pamphlet on the American Economy. That pamphlet was so scarified by the American press, so ridiculed by the experts of Wall Street, that Mr. Lane Leonard shook the dust of New York from his feet, transferred his bank balances to England, returned to his native Kent and bought Sevenways Castle and proceeded to put his theories into practice.

He met a pretty widow with a young child and married her. Within a few years she too had died. He changed the name of her little daughter by deed poll from Pamela Dolby to Pamela Lane Leonard, and designated her his heiress. It was necessary that he should have an heiress, though he would have preferred an heir.

In those days Lidgett was his junior chauffeur, a hatchet-faced boy, country born, shrewd, cunning, ruthless; but Mr. Lane Leonard knew nothing about his cunning or ruthlessness. He received from Lidgett a whole-hearted homage which was very pleasing to him. Lidgett did not prostrate himself on the ground every time he saw his employer—he just stopped short of that. He became the confidential servant and valet as well as chief chauffeur. Mr. Lane Leonard used to talk to him about the gold standard whilst he was dressing, and Lidgett used to shake his head in helpless admiration.

"What a brain you must have, Mr. Leonard! It beats me how you can keep these things in your mind! If I knew as much as you, I think I'd go mad!"

Crude stuff, but crude stuff is effective. To Lidgett Mr. Lane Leonard revealed his great plan for the creation of a gold reserve; it took three weeks for Lidgett to realise that his employer was talking about real gold. After that he became very alert.

Mr. Leonard was an assiduous church-goer, and invariably chose Evensong for his devotions. When they were in London Lidgett used to sit at the wheel of the Rolls parked outside St. George's, Hanover Square, wildly cursing the employer who was keeping him from a perfect evening's entertainment. There was a spieling club in Soho which was a second home to Mr. Lidgett, and as soon as his master was indoors and made comfortable for the night Lidgett lost no time in reaching the green table where they played chemin de fer.

His employer was a careless man, who never missed a five-pound note one way or the other, and Lidgett was a lucky man at the table, more lucky than the dignified and middle-aged gentleman he so often met at Dutch Harry's, and who seemed to come there only to lose.

Once he borrowed twenty pounds from Lidgett and found some difficulty in repaying it. Joe Lidgett got to know all about him; rather liked him, if the truth be told.

"You ought to give up this game, mister. You haven't got the right kind of nut."

"Very possible, very possible," said the other frigidly.

Sometimes in the early hours of the morning the little Cockney and his somewhat aristocratic friend would go to an all-night restaurant for a meal before they separated, the unfortunate loser to an early train which carried him into the country, Mr. Lidgett to his duties as chauffeur-valet. In the course of his confidences with Lidgett Mr. Leonard mentioned his brother-in-law, and enlarged upon his genius.

"He is one of the few men who really understand my theories, Lidgett," he said in an expansive moment. "Unfortunately, he and I quarrelled over a trifling matter, and I haven't heard from him for many years. A sound financier, Lidgett, a very sound financier! I have been tempted lately to get into touch with him; he is the one man I could trust to carry out my wishes if what this infernal doctor says has any foundation in fact."

"This infernal doctor" was a Harley Street specialist who had said something rather serious; or it would have been serious if Mr. Leonard had regarded himself as being completely mortal.

He saw little of his step-daughter. She was at a school, came home for dull holidays, and listened uncomprehendingly to Mr. Leonard's lectures on gold values. She saw the first treasure house built, inspected its steel doors, and thought that the vault was a little terrifying; she heard that all this was for her sake, but could never quite believe that.

One day Mr. Leonard had a fainting fit which lasted for an hour. When he recovered he sent for Lidgett.

"Lidgett, I want you to get in touch with Mr. Digby Olbude," he said. "I haven't his address, but you will probably find it in the telephone book. I have never troubled to look."

He explained just what he wanted of Mr. Olbude and Lidgett listened with interest, his agile mind working with great rapidity. Digby Olbude was to carry on the work of his brother-in-law, was to become for a number of years controller of untold wealth.

Lidgett went forth on his tour of investigation, wondering in what manner he might benefit from the change which most evidently was due.

Digby Olbude was not difficult to trace, though he seemed to have changed his name on two occasions and at his last address had no name at all. The shrewd little chauffeur came back to Sevenways a very preoccupied man. He found awaiting him a letter forwarded from London—a pathetic, pleading, incoherent letter, written in perfect English by his middle-aged gambler friend.

Joe Lidgett had an idea. A few days later his master was well enough to see him and he gave an account of his search for Digby Olbude.

"I would like to see him," said Leonard feebly. "I am afraid I'm in a bad way, Lidgett—where are you?"

"I'm here, sir," said Lidgett.

"It is rather difficult to see. My eyesight has become a little defective."

The gentleman Mr. Lidgett had found arrived by car the next morning. He went up more than a little nervously to the dying man's bedroom, and was introduced with pathetic formality to the lawyer Mr. Leonard had brought from London. He did not like lawyers, but the occasion demanded expert legal assistance.

"This is my brother-in-law, Digby Olbude..."

The will was signed and witnessed with some difficulty. It was characteristic of Lane Leonard that he did not even send for his heiress or leave any message of affection or tender farewell. To him she was a peg on which his theory was to hang—and it was not even his own theory.

She was notified of his passing in a formal letter from her new guardian, and she received the notification on the very day that Larry O'Ryan decided upon adopting a criminal career.

When Larry O'Ryan was expelled from a public school on a charge of stealing some eighty-five pounds from Mr. Farthingale's room, he could not only have cleared himself of the accusation, but he could also have named the culprit.

He had no parents, no friends, being maintained at the school by a small annuity left by his mother. If Creed's Bank had been a little more generous with his father, if the Panton Credit Trust had been honestly directed, if the Medway and Western had not forced a sale, Larry would have been rich.

It was no coincidence that these immensely rich corporations were patrons of the Monarch Security Steel Corporation—Monarchs had a monopoly in this kind of work—but we will talk about that later.

He hated the school, hated most the pompous pedagogue who was a friend of Mr. Farthingale and used his study when the house master was out—but he said nothing. After all, what chance had his word against a master's? He took his expulsion as an easy way of escaping from servitude, interviewed the lawyer who was his guardian and accepted the expressions of horror and abhorrence with which that gentleman favoured him.

Anyway, the eighty-five pounds was restored; before he left the school Larry saw the terrified thief and said a few plain words.

"I'll take the risk of being disbelieved," he said, "and I'll go to the head and say I saw you open the cash-box just as I was going into the study. I don't know why you wanted the money, but the people who investigate will find out."

The accused man thundered at him, reviled him, finally broke.

It was a grotesque situation, a middle-aged master and a lanky sixth-form boy, bullying and threatening one another alternately. Larry did not cry; on the other hand, his protagonist grew maudlin. But he restored the money. Everybody thought that it was Larry or Larry's lawyer-guardian who sent the notes by registered post; but it wasn't.

He went out into the world with the starkest outlook, looked round for work of sorts, was errand boy, office boy, clerk. No prospects. The army offered one, but the army stood for another kind of school discipline, house masters who wore stripes on their sleeves.

CHAPTER II

Larry thought it over one Saturday night and decided on burglary as a profession. For a year he went to night classes and polished up his knowledge of ballistics. At the end of the year he got a job at a safe-makers and locksmith's at Wolverhampton.

It was one of the most famous of all safe-makers, a firm world-renowned. All that a young man could learn of locks and safety devices Larry learned. He was an eager pupil; having a pleasant and engaging manner, he made friends with oldish men who, in return for the respect he paid them, told him many things about locks and safe construction.

He became an expert cutter of keys—had the use of a shed in the backyard of the widow with whom he lodged, and worked far into the night.

A gymnasium attached to a boys' club lent strength to skill.

When he left Wolverhampton his successes were startling and, in a newspaper sense, sensational. Creed's Bank lost forty thousand pounds in American currency held to liquidate certain demands which were due. Nobody saw the burglar come or go. The steel doors of the vault were opened with a key and locked with a key.

Then the Panton Credit Trust suffered. A matter of a hundred thousand pounds went in less than a hundred and twenty minutes.

At his third job he fell, due largely to the precautions taken on behalf of the Medway and Western Bank by a middle-aged detective who read the lessons of the earlier robberies aright; and had discovered that other banks had vault doors recently delivered and erected by the Monarch Safe Corporation.

Inquiries made at the works identified the enthusiastic young workman with a young gentleman who lived in a Jermyn Street flat and who had an account at the bank.

"It was," said Mr Reeder apologetically, "more by—um—luck than judgement that I succeeded in—er—anticipating this young man."

He liked Larry from the first interview he had with him, and that was in a cell at Bow Street. Larry was quite unlike any of the criminals with whom Mr. Reeder had been brought into contact. He neither whined nor lied, neither boasted nor was evasive. Mr. Reeder did not know his history and was unable to trace it.

"It's a great pity you're so clever, Mr. Reeder. This was to have been my final appearance as a burglar—hereafter I intended living the life of a well-to-do citizen, and hoped in course of time to become a Justice of the Peace!"

Mr, Reeder rarely smiled, but he did now.

"The other incursions into the burglar's profession were, I presume—um —Creed's Bank and the Panton Trust?"

It was Larry's turn to smile.

"That is a matter we will not discuss," he said politely.

Mr. Reeder, however, was more anxious to keep the matter in discussion, for there was a sum of a hundred and forty thousand pounds to be recovered.

"You will be ill advised, Mr. O'Ryan," he said gently, "to withhold these very important facts, particularly the whereabouts of—um—a very considerable sum which was taken from these two institutions. A complete disclosure will make a very considerable difference to you when you—er—come before the judge. I do not promise this," he added carefully; "I am merely going on precedents, but it is a fact that judges, in passing sentence, take into consideration the frankness with which an—um—accused person has dealt with his earlier depredations."

Larry O'Ryan laughed softly.

"That's a lovely word—depredations! It also makes me feel like one of the old robber barons of the Rhine. No, Mr. Reeder—nicely but firmly, no! In the first place, the two—depredations was the word, I think, you used?—to which you refer, are not and cannot be traceable to me. I have read about them and I know the facts which have been revealed in the newspapers. Beyond that I am not prepared to admit the slightest knowledge."

J.G. Reeder was insistent in his amiable way. He revealed his own information. He knew that O'Ryan had been employed by the Monarch Security Steel Corporation, he knew that it was possible he might have secured an understanding of the locks which had been so scientifically defied; and since all three institutions had obtained their steel vaults, their unbreakable doors, their gratings and secret locking arrangements from this company, there was no doubt in his mind (he said) that O'Ryan was responsible for both burglaries. But Larry shook his head.

"The burden of proof lies with the prosecution," he said with mock solemnity. "I should like very much indeed to help you, Mr. Reeder. I have heard of you, I admire you. Any man who in these days wears high-crowned felt hats and side-whiskers must have character, and I admire character. I hope that reference is not offensive to you; it is intended to be nothing but complimentary. I know quite a lot about you. You live in the Brockley Road, you keep chickens, you have an umbrella which you never open for fear it will be spoilt by the rain, and you smoke unspeakable cigarettes."

Again that rare smile of Mr. Reeder's.

"You're almost a detective," he said. "Now, let us talk about Creed's Bank—"

"Let us talk about the weather," said Larry.

All Scotland Yard, and the Public Prosecutor's Department, and Mr. Reeder, and various narks and noses, and the parasites of the underworld were concerned in the search for the missing hundred and forty thousand pounds, even though there was not sufficient evidence to indict Larry for these two crimes.

In due course he appeared before a judge at the Old Bailey, and pleaded guilty to being found on enclosed premises in possession of burglar's tools, and to house-breaking (he had entered the bank at four o'clock on a Saturday afternoon) and, after a rather acrimonious trial, was found guilty and sentenced to a term of twelve months in prison.

The trial was acrimonious because the counsel for the prosecution took a personal and violent dislike to the prisoner. Why, nobody knew; it was one of those prejudices which occasionally upset the judgement of intelligent men. It was probably some flippant remark which Larry made in cross-examination, a remark which counsel regarded as personally offensive to himself. He was not a big man, and he was rather a self-willed man. In his address to the jury he referred to the Creed's Bank robbery and the burglary at the Panton Trust. At the first reference to these affairs the judge stopped and warned him, but he was not to be warned. Although no evidence had been called, and no charge made, in relation to these crimes, he insisted upon drawing parallels. He emphasised the fact that the prisoner had been employed by the company which made the locks and steel doors of both vaults; and all the time Larry sat in the dock, his arms folded, listening with a smile, for he knew something about law.

There was an appeal; the conviction was quashed on a technical point, and Larry O'Ryan went free.

His first call was on Mr. J.G. Reeder, and he prefaced his visit with a short note asking whether his presence was acceptable. Reeder asked him to tea, which was the equivalent of being asked by the Lord Mayor to his most important banquet. Larry came it the highest spirits.

"May I say," asked Mr. Reeder, "that you are a very fortunate young man?"

"And how!" said Larry. "Yes, I was lucky. But who would imagine that the idiot would make a mistake like that! Are you sure you don't mind my calling?"

Mr. Reeder shook his head.

"If you hadn't come I should have invited you," he said.

With a pair of silver tongs he placed a muffin on Larry's plate.

"It would be a waste of time, Mr. O'Ryan, and I rather think a breach of—um—hospitality, if I made any further reference to those other unfortunate happenings, the—um—Creed's Bank and Panton Trust affairs. As a detective and an officer of state, I should be most happy if I could find one little string of a clue which would enable me to associate you with those—um—depredations is the word, I think, you like best?"

"Depredations is my favourite word," mumbled Larry through the muffin.

"Somehow, I don't think I shall ever be able to connect you," Mr. Reeder went on, "and in a sense I'm rather glad. That is a very immoral statement to make," he added hastily, "and against all my—um—principles, as you probably know. What are you going do for a living now, Mr. O'Ryan?"

"I am living on my income," said Larry calmly. "I have investments abroad which will bring me in, roughly, seven thousand a year."

Mr. Reeder nodded slowly.

"In other words, five per cent on a hundred and forty thousand pounds," he murmured. "A goodly sum—a very goodly sum." He sighed.

"You don't seem very happy about it." Larry's eyes twinkled.

Mr. Reeder shook his head.

"No, I am thinking of the poor shareholders of Creed's Bank—"

"There are no shareholders. The Creeds practically hold the shares between them. They tricked my father out of a hundred thousand pounds—a little more than that sum. I have never had the full particulars, but I know it was a hundred thousand—snapped it out of his pocket, and there was no possibility of getting back on them."

J.G. looked at the ceiling.

"So it was an act of poetic justice!" he said slowly. "And Panton's Trust?"

"You know the Panton crowd," said Larry quietly. "They have been living on the edge of highway robbery for the past twenty-five years. They've made most of their money out of crooked companies and tricky share dealing. They owe me much more than—they lost."

A beatific smile passed over Mr. Reeder's face. "You nearly said, 'than I took'," he said reproachfully.

"I nearly didn't say anything of the kind," said Larry. "No, don't waste your sympathy on them. And I could tell you something about the Medway and Western Bank that would interest you, but I won't."

"Poetic justice again, eh? You are almost a romantic figure!"

Mr. Reeder grasped the teapot and refilled the young man's cup.

"I'll promise you something; we'll not discuss this matter again, but I'll be very glad to see you any time you find life a little wearisome and would like to discover how really dull it can be. At the same time, I feel I should —um—warn you that if you—er—fall from grace and desire to wreak your poetic vengeance upon some other banking institution, these little visits will cease, and I shall do my best to put you behind locks which were not manufactured by the Monarch Security Steel Corporation!"

Larry became a fairly frequent visitor to the house in Brockley Road. Some people might have suspected Mr. Reeder of maintaining the acquaintance in order to secure further information about the earlier robberies. But Larry did not suspect Mr. Reeder of anything of the sort, and J.G. appreciated this compliment more than the young man knew.

Larry got into the habit of calling at night, and particularly when an interesting crime had been committed. He knew very little of the so-called underworld, and surprised Mr. Reeder when he told him that he had never met a crook until he was arrested.

This oddly matched pair had another interest in common, the British Museum. A visit to the museum was Larry's favourite recreation. Mr. Reeder, whenever he could find the time, invariably spent his Saturday afternoons in its heavily instructive atmosphere. And they both found their interest in the same psychology. Mr. Reeder loved to stand before the Elgin marbles and picture the studio in old Greece where these figures grew under the chisel of the master. He would stand for hours, looking down at a mummy, re-constructing the living woman who lay swathed behind the bandages. What was her life, her interests, her friends? How did she amuse herself? Had she children? What were they called? Did she find life boring or amusing? Did she have trouble with her servants?

Larry's mind ran in the same direction. They would stand before some ancient missal and conjure up a picture of the tonsured monk who worked in his cell, illuminating and writing with great labour the black lettering which was there under their eyes. When he opened the cell door and walked out into the world, what kind of a world was it? To whom did he speak?

Sometimes they varied their Saturday afternoons by a visit to the Tower. Who put that stone upon the other? What was his name? Where did he live? In what hovel? Who were his friends? A Norman artisan, brought by William across the seas. Possibly his name was Pierre, Mr. Reeder would hazard after a long, long silence.

"Gaston," suggested Larry.

Only once did they even speak of Larry's grisly past. It was an evening which they spent together in town. Mr. Reeder had just completed the evidence in the Central Bank robbery and was weary. They were dining in a little restaurant in Soho, when Larry asked:

"Do you know anything about the Lane Leonard estate?"

Mr. Reeder took off his glasses, polished them, put them on again and allowed them to sag and drop.

"Before I answer that question will you be good enough to tell me what you mean by that inquiry?"

Larry grinned.

"There's no need to be cautious. I'll tell you what brought the subject up —that iron grille before the cashier's desk. It's almost the same pattern as one we made for the Lane Leonard estate. I suppose they've got trust deeds to guard. They've certainly got one of the strongest steel vaults that's ever been supplied to a corporation that wasn't a bank."

Mr. Reeder beckoned a waiter and ordered coffee.

"The Lane Leonard estate is presumably the estate of the late John Lane Leonard. He was a millionaire who died three years ago, leaving an immense fortune to his step-daughter—I forget the exact amount, but it was somewhere between one and two million pounds."

"He wasn't a banker?" asked Larry curiously.

Mr. Reeder shook his head.

"No, he was not a banker. So far as I know, he was an American stockbroker, who was a very heavy speculator in shares, a man who had the intelligence to keep the money he had won on the Stock Exchange. He had a vault made, you say?"

Larry nodded.

"The strongest I've ever seen. Not large, but triple steel-plated walls and two doors, and all the tricks and safeguards that money could buy. I looked it over when it was completed, and I had a talk with the men who assembled it."

He thought for a moment.

"That must have been just before he died. It was just over three years ago. He must have had some pretty hefty securities, but why shouldn't they be kept at the bank?"

Mr. Reeder looked at him reproachfully.

"There are many reasons why securities should not be kept at the bank," he said, "and you are—er—one them."

Mr. Reeder thought of the Lane Leonard estate on his way back to Brockley. Unusual happenings fascinated him. He tried to recall the particulars of the Lane Leonard will. He had read it at the time, but he could not recall that there was anything remarkable about it.

When he got home he looked up a work of reference.

Miss Lane Leonard, the heiress, lived at Sevenways Castle, in Kent; Sevenways being a little village in the Isle of Thanet. He could recollect nothing about the family which was in any way interesting, or that had interested him. He had never seen the place, for duty had not brought him into the neighbourhood; but he remembered dimly having seen a photograph of an imposing mansion, and had a faint idea that at some time it had been a royal property, that of the seventh or eighth Henry.

CHAPTER III

It was shortly after this little talk that J.G. Reeder made the acquaintance of Mr. Buckingham. It was made in a public place, to Mr. Reeder's embarrassment, for he hated publicity. On that same day he had had an exchange of words with the Assistant Public Prosecutor. That official had sent for him and was a little embarrassed.

"I don't want to bother you, Mr. Reeder," he said, "particularly as I know you have your own peculiar method of working. But a report has come to this office that you have been seen very frequently in the company of the man who was charged at the Old Bailey and whose sentence was quashed on appeal. I think you ought to know this. I have told those concerned that you are probably trying to get information about the other two robberies. I suppose I am right in this?"

"No, sir," said Mr. Reeder, "you are most emphatically not right."

When Mr. Reeder was definite he was very definite.

"I am not even trying to keep this young man to the path of rectitude. A detective, sir, is like a journalist; he may be seen in any company without losing caste. I like Mr. O'Ryan; he is very interesting, and I shall see him just as often as I wish to see him, and if the department—um—feels that I am acting in any way derogatory to its dignity, or impairing its authority, I am prepared to place my resignation in its hands forthwith."

This was a Reeder which the Assistant Prosecutor did not know, but of which he had heard—Mr. Reeder the imperious, the dictatorial. It was not a pleasant experience.

"There is no reason why you should take that tone, Mr. Reeder—" he began.

"That is the tone I invariably employ with any person or persons who interfere in the slightest degree with my private life," said Mr. Reeder.

The Assistant Prosecutor telephoned his chief, who was in the country, and the Public Prosecutor replied very tersely and to the point.

"Let him do as he wishes. For God's sake don't interfere with him!" he said testily. "Reeder is quite capable of looking after himself and his own reputation."

So Mr. Reeder went in a sort of mild triumph to the Queen's Hall, where Larry was waiting for him, and together they sat and listened to a classical programme which was wholly incomprehensible to J.G. Reeder, but which he suffered rather than offend his companion.

"Wonderful!" breathed Larry, as the last trembling notes of a violin were engulfed in a thunder of applause.

"Extraordinary," agreed Mr. Reeder. "I didn't recognise the tune, but he seemed to play the fiddle rather nicely."

"You're a Philistine, Mr. Reeder," groaned Larry.

Mr. Reeder shook his head sadly.

"I'm afraid I shall never be able to appreciate these peculiar sounds which—um—so interest you," he said. "I have a liking for old songs; in fact, I think 'In the Gloaming' is one of the most beautiful pieces I have ever heard—"

"Come and have a drink," said Larry, in despair.

This was during the interval, and they made their way to the bar at the back of the stalls. It was here that Mr. Buckingham made his dramatic entrance.

He was a tall, broad-shouldered man, red of face, rough of speech; his hair was unruly, his eye a little wild, and he moved in a nidor of spirituous liquor. He stared glassily at Mr. Reeder, reached out a big and ugly hand.

"You're Mr. Reeder, ain't you?" he said thickly. "I've been thinking of coming to see you, and I would have come, only I've been busy. Fancy meeting you here! I've seen you often in court."

Mr. Reeder took the hand and dropped it. He hated moist hands. So far as he could recall, he had never met the man before, but evidently he was known to him. As though he read his thoughts, the other went on:

"My name's Buckingham. I used to be in 'L' Division." Leaning forward, he asked confidentially, "Have you ever heard such muck?"

Evidently this disrespectful reference was to the concert.

"I wouldn't have come, but my girl friend made me. She's highbrow!" He winked. "I'll introduce her."

He dived into the crowd and returned, dragging a pallid-looking girl with a long, unhealthy face, who was not so highbrow that she despised the source of Mr. Buckingham's inspiration, for her eyes too were a little glassy.

"One of these days I'll come and talk to you," said Buckingham. "I don't know whether I'll have to, but I may have to; and when I do you'll have something to talk about."

"I'm sure I shall," said Mr. Reeder.

"There's a time to be 'igh and mighty, and a time to be 'umble," Buckingham went on mysteriously. "That's all I've got to say—there's a time to be 'igh and mighty, and a time to be 'umble!"

The Oracle of Delphi could not have been more profound.

A second later Mr. Reeder saw him talking to a little man with a hard and unprepossessing face. Evidently the man was not a member of the audience, for later Mr. Reeder saw him going out through the main entrance.

"Who is he?" asked Larry when the man had gone.

"I haven't the least idea," said Reeder, and Larry chuckled.

"You've one thing in common at any rate," he said; "you both think classical music is muck. I'm going to give up trying to educate you."

Mr. Reeder was very apologetic after the concert. He liked music, but music of a kind. He had a weakness for the popular airs of twenty-five years ago, and confessed a little shamefacedly that he occasionally hummed these favourite tunes of his in his bath.

"Not that I can sing."

"I'm sure of that," said Larry.

Two days later Mr. Reeder saw the two men again. It was on the north side of Westminster Bridge. Immediately opposite the Houses of Parliament there was a traffic block. At this point the road was being repaired and the police were marshalling the traffic into a single line. Mr. Reeder was waiting to cross the road and was examining the vehicles that passed. To say that he was examining them idly would not have been true.

He never examined anything idly. He saw a new grey van and glanced up at the driver. It was the thin-faced man he had seen in the Queen's Hall bar, and by his side sat Buckingham.

Neither of the men saw him as they passed. Mr. Reeder could guess by the movement of the body that the van carried a fairly heavy load, for the springs were strained and the strain on the engine was almost perceptible.

Odd, thought Mr. Reeder... van drivers and their assistants do not as a rule choose concert halls as meeting places. But then, so many things in life were odd. For example:

It was a very curious friendship that had developed between himself and Larry. Reeder was the soul of rectitude. He had never in his life committed one act that could be regarded by the most rigid of moralists as dishonest. He had chosen, for the one friend he had ever had, a man who had only just escaped imprisonment, was undoubtedly a burglar, was undoubtedly the possessor of a large fortune which he had stolen from the interests which it was Mr. Reeder's duty to protect.

Such thoughts occurred to J.G. Reeder in such odd moments of contemplation as when he shaved himself or was brushing his teeth; but he had no misgiving, was unrepentant. He looked upon all criminals as a normal-minded doctor looks upon patients; they were beings who required specialised attention when they were in the grip of their peculiar malady, and were amongst the normals of life when they were cured.

And to be cured, from Mr. Reeder's point of view, was to undergo a special treatment in Wormwood Scrubbs, Dartmoor, Parkhurst, Maidstone, or whatever prison was adaptable for the treatment of those who suffered from, or caused, social disorders.

The next time Larry called, which was on a Sunday a fortnight later, he had an adventure to tell.

"Respect me as a reformed crook, and salute me as a hero," he said extravagantly, as he hung up his coat. "I've saved a distressed damsel from death! With that rare presence of mind which is the peculiar possession of the O'Ryans, I was able—"

"It wasn't so much presence of mind as a lamp-post," murmured Mr. Reeder; "though I grant that you were—um—quick on the—shall I say, uptake? In this case 'uptake' is the right word."

Larry stared at him.

"Did you see it?" he asked.

"I was an interested spectator," said Mr. Reeder. "It happened very near to my office, and I was looking out of the window at that moment. I fear I waste a great deal of time looking out of the window, but I find the traffic of Whitehall intensely interesting. A car got out of control and swerved on to the pavement. It was going beyond the ordinary speed limit, and the young lady would, I think, have been severely injured if you had not lifted her aside just before the car crashed into the lamp-post. As it was, she had a very narrow escape. I applauded you, but silently, because the rules of the office call for quiet. But I still think the lamp-post had almost as much to do with it—" "Of course it had, but she might have been hurt. Did you see her?" asked Larry eagerly. "She's lovely! God, how lovely!"

Mr. Reeder thought she was interesting, and said so. Larry scoffed.

"Interesting! She's marvellous! She has the face and figure of an angel —and don't tell me you've never met an angel—and she has a voice like custard. I was so knocked off my feet by her that she thought I was hurt."

Mr. Reeder nodded.

"I saw her. In fact, I—er—looked rather closely at her. I keep a small pair of field glasses on my desk, and I'm afraid I was rather inquisitive. Who is she?"

Larry shook his head.

"I don't know. I didn't ask her her name, naturally: she was rather upset by what had happened, and she hurried off. I saw her get into a Rolls-Royce that was evidently waiting for her—"

"Yes," said Mr. Reeder. "I saw the Rolls. It is a pity."

"It is a pity. If I'd had any sense I'd have told her my name. After all, the least she can do is to write and thank her brave preserver."

"She may yet—no, no, I wasn't thinking of that."

The housekeeper came in and laid the table, and during the operation Mr. Reeder was silent. When she had gone:

"I wasn't thinking of that," he went on, as though there had been no interruption of his thoughts. "I was thinking that if you had been properly introduced you might have asked her why such a strong safe was ordered."

Larry looked at him blankly.

"Strong safe? I don't know what you're talking about."

Mr. Reeder smiled. It pleased him to mystify this clever young man.

"The lady's name was Miss Lane Leonard," he said. Larry frowned.

"Do you know her?"

"I have never seen her before in my life."

"Then how the devil do you know she was Miss Lane Leonard? Have you seen her picture—?"

Mr. Reeder shook his head.

"I've never seen a picture of her. I have neither seen her since nor before; I have received no information from any person immediately concerning her identity."

"Then how the devil do you know?" asked the astonished Larry.

Mr. Reeder chuckled.

"A person who has a car number has also a name. I was interested to discover who she was, 'phoned across to Scotland Yard, and they supplied me with the name that is attached to that particular car number. Miss Lane Leonard, 409 Berkeley Square, and Sevenways Castle, Sevenways, Kent. 409 Berkeley Square, by the way, is an expensive block of residential flats, so that if you feel that she would be happier for knowing the name of her —um—brave deliverer—I think that was the phrase —you might drop her a line and explain, with whatever modesty you can command, just how much she owes to you."

Larry was very thoughtful.

"That's queer. Do you remember we were talking about the Lane Leonards' strong-room only a few weeks ago, and wondering why such an expensive contraption had been ordered. A lady worth a couple of millions."

"I'm sorry," Mr. Reeder smiled. "I've spoilt your romance. You would have preferred that she were poor—um—but honest. That her father, or preferably her mother, was in the grip of a cruel—um— usurer, and that you might have rescued her once more with the magnificent capital which you have acquired by illicit and altogether disreputable means."

Larry went red. He was a dreamer, and he was annoyed that anybody should know him as such, so annoyed that he abruptly changed the subject.

It was that night for the first time that J.G. Reeder learned the story of Larry O'Ryan's boyhood, and the circumstances which had determined him in his career.

"I'm glad you've told me, Mr. O'Ryan." (Curiously enough, during all the years he knew Larry he never addressed him in any other way.) "It makes you more understandable than I thought you were, and excuses, as far as abnormal tendencies can be excused, your subsequent—um—behaviour. You should, of course, have gone to the head master and told the truth, and probably in later years, since thinking the matter over, you have come to the same conclusion."

Larry nodded.

"Have you met the man since—the master who stole the money?"

"No," said Larry, "but I should have probably met him if I had made Wormwood Scrubbs en route to Dartmoor. Only a born crook could have stolen from Farthingale, who was a good-hearted soul and hadn't too much money. I sent him a monkey, by the way, last week. His wife's had an operation, and I know the little man hasn't a great deal of money."

"A monkey being twenty-five or five hundred pounds? I have never quite accustomed myself to these sporting terms," asked Mr. Reeder. "Five hundred pounds? Well, well, it is nice to be generous with other people's money, but we won't go into that."

He sat, drumming his fingers on the table.

"Once a crook, always a crook—that is your real belief Mr. O'Ryan? But at heart you're not a crook. You're just a young man who thought that he was taking the law into his own hands and was perfectly justified in doing so, which of course is absurd. If everybody thought as you do—but I am getting on to a very old and a tedious subject."

The telephone bell rang shrilly. Mr. Reeder walked to his desk, picked up the receiver and listened, answering monosyllabically. When he had finished:

"I'm afraid our evening is going to be spoilt, Mr. O'Ryan. I am wanted at the office."

"It must be something very important to take you up on Sunday evening," said O'Ryan.

"Everything that comes to me from the office is very important, on Sunday evening or even Monday evening," said Reeder.

He took up the telephone directory, called a number and gave explicit and urgent instructions.

"If you're hiring a car, it is important!"

Mr. Reeder inclined his head.

"It is rather a matter of urgency," he said. "It is, in fact—um —a murder."

CHAPTER IV

On this Sunday morning a policeman patrolling the very edge of the Metropolitan area, at that point near Slough where the County of Buckinghamshire and the County of London meet, had seen a foot sticking up apparently from the grass. It was in a place where no foot should have been, a rough, uneven field, crossed by an irrigation ditch which was now dry. The fact that there was a ditch there was unknown to the policeman until he opened a gate leading into the field and investigated.

As he opened the gate he noticed the marks of car wheels leading into the field, and saw that the padlocked chain which fastened the gate to a post had been broken. The policeman noticed this mechanically. He crossed the rough ground, wet with recent rain and came to the ditch, and the mystery of the foot was revealed. A man lay there on his back. He was dressed in his underclothes and a pair of socks, and one glance at the face told the policeman what had happened. He hailed a passing motorist and sent him off to the station to procure assistance. A police surgeon and an ambulance arrived, and the body was removed. Within an hour Scotland Yard was working on the case.

They had little guidance for their investigations. The man's clothes were innocent even of laundry marks; there was nothing whatever to assist in his identification. The curious fact which struck the investigating officers was that the underclothes were silk, though the man himself was evidently a workman, for his hands were rough and his general physique and appearance suggested that he belonged to the labouring rather than to the leisured classes.

Experts who examined the car tracks could throw no light upon the subject. It had been a big car, and presumably the hour at which the body had been deposited was between two and four o'clock in the morning. By the curve of the track the police decided that the car had come from the direction of London. That was all that was known about it. Cars on the Bath Road are frequent on a Saturday night, and no patrolling policeman had seen the vehicle turning into the field.

One thing was clear to Mr. Reeder the moment he had the facts in his possession, which was not until very late that afternoon, and it was that the car owner must have reconnoitred the spot and decided exactly where the body was to be deposited. He must have known of the existence of the chain which held the gate, and of the ditch beyond.

The field was the property of a small company which was buying land in the neighbourhood—the Land Development Corporation, which had an office in the City. Its business was to buy suitable building sites and to resell them on easy payments.

It was growing dark by the time Mr. Reeder finished his personal investigations.

"And now," he said, "I think I would like to see this unfortunate man."

They took him to the shed where the murdered man lay, and the Inspector in charge gave him the gist of the doctor's report.

"He was beaten over the head, his skull fractured; there is no other sign of injury, but the doctor said these are quite sufficient to cause almost instantaneous death. An iron bar must have been used, or something equally heavy."

Mr. Reeder said nothing. He went out of the shed, and waited while the door was padlocked.

"If we can only get him identified—" began the Inspector.

"I can identify him," said Mr. Reeder quietly. "His name is Buckingham —he is an ex-constable of the Metropolitan Police Force." Within two hours Reeder was examining Buckingham's record in the Inspector's office at Scotland Yard. It was not a particularly good one. The man had served for twelve years in the Metropolitan Police Force and had been six times reprimanded for conduct prejudicial to discipline and on one occasion had narrowly escaped expulsion from the force. He had a history of drunkenness, had twice been before the Commissioner accused of receiving bribes, once from a bookmaker and once from a man whom he had arrested and had subsequently released. Eventually he had retired, without pension, to take up a position in the country. Particulars of that position were not available, and the only information on file was his last address.

Reeder charged himself with this investigation; he went to a small house in Southwark, discovered Buckingham's wife living there and broke to her the news of her husband's death. She accepted the fact very calmly, indeed philosophically.

"I haven't seen him for three or four years," she said. "The only money he ever sent me was ten pounds last Christmas, and I wouldn't have got that only I met him in the street with a girl—and a sick-looking creature she was!—and had a row with him."

She was a little inconsistent in her indignation, for she told him quite calmly that she had married again, relying upon a law which is known only to the poor and certainly unknown to any lawyer, that if a husband deserts a wife and is not seen for two years she may marry again. And Mrs. Buckingham had undoubtedly married again.

Mr. Reeder was not concerned with this blatant act of bigamy, but pressed her as to where the man had been employed. Here he came against a blank wall. Her husband had told her nothing, and apparently throughout their married life his attitude had been one of reticence, particularly with regard to his financial position and his private affairs.

"He was a bad husband to me. He's dead; and I don't want to say anything against him. But I'm telling you, Mr. Whatever-your-name-is, that I'm not going into mourning for him. He's deserted me three times in my married life, and once he gave me a black eye, and I've never forgiven him for that. It was my right eye," she added.

Mr. Reeder could wonder if there were any greater enormity in blacking the right than the left eye, but he did not pursue inquiries in this direction.

All the woman could tell him was that her husband had taken a job in the country, that he was making a lot of money, and that when she had seen him in town he was "dressed flash, like a gentleman."

"When I say a gentleman," she said, "he might have been a waiter. He had a white shirt front on and a black tie, and he was looking as though he'd come into a fortune. Otherwise I wouldn't have asked him for any money."

So far as she knew, he had no friends; at any rate, she could not supply the name of any person from whom particulars of his life might be secured.

"When you say he worked in the country, which part of the country? Have you any idea what station he came from or went to?" he persisted.

She thought a while.

"Yes, Charing Cross. My brother saw him there one night, about two years ago."

She had none of his belongings, no notebook or papers of any kind. "Not even," she said, "as much as a tobacco tin."

She had cut herself completely and absolutely adrift from him, never wanted to hear from or see him again, and her accidental meeting with him in the street was only to be remembered because it was so profitable.

Mr. Reeder returned to headquarters, to consult with investigators who had followed other lines of inquiry, and learned that they too had come to a dead end. J.G. Reeder was puzzled and exhilarated, and could have wished that he controlled the inquiries instead of being an independent seeker after knowledge.

Here was a man, an ex-policeman, so prosperous that he could afford the finest silken underwear, found in a field, with no marks to identify him, obviously murdered, obviously conveyed from the scene of the murder by a car and deposited in the dark in a ditch which only those closely acquainted with the ground could have known existed.

There was another woman in London who could give him information: the "highbrow lady" with the pallid face, who loved classical music and strong drink. London would be combed for her; there was a possibility that she might easily be found.

The next morning he went early to the concert hall and interviewed the attendant. Mr. Reeder might know little about music, but he knew something about music-lovers, and if this woman was a regular concert-goer, the attendant might remember her. Fortune was with him, for two men knew her, one by name. She was a Miss Letzfeld and she was especially to be remembered because she suffered from an inferiority complex, believed that attendants deliberately slighted her and pestered the management with letters of complaint. By luck, one of these letters had been kept. Miss Letzfeld lived at Breddleston Mews in Kensington.

Mr. Reeder went straight to the address and, after repeated knockings, gained the attention of the occupant. She came down to open the door, rather unpleasant to see in the clean daylight. A thin, long-faced girl with sleepy eyes and an ugly mouth, wrapped in a dingy dressing gown.

To his surprise she recognised him.

"Your name's Reeder, isn't it? Didn't Billy introduce you—at the Queen's Hall? You're a detective, aren't you?" And then, quickly: "Is anything wrong?" "May I come up?" he asked.

She led the way up the narrow stairs, her high-heeled shoes drumming unmusically on the bare, uncarpeted treads.

The room into which he was ushered was expensively furnished, but most cheaply maintained. The untidy remnants of a meal were on a table. The room gave him the impression that it had neither been dusted nor swept for a week. Over one chair were a few articles of women's apparel, which she snatched up.

"I want to say this, Mr. Reeder," she said, almost before he was in the room, "that if there is anything wrong I know nothing about it. Billy's been very good to me, but he's trying. I don't know how he got his money, and I've never asked him."

To Mr. Reeder fell the unpleasant duty of telling her of the fate that had overtaken her man, and again he found that the tragic end of ex-Constable Buckingham evoked no very violent emotions. She was shocked, but impersonally shocked.

"That's terrible, isn't it?" she said breathlessly. "Billy was such a good boy" (the description sounded a little ludicrous even in that tragic moment), "though he wasn't what you might call particularly intellectual. I only saw him now and again, once a fortnight, sometimes once a week."

"Where did he come from?" asked Reeder. She shook her head.

"I don't know. He never told me things; he was very close about his private life. He worked in the country for a very rich man. I don't even know what part of the country it was."

"Had he plenty of money?"

"You mean Billy? Yes, he always had plenty of money, and lived well. He had an office in the city somewhere, something to do with land. I wouldn't have known that, but I saw a telegram that he left behind here one day. It was addressed to the Something Land Corporation, but it wasn't in his own name—"

"The Land Development Corporation?" asked Mr. Reeder quickly. "Do you remember the address?"

The girl wasn't sure, but she knew it was in the City.

She had nothing of the man's in her possession except—and here was the most important discovery—a photograph of Buckingham taken a year before. With this in his possession Mr. Reeder drove to the City.

The Land Development Corporation had an office in one of the big blocks near the Mansion House. It consisted of one room, in which a clerk and a typist worked, and a smaller room, very plainly furnished, where the Managing Director sat on his infrequent visits.

For an hour Mr. Reeder plied clerk and typist with questions, and when he got back to Scotland Yard he was in possession of so many facts that contradicted one another, so many that were entirely irreconcilable, that he found it difficult to put them in sequence.

The plain, matter-of-fact report which he put before his superior may be quoted in full.

"In the case of William Buckingham. Line of investigation, Land Development Corporation. This corporation was registered as a private company two years ago. It has a capital of 1000 pounds and debentures amounting to 300,000 pounds. The Directors are the clerk and the typist and a Mr. William Buck. The bank balance is 1300 pounds, and the company is proprietor of a large number of land blocks situated in the south of England, and evidently purchased with the object of development. A considerable number of these have been resold. Mr. Buck was undoubtedly Buckingham. He came to the office very rarely, only to sign cheques. Large sums of money have been paid into and withdrawn from the bank, and a superficial inspection of the books suggests that these were genuine transactions. A further examination, necessarily of a hurried character, reveals considerable gaps in the accounting. The field where the body of Buckingham was found is part of the property of this company, and obviously Buckingham would be well acquainted with the land, though it is a curious fact that he had been there recently twice by night..."

CHAPTER V

The next morning a portrait of Buckingham appeared in every London newspaper, together with such particulars as would assist in a further identification. No news came until the afternoon of that day. Mr. Reeder was in his office, examining documents in relation to a large and illicit importation of cocaine, when a messenger came in with a card. "Major Digby Olbude," it read, and in the left-hand corner: "Lane Leonard Estate Office, Sevenways Castle, Sevenways, Kent". Mr. Reeder sat back in his chair, adjusted his unnecessary glasses and read the card again.
"Ask Major Olbude to come up," he said.
Major Olbude was tall, florid, white of hair, rather pedantic of speech.
"I have come to see you about the man Buckingham. I understand you are in charge of the investigations?"
Mr. Reeder bowed. It was not the moment to direct what might prove an interesting and informative caller to the man who was legitimately entitled to have first-hand information.
"Will you sit down, Major?"
He rose, pushed a chair forward for the visitor, and Major Olbude pulled up the knees of his creased trousers carefully and sat down.
"I saw the portrait in this morning's newspaper—at least, my niece drew my attention to it—and I came up at once, because I feel it is my duty, and the duty, indeed, of every good citizen to assist the police even in the smallest particular in a case of this importance."
"Very admirable," murmured Mr. Reeder.
"Buckingham was in my service; he was one of the guards of what the local people call the treasure house of Sevenways Castle."
Again Mr. Reeder nodded, as though he knew all that was to be known about Sevenways Castle.
"As I say, my niece reads the newspapers, a practice in which I do not indulge, for in these days of sensationalism there is very little in newspapers in which an intellectual man finds the least pleasure and instruction. Buckingham had been in the employment of the late Mr. Lane Leonard, and on Mr. Lane Leonard's death his services were transferred to myself, Mr. Lane Leonard's brother-in-law and his sole trustee. I might say that Mr. Lane Leonard, as everybody knows, died very suddenly of heart failure and left behind a considerable fortune, eighty per cent of which was in bullion."
"In gold?" asked Mr. Reeder, surprised.
The major inclined his head.
"That was my brother-in-law's eccentricity. He had amassed this enormous sum of money by speculation, and lived in terror that it should be dissipated by his descendants—unhappily, he has only a daughter to carry on his name—in the same manner as it was amassed. He also took a very pessimistic view of the future of civilisation and particularly of the English race. He believed—and here I think he was justified— that for ten years there would be no industrial development in the country, and that English securities would fall steadily. He had a very rooted

objection to banks, and the upshot of it all was that he accumulated in his lifetime a sum in gold equivalent to over a million and a half pounds. This was kept, and is still kept, in a chamber which he had specially built practically within the walls of the castle, and to guard which he engaged a staff of ex-policemen, one of whom is on duty every hour of the day and night. It is unnecessary for me to tell you, Mr. Reeder, a man with a commercial knowledge, that by this method my brother-in-law was depriving his daughter of a very considerable income, the interest at five per cent on a million and a half pounds being seventy-five thousand pounds per annum. In ten years that would be three-quarters of a million, so that the provisions of this will mean that nearly four hundred thousand pounds is lost to my ward, and almost as much to the Treasury."

"Very distressing," said Mr. Reeder, and shook his head mournfully, as though the thought of the Treasury losing money cut him to the quick.

"There is a separate fund invested in high-class government security," the major went on, "on which my niece and myself live. Naturally, the custody of such an enormous sum is a source of constant anxiety to me—in fact, only two years ago I ordered an entirely new strong-room to be built at a very considerable cost."

He paused.

"And Buckingham?" asked Mr. Reeder gently.

"I will come to Buckingham," said the major with great dignity. "He was one of the guards employed. There are in all seven. Each lives in his own quarters, and it is against the rules I have instituted that these men should meet except when they relieve one another of their post. The practice is for the guard on duty to ring a bell communicating with the quarters of his relief, who immediately comes to the treasure house and, after being identified, is admitted. Buckingham should have come on duty at six o'clock on Saturday night. His predecessor at the post rang the bell as usual, but Buckingham did not appear. After an hour the man communicated with me, by telephone—there is a telephone connection between my study and the dome—I call it the dome because of its shape—and I set immediately to find the missing man. His room was empty, there was no sign of him, and I ordered the emergency man to take his place."

"Since then you have not seen him?"

The major shook his head.

"No, sir. Nor have I heard from him."

"What salary did you pay this man?"

"Ten pounds a week, quarters, lighting and food. All the guards were supplied from the kitchen of the castle."

"Had he any private means?"

"None," said the other emphatically.

"Would you be surprised to know that he has been speculating heavily in land?" asked Mr. Reeder.

The major rose to his feet, not quickly, but with a certain stately deliberation.

"I should be both surprised and horrified," he said.

"Is there any way by which he could have had access to the—um—treasure house?"

"No, sir," said Olbude, "no method whatever, except through the door, of which I hold the key. The wall is made of concrete twelve inches thick and lined with half-inch steel. The locks are unpickable."

"And the foundations?" suggested Mr. Reeder.

"Eight feet of solid concrete. It is absolutely impossible."

Mr. Reeder rubbed his chin, looking down at the desk, his lips drooping dismally.

"Do you often go into the—um—treasure house?"

"Yes, sir, I go in every month, on the first day of every month. In other words, I was there last Friday."

"And nothing had been disturbed?"

"Nothing," said the other emphatically.

"I presume the bullion is in steel boxes—"

"In large glass containers. That was another of Mr. Lane Leonard's eccentricities. There are about six hundred of these, each containing two thousand five hundred pounds' worth of gold. It is possible to see at a glance whether the money has been disturbed. The containers are hermetically closed and sealed. They stand on reinforced concrete shelves, in eight tiers, on three sides of the treasure house, each tier holding seventy-five containers. The treasure house, I may explain, consists of two buildings; the inner shell, which is the treasure house proper, and another separate building, as it were a box placed over this to give protection to the guard and sufficient space for them to promenade. The outer building contains a small kitchenette, with tables, chairs and the necessary accommodation for the comfort of the guard. Attached to this is a lobby, also guarded with a steel door, and beyond that an iron grille, above which is a powerful electric light to enable the inner guard to scrutinise his relief and make sure that he is the right man—that is to say, that he is not being impersonated."

Mr. Reeder was a little puzzled, but only a little. "Very extraordinary," he said, "Can you tell me any more about Buckingham?"

The major hesitated.

"No, except that he went to town more frequently than any of the other guards. For this I was responsible, I am afraid! I gave him greater freedom because he was the doyen of the guards in point of service."

"Extraordinary," said Mr. Reeder again.

The story had its fantastical and improbable side, and yet J.G. Reeder regarded it as being no more than—extraordinary. Misers there had been since there were valuable things to hoard. Every nation had its safe place where unproductive gold was hoarded. He knew of at least three similar cases of men who had maintained in vaults vast sums in bullion.

"I should like to come down to—to—um—Sevenways Castle and see this man's quarters," he said. "It will be necessary to go through his possessions. Had he any friends?"

The major nodded.

`"He had a friend, I believe, in London—a girl. I don't know who she was. To tell you the truth, Mr. Reeder, I have an idea that he was married, though he never spoke of his wife. But what were you telling me about his having money? That is news to me."

J.G. Reeder scratched his chin and hesitated.

"I am not quite sure whether I have absolute authority for saying that he was the head of a certain land corporation, but as his staff have recognised his photograph—"

He sketched the story of the Land Development Company, and Major Olbude listened without interruption.

"Then it was in one of his own fields that he was found? When I say his own fields, I mean on land which he himself owned. That is amazing. I am afraid I can tell you no more about him," he said, as he took up his hat and stick, "but of course I am available whenever you wish to question me. There may be some things about him that I have forgotten, but I will write my telephone number on your card and you may call me up."

He did this with his pencil, Mr. Reeder standing by and watching the process with interest.

He accompanied his guest down the stairs into Whitehall, and arrived in time to witness a peculiar incident. A Rolls was drawn up by the kerb and three persons were standing by it. He recognised the girl instantly. Larry's back was towards him, but he had no difficulty in identifying the broad shoulders of that young man. The third member of the party was evidently the chauffeur. He was red of face, talking and gesticulating violently. Mr. Reeder heard him say: "You've got no right to speak to the young lady, and if you want to talk, talk in English so as I can understand you."

The major quickened his pace, crossed to the group and spoke sharply to the chauffeur.

"Why are you making a scene?" he demanded.

Larry O'Ryan had walked away, a surprising circumstance, for Larry was the sort that never walked away from trouble of any kind.

Mr. Reeder came up to the group. The major could do no less than introduce him.

"This is my niece, Miss Lane Leonard," he said.

She was lovely; even Mr. Reeder, who was no connoisseur, acknowledged the fresh beauty of the girl. He thought she was rather pale, and wondered whether that was her natural colour.

"What is the trouble, my dear?" asked the major.

"I met a friend—the man who saved me from being run over by a motor car," she said jerkily. "I spoke to him in—in French."

"He speaks English all right," growled the unpleasant-looking chauffeur.

"Will you be quiet! Was that all, my dear?"

She nodded.

"You thanked him, I suppose? I remember you telling me that you did not have the opportunity of thanking him before. He went away before you could speak to him. Modesty in a young man is most admirable. And it was in Whitehall that it happened?"

"Yes," she nodded.

Mr. Reeder felt that she was looking at him, although her eyes were fixed upon her uncle. He saw something else; her gloved hand was trembling. She was trying hard to control it, but it trembled.

The major turned and shook hands with him.

"I shall probably be seeing you again, Mr. Reeder," he said.

He turned abruptly, helped the girl into the car and the machine drew away. Reeder looked round for Larry, saw him staring intently into a doorway, and as the car passed him, saw him turn so that his back was to the vehicle.

Larry walked quickly towards him.

"Sorry," he said; "but I wanted to see you and I was hanging around till you came out."

His eyes were bright; his whole attitude was tense, electric; he seemed charged with some suppressed excitement.

"You met the young lady?"

"Yes. Interesting, isn't she?"

"Why didn't you stay and meet her uncle?"

"Rather embarrassing—fine-looking old boy. Perhaps I was a little conscience-stricken. That chauffeur..."

He was not smiling; his eyes were hard, his lips were set straight.

"He never had a narrower escape than he did today. Have you ever wanted to kill somebody, Mr. Reeder? I've never had it before—just a brutal desire to maim and beat, and mutilate—"

"Why did you speak in French?"

"It's my favourite language," said Larry glibly. "Anyway, she might have been French; she's got the chic of a Parisienne and the loveliness of an Italian dawn."

Mr. Reeder looked at him oddly.

"Why are you being so mysterious?" he asked.

"Am I?" Larry laughed. There was a note of hysteria in that laugh. The bright look had come back to his eyes. "I wonder if he did?"

"Did what?" asked Mr. Reeder, but the young man answered him with a question.

"Are you going down to call on our friend? By the way, did he employ the man Buckingham?"

"What do you know about Buckingham?" asked Mr. Reeder slowly.

"It's in the papers this morning. I mean the man who was killed."

"Did you know him?"

Larry shook his head.

"No. I've seen his portrait—a commonplace-looking hombre, hardly worth murdering, do you think? Lord, Mr. Reeder, isn't it great to be alive!"

A few spots of rain were falling. Mr. Reeder was conscious of the fact that he was bare-headed.

"Come up to my office," he said. "I'll take the risk of being—um—reprimanded by my superior."

Larry hesitated.

"All right, I'm all for it," he said, and followed Mr. Reeder up the stairs.

J.G. shut the door and pointed to a chair.

"Why the excitement?" he asked. "Why the—um—champing of bits, as it were?"

Larry sat back in his chair and folded his arms tightly.

"I've got an idea I'm being six kinds of a fool for not taking you entirely into my confidence, but here's adventure, Mr. Reeder, the most glorious adventure that can come to a young man of courage and enterprise. And I think I'll spoil it a little if I tell you. I'll ask you one favour: was the major wearing his glasses when he came into the street?"

Mr. Reeder nodded.

"I don't remember that he took them off," he said. Larry frowned and bit his lip.

"I'll tell you something. Do you remember when I lifted that young lady out of the way of a car? It was right outside this office, wasn't it? She had just left her own car, and left it rather hurriedly, and was coming— where do you think? To this office, no less! She didn't tell me so, but I'm pretty sure that was where she was bound. And the chauffeur was flying after her. I didn't realise it at the time, but I realise it now. On the day before that happened there was an article in the Megaphone about you, rather a eulogistic one, and a pencil sketch of you. Do you remember?" Mr. Reeder blushed.

"There was rather a stupid—um—ill-informed— um—"

"Exactly. It was rather flattering. I don't know how flattering it was, but your own conscience will tell you. I worked it out in two seconds; that was why she was coming to see you. This misguided and ill-informed writer in the Megaphone said you were the greatest detective of the age, or something of the sort. It probably isn't true, though I'll hand you all sorts of bouquets on a gold plate, for you certainly embarrassed me on one never-to-be-forgotten occasion. And she read it, found out where your office was—anyway, she wants to see you now. She said that much."

"Wants to see me?" said Mr. Reeder incredulously. Larry nodded.

"Isn't it amazing! I couldn't have been speaking to her for more than a minute, and she's the beginning and end of life to me."

He got up and began to pace the room excitedly.

"To me, Mr. Reeder, a crook of crooks, a burglar. But she's worth a million and a half, and absolutely unreachable. I couldn't propose to her. But if she said, 'Walk into the middle of Westminster Bridge and jump into the river,' I'd do it!"

Mr. Reeder stared at him.

"It almost sounds as though you like her very much," he said.

"It almost does," said Larry savagely.

He stopped in his stride, pointed a finger of his extended hand towards Mr. Reeder.

"I'm not going to jump from the middle of Westminster Bridge. It's a far, far better thing that I do—or rather, I'm going to do a far, far better thing, and it's going to make all the difference in life to me if I succeed."

"If you will sit down," said Mr. Reeder mildly, "and talk a little less obscurely, perhaps I could assist you."

Larry shook his head.

"No; I've got to blaze my own trail." He chuckled. "My metaphors are a bit mixed, but then, so is my mind. When are you going to Sevenways Castle?"

"She told you she lived there, did she?" asked Mr. Reeder.
"When are you going?"
J.G. considered.
"Tomorrow—tomorrow afternoon probably." And then: "You don't know Buckingham?"
"No," said Larry. "I recognised him, of course, as the fellow who came up and spoke to you when we were at the Queen's Hall. Odd coincidence, meeting him at all, wasn't it?"
He walked to the door and opened it.
"I'll go now, Mr. Reeder, if you'll excuse me. Perhaps I'll call and see you tonight. By the way, are you in the American market?"
"I never speculate," said Reeder primly. "I don't think I have bought a stock or a share in my life, and certainly I should not buy now; I read the newspapers, of course, and I see the market is down."
"And how!" said Larry cryptically.
He was a little confusing. His reference to the stock market interested Mr. Reeder to the extent of inducing him to wade through the tape prices that night. Stock was falling rapidly in Wall Street; there was panic selling and gloomy forecasts of a complete collapse. He could only wonder how Larry's mercurial mind could have leapt to this mundane fact in his emotional moment.
He had a considerable amount of work to do that afternoon, inquiries to pursue at certain banks, reports to read and digest, and it was nearly nine o'clock before he went home, so tired that he fell asleep almost before he pulled the covers over his shoulders.

CHAPTER VI

Pamela Lane Leonard drove back into Kent that morning, silent, resentful, a little frightened.
"Why do you allow Lidgett to talk to you like that, Uncle Digby?" she asked.
Major Digby Olbude blinked and looked at her.
"Like what, my dear?" he asked irritably. "Lidgett is an old friend of the family, and retainers have certain privileges."
"Did you tell Mr. Reeder that he and Buckingham had quarrelled?"
Olbude did not answer for a while.
"I wasn't aware that they had quarrelled," he said, "and I certainly should not have told Mr. Reeder—how do you come to be acquainted with Mr. Reeder?"
She shook her head.
"I'm not acquainted with him. I've read a lot about him—he's very clever." And then: "Why do you allow Lidgett to talk to you so rudely, and why do you let him talk to me as if I were—well, a servant?"
The major drew a long breath.
"You're altogether mistaken, my dear. Lidgett is a little uncouth, but he's a very faithful servant. I will speak to him."
Another long silence.
"When did they quarrel—Buckingham and Lidgett, I mean?" asked Olbude.
"I saw them in the woods one day. Buckingham knocked him down."
Olbude ran his fingers through his grey hair.
"It is all very difficult," he said. "Your lamented father gave special instructions to me that on no account was Lidgett to be discharged; and until you are twenty-five I am afraid you have no voice in the matter, my dear."
Then, suddenly:
"What did you say to that young man?"
This was the second time he had asked the question.
"I've told you," she answered shortly. "He's the man who saved me from being killed by a car, and I thanked him."
She was not telling the truth, but her conscience was curiously clear.
There was something she wanted to tell him, but she could not. The very fact that the man she hated and feared was sitting within a yard of her, beyond the glass panel which separated chauffeur from passenger, was sufficient to stop her; it was Olbude who returned to the subject.
"Lidgett is a rough diamond. You've got to put his loyalty in the scale against his uncouthness, Pamela. He is devoted to the family—"
"He is devoted to me!" she said, her voice trembling with indignation. "Are you aware, Uncle Digby, that this man has asked me to marry him?"
He turned to her, open-mouthed.

"Asked you to marry him?" he said incredulously. "He actually asked you? I told him that in no circumstances was he to dare mention such a thing—"

It was her turn to be amazed.

"Surely he hasn't discussed it with you? And did you listen to him? Oh, no! Didn't you—uncle, what did you do?"

He moved uneasily, avoiding her eyes.

"He's a rough diamond," he repeated in a low voice. "There is a lot about Lidgett which is very admirable. Naturally, he is not particularly well educated, and he's twenty years older than you, but he's a man with many great qualities."

She could only subside helplessly in the corner of her seat and regard him with wondering eyes. He might have thought that she was impressed by his eulogy, for he went on.

"Lidgett is a man who has saved a lot of money. In fact, I think, thanks to the generosity of your stepfather, Lidgett is very rich. And the disparity of your ages isn't really as important as it appears."

Then, as a thought struck him, he asked quickly: "You didn't tell O'Ryan this?"

"O'Ryan?" she repeated. "Do you know him?"

"You seem to," he answered quickly. "Did he tell you his name in the few seconds you saw him?"

She nodded.

"Yes, he told me his name. Where did you meet him?"

He evaded the question.

"That's neither here nor there. I don't suppose he knows me. He was quite a child when I saw him last—he didn't say he knew me, did he?" he asked anxiously.

She shook her head.

"No, we hardly discussed you."

"What did you discuss?" he asked.

She hesitated.

"Nothing that would interest you," she said.

She went straight to her room when she arrived, and sat down to write a letter. It would probably go the way of other letters she had written; the servants of Sevenways were completely dominated by Lidgett, and she knew by experience that every letter she wrote passed through his hands.

The situation was an intolerable one, but she had grown up in it. Ever since she had returned from school, Lidgett had been master of the house, and her uncle the merest cipher. It was Lidgett who chose the servants, Lidgett who discharged them without reference to his employer; Lidgett took out the car when he wanted it, even ordered improvements to the estate without consulting his employer.

He had walked into the drawing-room one afternoon when she was reading, and without preliminary had put his monstrous proposal.

"I dare say this is going to shock you, Miss Pamela, but I've saved a bit of money and want to get married, and I'm in love with you, and that's the beginning and end of it."

"With me?" She could hardly believe her ears.

"That's the idea," he said coolly. "I haven't talked the matter over with the major, but don't think he'll object. Lots of ladies have married their chauffeurs, and I will make you as good a husband as any of these la-di-dah fellows you are likely to meet."

That had been the proposal, in almost exactly those words. She had been too staggered to make an adequate reply.

She was desperate now. Lidgett made no disguise of his dominant position. He had dared even in the presence of Larry to order her into her car and, even as she was writing, there came a knock at her door and his hateful voice called her. She put the letter hastily between sheets of blotting paper, unlocked the door and opened it.

"What was that fellow saying to you in French?" he asked.

"What he said was unimportant, Lidgett," she said quietly. "It is what I said that mattered. I told him that I was virtually a prisoner in this house, that you were in control and had asked me to marry you. I told him I was terribly afraid, and asked him to communicate with the police."

His face went red, livid, then a sickly white.

"Oh, you did, did you?" His voice was high and squeaky. "That's what you said—told lies about me!"

He was frightened; she recognised the symptoms and her heart leapt.

"The day I nearly had the accident," she went on, "I was on my way to see Mr. Reeder, the detective. I will not be treated as you are treating me. There's something wrong in this house and I'm going to find out what it is. Major Olbude has no authority; you govern him as you govern me, and there must be some reason. Mr. O'Ryan will find out what that reason is."

"Mr. O'Ryan will, will he? You know what he is, I suppose? A lag— he stood his trial for burglary. That's the kind of friend you want!"

He spoke breathlessly. Between rage and fear he was as near to being speechless as he had ever been.

"Well, we'll see about that!"

He turned on his heel and walked quickly away. She closed and locked the door. For the first time there came to her a feeling of hope. And who knew what the night would bring? For she had said something else to Larry O'Ryan, something she had not revealed to her gaoler.

* * * * *

Mr. Reeder slept soundly, invariably for the same length of time every night. He had gone to bed a little after ten: it was a little after four when he awoke, rose, put on the kettle for his tea, and turned on the water for his bath.

At half-past four he was working at his desk. At this hour his mind was crystal-clear, and he had fewer illusions.

He had an excellent library, dealing with the peculiarities of mankind. There was one volume which he took down and skimmed rapidly. Yes, there were any number of precedents for the gold store. There was the case of Schneider, and Mr. Van der Hyn, and the Polish baron Poduski, and the banker Lamonte, and that eccentric American millionaire Mr. John G. Grundewald—they had all been great hoarders of gold. Two of them had left wills similar to Mr. Lane Leonard's. One had made so many eccentric requests in his will that the court put it aside. There was nothing remarkable, then, about Lane Leonard's distrust of stock. Mr. Reeder had to confess that the latest news from America justified the caution of the dead millionaire.

He tried to reconstruct the business life of Buckingham. Here was a man who acted as a guard for treasure of immense value. It could not be truly said that he had opportunities for stealing, and yet in some way he had obtained immense sums of money, and that money had been paid into the bank in gold. That was the discovery that Reeder had made on the previous afternoon. Large sums of gold had been paid into the account of the Land Development Company, as much as fifty and sixty thousand pounds at a time; so much so that the company had been asked politely to account for its possession of so much bullion, and had retorted, less politely, that if the bank did not wish to act for the directors, other banking accommodation would be found.

When could it have been stolen? The man was found dead on the Sunday, and Major Olbude had visited the vault on the Friday. Probably that morning, when he again made an inspection, Mr. Reeder would receive an urgent telephone message calling him into Kent.

It began to get light. Mr. Reeder pulled up the blinds and looked out into the rain-sodden street. Overhead the skies were grey and leaden. J.G. brewed himself another cup of tea, and when it was made walked again to the window and stared down into the deserted thoroughfare.

He heard the whine of the car as it came round from the Lewisham High Road, pursuing a groggy course which suggested that the driver had over-stayed his supper. It was a red sports car, nearly new, with a long bonnet; to Mr. Reeder's surprise it finished its erratic course in front of his door. A little time passed before a man staggered out, clutching for support to the side of the car. He walked unsteadily through the gate and stumbled up the stone steps. Before he reached the door Mr. Reeder was down the stairs and had opened it. He caught Larry O'Ryan in his arms and steadied him.

"I'm all right," muttered Larry. "I want some water. Can I sit down for a minute?"

Mr. Reeder closed the door with his disengaged hand, and led the young man to the hall seat.

"I'll be all right in a second. I've lost a little blood," muttered Larry.

The shoulders of his light mackintosh were red with it, and his face was hardly distinguishable under the broad, red streaks.

"It's all right," he said again. "Just a little knight errantry." He chuckled feebly. "There's no fracture, though driving was rather a bother. I'm glad I didn't carry a gun—I should have used it. I think I can move now."

He got up, swaying. Mr. Reeder guided him up the stairs through his room into the bathroom, and, soaking a towel in water, cleaned his face and the long and ugly wound beneath his matted hair.

"I think it was the chauffeur; I'm not sure. I parked the car about half a mile from Sevenways Castle, and went on foot to reconnoitre."

All this jerkily, his head bent over a basin of red water whilst Mr. Reeder applied iodine and cut away long strands of hair with a pair of office scissors.

"Anyway, I saw her."

"You saw her?" asked Mr. Reeder in astonishment.

"Yes; only for a few seconds. She couldn't get out of the window— it was barred. And the door was locked. But we had a little talk. I took a light, collapsible ladder with me to reach the window. You'll find it in a plantation near the drive."

Mr. Reeder looked at him glumly.

"Are you suggesting she is a prisoner?"

"I'm not suggesting, I'm stating the fact. An absolute prisoner. There are servants in the house, but they've all been chosen by the same man. And the best part of his money is gone."

J.G. Reeder said nothing for a while.

"How do you know?" he asked.

"I went in and looked," was the calm reply. "The major will probably say that I pinched it, but that was a physical impossibility. I always intended to see that treasure house—I have photographs of every key to every strong room that the Monarch Company turned out in the last twenty years. There is a duplicate room in the office. I won't tell you how I got the photographs, because you would be pained, but I did. And I got into the treasure house as easily as falling asleep."

"The guards—?"

Larry incautiously shook his head and winced.

"Ouch! That hurt! There are no guards. That story is bunk. There probably were in Lane Leonard's time, but not now. I got in all right and I got out. More than half the containers are empty! I managed to get away from the park and I was within a few yards of my car when I was attacked; whoever it was must have spotted the car and waited for my return; and I always thought I was clever—prided myself upon my wideness. I saw nobody, but I heard a sound and turned round, and probably that saved my life. Cosh!"

"You didn't see the man that hit you?"

"No, it was quite dark, but I'll know him again, and he'll remember me for a long time. I carried a sword cane—one of those things you buy for a joke when you're in Spain and never expect to use. As I wasn't taking a gun because of my awful criminal record, I thought I'd be on the safe side and take that. Fortunately, I didn't lose hold of it, and before he could give me a second blow I gave him two slashes with it that made him yap and bolt. I couldn't see anything for blood, but I heard him smashing through a hedge. I don't know how I got back to the car and how I got to London."

"May I ask," said Mr. Reeder, "exactly why you went to Sevenways?"

"She asked me to see her last night—asked me in French; and she asked me in French because she didn't want the chauffeur to hear her. That's when she told me she wanted to see you. Her room is on the park side of the house—it's called a castle, but it's a Tudor house really— three windows on the right from the portico. As I say, the window was barred, so my plan came unstuck."

"What on earth were you going to do?" asked J.G.

"I was running away with her," said Larry calmly. "It was her idea."

Mr. Reeder was a picture of amazement.

"You were running away with her?" he said incredulously.

"That was the idea. She asked me to take her away. It sounds mad, but there it is. She must have trusted me, or she was desperate. I think a little of each."

Mr. Reeder went out to telephone, Larry protesting.

"Really, I don't want a doctor. A whack on the head is nothing."

"A whack on the head that cuts four inches of skin and exposes the scalp is a very important matter," said Mr. Reeder, "and I am one of the few remaining people who believe in doctors."

A surgeon came in half an hour and did a little fancy stitching. Mr. Reeder insisted that Larry should stay in the house; a very unusual request, for he never encouraged visitors, and this was the first guest he had had within the memory of his housekeeper.

It was early in the afternoon when Mr. Reeder reached Sevenways Castle. It stood in an extensive park and, as Larry had said, there was very little about it that had the appearance of a castle. Its architecture was Tudor, except that on one end there stuck out a rather ugly, modern addition which was built, it seemed, of dressed stone and visible from the drive. This must be the treasure house, he thought.

He had telephoned the hour he expected to arrive, and Major Olbude was waiting for him under the porch. He led him into the panelled library, where a red fire glowed on an open hearth.

"I've been trying to make up my mind whether I should wait for you to arrive or whether I should send for the local police. Some ruffian attacked a gamekeeper of mine with a sword last night. I've had to send him away to London to be medically treated. Really, Mr. Reeder, the events of the past few days have made me so nervous that I felt it prudent to send my niece to Paris. With one of my guards killed and my gamekeeper attacked, it almost looks as though there is some attempt being organised against the treasure house, and if I were not bound by the terms of the will I should send the whole contents of the place to the strong-room of a London bank. It is very disconcerting. By the way, you will be relieved to learn that I made a very careful inspection of the vault today, and none of the containers has been touched; all the seals are intact, as of course I expected they would be. I need hardly tell you that I am a little relieved, though there was no real cause for worrying. The strong-room is impregnable and, unless Buckingham was the most expert of thieves, he could not have forced the door without it being instantly detected. The key never leaves me day or night. I carry it, as a matter of fact, on a silver chain around my neck."

"And none of the containers has been touched?" asked Mr. Reeder.

"None. Would you like to see the vault?"

Mr. Reeder followed him along the broad corridor of the castle into a little room which apparently was the major's study, and through a steel door, which he unlocked, into a small lobby, illuminated by a skylight heavily criss-crossed with steel bars. There was another steel door, and beyond this they came to a narrow stone passage which led to the treasure house proper.

It was a huge concrete and steel safe, placed within four walls. The only adjunct to the building was a small kitchenette, where the guards sat, and this was immediately opposite the steel door of the vault.

"I think we're entitled to call it a vault," said the major, "because it is sunk some five feet below the level on which we are at present—one goes down steps to the interior—"

Mr. Reeder was looking round.

"Where is the guard?" he asked.

The major spread out his hands, despair in his good-looking face.

"I'm afraid I lost my head, after what you told me. I dismissed them with a month's wages and packed them off the moment I came back. It was stupid of me, because I'm sure they are trustworthy, but once you've become suspicious of men in whom you've placed the greatest confidence, I think it is best to make a clean sweep."

Mr. Reeder examined the steel door carefully.

He saw, however, at a glance that only the most expert of bank-smashers could have forced his way into the treasure chamber, and then only with the aid of modern scientific instruments. It was certainly not a one-man job, and decidedly no task for an amateur.

He came back to the house, his hands thrust into his pockets, the inevitable umbrella hooked on his arm, his high-crowned hat on the back of his head. He stopped to admire one of the pieces of statuary which lined the broad hall.

"A very old house," he said. "I am interested in the manor houses of England. Is there any possibility of looking over the place?"

Major Olbude hesitated.

"There's no reason why you shouldn't," he said. "Some of the rooms, of course, are locked up; in fact, we only use one wing."

They went from room to room. The drawing-room was empty. He saw on a low table a book. It was open in the middle, and lying face down on the table; a book that had been put aside by somebody who was so interested in the story that they were anxious to continue at the place they left off. Near by was a pair of reading glasses and a case. He made no comment, and went on to the dining-room, with its Elizabethan panels and deep mullioned windows; stopped to admire the carved crest of the original owner of the building, and listened intently while Major Olbude told him the history of Sevenways.

"You don't wish to see upstairs?"

"I should rather like to. The old sleeping apartments in these manor houses have a singular interest for me. I am—um—something of a student of architecture," said Mr. Reeder untruthfully.

CHAPTER VII

At the head of the grand stairway stretched a passage from which opened the principal bedrooms.
"This is my niece's room."
He threw open a door and showed a rather gloomy looking apartment with a four-poster bed.
"As I say, she went to Paris this morning—"
"And left everything very tidy," murmured Mr. Reeder. "It's such a pleasure to find that trait in a young lady."
There was no sign that the room had been lived in and there was a slight mustiness about it.
"There's little or nothing in this other wing, except my bedroom," said the major, leading the way past the staircase.
He was walking more quickly, but Mr. Reeder stopped opposite a doorway.
"There's one remark that was made by a Frenchman about an English manor house in the reign of Charles," he said sententiously. "Do you speak— er—French, Major?"
Now, the remarkable thing about Major Olbude was that he did not speak French. He had a knowledge of Greek and of Latin, but modern languages had never appealed to him, he said.
"His remark was this," said Mr. Reeder, and said something in French. He said it very loudly. "If you are in the room, move your blind when you hear me talking outside the house."
"I'm afraid that is unintelligible to me," said the major shortly.
"It means," said Mr. Reeder glibly, "that the Englishman's idea of a good house is a comfortable bed inside a fortress. Now," he said, as they went down the stairs together, "I would like to see the house from the outside."
They walked along the gravelled pathway running parallel with the front of the house. The major was growing obviously impatient; moreover, he was displaying a certain amount of anxiety, glancing round as though he were expecting an unwelcome visitor. Mr. Reeder noticed these things.
When he came opposite the third window from the right of the porch, he said loudly, pointing to a distant clump of trees:
"Was it there your gamekeeper was attacked?"
As he spoke, he glanced quickly backwards. The white blind that covered the third window to the right of the porch moved slightly.
"No, it was in the opposite direction, on the other side of the house," said the major shortly.
"Now would you like to see the sleeping quarters of Buckingham? The police have been here this morning—the Kentish police—and have made a thorough search, so I don't think it is worth while your examining the place. As far as I can gather, they found nothing."
Mr. Reeder looked at him thoughtfully.
"No, I don't think I want to see Buckingham's quarters, but there are one or two questions I would like to ask you. May I see the inside of the vault?"
"No, you may not."

Olbude's voice was sharp, frankly unfriendly. He seemed to realise this, for he added almost apologetically:

"You see, Mr. Reeder, I have a very heavy responsibility. This infernal trust is getting so much on my mind that I'm thinking of asking the courts to relieve me of my guardianship."

They were back in the library now. Mr. Reeder was no longer the languid, charming and rather timid gentleman. He was the hectoring, domineering Mr. Reeder, whom quite a number of people knew and disliked intensely.

"I want to see your niece," he said.

"She's gone to Paris."

"When did she go?"

"She went by car this morning."

"Let me ask you one question; is your niece short-sighted? Does she wear glasses?"

Olbude was taken off his guard.

"Yes; the doctor ordered her to wear glasses for reading."

"How many pairs of glasses has she?"

The major shrugged.

"What is the idea of these ridiculous questions?" he asked testily. "So far as I know, she has one pair, a sort of blue-shaded tortoise-shell—"

"Then will you explain why she took a long journey and left behind her the book in which she was so interested, and her reading glasses? You will find them in the drawing-room. I want to see her room."

"I have shown you her room," said Olbude, raising his voice.

"I want to see the third room from the left of the grand staircase."

Olbude looked at him for a second, and laughed. "My dear Mr. Reeder, surely this is not the method of the Public Prosecutor's Department?"

"It is my method," said Mr. Reeder curtly.

There was a pause.

"I will go upstairs and get her," said the major.

"If you don't mind, I will come with you."

Outside the door of the girl's room the major paused, key in hand.

"I will tell you the truth, though I don't see that this matter has anything to do with you," he said. "My niece has been very indiscreet. As far as I can gather, she made arrangements to run away with an unknown man, who, I have since ascertained, has a criminal record—you will be able to confirm this, for I understand you were in the case. Naturally, as her guardian, I have my duty to do, and as to my little fiction about her going to Paris—"

"Perhaps she will tell me all this herself," said Reeder.

The major snapped back the key and threw open the door.

"Come out, Pamela, please. Mr. Reeder wishes to see you."

She came out into the light, her eyes upon her guardian.

"I think it is true, is it not, that you had made arrangements to leave this house, Pamela, and that because of this I locked you in your room?"

She nodded. The girl was terrified, was in such fear that she could hardly stand. Yet, as Reeder sensed, it was not the major who inspired the fear.

"This is Mr. Reeder; I think you met him yesterday. Mr. Reeder seems to think there is something sinister in this act of discipline. Have I in any way ill-treated you?"

She shook her head, so slightly that the gesture was almost imperceptible.

"Is there anything you would like to say to Mr. Reeder—any complaint you wish to make? Mr. Reeder is a very important official in the Public Prosecutor's office." There was a note of pomposity in his tone. "You may be sure that if I have behaved in any way illegally, he will see that you are—"

"Quite unnecessary, isn't it, Major Olbude?" said Mr. Reeder's quiet voice. "I mean, all this—um—prompting and terrifying. Perhaps if I had a few minutes with the young lady in your library she might give me some information."

"About what? You would like to ask her a few questions about me, would you?" asked Olbude.

"Curiously enough, I have come down here to investigate the murder of a man called Buckingham. If you are concerned in the murder of that man, I shall certainly ask her questions about you." Reeder's eyes did not leave the man's face.

"If, on the other hand, that is a matter which does not concern you, the result of our conversation will be in no way embarrassing to you, Major Olbude. Did you know Buckingham, Miss Leonard?"

"Yes," she said. Her voice was low and sweet. "But not very well. I have seen him once or twice."

"We had better go back to the library," Olbude broke in; his voice was unsteady. "I don't suppose this young lady can tell you very much that you want to know, but since you're intent on cross-examining her, there's no reason in the world why I should put obstacles in your way. Naturally, I haven't any desire that a young girl should discuss a beastly business like murder, but if that is the method of the Public Prosecutor's office, by all means go ahead with it."

He took them back to the library, but made no attempt to leave them alone. Rather did he plant himself in the most comfortable chair in the room, within earshot.

She knew little about Buckingham. Mr. Reeder could not escape the conviction that she was not terribly interested in that unfortunate man. She had seen the picture in the newspaper and had drawn her uncle's attention to the tragedy. She knew nothing of the treasure house, had only seen it from the outside, and had met none of the guards.

She was not overawed by Olbude's presence, but with every answer she gave to the detective's inquiries she cast a frightened glance towards the door as though she expected somebody would come in. Mr. Reeder guessed who that somebody was.

He looked at his watch, and his attitude towards the girl suddenly changed. He had been gentle, almost grandmotherly with his "um's" and "er's", and now the hectoring Mr. Reeder reappeared.

"I'm not quite satisfied with your answers, Miss Leonard," he said, "and I am going to take you up to Scotland Yard to question you still further."

For a moment she was startled, looked at him in horror, and then she understood, and he saw the look of relief come into her eyes. The major had risen slowly to his feet.

"This is rather a high-handed proceeding." he quavered, "and I think I can save you a lot of trouble. I'll make a confession to you, Mr. Reeder; I have been shielding this man Buckingham. Why I should do so, heaven only knows, except that I didn't wish to incur undesirable publicity for my niece. When I visited the treasure house this morning I found that four of the containers were empty. You asked me if you might see the vault, and I refused. I think it was stupid of me; and now, if you wish, I can throw a great deal of light, not only upon the robbery, but upon the disappearance of this wretched man—"

"Let me tell you something," said Reeder. "It is an old story, part of which was told me by a boy from your school, and part I have unearthed in my own way."

The major licked his dry lips.

"It is a story about a namesake of yours," Reeder went on, "a rather clever man, who had a commission in the Territorial Army. He was, in fact, of your rank, and if I remember rightly, his Christian name was—um —Digby."

He saw the colour fade from Olbude's face and heard his quick breathing.

"He was, unhappily, a victim of the narcotic habit," said Mr. Reeder, not taking his eyes from the man's face, "and I will do him this justice, that he was heartily ashamed of his weakness and when he sank, as he did sink, to the level of a peddler of cocaine, he took another name. I was responsible for his arrest, with several other people engaged in that beastly traffic; and to me he confided that he had very rich relations who might help him. He even mentioned the name of a brother-in-law named Lane Leonard. At this time he had reached, as I say, a pretty low level. I am not a philanthropist, but I have a weakness for helping the hopeless, and the more hopeless they are —such is my peculiar—um—perversity—the more I endeavour to produce miracles. I rarely succeed. I did not succeed with Major Digby Olbude. I kept in touch with him after he came out of prison, but he managed to drift away beyond my reach, and I did not hear of him again till I learned that he had died in St. Pancras Infirmary. He was buried in the name of Smith, but, unhappily for everybody concerned, there was an old acquaintance of his in the hospital at the same time, and this old acquaintance formed the link by which Lidgett was able to trace this unfortunate man."

Olbude found his voice.

"There are quite a large number of Olbudes in the world," he said, "and Digby is a family name. He may have been a connection of mine."

"I don't think he was any relation of yours," said Mr. Reeder gently. "I think I had better see Lidgett, and then I would like to telephone to Scotland Yard and bring down the officer in charge of the Buckingham case. I'm afraid it is going to be a rather unpleasant experience for you, my friend."

"I know nothing about Buckingham," said the man huskily. "I had little to do with the guards. I saw them and paid them, and that is all."

"When you say 'guards' you mean 'guard'," said Mr. Reeder. "There have been no keepers of the treasure house since shortly after Mr. Lane Leonard's death, the only man employed being Buckingham. It only needed the most elementary of inquiries to dispose of that absurd story. You have the key of the treasure house, by the way?"

The other shook his head.

"Suspended round your neck by a silver chain?" suggested Mr. Reeder.

"No," said Olbude brusquely. "I have never had it. Lidgett has it."

Mr. Reeder smiled.

"Then there is all the more reason for interviewing that enterprising chauffeur," he said.

Pamela had stood silent through this exchange. There were significant gaps which she could fill.

"Lidgett is in his room," said Olbude at last. "I suppose it's going to be very serious for me?"

"I'm afraid it is," said Reeder.

The man bit his lip and stared out of the window.

"Nothing can be very much worse than the humiliating life I have lived for the past few years," he said. "I never dreamt that money and wealth could be purchased at such a ghastly price."

He looked at the girl with a quizzical smile.

"In this precious treasure house there is very nearly five hundred thousand pounds," he said. "I made a rough survey the other morning."

Lidgett was kind enough to let me have the keys—in fact, he had to allow this, because I flatly refused to make any statement concerning the condition of the Treasury until he let me satisfy myself that the money was not entirely gone. "He and Buckingham were fellow gamblers. I've never quite known how Buckingham came into his confidence, but I have a fancy that Buckingham was necessary for the transport of the gold. I will say this, that I was not aware that the money was being stolen, although I confess I was a little suspicious. When I taxed Lidgett with plundering the treasure house he very frankly admitted the fact, and defied me to take any action against him.

"I know they quarrelled a great deal, and, as Miss Lane Leonard will tell you, there was some fighting in which Lidgett got the worst of it. The murder was probably subsequent to this. And now I think I had better call Lidgett."

He went out of the room and up the stairs, past the far end of the left wing and knocked at the door. A surly voice asked who was there, and when he replied he heard the shuffle of slippered feet across the bare floor and the key was turned in the lock.

Lidgett was in a dressing-gown, his face covered with sticking plaster.

"Has he gone?" he growled.

Major Olbude shook his head, a smile on his good-looking face.

"No," he said lightly. "At the moment he is in the library with Miss Lane Leonard."

Lidgett gaped at him.

"With her? Talking to her? What the hell's the idea?"

"The idea is that I have told Mr. Reeder as much of the truth as I know. I naturally couldn't tell him exactly the circumstances leading to the murder of Buckingham, because I don't know what preceded it. I gather from your activity in the garage the next day, and the amount of washing down you did, that the murder was committed in the garage. I know you burnt clothes in the furnace, but all this is quite unimportant."

Lidgett stood, speechless. And then, as he realised all that was implied:

"You swine!" he screamed.

Mr. Reeder heard two quick shots and then a third. He flew up the stairs, arriving simultaneously with a manservant. When he came back to the girl his face was grave.

"I'm going to take you up to London, young lady," he said. "I have asked one of the maids to pack your things and bring them down."

"I can go up—" she began.

"There is no need."

"What has happened?" she asked.

"We'll talk about it in the car," said Reeder.

In truth he did nothing of the sort. He did not even tell her that the key attached to a silver chain, which he carried in his pocket, had been taken from the neck of the dead Lidgett and was still spotted with his blood.

* * * * *

"The story, so far as I can piece it together," said Mr. Reeder to his chief, "is somewhat complicated, but is not by any means as complicated as it appeared. Which, sir, is a peculiarity of most human stories.

"The real Major Olbude was a drug addict who died in St. Pancras Infirmary. He was a relative of Lane Leonard's, and at one time there had been certain business associations between them. When Lane Leonard found he was approaching his end, his mind went back to his brother-in-law and he sent Lidgett in search of him. By a stroke of luck Lidgett was able to trace Olbude, and discovered that he had died at St. Pancras Infirmary and been buried under the name of Smith.

"You must realise that Lidgett was a very shrewd and possibly a clever fellow. He was certainly cunning. He knew that unless a guardian were produced the estate would be thrown into Chancery and he would lose his employment, for he had never been a favourite with Miss Pamela. He conceived the idea of producing a spurious Major Olbude, and his choice fell upon a man he had met at a gambling house in Dean Street, a rather pompous schoolmaster who had this unfortunate failing, and was in the habit of coming to London every week-end to play at the club.

"Mr. Tasbitt was a master at Fernleigh College, a public school at which Larry O'Ryan was a scholar and from which he was expelled. There is no doubt whatever that the boy was innocent, and that the real thief was this same Tasbitt. Depending upon his master's failing senses, Lidgett took Tasbitt, who probably agreed to fraud with the greatest reluctance and in some terror, to Sevenways Castle. Tasbitt was introduced and accepted as Olbude; there was very little risk; few people knew Olbude. I have only today learned that his title of major was a piece of vanity on his part, and that he had only served some twelve months in the Territorial Army and had not risen beyond the rank of second lieutenant. But that is by the way.

"All might have gone well if Buckingham and Lidgett had not quarrelled, probably over the division of the loot. The two men were running a land development company, and though this was not very successful it was by no means a failure. I have now been able to trace Lidgett's account, and, a very considerable portion of the missing money will be in time restored to its owner when certain properties are liquidated.

"It was unfortunate for Tasbitt that O'Ryan was in the vicinity of my office the day he called on me, for he was instantly recognised and, as it appeared, the recognition was mutual."

When the Assistant Public Prosecutor heard the story he asked a pertinent question.

"Will this young lady marry O'Ryan?"

Mr. Reeder nodded.

"I think so," he said gravely.

"Isn't there a possibility that he's after her money?"

Mr. Reeder shook his head.

"He has quite a lot of money of his own," he said, a little regretfully.

Printed in Great Britain
by Amazon